A JAMES BOND QUARTET

by the same author

The adventures of James Bond

DIAMONDS ARE FOREVER
DR NO
GOLDFINGER
FOR YOUR EYES ONLY
THUNDERBALL
THE SPY WHO LOVED ME
ON HER MAJESTY'S SECRET SERVICE
YOU ONLY LIVE TWICE
THE MAN WITH THE GOLDEN GUN
OCTOPUSSY *AND* THE LIVING DAYLIGHTS

also by Ian Fleming

THE DIAMOND SMUGGLERS
THRILLING CITIES

for children

CHITTY-CHITTY-BANG-BANG: THE MAGICAL CAR

A JAMES BOND QUARTET

Casino Royale
Live and Let Die
Moonraker
From Russia, With Love

IAN FLEMING

JONATHAN CAPE
LONDON

This edition first published 1992
Jonathan Cape, 20 Vauxhall Bridge Road, London SW1V 2SA

A CIP catalogue record for this book
is available from the British Library

ISBN 0-224-03621-1

Typeset by Pure Tech Corporation, Pondicherry, India
Printed in Great Britain by
Mackays of Chatham PLC, Chatham, Kent

CONTENTS

CASINO ROYALE

I

THE SECRET AGENT

THE SCENT AND smoke and sweat of a casino are nauseating at three in the morning. Then the soul-erosion produced by high gambling — a compost of greed and fear and nervous tension — becomes unbearable and the senses awake and revolt from it.

James Bond suddenly knew that he was tired. He always knew when his body or his mind had had enough and he always acted on the knowledge. This helped him to avoid staleness and the sensual bluntness that breeds mistakes.

He shifted himself unobtrusively away from the roulette he had been playing and went to stand for a moment at the brass rail which surrounded breast-high the top table in the 'salle privée'.

Le Chiffre was still playing and still, apparently, winning. There was an untidy pile of flecked hundred-mille plaques in front of him. In the shadow of his thick left arm there nestled a discreet stack of the big yellow ones worth half a million francs each.

Bond watched the curious, impressive profile for a time, and then he shrugged his shoulders to lighten his thoughts and moved away.

The barrier surrounding the 'caisse' comes as high as your chin and the 'caissier', who is generally nothing more than a minor bank clerk, sits on a stool and dips into his piles of notes and plaques. These are ranged on shelves. They are on a level, behind the protecting barrier, with your groin. The caissier has a cosh and a gun to protect him, and to heave over the barrier and steal some notes and then vault back and get out of the casino through the passages and doors would be impossible. And the caissiers generally work in pairs.

Bond reflected on the problem as he collected the sheaf of hundred-thousand and then the sheaves of ten-thousand-franc notes. With another part of his mind, he had a vision of tomorrow's regular morning meeting of the casino committee.

'Monsieur Le Chiffre made two million. He played his usual game. Miss Fairchild made a million in an hour and then left. She executed three "bancos" of Monsieur Le Chiffre within an hour and then left. She played with coolness. Monsieur le Vicomte de Villorin made one million two at roulette. He was playing the maximum on the first and last dozens. He was lucky. Then the Englishman, Mister Bond, increased his winnings to exactly three million over the two days. He was playing a progressive system on red at table five. Duclos, the "chef de partie", has the details. It seems that he is persevering and plays in maximums. He has luck. His nerves seem good. On the "soirée", the chemin-de-fer won *x*, the baccarat won *y* and the roulette won *z*. The boule which was again badly frequented still makes its expenses.'

'Merci, Monsieur Xavier.'

'Merci, Monsieur le Président.'

Or something like that, thought Bond as he pushed his way through the swing doors of the salle privée and nodded to the bored man in evening clothes whose job it is to bar your entry and your exit with the electric foot-switch which can lock the doors at any hint of trouble.

And the casino committee would balance its books and break up to its homes or cafés for lunch.

As for robbing the caisse, in which Bond himself was not personally concerned, but only interested, he reflected that it would take ten good men, that they would certainly have to kill one or two employees, and that anyway you probably couldn't find ten non-squeal killers in France, or in any other country for the matter of that.

As he gave a thousand francs to the 'vestiaire' and walked down the steps of the casino, Bond made up his mind that Le Chiffre would in no circumstances try to rob the caisse and he put the contingency out of his mind. Instead he explored his present physical sensations. He felt the dry, uncomfortable gravel under his evening shoes, the bad, harsh taste in his mouth and the slight sweat under his arms. He could feel his eyes filling their sockets. The front of his face, his nose and antrum, were congested. He breathed the sweet night air deeply and focused his senses and his wits. He wanted to know if anyone had searched his room since he had left it before dinner.

He walked across the broad boulevard and through the gardens to the Hotel Splendide. He smiled at the concierge who gave him his key — No.45 on the first floor — and took the cable.

It was from Jamaica and read:

KINGSTONJA XXXX XXXXXX XXXX XXX
BOND SPLENDIDE ROYALE-LES-EAUX SEINE INFERIEURE HAVANA CIGAR PRODUCTION ALL CUBAN FACTORIES 1915 TEN MILLION REPEAT TEN MILLION STOP HOPE THIS FIGURE YOU REQUIRE REGARDS

DASILVA

This meant that ten million francs was on the way to him. It was the reply to a request Bond had sent that afternoon through Paris to his headquarters in London asking for more funds. Paris had spoken to London where Clements, the head of Bond's department, had spoken to M. who had smiled wryly and told 'The Broker' to fix it with the Treasury.

Bond had once worked in Jamaica and his cover on the Royale assignment was that of a very rich client of Messrs. Caffery, the principal import and export firm of Jamaica. So he was being controlled through Jamaica, through a taciturn man who was head of the picture desk on the *Daily Gleaner*, the famous newspaper of the Caribbean.

This man on the *Gleaner*, whose name was Fawcett, had been book-keeper for one of the leading turtle-fisheries on the Cayman Islands. One of the men from the Caymans who had volunteered on the outbreak of war, he had ended up as a Paymaster's clerk in a small naval intelligence organization in Malta. At the end of the war, when, with a heavy heart, he was due to return to the Caymans, he was spotted by the section of the Secret Service concerned with the Caribbean. He was strenuously trained in photography and in some other arts and, with the quiet connivance of an influential man in Jamaica, found his way to the picture desk of the *Gleaner*.

In the intervals between sifting photographs submitted by the great agencies — Keystone, Wide-World, Universal, I.N.P., and

Reuter-Photo — he would get peremptory instructions by telephone from a man he had never met to carry out certain simple operations requiring nothing but absolute discretion, speed, and accuracy. For these occasional services he received twenty pounds a month paid into his account with the Royal Bank of Canada by a fictitious relative in England.

Fawcett's present assignment was to relay immediately to Bond, full rates, the text of messages which he received at home by telephone from his anonymous contact. He had been told by this contact that nothing he would be asked to send would arouse the suspicion of the Jamaican post office. So he was not surprised to find himself suddenly appointed string correspondent for the 'Maritime Press and Photo Agency', with press-collect facilities to France and England, on a further monthly retainer of ten pounds.

He felt secure and encouraged, had visions of a B.E.M. and made the first payment on a Morris Minor. He also bought a green eye-shade which he had long coveted and which helped him to impose his personality on the picture desk.

Some of this background to his cable passed through Bond's mind. He was used to oblique control and rather liked it. He felt it feather-bedded him a little, allowed him to give or take an hour or two in his communications with M. He knew that this was probably a fallacy, that probably there was another member of the Service at Royale-les-Eaux who was reporting independently, but it did give the illusion that he wasn't only 150 miles across the Channel from that deadly office building near Regent's Park, being watched and judged by those few cold brains that made the whole show work. Just as Fawcett, the Cayman Islander in Kingston, knew that if he bought that Morris Minor outright instead of signing the hire-purchase agreement, someone in London would probably know and want to know where the money had come from.

Bond read the cable twice. He tore a telegraph form off the pad on the desk (why give them carbon copies?) and wrote his reply in capital letters:

THANKS INFORMATION SHOULD SUFFICE
BOND.

He handed this to the concierge and put the cable signed 'Dasilva' in his pocket. The employers (if any) of the concierge could bribe a copy out of the local post office, if the concierge hadn't already steamed the envelope open or read the cable upside down in Bond's hands.

He took his key and said good night and turned to the stairs, shaking his head at the liftman. Bond knew what an obliging danger-signal a lift could be. He didn't expect anyone to be moving on the first floor, but he preferred to be prudent.

Walking quietly up on the balls of his feet, he regretted the hubris of his reply to M. via Jamaica. As a gambler he knew it was a mistake to rely on too small a capital. Anyway, M. probably wouldn't let him have any more. He shrugged his shoulders and turned off the stairs into the corridor and walked softly to the door of his room.

Bond knew exactly where the switch was and it was with one flow of motion that he stood on the threshold with the door full open, the light on and a gun in his hand. The safe, empty room sneered at him. He ignored the half-open door of the bathroom and, after locking himself in, he turned up the bed-light and the mirror-light and threw his gun on the settee beside the window. Then he bent down and inspected one of his own black hairs which still lay undisturbed where he had left it before dinner, wedged into the drawer of the writing-desk.

Next he examined a faint trace of talcum powder on the inner rim of the porcelain handle of the clothes cupboard. It appeared immaculate. He went into the bathroom, lifted the cover of the lavatory cistern and verified the level of the water against a small scratch on the copper ball-cock.

Doing all this, inspecting these minute burglar-alarms, did not make him feel foolish or self-conscious. He was a secret agent, and still alive thanks to his exact attention to the detail of his profession. Routine precautions were to him no more unreasonable than they would be to a deep-sea diver or a test pilot, or to any man earning danger-money.

Satisfied that his room had not been searched while he was at the casino, Bond undressed and took a cold shower. Then he lit his seventieth cigarette of the day and sat down at the writing-table with the thick wad of his stake money and winnings beside him and entered some figures in a small note-book. Over the two days' play, he was up exactly three million francs. In London he had been issued with ten million, and he had asked London for a further ten. With this on its way to the local branch of the Crédit Lyonnais, his working capital amounted to twenty-three million francs, or some twenty-three thousand pounds.

For a few moments Bond sat motionless, gazing out of the window across the dark sea, then he shoved the bundle of banknotes under the pillow of the ornate single bed, cleaned his teeth, turned out the lights and climbed with relief between the harsh French sheets. For ten minutes he lay on his left side reflecting on the events of the day. Then he turned over and focused his mind towards the tunnel of sleep.

His last action was to slip his right hand under the pillow until it rested under the butt of the .38 Colt Police Positive with the sawn barrel. Then he slept, and with the warmth and humour of his eyes extinguished his features relapsed into a taciturn mask, ironical, brutal, and cold.

2

DOSSIER FOR M.

TWO WEEKS BEFORE, this memorandum had gone from Station S. of the Secret Service to M., who was then and is today head of this adjunct to the British defence ministries:

To: M.
From: Head of S.
Subject: A project for the destruction of Monsieur Le Chiffre (alias 'The Number', 'Herr Nummer', 'Herr Ziffer', etc.), one of the Opposition's chief agents in France and undercover Paymaster of the 'Syndicat des Ouvriers d'Alsace', the communist-controlled trade union in the heavy and transport industries of Alsace and, as we know, an important fifth column in the event of war with Redland.
Documentation: Head of Archives' biography of Le Chiffre is attached at *Appendix A*. Also, *Appendix B*, a note on SMERSH.

We have been feeling for some time that Le Chiffre is getting into deep water. In nearly all respects he is an admirable agent of the U.S.S.R., but his gross physical habits and predilections are an Achilles heel of which we have been able to take advantage from time to time and one of his mistresses is a Eurasian (No. 1860) controlled by Station F., who has recently been able to obtain some insight into his private affairs.

Briefly, it seems that Le Chiffre is on the brink of a financial crisis. Certain straws in the wind were noticed by 1860 — some discreet sales of jewellery, the disposal of a villa at Antibes, and a general tendency to check the loose spending which has always been a feature of his way of life. Further inquiries were made with the help of our friends of the Deuxième Bureau (with whom we have been working jointly on this case) and a curious story has come to light.

In January 1946 Le Chiffre bought control of a chain of brothels, known as the 'Cordon Jaune', operating in Normandy and Brittany. He was foolish enough to employ for this purpose some fifty million francs of the moneys entrusted to him by Leningrad Section III for the financing of S.O.D.A., the trade union mentioned above.

Normally the Cordon Jaune would have proved a most excellent investment and it is possible that Le Chiffre was motivated more by a desire to increase his union funds than by the hope of lining his own pocket by speculating with his employers' money. However that may be, it is clear that he could have found many investments more savoury than prostitution, if he had not been tempted by the by-product of unlimited women for his personal use.

Fate rebuked him with terrifying swiftness.

Barely three months later, on the 13th April, there was passed in France Law No. 46685 entitled *Loi Tendant à la Fermeture des Maisons de Tolérance et au Renforcement de la Lutte contre le Proxénitisme.*

(When M. came to this sentence he grunted and pressed a switch on the intercom.

'Head of S?'

'Sir.'

'What the hell does this word mean?' He spelt it out.

'Pimping, sir.'

'This is not the Berlitz School of Languages, Head of S. If you want to show off your knowledge of foreign jaw-breakers, be good enough to provide a crib. Better still, write in English.'

'Sorry, sir.'

M. released the switch and turned back to the memorandum.)

This law (he read), known popularly as 'La Loi Marthe Richard', closing all houses of ill-fame and forbidding the sale of pornographic books and films, knocked the bottom out of his investment almost overnight and suddenly Le Chiffre was faced with a serious deficit in his union funds. In desperation he turned his open houses into 'maisons de passe' where clandestine rendezvous could be arranged on the border-line of the law, and he continued to operate one or two 'cinémas bleus' underground, but these shifts in no way served to cover his overheads, and all attempts to sell his investment, even at a heavy loss, failed dismally. Meanwhile the Police des Mœurs were on his trail and in a short while twenty or more of his establishments were closed down.

The police were, of course, only interested in this man as a big-time brothel-keeper and it was not until we expressed an interest in his finances that the Deuxième Bureau unearthed the parallel dossier which was running with their colleagues of the police department.

The significance of the situation became apparent to us and to our French friends and, in the past few months, a veritable rat-hunt has been operated by the police after the establishments of the Cordon Jaune, with the result that today nothing remains of Le Chiffre's original investment and any routine inquiry would reveal a deficit of around fifty million francs in the trade union funds of which he is the treasurer and paymaster.

It does not seem that the suspicions of Leningrad have been aroused yet but, unfortunately for Le Chiffre, it is possible that at any rate SMERSH is on the scent. Last week a high-grade source of Station P. reported that a senior official of this efficient organ of Soviet vengeance had left Warsaw for Strasbourg via the Eastern sector of Berlin. There is no confirmation of this report from the Deuxième Bureau, nor from the authorities in Strasbourg (who are reliable and thorough), and there is also no news from Le Chiffre's headquarters there, which we have well covered by a double agent (in addition to 1860).

If Le Chiffre knew that SMERSH was on his tail or that they had the smallest suspicion of him, he would have no alternative but to commit suicide or attempt to escape, but his present plans suggest that while he is certainly desperate, he does not yet realize that his life may be at stake. It is these rather spectacular plans of his that have suggested to us a counter-operation which, though risky and unconventional, we submit at the end of this memorandum with confidence.

In brief, Le Chiffre plans, we believe, to follow the example of most other desperate till-robbers and make good the deficit in his accounts by gambling. The 'Bourse' is too slow. So are the various illicit traffics in drugs, or rare medicines, such as aureo- and streptomycin and cortisone. No race tracks could carry the sort of stakes he will have to play and, if he won, he would more likely be killed than paid off.

In any case, we know that he has withdrawn the final twenty-five million francs from the treasury of his union and that he has taken a small villa in the neighbourhood of Royale-les-Eaux, just north of Dieppe, for a week from a fortnight tomorrow.

Now, it is expected that the Casino at Royale will see the highest gambling in Europe this summer. In an effort to wrest the big money from Deauville and Le Touquet, the Société des Bains de Mers de Royale have leased the baccarat and the two top chemin-de-fer tables to the Mahomet Ali Syndicate, a group of émigré Egyptian bankers and businessmen with, it is said, a call on certain royal funds, who have for years been trying to cut in on the profits of Zographos and his Greek associates resulting from their monopoly of the highest French baccarat banks.

With the help of discreet publicity, a considerable number of the biggest operators in America and Europe have been encouraged to book at Royale this summer and it seems possible that this old-fashioned watering-place will regain some of its Victorian renown.

Be that as it may, it is here that Le Chiffre will, we are confident, endeavour on or after 15 June to make a profit at baccarat of fifty million francs on a working capital of twenty-five million. (And, incidentally, save his life.)

Proposed Counter-operation

It would be greatly in the interests of this country and of the other nations of the North Atlantic Treaty Organization that this powerful Soviet agent should be ridiculed and destroyed, that his communist trade union should be bankrupted and brought into disrepute, and that this potential fifth column, with a strength of 50,000, capable in time of war of controlling a wide sector of France's northern frontier, should lose faith and cohesion. All this would result if Le Chiffre could be defeated at the tables. (N.B. Assassination is pointless. Leningrad would quickly cover up his defalcations and make him into a martyr.)

We therefore recommend that the finest gambler available to the Service should be given the necessary funds and endeavour to out-gamble this man.

The risks are obvious and the possible loss to the Secret funds is high, but other operations on which large sums have been hazarded have had fewer chances of success, often for a smaller objective.

If the decision is unfavourable, the only alternative would be to place our information and our recommendations in the hands of the Deuxième Bureau or of our American colleagues of the Central Intelligence Agency in Washington. Both of these organizations would doubtless be delighted to take over the scheme.

Signed: S.

Appendix A.

Name: Le Chiffre.

Aliases: Variations on the words 'cypher' or 'number' in different languages; e.g. 'Herr Ziffer'.

Origin: Unknown.

First encountered as a displaced person, inmate of Dachau D.P. camp in the U.S. Zone of Germany, June 1945. Apparently suffering from amnesia and paralysis of vocal cords (? both feigned). Dumbness succumbed to therapy, but subject continued to claim total loss of memory except associations with Alsace Lorraine and Strasbourg whither he was transferred in September 1945, on Stateless Passport No. 304–596. Adopted the name 'Le Chiffre' ('since I am only a number on a passport'). No Christian names.

Age: About 45.

Description: Height 5 ft. 8 in. Weight 18 stone. Complexion very pale. Clean-shaven. Hair red-brown, 'en brosse'. Eyes very dark brown with whites showing all round iris. Small, rather feminine mouth. False teeth of expensive quality. Ears small, with large lobes, indicating some Jewish blood. Hands small, well-tended, hirsute. Feet small. Racially, subject is probably a mixture of Mediterranean with Prussian or Polish strains. Dresses well and meticulously, generally in dark double-breasted suits. Smokes incessantly Caporals, using a denicotinizing holder. At frequent intervals inhales from benzedrine inhaler. Voice soft and even. Bilingual in French and English. Good German. Traces of Marseillais accent. Smiles infrequently. Does not laugh.

Habits: Mostly expensive, but discreet. Large sexual appetites. Flagellant. Expert driver of fast cars. Adept with small arms and other forms of personal combat, including knives. Carries three Eversharp razor blades, in hat-band, heel of left shoe and cigarette case. Knowledge of accountancy and mathematics. Fine gambler. Always accompanied by two armed guards, well-dressed, one French, one German (details available).

Comment: A formidable and dangerous agent of the U.S.S.R., controlled by Leningrad Section III through Paris.

Signed: Archivist.

Appendix B.

Subject: SMERSH

Sources: Own archives and scanty material made available by Deuxième Bureau and C.I.A. Washington.

SMERSH is a conjunction of two Russian words: 'Smyert Shpionam', meaning roughly: 'Death to Spies'.

Ranks above M.V.D. (formerly N.K.V.D.) and is believed to come under the personal direction of Beria.

Headquarters: Leningrad (sub-station at Moscow).

Its task is the elimination of all forms of treachery and back-sliding within the various branches of the Soviet Secret Service and Secret Police at home and abroad. It is the most powerful and feared organization in the U.S.S.R. and is popularly believed never to have failed in a mission of vengeance.

It is thought that SMERSH was responsible for the assassination of Trotsky in Mexico (22 August 1940) and may indeed have made its name with this successful murder after attempts by other Russian individuals and organizations had failed.

SMERSH was next heard of when Hitler attacked Russia. It was then rapidly expanded to cope with treachery and double agents during the retreat of the Soviet forces in 1941. At that time it worked as an execution squad for the N.K.V.D. and its present selective mission was not so clearly defined.

The organization itself was thoroughly purged after the war and is now believed to consist of only a few hundred operatives of very high quality divided into five sections:

Department I: In charge of counter-intelligence among Soviet organizations at home and abroad.

Department II: Operations, including executions.

Department III: Administration and Finance.

Department IV: Investigations and legal work. Personnel.

Department V: Prosecutions: the section which passes final judgement on all victims.

Only one SMERSH operative has come into our hands since the war: Goytchev, alias Garrad-Jones. He shot Petchora, medical officer at the Yugoslav Embassy, in Hyde Park, 7 August 1948. During interrogation he committed suicide by swallowing a coat-button of compressed potassium cyanide. He revealed nothing beyond his membership of SMERSH, of which he was arrogantly boastful.

We believe that the following British double agents were victims of SMERSH: Donovan, Harthrop-Vane, Elizabeth Dumont, Ventnor, Mace, Savarin. (For details see Morgue: Section Q.)

Conclusion: Every effort should be made to improve our knowledge of this very powerful organization and destroy its operatives.

3

NUMBER 007

HEAD OF S. (the section of the Secret Service concerned with the Soviet Union) was so keen on his plan for the destruction of Le Chiffre, and it was basically his own plan, that he took the memorandum himself and went up to the top floor of the gloomy building overlooking Regent's Park and through the green baize door and along the corridor to the end room.

He walked belligerently up to M.'s chief of staff, a young sapper who had earned his spurs as one of the secretariat to the Chiefs of Staff committee after having been wounded during a sabotage operation in 1944, and had kept his sense of humour in spite of both experiences.

'Now look here, Bill. I want to sell something to the Chief. Is this a good moment?'

'What do you think, Penny?' The Chief of Staff turned to M.'s private secretary who shared the room with him.

Miss Moneypenny would have been desirable but for her eyes which were cool and direct and quizzical.

'Should be all right. He won a bit of a victory at the F.O. this morning and he's not got anyone for the next half an hour.' She smiled encouragingly at Head of S. whom she liked for himself and for the importance of his section.

'Well, here's the dope, Bill.' He handed over the black folder with the red star which stood for Top Secret. 'And for God's sake look enthusiastic when you give it him. And tell him I'll wait here and read a good code-book while he's considering it. He may want some more details, and anyway I want to see you two don't pester him with anything else until he's finished.'

'All right, sir.' The Chief of Staff pressed a switch and leant towards the intercom on his desk.

'Yes?' asked a quiet, flat voice.

'Head of S. has an urgent docket for you, sir.'

There was a pause.

'Bring it in,' said the voice.

The Chief of Staff released the switch and stood up.

'Thanks, Bill. I'll be next door,' said Head of S.

The Chief of Staff crossed his office and went through the double doors leading into M.'s room. In a moment he came out and over the entrance a small blue light burned the warning that M. was not to be disturbed.

Later, a triumphant Head of S. said to his Number Two: 'We nearly cooked ourselves with that last paragraph. He said it was subversion and blackmail. He got pretty sharp about it. Anyway, he approves. Says the idea's crazy, but worth trying if the Treasury will play and he thinks they will. He's going to tell them it's a better gamble than the money we're putting into deserting Russian colonels who turn double after a few months' asylum here. And he's longing to get at Le Chiffre, and anyway he's got the right man and wants to try him out on the job.'

'Who is it?' asked Number Two.

'One of the Double O's — I guess 007. He's tough and M. thinks there may be trouble with those gunmen of Le Chiffre's. He must be pretty good with the cards or he wouldn't have sat in the Casino in Monte Carlo for two months before the war watching that Roumanian team work their stuff with the invisible ink and the dark glasses. He and the Deuxième bowled them out in the end and 007 turned in a million francs he had won at shemmy. Good money in those days.'

James Bond's interview with M. had been short.

'What about it, Bond?' asked M. when Bond came back into his room after reading Head of S.'s memorandum and after gazing for ten minutes out of the waiting-room window at the distant trees in the park.

Bond looked across the desk into the shrewd, clear eyes.

'It's very kind of you, sir, I'd like to do it. But I can't promise to win. The odds at baccarat are the best-after "trente et quarante" — evens except for the tiny "cagnotte" — but I might get a bad run against me and get cleaned out. Play's going to be pretty high — opening'll go up to half a million, I should think.'

Bond was stopped by the cold eyes. M. knew all this already, knew the odds at baccarat as well as Bond. That was his job — knowing the odds at everything, and knowing men, his own and the opposition's. Bond wished he had kept quiet about his misgivings.

'He can have a bad run too,' said M. 'You'll have plenty of capital. Up to twenty-five million, the same as him. We'll start you on ten and send you another ten when you've had a look round. You can make the extra five yourself.' He smiled. 'Go over a few days before the big game starts and get your hand in. Have a talk to Q. about rooms and trains, and any equipment you want. The Paymaster will fix the funds. I'm going to ask the Deuxième to stand by. It's their territory and as it is we shall be lucky if they don't kick up rough. I'll try and persuade them to send Mathis. You seemed to get on well with him in Monte Carlo on that other Casino job. And I'm going to tell Washington because of the N.A.T.O. angle. C.I.A. have got one or two good men at Fontainebleau with the joint intelligence chaps there. Anything else?'

Bond shook his head. 'I'd certainly like to have Mathis, sir.'

'Well, we'll see. Try and bring it off. We're going to look pretty foolish if you don't. And watch out. This sounds an amusing job, but I don't think it's going to be. Le Chiffre is a good man. Well, best of luck.'

'Thank you, sir,' said Bond and went to the door.

'Just a minute.'

Bond turned.

'I think I'll keep you covered, Bond. Two heads are better than one and you'll need someone to run your communications. I'll think it over. They'll get in touch with you at Royale. You needn't worry. It'll be someone good.'

Bond would have preferred to work alone, but one didn't argue with M. He left the room hoping that the man they sent would be loyal to him and neither stupid nor, worse still, ambitious.

4

'L'ENNEMI ÉCOUTE'

AS, TWO WEEKS later, James Bond awoke in his room at the Hotel Splendide, some of this history passed through his mind.

He had arrived at Royale-les-Eaux in time for luncheon two days before. There had been no attempt to contact him and there had been no flicker of curiosity when he had signed the register 'James Bond, Port Maria, Jamaica'.

M. had expressed no interest in his cover.

'Once you start to make a set at Le Chiffre at the tables, you'll have had it,' he said. 'But wear a cover that will stick with the general public.'

Bond knew Jamaica well, so he asked to be controlled from there and to pass as a Jamaican plantocrat whose father had made his pile in tobacco and sugar and whose son chose to play it away on the stock markets and in casinos. If inquiries were made, he would quote Charles Da Silva of Caffery's, Kingston, as his attorney. Charles would make the story stick.

Bond had spent the last two afternoons and most of the nights at the Casino, playing complicated progression systems on the even chances at roulette. He made a high banco at chemin-de-fer whenever he heard one offered. If he lost, he would 'suivi' once and not chase it further if he lost the second time.

In this way he had made some three million francs and had given his nerves and card-sense a thorough work-out. He had got the geography of the Casino clear in his mind. Above all, he had been able to observe Le Chiffre at the tables and to note ruefully that he was a faultless and lucky gambler.

Bond liked to make a good breakfast. After a cold shower, he sat at the writing-table in front of the window. He looked out at the beautiful day and consumed half a pint of iced orange juice, three scrambled eggs and bacon and a double portion of coffee without sugar. He lit his first cigarette, a Balkan and

Turkish mixture made for him by Morlands of Grosvenor Street, and watched the small waves lick the long seashore and the fishing fleet from Dieppe string out towards the June heat-haze followed by a paperchase of herring-gulls.

He was lost in his thoughts when the telephone rang. It was the concierge announcing that a Director of Radio Stentor was waiting below with the wireless set he had ordered from Paris.

'Of course,' said Bond. 'Send him up.'

This was the cover fixed by the Deuxième Bureau for their liaison man with Bond. Bond watched the door, hoping that it would be Mathis.

When Mathis came in, a respectable business-man carrying a large square parcel by its leather handle, Bond smiled broadly and would have greeted him with warmth if Mathis had not frowned and held up his free hand after carefully closing the door.

'I have just arrived from Paris, monsieur, and here is the set you asked to have on approval — five valves, superhet, I think you call it in England, and you should be able to get most of the capitals of Europe from Royale. There are no mountains for forty miles in any direction.'

'It sounds all right,' said Bond, lifting his eyebrows at this mystery-making.

Mathis paid no attention. He placed the set, which he had unwrapped, on the floor beside the unlit panel electric fire below the mantelpiece.

'It is just past eleven,' he said, 'and I see that the "Compagnons de la Chanson" should now be on the medium wave from Rome. They are touring Europe. Let us see what the reception is like. It should be a fair test.'

He winked. Bond noticed that he had turned the volume on to full and that the red light indicating the long-wave band was illuminated, though the set was still silent.

Mathis fiddled at the back of the set. Suddenly an appalling roar of static filled the small room. Mathis gazed at the set for a few seconds with benevolence and then turned it off and his voice was full of dismay.

'My dear monsieur — forgive me please — badly tuned,' and he again bent to the dials. After a few adjustments the close harmony of the French came over the air and Mathis walked up and clapped Bond very hard on the back and wrung his hand until Bond's fingers ached.

Bond smiled back at him. 'Now what the hell?' he asked.

'My dear friend,' Mathis was delighted, 'you are blown, blown, blown. Up there,' he pointed at the ceiling, 'at this moment, either Monsieur Muntz or his alleged wife, allegedly bedridden with the *grippe*, is deafened, absolutely deafened, and I hope in agony.' He grinned with pleasure at Bond's frown of disbelief.

Mathis sat down on the bed and ripped open a packet of Caporal with his thumbnail. Bond waited.

Mathis was satisfied with the sensation his words had caused. He became serious.

'How it has happened I don't know. They must have been on to you for several days before you arrived. The opposition is here in real strength. Above you is the Muntz family. He is German. She is from somewhere in Central Europe, perhaps a Czech. This is an old-fashioned hotel. There are disused chimneys behind these electric fires. Just here,' he pointed a few inches above the panel fire, 'is suspended a very powerful radio pick-up. The wires run up the chimney to behind the Muntzes' electric fire where there is an amplifier. In their room is a wire-recorder and a pair of earphones on which the Muntzes listen in turn. That is why Madame Muntz has the grippe and takes all her meals in bed and why Monsieur Muntz has to be constantly at her side instead of enjoying the sunshine and the gambling of this delightful resort.

'Some of this we knew because in France we are very clever. The rest we confirmed by unscrewing your electric fire a few hours before you got here.'

Suspiciously Bond walked over and examined the screws which secured the panel to the wall. Their grooves showed minute scratches.

'Now it is time for a little more play-acting,' said Mathis. He walked over to the radio, which was still transmitting close harmony to its audience of three, and switched it off.

'Are you satisfied, monsieur?' he asked. 'You notice how clearly they come over. Are they not a wonderful team?' He made a winding motion with his right hand and raised his eyebrows.

'They are so good,' said Bond, 'that I would like to hear the rest of the programme.' He grinned at the thought of the angry glances which the Muntzes must be exchanging overhead. 'The machine itself seems splendid. Just what I was looking for to take back to Jamaica.'

Mathis made a sarcastic grimace and switched back to the Rome programme.

'You and your Jamaica,' he said, and sat down again on the bed.

Bond frowned at him. 'Well, it's no good crying over spilt milk,' he said. 'We didn't expect the cover to stick for long, but it's worrying that they bowled it out so soon.' He searched his mind in vain for a clue. Could the Russians have broken one of our ciphers? If so, he might just as well pack up and go home. He and his job would have been stripped naked.

Mathis seemed to read his mind. 'It can't have been a cipher,' he said. 'Anyway, we told London at once and they will have changed them. A pretty flap we caused, I can tell you.' He smiled with the satisfaction of a friendly rival. 'And now to business, before our good "Compagnons" run out of breath.

'First of all,' and he inhaled a thick lungful of Caporal, 'you will be pleased with your Number Two. She is very beautiful (Bond frowned), very beautiful indeed.' Satisfied with Bond's reaction, Mathis continued: 'She has black hair, blue eyes, and splendid . . . er . . . protuberances. Back and front,' he added. 'And she is a wireless expert which, though sexually less interesting, makes her a perfect employee of Radio Stentor and assistant to myself in my capacity as wireless salesman for this rich summer season down here.' He grinned. 'We are both staying in the hotel and my assistant will thus be on hand in case your new radio breaks down. All new machines, even French ones, are apt to have teething troubles in the first day or two. And occasionally at night,' he added with an exaggerated wink.

Bond was not amused. 'What the hell do they want to send me a woman for?' he said bitterly. 'Do they think this is a bloody picnic?'

Mathis interrupted. 'Calm yourself, my dear James. She is as serious as you could wish and as cold as an icicle. She speaks French like a native and knows her job backwards. Her cover's perfect and I have arranged for her to team up with you quite smoothly. What is more natural than that you should pick up a pretty girl here? As a Jamaican millionaire,' he coughed respectfully, 'what with your hot blood and all, you would look naked without one.'

Bond grunted dubiously.

'Any other surprises?' he asked suspiciously.

'Nothing very much,' answered Mathis. 'Le Chiffre is installed in his villa. It's about ten miles down the coast road. He has his two guards with him. They look pretty capable fellows. One of them has been seen visiting a little *pension* in the town where three mysterious and rather subhuman characters checked in two days ago. They may be part of the team. Their papers are in order — stateless Czechs apparently — but one of our men says the language they talk in their room is Bulgarian. We don't see many of those around. They're mostly used against the Turks and the Yugoslavs. They're stupid, but obedient. The Russians use them for simple killings or as fall-guys for more complicated ones.'

'Thanks very much. Which is mine to be?' asked Bond. 'Anything else?'

'No. Come to the bar of the Hermitage before lunch. I'll fix the introduction. Ask her to dinner this evening. Then it will be natural for her to come into the Casino with you. I'll be there too, but in the background. I've got one or two good chaps and we'll keep an eye on you. Oh, and there's an American called Leiter here, staying in the hotel. Felix Leiter. He's the C.I.A. chap from Fontainebleau. London told me to tell you. He looks okay. May come in useful.'

A torrent of Italian burst from the wireless set on the floor. Mathis switched it off and they exchanged some phrases about the set and about how Bond should pay for it. Then with effusive farewells and a final wink Mathis bowed himself out.

Bond sat at the window and gathered his thoughts. Nothing that Mathis had told him was reassuring. He was completely blown and under really professional surveillance. An attempt might be made to put him away even before he had a chance to pit himself against Le Chiffre at the tables. The Russians had no stupid prejudices about murder. And then there was this pest of a girl. He sighed. Women were for recreation. On a job, they got in the way and fogged things up with sex and hurt feelings and all the emotional baggage they carried around. One had to look out for them and take care of them.

'Bitch,' said Bond, and then remembering the Muntzes, he said 'bitch' again more loudly and walked out of the room.

5

THE GIRL FROM HEADQUARTERS

IT WAS TWELVE o'clock when Bond left the Splendide and the clock on the *mairie* was stumbling through its midday carillon. There was a strong scent of pine and mimosa in the air and the freshly watered gardens of the Casino opposite, interspersed with neat gravel parterres and paths, lent the scene a pretty formalism more appropriate to ballet than to melodrama.

The sun shone and there was a gaiety and sparkle in the air which seemed to promise well for the new era of fashion and prosperity for which the little seaside town, after many vicissitudes, was making its gallant bid.

Royale-les-Eaux, which lies near the mouth of the Somme before the flat coast-line soars up from the beaches of southern Picardy to the Brittany cliffs which run on to Le Havre, had experienced much the same fortunes as Trouville.

Royale (without the 'Eaux') also started as a small fishing-village and its rise to fame as a fashionable watering-place during the Second Empire was as meteoric as that of Trouville. But as Deauville killed Trouville, so, after a long period of decline, did Le Touquet kill Royale.

At the turn of the century, when things were going badly for the little seaside town and when the fashion was to combine pleasure with 'a cure', a natural spring in the hills behind Royale was discovered to contain enough diluted sulphur to have a beneficent effect on the liver. Since all French people suffer from liver complaints, Royale quickly became 'Royale-les-Eaux', and 'Eau Royale', in a torpedo-shaped bottle, grafted itself demurely on to the tail of the mineral-water lists in hotels and restaurant cars.

It did not long withstand the powerful combines of Vichy and Perrier and Vittel. There came a series of lawsuits, a number of people lost a lot of money and very soon its sale was again entirely local. Royale fell back on the takings from French and English families during the summer, on its fishing-fleet in winter and on the crumbs which fell to its elegantly dilapidated casino from the tables at Le Touquet.

But there was something splendid about the Negresco baroque of the Casino Royale, a strong whiff of Victorian elegance and luxury, and in 1950 Royale caught the fancy of a syndicate in Paris which disposed of large funds belonging to a group of expatriate Vichyites.

Brighton had been revived since the war, and Nice. Nostalgia for more spacious, golden times might be a source of revenue.

The Casino was repainted in its original white and gilt and the rooms decorated in the palest grey with wine-red carpets and curtains. Vast chandeliers were suspended from the ceilings. The gardens were spruced and the fountains played again and the two main hotels, the Splendide and the Hermitage, were prinked and furbished and restaffed.

Even the small town and the 'vieux-port' managed to fix welcoming smiles across their ravaged faces, and the main street became gay with the *vitrines* of great Paris jewellers and couturiers, tempted down for a butterfly season by rent-free sites and lavish promises.

Then the Mahomet Ali Syndicate was cajoled into starting a high game in the Casino and the 'Société des Bains de Mer de Royale' felt that now at last Le Touquet would have to yield up some of the treasure stolen over the years from its parent *plage*.

Against the background of this luminous and sparkling stage Bond stood in the sunshine and felt his mission to be incongruous and remote and his dark profession an affront to his fellow actors.

He shrugged away the momentary feeling of unease and walked round the back of his hotel and down the ramp to the garage. Before his rendezvous at the Hermitage he decided to take his car down the coast road and have a quick look at Le Chiffre's villa and then drive back by the inland road until it crossed the *route nationale* to Paris.

Bond's car was his only personal hobby. One of the last of the $4\frac{1}{2}$-litre Bentleys with the supercharger by Amherst Villiers, he had bought it almost new in 1933 and had kept it in careful storage through the war. It was still serviced every year and, in London, a former Bentley mechanic, who worked in a garage near Bond's Chelsea flat, tended it with jealous care. Bond drove it hard and well and with an almost sensual pleasure. It was a battleship-grey convertible coupé, which really did convert, and it was capable of touring at ninety with thirty miles an hour in reserve.

Bond eased the car out of the garage and up the ramp and soon the loitering drum-beat of the two-inch exhaust was echoing down the tree-lined boulevard, through the crowded main street of the little town, and off through the sand dunes to the south.

An hour later, Bond walked into the Hermitage bar and chose a table near one of the broad windows.

The room was sumptuous with those over-masculine trappings which, together with briar pipes and wire-haired terriers, spell luxury in France. Everything was brass-studded leather and polished mahogany. The curtains and carpets were in royal blue. The waiters wore striped waistcoats and green baize aprons. Bond ordered an Americano and examined the sprinkling of over-dressed customers, mostly from Paris he guessed, who sat talking with focus and vivacity, creating that theatrically clubbable atmosphere of 'l'heure de l'apéritif'.

The men were drinking inexhaustible quarter-bottles of champagne, the women dry martinis.

'Moi, j'adore le "Dry",' a bright-faced girl at the next table said to her companion, too neat in his unseasonable tweeds, who gazed at her with moist brown eyes over the top of an expensive shooting-stick from Hermès, 'fait avec du Gordon's, bien entendu.'

'D'accord, Daisy. Mais tu sais, un zeste de citron . . . '

Bond's eye was caught by the tall figure of Mathis on the pavement outside, his face turned in animation to a dark-haired girl in grey. His arm was linked in hers, high up above the elbow, and yet there was a lack of intimacy in their appearance, an ironical chill in the girl's profile, which made them seem two separate people rather than a couple. Bond waited for them to come through the street-door into the bar, but for appearances' sake continued to stare out of the window at the passers-by.

'But surely it is Monsieur Bond?' Mathis's voice behind him was full of surprised delight. Bond, appropriately flustered, rose to his feet. 'Can it be that you are alone? Are you awaiting someone? May I present my colleague, Mademoiselle Lynd? My dear, this is the gentleman from Jamaica with whom I had the pleasure of doing business this morning.'

Bond inclined himself with a reserved friendliness. 'It would be a great pleasure,' he addressed himself to the girl. 'I am alone. Would you both care to join me?' He pulled out a chair and while they sat down he beckoned to a waiter and despite Mathis's expostulations insisted on ordering the drinks — a 'fine à l'eau' for Mathis and a Bacardi for the girl.

Mathis and Bond exchanged cheerful talk about the fine weather and the prospects of a revival in the fortunes of Royale-les-Eaux. The girl sat silent. She accepted one of Bond's cigarettes, examined it and then smoked it appreciatively and without affectation, drawing the smoke deeply into her lungs with a little sigh and then exhaling it casually through her lips and nostrils. Her movements were economical and precise with no trace of self-consciousness.

Bond felt her presence strongly. While he and Mathis talked, he turned from time to time towards her, politely including her in the conversation, but adding up the impressions recorded by each glance.

Her hair was very black and she wore it cut square and low on the nape of the neck, framing her face to below the clear and beautiful line of her jaw. Although it was heavy and moved with the movements of her head, she did not constantly pat it back into place, but let it alone. Her eyes were wide apart and deep blue and they gazed candidly back at Bond with a touch of ironical disinterest which, to his annoyance, he found he would like to shatter, roughly. Her skin was lightly suntanned and bore no trace of make-up except on her mouth which was wide and sensual. Her bare arms and hands had a quality of repose and the general impression of restraint in her appearance and movements was carried even to her finger-nails which were unpainted and cut short. Round her neck she wore a plain gold chain of wide flat links and on the fourth finger of the right hand a broad topaz ring. Her medium-length dress was of grey 'soie sauvage' with a square-cut bodice, lasciviously tight across her fine breasts. The skirt was closely pleated and flowed down from a narrow, but not a thin, waist. She wore a three-inch, hand-stitched black belt. A hand-stitched black 'sabretache' rested on the chair beside her, together with a wide cartwheel hat of gold straw, its crown encircled by a thin black velvet ribbon which tied at the back in a short bow. Her shoes were square-toed of plain black leather.

Bond was excited by her beauty and intrigued by her composure. The prospect of working with her stimulated him. At the same time he felt a vague disquiet. On an impulse he touched wood.

Mathis had noticed Bond's preoccupation. After a time he rose.

'Forgive me,' he said to the girl, 'while I telephone to the Dubernes. I must arrange my rendezvous for dinner tonight. Are you sure you won't mind being left to your own devices this evening?'

She shook her head.

Bond took the cue and, as Mathis crossed the room to the telephone booth beside the bar, he said: 'If you are going to be alone tonight, would you care to have dinner with me?'

She smiled with the first hint of conspiracy she had shown. 'I would like to very much,' she said, 'and then perhaps you would chaperone me to the Casino where Monsieur Mathis tells me you are very much at home. Perhaps I will bring you luck.'

With Mathis gone, her attitude towards him showed a sudden warmth. She seemed to acknowledge that they were a team and, as they discussed the time and place of their meeting, Bond realized that it would be quite easy after all to plan the details of his project with her. He felt that after all she was interested and excited by her role and that she would work willingly with him. He had imagined many hurdles before establishing a rapport, but now he felt he could get straight down to professional details. He was quite honest to himself about the hypocrisy of his attitude towards her. As a woman, he wanted to sleep with her, but only when the job had been done.

When Mathis came back to the table Bond called for his bill. He explained that he was expected back at his hotel to have lunch with friends. When for a moment he held her hand in his he felt a warmth of affection and understanding pass between them that would have seemed impossible half an hour earlier.

The girl's eyes followed him out on to the boulevard.

Mathis moved his chair close to hers and said softly: 'That is a very good friend of mine. I am glad you have met each other. I can already feel the ice-floes on the two rivers breaking up.' He smiled. 'I don't think Bond has ever been melted. It will be a new experience for him. And for you.'

She did not answer him directly.

'He is very good-looking. He reminds me rather of Hoagy Carmichael, but there is something cold and ruthless in his . . .'

The sentence was never finished. Suddenly a few feet away the entire plate-glass window shivered into confetti. The blast of a terrific explosion, very near, hit them so that they were rocked back in their chairs. There was an instant of silence. Some objects pattered down on to the pavement outside. Bottles slowly toppled off the shelves behind the bar. Then there were screams and a stampede for the door.

'Stay there,' said Mathis.

He kicked back his chair and hurtled through the empty window-frame on to the pavement.

6

TWO MEN IN STRAW HATS

WHEN BOND LEFT the bar he walked purposefully along the pavement flanking the tree-lined boulevard towards his hotel a few hundred yards away. He was hungry.

The day was still beautiful, but by now the sun was very hot and the plane-trees, spaced about twenty feet apart on the grass verge between the pavement and the broad tarmac, gave a cool shade.

There were few people abroad and the two men standing quietly under a tree on the opposite side of the boulevard looked out of place.

Bond noticed them when he was still a hundred yards away and when the same distance separated them from the ornamental *porte-cochère* of the Splendide.

There was something rather disquieting about their appearance. They were both small and they were dressed alike in dark and, Bond reflected, rather hot-looking suits. They had the appearance of a variety turn waiting for a bus on the way to the theatre. Each wore a straw hat with a thick black ribbon as a concession, perhaps, to the holiday atmosphere of the resort, and the brims of these and the shadow from the tree under which they stood obscured their faces. Incongruously, each dark, squat little figure was illuminated by a touch of bright colour. They were both carrying square camera-cases slung from the shoulder.

And one case was bright red and the other case bright blue.

By the time Bond had taken in these details, he had come to within fifty yards of the two men. He was reflecting on the ranges of various types of weapon and the possibilities of cover when an extraordinary and terrible scene was enacted.

Red-man seemed to give a short nod to Blue-man. With a quick movement Blue-man unslung his blue camera-case. Blue-man, and Bond could not see exactly as the trunk of a plane-tree beside him just then intervened to obscure his vision, bent forward and seemed to fiddle with the case. Then with a blinding flash of white light there was the earsplitting crack of a monstrous explosion and Bond, despite the protection of the tree-trunk, was slammed down to the pavement by a solid bolt of hot air which dented his cheeks and stomach as if they had been made of paper. He lay, gazing up at the sun, while the air (or so it seemed to him) went on twanging with the explosion as if someone had hit the bass register of a piano with a sledge hammer.

When, dazed and half-conscious, he raised himself on one knee, a ghastly rain of pieces of flesh and shreds of blood-soaked clothing fell on him and around him, mingled with branches and gravel. Then a shower of small twigs and leaves. From all sides came the sharp tinkle of falling glass. Above in the sky hung a mushroom of black smoke which rose and dissolved as he drunkenly watched it. There was an obscene smell of high explosive, of burning wood, and of, yes, that was it — roast mutton. For fifty yards down the boulevard the trees were leafless and charred. Opposite, two of them had snapped off near the base and lay drunkenly across the road. Between them there was a still smoking crater. Of the two men in straw hats, there remained absolutely nothing. But there were red traces on the road, and on the pavements and against the trunks of the trees, and there were glittering shreds high up in the branches.

Bond felt himself starting to vomit.

It was Mathis who got to him first, and by that time Bond was standing with his arm round the tree which had saved his life.

Stupefied, but unharmed, he allowed Mathis to lead him off towards the Splendide from which guests and servants were pouring in chattering fright. As the distant clang of bells heralded the arrival of ambulances and fire-engines, they managed to push through the throng and up the short stairs and along the corridor to Bond's room.

Mathis paused only to turn on the radio in front of the fireplace, then, while Bond stripped off his blood-flecked clothes, Mathis sprayed him with questions.

When it came to the description of the two men, Mathis tore the telephone off its hook beside Bond's bed.

'. . . and tell the police,' he concluded, 'tell them that the Englishman from Jamaica who was knocked over by the blast is my affair. He is unhurt and they are not to worry him. I will explain to them in half an hour. They should tell the Press that it was apparently a vendetta between two Bulgarian communists and that one killed the other with a bomb. They need say nothing of the third Bulgar who must have been hanging about somewhere, but they must get him at all costs. He will certainly head for Paris. Road-blocks everywhere. Understood? *Alors, bonne chance.*'

Mathis turned back to Bond and heard him to the end.

'*Merde*, but you were lucky,' he said when Bond had finished. 'Clearly the bomb was intended for you. It must have been faulty. They intended to throw it and then dodge behind their tree. But it all came out the other way round. Never mind. We will discover the facts.' He paused. 'But certainly it is a curious affair. And these people appear to be taking you seriously.' Mathis looked affronted. 'But how did these *sacré* Bulgars intend to escape capture? And what was the significance of the red and the blue cases? We must try and find some fragments of the red one.'

Mathis bit his nails. He was excited and his eyes glittered. This was becoming a formidable and dramatic affair, in many aspects of which he was now involved personally. Certainly it was no longer just a case of holding Bond's coat while he had his private battle with Le Chiffre in the Casino. Mathis jumped up.

'Now get a drink and some lunch and a rest,' he ordered Bond. 'For me, I must get my nose quickly into this affair before the police have muddied the trail with their big black boots.'

Mathis turned off the radio and waved an affectionate farewell. The door slammed and silence settled on the room. Bond sat for a while by the window and enjoyed being alive.

Later, as Bond was finishing his first straight whisky 'on the rocks' and was contemplating the pâté de foie gras and cold langouste which the waiter had just laid out for him, the telephone rang.

'This is Mademoiselle Lynd.'

The voice was low and anxious.

'Are you all right?'

'Yes, quite.'

'I'm glad. Please take care of yourself.'

She rang off.

Bond shook himself, then he picked up his knife and selected the thickest of the pieces of hot toast.

He suddenly thought: two of them are dead, and I have got one more on my side. It's a start.

He dipped the knife into the glass of very hot water which stood beside the pot of Strasbourg porcelain and reminded himself to tip the waiter doubly for this particular meal.

7

'ROUGE ET NOIR'

BOND WAS DETERMINED to be completely fit and relaxed for a gambling session which might last most of the night. He ordered a masseur for three o'clock. After the remains of his luncheon had been removed, he sat at his window gazing out to sea until there came a knock on the door as the masseur, a Swede, presented himself.

Silently he got to work on Bond from his feet to his neck, melting the tensions in his body and calming his still twanging nerves. Even the long purpling bruises down Bond's left shoulder and side ceased to throb, and when the Swede had gone Bond fell into a dreamless sleep.

He awoke in the evening completely refreshed.

After a cold shower, Bond walked over to the Casino. Since the night before he had lost the mood of the tables. He needed to re-establish that focus which is half mathematical and half intuitive and which, with a slow pulse and a sanguine temperament, Bond knew to be the essential equipment of any gambler who was set on winning.

Bond had always been a gambler. He loved the dry riffle of the cards and the constant unemphatic drama of the quiet figures round the green tables. He liked the solid, studied comfort of card-rooms and casinos, the well-padded arms of the chairs, the glass of champagne or whisky at the elbow, the quiet unhurried attention of good servants. He was amused by the impartiality of the roulette ball and of the playing cards — and their eternal bias. He liked being an actor and a spectator and from his chair to take part in other men's dramas and decisions, until it came to his own turn to say that vital 'yes' or 'no', generally on a fifty-fifty chance.

Above all, he liked it that everything was one's own fault. There was only oneself to praise or blame. Luck was a servant and not a master. Luck had to be accepted with a shrug or taken advantage of up to the hilt. But it had to be understood and recognized for what it was and not confused with a faulty appreciation of the odds, for, at gambling, the deadly sin is to mistake bad play for bad luck. And luck in all its moods had to be loved and not feared. Bond saw luck as a woman, to be softly wooed or brutally ravaged, never pandered to or pursued. But he was honest enough to admit that he had never yet been made to suffer by cards or by women. One day, and he accepted the fact, he would be brought to his knees by love or by luck. When that happened he knew that he too would be branded with the deadly question-mark he recognized so often in others, the promise to pay before you have lost: the acceptance of fallibility.

But on this June evening when Bond walked through the 'kitchen' into the salle privée, it was with a sensation of confidence and cheerful anticipation that he changed a million francs into plaques of fifty mille and took a seat next to the chef de partie at Roulette Table Number 1.

Bond borrowed the chef's card and studied the run of the ball since the session had started at three o'clock that afternoon. He always did this although he knew that each turn of the wheel, each fall of the ball into a numbered slot, has absolutely no connexion with its predecessor. He accepted that the game begins afresh each time the croupier picks up the ivory ball with his right hand, gives one of the four spokes of the wheel a controlled twist clockwise with the same hand and, with a third motion, also with the right hand, flicks the ball round the outer rim of the wheel anti-clockwise, against its spin.

It was obvious that all this ritual and all the mechanical minutiae of the wheel, of the numbered slots and the cylinder, had been devised and perfected over the years so that neither the skill of the croupier nor any bias in the wheel could affect the fall of the ball. And yet it is a convention among roulette players, and Bond rigidly adhered to it, to take careful note of the past history of each session and to be guided by any peculiarities in the run of the wheel. To note, for instance, and consider significant, sequences of more than two on a single number or of more than four at the other chances down to evens.

Bond didn't defend the practice. He simply maintained that the more effort and ingenuity you put into gambling, the more you took out.

On the record of that particular table, after about three hours' play, Bond could see little of interest except that the last dozen had been out of favour. It was his practice to play always with the wheel, and only to turn against its previous pattern and start on a new tack after a zero had turned up. So he decided to play one of his favourite gambits and back two — in this case the first two — dozens, each with the maximum — one hundred thousand francs. He thus had two-thirds of the board covered (less the zero) and, since the dozens pay odds of two to one, he stood to win a hundred thousand francs every time any number lower than 25 turned up.

After seven coups he had won six times. He lost on the seventh when thirty came up. His net profit was half a million francs. He kept off the table for the eighth throw. Zero turned up. This piece of luck cheered him further and, accepting the thirty as a finger-post to the last dozen, he decided to back the first and last dozens until he had lost twice. Ten throws later the middle dozen came up twice, costing him four hundred thousand francs, but he rose from the table eleven hundred thousand francs to the good.

Directly Bond had started playing in maximums, his game had become the centre of interest at the table. As he seemed to be in luck, one or two pilot fish started to swim with the shark. Sitting directly opposite, one of these, whom Bond took to be an American, had shown more than the usual friendliness and pleasure at his share of the winning streak. He had smiled once or twice across the table, and there was something pointed in the way he duplicated Bond's movements, placing his two modest plaques of ten mille exactly opposite Bond's larger ones. When Bond rose, he too pushed back his chair and called cheerfully across the table:

'Thanks for the ride. Guess I owe you a drink. Will you join me?'

Bond had a feeling that this might be the C.I.A. man. He knew he was right as they strolled off together towards the bar, after Bond had thrown a plaque of ten mille to the croupier and had given a mille to the 'huissier' who drew back his chair.

'My name's Felix Leiter,' said the American. 'Glad to meet you.'

'Mine's Bond — James Bond.'

'Oh yes,' said his companion, 'and now let's see. What shall we have to celebrate?'

Bond insisted on ordering Leiter's Haig-and-Haig 'on the rocks' and then he looked carefully at the barman.

'A dry martini,' he said. 'One. In a deep champagne goblet.'

'Oui, monsieur.'

'Just a moment. Three measures of Gordon's, one of vodka, half a measure of Kina Lillet. Shake it very well until it's ice-cold, then add a large thin slice of lemon-peel. Got it?'

'Certainlv, monsieur.' The barman seemed pleased with the idea.

'Gosh, that's certainly a drink,' said Leiter.

Bond laughed. 'When I'm . . . er . . . concentrating,' he explained, 'I never have more than one drink before dinner. But I do like that one to be large and very strong and very cold and very well-made. I hate small portions of anything, particularly when they taste bad. This drink's my own invention. I'm going to patent it when I can think of a good name.'

He watched carefully as the deep glass became frosted with the pale golden drink, slightly aerated by the bruising of the shaker. He reached for it and took a long sip.

'Excellent,' he said to the barman, 'but if you can get a vodka made with grain instead of potatoes, you will find it still better.'

'Mais n'enculons pas des mouches,' he added in an aside to the barman. The barman grinned.

'That's a vulgar way of saying "we won't split hairs",' explained Bond.

But Leiter was still interested in Bond's drink. 'You certainly think things out,' he said with amusement as they carried their glasses to a corner of the room. He lowered his voice:

'You'd better call it the "Molotov Cocktail" after the one you tasted this afternoon.'

They sat down. Bond laughed.

'I see that the spot marked "X" has been roped off and they're making cars take a detour over the pavement. I hope it hasn't frightened away any of the big money.'

'People are accepting the communist story or else they think it was a burst gas-main. All the burnt trees are coming down tonight and if they work things here like they do at Monte Carlo, there won't be a trace of the mess left in the morning.'

Leiter shook a Chesterfield out of his pack. 'I'm glad to be working with you on this job,' he said, looking into his drink, 'so I'm particularly glad you didn't get blown to glory. Our people are definitely interested. They think it's just as important as your friends do and they don't think there's anything crazy about it at all. In fact, Washington's pretty sick we're not running the show, but you know what the big brass is like. I expect your fellows are much the same in London.'

Bond nodded. 'Apt to be a bit jealous of their scoops,' he admitted.

'Anyway, I'm under your orders and I'm to give you any help you ask for. With Mathis and his boys here, there may not be much that isn't taken care of already. But, anyway, here I am.'

'I'm delighted you are,' said Bond. 'The opposition has got me, and probably you and Mathis too, all weighed up and it seems no holds are going to be barred. I'm glad Le Chiffre seems as desperate as we thought he was. I'm afraid I haven't got anything very specific for you to do, but I'd be grateful if you'd stick around the Casino this evening. I've got an assistant, a Miss Lynd, and I'd like to hand her over to you when I start playing. You won't be ashamed of her. She's a good-looking girl.' He smiled at Leiter. 'And you might mark his two gunmen. I can't imagine he'll try a rough-house, but you never know.'

'I may be able to help,' said Leiter. 'I was a regular in our Marine Corps before I joined this racket, if that means anything to you.' He looked at Bond with a hint of self-deprecation.

'It does,' said Bond.

It turned out that Leiter was from Texas. While he talked on about his job with the Joint Intelligence Staff of N.A.T.O. and the difficulty of maintaining security in an organization where so many nationalities were represented, Bond reflected that good Americans were fine people and that most of them seemed to come from Texas.

Felix Leiter was about thirty-five. He was tall with a thin bony frame and his lightweight, tan-coloured suit hung loosely from his shoulders like the clothes of Frank Sinatra. His movements and speech were slow, but one had the feeling that there was plenty of speed and strength in him and that he would be a tough and cruel fighter. As he sat hunched over the table, he seemed to have some of the jack-knife quality of a falcon. There was this impression also in his face, in the sharpness of his chin and cheek-bones and the wide wry mouth. His grey eyes had a feline slant which was increased by his habit of screwing them up against the smoke of the Chesterfields which he tapped out of the pack in a chain. The permanent wrinkles which this habit had etched at the corners gave the impression that he smiled more with his eyes than with his mouth. A mop of straw-coloured hair lent his face a boyish look which closer examination contradicted. Although he seemed to talk quite openly about his duties in Paris, Bond soon noticed that he never spoke of his American colleagues in Europe or in Washington and he guessed that Leiter held the interests of his own organization far above the mutual concerns of the North Atlantic Allies. Bond sympathized with him.

By the time Leiter had swallowed another whisky and Bond had told him about the Muntzes and his short reconnaissance trip down the coast that morning, it was seven-thirty, and they decided to stroll over to their hotel together. Before leaving the Casino, Bond deposited his total capital of twenty-four million at the caisse, keeping only a few notes of ten mille as pocket-money.

As they walked across to the Splendide, they saw that a team of workmen was already busy at the scene of the explosion. Several trees were uprooted and hoses from three municipal tank cars were washing down the boulevard and pavements. The bomb-crater had disappeared and only a few passers-by had paused to gape. Bond assumed that similar face-lifting had already been carried out at the Hermitage and to the shops and frontages which had lost their windows.

In the warm blue dusk Royale-les-Eaux was once again orderly and peaceful.

'Who's the concierge working for?' asked Leiter as they approached the hotel. Bond was not sure, and said so.

Mathis had been unable to enlighten him. 'Unless you have bought him yourself,' he had said, 'you must assume that he has been bought by the other side. All concierges are venal. It is not their fault. They are trained to regard all hotel guests except maharajahs as potential cheats and thieves. They have as much concern for your comfort or well-being as crocodiles.'

Bond remembered Mathis's pronouncement when the concierge hurried up to inquire whether he had recovered from his most unfortunate experience of the afternoon. Bond thought it well to say that he still felt a little bit shaky. He hoped that if the intelligence were relayed, Le Chiffre would at any rate start playing that evening with a basic misinterpretation of his adversary's strength. The concierge proffered glycerine hopes for Bond's recovery.

Leiter's room was on one of the upper floors and they parted company at the lift after arranging to see each other at the Casino at around half-past ten or eleven, the usual hour for the high tables to begin play.

8

PINK LIGHTS AND CHAMPAGNE

BOND WALKED UP to his room, which again showed no sign of trespass, threw off his clothes, took a long hot bath followed by an ice-cold shower and lay down on his bed. There remained an hour in which to rest and compose his thoughts before he met the girl in the Splendide bar, an hour to examine minutely the details of his plans for the game, and for after the game, in all the various circumstances of victory or defeat. He had to plan the attendant roles of Mathis, Leiter, and the girl and visualize the reactions of the enemy in various contingencies. He closed his eyes and his thoughts pursued his imagination through a series of carefully constructed scenes as if he was watching the tumbling chips of coloured glass in a kaleidoscope.

At twenty minutes to nine he had exhausted all the permutations which might result from his duel with Le Chiffre. He rose and dressed, dismissing the future completely from his mind.

As he tied his thin, double-ended, black satin tie, he paused for a moment and examined himself levelly in the mirror. His grey-blue eyes looked calmly back with a hint of ironical inquiry and the short lock of black hair which would never stay in place slowly subsided to form a thick comma above his right eyebrow. With the thin vertical scar down his right cheek the general effect was faintly piratical. Not much of Hoagy Carmichael there, thought Bond, as he filled a flat, light gunmetal box with fifty of the Morland cigarettes with the triple gold band. Mathis had told him of the girl's comment.

He slipped the case into his pocket and snapped his black oxidized Ronson to see if it needed fuel. After pocketing the thin sheaf of ten-mille notes, he opened a drawer and took out a light chamois leather holster and slipped it over his left shoulder so that it hung about three inches below his armpit. He then took from under his shirts in another drawer a very flat

.25 Beretta automatic with a skeleton grip, extracted the clip and the single round in the barrel and whipped the action to and fro several times, finally pulling the trigger on the empty chamber. He charged the weapon again, loaded it, put up the safety catch and dropped it into the shallow pouch of the shoulder-holster. He looked carefully round the room to see if anything had been forgotten and slipped his single-breasted dinner-jacket coat over his heavy silk evening shirt. He felt cool and comfortable. He verified in the mirror that there was absolutely no sign of the flat gun under his left arm, gave a final pull at his narrow tie and walked out of the door and locked it.

When he turned at the foot of the short stairs towards the bar, he heard the lift-door open behind him and a cool voice call 'Good evening'.

It was the girl. She stood and waited for him to come up to her.

He had remembered her beauty exactly. He was not surprised to be thrilled by it again.

Her dress was of black velvet, simple and yet with the touch of splendour that only half a dozen couturiers in the world can achieve. There was a thin necklace of diamonds at her throat and a diamond clip in the low vee which just exposed the jutting swell of her breasts. She carried a plain black evening bag, a flat oblong which she now held, her arm akimbo, at her waist. Her jet black hair hung straight and simply to the final inward curl below the chin.

She looked quite superb and Bond's heart lifted.

'You look absolutely lovely. Business must be good in the radio world!'

She put her arm through his. 'Do you mind if we go straight into dinner?' she asked. 'I want to make a grand entrance and the truth is there's a horrible secret about black velvet. It marks when you sit down. And, by the way, if you hear me scream tonight, I shall have sat on a cane chair.'

Bond laughed. 'Of course, let's go straight in. We'll have a glass of vodka while we order our dinner.'

She gave him an amused glance and he corrected himself: 'Or a cocktail, of course, if you prefer it. The food here's the best in Royale.'

For an instant he felt nettled at the touch of irony, the lightest shadow of a snub, with which she had met his decisiveness, and at the way he had risen to her quick glance.

But it was only an infinitesimal clink of foils and as the bowing maitre d'hotel led them through the crowded room, it was forgotten as Bond in her wake watched the heads of the diners turn to look at her.

The fashionable part of the restaurant was beside the wide crescent of window built out like the broad stern of a ship over the hotel gardens, but Bond had chosen a table in one of the mirrored alcoves at the back of the great room. These had survived from Edwardian days and they were secluded and gay in white and gilt, with the red silk-shaded table and wall lights of the late Empire.

As they deciphered the maze of purple ink which covered the double folio menu, Bond beckoned to the 'sommelier'. He turned to his companion.

'Have you decided?'

'I would love a glass of vodka,' she said simply, and went back to her study of the menu.

'A small carafe of vodka, very cold,' ordered Bond. He said to her abruptly: 'I can't drink the health of your new frock without knowing your Christian name.'

'Vesper,' she said. 'Vesper Lynd.'

Bond gave her a look of inquiry.

'It's rather a bore always having to explain, but I was born in the evening, on a very stormy evening according to my parents. Apparently they wanted to remember it.' She smiled. 'Some people like it, others don't. I'm just used to it.'

'I think it's a fine name,' said Bond. An idea struck him. 'Can I borrow it?' He explained about the special martini he had invented and his search for a name for it. 'The Vesper,' he said. 'It sounds perfect and it's very appropriate to the violet hour when my cocktail will now be drunk all over the world. Can I have it?'

'So long as I can try one first,' she promised. 'It sounds a drink to be proud of.'

'We'll have one together when all this is finished,' said Bond. 'Win or lose. And now have you decided what you would like to have for dinner? Please be expensive,' he added as he sensed her hesitation, 'or you'll let down that beautiful frock.'

'I'd made two choices,' she laughed, 'and either would have been delicious, but behaving like a millionaire occasionally is a wonderful treat and if you're sure . . . well, I'd like to start with caviar and then have a plain grilled *rognon de veau* with *pommes soufflés*. And then I'd like to have *fraises des bois* with a lot of cream. Is it very shameless to be so certain and so expensive?' She smiled at him inquiringly.

'It's a virtue, and anyway it's only a good plain wholesome meal.' He turned to the maitre d'hotel, 'and bring plenty of toast.'

'The trouble always is,' he explained to Vesper, 'not how to get enough caviar, but how to get enough toast with it.'

'Now,' he turned back to the menu, 'I myself will accompany mademoiselle with the caviar, but then I would like a very small *tournedos*, underdone, with *sauce Béarnaise* and a *cœur d'artichaut*. While mademoiselle is enjoying the strawberries, I will have half an avocado pear with a little French dressing. Do you approve?'

The maitre d'hotel bowed.

'My compliments, mademoiselle and monsieur. Monsieur George,' he turned to the sommelier and repeated the two dinners for his benefit.

'Parfait,' said the sommelier, proffering the leather-bound wine list.

'If you agree,' said Bond, 'I would prefer to drink champagne with you tonight. It is a cheerful wine and it suits the occasion — I hope,' he added.

'Yes, I would like champagne,' she said.

With his finger on the page, Bond turned to the sommelier: 'The Taittinger 45?'

'A fine wine, monsieur,' said the sommelier. 'But if monsieur will permit,' he pointed with his pencil, 'the Blanc de Blanc Brut 1943 of the same marque is without equal.'

Bond smiled. 'So be it,' he said.

'That is not a well-known brand,' Bond explained to his companion, 'but it is probably the finest champagne in the world.' He grinned suddenly at the touch of pretension in his remark.

'You must forgive me,' he said. 'I take a ridiculous pleasure in what I eat and drink. It comes partly from being a bachelor, but mostly from a habit of taking a lot of trouble over details. It's very pernickety and old-maidish really, but then when I'm working I generally have to eat my meals alone and it makes them more interesting when one takes trouble.'

Vesper smiled at him.

'I like it,' she said. 'I like doing everything fully, getting the most out of everything one does. I think that's the way to live. But it sounds rather schoolgirlish when one says it,' she added apologetically.

The little carafe of vodka had arrived in its bowl of crushed ice and Bond filled their glasses.

'Well, I agree with you anyway,' he said, 'and now, here's luck for tonight, Vesper.'

'Yes,' said the girl quietly, as she held up her small glass and looked at him with a curious directness straight in the eyes. 'I hope all will go well tonight.'

She seemed to Bond to give a quick involuntary shrug of the shoulders as she spoke, but then she leant impulsively towards him.

'I have some news for you from Mathis. He was longing to tell you himself. It's about the bomb. It's a fantastic story.'

9
THE GAME IS BACCARAT

BOND LOOKED ROUND, but there was no possibility of being overheard, and the caviar would be waiting for the hot toast from the kitchens.

'Tell me.' His eyes glittered with interest.

'They got the third Bulgar, on the road to Paris. He was in a Citroën and he had picked up two English hikers as protective colouring. At the road-block his French was so bad that they asked for his papers and he brought out a gun and shot one of the motor-cycle patrol. But the other man got him, I don't know how, and managed to stop him committing suicide. Then they took him down to Rouen and extracted the story — in the usual French fashion, I suppose.

'Apparently they were part of a pool held in France for this sort of job — saboteurs, thugs, and so on — and Mathis's friends are already trying to round up the rest. They were to get two million francs for killing you and the agent who briefed them told them there was absolutely no chance of being caught if they followed his instructions exactly.'

She took a sip of vodka. 'But this is the interesting part.

'The agent gave them the two camera-cases you saw. He said the bright colours would make it easier for them. He told them that the blue case contained a very powerful smoke-bomb. The red case was the explosive. As one of them threw the red case, the other was to press a switch on the blue case and they would escape under cover of the smoke. In fact, the smoke-bomb was a pure invention to make the Bulgars think they could get away. Both cases contained an identical high-explosive bomb. There was no difference between the blue and the red cases. The idea was to destroy you and the bomb-throwers without trace. Presumably there were other plans for dealing with the third man.'

'Go on,' said Bond, full of admiration for the ingenuity of the double-cross.

'Well, apparently the Bulgars thought this sounded very fine, but cannily they decided to take no chances. It would be better, they thought, to touch off the smoke-bomb first and, from inside the cloud of smoke, hurl the explosive bomb at you. What you saw was the assistant bomb-thrower pressing down the lever on the phony smoke-bomb and, of course, they both went up together.

'The third Bulgar was waiting behind the Splendide to pick his two friends up. When he saw what had happened, he assumed they had bungled. But the police picked up some fragments of the unexploded red bomb and he was confronted with them. When he saw that they had been tricked and that his two friends were meant to be murdered with you, he started to talk. I expect he's still talking now. But there's nothing to link all this with Le Chiffre. They were given the job by some intermediary, perhaps one of Le Chiffre's guards, and Le Chiffre's name means absolutely nothing to the one who survived.'

She finished her story just as the waiters arrived with the caviar, a mound of hot toast, and small dishes containing finely chopped onion and grated hard-boiled egg, the white in one dish and the yolk in another.

The caviar was heaped on to their plates and they ate for a time in silence.

After a while Bond said: 'It's very satisfactory to be a corpse who changes places with his murderers. For them it certainly was a case of being hoist with their own petard. Mathis must be very pleased with the day's work — five of the opposition neutralized in twenty-four hours,' and he told her how the Muntzes had been confounded.

'Incidentally,' he asked, 'how did you come to get mixed up in this affair? What section are you in?'

'I'm personal assistant to Head of S,' said Vesper. 'As it was his plan, he wanted his section to have a hand in the operation and he asked M. if I could go. It seemed only to be a liaison job, so M. said yes although he told my chief that you would be furious at being given a woman to work with.' She paused and when Bond said nothing continued: 'I had to meet Mathis in Paris and come down with him. I've got a friend who is a *vendeuse* with Dior and somehow she managed to borrow me this and the frock I was wearing this morning, otherwise I couldn't possibly have competed with all these people.' She made a gesture towards the room.

'The office was very jealous although they didn't know what the job was. All they knew was that I was to work with a Double O. Of course you're our heroes. I was enchanted.'

Bond frowned. 'It's not difficult to get a Double O number if you're prepared to kill people,' he said. 'That's all the meaning it has. It's nothing to be particularly proud of. I've got the corpses of a Japanese cipher expert in New York and a Norwegian double agent in Stockholm to thank for being a Double O. Probably quite decent people. They just got caught up in the gale of the world like that Yugoslav that Tito bumped off. It's a confusing business, but if it's one's profession, one does what one's told. How do you like the grated egg with your caviar?'

'It's a wonderful combination,' she said. 'I'm loving my dinner. It seems a shame . . . ' She stopped, warned by a cold look in Bond's eye.

'If it wasn't for the job, we wouldn't be here,' he said.

Suddenly he regretted the intimacy of their dinner and of their talk. He felt he had said too much and that what was only a working relationship had become confused.

'Let's consider what has to be done,' he said in a matter-of-fact voice. 'I'd better explain what I'm going to try and do and how you can help. Which isn't very much I'm afraid,' he added.

'Now these are the basic facts.' He proceeded to sketch out the plan and enumerate the various contingencies which faced them.

The maitre d'hotel supervised the serving of the second course and then as they ate the delicious food, Bond continued.

She listened to him coldly, but with attentive obedience. She felt thoroughly deflated by his harshness, while admitting to herself that she should have paid more heed to the warnings of Head of S.

'He's a dedicated man,' her chief had said when he gave her the assignment. 'Don't imagine this is going to be any fun. He thinks of nothing but the job on hand and, while it's on, he's absolute hell to work for. But he's an expert and there aren't many about, so you won't be wasting your time. He's a good-looking chap, but don't fall for him. I don't think he's got much heart. Anyway, good luck and don't get hurt.'

All this had been something of a challenge and she was pleased when she felt she attracted and interested him, as she knew intuitively that she did. Then at a hint that they were finding pleasure together, a hint that was only the first words of a conventional phrase, he had suddenly turned to ice and had brutally veered away as if warmth were poison to him. She felt hurt and foolish. Then she gave a mental shrug and concentrated with all her attention on what he was saying. She would not make the same mistake again.

'. . . and the main hope is to pray for a run of luck for me, or against him.'

Bond was explaining just how baccarat is played.

'It's much the same as any other gambling game. The odds against the banker and the player are more or less even. Only a run against either can be decisive and "break the bank", or break the players.

'Tonight, Le Chiffre, we know, has bought the baccarat bank from the Egyptian syndicate which is running the high tables here. He paid a million francs for it and his capital has been reduced to twenty-four million. I have about the same. There will be ten players, I expect, and we sit round the banker at a kidney-shaped table.

'Generally, this table is divided into two tableaux. The banker plays two games, one against each of the tableaux to left and right of him. In that game the banker should be able to win by playing off one tableau against the other and by first-class accountancy. But there aren't enough baccarat players yet at Royale and Le Chiffre is just going to pit his luck against the other players at the single tableau. It's unusual because the odds in favour of the banker aren't so good, but they're a shade in his favour and, of course, he has control of the size of the stakes.

'Well, the banker sits there in the middle with a croupier to rake in the cards and call the amount of each bank and a chef de partie to umpire the game generally. I shall be sitting as near dead opposite Le Chiffre as I can get. In front of him he has a shoe containing six packs of cards, well shuffled. There's absolutely no chance of tampering with the shoe. The cards are shuffled by the croupier and cut by one of the players and put into the shoe in full view of the table. We've checked on the staff and they're all okay. It would be useful, but almost impossible, to mark all the cards, and it would mean the connivance at least of the croupier. Anyway, we shall be watching for that too.'

Bond drank some champagne and continued.

'Now what happens at the game is this. The banker announces an opening bank of five hundred thousand francs, or five hundred pounds as it is now. Each seat is numbered from the right of the banker and the player next to the banker, or Number 1, can accept this bet and push his money out on to the table, or pass it, if it is too much for him or he doesn't want to take it. Then Number 2 has the right to take it, and if he refuses, then Number 3, and so on round the table. If no single player takes it all, the bet is offered to the table as a whole and everyone chips in, including sometimes the spectators round the table, until the five hundred thousand is made up.

'That is a small bet which would immediately be met, but when it gets to a million or two, it's often difficult to find a taker or even, if the bank seems to be in luck, a group of takers to cover the bet. At that moment I shall always try and step in and accept the bet — in fact, I shall attack Le Chiffre's bank whenever I get a chance until either I've bust his bank or he's bust me. It may take some time, but in the end one of us two is bound to break the other, irrespective of the other players at the table, although they can, of course, make him richer or poorer in the meantime.

'Being the banker, he's got a slight advantage in the play, but knowing that I'm making a dead set at him and not knowing, I hope, my capital, is bound to play on his nerves a bit, so I'm hoping that we start about equal.'

He paused while the strawberries came and the avocado pear.

For a while they ate in silence, then they talked of other things while the coffee was served. They smoked. Neither of them drank brandy or a liqueur. Finally, Bond felt it was time to explain the actual mechanics of the game.

'It's a simple affair,' he said, 'and you'll understand it at once if you've ever played vingt-et-un, where the object is to get cards from the banker which add up more closely to a count of twenty-one than his do. In this game, I get two cards and the banker gets two and, unless anyone wins outright, either or both of us can get one more card. The object of the game is to hold two, or three cards which together count nine points, or as nearly nine as possible. Court cards and tens count nothing; aces one each; any other card its face value. It is only the last figure of your count that signifies. So nine plus seven equals six — not sixteen.

'The winner is the one whose count is nearest to nine. Draws are played over again.'

Vesper listened attentively, but she also watched the look of abstract passion on Bond's face.

'Now,' Bond continued, 'when the banker deals me my two cards, if they add up to eight or nine, they're a "natural" and I turn them up and I win, unless he has an equal or a better natural. If I haven't got a natural, I can stand on a seven or a six, perhaps ask for a card or perhaps not, on a five, and certainly ask for a card if my count is lower than five. Five is the turning point of the game. According to the odds, the chances of bettering or worsening your hand if you hold a five are exactly even.

'Only when I ask for a card or tap mine to signify that I stand on what I have, can the banker look at his. If he has a natural, he turns them up and wins. Otherwise he is faced with the same problems as I was. But he is helped in his decision to draw or not to draw a third card by my actions. If I have stood, he must assume that I have a five, six, or seven: if I have drawn, he will know that I had something less than a six and I may have improved my hand or not with the card he gave me. And this card was dealt to me face up. On its face value and a knowledge of the odds, he will know whether to take another card or to stand on his own.

'So he has a very slight advantage over me. He has a tiny help over his decision to draw or to stand. But there is always one problem card at this game — shall one draw or stand on a five and what will your opponent do with a five? Some players always draw or always stand. I follow my intuition.

'But in the end,' Bond stubbed out his cigarette and called for the bill, 'it's the natural eights and nines that matter, and I must just see that I get more of them than he does.'

10

THE HIGH TABLE

WHILE TELLING THE story of the game and anticipating the coming fight, Bond's face had lit up again. The prospect of at last getting to grips with Le Chiffre stimulated him and quickened his pulse. He seemed to have completely forgotten the brief coolness between them, and Vesper was relieved and entered into his mood.

He paid the bill and gave a handsome tip to the sommelier. Vesper rose and led the way out of the restaurant and out on to the steps of the hotel.

The big Bentley was waiting and Bond drove Vesper over, parking as close to the entrance as he could. As they walked through the ornate ante-rooms, he hardly spoke. She looked at him and saw that his nostrils were slightly flared. In other respects he seemed completely at ease, acknowledging cheerfully the greetings of the Casino functionaries. At the door to the salle privée they were not asked for their membership cards. Bond's high gambling had already made him a favoured client and any companion of his shared in the glory.

Before they had penetrated very far into the main room, Felix Leiter detached himself from one of the roulette tables and greeted Bond as an old friend. After being introduced to Vesper Lynd and exchanging a few remarks, Leiter said: 'Well, since you're playing baccarat this evening, will you allow me to show Miss Lynd how to break the bank at roulette? I've got three lucky numbers that are bound to show soon, and I expect Miss Lynd has some too. Then perhaps we could come and watch you when your game starts to warm up.'

Bond looked inquiringly at Vesper.

'I should love that,' she said, 'but will you give me one of your lucky numbers to play on?'

'I have no lucky numbers,' said Bond unsmilingly. 'I only bet on even chances, or as near them as I can get. Well, I shall leave you then.' He excused himself. 'You will be in excellent hands with my friend Felix Leiter.' He gave a short smile which embraced them both and walked with an unhurried gait towards the caisse.

Leiter sensed the rebuff.

'He's a very serious gambler, Miss Lynd,' he said. 'And I guess he has to be. Now come with me and watch Number 17 obey my extra-sensory perceptions. You'll find it quite a painless sensation being given plenty of money for nothing.'

Bond was relieved to be on his own again and to be able to clear his mind of everything but the task on hand. He stood at the caisse and took his twenty-four million francs against the receipt which had been given him that afternoon. He divided the notes into equal packets and put half the sum into his right-hand coat pocket and the other half into the left. Then he strolled slowly across the room between the thronged tables until he came to the top of the room where the broad baccarat table waited behind the brass rail.

The table was filling up and the cards were spread face down being stirred and mixed slowly in what is known as the 'croupiers' shuffle', supposedly the shuffle which is most effective and least susceptible to cheating.

The chef de partie lifted the velvet-covered chain which allowed entrance through the brass rail.

'I've kept Number 6 as you wished, Monsieur Bond.'

There were still three other empty places at the table. Bond moved inside the rail to where a huissier was holding out his chair. He sat down with a nod to the players on his right and left. He took out his wide gunmetal cigarette case and his black lighter and placed them on the green baize at his right elbow. The huissier wiped a thick glass ashtray with a cloth and put it beside them. Bond lit a cigarette and leant back in his chair.

Opposite him, the banker's chair was vacant. He glanced round the table. He knew most of the players by sight, but few of their names. At Number 7, on his right, there was a Monsieur Sixte, a wealthy Belgian with metal interests in the Congo. At Number 9 there was Lord Danvers, a distinguished but weak-looking man whose francs were presumably provided by his rich American wife, a middle-aged woman with the predatory mouth of a barracuda, who sat at Number 3. Bond reflected that they would probably play a pawky and nervous game and be amongst the early casualties. At Number 1, to the right of the bank, was a well-known Greek gambler who owned, as in Bond's experience apparently everyone does in the Eastern Mediterranean, a profitable shipping line. He would play coldly and well and would be a stayer.

Bond asked the huissier for a card and wrote on it, under a neat question-mark, the remaining numbers, 2, 4, 5, 8, 10, and asked the huissier to give it to the chef de partie.

Soon it came back with the names filled in.

Number 2, still empty, was to be Carmel Delane, the American film star with alimony from three husbands to burn and, Bond assumed, a call on still more from whoever her present companion at Royale might be. With her sanguine temperament she would play gaily and with panache and might run into a vein of luck.

Then came Lady Danvers at Number 3 and Numbers 4 and 5 were a Mr and Mrs Du Pont, rich-looking and might or might not have some of the real Du Pont money behind them. Bond guessed they would be stayers. They both had a business-like look about them and were talking together easily and cheerfully as if they felt very much at home at the big game. Bond was quite happy to have them next to him — Mrs Du Pont sat at Number 5 — and he felt prepared to share with them or with Monsieur Sixte on his right, if they found themselves faced with too big a bank.

At Number 8 was the Maharajah of a small Indian state, probably with all his wartime sterling balances to play with. Bond's experience told him that few of the Asiatic races were courageous gamblers, even the much-vaunted Chinese being inclined to lose heart if the going was bad. But the Maharajah would probably stay late in the game and stand some heavy losses if they were gradual.

Number 10 was a prosperous-looking young Italian, Signor Tomelli, who possibly had plenty of money from rack-rents in Milan and would probably play a dashing and foolish game. He might lose his temper and make a scene.

Bond had just finished his sketchy summing-up of the players when Le Chiffre, with the silence and economy of movement of a big fish, came through the opening in the brass rail and, with a cold smile of welcome for the table, took his place directly opposite Bond in the banker's chair.

With the same economy of movement, he cut the thick slab of cards which the croupier had placed on the table squarely between his blunt relaxed hands. Then, as the croupier fitted the six packs with one swift exact motion into the metal and wooden shoe, Le Chiffre said something quietly to him.

'Messieurs, mesdames, les jeux sont faits. Un banco de cinq cent mille,' and as the Greek at Number 1 tapped the table in front of his fat pile of hundred-mille plaques, 'le banco est fait.'

Le Chiffre crouched over the shoe. He gave it a short deliberate slap to settle the cards, the first of which showed its semicircular pale pink tongue through the slanting aluminium mouth of the shoe. Then, with a thick white forefinger he pressed gently on the pink tongue and slipped out the first card six inches or a foot towards the Greek on his right hand. Then he slipped out a card for himself, then another for the Greek, then one more for himself.

He sat immobile, not touching his own cards.

He looked at the Greek's face.

With his flat wooden spatula, like a long bricklayer's trowel, the croupier delicately lifted up the Greek's two cards and dropped them with a quick movement an extra few inches to the right so that they lay just before the Greek's pale hairy hands which lay inert like two watchful pink crabs on the table.

The two pink crabs scuttled out together and the Greek gathered the cards into his wide left hand and cautiously bent his head so that he could see, in the shadow made by his cupped hand, the value of the bottom of the two cards. Then he slowly inserted the forefinger of his right hand and slipped the bottom card slightly sideways so that the value of the top card was also just perceptible.

His face was quite impassive. He flattened out his left hand on the table and then withdrew it, leaving the two pink cards face down before him, their secret unrevealed.

Then he lifted his head and looked Le Chiffre in the eye.

'Non,' said the Greek flatly.

From the decision to stand on his two cards and not to ask for another, it was clear that the Greek had a five, or a six, or a seven. To be certain of winning, the bank had to reveal an eight or a nine. If the banker failed to show either figure, he also had the right to take another card which might or might not improve his count.

Le Chiffre's hands were clasped in front of him, his two cards three or four inches away. With his right hand he picked up the two cards and turned them face upwards on the table with a faint snap.

They were a four and a five, an undefeatable natural nine.

He had won.

'Neuf à la banque,' quietly said the croupier. With his spatula he faced the Greek's two cards. 'Et le sept,' he said unemotionally, lifting up gently the corpses of the seven and queen and slipping them through the wide slot in the table near his chair which leads into the big metal canister to which all dead cards are consigned. Le Chiffre's two cards followed them with the faint rattle which comes from the canister at the beginning of each session before the discards have made a cushion over the metal floor of their oubliette.

The Greek pushed forward five plaques of one hundred thousand and the croupier added these to Le Chiffre's half-million plaque which lay in the centre of the table. From each bet the Casino takes a tiny percentage, the cagnotte, but it is usual at a big game for the banker to subscribe this himself either in a prearranged lump sum or by contributions at the end of each hand, so that the amount of the bank's stake can always be a round figure. Le Chiffre had chosen the second course.

The croupier slipped some counters through the slot in the table which receives the cagnotte and announced quietly:

'Un banco d'un million.'

'Suivi,' murmured the Greek, meaning that he exercised his right to follow up his lost bet.

Bond lit a cigarette and settled himself in his chair. The long game was launched and the sequence of these gestures and the reiteration of this subdued litany would continue until the end came and the players dispersed. Then the enigmatic cards would be burnt or defaced, a shroud would be draped over the table and the grass-green baize battlefield would soak up the blood of its victims and refresh itself.

The Greek, after taking a third card, could achieve no better than a four to the bank's seven.

'Un banco de deux millions,' said the croupier.

The players on Bond's left remained silent.

'Banco,' said Bond.

11

MOMENT OF TRUTH

LE CHIFFRE LOOKED incuriously at him, the whites of his eyes, which showed all round the irises, lending something impassive and doll-like to his gaze.

He slowly removed one thick hand from the table and slipped it into the pocket of his dinner-jacket. The hand came out holding a small metal cylinder with a cap which Le Chiffre unscrewed. He inserted the nozzle of the cylinder, with an obscene deliberation, twice into each black nostril in turn, and luxuriously inhaled the benzedrine vapour.

Unhurriedly he pocketed the inhaler, then his hand came quickly back above the level of the table and gave the shoe its usual hard, sharp slap.

During this offensive pantomime Bond had coldly held the banker's gaze, taking in the wide expanse of white face surmounted by the short abrupt cliff of reddish-brown hair, the unsmiling wet red mouth and the impressive width of the shoulders, loosely draped in a massively cut dinner-jacket.

But for the high-lights on the satin of the shawl-cut lapels, he might have been faced by the thick bust of a black-fleeced Minotaur rising out of a green grass field.

Bond slipped a packet of notes on to the table without counting them. If he lost, the croupier would extract what was necessary to cover the bet, but the easy gesture conveyed that Bond didn't expect to lose and that this was only a token display from the deep funds at Bond's disposal.

The other players sensed a tension between the two gamblers and there was silence as Le Chiffre fingered the four cards out of the shoe.

The croupier slipped Bond's two cards across to him with the tip of his spatula. Bond, still with his eyes holding Le Chiffre's, reached his right hand out a few inches, glanced down very swiftly, then as he looked up again impassively at Le Chiffre, with a disdainful gesture he tossed the cards face upwards on the table.

They were a four and a five — an unbeatable nine.

There was a little gasp of envy from the table and the players to the left of Bond exchanged rueful glances at their failure to accept the two-million-franc bet.

With the hint of a shrug, Le Chiffre slowly faced his own two cards and flicked them away with his finger-nail. They were two valueless knaves.

'Le baccarat,' intoned the croupier as he spaded the thick chips over the table to Bond.

Bond slipped them into his right-hand pocket with the unused packet of notes. His face showed no emotion, but he was pleased with the success of his first coup and with the outcome of the silent clash of wills across the table.

The woman on his left, the American Mrs Du Pont, turned to him with a wry smile.

'I shouldn't have let it come to you,' she said. 'Directly the cards were dealt I kicked myself.'

'It's only the beginning of the game,' said Bond. 'You may be right the next time you pass it.'

Mr Du Pont leant forward from the other side of his wife: 'If one could be right every hand, none of us would be here,' he said philosophically.

'I would be,' his wife laughed. 'You don't think I do this for pleasure.'

As the game went on, Bond looked over the spectators leaning on the high brass rail round the table. He soon saw Le Chiffre's two gunmen. They stood behind and to either side of the banker. They looked respectable enough, but not sufficiently a part of the game to be unobtrusive.

The one more or less behind Le Chiffre's right arm was tall and funereal in his dinner-jacket. His face was wooden and grey, but his eyes flickered and gleamed like a conjurer's. His whole long body was restless and his hands shifted often on the brass rail. Bond guessed that he would kill without interest or concern for what he killed and that he would prefer strangling. He had something of Lennie in *Of Mice and Men*, but his inhumanity would not come from infantilism but from drugs. Marihuana, decided Bond.

The other man looked like a Corsican shopkeeper. He was short and very dark with a flat head covered with thickly greased hair. He seemed to be a cripple. A chunky malacca cane with a rubber tip hung on the rail beside him. He must have had permission to bring the cane into the Casino with him, reflected Bond, who knew that neither sticks nor any other objects were allowed in the rooms as a precaution against acts of violence. He looked sleek and well-fed. His mouth hung vacantly half-open and revealed very bad teeth. He wore a heavy black moustache and the backs of his hands on the rail were matted with black hair. Bond guessed that hair covered most of his squat body. Naked, Bond supposed, he would be an obscene object.

The game continued uneventfully, but with a slight bias against the bank.

The third coup is the 'sound barrier' at chemin-de-fer and baccarat. Your luck can defeat the first and second tests, but when the third deal comes along it most often spells disaster. Again and again at this point you find yourself being bounced back to earth. It was like that now. Neither the bank nor any of the players seemed to be able to get hot. But there was a steady and inexorable seepage against the bank, amounting after about two hours' play to ten million francs. Bond had no idea what profits Le Chiffre had made over the past two days. He estimated them at five million and guessed that now the banker's capital could not be more than twenty million.

In fact, Le Chiffre had lost heavily all that afternoon. At this moment he only had ten million left.

Bond, on the other hand, by one o'clock in the morning, had won four million, bringing his resources up to twenty-eight million.

Bond was cautiously pleased. Le Chiffre showed no trace of emotion. He continued to play like an automaton, never speaking except when he gave instructions in a low aside to the croupier at the opening of each new bank.

Outside the pool of silence round the high table, there was the constant hum of the other tables, chemin-de-fer, roulette and trente-et-quarante, interspersed with the clear calls of the croupiers and occasional bursts of laughter or gasps of excitement from different corners of the huge salle.

In the background there thudded always the hidden metronome of the Casino, ticking up its little treasure of one-percents with each spin of a wheel and each turn of a card — a pulsing fat-cat with a zero for a heart.

It was at ten minutes past one by Bond's watch when, at the high table, the whole pattern of play suddenly altered.

The Greek at Number 1 was still having a bad time. He had lost the first coup of half a million francs and the second. He passed the third time, leaving a bank of two millions. Carmel Delane at Number 2 refused it. So did Lady Danvers at Number 3.

The Du Ponts looked at each other.

'Banco,' said Mrs Du Pont, and promptly lost to the banker's natural eight.

'Un banco de quatre millions,' said the croupier.

'Banco,' said Bond, pushing out a wad of notes.

Again he fixed Le Chiffre with his eye. Again he gave only a cursory look at his two cards.

'No,' he said. He held a marginal five. The position was dangerous.

Le Chiffre turned up a knave and a four. He gave the shoe another slap. He drew a three.

'Sept à la banque,' said the croupier, 'et cinq,' he added as he tipped Bond's losing cards face upwards. He raked over Bond's money, extracted four million francs and returned the remainder to Bond.

'Un banco de huit millions.'

'Suivi,' said Bond.

And lost again, to a natural nine.

In two coups he had lost twelve million francs. By scraping the barrel, he had just sixteen million francs left, exactly the amount of the next banco.

Suddenly Bond felt the sweat on his palms. Like snow in sunshine his capital had melted. With the covetous deliberation of the winning gambler, Le Chiffre was tapping a light tattoo on the table with his right hand. Bond looked across into the eyes of murky basalt. They held an ironical question. 'Do you want the full treatment?' they seemed to ask.

'Suivi,' Bond said softly.

He took some notes and plaques out of his right-hand pocket and the entire stack of notes out of his left and pushed them forward. There was no hint in his movements that this would be his last stake.

His mouth felt suddenly as dry as flock wall-paper. He looked up and saw Vesper and Felix Leiter standing where the gunman with the stick had stood. He did not know how long they had been standing there. Leiter looked faintly worried, but Vesper smiled encouragement at him.

He heard a faint rattle on the rail behind him and turned his head. The battery of bad teeth under the black moustache gaped vacantly back at him.

'Le jeu est fait,' said the croupier, and the two cards came slithering towards him over the green baize — a green baize which was no longer smooth, but thick now, and furry and almost choking, its colour as livid as the grass on a fresh tomb.

The light from the broad satin-lined shades which had seemed so welcoming now seemed to take the colour out of his hand as he glanced at the cards. Then he looked again.

It was nearly as bad as it could have been — the king of hearts and an ace, the ace of spades. It squinted up at him like a black widow spider.

'A card.' He still kept all emotion out of his voice.

Le Chiffre faced his own two cards. He had a queen and a black five. He looked at Bond and pressed out another card with a wide forefinger. The table was absolutely silent. He faced it and flicked it away. The croupier lifted it delicately with his spatula and slipped it over to Bond. It was a good card, the five of hearts, but to Bond it was a difficult fingerprint in dried blood. He now had a count of six and Le Chiffre a count of five, but the banker having a five and giving a five, would and must draw another card and try and improve with a one, two, three, or four. Drawing any other card he would be defeated.

The odds were on Bond's side, but now it was Le Chiffre who looked across into Bond's eyes and hardly glanced at the card as he flicked it face upwards on the table.

It was, unnecessarily, the best, a four, giving the bank a count of nine. He had won, almost slowing up.

Bond was beaten and cleaned out.

12

THE DEADLY TUBE

BOND SAT SILENT, frozen with defeat. He opened his wide black case and took out a cigarette. He snapped open the tiny jaws of the Ronson and lit the cigarette and put the lighter back on the table. He took a deep lungful of smoke and expelled it between his teeth with a faint hiss.

What now? Back to the hotel and bed, avoiding the commiserating eyes of Mathis and Leiter and Vesper. Back to the telephone call to London, and then tomorrow the plane home, the taxi up to Regent's Park, the walk up the stairs and along the corridor, and M.'s cold face across the table, his forced sympathy, his 'better luck next time' and, of course, there couldn't be one, not another chance like this.

He looked round the table and up at the spectators. Few were looking at him. They were waiting while the croupier counted the money and piled up the chips in a neat stack in front of the banker, waiting to see if anyone would conceivably challenge this huge bank of thirty-two million francs, this wonderful run of banker's luck.

Leiter had vanished, not wishing to look Bond in the eye after the knock-out, he supposed. Yet Vesper looked curiously unmoved, she gave him a smile of encouragement. But then, Bond reflected, she knew nothing of the game. Had no notion, probably, of the bitterness of his defeat.

The huissier was coming towards Bond inside the rail. He stopped beside him. Bent over him. Placed a squat envelope beside Bond on the table. It was as thick as a dictionary. Said something about the caisse. Moved away again.

Bond's heart thumped. He took the heavy anonymous envelope below the level of the table and slit it open with his thumbnail, noticing that the gum was still wet on the flap.

Unbelieving and yet knowing it was true, he felt the broad wads of notes. He slipped them into his pockets, retaining the half-sheet of notepaper which was pinned to the topmost of them. He glanced at it in the shadow below the table. There was one line of writing in ink: 'Marshall Aid. Thirty-two million francs. With the compliments of the U.S.A.'

Bond swallowed. He looked over towards Vesper. Felix Leiter was again standing beside her. He grinned slightly and Bond smiled back and raised his hand from the table in a small gesture of benediction. Then he set his mind to sweeping away all traces of the sense of complete defeat which had swamped him a few minutes before. This was a reprieve, but only a reprieve. There could be no more miracles. This time he had to win — if Le Chiffre had not already made his fifty million — if he was going to go on!

The croupier had completed his task of computing the cagnotte, changing Bond's notes into plaques and making a pile of the giant stake in the middle of the table.

There lay thirty-two thousand pounds. Perhaps, thought Bond, Le Chiffre needed just one more coup, even a minor one of a few million francs, to achieve his object. Then he would have made his fifty million francs and would leave the table. By tomorrow his deficits would be covered and his position secure.

He showed no signs of moving and Bond guessed with relief that somehow he must have overestimated Le Chiffre's resources.

Then the only hope, thought Bond, was to stamp on him now. Not to share the bank with the table, or to take some minor part of it, but to go the whole hog. This would really jolt Le Chiffre. He would hate to see more than ten or fifteen million of the stake covered, and he could not possibly expect anyone to banco the entire thirty-two millions. He might not know that Bond had been cleaned out, but he must imagine that Bond had by now only small reserves. He could not know of the contents of the envelope. If he did, he would probably withdraw the bank and start all over again on the wearisome journey up from the five-hundred-thousand-franc opening bet.

The analysis was right.

Le Chiffre needed another eight million.

At last he nodded.

'Un banco de trente-deux millions.'

The croupier's voice rang out. A silence built itself up round the table.

'Un banco de trente-deux millions.'

In a louder, prouder voice the chef de partie took up the cry, hoping to draw big money away from the neighbouring chemin-de-fer tables. Besides, this was wonderful publicity. The stake had only once been reached in the history of baccarat — at Deauville in 1950. The rival Casino de la Forêt at Le Touquet had never got near it.

It was then that Bond leant slightly forward.

'Suivi,' he said quietly.

There was an excited buzz round the table. The word ran through the Casino. People crowded in. Thirty-two million! For most of them it was more than they had earned all their lives. It was their savings and the savings of their families. It was, literally, a small fortune.

One of the Casino directors consulted with the chef de partie. The chef de partie turned apologetically to Bond.

'Excusez moi, monsieur. La mise?'

It was an indication that Bond really must show he had the money to cover the bet. They knew, of course, that he was a very wealthy man, but after all, thirty-two millions! And it sometimes happened that desperate people would bet without a sou in the world and cheerfully go to prison if they lost.

'Mes excuses, Monsieur Bond,' added the chef de partie obsequiously.

It was when Bond shovelled the great wad of notes out on to the table and the croupier busied himself with the task of counting the pinned sheaves of ten-thousand-franc notes, the largest denomination issued in France, that he caught a swift exchange of glances between Le Chiffre and the gunman standing directly behind Bond.

Immediately he felt something hard press into the base of his spine, right into the cleft between his two buttocks on the padded chair.

At the same time a thick voice speaking southern French said softly, urgently, just behind his right ear:

'This is a gun, monsieur. It is absolutely silent. It can blow the base of your spine off without a sound. You will appear to have fainted. I shall be gone. Withdraw your bet before I count ten. If you call for help I shall fire.'

The voice was confident. Bond believed it. These people had

shown they would unhesitatingly go the limit. The thick walking stick was explained. Bond knew the type of gun. The barrel a series of soft rubber baffles which absorbed the detonation, but allowed the passage of the bullet. They had been invented and used in the war for assassinations. Bond had tested them himself.

'Un,' said the voice.

Bond turned his head. There was the man, leaning forward close behind him, smiling broadly under his black moustache as if he was wishing Bond luck, completely secure in the noise and the crowd.

The discoloured teeth came together. 'Deux,' said the grinning mouth.

Bond looked across. Le Chiffre was watching him. His eyes glittered back at Bond. His mouth was open and he was breathing fast. He was waiting, waiting for Bond's hand to gesture to the croupier, or else for Bond suddenly to slump backwards in his chair, his face grimacing with a scream.

'Trois.'

Bond looked over at Vesper and Felix Leiter. They were smiling and talking to each other. The fools. Where was Mathis? Where were those famous men of his?

'Quatre.'

And the other spectators. This crowd of jabbering idiots. Couldn't someone see what was happening? The chef de partie, the croupier, the huissier?

'Cinq.'

The croupier was tidying up the pile of notes. The chef de partie bowed smilingly towards Bond. Directly the stake was in order he would announce: 'Le jeux est fait,' and the gun would fire whether the gunman had reached ten or not.

'Six.'

Bond decided. It was a chance. He carefully moved his hands to the edge of the table, gripped it, edged his buttocks right back, feeling the sharp gun-sight grind into his coccyx.

'Sept.'

The chef de partie turned to Le Chiffre with his eyebrows lifted, waiting for the banker's nod that he was ready to play.

Suddenly Bond heaved backwards with all his strength. His momentum tipped the cross-bar of the chair-back down so quickly that it cracked across the malacca tube and wrenched it from the gunman's hand before he could pull the trigger.

Bond went head-over-heels on to the ground amongst the spectators' feet, his legs in the air. The back of the chair splintered with a sharp crack. There were cries of dismay. The spectators cringed away and then, reassured, clustered back. Hands helped him to his feet and brushed him down. The huissier bustled up with the chef de partie. At all costs a scandal must be avoided.

Bond held on to the brass rail. He looked confused and embarrassed. He brushed his hand across his forehead. 'A momentary faintness,' he said. 'It is nothing — the excitement, the heat.'

There were expressions of sympathy. Naturally, with this tremendous game. Would monsieur prefer to withdraw, to lie down, to go home? Should a doctor be fetched?

Bond shook his head. He was perfectly all right now. His excuses to the table. To the banker also.

A new chair was brought and he sat down. He looked across at Le Chiffre. Through his relief at being alive, he felt a moment of triumph at what he saw — some fear in the fat, pale face.

There was a buzz of speculation round the table. Bond's neighbours on both sides of him bent forward and spoke solicitously about the heat and the lateness of the hour and the smoke and the lack of air.

Bond replied politely. He turned to examine the crowd behind him. There was no trace of the gunman, but the huissier was looking for someone to claim the malacca stick. It seemed undamaged. But it no longer carried a rubber tip. Bond beckoned to him.

'If you will give it to that gentleman over there,' he indicated Felix Leiter, 'he will return it. It belongs to an acquaintance of his.'

The huissier bowed.

Bond grimly reflected that a short examination would reveal to Leiter why he had made such an embarrassing public display of himself.

He turned back to the table and tapped the green cloth in front of him to show that he was ready.

13

'A WHISPER OF LOVE, A WHISPER OF HATE'

'LA PARTIE CONTINUE,' announced the chef impressively. 'Un banco de trente-deux millions.'

The spectators craned forward. Le Chiffre hit the shoe with a flat-handed slap that made it rattle. As an afterthought he took out his benzedrine inhaler and sucked the vapour up his nose.

'Filthy brute,' said Mrs Du Pont on Bond's left.

Bond's mind was clear again. By a miracle he had survived a devastating wound. He could feel his armpits still wet with the fear of it. But the success of his gambit with the chair had wiped out all memories of the dreadful valley of defeat through which he had just passed.

He had made a fool of himself. The game had been interrupted for at least ten minutes, a delay unheard of in a respectable casino, but now cards were waiting for him in the shoe. They must not fail him. He felt his heart lift at the prospect of what was to come.

It was two o'clock in the morning. Apart from the thick crowd round the big game, play was still going on at three of the chemin-de-fer games and at the same number of roulette tables.

In the silence round his own table, Bond suddenly heard a distant croupier intone: 'Neuf. Le rouge gagne, impair et manque.'

Was this an omen for him or for Le Chiffre?

The two cards slithered towards him across the green sea.

Like an octopus under a rock, Le Chiffre watched him from the other side of the table.

Bond reached out a steady right hand and drew the cards towards him. Would it be the lift of the heart which a nine brings, or an eight brings?

He fanned the two cards under the curtain of his hand. The muscles of his jaw rippled as he clenched his teeth. His whole body stiffened in a reflex of self-defence.

He had two queens, two red queens.

They looked roguishly back at him from the shadows. They were the worst. They were nothing. Zero. Baccarat.

'A card,' said Bond fighting to keep hopelessness out of his voice. He felt Le Chiffre's eyes boring into his brain.

The banker slowly turned his own two cards face up.

He had a count of three — a king and a black three.

Bond softly exhaled a cloud of tobacco smoke. He still had a chance. Now he was really faced with the moment of truth. Le Chiffre slapped the shoe, slipped out a card, Bond's card, Bond's fate, and slowly turned it face up.

It was a nine, a wonderful nine of hearts, the card known in gipsy magic as 'a whisper of love, a whisper of hate', the card that meant almost certain victory for Bond.

The croupier slipped it delicately across. To Le Chiffre it meant nothing. Bond might have had a one, in which case he now had ten points, or nothing, or baccarat, as it is called. Or he might have had a two, three, four, or even five. In which case, with the nine, his maximum count would be four.

Holding a three and giving a nine is one of the moot situations at the game. The odds are so nearly divided between to draw or not to draw. Bond let the banker sweat it out. Since his nine could only be equalled by the banker drawing a six, he would normally have shown his count if it had been a friendly game.

Bond's cards lay on the table before him, the two impersonal pale pink-patterned backs and the faced nine of hearts. To Le Chiffre the nine might be telling the truth or many variations of lies.

The whole secret lay in the reverse of the two pink backs where the pair of queens kissed the green cloth.

The sweat was running down either side of the banker's beaky nose. His thick tongue came out slyly and licked a drop out of the corner of his red gash of a mouth. He looked at Bond's cards, and then at his own, and then back at Bond's.

Then his whole body shrugged and he slipped out a card for himself from the lisping shoe.

He faced it. The table craned. It was a wonderful card, a five.

'Huit à la banque,' said the croupier.

As Bond sat silent, Le Chiffre suddenly grinned wolfishly. He must have won.

The croupier's spatula reached almost apologetically across the table. There was not a man at the table who did not believe Bond was defeated.

The spatula flicked the two pink cards over on their backs. The gay red queens smiled up at the lights.

'Et le neuf.'

A great gasp went up round the table, and then a hubbub of talk.

Bond's eyes were on Le Chiffre. The big man fell back in his chair as if slugged above the heart. His mouth opened and shut once or twice in protest and his right hand felt at his throat. Then he rocked back. His lips were grey.

As the huge stack of plaques was shunted across the table to Bond the banker reached into an inner pocket of his jacket and threw a wad of notes on to the table.

The croupier riffled through them.

'Un banco de dix millions,' he announced. He slapped down their equivalent in ten plaques of a million each.

This is the kill, thought Bond. This man has reached the point of no return. This is the last of his capital. He has come to where I stood an hour ago and he is making the last gesture that I made. But if this man loses, there is no one to come to his aid, no miracle to help him.

Bond sat back and lit a cigarette. On a small table beside him half a bottle of Clicquot and a glass had materialized. Without asking who the benefactor was, Bond filled the glass to the brim and drank it down in two long draughts.

Then he leant back with his arms curled forward on the table in front of him like the arms of a wrestler seeking a hold at the opening of a bout of ju-jitsu.

The players on his left remained silent.

'Banco,' he said, speaking straight at Le Chiffre.

Once more the two cards were borne over to him and this time the croupier slipped them into the green lagoon between the outstretched arms.

Bond curled his right hand in, glanced briefly down and flipped the cards face up into the middle of the table.

'Le neuf,' said the croupier.

Le Chiffre was gazing down at his own two black kings.

'Et le baccarat,' and the croupier eased across the table the fat tide of plaques.

Le Chiffre watched them go to join the serried millions in the shadow of Bond's left arm, then he stood up slowly and without a word he brushed past the players to the break in the rail. He unhooked the velvet-covered chain and let it fall. The spectators opened a way for him. They looked at him curiously and rather fearfully as if he carried the smell of death on him. Then he vanished from Bond's sight.

Bond stood up. He took a hundred-mille plaque from the stacks beside him and slipped it across the table to the chef de partie. He cut short the effusive thanks and asked the croupier to have his winnings carried to the caisse. The other players were leaving their seats. With no banker, there could be no game, and by now it was half-past two. He exchanged some pleasant words with his neighbours to right and left and then ducked under the rail to where Vesper and Felix Leiter were waiting for him.

Together they walked over to the caisse. Bond was invited to come into the private office of the Casino directors. On the desk lay his huge pile of chips. He added the contents of his pockets to it.

In all there was over seventy million francs.

Bond took Felix Leiter's money in notes and took a cheque to cash on the Crédit Lyonnais for the remaining forty-odd million. He was congratulated warmly on his winnings. The directors hoped that he would be playing again that evening.

Bond gave an evasive reply. He walked over to the bar and handed Leiter's money to him. For a few minutes they discussed the game over a bottle of champagne. Leiter took a .45 bullet out of his pocket and placed it on the table.

'I gave the gun to Mathis,' he said. 'He's taken it away. He was as puzzled as we were by the spill you took. He was standing at the back of the crowd with one of his men when it happened. The gunman got away without difficulty. You can imagine how they kicked themselves when they saw the gun. Mathis gave me this bullet to show you what you escaped. The nose has been cut with a dum-dum cross. You'd have been in a terrible mess. But they can't tie it on to Le Chiffre. The man came in alone. They've got the form he filled up to get his entrance card. Of course, it'll all be phony. He got permission to bring the stick in with him. He had a certificate for a war-wound pension. These people certainly get themselves well organized. They've got his prints and they're on the Belinograph to Paris, so we may hear more about him in the morning.' Felix Leiter tapped out another cigarette. 'Anyway, all's well that ends well. You certainly took Le Chiffre for a ride at the end, though we had some bad moments. I expect you did too.'

Bond smiled. 'That envelope was the most wonderful thing that ever happened to me. I thought I was really finished. It wasn't at all a pleasant feeling. Talk about a friend in need. One day I'll try and return the compliment.'

He rose. 'I'll just go over to the hotel and put this away,' he said, tapping his pocket. 'I don't like wandering around with Le Chiffre's death warrant on me. He might get ideas. Then I'd like to celebrate a bit. What do you think?'

He turned to Vesper. She had hardly said a word since the end of the game.

'Shall we have a glass of champagne in the night club before we go to bed? It's called the Roi Galant. You get to it through the public rooms. It looks quite cheerful.'

'I think I'd love to,' said Vesper. 'I'll tidy up while you put your winnings away. I'll meet you in the entrance hall.'

'What about you, Felix?' Bond hoped he could be alone with Vesper.

Leiter looked at him and read his mind.

'I'd rather take a little rest before breakfast,' he said. 'It's been quite a day and I expect Paris will want me to do a bit of mopping-up tomorrow. There are several loose ends you won't have to worry about. I shall. I'll walk over to the hotel with you. Might as well convoy the treasure ship right into port.'

They strolled over through the shadows cast by the full moon. Both had their hands on their guns. It was three o'clock in the morning, but there were several people about and the courtyard of the Casino was still lined with motor-cars.

The short walk was uneventful.

At the hotel, Leiter insisted on accompanying Bond to his room. It was as Bond had left it six hours before.

'No reception committee,' observed Leiter, 'but I wouldn't put it past them to try a last throw. Do you think I ought to stay up and keep you two company?'

'You get your sleep,' said Bond. 'Don't worry about us. They won't be interested in me without the money and I've got an idea for looking after that. Thanks for all you've done. I hope we get on a job again one day.'

'Suits me,' said Leiter, 'so long as you can draw a nine when it's needed — and bring Vesper along with you,' he added dryly. He went out and closed the door.

Bond turned back to the friendliness of his room.

After the crowded arena of the big table and the nervous strain of the three hours' play, he was glad to be alone for a moment and to be welcomed by his pyjamas on the bed and his hair-brushes on the dressing-table. He went into the bathroom and dashed cold water over his face and gargled with a sharp mouthwash. He felt the bruises on the back of his head and on his right shoulder. He reflected cheerfully how narrowly he had twice that day escaped being murdered. Would he have to sit up all that night and wait for them to come again, or was Le Chiffre even now on his way to Le Havre or Bordeaux to pick up a boat for some corner of the world where he could escape the eyes and the guns of SMERSH?

Bond shrugged his shoulders. Sufficient unto that day had been its evil. He gazed for a moment into the mirror and wondered about Vesper's morals. He wanted her cold and arrogant body. He wanted to see tears and desire in her remote blue eyes and to take the ropes of her black hair in his hands and bend her long body back under his. Bond's eyes narrowed and his face in the mirror looked back at him with hunger.

He turned away and took out of his pocket the cheque for forty million francs. He folded this very small. Then he opened the door and looked up and down the corridor. He left the door wide open and with his ears cocked for footsteps or the sound of the lift, he set to work with a small screwdriver.

Five minutes later he gave a last-minute survey to his handiwork, put some fresh cigarettes in his case, closed and locked the door and went off down the corridor and across the hall and out into the moonlight.

14

'LA VIE EN ROSE?'

THE ENTRANCE TO the Roi Galant was a seven-foot golden picture-frame which had once, perhaps, enclosed the vast portrait of a noble European. It was in a discreet corner of the 'kitchen' — the public roulette and boule room, where several tables were still busy. As Bond took Vesper's arm and led her over the gilded step, he fought back a hankering to borrow some money from the caisse and plaster maximums over the nearest table. But he knew that this would be a brash and cheap gesture 'pour épater la bourgeoisie'. Whether he won or lost, it would be a kick in the teeth to the luck which had been given him.

The night club was small and dark, lit only by candles in gilded candelabra whose warm light was repeated in wall mirrors set in more gold picture-frames. The walls were covered in dark red satin and the chairs and 'banquettes' in matching red plush. In the far corner, a trio, consisting of a piano, an electric guitar and drums, was playing 'La Vie en Rose' with muted sweetness. Seduction dripped on the quietly throbbing air. It seemed to Bond that every couple must be touching with passion under the tables.

They were given a corner table near the door. Bond ordered a bottle of Veuve Clicquot and scrambled eggs and bacon.

They sat for a time listening to the music and then Bond turned to Vesper: 'It's wonderful sitting here with you and knowing the job's finished. It's a lovely end to the day — the prize-giving.'

He expected her to smile. She said: 'Yes, isn't it,' in a rather brittle voice. She seemed to be listening carefully to the music. One elbow rested on the table and her hand supported her chin, but on the back of her hand and not on the palm, and Bond noticed that her knuckles showed white as if her fist was tightly clenched.

Between the thumb and first two fingers of her right hand she held one of Bond's cigarettes, as an artist holds a crayon, and though she smoked with composure, she tapped the cigarette occasionally into an ashtray when the cigarette had no ash.

Bond noticed these small things because he felt intensely aware of her and because he wanted to draw her into his own feeling of warmth and relaxed sensuality. But he accepted her reserve. He thought it came from a desire to protect herself from him, or else it was her reaction to his coolness to her earlier in the evening, his deliberate coolness, which he knew had been taken as a rebuff.

He was patient. He drank champagne and talked a little about the happenings of the day and about the personalities of Mathis and Leiter and about the possible consequences for Le Chiffre. He was discreet and he only talked about the aspects of the case on which she must have been briefed by London.

She answered perfunctorily. She said that, of course, they had picked out the two gunmen, but had thought nothing of it when the man with the stick had gone to stand behind Bond's chair. They could not believe that anything would be attempted in the Casino itself. Directly Bond and Leiter had left to walk over to the hotel, she had telephoned Paris and told M.'s representative of the result of the game. She had had to speak guardedly and the agent had rung off without comment. She had been told to do this whatever the result. M. had asked for the information to be passed on to him personally at any time of the day or night.

This was all she said. She sipped at her champagne and rarely glanced at Bond. She didn't smile. Bond felt frustrated. He drank a lot of champagne and ordered another bottle. The scrambled eggs came and they ate in silence.

At four o'clock Bond was about to call for the bill when the maitre d'hotel appeared at their table and inquired for Miss Lynd. He handed her a note which she took and read hastily.

'Oh, it's only Mathis,' she said. 'He says would I come to the entrance hall. He's got a message for you. Perhaps he's not in evening clothes or something. I won't be a minute. Then perhaps we could go home.'

She gave him a strained smile. 'I'm afraid I don't feel very good company this evening. It's been rather a nerve-racking day. I'm so sorry.'

Bond made a perfunctory reply and rose, pushing back the table. 'I'll get the bill,' he said, and watched her take the few steps to the entrance.

He sat down and lit a cigarette. He felt flat. He suddenly realized that he was tired. The stuffiness of the room hit him as it had hit him in the Casino in the early hours of the previous day. He called for the bill and took a last mouthful of champagne. It tasted bitter, as the first glass too many always does. He would have liked to have seen Mathis's cheerful face and heard his news, perhaps even a word of congratulation.

Suddenly the note to Vesper seemed odd to him. It was not the way Mathis would do things. He would have asked them both to join him at the bar of the Casino or he would have joined them in the night club, whatever his clothes. They would have laughed together and Mathis would have been excited. He had much to tell Bond, more than Bond had to tell him. The arrest of the Bulgarian, who had probably talked some more; the chase after the man with the stick; Le Chiffre's movements when he left the Casino.

Bond shook himself. He hastily paid the bill, not waiting for the change. He pushed back his table and walked quickly through the entrance without acknowledging the good-nights of the maitre d'hotel and the doorman.

He hurried through the gaming-room and looked carefully up and down the long entrance hall. He cursed and quickened his step. There were only one or two officials and two or three men and women in evening clothes getting their things at the vestiaire.

No Vesper. No Mathis.

He was almost running. He got to the entrance and looked along the steps to left and right down and amongst the few remaining cars.

The commissionaire came towards him.

'A taxi, monsieur?'

Bond waved him aside and started down the steps, his eyes staring into the shadows, the night air cold on his sweating temples.

He was half-way down when he heard a faint cry, then the slam of a door away to the right. With a harsh growl and stutter from the exhaust a beetle-browed Citroën shot out of the shadows into the light of the moon, its front-wheel drive dry-skidding through the loose pebbles of the forecourt.

Its tail rocked on its soft springs as if a violent struggle was taking place on the back seat.

With a snarl it raced out to the wide entrance gate in a spray of gravel. A small black object shot out of an open rear window and thudded into a flower-bed. There was a scream of tortured rubber as the tyres caught the boulevard in a harsh left-handed turn, the deafening echo of a Citroën's exhaust in second gear, a crash into top, then a swiftly diminishing crackle as the car hared off between the shops on the main street towards the coast-road.

Bond knew he would find Vesper's evening bag among the flowers.

He ran back with it across the gravel to the brightly lit steps and scrabbled through its contents while the commissionaire hovered round him.

The crumpled note was there amongst the usual feminine baggage.

'Can you come out to the entrance hall for a moment? I have news for your companion.

RENÉ MATHIS.'

15

BLACK HARE AND GREY HOUND

IT WAS THE crudest possible forgery.

Bond leapt for the Bentley, blessing the impulse which had made him drive it over after dinner. With the choke full out, the engine answered at once to the starter and the roar drowned the faltering words of the commissionaire who jumped aside as the rear wheels whipped gravel at his piped trouser-legs.

As the car rocked to the left outside the gate, Bond ruefully longed for the front-wheel drive and low chassis of the Citroën. Then he went fast through the gears and settled himself for the pursuit, briefly savouring the echo of the huge exhaust as it came back at him from either side of the short main street through the town.

Soon he was out on the coast-road, a broad highway through the sand dunes which he knew from his morning's drive had an excellent surface and was well cat's-eyed on the bends. He pushed the revs up and up, hurrying the car to eighty then to ninety, his huge Marchal headlights boring a safe white tunnel, nearly half a mile long, between the walls of the night.

He knew the Citroën must have come this way. He had heard the exhaust penetrate beyond the town, and a little dust still hung on the bends. He hoped soon to see the distant shaft of its headlights. The night was still and clear. Only out at sea there must be a light summer mist for at intervals he could hear the fog-horns lowing like iron cattle down the coast.

As he drove, whipping the car faster and faster through the night, with the other half of his mind he cursed Vesper, and M. for having sent her on the job.

This was just what he had been afraid of. These blithering women who thought they could do a man's work. Why the hell couldn't they stay at home and mind their pots and pans and stick to their frocks and gossip and leave men's work to the men? And now for this to happen to him, just when the job had come off so beautifully. For Vesper to fall for an old trick like that and get herself snatched and probably held to ransom like some bloody heroine in a strip cartoon. The silly bitch.

Bond boiled at the thought of the fix he was in.

Of course. The idea was a straight swop. The girl against his cheque for forty million. Well, he wouldn't play: wouldn't think of playing. She was in the Service and knew what she was up against. He wouldn't even ask M. This job was more important than her. It was just too bad. She was a fine girl, but he wasn't going to fall for this childish trick. No dice. He would try and catch the Citroën and shoot it out with them and if she got shot in the process, that was too bad too. He would have done his stuff — tried to rescue her before they got her off to some hide-out — but if he didn't catch up with them he would get back to his hotel and go to sleep and say no more about it. The next morning he would ask Mathis what had happened to her and show him the note. If Le Chiffre put the touch on Bond for the money in exchange for the girl, Bond would do nothing and tell no one. The girl would just have to take it. If the commissionaire came along with the story of what he had seen, Bond would bluff it out by saying he had had a drunken row with the girl.

Bond's mind raged furiously on with the problem as he flung the great car down the coast-road, automatically taking the curves and watching out for carts or cyclists on their way into Royale. On straight stretches the Amherst Villiers supercharger dug spurs into the Bentley's twenty-five horses and the engine sent a high-pitched scream of pain into the night. Then the revolutions mounted until he was past 110 and on to the 120 m.p.h. mark on the speedometer.

He knew he must be gaining fast. Loaded as she was the Citroën could hardly better eighty even on this road. On an impulse he slowed down to seventy, turned on his fog-lights, and dowsed the twin Marchals. Sure enough, without the blinding curtain of his own lights, he could see the glow of another car a mile or two down the coast.

He felt under the dashboard and from a concealed holster took out a long-barrelled Colt Army Special .45 and laid it on the seat beside him. With this, if he was lucky with the surface of the road, he could hope to get their tyres or their petrol tank at anything up to a hundred yards.

Then he switched on the big lights again and screamed off in pursuit. He felt calm and at ease. The problem of Vesper's life was a problem no longer. His face in the blue light from the dashboard was grim but serene.

Ahead in the Citroën there were three men and the girl.

Le Chiffre was driving, his big fluid body hunched forward, his hands light and delicate on the wheel. Beside him sat the squat man who had carried the stick in the Casino. In his left hand he grasped a thick lever which protruded beside him almost level with the floor. It might have been a lever to adjust the driving-seat.

In the back seat was the tall thin gunman. He lay back relaxed, gazing at the ceiling, apparently uninterested in the wild speed of the car. His right hand lay caressingly on Vesper's left thigh which stretched out naked beside him.

Apart from her legs, which were naked to the hips, Vesper was only a parcel. Her long black velvet skirt had been lifted over her arms and head and tied above her head with a piece of rope. Where her face was, a small gap had been torn in the velvet so that she could breathe. She was not bound in any other way and she lay quiet, her body moving sluggishly with the swaying of the car.

Le Chiffre was concentrating half on the road ahead and half on the onrushing glare of Bond's headlights in the driving mirror. He seemed undisturbed when not more than a mile separated the hare from the hounds and he even brought the car down from eighty to sixty miles an hour. Now, as he swept round a bend he slowed down still further. A few hundred yards ahead a Michelin post showed where a small parochial road crossed with the highway.

'Attention,' he said sharply to the man beside him.

The man's hand tightened on the lever.

A hundred yards from the cross-roads he slowed to thirty. In the mirror Bond's great headlights were lighting up the bend.

Le Chiffre seemed to make up his mind.

'Allez.'

The man beside him pulled the lever sharply upwards. The boot at the back of the car yawned open like a whale's mouth. There was a tinkling clatter on the road and then a rhythmic jangling as if the car was towing lengths of chain behind it.

'Coupez.'

The man depressed the lever sharply and the jangling stopped with a final clatter.

Le Chiffre glanced again in the mirror. Bond's car was just entering the bend. Le Chiffre made a racing change and threw the Citroën left-handed down the narrow side-road, at the same time dowsing his lights.

He stopped the car with a jerk and all three men got swiftly out and doubled back under cover of a low hedge to the cross-roads, now fiercely illuminated by the lights of the Bentley. Each of them carried a revolver and the thin man also had what looked like a large black egg in his right hand.

The Bentley screamed down towards them like an express train.

16

THE CRAWLING OF THE SKIN

As BOND HURTLED round the bend, caressing the great car against the camber with an easy sway of body and hands, he was working out his plan of action when the distance between the two cars had narrowed still further. He imagined that the enemy driver would try to dodge off into a side-road if he got the chance. So when he had got round the bend and saw no lights ahead, it was a normal reflex to ease up on the accelerator and, when he saw the Michelin post, to prepare to brake.

He was only doing about sixty as he approached the black patch across the right-hand crown of the road which he assumed to be the shadow cast by a wayside tree. Even so, there was no time to save himself. There was suddenly a small carpet of glinting steel spikes right under his off-side wing. Then he was on top of it.

Bond automatically slammed the brakes full on and braced all his sinews against the wheel to correct the inevitable sharp slew to the left, but he only kept control for a split second. As the rubber was flayed from his off-side wheels and the rims for an instant tore up the tarmac, the heavy car whirled across the road in a tearing dry skid, slammed the left bank with a crash that knocked Bond out of the driving seat on to the floor, and then, facing back up the road, it reared slowly up, its front wheels spinning and its great headlights searching the sky. For a split second, resting on the petrol tank, it seemed to paw at the heavens like a giant praying-mantis. Then slowly it toppled over backwards and fell with a splintering crash of coachwork and glass.

In the deafening silence, the near-side front wheel whispered briefly on and then squeaked to a stop.

Le Chiffre and his two men only had to walk a few yards from their ambush.

'Put your guns away and get him out,' he ordered brusquely. 'I'll keep you covered. Be careful of him. I don't want a corpse. And hurry up, it's getting light.'

The two men got down on their knees. One of them took out a long knife and cut some of the fabric away from the side of the convertible hood and took hold of Bond's shoulders. He was unconscious and immovable. The other squeezed between the upturned car and the bank and forced his way through the crumpled window-frame. He eased Bond's legs, pinned between the steering wheel and the fabric roof of the car. Then they inched him out through a hole in the hood.

They were sweating and filthy with dust and oil by the time they had him lying in the road.

The thin man felt his heart and then slapped his face hard on either side. Bond grunted and moved a hand. The thin man slapped him again.

'That's enough,' said Le Chiffre. 'Tie his arms and put him in the car. Here,' he threw a roll of flex to the man. 'Empty his pockets first and give me his gun. He may have got some other weapons, but we can get them later.'

He took the objects the thin man handed him and stuffed them and Bond's Beretta into his wide pockets without examining them. He left the men to it and walked back to the car. His face showed neither pleasure nor excitement.

It was the sharp bite of the wire flex into his wrists that brought Bond to himself. He was aching all over as if he had been thrashed with a wooden club, but when he was yanked to his feet and pushed towards the narrow side-road where the engine of the Citroën was already running softly, he found that no bones were broken. But he felt in no mood for desperate attempts to escape and allowed himself to be dragged into the back seat of the car without resisting.

He felt thoroughly dispirited and weak in resolve as well as in his body. He had had to take too much in the past twenty-four hours and now this last stroke by the enemy seemed almost too final. This time there could be no miracles. No one knew where he was and no one would miss him until well on into the morning. The wreck of his car would be found before very long, but it would take hours to trace the ownership to him.

And Vesper. He looked to the right, past the thin man who was lying back with his eyes closed. His first reaction was one of scorn. Damn fool girl getting herself trussed up like a chicken, having her skirt pulled over her head as if the whole of this business was some kind of dormitory rag. But then he felt sorry for her. Her naked legs looked so childlike and defenceless.

'Vesper,' he said softly.

There was no answer from the bundle in the corner and Bond suddenly had a chill feeling, but then she stirred slightly.

At the same time the thin man caught him a hard back-handed blow over the heart.

'Silence.'

Bond doubled over with the pain and to shield himself from another blow, only to get a rabbit punch on the back of the neck which made him arch back again, the breath whistling through his teeth.

The thin man had hit him a hard professional cutting blow with the edge of the hand. There was something rather deadly about his accuracy and his lack of effort. He was now again lying back, his eyes closed. He was a man to make you afraid, an evil man. Bond hoped he might get a chance of killing him.

Suddenly the boot of the car was thrown open and there was a clanking crash. Bond guessed that they had been waiting for the third man to retrieve the carpet of spiked chain-mail. He assumed it must be an adaptation of the nail-studded devices used by the Resistance against German staff-cars.

Again he reflected on the efficiency of these people and the ingenuity of the equipment they used. Had M. underestimated their resourcefulness? He stifled a desire to place the blame on London. It was he who should have known. He who should have been warned by small signs and taken infinitely more precautions. He squirmed as he thought of himself washing down champagne in the Roi Galant while the enemy was busy preparing his counter-stroke. He cursed himself and cursed the hubris which had made him so sure that the battle was won and the enemy in flight.

All this time Le Chiffre had said nothing. Directly the boot was shut, the third man, whom Bond at once recognized, climbed in beside him and Le Chiffre reversed furiously back on to the main road. Then he banged the gear lever through the gate and was soon doing seventy on down the coast.

By now it was dawn — about five o'clock, Bond guessed — and he reflected that a mile or two on was the turning to Le Chiffre's villa. He had not thought that they would take Vesper there. Now that he realized that Vesper had only been a sprat to catch a mackerel the whole picture became clear.

It was an extremely unpleasant picture. For the first time since his capture, fear came to Bond and crawled up his spine.

Ten minutes later the Citroën lurched to the left, ran on a few hundred yards up a small side-road partly overgrown with grass and then between a pair of dilapidated stucco pillars into an unkempt forecourt surrounded by a high wall. They drew up in front of a peeling white door. Above a rusty bell-push in the door-frame, small zinc letters on a wooden base spelled out 'Les Noctambules' and, underneath, 'Sonnez SVP'.

From what Bond could see of the cement frontage, the villa was typical of the French seaside style. He could imagine the dead blue-bottles being hastily swept out for the summer let and the stale rooms briefly aired by a cleaning woman sent by the estate agent in Royale. Every five years one coat of white-wash would be slapped over the rooms and the outside wood-work, and for a few weeks the villa would present a smiling front to the world. Then the winter rains would get to work, and the imprisoned flies, and quickly the villa would take on again its abandoned look.

But, Bond reflected, it would admirably serve Le Chiffre's purpose this morning, if he was right in assuming what that was to be. They had passed no other house since his capture and from his reconnaissance of the day before he knew there was only an occasional farm for several miles to the south.

As he was urged out of the car with a sharp crack in the ribs from the thin man's elbow, he knew that Le Chiffre could have them both to himself, undisturbed, for several hours. Again his skin crawled.

Le Chiffre opened the door with a key and disappeared inside. Vesper, looking incredibly indecent in the early light of day, was pushed in after him with a torrent of lewd French from the man whom Bond knew to himself as 'the Corsican'. Bond followed without giving the thin man a chance to urge him.

The key of the front door turned in the lock.

Le Chiffre was standing in the doorway of a room on the right. He crooked a finger at Bond in a silent, spidery summons.

Vesper was being led down a passage towards the back of the house. Bond suddenly decided.

With a wild backward kick which connected with the thin man's shins and brought a whistle of pain from him, he hurled himself down the passage after her. With only his feet as weapons, there was no plan in his mind except to do as much damage as possible to the two gunmen and be able to exchange a few hurried words with the girl. No other plan was possible. He just wanted to tell her not to give in.

As the Corsican turned at the commotion Bond was on him and his right shoe was launched in a flying kick at the other man's groin.

Like lightning the Corsican slammed himself back against the wall of the passage and, as Bond's foot whistled past his hip, he very quickly, but somehow delicately, shot out his left hand, caught Bond's shoe at the top of its arc and twisted it sharply.

Completely off balance, Bond's other foot left the ground. In the air his whole body turned and with the momentum of his rush behind it crashed sideways and down on to the floor.

For a moment he lay there, all the breath knocked out of him. Then the thin man came and hauled him up against the wall by his collar. He had a gun in his hand. He looked Bond inquisitively in the eyes. Then unhurriedly he bent down and swiped the barrel viciously across Bond's shins. Bond grunted and caved at the knees.

'If there is a next time, it will be across your teeth,' said the thin man in bad French.

A door slammed. Vesper and the Corsican had disappeared. Bond turned his head to the right. Le Chiffre had moved a few feet out into the passage. He lifted his finger and crooked it again. Then for the first time he spoke.

'Come, my dear friend. We are wasting our time.'

He spoke in English with no accent. His voice was low and soft and unhurried. He showed no emotion. He might have been a doctor summoning the next patient from the waiting-room, a hysterical patient who had been expostulating feebly with a nurse.

Bond again felt puny and impotent. Nobody but an expert in ju-jitsu could have handled him with the Corsican's economy and lack of fuss. The cold precision with which the thin man had paid him back in his own coin had been equally unhurried, even artistic.

Almost docilely Bond walked back down the passage. He had nothing but a few more bruises to show for his clumsy gesture of resistance to these people.

As he preceded the thin man over the threshold he knew that he was utterly and absolutely in their power.

17

'MY DEAR BOY'

IT WAS A large bare room, sparsely furnished in cheap French 'art nouveau' style. It was difficult to say whether it was intended as a living- or dining-room for a flimsy-looking mirrored sideboard, sporting an orange crackle-ware fruit dish and two painted wooden candlesticks, took up most of the wall opposite the door and contradicted the faded pink sofa ranged against the other side of the room.

There was no table in the centre under the alabasterine ceiling light, only a small square of stained carpet with a futurist design in contrasting browns.

Over by the window was an incongruous-looking throne-like chair in carved oak with a red velvet seat, a low table on which stood an empty water carafe and two glasses, and a light armchair with a round cane seat and no cushion.

Half-closed venetian blinds obscured the view from the window, but cast bars of early sunlight over the few pieces of furniture and over part of the brightly papered wall and the brown stained floorboards.

Le Chiffre pointed at the cane chair.

'That will do excellently,' he said to the thin man. 'Prepare him quickly. If he resists, damage him only a little.'

He turned to Bond. There was no expression on his large face and his round eyes were uninterested. 'Take off your clothes. For every effort to resist, Basil will break one of your fingers. We are serious people and your good health is of no interest to us. Whether you live or die depends on the outcome of the talk we are about to have.'

He made a gesture towards the thin man and left the room.

The thin man's first action was a curious one. He opened the clasp-knife he had used on the hood of Bond's car, took the small armchair and with a swift motion he cut out its cane seat.

Then he came back to Bond, sticking the still open knife, like a fountain pen, in the vest pocket of his coat. He turned Bond round to the light and unwound the flex from his wrists. Then he stood quickly aside and the knife was back in his right hand.

'Vite.'

Bond stood chafing his swollen wrists and debating with himself how much time he could waste by resisting. He only delayed an instant. With a swift step and a downward sweep of his free hand, the thin man seized the collar of his dinner-jacket and dragged it down, pinning Bond's arms back. Bond made the traditional counter to this old policeman's hold by dropping down on one knee, but as he dropped the thin man dropped with him and at the same time brought his knife round and down behind Bond's back. Bond felt the back of the blade pass down his spine. There was the hiss of a sharp knife through cloth and his arms were suddenly free as the two halves of his coat fell forward.

He cursed and stood up. The thin man was back in his previous position, his knife again at the ready in his relaxed hand. Bond let the two halves of his dinner-jacket fall off his arms on to the floor.

'Allez,' said the thin man with a faint trace of impatience.

Bond looked him in the eye and then slowly started to take off his shirt.

Le Chiffre came quietly back into the room. He carried a pot of what smelt like coffee. He put it on the small table near the window. He also placed beside it on the table two other homely objects, a three-foot-long carpet-beater in twisted cane and a carving-knife.

He settled himself comfortably on the throne-like chair and poured some of the coffee into one of the glasses. With one foot he hooked forward the small armchair, whose seat was now an empty circular frame of wood, until it was directly opposite him.

Bond stood stark naked in the middle of the room, bruises showing livid on his white body, his face a grey mask of exhaustion and knowledge of what was to come.

'Sit down there.' Le Chiffre nodded at the chair in front of him.

Bond walked over and sat down.

The thin man produced some flex. With this he bound Bond's wrists to the arms of the chair and his ankles to the front legs. He passed a double strand across his chest, under the armpits and through the chair-back. He made no mistakes with the knots and left no play in any of the bindings. All of them bit sharply into Bond's flesh. The legs of the chair were broadly spaced and Bond could not even rock it.

He was utterly a prisoner, naked and defenceless.

His buttocks and the underpart of his body protruded through the seat of the chair towards the floor.

Le Chiffre nodded to the thin man who quietly left the room and closed the door.

There was a packet of Gauloises on the table and a lighter. Le Chiffre lit a cigarette and swallowed a mouthful of coffee from the glass. Then he picked up the cane carpet-beater and, resting the handle comfortably on his knee, allowed the flat trefoil base to lie on the floor directly under Bond's chair.

He looked Bond carefully, almost caressingly, in the eyes. Then his wrist sprang suddenly upwards on his knee.

The result was startling.

Bond's whole body arched in an involuntary spasm. His face contracted in a soundless scream and his lips drew right away from his teeth. At the same time his head flew back with a jerk showing the taut sinews of his neck. For an instant, muscles stood out in knots all over his body and his toes and fingers clenched until they were quite white. Then his body sagged and perspiration started to bead all over his skin. He uttered a deep groan.

Le Chiffre waited for his eyes to open.

'You see, dear boy?' He smiled a soft, fat smile. 'Is the position quite clear now?'

A drop of sweat fell off Bond's chin on to his naked chest.

'Now let us get down to business and see how soon we can be finished with this unfortunate mess you have got yourself into.' He puffed cheerfully at his cigarette and gave an admonitory tap on the floor beneath Bond's chair with his horrible and incongruous instrument.

'My dear boy,' Le Chiffre spoke like a father, 'the game of Red Indians is over, quite over. You have stumbled by mischance into a game for grown-ups and you have already found it a painful experience. You are not equipped, my dear boy, to play games with adults and it was very foolish of your nanny in London to have sent you out here with your spade and bucket. Very foolish indeed and most unfortunate for you.

'But we must stop joking, my dear fellow, although I am sure you would like to follow me in developing this amusing little cautionary tale.'

He suddenly dropped his bantering tone and looked at Bond sharply and venomously.

'Where is the money?'

Bond's bloodshot eyes looked emptily back at him.

Again the upward jerk of the wrist and again Bond's whole body writhed and contorted.

Le Chiffre waited until the tortured heart eased down its laboured pumping and until Bond's eyes dully opened again.

'Perhaps I should explain,' said Le Chiffre. 'I intend to continue attacking the sensitive parts of your body until you answer my question. I am without mercy and there will be no relenting. There is no one to stage a last-minute rescue and there is no possibility of escape for you. This is not a romantic adventure story in which the villain is finally routed and the hero is given a medal and marries the girl. Unfortunately these things don't happen in real life. If you continue to be obstinate, you will be tortured to the edge of madness and then the girl will be brought in and we will set about her in front of you. If that is still not enough, you will both be painfully killed and I shall reluctantly leave your bodies and make my way abroad to a comfortable house which is waiting for me. There I shall take up a useful and profitable career and live to a ripe and peaceful old age in the bosom of the family I shall doubtless create. So you see, my dear boy, that I stand to lose nothing. If you hand the money over, so much the better. If not, I shall shrug my shoulders and be on my way.'

He paused, and his wrist lifted slightly on his knee. Bond's flesh cringed as the cane surface just touched him.

'But you, my dear fellow, can only hope that I shall spare you further pain and spare your life. There is no other hope for you but that. Absolutely none.

'Well?'

Bond closed his eyes and waited for the pain. He knew that

the beginning of torture is the worst. There is a parabola of agony. A crescendo leading up to a peak and then the nerves are blunted and react progressively less until unconsciousness and death. All he could do was to pray for the peak, pray that his spirit would hold out so long and then accept the long free-wheel down to the final blackout.

He had been told by colleagues who had survived torture by the Germans and the Japanese that towards the end there came a wonderful period of warmth and languor leading into a sort of sexual twilight where pain turned to pleasure and where hatred and fear of the torturers turned to a masochistic infatuation. It was the supreme test of will, he had learnt, to avoid showing this form of punch-drunkenness. Directly it was suspected they would either kill you at once and save themselves further useless effort, or let you recover sufficiently so that your nerves had crept back to the other side of the parabola. Then they would start again.

He opened his eyes a fraction.

Le Chiffre had been waiting for this and like a rattlesnake the cane instrument leapt up from the floor. It struck again and again so that Bond screamed and his body jangled in the chair like a marionette.

Le Chiffre desisted only when Bond's tortured spasms showed a trace of sluggishness. He sat for a while sipping his coffee and frowning slightly like a surgeon watching a cardiograph during a difficult operation.

When Bond's eyes flickered and opened he addressed him again, but now with a trace of impatience.

'We know that the money is somewhere in your room,' he said. 'You drew a cheque to cash for forty million francs and I know that you went back to the hotel to hide it.'

For a moment Bond wondered how he had been so certain.

'Directly you left for the night club,' continued Le Chiffre, 'your room was searched by four of my people.'

The Muntzes must have helped, reflected Bond.

'We found a good deal in childish hiding-places. The ball-cock in the lavatory yielded an interesting little code-book and we found some more of your papers taped to the back of a drawer. All the furniture has been taken to pieces and your clothes and the curtains and bedclothes have been cut up. Every inch of the room has been searched and all the fittings removed. It is most unfortunate for you that we didn't find the cheque. If we had, you would now be comfortably in bed, perhaps with the beautiful Miss Lynd, instead of this.' He lashed upwards.

Through the red mist of pain, Bond thought of Vesper. He could imagine how she was being used by the two gunmen. They would be making the most of her before she was sent for by Le Chiffre. He thought of the fat wet lips of the Corsican and the slow cruelty of the thin man. Poor wretch to have been dragged into this. Poor little beast.

Le Chiffre was talking again.

'Torture is a terrible thing,' he was saying as he puffed at a fresh cigarette, 'but it is a simple matter for the torturer, particularly when the patient,' he smiled at the word, 'is a man. You see, my dear Bond, with a man it is quite unnecessary to indulge in refinements. With this simple instrument, or with almost any other object, one can cause a man as much pain as is possible or necessary. Do not believe what you read in novels or books about the war. There is nothing worse. It is not only the immediate agony, but also the thought that your manhood is being gradually destroyed and that at the end, if you will not yield, you will no longer be a man.

'That, my dear Bond, is a sad and terrible thought — a long chain of agony for the body and also for the mind, and then the final screaming moment when you will beg me to kill you. All that is inevitable unless you tell me where you hid the money.'

He poured some more coffee into the glass and drank it down leaving brown corners to his mouth.

Bond's lips were writhing. He was trying to say something. At last he got the word out in a harsh croak: 'Drink,' he said and his tongue came out and swilled across his dry lips.

'Of course, my dear boy, how thoughtless of me.' Le Chiffre poured some coffee into the other glass. There was a ring of sweat drops on the floor all round Bond's chair.

'We must certainly keep your tongue lubricated.'

He laid the handle of the carpet-beater down on the floor between his thick legs and rose from his chair. He went behind Bond and taking a handful of his soaking hair in one hand, he wrenched Bond's head sharply back. He poured the coffee down Bond's throat in small mouthfuls so that he would not choke. Then he released his head so that it fell forward again on his chest. He went back to his chair and picked up the carpet-beater.

Bond raised his head and spoke thickly.

'Money no good to you.' His voice was a laborious croak. 'Police trace it to you.'

Exhausted by the effort, his head sank forward again. He was a little, but only a little, exaggerating the extent of his physical collapse. Anything to gain time and anything to defer the next searing pain.

'Ah, my dear fellow, I had forgotten to tell you.' Le Chiffre smiled wolfishly. 'We met after our little game at the Casino and you were such a sportsman that you agreed we would have one more run through the pack between the two of us. It was a gallant gesture. Typical of an English gentleman.

'Unfortunately you lost and this upset you so much that you decided to leave Royale immediately for an unknown destination. Like the gentleman you are, you very kindly gave me a note explaining the circumstances so that I would have no difficulty in cashing your cheque. You see, dear boy, everything has been thought of and you need have no fears on my account.' He chuckled fatly.

'Now shall we continue? I have all the time in the world and truth to tell I am rather interested to see how long a man can stand this particular form of . . . er . . . encouragement.' He rattled the harsh cane on the floor.

So that was the score, thought Bond, with a final sinking of the heart. The 'unknown destination' would be under the ground or under the sea, or perhaps, more simple, under the crashed Bentley. Well, if he had to die anyway, he might as well try it the hard way. He had no hope that Mathis or Leiter would get to him in time, but at least there was a chance that they would catch up with Le Chiffre before he could get away. It must be getting on for seven. The car might have been found by now. It was a choice of evils, but the longer Le Chiffre continued the torture the more likely he would be revenged.

Bond lifted his head and looked Le Chiffre in the eyes.

The china of the whites was now veined with red. It was like looking at two blackcurrants poached in blood. The rest of the wide face was yellowish except where a thick black stubble covered the moist skin. The upward edges of black coffee at the corners of the mouth gave his expression a false smile and the whole face was faintly striped by the light through the venetian blinds.

'No,' he said flatly, '. . . you'.

Le Chiffre grunted and set to work again with savage fury. Occasionally he snarled like a wild beast.

After ten minutes Bond had fainted, blessedly.

Le Chiffre at once stopped. He wiped some sweat from his face with a circular motion of his disengaged hand. Then he looked at his watch and seemed to make up his mind.

He got up and stood behind the inert, dripping body. There was no colour in Bond's face or anywhere on his body above the waist. There was a faint flutter of his skin above the heart. Otherwise he might have been dead.

Le Chiffre seized Bond's ears and harshly twisted them. Then he leant forward and slapped his cheeks hard several times. Bond's head rolled from side to side with each blow. Slowly his breathing became deeper. An animal groan came from his lolling mouth.

Le Chiffre took a glass of coffee and poured some into Bond's mouth and threw the rest in his face. Bond's eyes slowly opened.

Le Chiffre returned to his chair and waited. He lit a cigarette and contemplated the spattered pool of blood on the floor beneath the inert body opposite.

Bond groaned again pitifully. It was an inhuman sound. His eyes opened wide and he gazed dully at his torturer.

Le Chiffre spoke.

'That is all, Bond. We will now finish with you. You understand? Not kill you, but finish with you. And then we will have in the girl and see if something can be got out of the remains of the two of you.'

He reached towards the table.

'Say good-bye to it, Bond.'

18

A CRAG-LIKE FACE

IT WAS EXTRAORDINARY to hear the third voice. The hour's ritual had only demanded a duologue against the horrible noise of the torture. Bond's dimmed senses hardly took it in. Then suddenly he was half-way back to consciousness. He found he could see and hear again. He could hear the dead silence after the one quiet word from the doorway. He could see Le Chiffre's head slowly come up and the expression of blank astonishment, of innocent amazement, slowly give way to fear.

'Shtop,' had said the voice, quietly.

Bond heard slow steps approaching behind his chair.

'Dhrop it,' said the voice.

Bond saw Le Chiffre's hand open obediently and the knife fall with a clatter to the floor.

He tried desperately to read into Le Chiffre's face what was happening behind him, but all he saw was blind incomprehension and terror. Le Chiffre's mouth worked, but only a high-pitched 'eek' came from it. His heavy cheeks trembled as he tried to collect enough saliva in his mouth to say something, ask something. His hands fluttered vaguely in his lap. One of them made a slight movement towards his pocket, but instantly fell back. His round staring eyes had lowered for a split second and Bond guessed there was a gun trained on him.

There was a moment's silence.

'SMERSH.'

The word came almost with a sigh. It came with a downward cadence as if nothing else had to be said. It was the final explanation. The last word of all.

'No,' said Le Chiffre. 'No. I . . . ' His voice tailed off.

Perhaps he was going to explain, to apologize, but what he must have seen in the other's face made it all useless.

'Your two men. Both dead. You are a fool and a thief and a traitor. I have been sent from the Soviet Union to eliminate you. You are fortunate that I have only time to shoot you. If it was possible, I was instructed that you should die most painfully. We cannot see the end of the trouble you have caused.'

The thick voice stopped. There was silence in the room save for the rasping breath of Le Chiffre.

Somewhere outside a bird began to sing and there were other small noises from the awakening countryside. The bands of sunlight were stronger and the sweat on Le Chiffre's face glistened brightly.

'Do you plead guilty?'

Bond wrestled with his consciousness. He screwed up his eyes and tried to shake his head to clear it, but his whole nervous system was numbed and no message was transmitted to his muscles. He could just keep his focus on the great pale face in front of him and on its bulging eyes.

A thin string of saliva crept from the open mouth and hung down from the chin.

'Yes,' said the mouth.

There was a sharp 'phut', no louder than a bubble of air escaping from a tube of toothpaste. No other noise at all, and suddenly Le Chiffre had grown another eye, a third eye on a level with the other two, right where the thick nose started to jut out below the forehead. It was a small black eye, without eyelashes or eyebrows.

For a second the three eyes looked out across the room and then the whole face seemed to slip and go down on one knee. The two outer eyes turned trembling up towards the ceiling. Then the heavy head fell sideways and the right shoulder and finally the whole upper part of the body lurched over the arm of the chair as if Le Chiffre were going to be sick. But there was only a short rattle of his heels on the ground and then no other movement.

The tall back of the chair looked impassively out across the dead body in its arms.

There was a faint movement behind Bond. A hand came from behind and grasped his chin and pulled it back.

For a moment Bond looked up into two glittering eyes behind a narrow black mask. There was the impression of a crag-like face under a hat-brim, the collar of a fawn mackintosh. He could take in nothing more before his head was pushed down again.

'You are fortunate,' said the voice. 'I have no orders to kill you. Your life has been saved twice in one day. But you can tell your organization that SMERSH is only merciful by chance or by mistake. In your case you were saved first by chance and now by mistake, for I should have had orders to kill any foreign spies who were hanging round this traitor like flies round a dog's-mess.

'But I shall leave you my visiting card. You are a gambler. You play at cards. One day perhaps you will play against one of us. It would be well that you should be known as a spy.'

Steps moved round to behind Bond's right shoulder. There was the click of a knife opening. An arm in some grey material came into Bond's line of vision. A broad hairy hand emerging from a dirty white shirt-cuff was holding a thin stiletto like a fountain pen. It poised for a moment above the back of Bond's right hand, immovably bound with flex to the arm of the chair. The point of the stiletto executed three quick straight slashes. A fourth slash crossed them where they ended, just short of the knuckles. Blood in the shape of an inverted 'M' welled out and slowly started to drip on to the floor.

The pain was nothing to what Bond was already suffering, but it was enough to plunge him again into unconsciousness.

The steps moved quietly away across the room. The door was softly closed.

In the silence, the cheerful small sounds of the summer's day crept through the closed window. High on the left-hand wall hung two small patches of pink light. They were reflections cast upwards from the floor by the zebra stripes of June sunshine, cast upwards from two separate pools of blood a few feet apart.

As the day progressed the pink patches marched slowly along the wall. And slowly they grew larger.

19

THE WHITE TENT

YOU ARE ABOUT to awake when you dream that you are dreaming.

During the next two days James Bond was permanently in this state without regaining consciousness. He watched the procession of his dreams go by without making any effort to disturb their sequence, although many of them were terrifying and all were painful. He knew that he was in a bed and that he was lying on his back and could not move and in one of his twilit moments he thought there were people round him, but he made no effort to open his eyes and re-enter the world.

He felt safer in the darkness and he hugged it to him.

On the morning of the third day a bloody nightmare shook him awake, trembling and sweating. There was a hand on his forehead which he associated with his dream. He tried to lift an arm and smash it sideways into the owner of the hand, but his arms were immovable, secured to the sides of his bed. His whole body was strapped down and something like a large white coffin covered him from chest to feet and obscured his view of the end of the bed. He shouted a string of obscenities, but the effort took all his strength and the words tailed off into a sob. Tears of forlornness and self-pity welled out of his eyes.

A woman's voice was speaking and the words gradually penetrated to him. It seemed to be a kind voice and it slowly came to him that he was being comforted and that this was a friend and not an enemy. He could hardly believe it. He had been so certain that he was still a captive and that the torture was about to begin again. He felt his face being softly wiped with a cool cloth which smelt of lavender and then he sank back into his dreams.

When he awoke again some hours later all his terrors had gone and he felt warm and languorous. Sun was streaming into the bright room and garden sounds came through the window. In the background there was the noise of small waves on a beach. As he moved his head he heard a rustle and a nurse who had been sitting beside his pillow rose and came into his line of vision. She was pretty and she smiled as she put her hand on his pulse.

'Well, I'm certainly glad you've woken up at last. I've never heard such dreadful language in my life.'

Bond smiled back at her.

'Where am I?' he asked and was surprised that his voice sounded firm and clear.

'You're in a nursing home at Royale and I've been sent over from England to look after you. There are two of us and I'm Nurse Gibson. Now just lie quiet and I'll go and tell doctor you're awake. You've been unconscious since they brought you in and we've been quite worried.'

Bond closed his eyes and mentally explored his body. The worst pain was in his wrists and ankles and in his right hand where the Russian had cut him. In the centre of the body there was no feeling. He assumed that he had been given a local anaesthetic. The rest of his body ached dully as if he had been beaten all over. He could feel the pressure of bandages everywhere and his unshaven neck and chin prickled against the sheets. From the feel of the bristles he knew that he must have been at least three days without shaving. That meant two days since the morning of the torture.

He was preparing a short list of questions in his mind when the door opened and the doctor came in followed by the nurse and in the background the dear figure of Mathis, a Mathis looking anxious behind his broad smile, who put a finger to his lips and walked on tiptoe to the window and sat down.

The doctor, a Frenchman with a young and intelligent face, had been detached from his duties with the Deuxième Bureau to look after Bond's case. He came and stood beside Bond and put his hand on Bond's forehead while he looked at the temperature chart behind the bed.

When he spoke he was forthright.

'You have a lot of questions to ask, my dear Mr Bond,' he said in excellent English, 'and I can tell you most of the answers. I do not want you to waste your strength, so I will give you the salient facts and then you may have a few minutes with Monsieur Mathis who wishes to obtain one or two details from you. It is really too early for this talk, but I wish to set your mind at rest so that we can proceed with the task of repairing your body without bothering too much about your mind.'

Nurse Gibson pulled up a chair for the doctor and left the room.

'You have been here about two days,' continued the doctor. 'Your car was found by a farmer on the way to market in Royale and he informed the police. After some delay Monsieur Mathis heard that it was your car and he immediately went to Les Noctambules with his men. You and Le Chiffre were found and also your friend, Miss Lynd, who was unharmed and according to her account suffered no molestation. She was prostrated with shock, but is now fully recovered and is at her hotel. She has been instructed by her superiors in London to stay at Royale under your orders until you are sufficiently recovered to go back to England.

'Le Chiffre's two gunmen are dead, each killed by a single .35 bullet in the back of the skull. From the lack of expression on their faces, they evidently never saw or heard their assailant. They were found in the same room as Miss Lynd. Le Chiffre is dead, shot with a similar weapon between the eyes. Did you witness his death?'

'Yes,' said Bond.

'Your own injuries are serious, but your life is not in danger though you have lost a lot of blood. If all goes well, you will recover completely and none of the functions of your body will be impaired.' The doctor smiled grimly. 'But I fear that you will continue to be in pain for several days and it will be my endeavour to give you as much comfort as possible. Now that you have regained consciousness your arms will be freed, but you must not move your body and when you sleep the nurse has orders to secure your arms again. Above all, it is important that you rest and regain your strength. At the moment you are suffering from a grave condition of mental and physical shock.' The doctor paused. 'For how long were you maltreated?'

'About an hour,' said Bond.

'Then it is remarkable that you are alive and I congratulate you. Few men could have supported what you have been through. Perhaps that is some consolation. As Monsieur Mathis can tell you, I have had in my time to treat a number of patients who have suffered similar handling and not one has come through it as you have done.'

The doctor looked at Bond for a moment and then turned brusquely to Mathis.

'You may have ten minutes and then you will be forcibly ejected. If you put the patient's temperature up, you will answer for it.'

He gave them both a broad smile and left the room.

Mathis came over and took the doctor's chair.

'That's a good man,' said Bond. 'I like him.'

'He's attached to the Bureau,' said Mathis. 'He is a very good man and I will tell you about him one of these days. He thinks you are a prodigy — and so do I.

'However, that can wait. As you can imagine, there is much to clear up and I am being pestered by Paris and, of course, London, and even by Washington via our good friend Leiter. Incidentally,' he broke off, 'I have a personal message from M. He spoke to me himself on the telephone. He simply said to tell you that he is much impressed. I asked if that was all and he said: "Well, tell him that the Treasury is greatly relieved." Then he rang off.'

Bond grinned with pleasure. What most warmed him was that M. himself should have rung up Mathis. This was quite unheard of. The very existence of M., let alone his identity, was never admitted. He could imagine the flutter this must have caused in the ultra-security-minded organization in London.

'A tall thin man with one arm came over from London the same day we found you,' continued Mathis, knowing from his own experience that these shop details would interest Bond more than anything else and give him most pleasure, 'and he fixed up the nurses and looked after everything. Even your car's being repaired for you. He seemed to be Vesper's boss. He spent a lot of time with her and gave her strict instructions to look after you.'

Head of S., thought Bond. They're certainly giving me the red carpet treatment.

'Now,' said Mathis, 'to business. Who killed Le Chiffre?'

'SMERSH,' said Bond.

Mathis gave a low whistle.

'My God,' he said respectfully. 'So they *were* on to him. What did he look like?'

Bond explained briefly what had happened up to the moment of Le Chiffre's death, omitting all but the most essential details. It cost him an effort and he was glad when it was done. Casting his mind back to the scene awoke the whole nightmare and the sweat began to pour off his forehead and a deep throb of pain started up in his body.

Mathis realized that he was going too far. Bond's voice was getting feebler and his eyes were clouding. Mathis snapped shut his shorthand book and laid a hand on Bond's shoulder.

'Forgive me, my friend,' he said. 'It is all over now and you are in safe hands. All is well and the whole plan has gone splendidly. We have announced that Le Chiffre shot his two accomplices and then committed suicide because he could not face an inquiry into the union funds. Strasbourg and the north are in an uproar. He was considered a great hero there and a pillar of the Communist Party in France. This story of brothels and casinos has absolutely knocked the bottom out of his organization and they're all running around like scalded cats. At the moment the Communist Party is giving out that he was off his head. But that hasn't helped much after Thorez's breakdown not long ago. They're just making it look as if all their big-shots were gaga. God knows how they're going to unscramble the whole business.'

Mathis saw that his enthusiasm had had the desired effect. Bond's eyes were brighter.

'One last mystery,' Mathis said, 'and then I promise I will go.' He looked at his watch. 'The doctor will be after my skin in a moment. Now, what about the money? Where is it? Where did you hide it? We too have been over your room with a tooth-comb. It isn't there.'

Bond grinned.

'It is,' he said, 'more or less. On the door of each room there is a small square of black plastic with the number of the room on it. On the corridor side, of course. When Leiter left me that night, I simply opened the door and unscrewed my number plate and put the folded cheque underneath it and screwed the plate back. It'll still be there.' He smiled. 'I'm glad there's something the stupid English can teach the clever French.'

Mathis laughed delightedly.

'I suppose you think that's paid me back for knowing what the Muntzes were up to. Well, I'll call it quits. Incidentally, we've got them in the bag. They were just some minor fry hired for the occasion. We'll see they get a few years.'

He rose hastily as the doctor stormed into the room and took one look at Bond.

'Out,' he said to Mathis. 'Out and don't come back.'

Mathis just had time to wave cheerfully to Bond and call some hasty words of farewell before he was hustled through the door. Bond heard a torrent of heated French diminishing down the corridor. He lay back exhausted, but heartened by all he had heard. He found himself thinking of Vesper as he quickly drifted off into a troubled sleep.

There were still questions to be answered, but they could wait.

20

THE NATURE OF EVIL

BOND MADE GOOD progress. When Mathis came to see him three days later he was propped up in bed and his arms were free. The lower half of his body was still shrouded in the oblong tent, but he looked cheerful and it was only occasionally that a twinge of pain narrowed his eyes.

Mathis looked crestfallen.

'Here's your cheque,' he said to Bond. 'I've rather enjoyed walking around with forty million francs in my pocket, but I suppose you'd better sign it and I'll put it to your account with the Crédit Lyonnais. There's no sign of our friend from SMERSH. Not a damn trace. He must have got to the villa on foot or on a bicycle because you heard nothing of his arrival and the two gunmen obviously didn't. It's pretty exasperating. We've got precious little on this SMERSH organization and neither has London. Washington said they had, but it turned out to be the usual waffle from refugee interrogation, and you know that's about as much good as interrogating an English man-in-the-street about his own Secret Service, or a Frenchman about the Deuxième.'

'He probably came from Leningrad to Berlin via Warsaw,' said Bond. 'From Berlin they've got plenty of routes open to the rest of Europe. He's back home by now being told off for not shooting me too. I fancy they've got quite a file on me in view of one or two of the jobs M.'s given me since the war. He obviously thought he was being smart enough cutting his initial in my hand.'

'What's that?' asked Mathis. 'The doctor said the cuts looked like a square M with a tail to the top. He said they didn't mean anything.'

'Well, I only got a glimpse before I passed out, but I've seen the cuts several times while they were being dressed and I'm pretty certain they are the Russian letter for SH. It's rather like an inverted M with a tail. That would make sense. SMERSH is short for SMYERT SHPIONAM — Death to Spies — and he thinks he's labelled me as a SHPION. It's a nuisance because M. will probably say I've got to go to hospital again when I get back to London and have new skin grafted over the whole of the back of my hand. It doesn't matter much. I've decided to resign.'

Mathis looked at him with his mouth open.

'Resign?' he asked incredulously. 'What the hell for?'

Bond looked away from Mathis. He studied his bandaged hands.

'When I was being beaten up,' he said, 'I suddenly liked the idea of being alive. Before Le Chiffre began, he used a phrase which stuck in my mind . . . "playing Red Indians". He said that's what I had been doing. Well, I suddenly thought he might be right.

'You see,' he said, still looking down at his bandages, 'when one's young, it seems very easy to distinguish between right and wrong, but as one gets older it becomes more difficult. At school it's easy to pick out one's own villains and heroes and one grows up wanting to be a hero and kill the villains.'

He looked obstinately at Mathis.

'Well, in the last few years I've killed two villains. The first was in New York — a Japanese cipher expert cracking our codes on the thirty-sixth floor of the R.C.A. building in the Rockefeller Center, where the Japs had their consulate. I took a room on the fortieth floor of the next-door skyscraper and I could look across the street into his room and see him working. Then I got a colleague from our organization in New York and a couple of Remington thirty-thirties with telescopic sights and silencers. We smuggled them up to my room and sat for days waiting for our chance. He shot at the man a second before me. His job was only to blast a hole through the window so that I could shoot the Jap through it. They have tough windows at the Rockefeller Center to keep the noise out. It worked very well. As I expected, his bullet got deflected by the glass and went God knows where. But I shot immediately after him, through the hole he had made. I got the Jap in the mouth as he turned to gape at the broken window.'

Bond smoked for a minute.

'It was a pretty sound job. Nice and clean too. Three hundred yards away. No personal contact. The next time in Stockholm wasn't so pretty. I had to kill a Norwegian who was doubling against us for the Germans. He'd managed to get two of our men captured — probably bumped off for all I know. For various reasons it had to be an absolutely silent job. I chose the bedroom of his flat and a knife. And, well, he just didn't die very quickly.

'For those two jobs I was awarded a Double o number in the Service. Felt pretty clever and got a reputation for being good and tough. A Double o number in our Service means you've had to kill a chap in cold blood in the course of some job.

'Now,' he looked up again at Mathis, 'that's all very fine. The hero kills two villains, but when the hero Le Chiffre starts to kill the villain Bond and the villain Bond knows he isn't a villain at all, you see the other side of the medal. The villains and heroes get all mixed up.

'Of course,' he added, as Mathis started to expostulate, 'patriotism comes along and makes it seem fairly all right, but this country-right-or-wrong business is getting a little out-of-date. Today we are fighting communism. Okay. If I'd been alive fifty years ago, the brand of conservatism we have today would have been damn near called communism and we should have been told to go and fight that. History is moving pretty quickly these days and the heroes and villains keep on changing parts.'

Mathis stared at him aghast. Then he tapped his head and put a calming hand on Bond's arm.

'You mean to say that this precious Le Chiffre who did his best to turn you into a eunuch doesn't qualify as a villain?' he asked. 'Anyone would think from the rot you talk that he had been battering your head instead of your . . . ' he gestured down the bed. 'You wait till M. tells you to get after another Le Chiffre. I bet you'll go after him all right. And what about SMERSH? I can tell you I don't like the idea of these chaps running around France killing anyone they feel has been a traitor to their precious political system. You're a bloody anarchist.'

He threw his arms in the air and let them fall helplessly to his sides.

Bond laughed.

'All right,' he said. 'Take our friend Le Chiffre. It's simple enough to say he was an evil man, at least it's simple enough for me because he did evil things to me. If he was here now, I wouldn't hesitate to kill him, but out of personal revenge and not, I'm afraid, for some high moral reason or for the sake of my country.'

He looked up at Mathis to see how bored he was getting with these introspective refinements of what, to Mathis, was a simple question of his duty.

Mathis smiled back at him.

'Continue, my dear friend. It is interesting for me to see this new Bond. Englishmen are so odd. They are like a nest of Chinese boxes. It takes a very long time to get to the centre of them. When one gets there the result is unrewarding, but the process is instructive and entertaining. Continue. Develop your arguments. There may be something I can use to my own chief the next time I want to get out of an unpleasant job.' He grinned maliciously.

Bond ignored him.

'Now in order to tell the difference between good and evil, we have manufactured two images representing the extremes — representing the deepest black and the purest white — and we call them God and the Devil. But in doing so we have cheated a bit. God is a clear image, you can see every hair on His beard. But the Devil. What does he look like?' Bond looked triumphantly at Mathis.

Mathis laughed ironically.

'A woman.'

'It's all very fine,' said Bond, 'but I've been thinking about these things and I'm wondering whose side I ought to be on. I'm getting very sorry for the Devil and his disciples such as the good Le Chiffre. The Devil has a rotten time and I always like to be on the side of the underdog. We don't give the poor chap a chance. There's a Good Book about goodness and how to be good and so forth, but there's no Evil Book about evil and how to be bad. The Devil had no prophets to write his Ten Commandments and no team of authors to write his biography. His case has gone completely by default. We know nothing about him but a lot of fairy stories from our parents and schoolmasters. He has no book from which we can learn the nature of evil in all its forms, with parables about evil people, proverbs about evil people, folklore about evil people. All we have is the living example of the people who are least good, or our own intuition.

'So,' continued Bond, warming to his argument, 'Le Chiffre was serving a wonderful purpose, a really vital purpose, perhaps the best and highest purpose of all. By his evil existence, which foolishly I have helped to destroy, he was creating a norm of badness by which, and by which alone, an opposite norm of goodness could exist. We were privileged, in our short knowledge of him, to see and estimate his wickedness and we emerge from the acquaintanceship better and more virtuous men.'

'Bravo,' said Mathis. 'I'm proud of you. You ought to be tortured every day. I really must remember to do something evil this evening. I must start at once. I have a few marks in my favour — only small ones, alas,' he added ruefully — 'but I shall work fast now that I have seen the light. What a splendid time I'm going to have. Now, let's see, where shall I start, murder, arson, rape? But no, these are peccadilloes. I must really consult the good Marquis de Sade. I am a child, an absolute child in these matters.'

His face fell.

'Ah, but our conscience, my dear Bond. What shall we do with him while we are committing some juicy sin? That is a problem. He is a crafty person this conscience and very old, as old as the first family of apes which gave birth to him. We must give that problem really careful thought or we shall spoil our enjoyment. Of course, we should murder him first, but he is a tough bird. It will be difficult, but if we succeed, we could be worse even than Le Chiffre.

'For you, dear James, it is easy. You can start off by resigning. That was a brilliant thought of yours, a splendid start to your new career. And so simple. Everyone has the revolver of resignation in his pocket. All you've got to do is pull the trigger and you will have made a big hole in your country and your conscience at the same time. A murder and a suicide with one bullet! Splendid! What a difficult and glorious profession. As for me, I must start embracing the new cause at once.'

He looked at his watch.

'Good. I've started already. I'm half an hour late for a meeting with the chief of police.'

He rose to his feet laughing.

'That was most enjoyable, my dear James. You really ought to go on the halls. Now about that little problem of yours, this business of not knowing good men from bad men and villains from heroes, and so forth. It is, of course, a difficult problem in the abstract. The secret lies in personal experience, whether you're a Chinaman or an Englishman.'

He paused at the door.

'You admit that Le Chiffre did you personal evil and that you would kill him if he appeared in front of you now?

'Well, when you get back to London you will find there are other Le Chiffres seeking to destroy you and your friends and your country. M. will tell you about them. And now that you have seen a really evil man, you will know how evil they can be and you will go after them to destroy them in order to protect yourself and the people you love. You won't wait to argue about it. You know what they look like now and what they can do to people. You may be a bit more choosy about the jobs you take on. You may want to be certain that the target really is black, but there are plenty of really black targets around. There's still plenty for you to do. And you'll do it. And when you fall in love and have a mistress or a wife and children to look after, it will seem all the easier.'

Mathis opened the door and stopped on the threshold.

'Surround yourself with human beings, my dear James. They are easier to fight for than principles.'

He laughed. 'But don't let me down and become human yourself. We would lose such a wonderful machine.'

With a wave of the hand he shut the door.

'Hey,' shouted Bond.

But the footsteps went quickly off down the passage.

21

VESPER

IT WAS ON the next day that Bond asked to see Vesper.

He had not wanted to see her before. He was told that every day she came to the nursing home and asked after him. Flowers had arrived from her. Bond didn't like flowers and he told the nurse to give them to another patient. After this had happened twice, no more flowers came. Bond had not meant to offend her. He disliked having feminine things around him. Flowers seemed to ask for recognition of the person who had sent them, to be constantly transmitting a message of sympathy and affection. Bond found this irksome. He disliked being cosseted. It gave him claustrophobia.

Bond was bored at the idea of having to explain some of this to Vesper. And he was embarrassed at having to ask one or two questions which mystified him, questions about Vesper's behaviour. The answers would almost certainly make her out to be a fool. Then he had his full report to M. to think about. In this he didn't want to have to criticize Vesper. It might easily cost her her job.

But above all, he admitted to himself, he shirked the answer to a more painful question.

The doctor had talked often to Bond about his injuries. He had always told him that there would be no evil effects from the terrible battering his body had received. He had said that Bond's full health would return and that none of his powers had been taken from him. But the evidence of Bond's eyes and his nerves refused these comforting assurances. He was still painfully swollen and bruised and whenever the injections wore off he was in agony. Above all, his imagination had suffered. For an hour in that room with Le Chiffre the certainty of impotence had been beaten into him and a scar had been left on his mind that could only be healed by experience.

From the day when Bond first met Vesper in the Hermitage

bar, he had found her desirable and he knew that if things had been different in the night club, if Vesper had responded in any way and if there had been no kidnapping, he would have tried to sleep with her that night. Even later, in the car and outside the villa when God knows he had had other things to think about, his eroticism had been hotly aroused by the sight of her indecent nakedness.

And now when he could see her again, he was afraid. Afraid that his senses and his body would not respond to her sensual beauty. Afraid that he would feel no stir of desire and that his blood would stay cool. In his mind he had made this first meeting into a test and he was shirking the answer. That was the real reason, he admitted, why he had waited to give his body a chance to respond, why he had put off their first meeting for over a week. He would like to have put off the meeting still further, but he explained to himself that his report must be written, that any day an emissary from London would come over and want to hear the full story, that today was as good as tomorrow, that anyway he might as well know the worst.

So on the eighth day he asked for her, for the early morning when he was feeling refreshed and strong after the night's rest.

For no reason at all, he had expected that she would show some sign of her experiences, that she would look pale and even ill. He was not prepared for the tall bronzed girl in a cream tussore frock with a black belt who came happily through the door and stood smiling at him.

'Good heavens, Vesper,' he said with a wry gesture of welcome, 'you look absolutely splendid. You must thrive on disaster. How have you managed to get such a wonderful sunburn?'

'I feel very guilty,' she said sitting down beside him. 'But I've been bathing every day while you've been lying here. The doctor said I was to and Head of S. said I was to, so, well, I just thought it wouldn't help you for me to be moping away all day long in my room. I've found a wonderful stretch of sand down the coast and I take my lunch and go there every day with a book and I don't come back till the evening. There's a bus that takes me there and back with only a short walk over the dunes, and I've managed to get over the fact that it's on the way down that road to the villa.'

Her voice faltered.

The mention of the villa had made Bond's eyes flicker.

She continued bravely, refusing to be defeated by Bond's lack of response.

'The doctor says it won't be long before you're allowed up. I thought perhaps . . . I thought perhaps I could take you down to this beach later on. The doctor says that bathing would be very good for you.'

Bond grunted.

'God knows when I'll be able to bathe,' he said. 'The doctor's talking through his hat. And when I can bathe it would probably be better for me to bathe alone for a bit. I don't want to frighten anybody. Apart from anything else,' he glanced pointedly down the bed, 'my body's a mass of scars and bruises. But you enjoy yourself. There's no reason why you shouldn't enjoy yourself.'

Vesper was stung by the bitterness and injustice in his voice.

'I'm sorry,' she said, 'I just thought . . . I was just trying . . .'

Suddenly her eyes filled with tears. She swallowed.

'I wanted . . . I wanted to help you get well.'

Her voice strangled. She looked piteously at him, facing the accusation in his eyes and in his manner.

Then she broke down and buried her face in her hands and sobbed.

'I'm sorry,' she said in a muffled voice. 'I'm really sorry.' With one hand she searched for a handkerchief in her bag. 'It's all my fault,' she dabbed at her eyes, 'I know it's all my fault.'

Bond at once relented. He put out a bandaged hand and laid it on her knee.

'It's all right, Vesper. I'm sorry I was so rough. It's just that I was jealous of you in the sunshine while I'm stuck here. Directly I'm well enough I'll come with you and you must show me your beach. Of course it's just what I want. It'll be wonderful to get out again.'

She pressed his hand and stood up and walked over to the window. After a moment she busied herself with her make-up. Then she came back to the bed.

Bond looked at her tenderly. Like all harsh, cold men, he was easily tipped over into sentiment. She was very beautiful and he felt warm towards her. He decided to make his questions as easy as possible.

He gave her a cigarette and for a time they talked of the visit of Head of S. and of the reactions in London to the rout of Le Chiffre.

From what she said it was clear that the final object of the plan had been more than fulfilled. The story was still being splashed all over the world and correspondents of most of the English and American papers had been at Royale trying to trace the Jamaican millionaire who had defeated Le Chiffre at the tables. They had got on to Vesper, but she had covered up well. Her story was that Bond had told her he was going on to Cannes and Monte Carlo to gamble with his winnings. The hunt had moved down to the South of France. Mathis and the police had obliterated all other traces and the papers were forced to concentrate on the Strasbourg angles and the chaos in the ranks of the French communists.

'By the way, Vesper,' said Bond after a time. 'What really happened to you after you left me in the night club? All I saw was the actual kidnapping.' He told her briefly of the scene outside the Casino.

'I'm afraid I must have lost my head,' said Vesper, avoiding Bond's eyes. 'When I couldn't see Mathis anywhere in the entrance hall I went outside and the commissionaire asked me if I was Miss Lynd, and then told me the man who had sent in the note was waiting in a car down on the right of the steps. Somehow I wasn't particularly surprised. I'd only known Mathis for a day or two and I didn't know how he worked, so I just walked down towards the car. It was away on the right and more or less in the shadows. Just as I was coming up to it, Le Chiffre's two men jumped out from behind one of the other cars in the row and simply scooped my skirt over my head.'

Vesper blushed.

'It sounds a childish trick,' she looked penitently at Bond, 'but it's really frightfully effective. One's a complete prisoner and although I screamed I don't expect any sound came out from under my skirt. I kicked out as hard as I could, but that was no use as I couldn't see and my arms were absolutely helpless. I was just a trussed chicken. They picked me up between them and shoved me into the back of the car. I went on struggling, of course, and when the car started and while they were trying to tie a rope or something round the top of my skirt over my head, I managed to get an arm free and throw my bag through the window. I hope it was some use.'

Bond nodded.

'It was really instinctive. I just thought you'd have no idea what had happened to me and I was terrified. I did the first thing I could think of.'

Bond knew that it was him they had been after and that if Vesper hadn't thrown her bag out, they would probably have thrown it out themselves directly they saw him appear on the steps.

'It certainly helped,' said Bond, 'but why didn't you make any sign when they finally got me after the car smash, when I spoke to you? I was dreadfully worried. I thought they might have knocked you out or something.'

'I'm afraid I must have been unconscious,' said Vesper. 'I fainted once from lack of air and when I came to they had cut a hole in front of my face. I must have fainted again. I don't remember much until we got to the villa. I really only gathered you had been captured when I heard you try and come after me in the passage.'

'And they didn't touch you?' asked Bond. 'They didn't try and mess about with you while I was being beaten up?'

'No,' said Vesper. 'They just left me in an armchair. They drank and played cards — "belotte" I think it was from what I heard — and then they went to sleep. I suppose that was how SMERSH got them. They bound my legs and put me on a chair in a corner facing the wall and I saw nothing of SMERSH. I heard some odd noises. I expect they woke me up. And then what sounded like one of them falling off his chair. Then there were some soft footsteps and a door closed and then nothing happened until Mathis and the police burst in hours later. I slept most of the time. I had no idea what had happened to you, but,' she faltered, 'I did once hear a terrible scream. It sounded very far away. At least, I think it must have been a scream. At the time I thought it might have been a nightmare.'

'I'm afraid that must have been me,' said Bond.

Vesper put out a hand and touched one of his. Her eyes filled with tears.

'It's horrible,' she said. 'The things they did to you. And it was all my fault. If only . . . '

She buried her face in her hands.

'That's all right,' said Bond comfortingly. 'It's no good crying over spilt milk. It's all over now and thank heavens they let you alone.' He patted her knee. 'They were going to start on you when they'd got me really softened up' (softened up is good, he thought to himself). 'We've got a lot to thank SMERSH for. Now, come on, let's forget about it. It certainly wasn't anything to do with you. Anybody could have fallen for that note. Anyway, it's all water over the dam,' he added cheerfully.

Vesper looked at him gratefully through her tears. 'You really promise?' she asked. 'I thought you would never forgive me. I . . . I'll try and make it up to you. Somehow.' She looked at him.

Somehow? thought Bond to himself. He looked at her. She was smiling at him. He smiled back.

'You'd better look out,' he said. 'I may hold you to that.'

She looked into his eyes and said nothing, but the enigmatic challenge was back. She pressed his hand and rose. 'A promise is a promise,' she said.

This time they both knew what the promise was.

She picked up her bag from the bed and walked to the door.

'Shall I come tomorrow?' She looked at Bond gravely.

'Yes, please, Vesper,' said Bond. 'I'd like that. Please do some more exploring. It will be fun to think of what we can do when I get up. Will you think of some things?'

'Yes,' said Vesper. 'Please get well quickly.'

They gazed at each other for a second. Then she went out and closed the door and Bond listened until the sound of her footsteps had disappeared.

22

THE HASTENING SALOON

FROM THAT DAY Bond's recovery was rapid.

He sat up in bed and wrote his report to M.

He made light of what he still considered amateurish behaviour on the part of Vesper. By juggling with the emphasis, he made the kidnapping sound much more Machiavellian than it had been. He praised Vesper's coolness and composure throughout the whole episode without saying that he had found some of her actions unaccountable.

Every day Vesper came to see him and he looked forward to these visits with excitement. She talked happily of her adventures of the day before, her explorations down the coast and the restaurants where she had eaten. She had made friends with the chief of police and with one of the directors of the Casino and it was they who took her out in the evening and occasionally lent her a car during the day. She kept an eye on the repairs to the Bentley which had been towed down to coachbuilders at Rouen, and she even arranged for some new clothes to be sent out from Bond's London flat. Nothing survived from his original wardrobe. Every stitch had been cut to ribbons in the search for the forty million francs.

The Le Chiffre affair was never mentioned between them. She occasionally told Bond amusing stories of Head of S.'s office. She had apparently transferred there from the W.R.N.S. And he told her of some of his adventures in the Service.

He found he could speak to her easily and he was surprised.

With most women his manner was a mixture of taciturnity and passion. The lengthy approaches to a seduction bored him almost as much as the subsequent mess of disentanglement. He found something grisly in the inevitability of the pattern of each affair. The conventional parabola — sentiment, the touch of the hand, the kiss, the passionate kiss, the feel of the body, the climax in the bed, then more bed, then less bed, then the boredom, the tears and the final bitterness — was to him shameful and hypocritical. Even more he shunned the 'mise-en-scène' for each of these acts in the play — the meeting at a party, the restaurant, the taxi, his flat, her flat, then the week-end by the sea, then the flats again, then the furtive alibis and the final angry farewell on some doorstep in the rain.

But with Vesper there could be none of this.

In the dull room and the boredom of his treatment her presence was each day an oasis of pleasure, something to look forward to. In their talk there was nothing but companionship with a distant undertone of passion. In the background there was the unspoken zest of the promise which, in due course and in their own time, would be met. Over all there brooded the shadow of his injuries and their tantalizingly slow healing.

Whether Bond liked it or not, the branch had already escaped his knife and was ready to burst into flower.

With enjoyable steps Bond recovered. He was allowed up. Then he was allowed to sit in the garden. Then he could go for a short walk, then for a long drive. And then the afternoon came when the doctor appeared on a flying visit from Paris and pronounced him well again. His clothes were brought round by Vesper, farewells were exchanged with the nurses, and a hired car drove them away.

It was three weeks from the day when he had been on the edge of death, and now it was July and the hot summer shimmered down the coast and out at sea. Bond clasped the moment to him.

Their destination was to be a surprise for him. He had not wanted to go back to one of the big hotels in Royale and Vesper said she would find somewhere away from the town. But she insisted on being mysterious about it and only said that she had found a place he would like. He was happy to be in her hands, but he covered up his surrender by referring to their destination as 'Trou sur Mer' (she admitted it was by the sea), and lauding the rustic delights of outside lavatories, bed-bugs, and cockroaches.

Their drive was spoiled by a curious incident.

While they followed the coast-road in the direction of Les Noctambules, Bond described to her his wild chase in the Bentley, finally pointing out the curve he had taken before the crash and the exact place where the vicious carpet of spikes had been laid. He slowed the car down and leant out to show her the deep cuts in the tarmac made by the rims of the wheels and the broken branches in the hedge and the patch of oil where the car had come to rest.

But all the time she was distrait and fidgety and commented only in monosyllables. Once or twice he caught her glancing in the driving-mirror, but when he had a chance to look back through the rear-window, they had just rounded a bend and he could see nothing.

Finally he took her hand.

'Something's on your mind, Vesper,' he said.

She gave him a taut, bright smile. 'It's nothing. Absolutely nothing. I had a silly idea we were being followed. It's just nerves, I suppose. This road is full of ghosts.'

Under cover of a short laugh she looked back again.

'Look.' There was an edge of panic in her voice.

Obediently Bond turned his head. Sure enough, a quarter of a mile away, a black saloon was coming after them at a good pace.

Bond laughed.

'We can't be the only people using this road,' he said. 'Anyway, who wants to follow us? We've done nothing wrong.' He patted her hand. 'It's a middle-aged commercial traveller in car-polish on his way to Le Havre. He's probably thinking of his lunch and his mistress in Paris. Really, Vesper, you mustn't think evil of the innocent.'

'I expect you're right,' she said nervously. 'Anyway, we're nearly there.'

She relapsed into silence and gazed out of the window.

Bond could still feel her tenseness. He smiled to himself at what he took to be simply a hangover from their recent adventures. But he decided to humour her and when they came to a small lane leading towards the sea and slowed to turn down it, he told the driver to stop directly they were off the main road.

Hidden by the tall hedge, they watched together through the rear-window.

Through the quiet hum of summer noises they could hear the car approaching. Vesper dug her fingers into his arm. The pace of the car did not alter as it approached their hiding-place and they had only a brief glimpse of a man's profile as a black saloon tore by.

It was true that he seemed to glance quickly towards them, but above them in the hedge there was a gaily painted sign pointing down the lane and announcing 'L'Auberge du Fruit Défendu, crustaces, fritures'. It was obvious to Bond that it was this that had caught the driver's eye.

As the rattle of the car's exhaust diminished down the road, Vesper sank back into her corner. Her face was pale.

'He looked at us,' she said. 'I told you so. I knew we were being followed. Now they know where we are.'

Bond could not contain his impatience. 'Bunkum,' he said. 'He was looking at that sign.' He pointed it out to Vesper.

She looked slightly relieved. 'Do you really think so?' she asked. 'Yes. I see. Of course, you must be right. Come on. I'm sorry to be so stupid. I don't know what came over me.'

She leant forward and talked to the driver through the partition, and the car moved on. She sank back and turned a bright face towards Bond. The colour had almost come back to her cheeks. 'I really am sorry. It's just that . . . it's that I can't believe everything's over and there's no one to be frightened of any more.' She pressed his hand. 'You must think me very stupid.'

'Of course not,' said Bond. 'But really nobody could be interested in us now. Forget it all. The whole job's finished, wiped up. This is our holiday and there's not a cloud in the sky. Is there?' he persisted.

'No, of course not.' She shook herself slightly. 'I'm mad. Now we'll be there in a second. I do hope you're going to like it.'

They both leant forward. Animation was back in her face and the incident left only the smallest question-mark hanging in the air. Even that faded as they came through the dunes and saw the sea and the modest little inn amongst the pines.

'It's not very grand, I'm afraid,' said Vesper. 'But it's very clean and the food's wonderful.' She looked at him anxiously.

She need not have worried. Bond loved the place at first sight — the terrace leading almost to the high-tide mark, the low two-storeyed house with gay brick-red awnings over the windows and the crescent-shaped bay of blue water and golden sand. How many times in his life would he have given anything to have turned off a main road to find a lost corner like this where he could let the world go by and live in the sea from dawn to dusk. And now he was to have a whole week of this. And of Vesper. In his mind he fingered the necklace of the days to come.

They drew up in the courtyard behind the house and the proprietor and his wife came out to greet them.

Monsieur Versoix was a middle-aged man with one arm. The other he had lost fighting with the Free French in Madagascar. He was a friend of the chief of police of Royale and it was the Commissaire who had suggested the place to Vesper and had spoken to the proprietor on the telephone. As a result, nothing was going to be too good for them.

Madame Versoix had been interrupted in the middle of preparing dinner. She wore an apron and held a wooden spoon in one hand. She was younger than her husband, chubby and handsome and warm-eyed. Instinctively Bond guessed that they had no children and that they gave their thwarted affection to their friends and some regular customers, and probably to some pets. He thought that their life was probably something of a struggle and that the inn must be very lonely in wintertime with the big seas and the noise of the wind in the pines.

The proprietor showed them to their rooms.

Vesper's was a double-room and Bond was next door, at the corner of the house, with one window looking out to sea and another with a view of the distant arm of the bay. There was a bathroom between them. Everything was spotless, and sparsely comfortable.

The proprietor was pleased when they both showed their delight. He said that dinner would be at seven-thirty and that Madame la patronne was preparing broiled lobsters with melted butter. He was sorry that they were so quiet just then. It was Tuesday. There would be more people at the week-end. The season had not been good. Generally they had plenty of English people staying, but times were difficult over there and the English just came for a week-end at Royale and then went home after losing their money at the Casino. It was not like the old days. He shrugged his shoulders philosophically. But then no day was like the day before, and no century like the previous one, and . . .

'Quite so,' said Bond.

23

TIDE OF PASSION

THEY WERE TALKING on the threshold of Vesper's room. When the proprietor left them, Bond pushed her inside and closed the door. Then he put his hands on her shoulders and kissed her on both cheeks.

'This is heaven,' he said.

Then he saw that her eyes were shining. Her hands came up and rested on his forearms. He stepped right up against her and his arms dropped round her waist. Her head went back and her mouth opened beneath his.

'My darling,' he said. He plunged his mouth down on to hers, forcing her teeth apart with his tongue and feeling her own tongue working at first shyly then more passionately. He slipped his hands down to her swelling buttocks and gripped them fiercely, pressing the centres of their bodies together. Panting, she slipped her mouth away from his and they clung together while he rubbed his cheek against hers and felt her hard breasts pressing into him. Then he reached up and seized her hair and bent her head back until he could kiss her again. She pushed him away and sank back exhausted on to the bed. For a moment they looked at each other hungrily.

'I'm sorry, Vesper,' he said. 'I didn't mean to then.'

She shook her head, dumb with the storm which had passed through her.

He came and sat beside her and they looked at each other with lingering tenderness as the tide of passion ebbed in their veins.

She leant over and kissed him on the corner of the mouth, then she brushed the black comma of hair back from his damp forehead.

'My darling,' she said. 'Give me a cigarette. I don't know where my bag is.' She looked vaguely round the room.

Bond lit one for her and put it between her lips. She took a deep lungful of smoke and let it pour out through her mouth with a slow sigh.

Bond put his arm round her, but she got up and walked over to the window. She stood there with her back to him.

Bond looked down at his hands and saw they were still trembling.

'It's going to take some time to get ready for dinner,' said Vesper still not looking at him. 'Why don't you go and bathe. I'll unpack for you.'

Bond left the bed and came and stood close against her. He put his arms round her and put a hand over each breast. They filled his hands and the nipples were hard against his fingers. She put her hands over his and pressed them into her, but she still looked away from him out of the window.

'Not now,' she said in a low voice.

Bond bent and burrowed his lips into the nape of her neck. For a moment he strained her hard to him then he let her go.

'All right, Vesper,' he said.

He walked over to the door and looked back. She had not moved. For some reason he thought she was crying. He took a step towards her and then realized that there was nothing to say between them then.

'My love,' he said.

Then he went out and shut the door.

Bond walked along to his room and sat down on the bed. He felt weak from the passion which had swept through his body. He was torn between the desire to fall back full-length on the bed and his longing to be cooled and revived by the sea. He played with the choice for a moment, then he went over to his suitcase and took out white linen bathing-drawers and a dark blue pyjama-suit.

Bond had always disliked pyjamas and had slept naked until in Hong Kong at the end of the war he came across the perfect compromise. This was a pyjama-coat which came almost down to the knees. It had no buttons, but there was a loose belt round the waist. The sleeves were wide and short, ending just above the elbow. The result was cool and comfortable and now when he slipped the coat on over his trunks, all his bruises and scars were hidden except the thin white bracelets on wrists and ankles and the mark of SMERSH on his right hand.

He slipped his feet into a pair of dark blue leather sandals and went downstairs and out of the house and across the terrace to the beach. As he passed across the front of the house he thought of Vesper, but he refrained from looking up to see if she was still standing at the window. If she saw him, she gave no sign.

He walked along the waterline on the hard golden sand until he was out of sight of the inn. Then he threw off his pyjama-coat and took a short run and a quick flat dive into the small waves. The beach shelved quickly and he kept under water as long as he could, swimming with powerful strokes and feeling the soft coolness all over him. Then he surfaced and brushed the hair out of his eyes. It was nearly seven and the sun had lost much of its heat. Before long it would sink beneath the further arm of the bay, but now it was straight in his eyes and he turned on his back and swam away from it so that he could keep it with him as long as possible.

When he came ashore nearly a mile down the bay the shadows had already engulfed his distant pyjamas but he knew he had time to lie on the hard sand and dry before the tide of dusk reached him.

He took off his bathing trunks and looked down at his body. There were only a few traces left of his injuries. He shrugged his shoulders and lay down with his limbs spread out in a star and gazed up at the empty blue sky and thought of Vesper.

His feelings for her were confused and he was impatient with the confusion. They had been so simple. He had intended to sleep with her as soon as he could, because he desired her and also because, and he admitted it to himself, he wanted coldly to put the repairs to his body to the final test. He thought they would sleep together for a few days and then he might see something of her in London. Then would come the inevitable disengagement which would be all the easier because of their positions in the Service. If it was not easy, he could go off on an assignment abroad or, which was also in his mind, he could resign and travel to different parts of the world as he had always wanted.

But somehow she had crept under his skin and over the last two weeks his feelings had gradually changed.

He found her companionship easy and unexacting. There was something enigmatic about her which was a constant stimulus. She gave little of her real personality away and he felt that however long they were together there would always be a private room inside her which he could never invade. She was thoughtful and full of consideration without being slavish and without compromising her arrogant spirit. And now he knew that she was profoundly, excitingly sensual, but that the conquest of her body, because of the central privacy in her, would each time have the sweet tang of rape. Loving her physically would each time be a thrilling voyage without the anticlimax of arrival. She would surrender herself avidly, he thought, and greedily enjoy all the intimacies of the bed without ever allowing herself to be possessed.

Naked, Bond lay and tried to push away the conclusions he read in the sky. He turned his head and looked down the beach and saw that the shadows of the headland were almost reaching for him.

He stood up and brushed off as much of the sand as he could reach. He reflected that he would have a bath when he got in and he absent-mindedly picked up his trunks and started walking back along the beach. It was only when he reached his pyjama-coat and bent to pick it up that he realized he was still naked. Without bothering about the trunks, he slipped on the light coat and walked on to the hotel.

At that moment his mind was made up.

24

'FRUIT DÉFENDU'

WHEN HE GOT back to his room he was touched to find all his belongings put away and in the bathroom his toothbrush and shaving things neatly arranged at one end of the glass shelf over the washbasin. At the other end was Vesper's toothbrush and one or two small bottles and a jar of face-cream.

He glanced at the bottles and was surprised to see that one contained Nembutal sleeping pills. Perhaps her nerves had been more shaken by the events at the villa than he had imagined.

The bath had been filled for him and there was a new flask of some expensive pine bath-essence on a chair beside it with his towel.

'Vesper,' he called.

'Yes?'

'You really are the limit. You make me feel like an expensive gigolo.'

'I was told to look after you. I'm only doing what I was told.'

'Darling, the bath's absolutely right. Will you marry me?'

She snorted. 'You need a slave, not a wife.'

'I want you.'

'Well, I want my lobster and champagne, so hurry up.'

'All right, all right,' said Bond.

He dried himself and dressed in a white shirt and dark blue slacks. He hoped that she would be dressed as simply and he was pleased when, without knocking, she appeared in the doorway wearing a blue linen shirt which had faded to the colour of her eyes and a dark red skirt in pleated cotton.

'I couldn't wait. I was famished. My room's over the kitchen and I've been tortured by the wonderful smells.'

He came over and put his arm round her.

She took his hand and together they went downstairs and out on to the terrace where their table had been laid in the light cast by the empty dining-room.

The champagne which Bond had ordered on their arrival stood in a plated wine-cooler beside their table and Bond poured out two full glasses. Vesper busied herself with a delicious home-made liver pâté and helped them both to the crisp French bread and the thick square of deep yellow butter set in chips of ice.

They looked at each other and drank deeply and Bond filled their glasses again to the rim.

While they ate Bond told her of his bathe and they talked of what they would do in the morning. All through the meal they left unspoken their feelings for each other, but in Vesper's eyes as much as in Bond's there was excited anticipation of the night. They let their hands and their feet touch from time to time as if to ease the tension in their bodies.

When the lobster had come and gone and the second bottle of champagne was half-empty and they had just ladled thick cream over their fraises des bois, Vesper gave a deep sigh of contentment.

'I'm behaving like a pig,' she said happily. 'You always give me all the things I like best. I've never been so spoiled before.' She gazed across the terrace at the moonlit bay. 'I wish I deserved it.' Her voice had a wry undertone.

'What do you mean?' asked Bond surprised.

'Oh, I don't know. I suppose people get what they deserve, so perhaps I do deserve it.'

She looked at him and smiled. Her eyes narrowed quizzically.

'You really don't know much about me,' she said suddenly.

Bond was surprised by the undertone of seriousness in her voice.

'Quite enough,' he said laughing. 'All I need until tomorrow and the next day and the next. You don't know much about me for the matter of that.' He poured out more champagne.

Vesper looked at him thoughtfully.

'People are islands,' she said. 'They don't really touch. However close they are, they're really quite separate. Even if they've been married for fifty years.'

Bond thought with dismay that she must be going into a 'vin triste'. Too much champagne had made her melancholy. But suddenly she gave a happy laugh. 'Don't look so worried.' She leaned forward and put her hand over his. 'I was only being sentimental. Anyway, my island feels very close to your island tonight.' She took a sip of champagne.

Bond laughed, relieved. 'Let's join up and make a peninsula,' he said. 'Now, directly we've finished the strawberries.'

'No,' she said, flirting. 'I must have coffee.'

'And brandy,' countered Bond.

The small shadow had passed. The second small shadow. This too left a tiny question-mark hanging in the air. It quickly dissolved as warmth and intimacy enclosed them again.

When they had had their coffee and Bond was sipping his brandy, Vesper picked up her bag and came and stood behind him.

'I'm tired,' she said, resting a hand on his shoulder.

He reached up and held it there and they stayed motionless for a moment. She bent down and lightly brushed his hair with her lips. Then she was gone and a few seconds later the light came on in her room.

Bond smoked and waited until it had gone out. Then he followed her, pausing only to say good night to the proprietor and his wife and thank them for the dinner. They exchanged compliments and he went upstairs.

It was only half-past nine when he stepped into her room from the bathroom and closed the door behind him.

The moonlight shone through the half-closed shutters and lapped at the secret shadows in the snow of her body on the broad bed.

Bond awoke in his own room at dawn and for a time he lay and stroked his memories.

Then he got quietly out of bed and in his pyjama-coat he crept past Vesper's door and out of the house to the beach.

The sea was smooth and quiet in the sunrise. The small pink waves idly licked the sand. It was cold, but he took off his jacket and wandered naked along the edge of the sea to the point where he had bathed the evening before, then he walked slowly and deliberately into the water until it was just below his chin. He took his feet off the bottom and sank, holding his nose with one hand and shutting his eyes, feeling the cold water comb his body and his hair.

The mirror of the bay was unbroken except where it seemed a fish had jumped. Under the water he imagined the tranquil scene and wished that Vesper could just then come through the pines and be astonished to see him suddenly erupt from the empty seascape.

When after a full minute he came to the surface in a froth of spray, he was disappointed. There was no one in sight. For a time he swam and drifted and then when the sun seemed hot enough, he came in to the beach and lay on his back and revelled in the body which the night had given back to him.

As on the evening before, he stared up into the empty sky and saw the same answer there.

After a while he rose and walked back slowly along the beach to his pyjama-coat.

That day he would ask Vesper to marry him. He was quite certain. It was only a question of choosing the right moment.

25

'BLACK-PATCH'

As he walked quietly from the terrace into the half darkness of the still shuttered dining-room, he was surprised to see Vesper emerge from the glass-fronted telephone booth near the front-door and softly turn up the stairs towards their rooms.

'Vesper,' he called, thinking she must have had some urgent message which might concern them both.

She turned quickly, a hand up to her mouth.

For a moment longer than necessary she stared at him, her eyes wide.

'What is it, darling?' he asked, vaguely troubled and fearing some crisis in their lives.

'Oh,' she said breathlessly, 'you made me jump. It was only . . . I was just telephoning to Mathis. To Mathis,' she repeated. 'I wondered if he could get me another frock. You know, from that girl-friend I told you about. The vendeuse. You see,' she talked quickly, her words coming out in a persuasive jumble, 'I've really got nothing to wear. I thought I'd catch him at home before he went to the office. I don't know my friend's telephone number and I thought it would be a surprise for you. I didn't want you to hear me moving and wake you up. Is the water nice? Have you bathed? You ought to have waited for me.'

'It's wonderful,' said Bond, deciding to relieve her mind, though irritated with her obvious guilt over this childish mystery. 'You must go in and then we'll have breakfast on the terrace. I'm ravenous. I'm sorry I made you jump. I was just startled to see anyone about at this hour of the morning.'

He put his arm round her, but she disengaged herself, and moved quickly on up the stairs.

'It was such a surprise to see you,' she said, trying to cover the incident up with a light touch.

'You looked like a ghost, a drowned man, with the hair down over your eyes like that.' She laughed harshly. Hearing the harshness, she turned the laugh into a cough.

'I hope I haven't caught cold,' she said.

She kept on patching up the edifice of her deceit until Bond wanted to spank her and tell her to relax and tell the truth. Instead he just gave her a reassuring pat on the back outside her room and told her to hurry up and have her bathe.

Then he went on to his room.

That was the end of the integrity of their love. The succeeding days were a shambles of falseness and hypocrisy, mingled with her tears and moments of animal passion to which she abandoned herself with a greed made indecent by the hollowness of their days.

Several times Bond tried to break down the dreadful walls of mistrust. Again and again he brought up the subject of the telephone call, but she obstinately bolstered up her story with embellishments which Bond knew she had thought out afterwards. She even accused Bond of thinking she had another lover.

These scenes always ended in her bitter tears and in moments almost of hysteria.

Each day the atmosphere became more hateful.

It seemed fantastic to Bond that human relationships could collapse into dust overnight and he searched his mind again and again for a reason.

He felt that Vesper was just as horrified as he was and, if anything, her misery seemed greater than his. But the mystery of the telephone conversation which Vesper angrily, almost fearfully it seemed to Bond, refused to explain was a shadow which grew darker with other small mysteries and reticences.

Already at luncheon on that day things got worse.

After a breakfast which was an effort for both of them, Vesper said she had a headache and would stay in her room out of the sun. Bond took a book and walked for miles down the beach. By the time he returned he had argued to himself that they would be able to sort the problem out over lunch.

Directly they sat down, he apologized gaily for having startled her at the telephone booth and then he dismissed the subject and went on to describe what he had seen on his walk. But Vesper was distrait and commented only in monosyllables. She toyed with her food and she avoided Bond's eyes and gazed past him with an air of preoccupation.

When she had failed once or twice to respond to some conversational gambit or other, Bond also relapsed into silence and occupied himself with his own gloomy thoughts.

All of a sudden she stiffened. Her fork fell with a clatter on to the edge of her plate and then noisily off the table on to the terrace.

Bond looked up. She had gone as white as a sheet and she was looking over his shoulder with terror in her face.

Bond turned his head and saw that a man had just taken his place at a table on the opposite side of the terrace, well away from them. He seemed ordinary enough, perhaps rather sombrely dressed, but in his first quick glance Bond put him down as some business-man on his way along the coast who had just happened on the inn or had picked it out of the Michelin.

'What is it, darling?' he asked anxiously.

Vesper's eyes never moved from the distant figure.

'It's the man in the car,' she said in a stifled voice. 'The man who was following us. I know it is.'

Bond looked again over his shoulder. The patron was discussing the menu with the new customer. It was a perfectly normal scene. They exchanged smiles over some item on the menu and apparently agreed that it would suit for the patron took the card and with, Bond guessed, a final exchange about the wine, he withdrew.

The man seemed to realize that he was being watched. He looked up and gazed incuriously at them for a moment. Then he reached for a brief-case on the chair beside him, extracted a newspaper and started to read it, his elbows propped up on the table.

When the man had turned his face towards them, Bond noticed that he had a black patch over one eye. It was not tied with a tape across the eye, but screwed in like a monocle. Otherwise he seemed a friendly middle-aged man, with dark brown hair brushed straight back and, as Bond had seen while he was talking to the patron, particularly large, white teeth.

He turned back to Vesper. 'Really, darling. He looks very innocent. Are you sure he's the same man? We can't expect to have this place entirely to ourselves.'

Vesper's face was still a white mask. She was clutching the edge of the table with both hands. He thought she was going to faint and almost rose to come round to her, but she made a gesture to stop him. Then she reached for a glass of wine and took a deep draught. The glass rattled on her teeth and she brought up her other hand to help. Then she put the glass down.

She looked at him with dull eyes.

'I know it's the same.'

He tried to reason with her, but she paid no attention. After glancing once or twice over his shoulder with eyes that held a curious submissiveness, she said that her headache was still bad and that she would spend the afternoon in her room. She left the table and walked indoors without a backward glance.

Bond was determined to set her mind at rest. He ordered coffee to be brought to the table and then he rose and walked swiftly through to the courtyard. The black Peugeot which stood there might indeed have been the saloon they had seen, but it might equally have been one of a million others on the French roads. He took a quick glance inside, but the interior was empty and when he tried the boot, it was locked. He made a note of the Paris number-plate, then he went quickly to the lavatory adjoining the dining-room, pulled the chain and walked out on to the terrace.

The man was eating and didn't look up.

Bond sat down in Vesper's chair so that he could watch the other table.

A few minutes later the man asked for the bill, paid it and left. Bond heard the Peugeot start up and soon the noise of its exhaust had disappeared in the direction of the road to Royale.

When the patron came back to his table, Bond explained that madame had unfortunately a slight touch of sunstroke. After the patron had expressed his regret and enlarged on the dangers of going out of doors in almost any weather, Bond casually asked about the other customer. 'He reminds me of a friend who also lost an eye. They wear similar black patches.'

The patron answered that the man was a stranger. He had been pleased with his lunch and had said that he would be passing that way again in a day or two and would take another meal at the auberge. Apparently he was Swiss, which could also be seen from his accent. He was a traveller in watches. It was shocking to have only one eye. The strain of keeping that patch in place all day long. He supposed one got used to it.

'It is indeed very sad,' said Bond. 'You also have been unlucky,' he gestured to the proprietor's empty sleeve, 'I myself was very fortunate.'

For a time they talked about the war. Then Bond rose.

'By the way,' he said, 'madame had an early telephone call which I must remember to pay for. Paris. An Elysée number, I think,' he added, remembering that that was Mathis's exchange.

'Thank you, monsieur, but the matter is regulated. I was speaking to Royale this morning and the exchange mentioned that one of my guests had put through a call to Paris and that there had been no answer. They wanted to know if madame would like the call kept in. I'm afraid the matter escaped my mind. Perhaps monsieur would mention it to madame. But, let me see, it was an Invalides number the exchange referred to.'

26

'SLEEP WELL, MY DARLING'

THE NEXT TWO days were much the same.

On the fourth day of their stay Vesper went off early to Royale. A taxi came and fetched her and brought her back. She said she needed some medicine.

That night she made a special effort to be gay. She drank a lot and when they went upstairs, she led him into her bedroom and made passionate love to him. Bond's body responded, but afterwards she cried bitterly into her pillow and Bond went to his room in grim despair.

He could hardly sleep and in the early hours he heard her door open softly. Some small sounds came from downstairs. He was sure she was in the telephone-booth. Very soon he heard her door softly close and he guessed that again there had been no reply from Paris.

This was Saturday.

On Sunday the man with the black patch was back again. Bond knew it directly he looked up from his lunch and saw her face. He had told her all that the patron had told him, withholding only the man's statement that he might be back. He had thought it would worry her.

He had also telephoned Mathis in Paris and checked on the Peugeot. It had been hired from a respectable firm two weeks before. The customer had had a Swiss triptique. His name was Adolph Gettler. He had given a bank in Zurich as his address.

Mathis had got on to the Swiss police. Yes, the bank had an account in this name. It was little used. Herr Gettler was understood to be connected with the watch industry. Inquiries could be pursued if there was a charge against him.

Vesper had shrugged her shoulders at the information.

This time when the man appeared she left her lunch in the middle and went straight up to her room.

Bond made up his mind. When he had finished, he followed her. Both her doors were locked and when he made her let him in, he saw that she had been sitting in the shadows by the window, watching, he presumed.

Her face was of cold stone. He led her to the bed and drew her down beside him. They sat stiffly, like people in a railway carriage.

'Vesper,' he said, holding her cold hands in his, 'we can't go on like this. We must finish with it. We are torturing each other and there is only one way of stopping it. Either you must tell me what all this is about or we must leave. At once.'

She said nothing and her hands were lifeless in his.

'My darling,' he said. 'Won't you tell me? Do you know, that first morning I was coming back to ask you to marry me. Can't we go back to the beginning again? What is this dreadful nightmare that is killing us?'

At first she said nothing, then a tear rolled slowly down her cheek.

'You mean you would have married me?'

Bond nodded.

'Oh my God,' she cried. 'My God.' She turned and clutched him, pressing her face against his chest.

He held her closely to him. 'Tell me, my love,' he said. 'Tell me what's hurting you.'

Her sobs became quieter.

'Leave me for a little,' she said and a new note had come into her voice. A note of resignation. 'Let me think for a little.' She kissed his face and held it between her hands. She looked at him with yearning. 'Darling, I'm trying to do what's best for us. Please believe me. But it's terrible. I'm in a frightful . . . ' She wept again, clutching him like a child with nightmares.

He soothed her, stroking the long black hair and kissing her softly.

'Go away now,' she said. 'I must have time to think. We've got to do something.'

She took his handkerchief and dried her eyes.

She led him to the door and there they held tightly to each other. Then he kissed her again and she shut the door behind him.

That evening most of the gayness and intimacy of their first night came back. She was excited and some of her laughter sounded brittle, but Bond was determined to fall in with her new mood and it was only at the end of dinner that he made a passing remark which made her pause.

She put her hand over his.

'Don't talk about it now,' she said. 'Forget it now. It's all past. I'll tell you about it in the morning.'

She looked at him and suddenly her eyes were full of tears. She found a handkerchief in her bag and dabbed at them.

'Give me some more champagne,' she said. She gave a queer little laugh. 'I want a lot more. You drink much more than me. It's not fair.'

They sat and drank together until the bottle was finished. Then she got to her feet. She knocked against her chair and giggled.

'I do believe I'm tight,' she said, 'how disgraceful. Please, James, don't be ashamed of me. I did so want to be gay. And I am gay.'

She stood behind him and ran her fingers through his black hair.

'Come up quickly,' she said. 'I want you badly tonight.'

She blew a kiss at him and was gone.

For two hours they made slow, sweet love in a mood of happy passion which the day before Bond would never have thought they could regain. The barriers of self-consciousness and mistrust seemed to have vanished and the words they spoke to each other were innocent and true again and there was no shadow between them.

'You must go now,' said Vesper when Bond had slept for a while in her arms.

As if to take back her words she held him more closely to her, murmuring endearments and pressing her body down the whole length of his.

When he finally rose and bent to smooth back her hair and finally kiss her eyes and her mouth good night, she reached out and turned on the light.

'Look at me,' she said, 'and let me look at you.'

He knelt beside her.

She examined every line of his face as if she was seeing him for the first time. Then she reached up and put an arm round his neck. Her deep blue eyes were swimming with tears as she drew his head slowly towards her and kissed him gently on the lips. Then she let him go and turned off the light.

'Good night, my dearest love,' she said.

Bond bent and kissed her. He tasted the tears on her cheek.

He went to the door and looked back.

'Sleep well, my darling,' he said. 'Don't worry, everything's all right now.'

He closed the door softly and walked to his room with a full heart.

27

THE BLEEDING HEART

THE PATRON BROUGHT him the letter in the morning. He burst into Bond's room, holding the envelope in front of him as if it was on fire.

'There has been a terrible accident. Madame . . . '

Bond hurled himself out of bed and through the bathroom, but the communicating door was locked. He dashed back and through his room and down the corridor past a shrinking, terrified maid.

Vesper's door was open. The sunlight through the shutters lit up the room. Only her black hair showed above the sheet and her body under the bedclothes was straight and moulded like a stone effigy on a tomb.

Bond fell on his knees beside her and drew back the sheet.

She was asleep. She must be. Her eyes were closed. There was no change in the dear face. She was just as she would look and yet, and yet she was so still, no movement, no pulse, no breath. That was it. There was no breath.

Later the patron came and touched him on the shoulder. He pointed at the empty glass on the table beside her. There were white dregs in the bottom of it. It stood beside her book and her cigarettes and matches and the small pathetic litter of her mirror and lipstick and handkerchief. And on the floor the empty bottle of sleeping-pills, the pills Bond had seen in the bathroom that first evening.

Bond rose to his feet and shook himself. The patron was still holding out the letter towards him. He took it.

'Please notify the Commissaire,' said Bond. 'I will be in my room when he wants me.'

He walked blindly away without a backward glance.

He sat on the edge of his bed and gazed out of the window at the peaceful sea. Then he stared dully at the envelope. It was addressed simply in a large round hand 'Pour Lui'.

The thought passed through Bond's mind that she must have left orders to be called early, so that it would not be he who found her.

He turned the envelope over. Not long ago it was her warm tongue which had sealed the flap.

He gave a sudden shrug and opened it.

It was not long. After the first few words he read it quickly, the breath coming harshly through his nostrils.

Then he threw it down on the bed as if it had been a scorpion.

My darling James [the letter opened],

I love you with all my heart and while you read these words I hope you still love me because, now, with these words, this is the last moment that your love will last. So good-bye, my sweet love, while we still love each other. Good-bye, my darling.

I am an agent of the M.V.D. Yes, I am a double agent for the Russians. I was taken on a year after the war and I have worked for them ever since. I was in love with a Pole in the R.A.F. Until you, I still was. You can find out who he was. He had two D.S.O.s and after the war he was trained by M. and dropped back into Poland. They caught him and by torturing him they found out a lot and also about me. They came after me and told me he could live if I would work for them. He knew nothing of this, but he was allowed to write to me. The letter arrived on the fifteenth of each month. I found I couldn't stop. I couldn't bear the idea of a fifteenth coming round without his letter. It would mean that I had killed him. I tried to give them as little as possible. You must believe me about this. Then it came to you. I told them you had been given this job at Royale, what your cover was and so on. That was why they knew about you before you arrived and why they had time to put the microphones in. They suspected Le Chiffre, but they didn't know what your assignment was except that it was something to do with him. That was all I told them.

Then I was told not to stand behind you in the Casino and to see that neither Mathis nor Leiter did. That was why the gunman was nearly able to shoot you. Then I had to stage that kidnapping. You may have wondered why I was so quiet in the night club. They didn't hurt me because I was working for M.V.D.

But when I found out what had been done to you, even though it was Le Chiffre who did it and he turned out to be a traitor, I decided I couldn't go on. By that time I had begun to fall in love with you. They wanted me to find out things from you while you were recovering, but I refused. I was controlled from Paris. I had to ring up an Invalides number twice a day. They threatened me, and finally they withdrew my control and I knew my lover in Poland would have to die. But they were afraid I would talk, I suppose, and I got a final warning that SMERSH would come for me if I didn't obey them. I took no notice. I was in love with you. Then I saw the man with the black patch in the Splendide and I found he had been making inquiries about my movements. This was the day before we came down here. I hoped I could shake him off. I decided that we would have an affair and I would escape to South America from Le Havre. I hoped I would have a baby of yours and be able to start again somewhere. But they followed us. You can't get away from them.

I knew it would be the end of our love if I told you. I realized that I could either wait to be killed by SMERSH and perhaps get you killed too, or I could kill myself.

There it is, my darling love. You can't stop me calling you that or saying that I love you. I am taking that with me and the memories of you.

I can't tell you much to help you. The Paris number was Invalides 55200. I never met any of them in London. Everything was done through an accommodation address, a newsagents at 450 Charing Cross Place.

At our first dinner together you talked about that man in Yugoslavia who was found guilty of treason. He said: 'I was carried away by the gale of the world.' That's my only excuse. That, and for love of the man whose life I tried to save.

It's late now and I'm tired, and you're just through two doors. But I've got to be brave. You might save my life, but I couldn't bear the look in your dear eyes.

My love, my love.

V.

Bond threw the letter down. Mechanically he brushed his fingers together. Suddenly he banged his temples with his fists and stood up. For a moment he looked out towards the quiet sea, then he cursed aloud, one harsh obscenity.

His eyes were wet and he dried them.

He pulled on a shirt and trousers and with a set cold face he walked down and shut himself in the telephone-booth.

While he was getting through to London, he calmly reviewed the facts of Vesper's letter. They all fitted. The little shadows and question-marks of the past four weeks, which his instinct had noted but his mind rejected, all stood out now like sign-posts.

He saw her now only as a spy. Their love and his grief were relegated to the boxroom of his mind. Later, perhaps they would be dragged out, dispassionately examined, and then bitterly thrust back with other sentimental baggage he would rather forget. Now he could only think of her treachery to the Service and to her country and of the damage it had done. His professional mind was completely absorbed with the consequences — the covers which must have been blown over the years, the codes which the enemy must have broken, the secrets which must have leaked from the centre of the very section devoted to penetrating the Soviet Union.

It was ghastly. God knew how the mess would be cleared up.

He ground his teeth. Suddenly Mathis's words came back to him: 'There are plenty of really black targets around,' and, earlier, 'What about SMERSH? I don't like the idea of these chaps running around France killing anyone they feel has been a traitor to their precious political system.'

Bond grinned bitterly to himself.

How soon Mathis had been proved right and how soon his own little sophistries had been exploded in his face!

While he, Bond, had been playing Red Indians through the years (yes, Le Chiffre's description was perfectly accurate), the real enemy had been working quietly, coldly, without heroics, right there at his elbow.

He suddenly had a vision of Vesper walking down a corridor with documents in her hand. On a tray. They just got it on a tray while the cool secret agent with a Double o number was gallivanting round the world — playing Red Indians.

His finger-nails dug into the palms of his hands and his body sweated with shame.

Well, it was not too late. Here was a target for him, right to hand. He would take on SMERSH and hunt it down. Without SMERSH, without this cold weapon of death and revenge, the M.V.D. would be just another bunch of civil servant spies, no better and no worse than any of the Western services.

SMERSH was the spur. Be faithful, spy well, or you die. Inevitably and without any question, you will be hunted down and killed.

It was the same with the whole Russian machine. Fear was the impulse. For them it was always safer to advance than to retreat. Advance against the enemy and the bullet might miss you. Retreat, evade, betray, and the bullet would never miss.

But now he would attack the arm that held the whip and the gun. The business of espionage could be left to the white-collar boys. They could spy and catch the spies. He would go after the threat behind the spies, the threat that made them spy.

The telephone rang and Bond snatched up the receiver.

He was on to 'the Link', the outside liaison officer who was the only man in London he might telephone from abroad. Then only in dire necessity.

He spoke quietly into the receiver.

'This is 007 speaking. This is an open line. It's an emergency. Can you hear me? Pass this on at once. 3030 was a double, working for Redland.

'Yes, dammit, I said "was". The bitch is dead now.'

LIVE AND LET DIE

I

THE RED CARPET

THERE ARE MOMENTS of great luxury in the life of a secret agent. There are assignments on which he is required to act the part of a very rich man; occasions when he takes refuge in good living to efface the memory of danger and the shadow of death; and times when, as was now the case, he is a guest in the territory of an allied Secret Service.

From the moment the BOAC Stratocruiser taxied up to the International Air Terminal at Idlewild, James Bond was treated like royalty.

When he left the aircraft with the other passengers he had resigned himself to the notorious purgatory of the US Health, Immigration and Customs machinery. At least an hour, he thought, of overheated, drab-green rooms smelling of last year's air and stale sweat and guilt and the fear that hangs round all frontiers, fear of those closed doors marked PRIVATE that hide the careful men, the files, the teleprinters chattering urgently to Washington, to the Bureau of Narcotics, Counter Espionage, the Treasury, the FBI.

As he walked across the tarmac in the bitter January wind he saw his own name going over the network: BOND, JAMES. BRITISH DIPLOMATIC PASSPORT 0094567, the short wait and the replies coming back on the different machines: NEGATIVE, NEGATIVE, NEGATIVE. And then, from the FBI; POSITIVE AWAIT CHECK. There would be some hasty traffic on the FBI circuit with the Central Intelligence Agency and then: FBI TO IDLEWILD: BOND OKAY OKAY, and the bland official out front would hand him back his passport with a 'Hope you enjoy your stay, Mr Bond.'

Bond shrugged his shoulders and followed the other passengers through the wire fence towards the door marked US HEALTH SERVICE.

In his case it was only a boring routine, of course, but he

disliked the idea of his dossier being in the possession of any foreign power. Anonymity was the chief tool of his trade. Every thread of his real identity that went on record in any file diminished his value and, ultimately, was a threat to his life. Here in America, where they knew all about him, he felt like a negro whose shadow has been stolen by the witch-doctor. A vital part of himself was in pawn, in the hands of others. Friends, of course, in this instance, but still . . .

'Mr Bond?'

A pleasant-looking nondescript man in plain clothes had stepped forward from the shadow of the Health Service building.

'My name's Halloran. Pleased to meet you!'

They shook hands.

'Hope you had a pleasant trip. Would you follow me please?'

He turned to the officer of the airport police on guard at the door.

'Okay, Sergeant.'

'Okay, Mr Halloran. Be seeing vou.'

The other passengers had passed inside. Halloran turned to the left, away from the building. Another policeman held open a small gate in the high boundary fence.

' 'Bye, Mr Halloran.'

' 'Bye, Officer. Thanks.'

Directly outside a black Buick waited, its engine sighing quietly. They climbed in. Bond's two light suitcases were in front next to the driver. Bond couldn't imagine how they had been extracted so quickly from the mound of passengers' luggage he had seen only minutes before being trolleyed over to Customs.

'Okay, Grady. Let's go.'

Bond sank back luxuriously as the big limousine surged forward, slipping quickly into top through the Dynaflow gears.

He turned to Halloran.

'Well, that's certainly one of the reddest carpets I've ever seen. I expected to be at least an hour getting through Immigration. Who laid it on? I'm not used to VIP treatment. Anyway, thanks very much for your part in it all.'

'You're very welcome, Mr Bond.' Halloran smiled and offered him a cigarette from a fresh pack of Luckies. 'We want to make your stay comfortable. Anything you want, just say so and it's yours. You've got some good friends in Washington. I don't myself know why you're here but it seems the authorities are keen that you should be a privileged guest of the Government. It's my job to see you get to your hotel as quickly and as comfortably as possible and then I'll hand over and be on my way. May I have your passport a moment, please.'

Bond gave it to him. Halloran opened a brief-case on the seat beside him and took out a heavy metal stamp. He turned the pages of Bond's passport until he came to the US Visa, stamped it, scribbled his signature over the dark blue circle of the Department of Justice cipher and gave it back to him. Then he took out his pocketbook and extracted a thick white envelope which he gave to Bond.

'There's a thousand dollars in there, Mr Bond.' He held up his hand as Bond started to speak. 'And it's Communist money we took in the Schmidt-Kinaski haul. We're using it back at them and you are asked to co-operate and spend this in any way you like on your present assignment. I am advised that it will be considered a very unfriendly act if you refuse. Let's please say no more about it and,' he added, as Bond continued to hold the envelope dubiously in his hand, 'I am also to say that the disposal of this money through your hands has the knowledge and approval of your own Chief.'

Bond eyed him narrowly and then grinned. He put the envelope away in his notecase.

'All right,' he said. 'And thanks. I'll try and spend it where it does most harm. I'm glad to have some working capital. It's certainly good to know it's been provided by the opposition.'

'Fine,' said Halloran, 'and now, if you'll forgive me, I'll just write up my notes for the report I'll have to put in. Have to remember to get a letter of thanks sent to Immigration and Customs and so forth for their co-operation. Routine.'

'Go ahead,' said Bond. He was glad to keep silent and gaze out at his first sight of America since the war. It was no waste of time to start picking up the American idiom again: the advertisements, the new car models and the prices of second-hand ones in the used-car lots; the exotic pungency of the road signs: SOFT SHOULDERS — SHARP CURVES — SQUEEZE AHEAD — SLIPPERY WHEN WET; the standard of driving; the number of women at the wheel, their menfolk docilely beside them; the men's clothes; the way the women were doing their hair; the Civil Defence warnings: IN CASE OF ENEMY ATTACK — KEEP MOVING — GET OFF BRIDGE; the thick rash of television aerials and the impact of TV on hoardings and shop windows; the occasional helicopter; the public appeals for cancer and polio funds: THE MARCH OF DIMES — all the small fleeting impressions that were as important to his trade as are broken bark and bent twigs to the trapper in the jungle.

The driver chose the Triborough Bridge and they soared across the breathtaking span into the heart of uptown Manhattan, the beautiful prospect of New York hastening towards them until they were down amongst the hooting, teeming, petrol-smelling roots of the stressed-concrete jungle.

Bond turned to his companion.

'I hate to say it,' he said, 'but this must be the fattest atomic bomb target on the whole face of the globe.'

'Nothing to touch it,' agreed Halloran. 'Keeps me awake nights thinking what would happen.'

They drew up at the best hotel in New York, the St Regis, at the corner of Fifth Avenue and 55th Street. A saturnine middle-aged man in a dark blue overcoat and black homburg came forward behind the commissionaire. On the sidewalk, Halloran introduced him.

'Mr Bond, meet Captain Dexter.' He was deferential. 'Can I pass him along to you now, Captain?'

'Sure, sure. Just have his bags sent up. Room 2100. Top floor. I'll go ahead with Mr Bond and see he has everything he wants.'

Bond turned to say goodbye to Halloran and thank him. For a moment Halloran had his back to him as he said something about Bond's luggage to the commissionaire. Bond looked past him across 55th Street. His eyes narrowed. A black sedan, a Chevrolet, was pulling sharply out into the thick traffic, right in front of a Checker cab that braked hard, its driver banging his fist down on the horn and holding it there. The sedan kept going, just caught the tail of the green light, and disappeared north up Fifth Avenue.

It was a smart, decisive bit of driving, but what startled Bond was that it had been a negress at the wheel, a fine-looking negress in a black chauffeur's uniform, and through the rear window he had caught a glimpse of the single passenger — a huge grey-black face which had turned slowly towards him and looked directly back at him, Bond was sure of it, as the car accelerated towards the Avenue.

Bond shook Halloran by the hand. Dexter touched his elbow impatiently.

'We'll go straight in and through the lobby to the elevators. Half-right across the lobby. And would you please keep your hat on, Mr Bond.'

As Bond followed Dexter up the steps into the hotel he reflected that it was almost certainly too late for these precautions. Hardly anywhere in the world will you find a negress driving a car. A negress acting as chauffeur is still more extraordinary. Barely conceivable even in Harlem, but that was certainly where the car was from.

And the giant shape in the back seat? That grey-black face? Mister Big?

'Hm,' said Bond to himself as he followed the slim back of Captain Dexter into the elevator.

The elevator slowed up for the twenty-first floor.

'We've got a little surprise ready for you, Mr Bond,' said Captain Dexter, without, Bond thought, much enthusiasm.

They walked down the corridor to the corner room.

The wind sighed outside the passage windows and Bond had a fleeting view of the tops of other skyscrapers and, beyond, the stark fingers of the trees in Central Park. He felt far out of touch with the ground and for a moment a strange feeling of loneliness and empty space gripped his heart.

Dexter unlocked the door of No 2100 and shut it behind them. They were in a small lighted lobby. They left their hats and coats on a chair and Dexter opened the door in front of them and held it for Bond to go through.

He walked into an attractive sitting-room decorated in Third Avenue 'Empire' — comfortable chairs and a broad sofa in pale yellow silk, a fair copy of an Aubusson on the floor, pale grey walls and ceiling, a bow-fronted French sideboard with bottles and glasses and a plated ice-bucket, a wide window through which the winter sun poured out of a Swiss-clear sky. The central heating was just bearable.

The communicating door with the bedroom opened.

'Arranging the flowers by your bed. Part of the famous CIA "Service With a Smile".' The tall thin young man came forward with a wide grin, his hand outstretched, to where Bond stood rooted with astonishment.

'Felix Leiter! What the hell are you doing here?' Bond grasped the hard hand and shook it warmly. 'And what the hell are you doing in my bedroom anyway? God it's good to see you. Why aren't you in Paris? Don't tell me they've put you on this job?'

Leiter examined the Englishman affectionately.

'You've said it. That's just exactly what they have done. What a break! At least it is for me. CIA thought we did all right together on the Casino job[1] so they hauled me away from the Joint Intelligence chaps in Paris, put me through the works in Washington and here I am. I'm sort of liaison between the Central Intelligence Agency and our friends of the FBI.' He waved towards Captain Dexter who was watching this unprofessional ebullience without enthusiasm. 'It's their case, of course, at least the American end of it is, but as you know there are some big overseas angles which are CIA's territory, so we're running it joint. Now you're here to handle the Jamaican end for the British and the team's complete. How does it look to you? Sit down and let's have a drink. I ordered lunch directly I got the word you were downstairs and it'll be on its way.' He went over to the sideboard and started mixing a martini.

'Well I'm damned,' said Bond. 'Of course that old devil M never told me. He just gives one the facts. Never tells one any good news. I suppose he thinks it might influence one's decision to take a case or not. Anyway, it's grand.'

Bond suddenly felt the silence of Captain Dexter. He turned to him.

'I shall be very glad to be under your orders here, Captain,' he said tactfully. 'As I understand it, the case breaks pretty neatly into two halves. The first half lies wholly on American territory. Your jurisdiction, of course. Then it looks as if we shall have to follow it into the Caribbean. Jamaica. And I understand I am to take over outside United States territorial waters. Felix here will

[1] This terrifying gambling case is described in the author's *Casino Royale*.

marry up the two halves so far as your government is concerned. I shall report to London through CIA while I'm here, and direct to London, keeping CIA informed, when I move to the Caribbean. Is that how you see it?'

Dexter smiled thinly. 'That's just about it, Mr Bond. Mr Hoover instructs me to say that he's very pleased to have you along. As our guest,' he added. 'Naturally we are not in any way concerned with the British end of the case and we're very happy that CIA will be handling that with you and your people in London. Guess everything should go fine. Here's luck,' and he lifted the cocktail Leiter had put into his hand.

They drank the cold hard drink appreciatively, Leiter with a faintly quizzical expression on his hawk-like face.

There was a knock on the door. Leiter opened it to let in the bellboy with Bond's suitcases. He was followed by two waiters pushing trolleys loaded with covered dishes, cutlery and snow-white linen which they proceeded to lay out on a folding table.

'Soft-shell crabs with tartare sauce, flat beef hamburgers, medium-rare, from the charcoal grill, French-fried potatoes, broccoli, mixed salad with thousand-island dressing, ice cream with melted butterscotch, and as good a Liebfraumilch as you can get in America. Okay?'

'It sounds fine,' said Bond with a mental reservation about the melted butterscotch.

They sat down and ate steadily through each delicious course of American cooking at its rare best.

They said little, and it was only when the coffee had been brought and the table cleared away that Captain Dexter took the fifty-cent cigar from his mouth and cleared his throat decisively.

'Mr Bond,' he said, 'now perhaps you would tell us what you know about this case.'

Bond slit open a fresh pack of King Size Chesterfields with his thumbnail and, as he settled back in his comfortable chair in the warm luxurious room, his mind went back two weeks to the bitter raw day in early January when he had walked out of his Chelsea flat into the dreary half-light of a London fog.

2

INTERVIEW WITH M

THE GREY BENTLEY convertible, the 1933 $4\frac{1}{2}$ -litre with the Amherst-Villiers supercharger, had been brought round a few minutes earlier from the garage where he kept it and the engine had kicked directly he pressed the self-starter. He had turned on the twin fog lights and had driven gingerly along King's Road and then up Sloane Street into Hyde Park.

M's Chief of Staff had telephoned at midnight to say that M wanted to see Bond at nine the next morning. 'Bit early in the day,' he had apologized, 'but he seems to want some action from somebody. Been brooding for weeks. Suppose he's made up his mind at last.'

'Any line you can give me over the telephone?'

'A for Apple and C for Charlie,' said the Chief of Staff, and rang off.

That meant that the case concerned Stations A and C, the sections of the Secret Service dealing respectively with the United States and the Caribbean. Bond had worked for a time under Station A during the war, but he knew little of C or its problems.

As he crawled beside the kerb up through Hyde Park, the slow drumbeat of his two-inch exhaust keeping him company, he felt excited at the prospect of his interview with M, the remarkable man who was then, and still is, head of the Secret Service. He had not looked into those cold, shrewd eyes since the end of the summer. On that occasion M had been pleased.

'Take some leave,' he had said. 'Plenty of leave. Then get some new skin grafted over the back of that hand. "Q" will put you on to the best man and fix a date. Can't have you going round with that damn Russian trade-mark on you. See if I can find you a good target when you've got cleaned up. Good luck.'

The hand had been fixed, painlessly but slowly. The thin scars, the single Russian letter which stands for SCH, the first letter of *Spion*, a spy, had been removed and as Bond thought of the man with the stiletto who had cut them he clenched his hands on the wheel.

What was happening to the brilliant organization of which the man with the knife had been an agent, the Soviet organ of vengeance, SMERSH, short for *Smyert Spionam* — Death to Spies? Was it still as powerful, still as efficient? Who controlled it now that Beria was gone? After the great gambling case in which he had been involved at Royale-les-Eaux, Bond had sworn to get back at them. He had told M as much at that last interview. Was this appointment with M to start him on his trail of revenge?

Bond's eyes narrowed as he gazed into the murk of Regent's Park and his face in the faint dashlight was cruel and hard.

He drew up in the mews behind the gaunt high building, handed his car over to one of the plain-clothes drivers from the pool and walked round to the main entrance. He was taken up in the lift to the top floor and along the thickly carpeted corridor he knew so well to the door next to M's. The Chief of Staff was waiting for him and at once spoke to M on the intercom.

'007's here now, Sir.'

'Send him in.'

The desirable Miss Moneypenny, M's all-powerful private secretary, gave him an encouraging smile and he walked through the double doors. At once the green light came on, high on the wall in the room he had left. M was not to be disturbed as long as it burned.

A reading lamp with a green glass shade made a pool of light across the red leather top of the broad desk. The rest of the room was darkened by the fog outside the windows.

'Morning, 007. Let's have a look at the hand. Not a bad job. Where did they take the skin from?'

'High up on the forearm, Sir.'

'Hm. Hairs'll grow a bit thick. Crooked too. However. Can't be helped. Looks all right for the time being. Sit down.'

Bond walked round to the single chair which faced M across the desk. The grey eyes looked at him, through him.

'Had a good rest?'

'Yes thank you, Sir.'

'Ever seen one of these?' M abruptly fished something out of his waistcoat pocket. He tossed it half way across the desk towards Bond. It fell with a faint clang on the red leather and lay, gleaming richly, an inch-wide, hammered gold coin.

Bond picked it up, turned it over, weighed it in his hand.

'No, Sir. Worth about five pounds, perhaps.'

'Fifteen to a collector. It's a Rose Noble of Edward IV.'

M fished again in his waistcoat pocket and tossed more magnificent gold coins on to the table in front of Bond. As he did so, he glanced at each one and identified it.

'Double Excellente, Spanish, Ferdinand and Isabella, 1510; Ecu au Soleil, French, Charles IX, 1574; Double Ecu d'or, French, Henry IV, 1600; Double Ducat, Spanish, Philip II, 1560; Ryder, Dutch, Charles d'Egmond, 1538; Quadruple, Genoa, 1617; Double louis, à la mèche courte, French, Louis XIV, 1644. Worth a lot of money melted down. Much more to collectors, ten to twenty pounds each. Notice anything common to them all?'

Bond reflected. 'No, Sir.'

'All minted before 1650. Bloody Morgan, the pirate, was Governor and Commander-in-Chief of Jamaica from 1674 to 1683. The English coin is the joker in the pack. Probably shipped out to pay the Jamaica garrison. But for that and the dates, these could have come from any other treasure-trove put together by the great pirates — L'Ollonais, Pierre le Grand, Sharp, Sawkins, Blackbeard. As it is, and both Spinks and the British Museum agree, this is almost certainly part of Bloody Morgan's treasure.'

M paused to fill his pipe and light it. He didn't invite Bond to smoke and Bond would not have thought of doing so uninvited.

'And the hell of a treasure it must be. So far nearly a thousand of these and similar coins have turned up in the United States in the last few months. And if the Special Branch of the Treasury, and the FBI, have traced a thousand, how many more have been melted down or disappeared into private collections? And they keep on coming in, turning up in banks, bullion merchants, curio shops, but mostly pawnbrokers of course. The FBI are in a proper fix. If they put these on the police notices of stolen property they know the source will dry up. They'd be melted down into gold bars and channelled straight into the black bullion market. Have to sacrifice the rarity value of the coins, but the gold would go straight underground. As it is, someone's using the negroes — porters, sleeping-car attendants, truck-drivers — and getting the money well spread over the States. Quite innocent people. Here's a typical case.' M opened a brown folder bearing the Top Secret red star and selected a single sheet of paper. Through the reverse side, as M held it up, Bond could see the engraved heading: 'Department of Justice. Federal Bureau of Investigation.' M read from it:

'Zachary Smith, 35, Negro, Member of the Sleeping Car Porters Brotherhood, address 90b West 126th Street, New York City.' (M looked up: 'Harlem,' he said.) 'Subject was identified by Arthur Fein of Fein Jewels Inc., 870 Lenox Avenue, as having offered for sale on November 21st last four gold coins of the sixteenth and seventeenth century (details attached). Fein offered a hundred dollars which was accepted. Interrogated later, Smith said they had been sold to him in Seventh Heaven Bar-B-Q (a well-known Harlem bar) for twenty dollars each by a negro he had never seen before or since. Vendor had said they were worth fifty dollars each at Tiffany's, but that he, the vendor, wanted ready cash and Tiffany's was too far anyway. Smith bought one for twenty dollars and on finding that a neighbouring pawnbroker would offer him twenty-five dollars for it, returned to the bar and purchased the remaining three for sixty dollars. The next morning he took them to Fein's. Subject has no criminal record.'

M returned the paper to the brown folder.

'That's typical,' he said. 'Several times they've caught up with the next link, the middle man who bought them a bit cheaper and they find that he bought a handful, in one case a hundred of them, from some man who presumably got them cheaper still. All these larger transactions have taken place in Harlem or Florida. Always the next man in the link was an unknown negro, in all cases a white-collar man, prosperous, educated, who said he guessed they were treasure-trove, Blackbeard's treasure.

'This Blackbeard story would stand up to most investigations,' continued M, 'because there is reason to believe that part of his hoard was dug up around Christmas Day, 1928, at a place called Plum Point. It's a narrow neck of land in Beaufort

County, North Carolina, where a stream called Bath Creek flows into the Pamlico River. Don't think I'm an expert,' he smiled, 'you can read all about this in the dossier. So, in theory, it would be quite reasonable for those lucky treasure-hunters to have hidden the loot until everyone had forgotten the story and then thrown it fast on the market. Or else they could have sold it en bloc at the time, or later, and the purchaser has just decided to cash in. Anyway it's a good enough cover except on two counts.'

M paused and relit his pipe.

'Firstly, Blackbeard operated from about 1690 to 1710 and it's improbable that none of his coin should have been minted later than 1650. Also, as I said before, it's very unlikely that his treasure would contain Edward IV Rose Nobles, since there's no record of an English treasure-ship being captured on its way to Jamaica. The Brethren of the Coast wouldn't take them on. Too heavily escorted. There were much easier pickings if you were sailing in those days "on the plundering account" as they called it.

'Secondly,' and M looked at the ceiling and then back at Bond, 'I know where the treasure is. At least I'm pretty sure I do. And it's not in America. It's in Jamaica, and it is Bloody Morgan's, and I guess it's one of the most valuable treasure-troves in history.'

'Good Lord,' said Bond. 'How . . . where do we come into it?'

M held up his hand. 'You'll find all the details in here.' He let his hand come down on the brown folder. 'Briefly, Station C has been interested in a Diesel yacht, the *Secatur*, which has been running from a small island on the north coast of Jamaica through the Florida Keys into the Gulf of Mexico, to a place called St Petersburg. Sort of pleasure resort, near Tampa. West coast of Florida. With the help of the FBI we've traced the ownership of this boat and of the island to a man called Mr Big, a negro gangster. Lives in Harlem. Ever heard of him?'

'No,' said Bond.

'And curiously enough,' M's voice was softer and quieter, 'a twenty-dollar bill which one of these casual negroes had paid for a gold coin and whose number he had noted for Peaka Peow, the Numbers game, was paid out by one of Mr Big's lieutenants. And it was paid,' M pointed the stem of his pipe at Bond, 'for information received, to an FBI double-agent who is a member of the Communist Party.'

Bond whistled softly.

'In short,' continued M, 'we suspect that this Jamaican treasure is being used to finance the Soviet espionage system, or an important part of it, in America. And our suspicion becomes a certainty when I tell you who this Mr Big is.'

Bond waited, his eyes fixed on M's.

'Mr Big,' said M, weighing his words, 'is probably the most powerful negro criminal in the world. He is,' and he enumerated carefully, 'the head of the Black Widow Voodoo cult and believed by that cult to be the Baron Samedi himself. You'll find all about that here,' he tapped the folder, 'and it'll frighten the daylights out of you. He is also a Soviet agent. And finally he is, and this will particularly interest you, Bond, a known member of SMERSH.'

'Yes,' said Bond slowly, 'I see now.'

'Quite a case,' said M looking keenly at him. 'And quite a man, this Mr Big.'

'I don't think I've ever heard of a great negro criminal before,' said Bond, 'Chinamen, of course, the men behind the opium trade. There've been some big-time Japs, mostly in pearls and drugs. Plenty of negroes mixed up in diamonds and gold in Africa, but always in a small way. They don't seem to take to big business. Pretty law-abiding chaps I should have thought except when they've drunk too much.'

'Our man's a bit of an exception,' said M. 'He's not pure negro. Born in Haiti. Good dose of French blood. Trained in Moscow, too, as you'll see from the file. And the negro races are just beginning to throw up geniuses in all the professions — scientists, doctors, writers. It's about time they turned out a great criminal. After all, there are 250,000,000 of them in the world. Nearly a third of the white population. They've got plenty of brains and ability and guts. And now Moscow's taught one of them the technique.'

'I'd like to meet him,' said Bond. Then he added, mildly, 'I'd like to meet any member of SMERSH.'

'All right then, Bond. Take it away.' M handed him the thick brown folder. 'Talk it over with Plender and Damon. Be ready to start in a week. It's a joint CIA and FBI job. For God's sake don't step on the FBI's toes. Covered with corns. Good luck.'

Bond had gone straight down to Commander Damon, Head of Station A, an alert Canadian who controlled the link with the Central Intelligence Agency, America's Secret Service.

Damon looked up from his desk. 'I see you've bought it,' he said looking at the folder. 'Thought you would. Sit down.' He waved to an armchair beside the electric fire. 'When you've waded through it all, I'll fill in the gaps.'

3

A VISITING CARD

AND NOW IT was ten days later and the talk with Dexter and Leiter had not added much, reflected Bond as he awoke slowly and luxuriously in his bedroom at the St Regis the morning after his arrival in New York.

Dexter had had plenty of detail on Mr Big, but nothing that threw any new light on the case. Mr Big was forty-five years old, born in Haiti, half negro and half French. Because of the initial letters of his fanciful name, Buonaparte Ignace Gallia, and because of his huge height and bulk, he came to be called, even as a youth, 'Big Boy' or just 'Big'. Later this became 'The Big Man' or 'Mr Big', and his real names lingered only on a parish register in Haiti and on his dossier with the FBI. He had no known vices except women, whom he consumed in quantities. He didn't drink or smoke and his only Achilles heel appeared to be a chronic heart disease which had, in recent years, imparted a greyish tinge to his skin.

The Big Boy had been initiated into Voodoo as a child, earned his living as a truck driver in Port au Prince, then emigrated to America and worked successfully for a hijacking team in the Legs Diamond gang. With the end of Prohibition he had moved to Harlem and bought half-shares in a small nightclub and a string of coloured call-girls. His partner was found in a barrel of cement in the Harlem River in 1938 and Mr Big automatically became sole proprietor of the business. He was called up in 1943 and, because of his excellent French, came to the notice of the Office of Strategic Services, the wartime secret service of America, who trained him with great thoroughness and put him into Marseilles as an agent against the Pétain collaborationists. He merged easily with African negro dock-hands, and worked well, providing good and accurate naval intelligence. He operated closely with a Soviet spy who was doing a similar job for the Russians. At the end of the war he was demobilized in

France (and decorated by the Americans and the French) and then he disappeared for five years, probably to Moscow. He returned to Harlem in 1950 and soon came to the notice of the FBI as a suspected Soviet agent. But he never incriminated himself or fell into any of the traps laid by the FBI. He bought up three nightclubs and a prosperous chain of Harlem brothels. He seemed to have unlimited funds and paid all his lieutenants a flat rate of twenty thousand dollars a year. Accordingly, and as a result of weeding by murder, he was expertly and diligently served. He was known to have originated an underground Voodoo temple in Harlem and to have established a link between it and the main cult in Haiti. The rumour had started that he was the Zombie or living corpse of Baron Samedi himself, the dreaded Prince of Darkness, and he fostered the story so that now it was accepted through all the lower strata of the negro world. As a result, he commanded real fear, strongly substantiated by the immediate and often mysterious deaths of anyone who crossed him or disobeyed his orders.

Bond had questioned Dexter and Leiter very closely on the evidence connecting the giant negro with SMERSH. It certainly seemed conclusive.

In 1951, by the promise of one million dollars in gold and a safe refuge after six months' work for them, the FBI had at last persuaded a known Soviet agent of the MWD to turn double. All went well for a month and the results exceeded the highest expectations. The Russian spy held the appointment of an economic expert on the Soviet delegation to the United Nations. One Saturday, he had gone to take the subway to Pennsylvania Station en route for the Soviet week-end rest camp at Glen Cove, the former Morgan estate on Long Island.

A huge negro, positively identified from photographs as The Big Man, had stood beside him on the platform as the train came in and was seen walking towards the exit even before the first coach had come to a standstill over the bloody vestiges of the Russian. He had not been seen to push the man, but in the crowd it would not have been difficult. Spectators said it could not have been suicide. The man screamed horribly as he fell and he had had (melancholy touch!) a bag of golf clubs over his shoulder. The Big Man, of course, had had an alibi as solid as

Fort Knox. He had been held and questioned, but was quickly sprung by the best lawyer in Harlem.

The evidence was good enough for Bond. He was just the man for SMERSH, with just the training. A real, hard weapon of fear and death. And what a brilliant setup for dealing with the smaller fry of the negro underworld and for keeping a coloured information network well up to the mark! — the fear of Voodoo and the supernatural, still deeply, primevally ingrained in the negro subconscious! And what genius to have, as a beginning, the whole transport system of America under surveillance, the trains, the porters, the truck drivers, the stevedores! To have at his disposal a host of key men who would have no idea that the questions they answered had been asked by Russia. Small-time professional men who, if they thought at all, would guess that the information on freights and schedules was being sold to rival transport concerns.

Not for the first time, Bond felt his spine crawl at the cold brilliant efficiency of the Soviet machine, and at the fear of death and torture which made it work and of which the supreme engine was SMERSH — SMERSH, the very whisper of death.

Now, in his bedroom at the St Regis, Bond shook away his thoughts and jumped impatiently out of bed. Well, there was one of them at hand, ready for the crushing. At Royale he had only caught a glimpse of his man. This time it would be face to face. Big Man? Then let it be a giant, a homeric slaying.

Bond walked over to the window and pulled back the curtains. His room faced north, towards Harlem. Bond gazed for a moment towards the northern horizon, where another man would be in his bedroom asleep, or perhaps awake and thinking conceivably of him, Bond, whom he had seen with Dexter on the steps of the hotel. Bond looked at the beautiful day and smiled. And no man, not even Mr Big, would have liked the expression on his face.

Bond shrugged his shoulders and walked quickly to the telephone.

'St Regis Hotel. Good morning,' said a golden voice.

'Room Service, please,' said Bond.

'Room Service? I'd like to order breakfast. Half a pint of orange juice, three eggs, lightly scrambled, with bacon, a double portion of café Espresso with cream. Toast. Marmalade. Got it?'

The order was repeated back to him. Bond walked out into the lobby and picked up the five pounds' weight of newspapers which had been placed quietly inside the door earlier in the morning. There was also a pile of parcels on the hall table which Bond disregarded.

The afternoon before he had had to submit to a certain degree of Americanization at the hands of the FBI. A tailor had come and measured him for two single-breasted suits in dark blue lightweight worsted (Bond had firmly refused anything more dashing) and a haberdasher had brought chilly white nylon shirts with long points to the collars. He had had to accept half a dozen unusually patterned foulard ties, dark socks with fancy clocks, two or three 'display kerchiefs' for his breast pocket, nylon vests and pants (called T-shirts and shorts), a comfortable lightweight camel-hair overcoat with over-buttressed shoulders, a plain grey snap-brim Fedora with a thin black ribbon and two pairs of hand-stitched and very comfortable black Moccasin 'casuals'.

He also acquired a 'Swank' tie-clip in the shape of a whip, an alligator-skin billfold from Mark Cross, a plain Zippo lighter, a plastic 'Travel-Pak' containing razor, hairbrush and toothbrush, a pair of horn-rimmed glasses with plain lenses, various other oddments and, finally, a lightweight Hartmann 'Skymate' suit-case to contain all these things.

He was allowed to retain his own Beretta .25 with the skeleton grip and the chamois leather shoulder-holster, but all his other possessions were to be collected at midday and forwarded down to Jamaica to await him.

He was given a military haircut and was told that he was a New Englander from Boston and that he was on holiday from his job with the London office of the Guaranty Trust Company. He was reminded to ask for the 'check' rather than the 'bill', to say 'cab' instead of 'taxi' and (this from Leiter) to avoid words of more than two syllables. ('You can get through any American conversation,' advised Leiter, 'with "Yeah", "Nope" and "Sure".') The English word to be avoided at all costs, added Leiter, was 'Ectually'. Bond had said that this word was not part of his vocabulary.

Bond looked grimly at the pile of parcels which contained his new identity, stripped off his pyjamas for the last time ('We mostly sleep in the raw in America, Mr Bond') and gave himself a sizzling cold shower. As he shaved he examined his face in the glass. The thick comma of black hair above his right eyebrow had lost some of its tail and his hair was trimmed close across the temples. Nothing could be done about the thin vertical scar down his right cheek, although the FBI had experimented with 'Cover-Mark', or about the coldness and hint of anger in his grey-blue eyes, but there was the mixed blood of America in the black hair and high cheekbones and Bond thought he might get by — except, perhaps, with women.

Naked, Bond walked out into the lobby and tore open some of the packages. Later, in white shirt and dark blue trousers, he went into the sitting-room, pulled a chair up to the writing desk near the window and opened *The Traveller's Tree*, by Patrick Leigh Fermor.*

This extraordinary book had been recommended to him by M. 'It's by a chap who knows what he's talking about,' he said, 'and don't forget that he was writing about what was happening in Haiti in 1950. This isn't medieval black magic stuff. It's being practised every day.'

Bond was half way through the section on Haiti.

> The next step [he read] is the invocation of evil denizens of the Voodoo pantheon — such as Don Pedro, Kitta, Mondongue, Bakalou and Zandor — for harmful purposes, for the reputed practice (which is of Congolese origin) of turning people into zombies in order to use them as slaves, the casting of maleficent spells, and the destruction of enemies. The effects of the spell, of which the outward form may be an image of the intended victim, a miniature coffin or a toad, are frequently stiffened by the separate use of poison. Father Cosme enlarged on the superstitions that maintain that men with certain powers change themselves into snakes; on the 'Loups-Garoups' that fly at night in the form of vampire bats and suck the blood of children; on men who reduce themselves to infinitesimal size and roll

* Fleming called this 'one of the great travel books', now published by Penguin.

about the countryside in calabashes. What sounded far more sinister were a number of mystico-criminal secret societies of wizards, with nightmarish titles — 'les Mackanda', named after the poison campaign of the Haitian hero; 'les Zobop', who were also robbers; the 'Mazanxa', the 'Caporelata' and the 'Vlinbindingue'. These, he said, were the mysterious groups whose gods demand — instead of a cock, a pigeon, a goat, a dog or a pig, as in the normal rites of Voodoo — the sacrifice of a 'cabrit sans cornes'. This hornless goat, of course, means a human being . . .

Bond turned over the pages, occasional passages combining to form an extraordinary picture in his mind of a dark religion and its terrible rites.

. . . Slowly, out of the turmoil and the smoke and the shattering noise of the drums, which, for a time, drove everything except their impact from the mind, the details began to detach themselves . . .

. . . Backwards and forwards, very slowly, the dancers shuffled, and at each step their chins shot out and their buttocks jerked upwards, while their shoulders shook in double time. Their eyes were half closed and from their mouths came again and again the same incomprehensible words, the same short line of chanted song, repeated after each iteration, half an octave lower. At a change in the beat of the drums, they straightened their bodies, and, flinging their arms in the air while their eyes rolled upwards, spun round and round . . .

. . . At the edge of the crowd we came upon a little hut, scarcely larger than a dog kennel: 'Le caye Zombi'. The beam of a torch revealed a black cross inside and some rags and chains and shackles and whips: adjuncts used at the Ghédé ceremonies, which Haitian ethnologists connect with the rejuvenation rites of Osiris recorded in the Book of the Dead. A fire was burning, in which two sabres and a large pair of pincers were standing, their lower parts red with the heat: 'le Feu Marinette', dedicated to a goddess who is the evil obverse of the bland and amorous Maîtresse Erzulie Fréda Dahomin, the Goddess of Love.

Beyond, with its base held fast in a socket of stone, stood a large black wooden cross. A white death's head was painted near the base, and over the cross-bar were pulled the sleeves of a very old morning coat. Here also rested the brim of a battered bowler hat, through the torn crown of which the top of the cross projected. This totem, with which every peristyle must be equipped, is not a lampoon of the central event of the Christian faith, but represents the God of the Cemeteries and the Chief of the Legion of the Dead, Baron Samedi. The Baron is paramount in all matters immediately beyond the tomb. He is Cerberus and Charon as well as Aeacus, Rhadamanthus and Pluto . . .

. . . The drums changed and the Houngenikon came dancing on to the floor, holding a vessel filled with some burning liquid from which sprang blue and yellow flames. As he circled the pillar and spilt three flaming libations, his steps began to falter. Then, lurching backwards with the same symptoms of delirium that had manifested themselves in his forerunner, he flung down the whole blazing mass. The houncis caught him as he reeled, and removed his sandals and rolled his trousers up, while the kerchief fell from his head and laid bare his young woolly skull. The other houncis knelt to put their hands in the flaming mud, and rub it over their hands and elbows and faces. The Houngan's bell and 'açon' rattled officiously and the young priest was left by himself, reeling and colliding against the pillar, helplessly catapulting across the floor, and falling among the drums. His eyes were shut, his forehead screwed up and his chin hung loose. Then, as though an invisible fist had dealt him a heavy blow, he fell to the ground and lay there, with his head stretching backwards in a rictus of anguish until the tendons of his neck and shoulders projected like roots. One hand clutched at the other elbow behind his hollowed back as though he were striving to break his own arm, and his whole body, from which the sweat was streaming, trembled and shuddered like a dog in a dream. Only the whites of his eyes were visible as, although his eye-sockets were now wide open, the pupils had vanished under the lids. Foam collected on his lips . . .

. . . Now the Houngan, dancing a slow step and brandish-

> ing a cutlass, advanced from the fireside, flinging the weapon again and again into the air, and catching it by the hilt. In a few minutes he was holding it by the blunted end of the blade. Dancing slowly towards him, the Houngenikon reached out and grasped the hilt. The priest retired, and the young man, twirling and leaping, spun from side to side of the 'tonnelle'. The ring of spectators rocked backwards as he bore down upon them whirling the blade over his head, with the gaps in his bared teeth lending to his mandril face a still more feral aspect. The 'tonnelle' was filled for a few seconds with genuine and unmitigated terror. The singing had turned to a universal howl and the drummers, rolling and lolling with the furious and invisible motion of their hands, were lost in a transport of noise. Flinging back his head, the novice drove the blunt end of the cutlass into his stomach. His knees sagged, and his head fell forward . . .

There came a knock on the door and a waiter came in with breakfast. Bond was glad to put the dreadful tale aside and re-enter the world of normality. But it took him minutes to forget the atmosphere, heavy with terror and the occult, that had surrounded him as he read.

With breakfast came another parcel, about a foot square, expensive-looking, which Bond told the waiter to put on the sideboard. Some afterthought of Leiter's, he supposed. He ate his breakfast with enjoyment. Between mouthfuls he looked out of the wide window and reflected on what he had just read.

It was only when he had swallowed his last mouthful of coffee and had lit his first cigarette of the day that he suddenly became aware of the tiny noise in the room behind him.

It was a soft, muffled ticking, unhurried, metallic. And it came from the direction of the sideboard.

'Tick-tock . . . tick-tock . . . tick-tock.'

Without a moment's hesitation, without caring that he looked a fool, he dived to the floor behind his armchair and crouched, all his senses focused on the noise from the square parcel. 'Steady,' he said to himself. 'Don't be an idiot. It's just a clock.' But why a clock? Why should he be given a clock? Who by?

'Tick-tock . . . Tick-tock . . . Tick-tock.'

It had become a huge noise against the silence of the room. It seemed to be keeping time with the thumping of Bond's heart. 'Don't be ridiculous. That Voodoo stuff of Leigh Fermor's has put your nerves on edge. Those drums . . .'

'Tick-tock . . . tick-tock . . . tick — '

And then, suddenly, the alarm went off with a deep, melodious, urgent summons.

'Tongtongtongtongtongtong . . .'

Bond's muscles relaxed. His cigarette was burning a hole in the carpet. He picked it up and put it in his mouth. Bombs in alarm clocks go off when the hammer first comes down on the alarm. The hammer hits a pin in a detonator, the detonator fires the explosive and WHAM . . .

Bond raised his head above the back of the chair and watched the parcel.

'Tongtongtongtongtong. . .'

The muffled gonging went on for half a minute, then it started to slow down.

'tong . . tong . . . tong . . . . . tong . . . . tong . . . . ,

'C-R-R-R-A-CK . . .'

It was not louder than a 12-bore cartridge, but in the confined space it was an impressive explosion.

The parcel, in tatters, had fallen to the ground. The glasses and bottles on the sideboard were smashed and there was a black smudge of smoke on the grey wall behind them. Some pieces of glass tinkled down on to the floor. There was a strong smell of gunpowder in the room.

Bond got slowly to his feet. He went to the window and opened it. Then he dialled Dexter's number. He spoke levelly.

'Pineapple . . . No, a small one . . . only some glasses . . . okay, thanks . . . of course not . . .'bye.'

He skirted the debris, walked through the small lobby to the door leading into the passage, opened it, hung the DON'T DISTURB sign outside, locked it, and went through into his bedroom.

By the time he had finished dressing there was a knock on the door.

'Who is it?' he called.

'Okay. Dexter.'

Dexter hustled in, followed by a sallow young man with a black box under his arm.

'Trippe, from Sabotage,' announced Dexter.

They shook hands and the young man at once went on his knees beside the charred remnants of the parcel.

He opened his box and took out some rubber gloves and a handful of dentist's forceps. With his tools he painstakingly extracted small bits of metal and glass from the charred parcel and laid them out on a broad sheet of blotting paper from the writing desk.

While he worked, he asked Bond what had happened.

'About a half-minute alarm? I see. Hullo, what's this?' He delicately extracted a small aluminium container such as is used for exposed film. He put it aside.

After a few minutes he sat up on his haunches.

'Half-minute acid capsule,' he announced. 'Broken by the first hammer-stroke of the alarm. Acid eats through thin copper wire. Thirty seconds later wire breaks, releases plunger on to cap of this.' He held up the base of a cartridge. '4-bore elephant gun. Black powder. Blank. No shot. Lucky it wasn't a grenade. Plenty of room in the parcel. You'd have been damaged. Now let's have a look at this.' He picked up the aluminium cylinder, unscrewed it, extracted a small roll of paper, and unravelled it with his forceps.

He carefully flattened it out on the carpet, holding its corners down with four tools from his black box. It contained three typewritten sentences. Bond and Dexter bent forward.

'THE HEART OF THIS CLOCK HAS STOPPED TICKING,' they read. 'THE BEATS OF YOUR OWN HEART ARE NUMBERED. KNOW THAT NUMBER AND I HAVE STARTED TO COUNT.'

The message was signed '1234567 . . ?'

They stood up.

'Hm,' said Bond. 'Bogeyman stuff.'

'But how the hell did he know you were here?' asked Dexter.

Bond told him of the black sedan on 55th Street.

'But the point is,' said Bond, 'how did he know what I was here *for*? Shows he's got Washington pretty well sewn up. Must be a leak the size of the Grand Canyon somewhere.'

'Why should it be Washington?' asked Dexter testily. 'Anyway,' he controlled himself with a forced laugh, 'hell and damnation. Have to make a report to Headquarters on this. So long, Mr Bond. Glad you came to no harm.'

'Thanks,' said Bond. 'It was just a visiting card. I must return the compliment.'

4

THE BIG SWITCHBOARD

WHEN DEXTER AND his colleague had gone, taking the remains of the bomb with them, Bond took a damp towel and rubbed the smoke-mark off the wall. Then he rang for the waiter and, without explanation, told him to put the broken glass on his check and clear away the breakfast things. Then he took his hat and coat and went out on the street.

He spent the morning on Fifth Avenue and on Broadway, wandering aimlessly, gazing into the shop windows and watching the passing crowds. He gradually assimilated the casual gait and manners of a visitor from out of town and when he tested himself out in a few shops and asked the way of several people he found that nobody looked at him twice.

He had a typical American meal at an eating house called 'Gloryfried Ham-N-Eggs' ('The Eggs We Serve Tomorrow Are Still in the Hens') on Lexington Avenue and then took a cab downtown to police headquarters where he was due to meet Leiter and Dexter at 2.30.

A Lieutenant Binswanger of Homicide, a suspicious and crusty officer in his late forties, announced that Commissioner Monahan had said that they were to have complete co-operation from the Police Department. What could he do for them? They examined Mr Big's police record, which more or less duplicated Dexter's information, and they were shown the records and photographs of most of his known associates.

They went over the reports of the US Coastguard Service on the comings and goings of the yacht *Secatur* and also the comments of the US Customs Service, who had kept a close watch on the boat each time she had docked at St Petersburg.

These confirmed that the yacht had put in at irregular intervals over the previous six months and that she always tied up in the Port of St Petersburg at the wharf of the 'Ourobouros Worm and Bait Shippers Inc.', an apparently innocent concern whose main business was to sell live bait to fishing clubs throughout Florida, the Gulf of Mexico and further afield. The company also had a profitable sideline in sea-shells and coral for interior decoration, and a further sideline in tropical aquarium fish — particularly rare poisonous species for the research departments of medical and chemical foundations.

According to the proprietor, a Greek sponge-fisher from the neighbouring Tarpon Springs, the *Secatur* did big business with his company, bringing in cargoes of queen conchs and other shells from Jamaica and also highly prized varieties of tropical fish. These were purchased by Ourobouros Inc., stored in their warehouse and sold in bulk to wholesalers and retailers up and down the coast. The name of the Greek was Papagos. No criminal record.

The FBI, with the help of Naval Intelligence, had tried listening in to the *Secatur*'s wireless. But she kept off the air except for short messages before she sailed from Cuba or Jamaica and then transmitted *en clair* in a language which was unknown and completely indecipherable. The last notation on the file was to the effect that the operator was talking in 'Langage', the secret Voodoo speech only used by initiates, and that every effort would be made to hire an expert from Haiti before the next sailing.

'More gold been turning up lately,' announced Lieutenant Binswanger as they walked back to his office from the Identification Bureau across the street. ''Bout a hundred coins a week in Harlem and New York alone. Want us to do anything about it? If you're right and these are Commie funds, they must be pulling it in pretty fast while we sit on our asses doin' nothing.'

'Chief says to lay off,' said Dexter. 'Hope we'll see some action before long.'

'Well, the case is all yours,' said Binswanger, grudgingly. 'But the Commissioner sure don't like having this bastard crappin' away on his own front doorstep while Mr Hoover sits down in Washington well to leeward of the stink. Why don't we pull him in on tax evasion or misuse of the mails or parkin' in front of a hydrant or sumpn? Take him down to the Tombs and give 'em the works? If the Feds won't do it, we'd be glad to oblige.'

'D'you want a race riot?' objected Dexter sourly. 'There's nothing against him and you know it, and we know it. If he wasn't sprung in half an hour by that black mouthpiece of his, those Voodoo drums would start beating from here to the Deep South. When they're full of that stuff we all know what happens. Remember '35 and '43? You'd have to call out the Militia. We didn't ask for the case. The President gave it us and we've got to stick with it.'

They were back in Binswanger's drab office. They picked up their coats and hats.

'Anyway, thanks for the help, Lootenant,' said Dexter with forced cordiality, as they made their farewells. 'Been most valuable.'

'You're welcome,' said Binswanger stonily. 'Elevator's to your right.' He closed the door firmly behind them.

Leiter winked at Bond behind Dexter's back. They rode down to the main entrance on Center Street in silence.

On the sidewalk, Dexter turned to them.

'Had some instructions from Washington this morning,' he said unemotionally. 'Seems I'm to look after the Harlem end, and you two are to go down to St Petersburg tomorrow. Leiter's to find out what he can there and then move right on to Jamaica with you, Mr Bond. That is,' he added, 'if you'd care to have him along. It's your territory.'

'Of course,' said Bond. 'I was going to ask if he could come anyway.'

'Fine,' said Dexter. 'Then I'll tell Washington everything's fixed. Anything else I can do for you? All communications with FBI, Washington, of course. Leiter's got the names of our men in Florida, knows the Signals routine and so forth.'

'If Leiter's interested and if you don't mind,' said Bond, 'I'd like very much to get up to Harlem this evening and have a look round. Might help to have some idea of what it looks like in Mr Big's back yard.'

Dexter reflected.

'Okay,' he said finally. 'Probably no harm. But don't show yourselves too much. And don't get hurt,' he added. 'There's no one to help you up there. And don't go stirring up a lot of trouble for us. This case isn't ripe yet. Until it is, our policy with Mr Big is "live and let live".'

Bond looked quizzically at Captain Dexter.

'In my job,' he said, 'when I come up against a man like this one, I have another motto. It's "live and let die".'

Dexter shrugged his shoulders. 'Maybe,' he said, 'but you're under my orders here, Mr Bond, and I'd be glad if you'd accept them.'

'Of course,' said Bond, 'and thanks for all your help. Hope you have luck with your end of the job.'

Dexter flagged a cab. They shook hands.

''Bye fellers,' said Dexter briefly. 'Stay alive.' His cab pulled out into the uptown traffic.

Bond and Leiter smiled at each other.

'Able guy, I should say,' said Bond.

'They're all that in his show,' said Leiter. 'Bit inclined to be stuffed shirts. Very touchy about their rights. Always bickering with us or with the police. But I guess you have much the same problem in England.'

'Oh of course,' said Bond. 'We're always rubbing MI5 up the wrong way. And they're always stepping on the corns of the Special Branch. Scotland Yard,' he explained. 'Well, how about going up to Harlem tonight?'

'Suits me,' said Leiter. 'I'll drop you at the St Regis and pick you up again about six-thirty. Meet you in the King Cole Bar, on the ground floor. Guess you want to take a look at Mr Big,' he grinned. 'Well, so do I, but it wouldn't have done to tell Dexter so.' He flagged a Yellow Cab.

'St Regis Hotel. Fifth at 55th.'

They climbed into the overheated tin box reeking of last week's cigar-smoke.

Leiter wound down a window.

'Whaddya want ter do?' asked the driver over his shoulder. 'Gimme pneumony?'

'Just that,' said Leiter, 'if it means saving us from this gas chamber.'

'Wise guy, hn?' said the driver, crashing tinnily through his gears. He took the chewed end of a cigar from behind his ear and held it up. 'Two bits for three,' he said in a hurt voice.

'Twenty-four cents too much,' said Leiter. The rest of the drive was passed in silence.

They parted at the hotel and Bond went up to his room. It was four o'clock. He asked the telephone operator to call him at six. For a while he looked out of the window of his bedroom. To his left, the sun was setting in a blaze of colour. In the skyscrapers the lights were coming on, turning the whole town into a golden honeycomb. Far below the streets were rivers of neon lighting, crimson, blue, green. The wind sighed sadly outside in the velvet dusk, lending his room still more warmth and security and luxury. He drew the curtains and turned on the soft lights over his bed. Then he took off his clothes and climbed between the fine percale sheets. He thought of the bitter weather in the London streets, the grudging warmth of the hissing gas-fire in his office at Headquarters, the chalked-up menu on the pub he had passed on his last day in London: 'Giant Toad & 2 Veg.'

He stretched luxuriously. Very soon he was asleep.

Up in Harlem, at the big switchboard, 'The Whisper' was dozing over his racing form. All his lines were quiet. Suddenly a light shone on the right of the board — an important light.

'Yes, Boss,' he said softly into his headphone. He couldn't have spoken any louder if he had wished to. He had been born on 'Lung Block', on Seventh Avenue, at 142nd Street, where death from TB is twice as high as anywhere in New York. Now, he only had part of one lung left.

'Tell all "Eyes",' said a slow, deep voice, 'to watch out from now on. Three men.' A brief description of Leiter, Bond and Dexter followed. 'May be coming in this evening or tomorrow. Tell them to watch particularly on First to Eighth and the other Avenues. The night spots too, in case they're missed coming in. They're not to be molested. Call me when you get a sure fix. Got it?'

'Yes, Sir, Boss,' said The Whisper, breathing fast. The voice went quiet. The operator took the whole handful of plugs, and soon the big switchboard was alive with winking lights. Softly, urgently, he whispered on into the evening.

At six o'clock Bond was awakened by the soft burr of the telephone. He took a cold shower and dressed carefully. He put on a garishly striped tie and allowed a broad wedge of bandana to protrude from his breast pocket. He slipped the chamois leather holster over his shirt so that it hung three inches below his left armpit. He whipped at the mechanism of the Beretta until all eight bullets lay on the bed. Then he packed them back into the magazine, loaded the gun, put up the safety-catch and slipped it into the holster.

He picked up the pair of Moccasin casuals, felt their toes and weighed them in his hand. Then he reached under the bed and pulled out a pair of his own shoes he had carefully kept out of the suitcase full of his belongings the FBI had taken away from him that morning.

He put them on and felt better equipped to face the evening.

Under the leather, the toe-caps were lined with steel.

At six twenty-five he went down to the King Cole Bar and chose a table near the entrance and against the wall. A few minutes later Felix Leiter came in. Bond hardly recognized him. His mop of straw-coloured hair was now jet black and he wore a dazzling blue suit with a white shirt and a black and white polka-dot tie.

Leiter sat down with a broad grin.

'I suddenly decided to take these people seriously,' he explained. 'This stuff's only a rinse. It'll come off in the morning. I hope,' he added.

Leiter ordered medium-dry martinis with a slice of lemon peel. He stipulated House of Lords gin and Martini Rossi. The American gin, a much higher proof than English gin, tasted harsh to Bond. He reflected that he would have to be careful what he drank that evening.

'We'll have to keep on our toes, where we're going,' said Felix Leiter, echoing his thoughts. 'Harlem's a bit of a jungle these days. People don't go up there any more like they used to. Before the war, at the end of an evening, one used to go to Harlem just as one goes to Montmartre in Paris. They were glad to take one's money. One used to go to the Savoy Ballroom and watch the dancing. Perhaps pick up a high-yaller and risk the doctor's bills afterwards. Now that's all changed. Harlem doesn't like being stared at any more. Most of the places have closed and you go to the others strictly on sufferance. Often you get tossed out on your ear, simply because you're white. And you don't get any sympathy from the police either.'

Leiter extracted the lemon peel from his martini and chewed it reflectively. The bar was filling up. It was warm and companionable — a far cry, Leiter reflected, from the inimical, electric climate of the negro pleasure-spots they would be drinking in later.

'Fortunately,' continued Leiter, 'I like the negroes and they know it somehow. I used to be a bit of an aficionado of Harlem. Wrote a few pieces on Dixieland Jazz for the *Amsterdam News*, one of the local papers. Did a series for the North American Newspaper Alliance on the negro theatre about the time Orson Welles put on his *Macbeth* with an all-negro cast at the Lafayette. So I know my way about up there. And I admire the way they're getting on in the world, though God knows I can't see the end of it.'

They finished their drinks and Leiter called for the check.

'Of course there are some bad ones,' he said. 'Some of the worst anywhere. Harlem's the capital of the negro world. In any half a million people of any race you'll get plenty of stinkeroos. The trouble with our friend Mr Big is that he's the hell of a good technician, thanks to his OSS and Moscow training. And he must be pretty well organized up there.'

Leiter paid. He shrugged his shoulders.

'Let's go,' he said. 'We'll have ourselves some fun and try and get back in one piece. After all, this is what we're paid for. We'll take a bus on Fifth Avenue. You won't find many cabs that want to go up there after dark.'

They walked out of the warm hotel and took the few steps to the bus stop on the Avenue.

It was raining. Bond turned up the collar of his coat and gazed up the Avenue to his right, towards Central Park, towards the dark citadel that housed The Big Man.

Bond's nostrils flared slightly. He longed to get in there after him. He felt strong and compact and confident. The evening awaited him, to be opened and read, page by page, word by word.

In front of his eyes, the rain came down in swift, slanting strokes — italic script across the unopened black cover that hid the secret hours that lay ahead.

5

NIGGER HEAVEN

AT THE BUS stop at the corner of Fifth and Cathedral Parkway three negroes stood quietly under the light of a street lamp. They looked wet and bored. They were. They had been watching the traffic on Fifth since the call went out at four-thirty.

'Yo next, Fatso,' said one of them as the bus came up out of the rain and stopped with a sigh from the great vacuum brakes.

'Ahm tahd,' said the thick-set man in the mackintosh. But he pulled his hat down over his eyes and climbed aboard, slotted his coins and moved down the bus, scanning the occupants. He blinked as he saw the two white men, walked on and took the seat directly behind them.

He examined the backs of their necks, their coats and hats and their profiles. Bond sat next to the window. The negro saw the reflection of his scar in the dark glass.

He got up and moved to the front of the bus without looking back. At the next stop he got off the bus and made straight for the nearest drugstore. He shut himself into the paybox.

Whisper questioned him urgently, then broke the connection.

He plugged in on the right of the board.

'Yes?' said the deep voice.

'Boss, one of them's just come in on Fifth. The Limey with the scar. Got a friend with him, but he don't seem to fit the dope on the other two.' Whisper passed on an accurate description of Leiter. 'Coming north, both of them.' He gave the number and probable timing of the bus.

There was a pause.

'Right,' said the quiet voice. 'Call off all Eyes on the other avenues. Warn the night spots that one of them's inside and get this to Tee-Hee Johnson, McThing, Blabbermouth Foley, Sam Miami and The Flannel . . .'

The voice spoke for five minutes.

'Got that? Repeat.'

'Yes, Sir, Boss,' said The Whisper. He glanced at his shorthand pad and whispered fluently and without a pause into the mouthpiece.

'Right.' The line went dead.

His eyes bright, The Whisper took up a fistful of plugs and started talking to the town.

From the moment that Bond and Leiter walked under the canopy of Sugar Ray's on Seventh Avenue at 123rd Street there was a team of men and women watching them or waiting to watch them, speaking softly to The Whisper at the big switchboard on the Riverside Exchange, handing them on towards the rendezvous. In a world where they were naturally the focus of attention, neither Bond nor Leiter felt the hidden machine nor sensed the tension around them.

In the famous night spot the stools against the long bar were crowded, but one of the small booths against the wall was empty and Bond and Leiter slipped into the two seats with the narrow table between them.

They ordered Scotch-and-soda — Haig and Haig Pinchbottle. Bond looked the crowd over. It was nearly all men. There were two or three whites, boxing fans or reporters for the New York sports columns, Bond decided. The atmosphere was warmer, louder than downtown. The walls were covered with boxing photographs, mostly of Sugar Ray Robinson and of scenes from his great fights. It was a cheerful place, doing great business.

'He was a wise guy, Sugar Ray,' said Leiter. 'Let's hope we both know when to stop when the time comes. He stashed plenty away and now he's adding to his pile on the music halls. His percentage of this place must be worth a packet and he owns a lot of real estate around here. He works hard still, but it's not the sort of work that sends you blind or gives you a haemorrhage of the brain. He quit while he was still alive.'

'He'll probably back a Broadway show and lose it all,' said Bond. 'If I quit now and went in for fruit-farming in Kent, I'd most likely hit the worst weather since the Thames froze over, and be cleaned out. One can't plan for everything.'

'One can try,' said Leiter. 'But I know what you mean — better the frying pan you know than the fire you don't. It isn't a bad life when it consists of sitting in a comfortable bar drinking good whisky. How do you like this corner of the jungle?' He leant forward. 'Just listen in to the couple behind you. From what I've heard they're straight out of "Nigger Heaven".'

Bond glanced carefully over his shoulder.

The booth behind him contained a handsome young negro in an expensive fawn suit with exaggerated shoulders. He was lolling back against the wall with one foot up on the bench beside him. He was paring the nails of his left hand with a small silver pocket-knife, occasionally glancing in bored fashion towards the animation at the bar. His head rested on the back of the booth just behind Bond and a whiff of expensive hair-straightener came from him. Bond took in the artificial parting traced with a razor across the left side of the scalp, through the almost straight hair which was a tribute to his mother's constant application of the hot comb since childhood. The plain black silk tie and the white shirt were in good taste.

Opposite him, leaning forward with concern on her pretty face, was a sexy little negress with a touch of white blood in her. Her jet-black hair, as sleek as the best permanent wave, framed a sweet almond-shaped face with rather slanting eyes under finely drawn eyebrows. The deep purple of her parted, sensual lips was thrilling against the bronze skin. All that Bond could see of her clothes was the bodice of a black satin evening dress, tight and revealing across the firm, small breasts. She wore a plain gold chain round her neck and a plain gold band round each thin wrist.

She was pleading anxiously and paid no heed to Bond's quick embracing glance.

'Listen and see if you can get the hang of it,' said Leiter. 'It's straight Harlem — Deep South with a lot of New York thrown in.'

Bond picked up the menu and leant back in the booth, studying the Special Fried Chicken Dinner at $3.75.

'Cmon honey,' wheedled the girl. 'How come yuh-all's actin' so tahd tonight?'

'Guess ah jist nacherlly gits tahd listenin' at yuh,' said the man languidly. 'Why'nt yuh hush yo' mouff'n let me 'joy mahself 'n peace 'n qui-yet.'

'Is yuh wan' me to go 'way, honey?'

'Yuh kin suit yo sweet self.'

'Aw honey,' pleaded the girl. 'Don' ack mad at me, honey. Ah was fixin' tuh treat yuh tonight. Take yuh to Smalls Par'dise, mebbe. See dem high-yallers shakin' 'n truckin'. Dat Birdie Johnson, da maitre d', he permis me a ringside whenebber Ah come nex'.'

The man's voice suddenly sharpened. 'Wha' dat Birdie he mean tuh yuh, hey?' he asked suspiciously. 'Perzackly,' he paused to let the big word sink in, 'perzackly wha' goes 'tween yuh 'n dat lowdown ornery wuthless Nigguh? Yuh sleepin' wid him mebbe? Guess Ah gotta study 'bout dat little situayshun 'tween yuh an' Birdie Johnson. Mebbe git mahself a betterer gal. Ah jist don' lak gals which runs off ever' which way when Ah jist happen be busticated temporaneously. Yesmam. Ah gotta study 'bout dat little situayshun.' He paused threateningly. 'Sure have,' he added.

'Aw honey,' the girl was anxious. 'dey ain't no use tryin' to git mad at me. Ah done nuthen tuh give yuh recasion tuh ack dat way. Ah jist thunk you mebbe preshiate a ringside at da Par'dise 'nstead of settin' hyah countin' yo troubles. Why, honey, yuh all knows ah wudden fall fo' dat richcrat ack' of Birdie Johnson. No sir. He don' mean nuthen tuh me. Him duh wusstes' man 'n Harlem, dawg bite me effn he ain't. All da same, he permis me da bestess seats 'nda house 'n Ah sez lets us go set 'n dem, 'n have us a beer 'n a good time. Cmon, honey. Let's us git out of hyah. Yuh done look so swell 'n Ah jist wan' mah frens tuh see usn together.'

'Yuh done look okay yoself, honeychile,' said the man, mollified by the tribute to his elegance, 'an' dats da troof. But Ah mus' spressify dat yuh stays close up tuh me an keeps yo eyes offn dat lowdown trash 'n his hot pants. 'N Ah may say,' he added threateningly, 'dat ef Ah ketches yuh makin' up tuh dat dope Ah'll jist nachrally whup da hide offn yo sweet ass.'

'Shoh ting, honey,' whispered the girl excitedly.

Bond heard the man's foot scrape off the seat to the ground.

'Cmon, baby, lessgo. Waiduh!'

Bond put down the menu. 'Got the gist of it,' he said. 'Seems they're interested in much the same things as everyone else — sex, having fun, and keeping up with the Joneses. Thank God they're not genteel about it.'

'Some of them are,' said Leiter. 'Tea cups, aspidistras and tut-tutting all over the place. The Methodists are almost their strongest sect. Harlem's riddled with social distinctions, the same as any other big city, but with all the colour variations added. Come on,' he suggested, 'let's go and get ourselves something to eat.'

They finished their drinks and Bond called for the check.

'All this evening's on me,' he said. 'I've got a lot of money to get rid of and I've brought three hundred dollars of it along with me.'

'Suits me,' said Leiter, who knew about Bond's thousand dollars.

As the waiter was picking up the change, Leiter suddenly said, 'Know where The Big Man's operating tonight?'

The waiter showed the whites of his eyes.

He leant forward and flicked the table down with his napkin.

'I've got a wife 'n kids, Boss,' he muttered out of the corner of his mouth. He stacked the glasses on his tray and went back to the bar.

'Mr Big's got the best protection of all,' said Leiter. 'Fear.'

They went out on to Seventh Avenue. The rain had stopped, but 'Hawkins', the bone-chilling wind from the north which the negroes greet with a reverent 'Hawkins is here', had come instead to keep the streets free of their usual crowds. Leiter and Bond moved with the trickle of couples on the sidewalk. The looks they got were mostly contemptuous or frankly hostile. One or two men spat in the gutter when they had passed.

Bond suddenly felt the force of what Leiter had told him. They were trespassing. They just weren't wanted. Bond felt the uneasiness that he had known so well during the war, when he had been working for a time behind the enemy lines. He shrugged the feeling away.

'We'll go to Ma Frazier's, further up the Avenue,' said Leiter. 'Best food in Harlem, or at any rate it used to be.'

As they went along Bond gazed into the shop windows.

He was struck by the number of barbers' saloons and 'beauticians'. They all advertised various forms of hair-straightener — 'Apex Glossatina, for use with the hot comb', 'Silky Strate. Leaves no redness, no burn' — or nostrums for bleaching the skin. Next in frequency were the haberdashers and clothes shops, with fantastic men's snakeskin shoes, shirts with small aeroplanes as a pattern, peg-top trousers with inch-wide stripes, zoot suits. All the book shops were full of educational literature — how to learn this, how to do that — and comics. There were several shops devoted to lucky charms and various occultisms — *Seven Keys to Power*, 'The strangest book ever written', with sub-titles such as: 'If you are CROSSED, shows you how to remove and cast it back.' 'Chant your desires in the Silent Tongue.' 'Cast a Spell on Anyone, no matter where.' 'Make any person Love you.' Among the charms were 'High John the Conqueror Root', 'Money Drawing Brand Oil', 'Sachet Powders, Uncrossing Brand', 'Incense, Jinx removing Brand', and the 'Lucky Whamie Hand Charm, giving Protection from Evil. Confuses and Baffles Enemies'.

Bond reflected it was no wonder that the Big Man found Voodooism such a powerful weapon on minds that still recoiled at a white chicken's feather or crossed sticks in the road — right in the middle of the shining capital city of the Western world.

'I'm glad we came up here,' said Bond. 'I'm beginning to get the hang of Mr Big. One just doesn't catch the smell of all this in a country like England. We're a superstitious lot there of course — particularly the Celts, but here one can almost hear the drums.'

Leiter grunted. 'I'll be glad to get back to my bed,' he said. 'But we need to size up this guy before we decide how to get at him.'

Ma Frazier's was a cheerful contrast to the bitter streets. They had an excellent meal of Little Neck Clams and Fried Chicken Maryland with bacon and sweet corn. 'We've got to have it,' said Leiter. 'It's the national dish.'

It was very civilized in the warm restaurant. Their waiter seemed glad to see them and pointed out various celebrities, but when Leiter slipped in a question about Mr Big the waiter seemed not to hear. He kept away from them until they called for their bill.

Leiter repeated the question.

'Sorry, Sah,' said the waiter briefly. 'Ah caint recall a gemmun of dat name.'

By the time they left the restaurant it was ten-thirty and the Avenue was almost deserted. They took a cab to the Savoy Ballroom, had a Scotch-and-soda, and watched the dancers.

'Most modern dances were invented here,' said Leiter. 'That's how good it is. The Lindy Hop, Truckin', the Susie Q, the Shag. All started on that floor. Every big American band you've ever heard of is proud that it once played here — Duke Ellington, Louis Armstrong, Cab Calloway, Noble Sissle, Fletcher Henderson. It's the Mecca of jazz and jive.'

They had a table near the rail round the huge floor. Bond was spellbound. He found many of the girls very beautiful. The music hammered its way into his pulse until he almost forgot what he was there for.

'Gets you, doesn't it?' said Leiter at last. 'I could stay here all night. Better move along. We'll miss out Small's Paradise. Much the same as this, but not quite in the same class. Think I'll take you to Yeah Man, back on Seventh. After that we must get moving to one of Mr Big's own joints. Trouble is, they don't open till midnight. I'll pay a visit to the washroom while you get the check. See if I can get a line on where we're likely to find him tonight. We don't want to have to go to all his places.'

Bond paid the check and met Leiter downstairs in the narrow entrance hall.

Leiter drew him outside and they walked up the street looking for a cab.

'Cost me twenty bucks,' said Leiter, 'but the word is he'll be at The Boneyard. Small place on Lenox Avenue. Quite close to his headquarters. Hottest strip in town. Girl called G-G Sumatra. We'll have another drink at Yeah Man and hear the piano. Move on at about twelve-thirty.'

The big switchboard, now only a few blocks away, was almost quiet. The two men had been checked in and out of Sugar Ray's, Ma Frazier's and the Savoy Ballroom. Midnight had them entering Yeah Man. At twelve-thirty the final call came and then the board was silent.

Mr Big spoke on the house-phone. First to the head waiter.

'Two white men coming in in five minutes. Give them the Z table.'

'Yes, Sir, Boss,' said the head waiter. He hurried across the dance floor to a table away on the right, obscured from most of the room by a wide pillar. It was next to the service entrance but with a good view of the floor and the band opposite.

It was occupied by a party of four, two men and two girls.

'Sorry folks,' said the head waiter. 'Been a mistake. Table's reserved. Newspaper men from downtown.'

One of the men began to argue.

'Move, Bud,' said the head waiter crisply. 'Lofty, show these folks to table F. Drinks is on the house. Sam,' he beckoned to another waiter, 'clear the table. Two covers.' The party of four moved docilely away, mollified by the prospect of free liquor. The head waiter put a Reserved sign on table Z, surveyed it and returned to his post at his table-plan on the high desk beside the curtained entrance.

Meanwhile Mr Big had made two more calls on the house-phone. One to the Master of Ceremonies.

'Lights out at the end of G-G's act.'

'Yes, Sir, Boss,' said the MC with alacrity.

The other call was to four men who were playing craps in the basement. It was a long call, and very detailed.

6

TABLE Z

AT TWELVE FORTY-FIVE Bond and Leiter paid off their cab and walked in under the sign which announced 'The Boneyard' in violet and green neon.

The thudding rhythm and the sour-sweet smell rocked them as they pushed through the heavy curtains inside the swing door. The eyes of the hat-check girls glowed and beckoned.

'Have you reserved, Sir?' asked the head waiter.

'No,' said Leiter. 'We don't mind sitting at the bar.'

The head waiter consulted his table-plan. He seemed to decide. He put his pencil firmly through a space at the end of the card.

'Party hasn't shown. Guess Ah caint hold their res'vation all night. This way, please.' He held his card high over his head and led them round the small crowded dance floor. He pulled out one of the two chairs and removed the 'Reserved' sign.

'Sam,' he called a waiter over. 'Look after these gemmums' order.' He moved away.

They ordered Scotch-and-soda and chicken sandwiches.

Bond sniffed. 'Marihuana,' he commented.

'Most of the real hep-cats smoke reefers,' explained Leiter. 'Wouldn't be allowed most places.'

Bond looked round. The music had stopped. The small four-piece band, clarinet, double-bass, electric guitar and drums, was moving out of the corner opposite. The dozen or so couples were walking and jiving to their tables and the crimson light was turned off under the glass dance floor. Instead, pencil-thin lights in the roof came on and hit coloured glass witchballs, larger than footballs, that hung at intervals round the wall. They were of different hues, golden, blue, green, violet, red. As the beams of light hit them, they glowed like coloured suns. The walls, varnished black, mirrored their reflections as did the sweat on the ebony faces of the men. Sometimes a man sitting between two lights showed cheeks of different colour, green on one side, perhaps, and red on the other. The lighting made it impossible to distinguish features unless they were only a few feet away. Some of the lights turned the girls' lipstick black, others lit their whole faces in a warm glow on one side and gave the other profile the luminosity of a drowned corpse.

The whole scene was macabre and livid, as if El Greco had done a painting by moonlight of an exhumed graveyard in a burning town.

It was not a large room, perhaps sixty feet square. There were about fifty tables and the customers were packed in like black olives in a jar. It was hot and the air was thick with smoke and the sweet, feral smell of two hundred negro bodies. The noise was terrific — an undertone of the jabber of negroes enjoying themselves without restraint, punctuated by sharp bursts of noise, shouts and high giggles, as loud voices called to each other across the room.

'Sweet Jeessus, look who's hyar . . . '

'Where you been keepin yoself, baby . . . '

'Gawd's troof. It's Pinkus . . . Hi Pinkus . . . '

'Cmon over . . . '

'Lemme be . . . Lemme be, I'se telling ya . . . ' (The noise of a slap.)

'Where's G-G. Cmon G-G. Strut yo stuff . . . '

From time to time a man or girl would erupt on to the dance floor and start a wild solo jive. Friends would clap the rhythm. There would be a burst of catcalls and whistles. If it was a girl, there would be cries of 'Strip, Strip, Strip,' 'Get hot, baby!' 'Shake it, Shake it,' and the MC would come out and clear the floor amidst groans and shouts of derision.

The sweat began to bead on Bond's forehead. Leiter leant over and cupped his hands. 'Three exits. Front. Service behind us. Behind the band.' Bond nodded. At that moment he felt it didn't matter. This was nothing new to Leiter, but for Bond it was a close-up of the raw material on which The Big Man worked, the clay in his hands. The evening was gradually putting flesh on the dossiers he had read in London and New York. If the evening ended now, without any closer sight of Mr Big himself, Bond still felt his education in the case would be almost complete. He took a deep draught of his whisky. There was a burst of applause. The MC had come out on to the dance floor, a tall negro in immaculate tails with a red carnation in his buttonhole. He stood, holding up his hands. A single white spotlight caught him. The rest of the room went dark.

There was silence.

'Folks,' announced the MC with a broad flash of gold and white teeth. 'This is it.'

There was excited clapping.

He turned to the left of the floor, directly across from Leiter and Bond.

He flung out his right hand. Another spot came on.

'Mistah Jungles Japhet 'n his drums.'

A crash of applause, catcalls, whistles.

Four grinning negroes in flame-coloured shirts and peg-top white trousers were revealed, squatting astride four tapering barrels with rawhide membranes. The drums were of different sizes. The negroes were all gaunt and stringy. The one sitting astride the bass drum rose briefly and shook clasped hands at the spectators.

'Voodoo drummers from Haiti,' whispered Leiter.

There was silence. With the tips of their fingers the drummers began a slow, broken beat, a soft rumba shuffle.

'And now, friends,' announced the MC, still turned towards the drums, 'G-G . . . ' he paused, 'SUMATRA.'

The last word was a yell. He began to clap. There was pandemonium in the room, a frenzy of applause. The door behind the drums burst open and two huge negroes, naked except for gold loincloths, ran out on to the floor carrying between them, her arms round their necks, a tiny figure, swathed completely in black ostrich feathers, a black domino across her eyes.

They put her down in the middle of the floor. They bowed down on either side of her until their foreheads met the ground. She took two paces forward. With the spotlight off them, the two negroes melted away into the shadows and through the door.

The MC had disappeared. There was absolute silence save for the soft thud of the drums.

The girl put her hand up to her throat and the cloak of black feathers came away from the front of her body and spread out into a five-foot black fan. She swirled it slowly behind her until it stood up like a peacock's tail. She was naked except for a brief vee of black lace and a black sequin star in the centre of each breast and the thin black domino across her eyes. Her body was small, hard, bronze, beautiful. It was slightly oiled and glinted in the white light.

The audience was silent. The drums began to step up the tempo. The bass drum kept its beat dead on the timing of the human pulse.

The girl's naked stomach started slowly to revolve in time with the rhythm. She swept the black feathers across and behind her again, and her hips started to grind in time with the bass drum. The upper part of her body was motionless. The black feathers swirled again, and now her feet were shifting and her shoulders. The drums beat louder. Each part of her body seemed to be keeping a different time. Her lips were bared slightly from her teeth. Her nostrils began to flare. Her eyes glinted hotly through the diamond slits. It was a sexy pug-like face — *chienne* was the only word Bond could think of.

The drums thudded faster, a complexity of interlaced rhythms. The girl tossed the big fan off the floor, held her arms up above her head. Her whole body began to shiver. Her belly moved faster. Round and round, in and out. Her legs straddled. Her hips began to revolve in a wide circle. Suddenly she plucked the sequin star off her right breast and threw it into the audience. The first noise came from the spectators, a quiet growl. Then they were silent again. She plucked off the other star. Again the growl and then silence. The drums began to crash and roll. Sweat poured off the drummers. Their hands fluttered like grey flannel on the pale membranes. Their eyes were bulging, distant. Their heads were slightly bent to one side as if they were listening. They hardly glanced at the girl. The audience panted softly, liquid eyes bulging and rolling.

The sweat was shining all over her now. Her breasts and stomach glistened with it. She broke into great shuddering jerks. Her mouth opened and she screamed softly. Her hands snaked down to her sides and suddenly she had torn away the strip of lace. She threw it into the audience. There was nothing now but a single black G-string. The drums went into a hurricane of sexual rhythm. She screamed softly again and then, her arms stretched before her as a balance, she started to lower her body down to the floor and up again. Faster and faster. Bond could hear the audience panting and grunting like pigs at the trough. He felt his own hands gripping the tablecloth. His mouth was dry.

The audience began to shout at her. 'Cmon, G-G. Take it away, Baby. Cmon. Grind, Baby, grind.'

She sank to her knees and as the rhythm slowly died so she too went into a last series of juddering spasms, mewing softly.

The drums came down to a slow tom-tom beat and shuffle. The audience howled for her body. Harsh obscenities came from different corners of the room.

The MC came on to the floor. A spot went on him.

'Okay, folks, okay.' The sweat was pouring off his chin. He spread his arms in surrender.

'Da G-G AGREES!'

There was a delighted howl from the audience. Now she would be quite naked. 'Take it off, G-G. Show yoself, Baby. Cmon, cmon.'

The drums growled and stuttered softly.

'But, mah friends,' yelled the MC, 'she stipperlates — With da lights OUT!'

There was a frustrated groan from the audience. The whole room was plunged in darkness.

Must be an old gag, thought Bond to himself.

Suddenly all his senses were alert.

The howling of the mob was disappearing, rapidly. At the same time he felt cold air on his face. He felt as if he was sinking.

'Hey,' shouted Leiter. His voice was close but it sounded hollow.

Christ! thought Bond.

Something snapped shut above his head. He put his hand out behind him. It touched a moving wall a foot from his back.

'Lights,' said a voice, quietly.

At the same time both his arms were gripped. He was pressed down in his chair.

Opposite him, still at the table, sat Leiter, a huge negro grasping his elbows. They were in a tiny square cell. To right and left were two more negroes in plain clothes with guns trained on them.

There was the sharp hiss of a hydraulic garage lift and the table settled quietly to the floor. Bond glanced up. There was the faint join of a broad trapdoor a few feet above their heads. No sound came through it.

One of the negroes grinned.

'Take it easy, folks. Enjoy da ride?'

Leiter let out one single harsh obscenity. Bond relaxed his muscles, waiting.

'Which is da Limey?' asked the negro who had spoken. He seemed to be in charge. The pistol he held trained lazily on Bond's heart was very fancy. There was a glint of mother-of-pearl between his black fingers on the stock and the long octagonal barrel was finely chased.

'Dis one, Ah guess,' said the negro who was holding Bond's arms. 'He's got da scar.'

The negro's grip on Bond's arm was terrific. It was as if he had two fierce tourniquets applied above the elbows. His hands were beginning to go numb.

The man with the fancy gun came round the corner of the table. He shoved the muzzle of his gun into Bond's stomach. The hammer was back.

'You oughtn't to miss at that range,' said Bond.

'Shaddap,' said the negro. He frisked Bond expertly with his left hand — legs, thighs, back, sides. He dug out Bond's gun and handed it to the other armed man.

'Give dat to da Boss, Tee-Hee,' he said. 'Take da Limey up. Yuh go 'long wid em. Da other guy stays wid me.'

'Yassuh,' said the man called Tee-Hee, a paunchy negro in a chocolate shirt and lavender-coloured peg-top trousers.

Bond was hauled to his feet. He had one foot hooked under a leg of the table. He yanked hard. There was a crash of glass and silverware. At the same moment, Leiter kicked out backwards round the leg of his chair. There was a satisfactory 'klonk' as his heel caught his guard's shin. Bond did the same but missed. There was a moment of chaos, but neither of the guards slackened his grip. Leiter's guard picked him bodily out of the chair as if he had been a child, faced him to the wall and slammed him into it. It nearly smashed Leiter's nose. The guard swung him round. Blood was streaming down over his mouth.

The two guns were still trained unwaveringly on them. It had been a futile effort, but for a split second they had regained the initiative and effaced the sudden shock of capture.

'Don' waste yo breff,' said the negro who had been giving the orders. 'Take da Limey away.' He addressed Bond's guard. 'Mr Big's waiten'.' He turned to Leiter. 'Yo kin tell yo fren' good-bye,' he said. 'Yo is unlikely be seein' yoselves agin.'

Bond smiled at Leiter. 'Lucky we made a date for the police to meet us here at two,' he said. 'See you at the line-up.'

Leiter grinned back. His teeth were red with blood. 'Commissioner Monahan's going to be pleased with this bunch. Be seeing you.'

'Crap,' said the negro with conviction. 'Get goin'.'

Bond's guard whipped him round and shoved him against a section of the wall. It opened on a pivot into a long bare passage. The man called Tee-Hee pushed past them and led the way.

The door swung to behind them.

7
MISTER BIG

THEIR FOOTSTEPS ECHOED down the stone passage. At the end there was a door. They went through into another long passage lit by an occasional bare bulb in the roof. Another door and they found themselves in a large warehouse. Cases and bales were stacked in neat piles. There were runways for overhead cranes. From the markings on the crates it seemed to be a liquor store. They followed an aisle across to an iron door. The man called Tee-Hee rang a bell. There was absolute silence. Bond guessed they must have walked at least a block away from the nightclub.

There was a clang of bolts and the door opened. A negro in evening dress with a gun in his hand stepped aside and they went through into a carpeted hallway.

'Yo kin go on in, Tee-Hee,' said the man in evening dress.

Tee-Hee knocked on a door facing them, opened it and led the way through.

In a high-backed chair, behind an expensive desk, Mr Big sat looking quietly at them.

'Good morning, Mister James Bond.' The voice was deep and soft. 'Sit down.'

Bond's guard led him across the thick carpet to a low armchair in leather and tubular steel. He released Bond's arms and Bond sat down and faced The Big Man across the wide desk.

It was a blessed relief to be rid of the two vice-like hands. All sensation had left Bond's forearms. He let them hang beside him and welcomed the dull pain as the blood started to flow again.

Mr Big sat looking at him, his huge head resting against the back of the tall chair. He said nothing.

Bond at once realized that the photographs had conveyed nothing of this man, nothing of the power and the intellect which seemed to radiate from him, nothing of the over-size features.

It was a great football of a head, twice the normal size and very nearly round. The skin was grey-black, taut and shining like the face of a week-old corpse in the river. It was hairless, except for some grey-brown fluff above the ears. There were no eyebrows and no eyelashes and the eyes were extraordinarily far apart so that one could not focus on them both, but only on one at a time. Their gaze was very steady and penetrating. When they rested on something, they seemed to devour it, to encompass the whole of it. They bulged slightly and the irises were golden round black pupils which were now wide. They were animal eyes, not human, and they seemed to blaze.

The nose was wide without being particularly negroid. The nostrils did not gape at you. The lips were only slightly everted, but thick and dark. They opened only when the man spoke and then they opened wide and drew back from the teeth and the pale pink gums.

There were few wrinkles or creases on the face, but there were two deep clefts above the nose, the clefts of concentration. Above them the forehead bulged slightly before merging with the polished, hairless crown.

Curiously, there was nothing disproportionate about the monstrous head. It was carried on a wide, short neck supported by the shoulders of a giant. Bond knew from the records that he was six and a half feet tall and weighed twenty stone, and that little of it was fat. But the total impression was awe-inspiring, even terrifying, and Bond could imagine that so ghastly a misfit must have been bent since childhood on revenge against fate and against the world that hated because it feared him.

The Big Man was draped in a dinner jacket. There was a hint of vanity in the diamonds that blazed on his shirt-front and at his cuffs. His huge flat hands rested half-curled on the table in front of him. There were no signs of cigarettes or an ash tray and the smell of the room was neutral. There was nothing on the desk save a large intercom with about twenty switches and, incongruously, a very small ivory riding crop with a long thin white lash.

Mr Big gazed with silent and deep concentration across the table at Bond.

After inspecting him carefully in return, Bond glanced round the room.

It was full of books, spacious and restful and very quiet, like the library of a millionaire.

There was one high window above Mr Big's head but otherwise the walls were solid with bookshelves. Bond turned round in his chair. More bookshelves, packed with books. There was no sign of a door, but there might have been any number of doors faced with dummy books. The two negroes who had brought him to the room stood rather uneasily against the wall behind his chair. The whites of their eyes showed. They were not looking at Mr Big, but at a curious effigy which stood on a table in an open space of floor to the right, and slightly behind Mr Big.

Even with his slight knowledge of Voodoo, Bond recognized it at once from Leigh Fermor's description.

A five-foot white wooden cross stood on a raised white pedestal. The arms of the cross were thrust into the sleeves of a dusty black frock-coat whose tails hung down behind the table towards the floor. Above the neck of the coat a battered bowler hat gaped at him, its crown pierced by the vertical bar of the cross. A few inches below the rim, round the neck of the cross, resting on the cross-bar, was a deep starched clergyman's collar.

At the base of the white pedestal, on the table, lay an old pair of lemon-coloured gloves. A short malacca stick with a gold knob, its ferrule resting beside the gloves, rose against the left shoulder of the effigy. Also on the table was a battered black top hat.

This evil scarecrow gazed out across the room — God of the Cemeteries and Chief of the Legion of the Dead — Baron Samedi. Even to Bond it seemed to carry a dreadful gaping message.

Bond looked away, back to the great grey-black face across the desk.

Mr Big spoke.

'I want you, Tee-Hee.' His eyes shifted. 'You can go, Miami.'

'Yes, Sir, Boss,' they both said together.

Bond heard a door open and close.

Silence fell again. At first, Mr Big's eyes had been focused sharply on Bond. They had examined him minutely. Now, Bond noticed that though the eyes rested on him they had become slightly opaque. They gazed upon Bond without perception. Bond had the impression that the brain behind them was occupied elsewhere.

Bond was determined not to be disconcerted. Feeling had returned to his hands and he moved them towards his body to reach for his cigarettes and lighter.

Mr Big spoke.

'You may smoke, Mister Bond. In case you have any other intentions you may care to lean forward and inspect the keyhole of the drawer in this desk facing your chair. I shall be ready for you in a moment.'

Bond leant forward. It was a large keyhole. In fact Bond estimated, .45 centimetres in diameter. Fired, Bond supposed, by a foot-switch under the desk. What a bunch of tricks this man was. Puerile. Puerile? Perhaps, after all, not to be dismissed so easily. The tricks — the bomb, the disappearing table — had worked neatly, efficiently. They had not been just empty conceits, designed to impress. Again, there was nothing absurd about this gun. Rather painstaking, perhaps, but, he had to admit, technically sound.

He lit a cigarette and gratefully drew the smoke deep into his lungs. He did not feel particularly worried by his position. He refused to believe he would come to any harm. It would be a clumsy affair to have him disappear a couple of days after he arrived from England unless a very expert accident could be contrived. And Leiter would have to be disposed of at the same time. That would be altogether too much for their two Services and Mr Big must know it. But he was worried about Leiter in the hands of those clumsy black apes.

The Big Man's lips rolled slowly back from his teeth.

'I have not seen a member of the Secret Service for many years, Mister Bond. Not since the war. Your Service did well in the war. You have some able men. I learn from my friends that you are high up in your Service. You have a double-o number, I believe — 007, if I remember right. The significance of that double-o number, they tell me, is that you have had to kill a man in the course of some assignment. There cannot be many double-o numbers in a Service which does not use assassination as a weapon. Whom have you been sent over to kill here, Mister Bond? Not me by any chance?'

The voice was soft and even, without expression. There was a slight mixture of accents, American and French, but the English was almost pedantically accurate, without a trace of slang.

Bond remained silent. He assumed that Moscow had signalled his description.

'It is necessary for you to reply, Mister Bond. The fate of both of you depends upon your doing so. I have confidence in the sources of my information. I know much more than I have said. I shall easily detect a lie.'

Bond believed him. He chose a story he could support and which would cover the facts.

'There are English gold coins circulating in America. Edward IV Rose Nobles,' he said. 'Some have been sold in Harlem. The American Treasury asked for assistance in tracing them since they must come from a British source. I came up to Harlem to see for myself, with a representative of the American Treasury, who I hope is now safely on his way back to his hotel.'

'Mr Leiter is a representative of the Central Intelligence Agency, not of the Treasury,' said Mr Big without emotion. 'His position at this moment is extremely precarious.'

He paused and seemed to reflect. He looked past Bond.

'Tee-Hee.'

'Yassuh, Boss.'

'Tie Mister Bond to his chair.'

Bond half rose to his feet.

'Don't move, Mister Bond,' said the voice softly. 'You have a bare chance of survival if you stay where you are.'

Bond looked at The Big Man, at the golden, impassive eyes.

He lowered himself back into his chair. Immediately a broad strap was passed round his body and buckled tight. Two short straps went round his wrists and tied them to the leather and metal arms. Two more went round his ankles. He could hurl himself and the chair to the floor, but otherwise he was powerless.

Mr Big pressed down a switch on the intercom.

'Send in Miss Solitaire,' he said and centred the switch again.

There was a moment's pause and then a section of the bookcase to the right of the desk swung open.

One of the most beautiful women Bond had ever seen came slowly in and closed the door behind her. She stood just inside the room and stood looking at Bond, taking him in slowly inch by inch, from his head to his feet. When she had completed her detailed inspection, she turned to Mr Big.

'Yes?' she inquired flatly.

Mr Big had not moved his head. He addressed Bond.

'This is an extraordinary woman, Mister Bond,' he said in the same quiet soft voice, 'and I am going to marry her because she is unique. I found her in a cabaret, in Haiti, where she was born. She was doing a telepathic act which I could not understand. I looked into it and I still could not understand. There was nothing to understand. It was telepathy.'

Mr Big paused.

'I tell you this to warn you. She is my inquisitor. Torture is messy and inconclusive. People tell you what will ease the pain. With this girl it is not necessary to use clumsy methods. She can divine the truth in people. That is why she is to be my wife. She is too valuable to remain at liberty. And,' he continued blandly, 'it will be interesting to see our children.'

Mr Big turned towards her and gazed at her impassively.

'For the time being she is difficult. She will have nothing to do with men. That is why, in Haiti, she was called "Solitaire".'

'Draw up a chair,' he said quietly to her. 'Tell me if this man lies. Keep clear of the gun,' he added.

The girl said nothing but took a chair similar to Bond's from beside the wall and pushed it towards him. She sat down almost touching his right knee. She looked into his eyes.

Her face was pale, with the pallor of white families that have lived long in the tropics. But it contained no trace of the usual exhaustion which the tropics impart to the skin and hair. The eyes were blue, alight and disdainful, but, as they gazed into his with a touch of humour, he realized they contained some message for him personally. It quickly vanished as his own eyes answered. Her hair was blue-black and fell heavily to her shoulders. She had high cheekbones and a wide, sensual mouth which held a hint of cruelty. Her jawline was delicate and finely cut. It showed decision and an iron will which were repeated in the straight, pointed nose. Part of the beauty of the face lay in its lack of compromise. It was a face born to command. The face of the daughter of a French Colonial slave-owner.

She wore a long evening dress of heavy white matt silk whose classical line was broken by the deep folds which fell from her shoulders and revealed the upper half of her breasts. She wore diamond earrings, square-cut in broken bands, and a thin diamond bracelet on her left wrist. She wore no rings. Her nails were short and without enamel.

She watched his eyes on her and nonchalantly drew her forearms together in her lap so that the valley between her breasts deepened.

The message was unmistakable and an answering warmth must have showed on Bond's cold, drawn face, for suddenly The Big Man picked up the small ivory whip from the desk beside him and lashed across at her, the thong whistling through the air and landing with a cruel bite across her shoulders.

Bond winced even more than she did. Her eyes blazed for an instant and then went opaque.

'Sit up,' said The Big Man softly, 'you forget yourself.'

She sat slowly more upright. She had a pack of cards in her hands and she started to shuffle them. Then, out of bravado perhaps, she sent him yet another message — of complicity and of more than complicity.

Between her hands, she faced the knave of hearts. Then the queen of spades. She held the two halves of the pack in her lap so that the two court cards looked at each other. She brought the two halves of the pack together until they kissed. Then she riffled the cards and shuffled them again.

At no moment of this dumb show did she look at Bond and it was all over in an instant. But Bond felt a glow of excitement and a quickening of the pulse. He had a friend in the enemy's camp.

'Are you ready, Solitaire?' asked The Big Man.

'Yes, the cards are ready,' said the girl, in a low, cool voice.

'Mister Bond, look into the eyes of this girl and repeat the reason for your presence here which you gave me just now.'

Bond looked into her eyes. There was no message. They were not focused on his. They looked through him.

He repeated what he had said.

For a moment he felt an uncanny thrill. Could this girl tell? If she could tell, would she speak for him or against him?

For a moment there was dead silence in the room. Bond tried to look indifferent. He gazed up at the ceiling — then back at her.

Her eyes came back into focus. She turned away from him and looked at Mr Big.

'He speaks the truth,' she said coldly.

8
NO SENSAYUMA

MR BIG REFLECTED for a moment. He seemed to decide. He pressed a switch on the intercom.

'Blabbermouth?'

'Yassuh, Boss.'

'You're holding that American, Leiter.'

'Yassuh.'

'Hurt him considerably. Ride him down to Bellevue Hospital and dump him nearby. Got that?'

'Yassuh.'

'Don't be seen.'

'Nossuh.'

Mr Big centred the switch.

'God damn your bloody eyes,' said Bond viciously. 'The CIA won't let you get away with this!'

'You forget, Mister Bond. They have no jurisdiction in America. The American Secret Service has no power in America — only abroad. And the FBI are no friends of theirs. Tee-Hee, come here.'

'Yassuh, Boss.' Tee-Hee came and stood beside the desk.

Mr Big looked across at Bond.

'Which finger do you use least, Mister Bond?'

Bond was startled by the question. His mind raced.

'On reflection, I expect you will say the little finger of the left hand,' continued the soft voice. 'Tee-Hee, break the little finger of Mister Bond's left hand.'

The negro showed the reason for his nickname.

'Hee-hee,' he gave a falsetto giggle, 'hee-hee.'

He walked jauntily over to Bond. Bond clutched madly at the arms of his chair. Sweat started to break out on his forehead. He tried to imagine the pain so that he could control it.

The negro slowly unhinged the little finger of Bond's left hand, immovably bound to the arm of his chair.

He held the tip between finger and thumb and very deliberately started to bend it back, giggling inanely to himself.

Bond rolled and heaved, trying to upset the chair, but Tee-Hee put his other hand on the chair-back and held it there. The sweat poured off Bond's face. His teeth started to bare in an involuntary rictus. Through the increasing pain he could just see the girl's eyes wide upon him, her red lips slightly parted.

The finger stood upright, away from the hand. Started to bend slowly backwards towards his wrist. Suddenly it gave. There was a sharp crack.

'That will do,' said Mr Big.

Tee-Hee released the mangled finger with reluctance.

Bond uttered a soft animal groan and fainted.

'Da guy ain't got no sensayuma,' commented Tee-Hee.

Solitaire sat limply back in her chair and closed her eyes.

'Did he have a gun?' asked Mr Big.

'Yassuh.' Tee-Hee took Bond's Beretta out of his pocket and slipped it across the desk. The Big Man picked it up and looked at it expertly. He weighed it in his hand, testing the feel of the skeleton grip. Then he pumped the shells out on to the desk, verified that he had also emptied the chamber and slid it over towards Bond.

'Wake him up,' he said, looking at his watch. It said three o'clock.

Tee-Hee went behind Bond's chair and dug his nails into the lobes of Bond's ears.

Bond groaned and lifted his head.

His eyes focused on Mr Big and he uttered a string of obscenities.

'Be thankful you're not dead,' said Mr Big without emotion. 'Any pain is preferable to death. Here is your gun. I have the shells. Tee-Hee, give it back to him.'

Tee-Hee took it off the desk and slipped it back into Bond's holster.

'I will explain to you briefly,' continued The Big Man, 'why it is that you are not dead; why you have been permitted to enjoy the sensation of pain instead of adding to the pollution of the Harlem River from the folds of what is jocularly known as a cement overcoat.'

He paused for a moment and then spoke.

'Mister Bond, I suffer from boredom. I am a prey to what the early Christians called "accidie", the deadly lethargy that envelops those who are sated, those who have no more desires. I am absolutely pre-eminent in my chosen profession, trusted by those who occasionally employ my talents, feared and instantly obeyed by those whom I myself employ. I have, literally, no more worlds to conquer within my chosen orbit. Alas, it is too late in my life to change that orbit for another one, and since power is the goal of all ambition, it is unlikely that I could possibly acquire more power in another sphere than I already possess in this one.'

Bond listened with part of his mind. With the other half he was already planning. He sensed the presence of Solitaire, but he kept his eyes off her. He gazed steadily across the table at the great grey face with its unwinking golden eyes.

The soft voice continued.

'Mister Bond, I take pleasure now only in artistry, in the polish and finesse which I can bring to my operations. It has become almost a mania with me to impart an absolute rightness, a high elegance, to the execution of my affairs. Each day, Mister Bond, I try and set myself still higher standards of subtlety and technical polish so that each of my proceedings may be a work of art, bearing my signature as clearly as the creations of, let us say, Benvenuto Cellini. I am content, for the time being, to be my only judge, but I sincerely believe, Mister Bond, that the approach to perfection which I am steadily achieving in my operations will ultimately win recognition in the history of our times.'

Mr Big paused. Bond saw that his great yellow eyes were wide, as if he saw visions. He's a raving megalomaniac, thought Bond. And all the more dangerous because of it. The fault in most criminal minds was that greed was their only impulse. A dedicated mind was quite another matter. This man was no gangster. He was a menace. Bond was fascinated and slightly awestruck.

'I accept anonymity for two reasons,' continued the low voice. 'Because the nature of my operations demands it and because I admire the self-negation of the anonymous artist. If you will allow the conceit, I see myself sometimes as one of those great Egyptian fresco painters who devoted their lives to producing masterpieces in the tombs of kings, knowing that no living eye would ever see them.'

The great eyes closed for a moment.

'However, let us return to the particular. The reason, Mister Bond, why I have not killed you this morning is because it would give me no aesthetic pleasure to blow a hole in your stomach. With this engine,' he gestured towards the gun trained on Bond through the desk drawer, 'I have already blown many holes in many stomachs, so I am quite satisfied that my little mechanical toy is a sound technical achievement. Moreover, as no doubt you rightly surmise, it would be a nuisance for me to have a lot of busybodies around here asking questions about the disappearance of yourself and your friend Mr Leiter. Not more than a nuisance; but for various reasons I wish to concentrate on other matters at the present time.

'So,' Mr Big looked at his watch, 'I decided to leave my card upon each of you and to give you one more solemn warning. You must leave the country today, and Mr Leiter must transfer to another assignment. I have quite enough to bother me without having a lot of agents from Europe added to the considerable strength of local busybodies with which I have to contend.

'That is all,' he concluded. 'If I see you again, you will die in a manner as ingenious and appropriate as I can devise on that day.

'Tee-Hee, take Mister Bond to the garage. Tell two of the men to take him to Central Park and throw him in the ornamental water. He may be damaged but not killed if he resists. Understood?'

'Yassuh, Boss,' said Tee-Hee, giggling in a high falsetto.

He undid Bond's ankles, then his wrists. He took Bond's injured hand and twisted it right up his back. Then with his other hand he undid the strap round his waist. He yanked Bond to his feet.

'Giddap,' said Tee-Hee.

Bond gazed once more into the great grey face.

'Those who deserve to die,' he paused, 'die the death they deserve. Write that down,' he added. 'It's an original thought.'

Then he glanced at Solitaire. Her eyes were bent on the hands in her lap. She didn't look up.

'Git goin,' said Tee-Hee. He turned Bond round towards the wall and pushed him forward, twisting Bond's wrist up his back until his forearm was almost dislocated. Bond uttered a realistic groan and his footsteps faltered. He wanted Tee-Hee to believe that he was cowed and docile. He wanted the torturing grip to ease just a little on his left arm. As it was, any sudden movement would only result in his arm being broken.

Tee-Hee reached over Bond's shoulder and pressed on one of the books in the serried shelves. A large section opened on a central pivot. Bond was pushed through and the negro kicked the heavy section back into place. It closed with a double click. From the thickness of the door, Bond guessed it would be sound-proof. They were faced by a short carpeted passage ending in some stairs that led downwards. Bond groaned.

'You're breaking my arm,' he said. 'Look out. I'm going to faint.'

He stumbled again, trying to measure exactly the negro's position behind him. He remembered Leiter's injunction: 'Shins, groin, stomach, throat. Hit 'em anywhere else and you'll just break your hand.'

'Shut yo mouf,' said the negro, but he pulled Bond's hand an inch or two down his back.

This was all Bond needed.

They were half way down the passage with only a few feet more to the top of the stairs. Bond faltered again, so that the negro's body bumped into his. This gave him the range and direction he needed.

He bent a little and his right hand, straight and flat as a board, whipped round and inwards. He felt it thud hard into the target. The negro screamed shrilly like a wounded rabbit. Bond felt his left arm come free. He whirled round, pulling out his empty gun with his right hand. The negro was bent double, his hands between his legs, uttering little panting screams. Bond whipped the gun down hard on the back of the woolly skull. It gave back a dull klonk as if he had hammered on a door, but the negro groaned and fell forward on his knees, throwing out his hands for support. Bond got behind him and with all the force he could put behind the steel-capped shoe, he gave one mighty kick below the lavender-coloured seat of the negro's pants.

A final short scream was driven out of the man as he sailed

the few feet to the stairs. His head hit the side of the iron banisters and then, a twisting wheel of arms and legs, he disappeared over the edge, down into the well. There was a short crash as he caromed off some obstacle, then a pause, then a mingled thud and crack as he hit the ground. Then silence.

Bond wiped the sweat out of his eyes and stood listening. He thrust his wounded left hand into his coat. It was throbbing with pain and swollen to almost twice its normal size. Holding his gun in his right hand, he walked to the head of the stairs and slowly down, moving softly on the balls of his feet.

There was only one floor between him and the spread-eagled body below. When he reached the landing, he stopped again and listened. Quite close, he could hear the high-pitched whine of some form of fast wireless transmitter. He verified that it came from behind one of the two doors on the landing. This must be Mr Big's communications centre. He longed to carry out a quick raid. But his gun was empty and he had no idea how many men he would find in the room. It could only have been the earphones on their ears that had prevented the operators from hearing the sounds of Tee-Hee's fall. He crept on down.

Tee-Hee was either dead or dying. He lay spread-eagled on his back. His striped tie lay across his face like a squashed adder. Bond felt no remorse. He frisked the body for a gun and found one stuck in the waistband of the lavender trousers, now stained with blood. It was a Colt .38 Detective Special with a sawn barrel. All chambers were loaded. Bond slipped the useless Beretta back in its holster. He nestled the big gun into his palm and smiled grimly.

A small door faced him, bolted on the inside. Bond put his ear to it. The muffled sound of an engine reached him. This must be the garage. But the running engine? At that time of the morning? Bond ground his teeth. Of course. Mr Big would have spoken on the intercom and warned them that Tee-Hee was bringing him down. They must be wondering what was holding him. They were probably watching the door for the negro to emerge.

Bond thought for a moment. He had the advantage of surprise. If only the bolts were well-oiled.

His left hand was almost useless. With the Colt in his right, he tested the first bolt with the edge of his damaged hand. It slipped easily back. So did the second. There remained only a press-down handle. He eased it down and pulled the door softly towards him.

It was a thick door and the noise of the engine got louder as the crack widened. The car must be just outside. Any further movement of the door would betray him. He whipped it open and stood facing sideways like a fencer so as to offer as small a target as possible. The hammer lay back on his gun.

A few feet away stood a black sedan, its engine running. It faced the open double doors of the garage. Bright arc-lights lit up the shining bodywork of several other cars. There was a big negro at the wheel of the sedan and another stood near him, leaning against the rear door. No one else was in view.

At sight of Bond the negroes' mouths fell open in astonishment. A cigarette dropped from the mouth of the man at the wheel. Then they both dived for their guns.

Instinctively, Bond shot first at the man standing, knowing he would be quickest on the draw.

The heavy gun roared hollowly in the garage.

The negro clutched his stomach with both hands, staggered two steps towards Bond, and collapsed on his face, his gun clattering on to the concrete.

The man at the wheel screamed as Bond's gun swung on to him. Hampered by the wheel the negro's shooting hand was still inside his coat.

Bond shot straight into the screaming mouth and the man's head crashed against the side window.

Bond ran round the car and opened the door. The negro sprawled horribly out. Bond threw his revolver on to the driving seat and yanked the body out on to the ground. He tried to avoid the blood. He got into the seat and blessed the running engine and the steering wheel gear-lever. He slammed the door, rested his injured hand on the left of the wheel and crashed the lever forward.

The hand-brake was still on. He had to lean under the wheel to release it with his right hand.

It was a dangerous pause. As the heavy car surged forward out of the wide doors there was the boom of a gun and a bullet hammered into the bodywork. He tore the wheel round right-handed and there was another shot that missed high. Across the street a window splintered.

The flash came from low down near the floor and Bond guessed that the first negro had somehow managed to reach his gun.

There were no other shots and no sound came from the blank faces of the buildings behind him. As he went through the gears he could see nothing in the driving-mirror except the broad bar of light from the garage shining out across the dark empty street.

Bond had no idea where he was or where he was heading. It was a wide featureless street and he kept going. He found himself driving on the left-hand side and quickly swerved over to the right. His hand hurt terribly but the thumb and forefinger helped to steady the wheel. He tried to remember to keep his left side away from the blood on the door and window. The endless street was populated only by the little ghosts of steam that wavered up out of the gratings in the asphalt that gave access to the piped heat system of the city. The ugly bonnet of the car mowed them down one by one, but in the driving-mirror Bond could see them rising again behind him in a diminishing vista of mildly gesticulating white wraiths.

He kept the big car at fifty. He came to some red traffic lights and jumped them. Several more dark blocks and then there was a lighted avenue. There was traffic and he paused until the lights went green. He turned left and was rewarded by a succession of green lights, each one sweeping him on and further away from the enemy. He checked at an intersection and read the signs. He was on Park Avenue and 116th Street. He slowed again at the next street. It was 115th. He was heading downtown, away from Harlem, back into the city. He kept going. He turned off at 60th Street. It was deserted. He switched off the engine and left the car opposite a fire hydrant. He took the gun off the seat, shoved it down the waistband of his trousers and walked back to Park Avenue.

A few minutes later he flagged a prowling cab and then suddenly he was walking up the steps of the St Regis.

'Message for you, Mr Bond,' said the night porter. Bond kept his left side away from him. He opened the message with his right hand. It was from Felix Leiter, timed at four a.m. 'Call me at once,' it said.

Bond walked to the elevator and was carried up to his floor. He let himself into 2100 and went through into the sitting-room.

So both of them were alive. Bond fell into a chair beside the telephone.

'God Almighty,' said Bond with deep gratitude. 'What a break.'

9

TRUE OR FALSE?

BOND LOOKED AT the telephone, then he got up and walked over to the sideboard. He put a handful of wilted ice cubes into a tall glass, poured in three inches of Haig and Haig and swilled the mixture round in the glass to cool and dilute it. Then he drank down half the glass in one long swallow. He put the glass down and eased himself out of his coat. His left hand was so swollen that he could only just get it through the sleeve. His little finger was still crooked back and the pain was vicious as it scraped against the cloth. The finger was nearly black. He pulled down his tie and undid the top of his shirt. Then he picked up his glass, took another deep swallow, and walked back to the telephone.

Leiter answered at once.

'Thank God,' said Leiter with real feeling. 'What's the damage?'

'Broken finger,' said Bond. 'How about you?'

'Blackjack. Knocked out. Nothing serious. They started off by considering all sorts of ingenious things. Wanted to couple me to the compressed air pump in the garage. Start on the ears and then proceed elsewhere. When no instructions came from The Big Man they got bored and I got to arguing the finer points of jazz with Blabbermouth, the man with the fancy six-shooter. We got on to Duke Ellington and agreed that we liked our band-leaders to be percussion men, not wind. We agreed the piano or the drums held the band together better than any other solo instrument — Jelly-roll Morton, for instance. Apropos the Duke, I told him the crack about the clarinet — "an ill woodwind that nobody blows good". That made him laugh fit to bust. Suddenly we were friends. The other man — The Flannel, he was called — got sour and Blabbermouth told him he could go off duty, he'd look after me. Then The Big Man rang down.'

'I was there,' said Bond. 'It didn't sound so hot.'

'Blabbermouth was worried as hell. He wandered round the room talking to himself. Suddenly he used the blackjack, hard, and I went out. Next thing I knew we were outside Bellevue Hospital. About half after three. Blabbermouth was very apologetic, said it was the least he could have done. I believe him. He begged me not to give him away. Said he was going to report that he'd left me half dead. Of course I promised to leak back some very lurid details. We parted on the best of terms. I got some treatment at the Emergency ward and came home. I was worried to hell an' gone about you, but after a while the telephone started ringing. Police and FBI. Seems The Big Man has complained that some fool Limey went berserk at The Boneyard early this morning, shot three of his men — two chauffeurs and a waiter, if you please — stole one of his cars and got away, leaving his overcoat and hat in the cloakroom. The Big Man's yelling for action. Of course I warned off the dicks and the FBI, but they're madder'n hell and we've got to get out of town at once. It'll miss the mornings but it'll be splashed all over the afternoon blatts and radio and TV'll have it. Apart from all that, Mr Big will be after you like a nest of hornets. Anyway, I've got some plans fixed. Now you tell, and God, am I glad to hear your voice!'

Bond gave a detailed account of all that had happened. He forgot nothing. When he had finished, Leiter gave a low whistle.

'Boy,' he said with admiration. 'You certainly made a dent in The Big Man's machine. But were you lucky. That Solitaire dame certainly seems to have saved your bacon. D'you think we can use her?'

'Could if we could get near her,' said Bond. 'I should think he keeps her pretty close.'

'We'll have to think about that another day,' said Leiter. 'Now we better get moving. I'll hang up and call you back in a few minutes. First I'll get the police surgeon round to you right away. Be along in a quarter of an hour or so. Then I'll talk to the Commissioner myself and sort out some of the police angles. They can stall a bit by discovering the car. The FBI'll have to tip off the radio and newspaper boys so that at least we can keep your name out of it and all this Limey talk. Otherwise we shall have the British Ambassador being hauled out of bed and parades by the National Association for the Advancement of Coloured People and God knows what all.' Leiter chuckled down the telephone. 'Better have a word with your chief in London. It's about half after ten their time. You'll need a bit of protection. I can look after the CIA, but the FBI have got a bad attack of "see-here-young-man" this morning. You'll need some more clothes. I'll see to that. Keep awake. We'll get plenty of sleep in the grave. Be calling you.'

He hung up. Bond smiled to himself. Hearing Leiter's cheerful voice and knowing everything was being taken care of had wiped away his exhaustion and his black memories.

He picked up the telephone and talked to the Overseas operator. Ten minutes' delay, she said.

Bond walked into his bedroom and somehow got out of his clothes. He gave himself a very hot shower and then an ice-cold one. He shaved and managed to pull on a clean shirt and trousers. He put a fresh clip in his Beretta and wrapped the Colt in his discarded shirt and put it in his suitcase. He was half way through his packing when the telephone rang.

He listened to the zing and echo on the line, the chatter of distant operators, the patches of Morse from aircraft and ships at sea, quickly suppressed. He could see the big, grey building near Regent's Park and imagine the busy switchboard and the cups of tea and a girl saying, 'Yes, this is Universal Export,' the address Bond had asked for, one of the covers used by agents for emergency calls on open lines from abroad. She would tell the Supervisor, who would take the call over.

'You're connected, caller,' said the Overseas operator. 'Go ahead please. New York calling London.'

Bond heard the calm English voice. 'Universal Export. Who's speaking, please?'

'Can I speak to the Managing Director?' said Bond. 'This is his nephew James speaking from New York.'

'Just a moment, please.' Bond could follow the call to Miss Moneypenny and see her press the switch on the intercom. 'It's New York, Sir,' she would say. 'I think it's 007.' 'Put him through,' M would say.

'Yes?' said the cold voice that Bond loved and obeyed.

'It's James, Sir,' said Bond. 'I may need a bit of help over a difficult consignment.'

'Go ahead,' said the voice.

'I went uptown to see our chief customer last night,' said Bond. 'Three of his best men went sick while I was there.'

'How sick?' asked the voice.

'As sick as can be, Sir,' said Bond. 'There's a lot of 'flu about.'

'Hope you didn't catch any.'

'I've got a slight chill, Sir,' said Bond, 'but absolutely nothing to worry about. I'll write to you about it. The trouble is that with all this 'flu about Federated think I will do better out of town.' (Bond chuckled to himself at the thought of M's grin.) 'So I'm off right away with Felicia.'

'Who?' asked M.

'Felicia.' Bond spelled it out. 'My new secretary from Washington.'

'Oh yes.'

'Thought I'd try that factory you advised at San Pedro.'

'Good idea.'

'But Federated may have other ideas and I hoped you'd give me your support.'

'I quite understand,' said M. 'How's business?'

'Rather promising, Sir. But tough going. Felicia will be typing my full report today.'

'Good,' said M. 'Anything else?'

'No, that's all, Sir. Thanks for your support.'

'That's all right. Keep fit. Goodbye.'

'Goodbye, Sir.'

Bond put down the telephone. He grinned. He could imagine M calling in the Chief of Staff. '007's already tangled up with the FBI. Dam' fool went up to Harlem last night and bumped off three of Mr Big's men. Got hurt himself, apparently, but not much. Got to get out of town with Leiter, the CIA man. Going down to St Petersburg. Better warn A and C. Expect we'll have Washington round our ears before the day's over. Tell A to say I fully sympathize, but that 007 has my full confidence and I'm sure he acted in self-defence. Won't happen again, and so forth. Got that?' Bond grinned again as he thought of Damon's exasperation at having to dish out a lot of soft soap to Washington when he probably had plenty of other Anglo-American snarls to disentangle.

The telephone rang. It was Leiter again.

'Now listen,' he said. 'Everybody's calming down somewhat. Seems the men you got were a pretty nasty trio — Tee-Hee Johnson, Sam Miami and a man called McThing. All wanted on various counts. The FBI's covering up for you. Reluctantly of course, and the police are stalling like mad. The FBI big brass had already asked my Chief for you to be sent home — got him out of bed, if you please — mostly jealousy I guess — but we've killed all that. Same time, we've both got to quit town at once. That's all fixed too. We can't go together, so you're taking the train and I'll fly. Jot this down.'

Bond cradled the telephone against his shoulder and reached for a pencil and paper. 'Go ahead,' he said.

'Pennsylvania Station. Track 14. Ten-thirty this morning. "The Silver Phantom". Through train to St Petersburg via Washington, Jacksonville and Tampa. I've got you a compartment. Very luxurious. Car 245, Compartment H. Ticket'll be on the train. Conductor will have it. In the name of Bryce. Just go to Gate 14 and down to the train. Then straight to your compartment and lock yourself in till the train starts. I'm flying down in an hour by Eastern, so you'll be alone from now on. If you get stuck call Dexter, but don't be surprised if he bites your head off. Train gets in around midday tomorrow. Take a cab and go to the Everglades Cabanas, Gulf Boulevard West, on Sunset Beach. That's on a place called Treasure Island where all the beach hotels are. Connected with St Petersburg by a causeway. Cabby'll know it.

'I'll be waiting for you. Got all that? And for God's sake watch out. And I mean it. The Big Man'll get you if he possibly can and a police escort to the train would only put the finger on you. Take a cab and keep out of sight. I'm sending you up another hat and a fawn raincoat. The check's taken care of at the St Regis. That's the lot. Any questions?'

'Sounds fine,' said Bond. 'I've talked to M and he'll square Washington if there's any trouble. Look after yourself too,' he added. 'You'll be next on the list after me. See you tomorrow. So long.'

'I'll watch out,' said Leiter. 'Bye.'

It was half past six and Bond pulled back the curtains in the sitting-room and watched the dawn come up over the city. It was still dark down in the caverns below but the tips of the great concrete stalagmites were pink and the sun lit up the windows floor by floor as if an army of descending janitors was at work in the buildings.

The police surgeon came, stayed for a painful quarter of an hour and left.

'Clean fracture,' he had said. 'Take a few days to heal. How did you come by it?'

'Caught it in a door,' said Bond.

'You ought to keep away from doors,' commented the surgeon. 'They're dangerous things. Ought to be forbidden by law. Lucky you didn't catch your neck in this one.'

When he had gone, Bond finished his packing. He was wondering how soon he could order breakfast when the telephone rang.

Bond was expecting a harsh voice from the police or the FBI. Instead, a girl's voice, low and urgent, asked for Mr Bond.

'Who's calling?' asked Bond, gaining time. He knew the answer.

'I know it's you,' said the voice, and Bond could feel that it was right up against the mouthpiece. 'This is Solitaire.' The name was scarcely breathed into the telephone.

Bond waited, all his senses pricked to what might be the scene at the other end of the line. Was she alone? Was she speaking foolishly on a house-phone with extensions to which other listeners were now coldly, intently glued? Or was she in a room with only Mr Big's eyes bent carefully on her, a pencil and pad beside him so that he could prompt the next question?

'Listen,' said the voice. 'I've got to be quick. You must trust me. I'm in a drugstore, but I must get back at once to my room. Please believe me.'

Bond had his handkerchief out. He spoke into it. 'If I can reach Mr Bond what shall I tell him?'

'Oh damn you,' said the girl with what sounded like a genuine touch of hysteria. 'I swear by my mother, by my unborn children. I've got to get away. And so have you. You've got to take me. I'll help you. I know a lot of his secrets. But be quick. I'm risking my life here talking to you.' She gave a sob of exasperation and panic. 'For God's sake trust me. You must. You must!'

Bond still paused, his mind working furiously.

'Listen.' She spoke again, but this time dully, almost hopelessly. 'If you don't take me, I shall kill myself. Now will you? Do you want to murder me?'

If it was acting, it was too good acting. It was still an unpardonable gamble, but Bond decided. He spoke directly into the telephone, his voice low.

'If this is a double-cross, Solitaire, I'll get at you and kill you if it's the last thing I do. Have you got a pencil and paper?'

'Wait,' said the girl, excitedly. 'Yes, yes.'

If it had been a plant, reflected Bond, all that would have been ready.

'Be at Pennsylvania Station at ten-twenty exactly. The Silver Phantom to . . . ' he hesitated. ' . . . to Washington. Car 245, Compartment H. Say you're Mrs Bryce. Conductor has the ticket in case I'm not there already. Go straight to the compartment and wait for me. Got that?'

'Yes,' said the girl, 'and thank you, thank you.'

'Don't be seen,' said Bond. 'Wear a veil or something.'

'Of course,' said the girl. 'I promise. I really promise. I must go.' She rang off.

Bond looked at the dead receiver then put it down on the cradle. 'Well,' he said aloud. 'That's torn it.'

He got up and stretched. He walked to the window and looked out, seeing nothing. His thoughts raced. Then he shrugged and turned back to the telephone. He looked at his watch. It was seven-thirty.

'Room Service, good morning,' said the golden voice.

'Breakfast, please,' said Bond. 'Pineapple juice, double. Cornflakes and cream. Shirred eggs with bacon. Double portion of Café Espresso. Toast and marmalade.'

'Yes, Sir,' said the girl. She repeated the order. 'Right away.'

'Thank you.'

'You're welcome.'

Bond grinned to himself.

'The condemned man made a hearty breakfast,' he reflected. He sat down by the window and gazed up at the clear sky, into the future.

Up in Harlem, at the big switchboard, The Whisper was talking to the town again, passing Bond's description again to all Eyes: 'All de railroads, all de airports. Fifth Avenue an' 55th Street doors of da San Regis. Mr Big sez we gotta chance da highways. Pass it down da line. All de railroads, all de airports. . . '

10

THE SILVER PHANTOM

BOND, THE COLLAR of his new raincoat up round his ears, was missed as he came out of the entrance of the St Regis Drugstore on 55th Street, which has a connecting door into the hotel.

He waited in the entrance and leaped at a cruising cab, hooking the door open with the thumb of his injured hand and throwing his light suitcase in ahead of him. The cab hardly checked. The negro with the collecting-box for the Coloured Veterans of Korea and his colleague fumbling under the bonnet of his stalled car stayed on the job until, much later, they were called off by a man who drove past and sounded two shorts and a long on his horn.

But Bond was immediately spotted as he left his cab at the drive-in to the Pennsylvania Station. A lounging negro with a wicker basket walked quickly into a call-box. It was ten-fifteen.

Only fifteen minutes to go and yet, just before the train started, one of the waiters in the diner reported sick and was hurriedly replaced by a man who had received a full and careful briefing on the telephone. The chef swore there was something fishy, but the new man said a word or two to him and the chef showed the whites of his eyes and went silent, surreptitiously touching the lucky bean that hung round his neck on a string.

Bond had walked quickly through the great glass-covered concourse and through Gate 14 down to his train.

It lay, a quarter of a mile of silver carriages, quietly in the dusk of the underground station. Up front, the auxiliary generators of the 4000 horsepower twin Diesel electric units ticked busily. Under the bare electric bulbs the horizontal purple and gold bands, the colours of the Seaboard Railroad, glowed regally on the streamlined locomotives. The engineman and fireman who would take the great train on the first two-hundred-mile lap into the south lolled in the spotless aluminium cabin, twelve feet above the track, watching the ammeter and the air-pressure dial, ready to go.

It was quiet in the great concrete cavern below the city and every noise threw an echo.

There were not many passengers. More would be taken on at Newark, Philadelphia, Baltimore and Washington. Bond walked a hundred yards, his feet ringing on the empty platform, before he found Car 245, towards the rear of the train. A Pullman porter stood at the door. He wore spectacles. His black face was bored but friendly. Below the windows of the carriage, in broad letters of brown and gold, was written 'Richmond, Fredericksburg and Potomac', and below that 'Bellesylvania', the name of the Pullman car. A thin wisp of steam rose from the couplings of the central heating near the door.

'Compartment H,' said Bond.

'Mr Bryce, Suh? Yassuh. Mrs Bryce just come aboard. Straight down da cyar.'

Bond stepped on to the train and turned down the drab olive green corridor. The carpet was thick. There was the usual American train-smell of old cigar-smoke. A notice said 'Need a second pillow? For any extra comfort ring for your Pullman Attendant. His name is,' then a printed card, slipped in: 'Samuel D. Baldwin.'

H was more than half way down the car. There was a respectable-looking American couple in E, otherwise the rooms were empty. The door of H was closed. He tried it and it was locked.

'Who's that?' asked a girl's voice, anxiously.

'It's me,' said Bond.

The door opened. Bond walked through, put down his bag and locked the door behind him.

She was in a black tailor-made. A wide-mesh veil came down from the rim of a small black straw hat. One gloved hand was up to her throat and through the veil Bond could see that her face was pale and her eyes were wide with fear. She looked rather French and very beautiful.

'Thank God,' she said.

Bond gave a quick glance round the room. He opened the lavatory door and looked in. It was empty.

A voice on the platform outside called 'Board!' There was a clang as the attendant pulled up the folding iron step and shut the door and then the train was rolling quietly down the track. A bell clanged monotonously as they passed the automatic signals. There was a slight clatter from the wheels as they crossed some points and then the train began to accelerate. For better or for worse, they were on their way.

'Which seat would you like?' asked Bond.

'I don't mind,' she said anxiously. 'You choose.'

Bond shrugged and sat down with his back to the engine. He preferred to face forwards.

She sat down nervously facing him. They were still in the long tunnel that takes the Philadelphia lines out of the city.

She took off her hat and unpinned the broad-mesh veil and put them on the seat beside her. She took some hairpins out of the back of her hair and shook her head so that the heavy black hair fell forward. There were blue shadows under her eyes and Bond reflected that she too must have gone without sleep that night.

There was a table between them. Suddenly she reached forward and pulled his right hand towards her on the table. She held it in both her hands and bent forward and kissed it. Bond frowned and tried to pull his hand away, but for a moment she held it tight in both of hers.

She looked up and her wide blue eyes looked candidly into his.

'Thank you,' she said. 'Thank you for trusting me. It was difficult for you.' She released his hand and sat back.

'I'm glad I did,' said Bond inadequately, his mind trying to grapple with the mystery of this woman. He dug in his pocket for his cigarettes and lighter. It was a new pack of Chesterfields and with his right hand he scrabbled at the cellophane wrapper.

She reached over and took the pack from him. She slit it with her thumbnail, took out a cigarette, lit it and handed it to him. Bond took it from her and smiled into her eyes, tasting the hint of lipstick from her mouth.

'I smoke about three packs a day,' he said. 'You're going to be busy.'

'I'll just help with the new packs,' she said. 'Don't be afraid I'm going to fuss over you the whole way to St Petersburg.'

Bond's eyes narrowed and the smile went out of them.

'You don't believe I thought we were only going as far as Washington,' she said. 'You weren't very quick on the telephone this morning. And anyway, Mr Big was certain you would make for Florida. I heard him warning his people down there about you. He spoke to a man called "The Robber", long distance. Said to watch the airport at Tampa and the trains. Perhaps we ought to get off the train earlier, at Tarpon Springs or one of the small stations up the coast. Did they see you getting on the train?'

'Not that I know of,' said Bond. His eyes had relaxed again. 'How about you? Have any trouble getting away?'

'It was my day for a singing lesson. He's trying to make a torch singer out of me. Wants me to go on at The Boneyard. One of his men took me to my teacher as usual and was due to pick me up again at midday. He wasn't surprised I was having a lesson so early. I often have breakfast with my teacher so as to get away from Mr Big. He expects me to have all my meals with him.' She looked at her watch. He noted cynically that it was an expensive one — diamonds and platinum, Bond guessed. 'They'll be missing me in about an hour. I waited until the car had gone, then I walked straight out again and called you. Then I took a cab downtown. I bought a toothbrush and a few other things at a drugstore. Otherwise I've got nothing except my jewellery and the mad money I've always kept hidden from him. About five thousand dollars. So I won't be a financial burden.' She smiled. 'I thought I'd get my chance one day.' She gestured towards the window. 'You've given me a new life. I've been shut up with him and his nigger gangsters for nearly a year. This is heaven.'

The train was running through the unkempt barren plains and swamps between New York and Trenton. It wasn't an attractive prospect. It reminded Bond of some of the stretches on the pre-war Trans-Siberian Railway except for the huge lonely hoardings advertising the current Broadway shows and the occasional dumps of scrapiron and old motor cars.

'I hope I can find you something better than that,' he said smiling. 'But don't thank me. We're quits now. You saved my life last night. That is,' he added looking at her curiously, 'if you really have got second sight.'

'Yes,' she said, 'I have. Or something very like it. I can often see what's going to happen, particularly to other people. Of course I embroider on it and when I was earning my living doing it in Haiti it was easy to turn it into a good cabaret act. They're riddled with Voodoo and superstitions there and they were quite certain I was a witch. But I promise that when I first saw you in that room I knew you had been sent to save me. I,' she blushed, 'I saw all sorts of things.'

'What sort of things?'

'Oh I don't know,' she said, her eyes dancing. 'Just things. Anyway, we'll see. But it's going to be difficult,' she added seriously, 'and dangerous. For both of us.' She paused. 'So will you please take good care of us?'

'I'll do my best,' said Bond. 'The first thing is for us both to get some sleep. Let's have a drink and some chicken sandwiches and then we'll get the porter to put our beds down. You mustn't be embarrassed,' he added, seeing her eyes recoil. 'We're in this together. We have to spend twenty-four hours in a double bedroom together, and it's no good being squeamish. Anyway, you're Mrs Bryce,' he grinned, 'and you must just act like her. Up to a point anyway,' he added.

She laughed. Her eyes speculated. She said nothing but rang the bell below the window.

The conductor arrived at the same time as the Pullman attendant. Bond ordered Old Fashioneds, and stipulated Old Grandad bourbon, chicken sandwiches, and decaffeined Sanka coffee so that their sleep would not be spoilt.

'I have to collect another fare from you, Mr Bryce,' said the conductor.

'Of course,' said Bond. Solitaire made a movement towards her handbag. 'It's all right, darling,' said Bond, pulling out his notecase. 'You've forgotten you gave me your money to look after before we left the house.'

'Guess the lady'll need plenty for her summer frocks,' said the conductor. 'Shops is plenty expensive in St Pete. Plenty hot down there too. You folks been to Florida before?'

'We always go at this time of year,' said Bond.

'Hope you have a pleasant trip,' said the conductor.

When the door shut behind him, Solitaire laughed delightedly.

'You can't embarrass me,' she said. 'I'll think up something really fierce if you're not careful. To begin with, I'm going in there,' she gestured towards the door behind Bond's head. 'I must look terrible.'

'Go ahead, darling,' laughed Bond as she disappeared.

Bond turned to the window and watched the pretty clapboard houses slip by as they approached Trenton. He loved trains and he looked forward with excitement to the rest of the journey.

The train was slowing down. They slid past sidings full of empty freight cars bearing names from all over the States — 'Lackawanna', 'Chesapeake and Ohio', 'Lehigh Valley', 'Seaboard Fruit Express', and the lilting 'Acheson, Topeka and Santa Fe' — names that held all the romance of the American railroads.

British Railways? thought Bond. He sighed and turned his thoughts back to the present adventure.

For better or worse he had decided to accept Solitaire, or rather, in his cold way, to make the most of her. There were many questions to be answered but now was not the time to ask them. All that immediately concerned him was that another blow had been struck at Mr Big — where it would hurt most, in his vanity.

As for the girl, as a girl, he reflected that it was going to be fun teasing her and being teased back and he was glad that they had already crossed the frontiers into comradeship and even intimacy.

Was it true what The Big Man had said, that she would have nothing to do with men? He doubted it. She seemed open to love and to desire. At any rate he knew she was not closed to him. He wanted her to come back and sit down opposite him again so that he could look at her and play with her and slowly discover her. Solitaire. It was an attractive name. No wonder they had christened her that in the sleazy nightclubs of Port au Prince. Even in her present promise of warmth towards him there was much that was withdrawn and mysterious. He sensed a lonely childhood on some great decaying plantation, an echoing 'Great House' slowly falling into disrepair and being encroached on by the luxuriance of the tropics. The parents dying, and the property being sold. The companionship of a servant or two and an equivocal life in lodgings in the capital.

The beauty which was her only asset and the struggle against the shady propositions to be a 'governess', a 'companion', a 'secretary', all of which meant respectable prostitution. Then the dubious, unknown steps into the world of entertainment. The evening stint at the nightclub with the mysterious act which, among people dominated by magic, must have kept many away from her and made her a person to be feared. And then, one evening, the huge man with the grey face sitting at a table by himself. The promise that he would put her on Broadway. The chance of a new life, of an escape from the heat and the dirt and the solitude.

Bond turned brusquely away from the window. A romantic picture, perhaps. But it must have been something like that.

He heard the door unlock. The girl came back and slid into the seat opposite him. She looked fresh and gay. She examined him carefully.

'You have been wondering about me,' she said. 'I felt it. Don't worry. There is nothing very bad to know. I will tell you all about it some day. When we have time. Now I want to forget about the past. I will just tell you my real name. It is Simone Latrelle, but you can call me what you like. I am twenty-five. And now I am happy. I like this little room. But I am hungry and sleepy. Which bed will you have?'

Bond smiled at the question. He reflected.

'It's not very gallant,' he said, 'but I think I'd better have the bottom one. I'd rather be close to the floor — just in case. Not that there's anything to worry about,' he added, seeing her frown, 'but Mr Big seems to have a pretty long arm, particularly in the negro world. And that includes the railroads. Do you mind?'

'Of course not,' she said. 'I was going to suggest it. And you couldn't climb into the top one with your poor hand.'

Their lunch arrived, brought from the diner by a preoccupied negro waiter. He seemed anxious to be paid and get back to his work.

When they had finished and Bond rang for the Pullman porter, he also seemed distrait and avoided looking at Bond. He took his time getting the beds made up. He made much show of not having enough room to move around in.

Finally, he seemed to pluck up courage.

'Praps Mistress Bryce like set down nex' door while Ah git the room fixed,' he said looking over Bond's head. 'Nex' room goin' to be empty all way to St Pete.' He took out a key and unlocked the communicating door without waiting for Bond's reply.

At a gesture from Bond, Solitaire took the hint. He heard her lock the door into the corridor. The negro bumped the communicating door shut.

Bond waited for a moment. He remembered the negro's name.

'Got something on your mind, Baldwin?' he asked.

Relieved, the attendant turned and looked straight at him.

'Sho have, Mister Bryce. Yassuh.' Once started, the words came in a torrent. 'Shouldn be tellin yuh this, Mister Bryce, but deres plenty trouble 'n this train, this trip. Yuh gotten yoself a henemy 'n dis train, Mister Bryce. Yassuh. Ah hears tings which Ah don' like at all. Caint say much. Get mahself'n plenty trouble. But yuh all want to watch yo step plenty good. Yassuh. Certain party got da finger'n yuh, Mister Bryce, 'n dat man is bad news. Better take dese hyah,' he reached in his pocket and brought out two wooden window wedges. 'Push dem under the doors,' he said. 'Ah caint do nuthen else. Git mah throat cut. But Ah don like any foolin' aroun' wid da customers 'n my cyar. Nossuh.'

Bond took the wedges from him. 'But . . . '

'Caint help yuh no more, Sah,' said the negro with finality, his hand on the door. 'Ef yuh ring fo me dis evenin, Ah'll fetch yo dinner. Doan yuh go lettin' any person else in the room.'

His hand came out to take the twenty-dollar bill. He crumpled it into his pocket.

'Ah'll do all ah can, Sah,' he said. 'But dey'll git me ef Ah don' watch it. Sho will.' He went out and quickly shut the door behind him.

Bond thought for a moment then he opened the communicating door. Solitaire was reading.

'He's fixed everything,' he said. 'Took a long time about it. Wanted to tell me all his life story as well. I'll keep out of your way until you've climbed up to your nest. Call me when you're ready.'

He sat down next door in the seat she had left and watched the grim suburbs of Philadelphia showing their sores, like beggars, to the rich train.

No object in frightening her until it had to be. But the new threat had come sooner than he expected and her danger if the watcher on the train discovered her identity would be as great as his.

She called and he went in.

The room was in darkness save for his bed-light which she had turned on.

'Sleep well,' she said.

Bond got out of his coat. He quietly slipped the wedges firmly under both doors. Then he lay down carefully on his right side on the comfortable bed and without a thought for the future fell into a deep sleep, lulled by the pounding gallop of the train.

A few cars away, in the deserted diner, a negro waiter read again what he had written on a telegraph blank and waited for the ten-minute stop at Philadelphia.

11

ALLUMEUSE

THE CRACK TRAIN thundered on through the bright afternoon towards the south. They left Pennsylvania behind, and Maryland. There came a long halt at Washington where Bond heard through his dreams the measured clang of the warning bells on the shunting engines and the soft think-speak of the public address system on the station. Then on into Virginia. Here the air was already softer and the dusk, only five hours away from the bright frosty breath of New York, smelled almost of spring.

An occasional group of negroes, walking home from the fields, would hear the distant rumble on the silent sighing silver rails and one would pull out his watch and consult it and announce, 'Hyah comes da Phantom. Six o'clock. Guess ma watch is right on time.' 'Sho nuff,' one of the others would say as the great beat of the Diesels came nearer and the lighted coaches streaked past and on towards North Carolina.

They awoke around seven to the hasty ting of a grade-crossing alarm bell as the big train nosed its way out of the fields into the suburbs of Raleigh. Bond pulled the wedges from under the doors before he turned on the lights and rang for the attendant.

He ordered dry martinis and when the two little 'personalized' bottles appeared with the glasses and the ice they seemed so inadequate that he at once ordered four more.

They argued over the menu. The fish was described as being 'Made From Flaky Tender Boneless Filets' and the chicken as 'Delicious French Fried to a Golden Brown, Served Disjointed'.

'Eyewash,' said Bond, and they finally ordered scrambled eggs and bacon and sausages, a salad, and some of the domestic Camembert that is one of the most welcome surprises on American menus.

It was nine o'clock when Baldwin came to clear the dishes away. He asked if there was anything else they wanted.

Bond had been thinking. 'What time do we get into Jacksonville?' he asked.

'Aroun' five 'n the morning, Suh.'

'Is there a subway on the platform?'

'Yassuh. Dis cyar stops right alongside.'

'Could you have the door open and the steps down pretty quick?'

The negro smiled. 'Yassuh. Ah kin take good care of that.'

Bond slipped him a ten-dollar bill. 'Just in case I miss you when we arrive in St Petersburg,' he said.

The negro grinned. 'Ah greatly preeshiate yo kindness, Suh. Goodnight, Suh. Goodnight, Mam.'

He went out and closed the door.

Bond got up and pushed the wedges firmly under the two doors.

'I see,' said Solitaire. 'So it's like that.'

'Yes,' said Bond. 'I'm afraid so.' He told her of the warning he had had from Baldwin.

'I'm not surprised,' said the girl when he had finished. 'They must have seen you coming into the station. He's got a whole team of spies called "The Eyes" and when they're put out on a job it's almost impossible to get by them. I wonder who he's got on the train. You can be certain it's a negro, either a Pullman attendant or someone in the diner. He can make these people do absolutely anything he likes.'

'So it seems,' said Bond. 'But how does it work? What's he got on them?'

She looked out of the window into the tunnel of darkness through which the lighted train was burning its thundering path. Then she looked back across the table into the cool wide grey-blue eyes of the English agent. She thought: how can one explain to someone with that certainty of spirit, with that background of common sense, brought up with clothes and shoes among the warm houses and the lighted streets? How can one explain to someone who hasn't lived close to the secret heart of the tropics, at the mercy of their anger and stealth and poison; who hasn't experienced the mystery of the drums, seen the quick workings of magic and the mortal dread it inspires? What can he know of catalepsy, and thought-transference and the sixth sense of fish, of birds, of negroes; the deadly meaning of a white chicken's feather, a crossed stick in the road, a little leather bag of bones and herbs? What of Mialism, of shadow-taking, of the death by swelling and the death by wasting?

She shivered and a whole host of dark memories clustered round her. Above all, she remembered that first time in the Houmfor where her black nurse had once taken her as a child. 'It do yuh no harm, Missy. Dis powerful good juju. Care fe yuh res 'f yo life.' And the disgusting old man and the filthy drink he had given her. How her nurse had held her jaws open until she had drunk the last drop and how she had lain awake screaming every night for a week. And how her nurse had been worried and then suddenly she had slept all right until, weeks later, shifting on her pillow, she had felt something hard and had dug it out from the pillowcase, a dirty little packet of muck. She had thrown it out of the window, but in the morning she could not find it. She had continued to sleep well and she knew it must have been found by the nurse and secreted somewhere under the floorboards.

Years later, she had found out about the Voodoo drink — a concoction of rum, gunpowder, grave-dirt and human blood. She almost retched as the taste came back to her mouth.

What could this man know of these things or of her half-belief in them?

She looked up and found Bond's eyes fixed quizzically on her.

'You're thinking I shan't understand,' he said. 'And you're right up to a point. But I know what fear can do to people and I know that fear can be caused by many things. I've read most of the books on Voodoo and I believe that it works. I don't think it would work on me because I stopped being afraid of the dark when I was a child and I'm not a good subject for suggestion or hypnotism. But I know the jargon and you needn't think I shall laugh at it. The scientists and doctors who wrote the books don't laugh at it.'

Solitaire smiled. 'All right,' she said. 'Then all I need tell you is that they believe The Big Man is the Zombie of Baron Samedi. Zombies are bad enough by themselves. They're animated corpses that have been made to rise from the dead and obey the commands of the person who controls them. Baron Samedi is the most dreadful spirit in the whole of Voodooism. He is the spirit of darkness and death. So for Baron Samedi to be in control of his own Zombie is a very dreadful conception. You know what Mr Big looks like. He is huge and grey and he has great psychic power. It is not difficult for a negro to believe that he is a Zombie and a very bad one at that. The step to Baron Samedi is simple. Mr Big encourages the idea by having the Baron's fetish at his elbow. You saw it in his room.'

She paused. She went on quickly, almost breathlessly. 'And I can tell you that it works and that there's hardly a negro who has seen him and heard the story who doesn't believe it and who doesn't regard him with complete and absolute dread. And they are right,' she added. 'And you would say so too if you knew the way he deals with those who haven't obeyed him completely, the way they are tortured and killed.'

'Where does Moscow come in?' asked Bond. 'Is it true he's an agent of SMERSH?'

'I don't know what SMERSH is,' said the girl, 'but I know he works for Russia, at least I've heard him talking Russian to people who come from time to time. Occasionally he's had me into that room and asked me afterwards what I thought of his visitors. Generally it seemed to me they were telling the truth although I couldn't understand what they said. But don't forget I've only known him for a year and he's fantastically secretive. If Moscow does use him they've got hold of one of the most powerful men in America. He can find out almost anything he wants to and if he doesn't get what he wants somebody gets killed.'

'Why doesn't someone kill him?' asked Bond.

'You can't kill him,' she said. 'He's already dead. He's a Zombie.'

'Yes, I see,' said Bond slowly. 'It's quite an impressive arrangement. Would you try?'

She looked out of the window, then back at him.

'As a last resort,' she admitted unwillingly. 'But don't forget I come from Haiti. My brain tells me I could kill him, but . . .' she made a helpless gesture with her hands. ' . . . my instinct tells me I couldn't.'

She smiled at him docilely. 'You must think me a hopeless fool,' she said.

Bond reflected. 'Not after reading all those books,' he admitted. He put his hand across the table and covered hers with it. 'When the time comes,' he said smiling, 'I'll cut a cross in my bullet. That used to work in the old days.'

She looked thoughtful. 'I believe that if anybody can do it, you can,' she said. 'You hit him hard last night in exchange for what he did to you.' She took his hand in hers and pressed it. 'Now tell me what I must do.'

'Bed,' said Bond. He looked at his watch. It was ten o'clock. 'Might as well get as much sleep as we can. We'll slip off the train at Jacksonville and chance being spotted. Find another way down to the coast.'

They got up. They stood facing each other in the swaying train.

Suddenly Bond reached out and took her in his right arm. Her arms went round his neck and they kissed passionately. He pressed her up against the swaying wall and held her there. She took his face between her two hands and held it away, panting. Her eyes were bright and hot. Then she brought his lips against hers again and kissed him long and lasciviously, as if she was the man and he the woman.

Bond cursed the broken hand that prevented him exploring her body, taking her. He freed his right hand and put it between their bodies, feeling her hard breasts, each with its pointed stigma of desire. He slipped it down her back until it came to the cleft at the base of her spine and he let it rest there, holding the centre of her body hard against him until they had kissed enough.

She took her arms away from around his neck and pushed him away.

'I hoped I would one day kiss a man like that,' she said. And when I first saw you, I knew it would be you.'

Her arms were down by her sides and her body stood there, open to him, ready for him.

'You're very beautiful,' said Bond. 'You kiss more wonderfully than any girl I have ever known.' He looked down at the bandages on his left hand. 'Curse this arm,' he said. 'I can't hold you properly or make love to you. It hurts too much. That's something else Mr Big's got to pay for.'

She laughed.

She took a handkerchief out of her bag and wiped the lipstick off his mouth. Then she brushed the hair away from his forehead, and kissed him again, lightly and tenderly.

'It's just as well,' she said. 'There are too many other things on our minds.'

The train rocked him back against her.

He put his hand on her left breast and kissed her white throat. Then he kissed her mouth.

He felt the pounding of his blood softening. He took her by the hand and drew her out into the middle of the little swaying room.

He smiled. 'Perhaps you're right,' he said. 'When the time comes I want to be alone with you, with all the time in the world. Here there is at least one man who will probably disturb our night. And we'll have to be up at four in the morning anyway. So there simply isn't time to begin making love to you now. You get ready for bed and I'll climb up after you and kiss you good night.'

They kissed once more, slowly, then he stepped away.

'We'll just see if we have company next door,' he said.

He softly pulled the wedge away from under the communicating door and gently turned the lock. He took the Beretta out of its holster, thumbed back the safety-catch and gestured to her to pull open the door so that she was behind it. He gave the signal and she wrenched it quickly open. The empty compartment yawned sarcastically at them.

Bond smiled at her and shrugged his shoulders.

'Call me when you're ready,' he said and went in and closed the door.

The door to the corridor was locked. The room was identical with theirs. Bond went over it very carefully for vulnerable points. There was only the air-conditioning vent in the ceiling and Bond, who was prepared to consider any possibility, dismissed the employment of gas in the system. It would slay all the other occupants of the car. There only remained the waste pipes in the small lavatory and while these certainly could be used to insert some death-dealing medium from the underbelly of the train, the operator would have to be a daring and skilled acrobat. There was no ventilating grill into the corridor.

Bond shrugged his shoulders. If anyone came, it would be through the doors. He would just have to stay awake.

Solitaire called for him. The room smelled of Balmain's Vent

Vert. She was leaning on her elbow and looking down at him from the upper berth.

The bedclothes were pulled up round her shoulder. Bond guessed that she was naked. Her black hair fell away from her head in a dark cascade. With only the reading-lamp on behind her, her face was in shadow. Bond climbed up the little aluminium ladder and leant towards her. She reached towards him and suddenly the bedclothes fell away from her shoulders.

'Damn you,' said Bond. 'You . . . '

She put her hand over his mouth.

' "Allumeuse," is the nice word for it,' she said. 'It is fun for me to be able to tease such a strong silent man. You burn with such an angry flame. It is the only game I have to play with you and I shan't be able to play it for long. How many days until your hand is well again?'

Bond bit hard into the soft hand over his mouth. She gave a little scream.

'Not many,' said Bond. 'And then one day when you're playing your little game you'll suddenly find yourself pinned down like a butterfly.'

She put her arms round him and they kissed, long and passionately.

Finally she sank back among the pillows.

'Hurry up and get well,' she said. 'I'm tired of my game already.'

Bond climbed down to the floor and pulled her curtains across the berth.

'Try and get some sleep now,' he said. 'We've got a long day tomorrow.'

She murmured something and he heard her turn over. She switched off the light.

Bond verified that the wedges were in place under the doors. Then he took off his coat and tie and lay down on the bottom berth. He turned off his own light and lay thinking of Solitaire and listening to the steady gallop of the wheels beneath his head and the comfortable small noises in the room, the gentle rattles and squeaks and murmurs in the coachwork that bring sleep so quickly on a train at night-time.

It was eleven o'clock and the train was on the long stretch between Columbia and Savannah, Georgia. There were another six hours or so to Jacksonville, another six hours of darkness during which The Big Man would almost certainly have instructed his agent to make some move, while the whole train was asleep and while a man could use the corridors without interference.

The great train snaked on through the dark, pounding out the miles through the empty plains and mingy hamlets of Georgia, the 'Peach State', the angry moan of its four-toned wind-horn soughing over the wide savannah and the long shaft of its single searchlight ripping the black calico of the night.

Bond turned on his light again and read for a while, but his thoughts were too insistent and he soon gave up and switched the light off. Instead, he thought of Solitaire and of the future and of the more immediate prospects of Jacksonville and St Petersburg and of seeing Leiter again.

Much later, around one o'clock in the morning, he was dozing and on the edge of sleep, when a soft metallic noise quite close to his head brought him wide awake with his hand on his gun.

There was someone at the passage door and the lock was being softly tried.

Bond was immediately on the floor and moving silently on his bare feet. He gently pulled the wedge away from under the door to the next compartment and as gently pulled the bolt and opened the door. He crossed the next compartment and softly began to open the door to the corridor.

There was a deafening click as the bolt came back. He tore the door open and threw himself into the corridor, only to see a flying figure already nearing the forward end of the car.

If his two hands had been free he could have shot the man, but to open the doors he had had to tuck his gun into the waistband of his trousers. Bond knew that pursuit would be hopeless. There were too many empty compartments into which the man could dodge and quietly close the door. Bond had worked all this out beforehand. He knew his only chance would be surprise and either a quick shot or the man's surrender.

He walked a few steps to Compartment H. A tiny diamond of paper protruded into the corridor.

He went back and into their room, locking the doors behind him. He softly turned on his reading light. Solitaire was still asleep. The rest of the paper, a single sheet, lay on the carpet against the passage door. He picked it up and sat on the edge of his bed.

It was a sheet of cheap ruled notepaper. It was covered with irregular lines of writing in rough capitals, in red ink. Bond handled it gingerly, without much hope that it would yield any prints. These people weren't like that.

Oh Witch [he read] *do not slay me,*
Spare me. His is the body.

The divine drummer declares that
When he rises with the dawn
He will sound his drums for YOU *in the morning.*
Very early, very early, very early, very early.
Oh Witch that slays the children of men before they are fully matured
Oh Witch that slays the children of men before they are fully matured
The divine drummer declares that
When he rises with the dawn
He will sound his drums for YOU *in the morning*
Very early, very early, very early, very early.
We are addressing YOU
And YOU *will understand.*

Bond lay down on his bed and thought.
Then he folded the paper and put it in his pocketbook.
He lay on his back and looked at nothing, waiting for daybreak.

12

THE EVERGLADES

IT WAS AROUND five o'clock in the morning when they slipped off the train at Jacksonville.

It was still dark and the naked platforms of the great Florida junction were sparsely lit. The entrance to the subway was only a few yards from Car 245 and there was no sign of life on the sleeping train as they dived down the steps. Bond had told the attendant to keep the door of their compartment locked after they had gone and the blinds drawn and he thought there was quite a chance they would not be missed until the train reached St Petersburg.

They came out of the subway into the booking-hall. Bond verified that the next express for St Petersburg would be the Silver Meteor, the sister train of the Phantom, due at about nine o'clock, and he booked two Pullman seats on it. Then he took Solitaire's arm and they walked out of the station into the warm dark street.

There were two or three all-night diners to choose from and they pushed through the door that announced 'Good Eats' in the brightest neon. It was the usual sleazy food-machine — two tired waitresses behind a zinc counter loaded with cigarettes and candy and paper-backs and comics. There was a big coffee percolator and a row of butane gas-rings. A door marked 'Rest-room' concealed its dreadful secrets next to a door marked 'Private' which was probably the back entrance. A group of overalled men at one of the dozen stained crueted tables looked up briefly as they came in and then resumed their low conversation. Relief crews for the Diesels, Bond guessed.

There were four narrow booths on the right of the entrance and Bond and Solitaire slipped into one of them. They looked dully at the stained menu card.

After a time, one of the waitresses sauntered over and stood leaning against the partition, running her eyes over Solitaire's clothes.

'Orange juice, coffee, scrambled eggs, twice,' said Bond briefly.

' 'Kay,' said the girl. Her shoes lethargically scuffed the floor as she sauntered away.

'The scrambled eggs'll be cooked with milk,' said Bond. 'But one can't eat boiled eggs in America. They look so disgusting without their shells, mixed up in a tea-cup the way they do them here. God knows where they learned the trick. From Germany I suppose. And bad American coffee's the worst in the world, worse even than in England. I suppose they can't do much harm to the orange juice. After all we are in Florida now.' He suddenly felt depressed by the thought of their four-hour wait in this unwashed, dog-eared atmosphere.

'Everybody's making easy money in America these days,' said Solitaire. 'That's always bad for the customer. All they want is to strip a quick dollar off you and toss you out. Wait till you get down to the coast. At this time of the year, Florida's the biggest sucker-trap on earth. On the East Coast they fleece the millionaires. Where we're going they just take it off the little man. Serves him right, of course. He goes there to die. He can't take it with him.'

'For heaven's sake,' said Bond, 'what sort of a place are we going to?'

'Everybody's nearly dead in St Petersburg,' explained Solitaire. 'It's the Great American Graveyard. When the bank clerk or the post office worker or the railroad conductor reaches sixty he collects his pension or his annuity and goes to St Petersburg to get a few years' sunshine before he dies. It's called "The Sunshine City". The weather's so good that the evening paper there, *The Independent*, is given away free any day the sun hasn't shone by edition time. It only happens three or four times a year and it's a fine advertisement. Everybody goes to bed around nine o'clock in the evening and during the day the old folks play shuffleboard and bridge, herds of them. There's a couple of baseball teams down there, the "Kids" and the "Kubs", all over seventy-five! Then they play bowls, but most of the time they sit squashed together in droves on things called "Sidewalk Davenports", rows of benches up and down the sidewalks of the main streets. They just sit in the sun and gossip and doze. It's a terrifying sight, all these old people with their spectacles and hearing-aids and clicking false-teeth.'

'Sounds pretty grim,' said Bond. 'Why the hell did Mr Big choose this place to operate from?'

'It's perfect for him,' said Solitaire seriously. 'There's practically no crime, except cheating at bridge and Canasta. So there's a very small police force. There's quite a big Coastguard Station but it's mainly concerned with smuggling between Tampa and Cuba, and sponge-fishing out of season at Tarpon Springs. I don't really know what he does there except that he's got a big agent called "The Robber". Something to do with Cuba, I expect,' she added thoughtfully. 'Probably mixed up with Communism. I believe Cuba comes under Harlem and runs red agents all through the Caribbean.

'Anyway,' she went on, 'St Petersburg is probably the most innocent town in America. Everything's very "folksy" and "gracious". It's true there's a place called "The Restorium", a hospital for alcoholics. But very old ones I suppose,' she laughed, 'and I expect they're past doing anyone any harm. You'll love it,' she smiled maliciously at Bond. 'You'll probably want to settle down there for life and be an "Oldster" too. That's the great word down there . . . "oldster".'

'God forbid,' said Bond fervently. 'It sounds rather like Bournemouth or Torquay. But a million times worse. I hope we don't get into a shooting match with "The Robber" and his friends. We'd probably hurry a few hundred oldsters off to the cemetery with heart-failure. But isn't there anyone young in this place?'

'Oh yes,' laughed Solitaire. 'Plenty of them. All the local inhabitants who take the money off the oldsters, for instance. The people who own the motels and the trailer-camps. You could make plenty of money running the bingo tournaments. I'll be your "barker" — the girl outside who gets the suckers in. Dear Mr Bond,' she reached over and pressed his hand, 'will you settle down with me and grow old gracefully in St Petersburg?'

Bond sat back and looked at her critically. 'I want a long time of disgraceful living with you first,' he said with a grin. 'I'm probably better at that. But it suits me that they go to bed at nine down there.'

Her eyes smiled back at him. She took her hand away from his as their breakfast arrived. 'Yes,' she said. 'You go to bed at nine. Then I shall slip out by the back door and go on the tiles with the Kids and the Kubs.'

The breakfast was as bad as Bond had prophesied.

When they had paid they wandered over to the station waiting-room.

The sun had risen and the light swarmed in dusty bars into the vaulted, empty hall. They sat together in a corner and until the Silver Meteor came in Bond plied her with questions about The Big Man and all she could tell him about his operations.

Occasionally he made a note of a date or a name but there was little she could add to what he knew. She had an apartment to herself in the same Harlem block as Mr Big and she had been kept virtually a prisoner there for the past year. She had two tough negresses as 'companions' and was never allowed out without a guard.

From time to time Mr Big would have her brought over to the room where Bond had seen him. There she would be told to divine whether some man or woman, generally bound to the chair, was lying or not. She varied her replies according to whether she sensed these people were good or evil. She knew that her verdict might often be a death sentence but she felt indifferent to the fate of those she judged to be evil. Very few of them were white.

Bond jotted down the dates and details of all these occasions.

Everything she told him added to the picture of a very powerful and active man, ruthless and cruel, commanding a huge network of operations.

All she knew of the gold coins was that she had several times had to question men on how many they had passed and the price they had been paid for them. Very often, she said, they were lying on both counts.

Bond was careful to divulge very little of what he himself knew or guessed. His growing warmth towards Solitaire and his desire for her body were in a compartment which had no communicating door with his professional life.

The Silver Meteor came in on time and they were both relieved to be on their way again and to get away from the dreary world of the big junction.

The train sped on down through Florida, through the forests and swamps, stark and bewitched with Spanish moss, and through the mile upon mile of citrus groves.

All through the centre of the state the moss lent a dead, spectral feeling to the landscape. Even the little townships through which they passed had a grey skeletal aspect with their dried-up, sun-sucked clapboard houses. Only the citrus groves laden with fruit looked green and alive. Everything else seemed baked and desiccated with the heat.

Looking out at the gloomy silent withered forests, Bond thought that nothing could be living in them except bats and scorpions, horned toads and black widow spiders.

They had lunch and then suddenly the train was running along the Gulf of Mexico, through the mangrove swamps and palm groves, endless motels and caravan sites, and Bond caught the smell of the other Florida, the Florida of the advertisements, the land of 'Miss Orange Blossom 1954'.

They left the train at Clearwater, the last station before St Petersburg. Bond took a cab and gave the address on Treasure Island, half an hour's drive away. It was two o'clock and the sun blazed down out of a cloudless sky. Solitaire insisted on taking off her hat and veil. 'It's sticking to my face,' she said. 'Hardly a soul has ever seen me down here.'

A big negro with a face pitted with ancient smallpox was held up in his cab at the same time as they were checked at the intersection of Park Street and Central Avenue, where the Avenue runs on to the long Treasure Island causeway across the shallow waters of Boca Ciega Bay.

When the negro saw Solitaire's profile his mouth fell open. He pulled his cab into the kerb and dived into a drugstore. He called a St Petersburg number.

'Dis is Poxy,' he said urgently into the mouthpiece. 'Gimme da Robber 'n step on it. Dat you, Robber? Lissen, Da Big Man muss be n'town. Whaddya mean yuh jes talked wit him n' New York? Ah jes seen his gal 'n a Clearwater cab, one of da Stassen Company's. Headin' over da Causeway. Sho ahm sartin. Cross ma heart. Couldn mistake dat eyeful. Wid a man 'n a blue suit, grey Stetson. Seemed like a scar down his face. Whaddya mean, follow em? Ah jes couldn believe yuh wouldn tell me Da Big

Man wuz 'n town ef he wuz. Thought mebbe Ahd better check 'n make sho. Okay, okay. Ah'll ketch da cab when he comes back over da Causeway, else at Clearwater. Okay, okay. Keep yo shirt on. Ah aint done nuthen wrong.'

The man called 'The Robber' was through to New York in five minutes. He had been warned about Bond but he couldn't understand where Solitaire tied in to the picture. When he had finished talking to The Big Man he still didn't know, but his instructions were quite definite.

He rang off and sat for a while drumming his fingers on his desk. Ten grand for the job. He'd need two men. That would leave eight grand for him. He licked his lips and called a pool-room in a downtown bar in Tampa.

Bond paid off the cab at the Everglades, a group of neat white and yellow clapboard cottages set on three sides of a square of Bahama grass which ran fifty yards down to a bone-white beach and then to the sea. From there, the whole Gulf of Mexico stretched away, as calm as a mirror, until the heat-haze on the horizon married it into the cloudless sky.

After London, after New York, after Jacksonville, it was a sparkling transition.

Bond went through a door marked 'Office' with Solitaire demurely at his heels. He rang a bell that said, 'Manageress: Mrs Stuyvesant,' and a withered shrimp of a woman with blue-rinsed hair appeared and smiled with her pinched lips. 'Yes?'

'Mr Leiter?'

'Oh yes, you're Mr Bryce. Cabana Number One, right down on the beach. Mr Leiter's been expecting you since lunchtime. And . . . ?' She heliographed with her pince-nez towards Solitaire.

'Mrs Bryce,' said Bond.

'Ah yes,' said Mrs Stuyvesant, wishing to disbelieve. 'Well, if you'd care to sign the register, I'm sure you and Mrs Bryce would like to freshen up after the journey. The full address, please. Thank you.'

She led them out and down the cement path to the end cottage on the left. She knocked and Leiter appeared. Bond had looked forward to a warm welcome, but Leiter seemed staggered to see him. His mouth hung open. His straw-coloured hair, still faintly black at the roots, looked like a haystack.

'You haven't met my wife, I think,' said Bond.

'No, no, I mean, yes. How do you do?'

The whole situation was beyond him. Forgetting Solitaire, he almost dragged Bond through the door. At the last moment he remembered the girl and seized her with his other hand and pulled her in too, banging the door shut with his heel so that Mrs Stuyvesant's 'I hope you have a happy . . .' was guillotined before the 'stay'.

Once inside, Leiter could still not take them in. He stood and gaped from one to the other.

Bond dropped his suitcase on the floor of the little lobby. There were two doors. He pushed open the one on his right and held it for Solitaire. It was a small living-room that ran the width of the cottage and faced across the beach to the sea. It was pleasantly furnished with bamboo beach chairs upholstered in foam rubber covered with a red and green hibiscus chintz. Palm-leaf matting covered the floor. The walls were duck's-egg blue and in the centre of each was a colour print of tropical flowers in a bamboo frame. There was a large drum-shaped table in bamboo with a glass top. It held a bowl of flowers and a white telephone. There were broad windows facing the sea and to the right of them a door leading on to the beach. White plastic jalousies were drawn half up the windows to cut the glare from the sand.

Bond and Solitaire sat down. Bond lit a cigarette and threw the pack and his lighter on to the table.

Suddenly the telephone rang. Leiter came out of his trance and walked over from the door and picked up the receiver.

'Speaking,' he said. 'Put the Lieutenant on. That you, Lieutenant? He's here. Just walked in. No, all in one piece.' He listened for a moment then turned to Bond. 'Where did you leave the Phantom?' he asked. Bond told him. 'Jacksonville,' said Leiter into the telephone. 'Yeah, I'll say. Sure. I'll get the details from him and call you back. Will you call off Homicide? I'd sure appreciate it. And New York. Much obliged, Lieutenant. Orlando 9000. Okay. And thanks again. Bye.' He put down the receiver. He wiped the sweat off his forehead and sat down opposite Bond.

Suddenly he looked at Solitaire and grinned apologetically. 'I guess you're Solitaire,' he said. 'Sorry for the rough welcome. It's been quite a day. For the second time in around twenty-four hours I didn't expect to see this guy again.' He turned back to Bond. 'Okay to go ahead?' he asked.

'Yes,' said Bond. 'Solitaire's on our side now.'

'That's a break,' said Leiter. 'Well you won't have seen the papers or heard the radio so I'll give you the headlines first. The Phantom was stopped soon after Jacksonville. Between Waldo and Ocala. Your compartment was tommy-gunned and bombed. Blown to bits. Killed the Pullman porter who was in the corridor at the time. No other casualties. Bloody uproar going on. Who did it? Who's Mr Bryce and who's Mrs Bryce? Where are they? Of course we were sure you'd been snatched. The police at Orlando are in charge. Traced the bookings back to New York. Found the FBI had made them. Everyone comes down on me like a load of bricks. Then you walk in with a pretty girl on your arm looking as happy as a clam.'

Leiter burst out laughing. 'Boy! You should have heard Washington a while back. Anybody would have thought it was me that bombed the goddam train.'

He reached for one of Bond's cigarettes and lit it.

'Well,' he said. 'That's the synopsis. I'll hand over the shooting script when I've heard your end. Give.'

Bond described in detail what had happened since he had spoken to Leiter from the St Regis. When he came to the night on the train he took the piece of paper out of his pocketbook and pushed it across the table.

Leiter whistled. 'Voodoo,' he said. 'This was meant to be found on the corpse, I guess. Ritual murder by friends of the men you bumped in Harlem. That's how it was supposed to look. Take the heat right away from The Big Man. They certainly think out all the angles. We'll get after that thug they had on the train. Probably one of the help in the diner. He must have been the man who put the finger on your compartment. You finish. Then I'll tell you how he did it.'

'Let me see,' said Solitaire. She reached across for the paper.

'Yes,' she said quietly. 'It's an *ouanga*, a Voodoo fetish. It's the invocation to the Drum Witch. It's used by the Ashanti tribe in Africa when they want to kill someone. They use something like it in Haiti.' She handed it back to Bond. 'It was lucky you didn't tell me about it,' she said seriously. 'I would still be having hysterics.'

'I didn't care for it myself,' said Bond. 'I felt it was bad news. Lucky we got off at Jacksonville. Poor Baldwin. We owe him a lot.'

He finished the story of the rest of their trip.

'Anyone spot you when you left the train?' asked Leiter.

'Shouldn't think so,' said Bond. 'But we'd better keep Solitaire under cover until we can get her out. Thought we ought to fly her over to Jamaica tomorrow. I can get her looked after there till we come on.'

'Sure,' agreed Leiter. 'We'll put her in a charter plane at Tampa. Get her down to Miami by tomorrow lunchtime and she can take one of the afternoon services — KLM or Panam. Get her in by dinner-time tomorrow. Too late to do anything this afternoon.'

'Is that all right, Solitaire?' Bond asked her.

The girl was staring out of the window. Her eyes had the far-away look that Bond had seen before.

Suddenly she shivered.

Her eyes came back to Bond. She put out a hand and touched his sleeve.

'Yes,' she said. She hesitated. 'Yes, I guess so.'

13
DEATH OF A PELICAN

SOLITAIRE STOOD UP.

'I must go and tidy myself,' she said, 'I expect you've both got plenty to talk about.'

'Of course,' said Leiter jumping up. 'Crazy of me! You must be dead beat. Guess you'd better take James's room and he can bed down with me.'

Solitaire followed him out into the little hall and Bond heard Leiter explaining the arrangement of the rooms.

In a moment Leiter came back with a bottle of Haig and Haig and some ice.

'I'm forgetting my manners,' he said. 'We could both do with a drink. There's a small pantry next the bathroom and I've stocked it with all we're likely to need!'

He fetched some soda water and they both took a long drink.

'Let's have the details,' said Bond, sitting back. 'Must have been the hell of a fine job.'

'Sure was,' agreed Leiter, 'except for the shortage of corpses.'

He put his feet on the table and lit a cigarette.

'Phantom left Jacksonville around five,' he began. 'Got to Waldo around six. Just after leaving Waldo — and here I'm guessing — Mr Big's man comes along to your car, gets into the next compartment to yours and hangs a towel between the drawn blind and the window, meaning — and he must have done a good deal of telephoning at stations on the way down — meaning "the window to the right of this towel is it".

'There's a long stretch of straight track between Waldo and Ocala,' continued Leiter, 'running through forest and swamp land. State highway right alongside the track. About twenty minutes outside Waldo, Wham! goes a dynamite emergency signal under the leading Diesel. Driver comes down to forty. Wham! And another Wham! Three in line! Emergency! Halt at once! He halts the train wondering what the hell. Straight track. Last signal green over green. Nothing in sight. It's around quarter after six and just getting light. There's a sedan, clouted heap I expect [Bond raised an eyebrow. 'Stolen car' explained Leiter], grey, thought to have been a Buick, no lights, engine running, waiting on the highway opposite the centre of the train. Three men get out. Coloured. Probably negro. They walk slowly in line abreast along the grass verge between the road and the track. Two on the outside carry rippers — tommy-guns. Man in the centre has something in his hand. Twenty yards and they stop outside Car 245. Men with the rippers give a double squirt at your window. Open it up for the pineapple. Centre man tosses in the pineapple and all three run back to the car. Two seconds fuse. As they reach the car, BOOM! Fricassee of Compartment H. Fricassee, presumably, of Mr and Mrs Bryce. In fact fricassee of your Baldwin who runs out and crouches in corridor directly he sees men approaching his car. No other casualties except multiple shock and hysterics throughout train. Car drives away very fast towards limbo where it still is and will probably remain. Silence, mingled with screams, falls. People run to and fro. Train limps gingerly into Ocala. Drops Car 245. Is allowed to proceed three hours later. Scene II. Leiter sits alone in cottage, hoping he has never said an unkind word to his friend James, and wondering how Mr Hoover will have Mr Leiter served for his dinner tonight. That's all, folks.'

Bond laughed. 'What an organization!' he said. 'I'm sure it's all beautifully covered up and alibied. What a man! He certainly seems to have the run of this country. Just shows how one can push a democracy around, what with *habeas corpus* and human rights and all the rest. Glad we haven't got him on our hands in England. Wooden truncheons wouldn't make much of a dent in him. Well,' he concluded, 'that's three times I've managed to get away with it. The pace is beginning to get a bit hot.'

'Yes,' said Leiter thoughtfully. 'Before you arrived over here you could have counted the mistakes Mr Big has ever made on one thumb. Now he's made three all in a row. He won't like that. We've got to put the heat on him while he's still groggy and then get out, quick. Tell you what I've got in mind. There's no doubt that gold gets into the States through this place. We've tracked the *Secatur* again and again and she just comes straight over from Jamaica to St Petersburg and docks at that worm and bait factory — Rubberus or whatever it's called.'

'Ourobouros,' said Bond. 'The Great Worm of mythology. Good name for a worm and bait factory.' Suddenly a thought struck him. He hit the glass table-top with the flat of his hand. 'Felix! Of course. Ourobouros — "The Robber" — don't you see. Mr Big's man down here. It must be the same.'

Leiter's face lit up. 'Christ Almighty,' he exclaimed. 'Of course it's the same. That Greek who's supposed to own it, the man in Tarpon Springs that figures in the reports that blockhead showed us in New York, Binswanger. He's probably just a figurehead. Probably doesn't even know there's anything phoney about it. It's his manager here we've got to get after. "The Robber". Of course that's who it is.'

Leiter jumped up.

'C'mon. Let's get going. We'll go right along and look the place over. I was going to suggest it anyway, seeing the *Secatur* always docks at their wharf. She's in Cuba now, by the way,' he added, 'Havana. Cleared from here a week ago. They searched her good and proper when she came in and when she left. Didn't find a thing of course. Thought she might have a false keel. Almost tore it off. She had to go into dock before she could sail again. Nix. Not a shadow of anything wrong. Let alone a stack of gold coins. Anyway, we'll go and smell around. See if we can get a look at our Robber friend. I'll just have to talk to Orlando and Washington. Tell 'em all we know. They must catch up quick with The Big Man's fellow on the train. Probably too late by now. You go and see how Solitaire's getting on. Tell her she's not to move till we get back. Lock her in. We'll take her out to dinner in Tampa. They've got the best restaurant on the whole coast, Cuban, Los Novedades. We'll stop at the airport on the way and fix her flight for tomorrow.'

Leiter reached for the telephone and asked for Long Distance. Bond left him to it.

Ten minutes later they were on their way.

Solitaire had not wanted to be left. She had clung to Bond. 'I want to get away from here,' she said, her eyes frightened. 'I have a feeling . . . ' She didn't end the sentence. Bond kissed her.

'It's all right,' he said. 'We'll be back in an hour or so. Nothing can happen to you here. Then I shan't leave you until you're on the plane. We can even stay the night in Tampa and get you off at first light.'

'Yes please,' said Solitaire anxiously. 'I'd rather do that. I'm frightened here. I feel in danger.' She put her arms round his neck. 'Don't think I'm being hysterical.' She kissed him. 'Now you can go. I just wanted to see you. Come back quickly.'

Leiter had called and Bond had closed the door on her and locked it.

He followed Leiter to his car on the Parkway feeling vaguely troubled. He couldn't imagine that the girl could come to any harm in this peaceful, law-abiding place, or that The Big Man could conceivably have traced her to The Everglades which was only one of a hundred similar beach establishments on Treasure Island. But he respected the extraordinary power of her intuitions and her attack of nerves made him uneasy.

The sight of Leiter's car put these thoughts out of his mind.

Bond liked fast cars and he liked driving them. Most American cars bored him. They lacked personality and the patina of individual craftsmanship that European cars have. They were just 'vehicles', similar in shape and in colour, and even in the tone of their horns. Designed to serve for a year and then be turned in in part exchange for the next year's model. All the fun of driving had been taken out of them with the abolition of a gear-change, with hydraulic-assisted steering and spongy suspension. All effort had been smoothed away and all of that close contact with the machine and the road that extracts skill and nerve from the European driver. To Bond, American cars were just beetle-shaped dodgems in which you motored along with one hand on the wheel, the radio full on, and the power-operated windows closed to keep out the draughts.

But Leiter had got hold of an old Cord, one of the few American cars with a personality, and it cheered Bond to climb into the low-hung saloon, to hear the solid bite of the gears and the masculine tone of the wide exhaust. Fifteen years old, he reflected, yet still one of the most modern-looking cars in the world.

They swung on to the causeway and across the wide expanse of unrippled water that separates the twenty miles of narrow island from the broad peninsula sprawling with St Petersburg and its suburbs.

Already as they idled up Central Avenue on their way across the town to the yacht basin and the main harbour and the big hotels, Bond caught a whiff of the atmosphere that makes the town the 'Old Folks Home' of America. Everyone on the sidewalks had white hair, white or blue, and the famous Sidewalk Davenports that Solitaire had described were thick with oldsters sitting in rows like the starlings in Trafalgar Square.

Bond noted the small grudging mouths of the women, the sun gleaming on their pince-nez; the stringy, collapsed chests and arms of the men displayed to the sunshine in Truman shirts. The fluffy, sparse balls of hair on the women showing the pink scalp. The bony bald heads of the men. And, everywhere, a prattling camaraderie, a swapping of news and gossip, a making of folksy dates for the shuffleboard and the bridge-table, a handing round of letters from children and grandchildren, a tut-tutting about prices in the shops and the motels.

You didn't have to be amongst them to hear it all. It was all in the nodding and twittering of the balls of blue fluff, the back-slapping and hawk-an-spitting of the little old baldheads.

'It makes you want to climb right into the tomb and pull the lid down,' said Leiter at Bond's exclamations of horror. 'You wait till we get out and walk. If they see your shadow coming up the sidewalk behind them they jump out of the way as if you were the Chief Cashier coming to look over their shoulders in the bank. It's ghastly. Makes me think of the bank clerk who went home unexpectedly at midday and found the President of the bank sleeping with his wife. He went back and told his pals in the ledger department and said, "Gosh, fellers, he nearly caught me!" '

Bond laughed.

'You can hear all the presentation gold watches ticking in their pockets,' said Leiter. 'Place is full of undertakers, and pawnshops stuffed with gold watches and masonic rings and bits of jet and lockets full of hair. Makes you shiver to think of it all. Wait till you go to Aunt Milly's Place and see them all in droves mumbling over their corn beef hash and cheeseburgers, trying to keep alive till ninety. It'll frighten the life out of you. But they're not all old down here. Take a look at that ad over there.' He pointed towards a big hoarding on a deserted lot.

It was an advertisement for maternity clothes. 'STUTZHEIMER & BLOCK,' it said, 'IT'S NEW! OUR ANTICIPATION DEPARTMENT, AND AFTER! CLOTHES FOR CHIPS (1–4) AND TWIGS (4–8).'

Bond groaned. 'Let's get away from here,' he said. 'This is really beyond the call of duty.'

They came down to the waterfront and turned right until they came to the seaplane base and the coastguard station. The streets were free of oldsters and here there was the normal life of a harbour — wharves, warehouses, a ships' chandler, some up-turned boats, nets drying, the cry of seagulls, the rather fetid smell coming in off the bay. After the teeming boneyard of the town the sign over the garage: 'Drive-ur-Self. Pat Grady. The Smiling Irishman. Used cars', was a cheerful reminder of a livelier, bustling world.

'Better get out and walk,' said Leiter. 'The Robber's place is in the next block.'

They left the car beside the harbour and sauntered along past a timber warehouse and some oil storage tanks. Then they turned left again towards the sea.

The side-road ended at a small weather-beaten wooden jetty that reached out twenty feet on barnacled piles into the bay. Right up against its open gate was a long low corrugated iron warehouse. Over its wide double doors was painted, black on white, 'Ourobouros Inc. Live Worm and Bait Merchants. Coral, Shells, Tropical Fish. Wholesale only'. In one of the double doors there was a smaller door with a gleaming Yale lock. On the door was a sign: 'Private. Keep Out'.

Against this a man sat on a kitchen chair, its back tilted so that the door supported his weight. He was cleaning a rifle, a Remington 30 it looked like to Bond. He had a wooden toothpick sticking out of his mouth and a battered baseball cap on the back of his head. He was wearing a stained white singlet that revealed tufts of black hair under his arms, and slept-in white canvas trousers and rubber-soled sneakers. He was around forty and his face was as knotted and seamed as the mooring posts on the jetty. It was a thin, hatchet face, and the lips were thin too, and bloodless. His complexion was the colour of tobacco dust, a sort of yellowy-beige. He looked cruel and cold, like the bad man in a film about poker-players and gold mines.

Bond and Leiter walked past him and on to the pier. He didn't look up from his rifle as they went past but Bond sensed that his eyes were following them.

'If that isn't The Robber,' said Leiter, 'it's a blood relation.'

A pelican, grey with a pale yellow head, was hunched on one of the mooring posts at the end of the jetty. He let them get very close then reluctantly gave a few heavy beats of his wings and planed down towards the water. The two men stood and watched him flying slowly along just above the surface of the harbour. Suddenly he crashed clumsily down, his long bill snaking out and down in front of him. It came up clutching a small fish which he moodily swallowed. Then the heavy bird got up again and went on fishing, flying mostly into the sun so that its big shadow would give no warning. When Bond and Leiter turned to walk back down the jetty it gave up fishing and glided back to its post. It settled with a clatter of wings and resumed its thoughtful consideration of the late afternoon.

The man was still bent over his gun, wiping the mechanism with an oily rag.

'Good afternoon,' said Leiter. 'You the manager of this wharf?'

'Yep,' said the man without looking up.

'Wondered if there was any chance of mooring my boat here. Basin's pretty crowded.'

'Nope.'

Leiter took out his notecase. 'Would twenty talk?'

'Nope.' The man gave a rattling hawk in his throat and spat directly between Bond and Leiter.

'Hey,' said Leiter. 'You want to watch your manners.'

The man deliberated. He looked up at Leiter. He had small, close-set eyes as cruel as a painless dentist's.

'What's a name of your boat?'

'The *Sybil*,' said Leiter.

'Ain't no sich boat in the basin,' said the man. He clicked the breech shut on his rifle. It lay casually on his lap pointing down the approach to the warehouse, away from the sea.

'You're blind,' said Leiter. 'Been there a week. Sixty-foot twin-screw Diesel. White with a green awning. Rigged for fishing.'

The rifle started to move lazily in a low arc. The man's left hand was at the trigger, his right just in front of the trigger-guard, pivoting the gun.

They stood still.

The man sat lazily looking down at the breech, his chair still tilted against the small door with the yellow Yale lock.

The gun slowly traversed Leiter's stomach, then Bond's. The two men stood like statues, not risking a move of the hand. The gun stopped pivoting. It was pointing down the wharf. The Robber looked briefly up, narrowed his eyes and pulled the trigger. The pelican gave a faint squawk and they heard its heavy body crash into the water. The echo of the shot boomed across the harbour.

'What the hell d'you do that for?' asked Bond, furiously.

'Practice,' said the man, pumping another bullet into the breech.

'Guess there's a branch of the ASPCA in this town,' said Leiter. 'Let's get along there and report this guy.'

'Want to be prosecuted for trespass?' asked The Robber, getting slowly up and shifting the gun under his arm. 'This is private property. Now,' he spat the words out, 'git the hell out of here.' He turned and yanked the chair away from the door, opened the door with a key and turned with one foot on the threshold. 'You both got guns,' he said. 'I kin smell 'em. You come aroun' here again and you follow the boid 'n I plead self-defence. I've had a bellyful of you lousy dicks aroun' here lately breathin' down my neck. *Sybil* my ass!' He turned contemptuously through the door and slammed it so that the frame rattled.

They looked at each other. Leiter grinned ruefully and shrugged his shoulders.

'Round One to The Robber,' he said.

They moved off down the dusty side-road. The sun was setting and the sea behind them was a pool of blood. When they got to the main road, Bond looked back. A big arc light had come on over the door and the approach to the warehouse was stripped of shadows.

'No good trying anything from the front,' said Bond. 'But there's never been a warehouse with only one entrance.'

'Just what I was thinking,' said Leiter. 'We'll save that for the next visit.'

They got into the car and drove slowly home across Central Avenue.

On their way home Leiter asked a string of questions about Solitaire. Finally he said casually: 'By the way, hope I fixed the rooms like you want them.'

'Couldn't be better,' said Bond cheerfully.

'Fine,' said Leiter. 'Just occurred to me you two might be hyphenating.'

'You read too much Winchell,' said Bond.

'It's just a delicate way of putting it,' said Leiter. 'Don't forget the walls of those cottages are pretty thin. I use my ears for hearing with — not for collecting lipstick.'

Bond grabbed for a handkerchief. 'You lousy, goddam sleuth,' he said furiously.

Leiter watched him scrubbing at himself out of the corner of his eye. 'What are you doing?' he asked innocently. 'I wasn't for a moment suggesting the colour of your ears was anything but a natural red. However . . .' He put a wealth of meaning into the word.

'If you find yourself dead in your bed tonight,' laughed Bond, 'you'll know who did it.'

They were still chaffing each other when they arrived at The Everglades and they were laughing when the grim Mrs Stuyvesant greeted them on the lawn.

'Pardon me, Mr Leiter,' she said. 'But I'm afraid we can't allow music here. I can't have the other guests disturbed at all hours.'

They looked at her in astonishment. 'I'm sorry, Mrs Stuyvesant,' said Leiter. 'I don't quite get you.'

'That big radiogram you had sent round,' said Mrs Stuyvesant. 'The men could hardly get the packing-case through the door.'

14

'HE DISAGREED WITH SOMETHING THAT ATE HIM'

THE GIRL HAD not put up much of a struggle.

When Leiter and Bond, leaving the manageress gaping on the lawn, raced down to the end cottage, they found her room untouched and the bedclothes barely rumpled.

The lock of her room had been forced with one swift wrench of a jemmy and then the two men must have just stood there with guns in their hands.

'Get going, lady. Get your clothes on. Try any tricks and we'll let the fresh air into you.'

Then they must have gagged her or knocked her out and doubled her into the packing-case and nailed it up. There were tyre marks at the back of the cottage where the truck had stood. Almost blocking the entrance hall was a huge old-fashioned radiogram. Second-hand it must have cost them under fifty bucks.

Bond could see the expression of blind terror on Solitaire's face as if she was standing before him. He cursed himself bitterly for leaving her alone. He couldn't guess how she had been traced so quickly. It was just another example of The Big Man's machine.

Leiter was talking to the FBI headquarters at Tampa. 'Airports, railroad terminals and the highways,' he was saying. 'You'll get blanket orders from Washington just as soon as I've spoken to them. I guarantee they'll give this top priority. Thanks a lot. Much appreciated. I'll be around. Okay.'

He hung up. 'Thank God they're co-operating,' he said to Bond who was standing gazing with hard blank eyes out to sea. 'Sending a couple of their men round right away and throwing as wide a net as they can. While I sew this up with Washington and New York, get what you can from that old battle-axe. Exact time, descriptions, etc. Better make out it was a burglary and that Solitaire has skipped with the men. She'll understand that. It'll keep the whole thing on the level of the usual hotel crimes. Say the police are on the way and that we don't blame The Everglades. She'll want to avoid a scandal. Say we feel the same way.'

Bond nodded. 'Skipped with the men?' That was possible too. But somehow he didn't think so. He went back to Solitaire's room and searched it minutely. It still smelled of her, of the Vent Vert that reminded him of their journey together. Her hat and veil were in the cupboard and her few toilet articles on the shelf in the bathroom. He soon found her bag and knew that he was right to have trusted her. It was under the bed and he visualized her kicking it there as she got up with the guns trained on her. He emptied it out on the bed and felt the lining. Then he took out a small knife and carefully cut a few threads. He took out the five thousand dollars and slipped them into his pocketbook. They would be safe with him. If she was killed by Mr Big, he would spend them on avenging her. He covered up the torn lining as best he could, replaced the other contents of the bag and kicked it back under the bed.

Then he went up to the office.

It was eight o'clock by the time the routine work was finished. They had a stiff drink together and then went to the central dining-room where the handful of other guests were just finishing their dinner. Everyone looked curiously and rather fearfully at them. What were these two rather dangerous-looking young men doing in this place? Where was the woman who had come with them? Whose wife was she? What had all those goings-on meant that evening? Poor Mrs Stuyvesant running about looking quite distracted. And didn't they realize that dinner was at seven o'clock? The kitchen staff would be just going home. Serve them right if their food was quite cold. People must have consideration for others. Mrs Stuyvesant had said she thought they were government men, from Washington. Well, what did that mean?

The consensus of opinion was that they were bad news and no credit to the carefully restricted clientele of The Everglades.

Bond and Leiter were shown to a bad table near the service door. The set dinner was a string of inflated English and pidgin

French. What it came down to was tomato juice, boiled fish with a white sauce, a strip of frozen turkey with a dab of cranberry, and a wedge of lemon curd surmounted by a whorl of stiff cream substitute. They munched it down gloomily while the dining-room emptied of its oldster couples and the table lights went out one by one. Fingerbowls, in which floated one hibiscus petal, was the final gracious touch to their meal.

Bond ate silently and when they had finished Leiter made a determined effort to be cheerful.

'Come and get drunk,' he said. 'This is the bad end to a worse day. Or do you want to play bingo with the oldsters? It says there's a bingo tournament in the "romp room" this evening.'

Bond shrugged his shoulders and they went back to their sitting-room and sat gloomily for a while, drinking and staring out across the sand, bone-white in the light of the moon, towards the endless dark sea.

When Bond had drunk enough to drown his thoughts he said good night and went off to Solitaire's room which he had now taken over as his bedroom. He climbed between the sheets where her warm body had lain and, before he slept, he had made up his mind. He would go after The Robber as soon as it was light and strangle the truth out of him. He had been too preoccupied to discuss the case with Leiter but he was certain that The Robber must have had a big hand in the kidnapping of Solitaire. He thought of the man's little cruel eyes and the pale thin lips. Then he thought of the scrawny neck rising like a turtle's out of the dirty sweat-shirt. Under the bedclothes the muscles of his arms went taut. Then, his mind made up, he relaxed his body into sleep.

He slept until eight. When he saw the time on his watch he cursed. He quickly took a shower, holding his eyes open into the needles of water until they smarted. Then he put a towel round his waist and went into Leiter's room. The slats of the jalousies were still down but there was light enough to see that neither bed had been slept in.

He smiled, thinking that Leiter had probably finished the bottle of whisky and fallen asleep on the couch in the living-room. He walked through. The room was empty. The bottle of whisky, still half full, was on the table and a pile of cigarette butts overflowed the ashtray.

Bond went to the window, pulled up the jalousies and opened it. He caught a glimpse of a beautiful clear morning before he turned back into the room.

Then he saw the envelope. It was on a chair in front of the door through which he had come. He picked it up. It contained a note scribbled in pencil.

> Got to thinking and don't feel like sleep. It's about five a.m. Going to visit the worm-and-bait store. All same early bird. Odd that trick-shot artist was sitting there while S. was being snatched. As if he knew we were in town and was ready for trouble in case the snatch went wrong. If I'm not back by ten, call out the militia. Tampa 88.
>
> FELIX

Bond didn't wait. While he shaved and dressed he ordered some coffee and rolls and a cab. In just over ten minutes he had got them all and had scalded himself with the coffee. He was leaving the cottage when he heard the telephone ring in the living-room. He ran back.

'Mr Bryce? Mound Park Hospital speaking,' said a voice. 'Emergency ward. Dr Roberts. We have a Mr Leiter here who's asking for you. Can you come right over?'

'God Almighty,' said Bond, gripped with fear. 'What's the matter with him. Is he bad?'

'Nothing to worry about,' said the voice. 'Automobile accident. Looks like a hit-and-run job. Slight concussion. Can you come over? He seems to want you.'

'Of course,' said Bond relieved. 'Be there right away.'

Now what the hell, he wondered as he hurried across the lawn. Must have been beaten up and left in the road. On the whole Bond was glad it was no worse.

As they turned across Treasure Island Causeway an ambulance passed them, its bell clanging.

More trouble, thought Bond. Don't seem to be able to move without running into it.

They crossed St Petersburg by Central Avenue and turned right down the road he and Leiter had taken the day before. Bond's suspicions seemed to be confirmed when he found the hospital was only a couple of blocks from Ourobouros Inc.

Bond paid off the cab and ran up the steps of the impressive building. There was a reception desk in the spacious entrance hall. A pretty nurse sat at the desk reading the ads in the *St Petersburg Times*.

'Dr Roberts?' inquired Bond.

'Dr which?' asked the girl looking at him with approval.

'Dr Roberts, Emergency ward,' said Bond impatiently. 'Patient called Leiter, Felix Leiter. Brought in this morning.'

'No doctor called Roberts here,' said the girl. She ran a finger down a list on the desk. 'And no patient called Leiter. Just a moment and I'll call the ward. What did you say your name was?'

'Bryce,' said Bond. 'John Bryce.' He started to sweat profusely although it was quite cool in the hall. He wiped his wet hands on his trousers, fighting to keep from panic. The damn girl just didn't know her job. Too pretty to be a nurse. Ought to have someone competent on the desk. He ground his teeth as she talked cheerfully into the telephone.

She put down the receiver. 'I'm sorry, Mr Bryce. Must be some mistake. No cases during the night and they've never heard of a Dr Roberts or a Mr Leiter. Sure you've got the right hospital?'

Bond turned away without answering her. Wiping the sweat from his forehead, he made for the exit.

The girl made a face at his back and picked up her paper.

Mercifully, a cab was just drawing up with some other visitors. Bond took it and told the driver to get him back quick to The Everglades. All he knew was that they had got Leiter and had wanted to draw Bond away from the cottage. Bond couldn't make it out, but he knew that suddenly everything was going bad on them and that the initiative was back in the hands of Mr Big and his machine.

Mrs Stuyvesant hurried out when she saw him leave the cab.

'Your poor friend,' she said without sympathy. 'Really he should be more careful.'

'Yes, Mrs Stuyvesant. What is it?' said Bond impatiently.

'The ambulance came just after you left.' The woman's eyes were gleaming with the bad news. 'Seems Mr Leiter was in an accident with his car. They had to carry him to the cottage on a stretcher. Such a nice coloured man was in charge. He said Mr Leiter would be quite all right but he mustn't be disturbed on any account. Poor boy. Face all covered with bandages. They said they'd make him comfortable and a doctor would be coming later. If there's anything I can . . .'

Bond didn't wait for more. He ran down the lawn to the cottage and dashed through the lobby into Leiter's room.

There was the shape of a body on Leiter's bed. It was covered with a sheet. Over the face, the sheet seemed to be motionless.

Bond gritted his teeth as he leant over the bed. Was there a tiny flutter of movement?

Bond snatched the shroud down from the face. There was no face. Just something wrapped round and round with dirty bandages, like a white wasps' nest.

He softly pulled the sheet down further. More bandages, still more roughly wound, with wet blood seeping through. Then the top of a sack which covered the lower half of the body. Everything soaked in blood.

There was a piece of paper protruding from a gap in the bandages where the mouth should have been.

Bond pulled it away and leant down. There was the faintest whisper of breath against his cheek. He snatched up the bedside telephone. It took minutes before he could make Tampa understand. Then the urgency in his voice got through. They would get to him in twenty minutes.

He put down the receiver and looked vaguely at the paper in his hand. It was a rough piece of white wrapping paper. Scrawled in pencil in ragged block letters were the words:

HE DISAGREED WITH SOMETHING THAT ATE HIM

And underneath in brackets:

(PS. WE HAVE PLENTY MORE JOKES AS GOOD AS THIS)

With the movements of a sleep-walker, Bond put the piece of paper down on the bedside table. Then he turned back to the body on the bed. He hardly dared touch it for fear that the tiny fluttering breath would suddenly cease. But he had to find out something. His fingers worked softly at the bandages on top of the head. Soon he uncovered some strands of hair. The hair was wet and he put his fingers to his mouth. There was a salt taste.

He pulled out some strands of hair and looked closely at them. There was no more doubt.

He saw again the pale straw-coloured mop that used to hang down in disarray over the right eye, grey and humorous, and below it the wry, hawk-like face of the Texan with whom he had shared so many adventures. He thought of him for a moment, as he had been. Then he tucked the lock of hair back into the bandages and sat on the edge of the other bed and quietly watched over the body of his friend and wondered how much of it could be saved.

When the two detectives and the police surgeon arrived he told them all he knew in a quiet flat voice. Acting on what Bond had already told them on the telephone they had sent a squad car down to The Robber's place and they waited for a report while the surgeon worked next door.

He was finished first. He came back into the sitting-room looking anxious. Bond jumped to his feet. The police surgeon slumped into a chair and looked up at him.

'I think he'll live,' he said. 'But it's fifty-fifty. They certainly did a job on the poor guy. One arm gone. Half the left leg. Face in a mess, but only superficial. Darned if I know what did it. Only thing I can think of is an animal or a big fish. Something's been tearing at him. Know a bit more when I can get him to the hospital. There'll be traces left from the teeth of whatever it was. Ambulance should be along any time.'

They sat in gloomy silence. The telephone rang intermittently. New York, Washington. The St Petersburg Police Department wanted to know what the hell was going on down at the wharf and were told to keep out of the case. It was a Federal job. Finally, from a call-box, there was the lieutenant in charge of the squad car reporting.

They had been over The Robber's place with a toothcomb. Nothing but tanks of fish and bait and cases of coral and shells. The Robber and two men who were down there in charge of the pumps and the water-heating had been taken in custody and grilled for an hour. Their alibis had been checked and found to be solid as the Empire State. The Robber had angrily demanded his mouthpiece and when the lawyer had finally been allowed to get to them they had been automatically sprung. No charge and no evidence to base one on. Dead-ends everywhere except that Leiter's car had been found the other side of the yacht basin, a mile away from the wharf. A mass of fingerprints, but none that fitted the three men. Any suggestions?

Keep with it,' said the senior man in the cottage who had introduced himself as Captain Franks. 'Be along presently. Washington says we've got to get these men if it's the last thing we do. Two top operatives flying down tonight. Time to get co-operation from the police. I'll tell 'em to get their stoolies working in Tampa. This isn't only a St Petersburg job. Bye now.'

It was three o'clock. The police ambulance came and left again with the surgeon and the body that was so near to death. The two men left. They promised to keep in touch. They were anxious to know Bond's plans. Bond was evasive. Said he'd have to talk to Washington. Meanwhile, could he have Leiter's car? Yes, it would be brought round directly Records had finished with it.

When they had gone, Bond sat lost in thought. They had made sandwiches from the well-stocked pantry and Bond now finished these and had a stiff drink.

The telephone rang. Long Distance. Bond found himself speaking to the head of Leiter's Section of the Central Intelligence Agency. The gist of it was that they'd be very glad if Bond would move on to Jamaica at once. All very polite. They had spoken to London who had agreed. When should they tell London that Bond would arrive in Jamaica?

Bond knew there was a Transcarib plane via Nassau due out next day. He said he'd be taking it. Any other news? Oh yes, said the CIA. The gentleman from Harlem and his girl friend had left by plane for Havana, Cuba, during the night. Private charter from a little place up the East Coast called Vero Beach. Papers were in order and the charter company was such a small one the FBI had not bothered to include them when they put the watch on all airports. Arrival had been reported by the CIA man in Cuba. Yes, too bad. Yes, the *Secatur* was still there. No sailing date. Well, too bad about Leiter. Fine man. Hope he makes out. So Bond would be in Jamaica tomorrow? Okay. Sorry things been so hectic. Bye.

Bond thought for a while then he picked up the telephone and spoke briefly to a man at the Eastern Garden Aquarium at

Miami and consulted him about buying a live shark to keep in an ornamental lagoon.

'Only place I ever heard of is right near you now, Mr Bryce,' said the helpful voice. ' Ourobouros Worm and Bait. They got sharks. Big ones. Do business with foreign zoos and suchlike. White, tiger, even hammerheads. They'll be glad to help you. Costs a lot to feed 'em. You're welcome. Any time you're passing. Bye.'

Bond took out his gun and cleaned it, waiting for the night.

15
MIDNIGHT AMONG THE WORMS

AROUND SIX BOND packed his bag and paid the check. Mrs Stuyvesant was glad to see the last of him. The Everglades hadn't experienced such alarums since the last hurricane.

Leiter's car was back on the Boulevard and he drove it over to the town. He visited a hardware store and made various purchases. Then he had the biggest steak, rare, with French fries, he had ever seen. It was a small grill called Pete's, dark and friendly. He drank a quarter of a pint of Old Grandad with the steak and had two cups of very strong coffee. With all this under his belt he began to feel more sanguine.

He spun out the meal and the drinks until nine o'clock. Then he studied a map of the city and took the car and made a wide detour that brought him within a block of The Robber's wharf from the south. He ran the car down to the sea and got out.

It was a bright moonlit night and the buildings and warehouses threw great blocks of indigo shadow. The whole section seemed deserted and there was no sound except the quiet lapping of the small waves against the sea-wall and water gurgling under the empty wharves.

The top of the low sea-wall was about three feet wide. It was in shadow for the hundred yards or more that separated him from the long black outline of the Ourobouros warehouse.

Bond climbed on to it and walked carefully and silently along between the buildings and the sea. As he got nearer a steady, high-pitched whine became louder and by the time he dropped down on the wide cement parking space at the back of the building it was a muted scream. Bond had expected something of the sort. The noise came from the air-pumps and heating system which he knew would be necessary to keep the fish healthy through the chill of the night hours. He had also relied on the fact that most of the roof would certainly be of glass to admit sunlight during the day. Also that there would be good ventilation.

He was not disappointed. The whole of the south wall of the warehouse, from just above the level of his head, was of plate glass, and through it he could see the moonlight shining down through half an acre of glass roofing. High up above him and well out of reach, broad windows were open to the night air. There was, as he and Leiter had expected, a small door low down, but it was locked and bolted and leaded wires near the hinges suggested some form of burglar-alarm.

Bond was not interested in the door. Following his hunch, he had come equipped for an entry through glass. He cast about for something that would raise him an extra two feet. In a land where litter and junk is so much a part of the landscape he soon found what he wanted. It was a discarded heavy-gauge tyre. He rolled it to the wall of the warehouse away from the door and took off his shoes.

He put bricks against the bottom edges of the tyre to hold it steady and hoisted himself up. The steady scream of the pumps gave him protection and he at once set to work with a small glass-cutter which he had bought, together with a hunk of putty, on his way to dinner. When he had cut down the two vertical sides of one of the yard-square panes, he pressed the putty against the centre of the glass and worked it to a protruding knob. He then went to work on the lateral edges of the pane.

While he worked he gazed through into the moonlit vistas of the huge repository. The endless rows of tanks stood on wooden trestles with narrow passages between. Down the centre of the building there was a wider passage. Under the trestles Bond could see long tanks and trays let into the floor. Just below him, broad racks covered with regiments of sea-shells jutted out from the walls. Most of the tanks were dark but in some a tiny strip of electric light glimmered spectrally and glinted on little fountains of bubbles rising from the weeds and sand. There was a light metal runway suspended from the roof over each row of tanks and Bond guessed that any individual tank could be lifted out and brought to the exit for shipment or to extract sick fish for quarantine. It was a window into a queer world and into a queer business. It was odd to think of all the worms and eels and fish stirring quietly in the night, the thousands of gills sighing and the multitude of antennae waving and pointing and transmitting their tiny radar signals to the dozing nerve-centres.

After a quarter of an hour's meticulous work there was a slight cracking noise and the pane came away attached to the putty knob in his hand.

He climbed down and put the pane carefully on the ground away from the tyre. Then he stuffed his shoes inside his shirt. With only one good hand they might be vital weapons. He listened. There was no sound but the unfaltering whine of the pumps. He looked up to see if by chance there were any clouds about to cross the moon, but the sky was empty save for its canopy of brightly burning stars. He got back on top of the tyre and with an easy heave half his body was through the wide hole he had made.

He turned and grasped the metal frame above his head and putting all his weight on his arms he jack-knifed his legs through and down so that they were hanging a few inches above the racks full of shells. He lowered himself until he could feel the backs of the shells with his stockinged toes then he softly separated them with his toes until he had exposed a width of board. Then he let his whole weight subside softly on to the tray. It held, and in a moment he was down on the floor listening with all his senses for any noise behind the whine of the machinery.

But there was none. He took his steel-tipped shoes out of his shirt and left them on the cleared board, then he moved off on the concrete floor with a pencil flashlight in his hand.

He was in the aquarium-fish section and as he examined the labels he caught flashes of coloured light from the deep tanks and occasionally a piece of living jewellery would materialize and briefly goggle at him before he moved on.

There were all kinds, swordtails, guppies, platys, terras, neons, cichlids, labyrinth and paradise fish, and every variety of exotic goldfish. Underneath, sunk in the floor, and most of them covered with chicken wire, there were tray upon tray swarming and heaving with worms and baits, white worms, micro worms, Daphnia, shrimp, and thick slimy clam worms. From these ground tanks, forests of tiny eyes looked up at his torch.

There was the fetid smell of a mangrove swamp in the air and the temperature was in the high seventies. Soon Bond began to sweat slightly and to long for the clean night air.

He had moved to the central passageway before he found the poison fish which were one of his objectives. When he had read about them in the files of the Police Headquarters in New York, he had made a mental note that he would like to know more about this sideline of the peculiar business of Ourobouros Inc.

Here the tanks were smaller and there was generally only one specimen in each. Here the eyes that looked sluggishly at Bond were cold and hooded and an occasional fang was bared at the torch or a spined backbone slowly swelled.

Each tank bore an ominous skull-and-cross-bones in chalk and there were large labels that said VERY DANGEROUS and KEEP OFF.

There must have been at least a hundred tanks of various sizes, from the large ones to hold torpedo skates and the sinister guitar fish, to smaller ones for the horse-killer eel, mud fish from the Pacific, and the monstrous West Indian scorpion fish each of whose spines has a poison sac as powerful as a rattlesnake's.

Bond's eyes narrowed as he noticed that in all the dangerous tanks the mud or sand on the bottom occupied nearly half the tank.

He chose a tank containing a six-inch scorpion fish. He knew something of the habits of this deadly species and in particular that they do not strike, but poison only on contact.

The top of the tank was on a level with his waist. He took out a strong pocket-knife he had purchased and opened the longest blade. Then he leant over the tank and with his sleeve rolled up he deliberately aimed his knife at the centre of the craggy head between the overhung grottoes of the eyesockets. As his hand broke the surface of the water the white dinosaur spines stood threateningly erect and the mottled stripes of the fish turned to a uniform muddy brown. Its broad, winglike pectorals rose slightly, poised for flight.

Bond lunged swiftly, correcting his aim for the refraction from the surface of the tank. He pinned the bulging head down as the tail threshed wildly and slowly drew the fish towards him and up the glass side of the tank. He stood aside and whipped it out on to the floor where it continued flapping and jumping despite its shattered skull.

He leant over the tank and plunged his hand deep into the centre of the mud and sand.

Yes, they were there. His hunch about the poison fish had been right. His fingers felt the close rows of coin deep under the mud, like counters in a box. They were in a flat tray. He could feel the wooden partitions. He pulled out a coin, rinsing it and his hand in the cleaner surface water as he did so. He shone his torch on it. It was as big as a modern five-shilling piece and nearly as thick and it was gold. It bore the arms of Spain and the head of Philip II.

He looked at the tank, measuring it. There must be a thousand coins in this one tank that no customs officer would think of disturbing. Ten to twenty thousand dollars' worth, guarded by one poison-fanged Cerberus. These must be the cargo brought in by the *Secatur* on her last trip a week ago. A hundred tanks. Say one hundred and fifty thousand dollars' worth of gold per trip. Soon the trucks would be coming for the tanks and somewhere down the road men with rubber-coated tongs would extract the deadly fish and throw them back in the sea or burn them. The water and the mud would be emptied out and the gold coin washed and poured into bags. Then the bags would go to agents and the coins would trickle out on the market, each one strictly accounted for by Mr Big's machine.

It was a scheme after Mr Big's philosophy, effective, technically brilliant, almost foolproof.

Bond was full of admiration as he bent to the floor and speared the scorpion fish in the side. He dropped it back in the tank. There was no point in divulging his knowledge to the enemy.

It was as he turned away from the tank that all the lights in the warehouse suddenly blazed on and a voice of sharp authority said, 'Don't move an inch. Stick 'em up.'

As Bond took a rolling dive under the tank he caught a glimpse of the lank figure of The Robber squinting down the sights of his rifle about twenty yards away, up against the main entrance. As he dived he prayed that The Robber would miss, but also he prayed that the floor tank which was to take his dive would be one of the covered ones. It was. It was covered with chicken wire. Something snapped up at him as he hit the wire and sprawled clear in the next passageway. As he dived, the rifle cracked and the scorpion fish tank above his head splintered sharply and water gushed down.

Bond sprinted fast between the tanks back towards his only means of retreat. Just as he turned the corner there was a shot and a tank of angel fish exploded like a bomb just beside his ear.

He was now at his end of the warehouse with The Robber at the other, fifty yards away. There was no possible chance of jumping for his window on the other side of the central passageway. He stood for a moment gaining his breath and thinking. He realized that the lines of tanks would only protect him to the knees and that between the tanks he would be in full view down the narrow passages. Either way, he could not stand still. He was reminded of the fact as a shot whammed between his legs into a pile of conchs, sending splinters of their hard china buzzing round him like wasps. He ran to his right and another shot came at his legs. It hit the floor and zoomed into a huge carboy of clams that split in half and emptied a hundred shell-fish over the floor. Bond raced back taking long quick strides. He had his Beretta out and loosed off two shots as he crossed the central passageway. He saw The Robber jump for shelter as a tank shattered above his head.

Bond grinned as he heard a shout drowned by the crash of glass and water.

He immediately dropped to one knee and fired two shots at The Robber's legs, but fifty yards for his small-calibre pistol was too much. There was the crash of another tank but the second shot clanged emptily into the iron entrance gates.

Then The Robber was shooting again and Bond could only dodge to and fro behind the cases and wait to be caught in the kneecap. Occasionally he fired a shot in return to make The Robber keep his distance but he knew the battle was lost. The other man seemed to have endless ammunition. Bond had only two shots left in his gun and one fresh clip in his pocket.

As he shuttled to and fro, slipping on the rare fish that flapped wildly on the concrete, he even stooped to snatching up heavy queen conchs and helmet shells and hurling them towards the enemy. Often they burst impressively on top of some tank at The Robber's end and added to the appalling racket inside the corrugated iron shed. But they were quite ineffective. He thought of shooting out the lights but there were at least twenty of them in two rows.

Finally Bond decided to give up. He had one ruse to fall back on and any change in the battle was better than exhausting himself at the wrong end of this deadly coconut-shy.

As he passed a row of cases of which the one near him was shattered, he pushed it on to the floor. It was still half full of rare Siamese fighting fish and Bond was pleased with the expensive crash as the remains of the tank burst in fragments on the floor. A wide space was cleared on the trestle table and after making two quick darts to pick up his shoes he dashed back to the table and jumped up.

With no target for The Robber to shoot at there was a moment's silence save for the whine of the pumps, the sound of water dripping out of broken tanks and the flapping of dying fish. Bond slipped his shoes on and laced them tight.

'Hey, Limey,' called The Robber patiently. 'Come on out or I start using pineapples. I been expectin' you an' I got plenty ammo.'

'Guess I got to give up,' answered Bond through cupped hands. 'But only because you smashed one of my ankles.'

'I'll not shoot,' called The Robber. 'Drop your gun on the floor and come down the central passage with your hands up. We'll have a quiet little talk.'

'Guess I got no option,' said Bond putting hopelessness into his voice. He dropped his Beretta with a clatter on to the cement floor. He took the gold coin out of his pocket and clenched it in his bandaged left hand.

Bond groaned as he put his feet to the floor. He dragged his left leg behind him as he limped heavily up the central passage, his hands held level with his shoulders. He stopped half way up the passage.

The Robber came slowly towards him, half-crouching, his rifle pointed at Bond's stomach. Bond was glad to see that his shirt was soaked and that he had a cut over the left eye.

The Robber walked well to the left of the passageway. When he was about ten yards away from Bond he paused with one stockinged foot casually resting on a small obstruction in the cement floor.

He gestured with his rifle. 'Higher,' he said harshly.

Bond groaned and lifted his hands a few inches so that they were almost across his face, as if in defence.

Between the fingers he saw The Robber's toes kick something sharply sideways and there was a faint clang as if a bolt had been drawn. Bond's eyes glinted behind his hands and his jaw tightened. He knew now what had happened to Leiter.

The Robber came on, his hard, thin frame obscuring the spot where he had paused.

'Christ,' said Bond, 'I gotta sit down. My leg won't hold me.'

The Robber stopped a few feet away. 'Go ahead and stand while I ask you a few questions, Limey.' He bared his tobacco-stained teeth. 'You'll soon be lying down, and for keeps.' The Robber stood and looked him over. Bond sagged. Behind the defeat in his face his brain was measuring in inches.

'Nosey bastard,' said The Robber . . .

At that moment Bond dropped the gold coin out of his left hand. It clanged on the cement floor and started to roll.

In the fraction of a second that The Robber's eyes flickered down, Bond's right foot in its steel-capped shoe lashed out to its full length. It kicked the rifle almost out of The Robber's hands. At the same moment that The Robber pulled the trigger and the bullet crashed harmlessly through the glass ceiling, Bond launched himself in a dive at the man's stomach, his two arms flailing.

Both hands connected with something soft and brought a grunt of agony. Pain shot through Bond's left hand and he winced as the rifle crashed down across his back. He bore on into the man, blind to pain, hitting with both hands, his head down between hunched shoulders, forcing the man back and off his balance. As he felt the balance yield he straightened himself slightly and lashed out again with his steel-capped foot. It connected with The Robber's kneecap. There was a scream of agony and the rifle clattered to the ground as The Robber tried to save himself. He was half way to the floor when Bond's uppercut hit him and projected the body another few feet.

The Robber fell in the centre of the passage just opposite what Bond could now see was a drawn bolt in the floor.

As the body hit the ground a section of the floor turned swiftly on a central pivot and the body almost disappeared down the black opening of a wide trapdoor in the concrete.

As he felt the floor give under his weight The Robber gave a shrill scream of terror and his hands scrabbled for a hold. They caught the edge of the floor and clutched it just as his whole body slid into space and the six-foot panel of reinforced concrete revolved smoothly until it rested upright on its pivot, a black rectangle yawning on either side.

Bond gasped for air. He put his hands on his hips and got back some of his breath. Then he walked to the edge of the right-hand hole and looked down.

The Robber's terrified face, the lips drawn back from the teeth and the eyes madly distended, jabbered up at him.

Looking beyond him, Bond could see nothing, but he heard the lapping of water against the foundations of the building and there was a faint luminescence on the seaward side. Bond guessed that there was access to the sea through wire or narrow bars.

As The Robber's voice died down to a whimper, Bond could hear something stirring down there, awoken by the light. A hammerhead or a tiger shark he guessed, with their sharper reactions.

'Pull me out, friend. Give me a break. Pull me out. I can't hold much longer. I'll do anything you want. Tell you anything.' The Robber's voice was a hoarse whisper of supplication.

'What happened to Solitaire?' Bond stared down into the frenzied eyes.

'The Big Man did it. Told me to fix a snatch. Two men in Tampa. Ask for Butch and The Lifer. Poolroom behind the Oasis. She came to no harm. Lemme out, pal.'

'And the American, Leiter?'

The agonized face pleaded. 'It was his fault. Called me out early this mornin'. Said the place was on fire. Seen it passing in his car. Held me up and brought me back in here. Wanted to search the place. Just fell through the trap. Accident. I swear it was his fault. We pulled him out before he was finished. He'll be okay.'

Bond looked down coldly at the white fingers desperately clinging to the sharp edge of concrete. He knew that The Robber must have got the bolt back and somehow engineered Leiter over the trap. He could hear the man's laugh of triumph as the floor swung open, could see the cruel smile as he pencilled the note and stuck it into the bandages when they had fished the half-eaten body out.

For a moment blind rage seized him.

He kicked out sharply, twice.

One short scream came up out of the depths. There was a splash and then a great commotion in the water.

Bond walked to the side of the trapdoor and pushed the upright concrete slab. It revolved easily on its central pivot.

Just before its edges shut out the blackness below, Bond heard one terrible snuffling grunt as if a great pig was getting its mouth full. He knew it for the grunt that a shark makes as its hideous flat nose comes up out of the water and its sickle-shaped mouth closes on a floating carcase. He shuddered and kicked the bolt home with his foot.

Bond collected the gold coin off the floor and picked up his Beretta. He went to the main entrance and looked back for a moment at the shambles of the battlefield.

He reflected that there was nothing to show that the secret of the treasure had been discovered. The top had been shot off the scorpion fish tank under which Bond had dived and when the other men came in the morning they would not be surprised to find the fish dead in the tank. They would get the remains of The Robber out of the shark tank and report to Mr Big that he'd been worsted in a gun battle and that there were X thousand dollars' worth of damage which would have to be repaired before the *Secatur* could bring over its next cargo. They would find some of Bond's bullets and soon guess that it was his work.

Bond grimly shut his mind to the horror beneath the floor of the warehouse. He turned off the lights and let himself out by the main entrance.

A small payment had been made on account of Solitaire and Leiter.

16

THE JAMAICA VERSION

IT WAS TWO o'clock in the morning. Bond eased his car away from the sea-wall and moved off through the town on to 4th Street, the highway to Tampa.

He dawdled along down the four-lane concrete highway through the endless gauntlet of motels, trailer camps and roadside emporia selling beach furniture, sea-shells and concrete gnomes.

He stopped at the Gulf Winds Bar and Snacks and ordered a double Old Grandad on the rocks. While the barman poured it he went into the washroom and cleaned himself up. The bandages on his left hand were covered with dirt and the hand throbbed painfully. The splint had broken on the The Robber's stomach. There was nothing Bond could do about it. His eyes were red with strain and lack of sleep. He went back to the bar, drank down the bourbon and ordered another one. The barman looked like a college kid spending his holidays the hard way. He wanted to talk but there was no talk left in Bond. Bond sat and looked into his glass and thought about Leiter and The Robber and heard the sickening grunt of the feeding shark.

He paid and went out and on again over the Gandy Bridge and the air of the Bay was cool on his face. At the end of the bridge he turned left towards the airport and stopped at the first motel that looked awake.

The middle-aged couple that owned the place were listening to late rhumba music from Cuba with a bottle of rye between them. Bond told a story of a blow-out on his way from Sarasota to Silver Springs. They weren't interested. They were just glad to take his ten dollars. He drove his car up to the door of Room 5 and the man unlocked the door and turned on the light. There was a double bed and a shower and a chest of drawers and two chairs. The motif was white and blue. It looked clean and Bond put his bag down thankfully and said good night. He stripped and threw his clothes unfolded on to a chair. Then he took a quick shower, cleaned his teeth and gargled with a sharp mouthwash and climbed into bed.

He plunged at once into a calm untroubled sleep. It was the first night since he had arrived in America that did not threaten a fresh battle with his stars on the morrow.

He awoke at midday and walked down the road to a cafeteria where the short-order cook fixed him a delicious three-decker western sandwich and coffee. Then he came back to his room and wrote a detailed report to the FBI at Tampa. He omitted all reference to the gold in the poison tanks for fear that The Big Man would close down his operations in Jamaica. The nature of these had still to be discovered. Bond knew that the damage he had done to the machine in America had no bearing on the heart of his assignment — the discovery of the source of the gold, its seizure, and the destruction, if possible, of Mr Big himself.

He drove to the airport and caught the silver, four-engined plane with a few minutes to spare. He left Leiter's car in the parking space as in his report he had told the FBI he would. He guessed that he need not have mentioned it to the FBI when he saw a man in an unnecessary raincoat hanging round the souvenir shop, buying nothing. Raincoats seemed almost the badge of office of the FBI. Bond was certain they wanted to see he caught the plane. They would be glad to see the last of him. Wherever he had gone in America he had left dead bodies. Before he boarded the plane he called the hospital in St Petersburg. He wished he hadn't; Leiter was still unconscious and there was no news. Yes, they would cable him when they had something definite.

It was five in the evening when they circled over Tampa Bay and headed east. The sun was low on the horizon. A big jet from Pensacola swept by, well to port, leaving four trails of vapour that hung almost motionless in the still air. Soon it would complete its training circuit and go in to land, back to the Gulf Coast packed with oldsters in Truman shirts. Bond was glad to be on his way to the soft green flanks of Jamaica and to be leaving behind the great hard continent of Eldollarado.

The plane swept on across the waist of Florida, across the acres of jungle and swamp without sign of human habitation, its wing-lights blinking green and red in the gathering dark. Soon they were over Miami and the monster chump-traps of the Eastern Seaboard, their arteries ablaze with neon. Away to port, State Highway No. 1 disappeared up the coast in a golden ribbon of motels, gas stations and fruit-juice stands, up through Palm Beach and Daytona to Jacksonville, three hundred miles away. Bond thought of the breakfast he had had at Jacksonville not three days before and of all that had happened since. Soon, after a short stop at Nassau, he would be flying over Cuba, perhaps over the hideout where Mr Big had put her away. She would hear the noise of the plane and perhaps her instincts would make her look up towards the sky and feel that for a moment he was nearby.

Bond wondered if they would ever meet again and finish what they had begun. But that would have to come later when his work was over — the prize at the end of the dangerous road that had started three weeks before in the fog of London.

After a cocktail and an early dinner they came in to Nassau and spent half an hour on the richest island in the world, the sandy patch where a thousand million pounds of frightened sterling lies buried beneath the Canasta tables and where bungalows surrounded by a thin scurf of screwpine and casuarina change hands at fifty thousand pounds apiece.

They left the platinum whistle-stop behind and were soon crossing the twinkling mother-of-pearl lights of Havana, so different in their pastel modesty from the harsh primary colours of American cities at night.

They were flying at 15,000 feet when, just after crossing Cuba, they ran into one of those violent tropical storms that suddenly turn aircraft from comfortable drawing-rooms into bucketing death-traps. The great plane staggered and plunged, its screws now roaring in vacuum and now biting harshly into walls of solid air. The thin tube shuddered and swung. Crockery crashed in the pantry and huge rain hammered on the perspex windows.

Bond gripped the arms of his chair so that his left hand hurt and cursed softly to himself.

He looked at the racks of magazines and thought: they won't help much when the steel tires at 15,000 feet, nor will the eau-de-cologne in the washroom, nor the personalized meals, the free razor, the 'orchid for your lady' now trembling in the ice-box. Least of all the safety-belts and the life-jackets with the whistle that the steward demonstrates will really blow, nor the cute little rescue-lamp that glows red.

No, when the stresses are too great for the tired metal, when the ground mechanic who checks the de-icing equipment is crossed in love and skimps his job, way back in London, Idlewild, Gander, Montreal; when those or many things happen, then the little warm room with propellers in front falls straight down out of the sky into the sea or on to the land, heavier than air, fallible, vain. And the forty little heavier-than-air people, fallible within the plane's fallibility, vain within its larger vanity, fall down with it and make little holes in the land or little splashes in the sea. Which is anyway their destiny, so why worry? You are linked to the ground mechanic's careless fingers in Nassau just as you are linked to the weak head of the little man in the family saloon who mistakes the red light for the green and meets you head-on, for the first and last time, as you are motoring quietly home from some private sin. There's nothing to do about it. You start to die the moment you are born. The whole of life is cutting through the pack with death. So take it easy. Light a cigarette and be grateful you are still alive as you suck the smoke deep into your lungs. Your stars have already let you come quite a long way since you left your mother's womb and whimpered at the cold air of the world. Perhaps they'll even let you get to Jamaica tonight. Can't you hear those cheerful voices in the control tower that have said quietly all day long, 'Come in BOAC. Come in Panam. Come in KLM'? Can't you hear them calling you down too: 'Come in Transcarib. Come in Transcarib'? Don't lose faith in your stars. Remember that hot stitch of time when you faced death from The Robber's gun last night. You're still alive aren't you? There, we're out of it already. It was just to remind you that being quick with a gun doesn't mean you're really tough. Just don't forget it. This happy landing at Palisadoes Airport comes to you by courtesy of your stars. Better thank them.

Bond unfastened his seat-belt and wiped the sweat off his face.

To hell with it he thought as he stepped down out of the huge strong plane.

Strangways, the chief Secret Service agent for the Caribbean, was at the airport to meet him and he was quickly through Customs and Immigration and Finance Control.

It was nearly eleven and the night was quiet and hot. There was the shrill sound of crickets from the dildo cactus on both sides of the airport road and Bond gratefully drank in the sounds and smells of the tropics as the military pick-up cut across the corner of Kingston and took them up towards the gleaming, moonlit foothills of the Blue Mountains.

They talked in monosyllables until they were settled on the comfortable veranda of Strangways's neat white house on the Junction Road below Stony Hill.

Strangways poured a strong whisky-and-soda for both of them and then gave a concise account of the whole of the Jamaica end of the case.

He was a lean, humorous man of about thirty-five, a former Lieutenant-Commander in the Special Branch of the RNVR. He had a black patch over one eye and the sort of aquiline good looks that are associated with the bridges of destroyers. But his face was heavily lined under its tan and Bond sensed from his quick gestures and clipped sentences that he was nervous and highly strung. He was certainly efficient and he had a sense of humour, and he showed no signs of jealousy at someone from headquarters butting in on his territory. Bond felt that they would get on well together and he looked forward to the partnership.

This was the story that Strangways had to tell.

It had always been rumoured that there was treasure on the Isle of Surprise and everything that was known about Bloody Morgan supported the rumour.

The tiny island lay in the exact centre of Shark Bay, a small harbour that lies at the end of the Junction Road that runs across the thin waist of Jamaica from Kingston to the north coast.

The great buccaneer had made Shark Bay his headquarters. He liked to have the whole width of the island between himself and the Governor at Port Royal so that he could slip in and out of Jamaican waters in complete secrecy. The Governor also liked the arrangement. The Crown wished a blind eye to be turned on Morgan's piracy until the Spaniards had been cleared out of the Caribbean. When this was accomplished, Morgan was rewarded with a knighthood and the Governorship of Jamaica. Till then, his actions had to be disavowed to avoid a European war with Spain.

So, for the long period before the poacher turned gamekeeper, Morgan used Shark Bay as his sallyport. He built three houses on the neighbouring estate, christened Llanrumney after his birthplace in Wales. These houses were called 'Morgan's', 'The Doctor's', and 'The Lady's'. Buckles and coins are still turned up in the ruins of them.

His ships always anchored in Shark Bay and he careened them in the lee of the Isle of Surprise, a precipitous lump of coral and limestone that surges straight up out of the centre of the bay and is surmounted by a jungly plateau of about an acre.

When, in 1683, he left Jamaica for the last time, it was under open arrest to be tried by his peers for flouting the Crown. His treasure was left behind somewhere in Jamaica and he died in penury without revealing its whereabouts. It must have been a vast hoard, the fruits of countless raids on Hispaniola, of the capture of innumerable treasure ships sailing for The Plate, of the sacking of Panama and the looting of Maracaibo. But it vanished without trace.

It was always thought that the secret lay somewhere on the Isle of Surprise, but for two hundred years the diving and digging of treasure-hunters yielded nothing. Then, said Strangways, just six months before, two things had happened within a few weeks. A young fisherman disappeared from the village of Shark Bay, and had not been heard of since, and an anonymous New York syndicate purchased the island for a thousand pounds from the present owner of the Llanrumney Estate, which was now a rich banana and cattle property.

A few weeks after the sale, the yacht *Secatur* put in to Shark Bay and dropped anchor in Morgan's old anchorage in the lee of the island. It was manned entirely by negroes. They went to work and cut a stairway in the rock face of the island and erected on the summit a number of low-lying shacks in the fashion known in Jamaica as 'wattle-and-daub'.

They appeared to be completely equipped with provisions and all they purchased from the fishermen of the bay was fresh fruit and water.

They were a taciturn and orderly lot who gave no trouble. They explained to the Customs which they had cleared in the neighbouring Port Maria that they were there to catch tropical fish, especially the poisonous varieties, and collect rare shells for Ourobouros Inc. in St Petersburg. When they had established themselves they purchased large quantities of these from the Shark Bay, Port Maria and Oracabessa fishermen.

For a week they carried out blasting operations on the island and it was given out that these were for the purpose of excavating a large fish-tank.

The *Secatur* began a fortnightly shuttle-service with the Gulf of Mexico and watchers with binoculars confirmed that, before each sailing, consignments of portable fish-tanks were taken aboard. Always half a dozen men were left behind. Canoes approaching the island were warned off by a watchman at the base of the steps in the cliff who fished all day from a narrow jetty alongside which the *Secatur* on her visits moored with two anchors out, well sheltered from the prevailing north-easterly winds.

No one succeeded in landing on the island by daylight and, after two tragic attempts, nobody tried to gain access by night.

The first attempt was made by a local fisherman spurred on by the rumours of buried treasure that no talk of tropical fish could suppress. He had swum out one dark night and his body had been washed back over the reef next day. Sharks and barracuda had left nothing but the trunk and the remains of a thigh.

At about the time he should have reached the island the whole village of Shark Bay was awakened by the most horrible drumming noise. It seemed to come from inside the island. It was recognized as the beating of Voodoo drums. It started softly and rose slowly to a thunderous crescendo. Then it died down again and stopped. It lasted about five minutes.

From that moment the island was ju-ju, or obeah, as it is called in Jamaica, and even in daylight canoes kept at a safe distance.

By this time Strangways was interested and he made a full report to London. Since 1950 Jamaica had become an important strategic target thanks to the development by Reynolds Metal and the Kaiser Corporation of huge bauxite deposits found on the island. So far as Strangways was concerned, the activities on Surprise might easily be the erection of a base for one-man submarines in the event of war, particularly since Shark Bay was within range of the route followed by the Reynolds ships to the new bauxite harbour at Ocho Rios, a few miles down the coast.

London followed the report up with Washington and it came to light that the New York syndicate that had purchased the island was wholly owned by Mr Big.

This was three months ago. Strangways was ordered to penetrate the island at all costs and find out what was going on. He mounted quite an operation. He rented a property on the western arm of Shark Bay called Beau Desert. It contained the ruins of one of the famous Jamaican Great Houses of the early nineteenth century and also a modern beach-house directly across from the *Secatur*'s anchorage up against Surprise.

He brought down two very fine swimmers from the naval base at Bermuda and set up a permanent watch on the island through day- and night-glasses. Nothing of a suspicious nature was seen and on a dark calm night he sent out the two swimmers with instructions to make an underwater survey of the foundations of the island.

Strangways described his horror when, an hour after they had left to swim across the three hundred yards of water, the terrible drumming had started up somewhere inside the cliffs of the island.

That night the two men did not return.

On the next day they were both washed up at different parts of the bay. Or rather, the remains left by the shark and barracuda.

At this point in Strangway's narrative, Bond interrupted him.

'Just a minute,' he said. 'What's all this about shark and barracuda? They're not generally savage in these waters. There aren't very many of them round Jamaica and they don't often feed at night. Anyway, I don't believe either of them attack humans unless there's blood in the water. Occasionally they might snap at a white foot out of curiosity. Have they ever behaved like this round Jamaica before?'

'Never been a case since a girl got a foot bitten off in Kingston harbour in 1942,' said Strangways. 'She was being towed by a speedboat, flipping her feet up and down. The white feet must have looked particularly appetizing. Travelling at just the right speed too. Everyone agrees with your theory. And my men had harpoons and knives. I thought I'd done everything to protect them. Dreadful business. You can imagine how I felt about it. Since then we've done nothing except try to get legitimate access to the island via the Colonial Office and Washington. You see, it belongs to an American now. Damn slow business, particularly as there's nothing against these people. They seem to have pretty good protection in Washington and some smart international lawyers. We're absolutely stuck. London told me to hang on until you came.' Strangways took a pull at his whisky and looked expectantly at Bond.

'What are the *Secatur*'s movements?' asked Bond.

'Still in Cuba. Sailing in about a week, according to the CIA.'

'How many trips has she done?'

'About twenty.'

Bond multiplied one hundred and fifty thousand dollars by twenty. If his guess was right, Mr Big had already taken a million pounds in gold out of the island.

'I've made some provisional arrangements for you,' said Strangways. 'There's the house at Beau Desert. I've got you a car, Sunbeam Talbot coupé. New tyres. Fast. Right car for these roads. I've got a good man to act as your factotum. A Cayman Islander called Quarrel. Best swimmer and fisherman in the Caribbean. Terribly keen. Nice chap. And I've borrowed the West Indian Citrus Company's rest-house at Manatee Bay. It's the other end of the island. You could rest up there for a week and get in a bit of training until the *Secatur* comes in. You'll need to be fit if you're going to try to get over to Surprise and I honestly believe that's the only answer. Anything else I can do? I'll be about, of course, but I'll have to stay around Kingston to keep up communications with London and Washington. They'll want to know everything we do. Anything else you'd like me to fix up?'

Bond had been making up his mind.

'Yes,' he said. 'You might ask London to get the Admiralty to lend us one of their frogmen suits complete with compressed-air bottles. Plenty of spares. And a couple of good underwater harpoon guns. The French ones called "Champion" are the best.

Good underwater torch. A commando dagger. All the dope they can get from the Natural History Museum on barracuda and shark. And some of that shark repellent stuff the Americans used in the Pacific. Ask BOAC to fly it all out on their direct service.'

Bond paused. 'Oh yes,' he said. 'And one of those things our saboteurs used against ships in the war. Limpet mine, with assorted fuses.'

17
THE UNDERTAKER'S WIND

PAW-PAW WITH A slice of green lime, a dish piled with red bananas, purple star-apples and tangerines, scrambled eggs and bacon, Blue Mountain coffee, the most delicious in the world, Jamaican marmalade, almost black, and guava jelly.

As Bond, wearing shorts and sandals, had his breakfast on the veranda and gazed down on the sunlit panorama of Kingston and Port Royal, he thought how lucky he was and what wonderful moments of consolation there were for the darkness and danger of his profession.

Bond knew Jamaica well. He had been there on a long assignment just after the war when the Communist headquarters in Cuba was trying to infiltrate the Jamaican labour unions. It had been an untidy and inconclusive job but he had grown to love the great green island and its staunch, humorous people. Now he was glad to be back and to have a whole week of respite before the grim work began again.

After breakfast, Strangways appeared on the veranda with a tall brown-skinned man in a faded blue shirt and old brown twill trousers.

This was Quarrel, the Cayman Islander, and Bond liked him immediately. There was the blood of Cromwellian soldiers and buccaneers in him and his face was strong and angular and his mouth was almost severe. His eyes were grey. It was only the spatulate nose and the pale palms of his hands that were negroid.

Bond shook him by the hand.

'Good morning, Captain,' said Quarrel. Coming from the most famous race of seamen in the world, this was the highest title he knew. But there was no desire to please, or humility, in his voice. He was speaking as mate of the ship and his manner was straightforward and candid.

That moment defined their relationship. It remained that of a

Scots laird with his head stalker; authority was unspoken and there was no room for servility.

After discussing their plans, Bond took the wheel of the little car Quarrel had brought up from Kingston and they started on up the Junction Road leaving Strangways to busy himself with Bond's requirements.

They had got off before nine and it was still cool as they crossed the mountains that run along Jamaica's back like the central ridges of a crocodile's armour. The road wound down towards the northern plains through some of the most beautiful scenery in the world, the tropical vegetation changing with the altitude. The green flanks of the uplands, all feathered with bamboo interspersed with the dark, glinting green of breadfruit and the sudden Bengal fire of Flame of the Forest, gave way to the lower forests of ebony, mahogany, mahoe and logwood. And when they reached the plains of Agualta Vale the green sea of sugar-cane and bananas stretched away to where the distant fringe of glittering shrapnel bursts marked the palm groves along the north coast.

Quarrel was a good companion on the drive and a wonderful guide. He talked about the trapdoor spiders as they passed through the famous palm gardens of Castleton, he told about a fight he had witnessed between a giant centipede and a scorpion and he explained the difference between the male and female paw-paw. He described the poisons of the forest and the healing properties of tropical herbs, the pressure the palm kernel develops to break open its coconut, the length of a humming-bird's tongue, and how crocodiles carry their young in their mouths laid lengthways like sardines in a tin.

He spoke exactly but without expertise, using Jamaican language in which plants 'strive' or 'quail', moths are 'bats', and 'love' is used instead of 'like'. As he talked he would raise his hand in greeting to the people on the road and they would wave back and shout his name.

'You seem to know a lot of people,' said Bond as the driver of a bulging bus with ROMANCE in large letters over the windshield gave him a couple of welcoming blasts on his wind-horn.

'I bin watching Surprise for tree muns, Cap'n,' answered Quarrel, ''n I been travelling this road twice a week. Everyone soon know you in Jamaica. They got good eyes.'

By half past ten they had passed through Port Maria and branched off along the little parochial road that runs down to Shark Bay. Round a turning they suddenly came on it below them and Bond stopped the car and they got out.

The bay was crescent-shaped, perhaps three quarters of a mile wide at its arms. Its blue surface was ruffled by a light breeze blowing from the north-east, the edge of the trade winds that are born five hundred miles away in the Gulf of Mexico and then go on their long journey round the world.

A mile from where they stood, a long line of breakers showed the reef just outside the bay and the narrow untroubled waters of the passage which was the only entrance to the anchorage. In the centre of the crescent, the Isle of Surprise rose a hundred feet sheer out of the water, small waves creaming against its easterly base, calm waters in its lee.

It was nearly round, and it looked like a tall grey cake topped with green icing on a blue china plate.

They had stopped about a hundred feet above the little cluster of fishermen's huts behind the palm-fringed beach of the bay and they were level with the flat green top of the island, half a mile away. Quarrel pointed out the thatched roofs of the wattle-and-daub shanties among the trees in the centre of the island. Bond examined them through Quarrel's binoculars. There was no sign of life except a thin wisp of smoke blowing away with the breeze.

Below them, the water of the bay was pale green on the white sand. Then it deepened to dark blue just before the broken brown of a submerged fringe of inner reef that made a wide semicircle a hundred yards from the island. Then it was dark blue again with patches of lighter blue and aquamarine. Quarrel said that the depth of the *Secatur*'s anchorage was about thirty feet.

To their left, in the middle of the western arm of the bay, deep among the trees behind a tiny white sand beach, was their base of operations, Beau Desert. Quarrel described its layout and Bond stood for ten minutes examining the three-hundred-yard stretch of sea between it and the *Secatur*'s anchorage up against the island.

In all, Bond spent an hour reconnoitring the place, then, without going near their house or the village, they turned the car and got back on the main coast road.

They drove on through the beautiful little banana port of Oracabessa and Ocho Rios with its huge new bauxite plant, along the north shore to Montego Bay, two hours away. It was now February and the season was in full swing. The little village and the straggle of large hotels were bathed in the four months' gold-rush that sees them through the whole year. They stopped at a rest-house on the other side of the wide bay and had lunch and then drove on through the heat of the afternoon to the western tip of the island, two hours further on.

Here, because of the huge coastal swamps, nothing has happened since Columbus used Manatee Bay as a casual anchorage. Jamaican fishermen have taken the place of the Arawak Indians, but otherwise there is the impression that time has stood still.

Bond thought it the most beautiful beach he had ever seen, five miles of white sand sloping easily into the breakers and, behind, the palm trees marching in graceful disarray to the horizon. Under them, the grey canoes were pulled up beside pink mounds of discarded conch shells and among them smoke rose from the palm thatch cabins of the fishermen in the shade between the swamplands and the sea.

In a clearing among the cabins, set on a rough lawn of Bahama grass, was the house on stilts built as a weekend cottage for the employees of the West Indian Citrus Company. It was built on stilts to keep the termites at bay and it was closely wired against mosquito and sandfly. Bond drove off the rough track and parked under the house. While Quarrel chose two rooms and made them comfortable Bond put a towel round his waist and walked through the palm trees to the sea, twenty yards away.

For an hour he swam and lazed in the warm buoyant water, thinking of Surprise and its secret, fixing these three hundred yards in his mind, wondering about the shark and barracuda and the other hazards of the sea, that great library of books one cannot read.

Walking back to the little wooden bungalow, Bond picked up his first sandfly bites. Quarrel chuckled when he saw the flat bumps on his back that would soon start to itch maddeningly.

'Can't do nuthen to keep them away, Cap'n,' he said. 'But Ah kin stop them ticklin. You best take a shower first to git the salt off. They only bites hard for an hour in the evenin' and then they likes salt with their dinner.'

When Bond came out of the shower Quarrel produced an old medicine bottle and swabbed the bites with a brown liquid that smelled of creosote.

'We get more skeeters and sandfly in the Caymans than anywheres else in the world,' he said, 'but we gives them no attention so long as we got this medicine.'

The ten minutes of tropical twilight brought its quick melancholy and then the stars and the three-quarter moon blazed down and the sea died to a whisper. There was the short lull between the two great winds of Jamaica, and then the palms began to whisper again.

Quarrel jerked his head towards the window.

'De "Undertaker's Wind",' he commented.

'How's that?' asked Bond, startled.

'On-and-off-shore breeze de sailors call it,' said Quarrel. 'De Undertaker blow de bad air out of de island night-times from six till six. Then every morning de "Doctor's Wind" come and blow de sweet air in from de sea. Leastwise dats what we calls dem in Jamaica.'

Quarrel looked quizzically at Bond.

'Guess you and de Undertaker's Wind got much de same job, Cap'n,' he said half-seriously.

Bond laughed shortly. 'Glad I don't have to keep the same hours,' he said.

Outside, the crickets and the tree-frogs started to zing and tinkle and the great hawkmoths came to the wire-netting across the windows and clutched it, gazing with trembling ecstasy at the two oil lamps that hung from the cross-beams inside.

Occasionally a pair of fishermen, or a group of giggling girls, would walk by down the beach on their way to the single tiny rum-shop at the point of the bay. No man walked alone for fear of the duppies under the trees, or the rolling calf, the ghastly animal that comes rolling towards you along the ground, its legs in chains and flames coming out of its nostrils.

While Quarrel prepared one of the succulent meals of fish and eggs and vegetables that were to be their staple diet, Bond sat under the light and pored over the books that Strangways had borrowed from the Jamaica Institute, books on the tropical sea and its denizens by Beebe and Allyn and others, and on submarine hunting by Cousteau and Hass. When he set out to cross those three hundred yards of sea, he was determined to do it expertly and to leave nothing to chance. He knew the calibre of Mr Big and he guessed that the defences of Surprise would be technically brilliant. He thought they would not involve simple weapons like guns and high explosives. Mr Big needed to work undisturbed by the police. He had to keep out of reach of the law. He guessed that somehow the forces of the sea had been harnessed to do The Big Man's work for him and it was on these that he concentrated, on murder by shark and barracuda, perhaps by manta ray and octopus.

The facts set out by the naturalists were chilling and awe-inspiring, but the experiences of Cousteau in the Mediterranean and of Hass in the Red Sea and Caribbean were more encouraging.

That night Bond's dreams were full of terrifying encounters with giant squids and stingrays, hammerheads and the saw-teeth of barracuda, so that he whimpered and sweated in his sleep.

On the next day he started his training under the critical, appraising eyes of Quarrel. Every morning he swam a mile up the beach before breakfast and then ran back along the firm sand to the bungalow. At about nine they would set out in a canoe, the single triangular sail taking them fast through the water up the coast to Bloody Bay and Orange Bay where the sand ends in cliffs and small coves and the reef is close in against the coast.

Here they would beach the canoe and Quarrel would take him out with spears and masks and an old underwater harpoon gun on breathtaking expeditions in the sort of waters he would encounter in Shark Bay.

They hunted quietly, a few yards apart, Quarrel moving effortlessly in an element in which he was almost at home. Soon Bond too learned not to fight the sea but always to give and take with the currents and eddies and not to struggle against them, to use judo tactics in the water.

On the first day he came home cut and poisoned by the coral and with a dozen sea-egg spines in his side. Quarrel grinned and treated the wounds with merthiolate and Milton. Then, as every evening, he massaged Bond for half an hour with palm oil, talking quietly the while about the fish they had seen that day, explaining the habits of the carnivores and the ground-feeders, the camouflage of fish and their machinery for changing colour through the bloodstream.

He also had never known fish to attack a man except in desperation or because there was blood in the water. He explained that fish are rarely hungry in tropical waters and that most of their weapons are for defence and not for attack. The only exception, he admitted, was the barracuda. 'Mean fish,' he called them, fearless since they knew no enemy except disease, capable of fifty miles an hour over short distances, and with the worst battery of teeth of any fish in the sea.

One day they shot a ten-pounder that had been hanging round them, melting into the grey distances and then reappearing, silent, motionless in the upper water, its angry tiger's eyes glaring at them so close that they could see its gills working softly and the teeth glinting like a wolf's along its cruel underslung jaw.

Quarrel finally took the harpoon gun from Bond and shot it, badly, through the streamlined belly. It came straight for them, its jaws on their great hinges wide open like a striking rattlesnake. Bond made a wild lunge at it with his spear just as it was on to Quarrel. He missed but the spear went between its jaws. They immediately snapped shut on the steel shaft and as the fish tore the spear out of Bond's hand, Quarrel stabbed at it with his knife and it went mad, dashing through the water with its entrails hanging out, the spear clenched between its teeth, and the harpoon dangling from its body. Quarrel could scarcely hold the line as the fish tried to tear the wide barb through the walls of its stomach, but he moved with it towards a piece of submerged reef and climbed on to it and slowly pulled the fish in.

When Quarrel had cut its throat and they twisted the spear out of its jaws they found bright, deep scratches in the steel.

They took the fish ashore and Quarrel cut its head off and opened the jaws with a piece of wood. The upper jaw rose in an enormous gape, almost at right angles to the lower, and revealed a fantastic battery of razor-sharp teeth, so crowded that they overlapped like shingles on a roof. Even the tongue had several runs of small pointed recurved teeth and, in front, there were two huge fangs that projected forward like a snake's.

Although it only weighed just over ten pounds, it was over four feet long, a nickel bullet of muscle and hard flesh.

'We shoot no more cudas,' said Quarrel. 'But for you I been in hospital for a month and mebbe lost ma face. It was foolish of me. If we swim towards it, it gone away. Dey always do. Dey cowards like all fish. Doan you worry bout those.' He pointed at the teeth. 'You never see dem again.'

'I hope not,' said Bond. 'I haven't got a face to spare.'

By the end of the week, Bond was sunburned and hard. He had cut his cigarettes down to ten a day and had not had a single drink. He could swim two miles without tiring, his hand was completely healed and all the scales of big city life had fallen from him.

Quarrel was pleased. 'You ready for Surprise, Cap'n,' he said, 'and I not like be de fish what tries to eat you.'

Towards nightfall on the eighth day they came back to the rest-house to find Strangways waiting for them.

'I've got some good news for you,' he said, 'your friend Felix Leiter's going to be all right. At all events he's not going to die. They've had to amputate the remains of an arm and a leg. Now the plastic surgery chaps have started building up his face. They called me up from St Petersburg yesterday. Apparently he insisted on getting a message to you. First thing he thought of when he could think at all. Says he's sorry not to be with you and to tell you not to get your feet wet — or at any rate, not as wet as he did.'

Bond's heart was full. He looked out of the window. 'Tell him to get well quickly,' he said abruptly. 'Tell him I miss him.' He looked back into the room. 'Now what about the gear? Everything okay?'

'I've got it all,' said Strangways, 'and the *Secatur* sails tomorrow for Surprise. After clearing at Port Maria, they should anchor before nightfall. Mr Big's on board — only the second time he's been down here. Oh and they've got a woman with them. Girl called Solitaire according to the CIA. Know anything about her?'

'Not much,' said Bond. 'But I'd like to get her away from him. She's not one of his team.'

'Sort of damsel in distress,' said the romantic Strangways. 'Good show. According to the CIA she's a corker.'

But Bond had gone out on the veranda and was gazing up at his stars. Never before in his life had there been so much to play for. The secret of the treasure, the defeat of a great criminal, the smashing of a Communist spy ring, and the destruction of a tentacle of SMERSH, the cruel machine that was his own private target. And now Solitaire, the ultimate personal prize.

The stars winked down their cryptic morse and he had no key to their cipher.

18

BEAU DESERT

STRANGWAYS WENT BACK alone after dinner and Bond agreed that they would follow at first light. Strangways left him a fresh pile of books and pamphlets on shark and barracuda and Bond went through them with rapt attention.

They added little to the practical lore he had picked up from Quarrel. They were all by scientists and much of the data on attacks was from the beaches of the Pacific where a flashing body in the thick surf would excite any inquisitive fish.

But there seemed to be general agreement that the danger to underwater swimmers with breathing equipment was far less than to surface swimmers. They might be attacked by almost any of the shark family, particularly when the shark was stimulated and excited by blood in the water, by the smell of a swimmer, or by the sensory vibration set up by an injured person in the water. But they could sometimes be frightened off, he read, by loud noises in the water — even by shouting below the surface, and they would often flee if a swimmer chased them.

The most successful form of shark repellent, according to US Naval Research Laboratory tests, was a combination of copper acetate and a dark nigrosine dye, and cakes of this mixture were apparently now attached to the Mae Wests of all the US Armed Forces.

Bond called in Quarrel. The Cayman Islander was scornful until Bond read out to him what the Navy Department had to say about their researches at the end of the war among packs of sharks stimulated by what was described as 'extreme mob behaviour conditions': ' . . . Sharks were attracted to the back of the shrimp boat with trash fish,' read out Bond. 'Sharks appeared as a slashing, splashing shoal. We prepared a tub of fresh fish and another tub of fish mixed with repellent powder. We got up to the shoal of sharks and the photographer started his camera. I shovelled over the plain fish for 30 seconds while the sharks with much splashing, ate them. Then I started on the repellent fish and shovelled for 30 seconds repeating the procedure 3 times. On the first trial the sharks were quite ferocious in feeding on plain fish right at the stern of the boat. They cut fish for only about 5 seconds after the repellent mixture was thrown over. A few came back when the plain fish were put out immediately following the repellent. On a second trial 30 minutes later, a ferocious school fed for the 30 seconds that plain fish were supplied, but left as soon as the repellent struck the water. There were no attacks on fish while the repellent was in the water. On the third trial we could not get the sharks nearer than 20 yards of the stern of the boat.'

'What do you make of that?' asked Bond.

'You better have some of dat stuff,' said Quarrel, impressed against his will.

Bond was inclined to agree with him. Washington had cabled that cakes of the stuff were on the way. But they had not yet arrived and were not expected for another forty-eight hours. If the repellent did not arrive, Bond was not dismayed. He could not imagine that he would encounter such dangerous conditions in his underwater swim to the island.

Before he went to bed, he finally decided that nothing would attack him unless there was blood in the water or unless he communicated fear to a fish that threatened. As for octopus, scorpion fish and morays, he would just have to watch where he put his feet. To his mind, the three-inch spines of the black sea-eggs were the greatest hazard to normal underwater swimming in the tropics and the pain they caused would not be enough to interfere with his plans.

They left before six in the morning and were at Beau Desert by half past ten.

The property was a beautiful old plantation of about a thousand acres with the ruins of a fine Great House commanding the bay. It was given over to pimento and citrus inside a fringe of hardwoods and palms and had a history dating back to the time of Cromwell. The romantic name was in the fashion of the eighteenth century when Jamaican properties were called Bellair, Bellevue, Boscobel, Harmony, Nymphenburg or had names like Prospect, Content or Repose.

A track, out of sight of the island in the bay, led them among the trees down to the little beach-house. After the week's picnic at Manatee Bay, the bathrooms and comfortable bamboo furniture seemed very luxurious and the brightly coloured rugs were like velvet under Bond's hardened feet.

Through the slats of the jalousies Bond looked across the little garden, aflame with hibiscus, bougainvillaea and roses, which ended in the tiny crescent of white sand half obscured by the trunks of the palms. He sat on the arm of a chair and let his eyes go on, inch by inch, across the different blues and browns of sea and reef until they met the base of the island. The upper half of it was obscured by the dipping feathers of the palm trees in the foreground, but the stretch of vertical cliff within his vision looked grey and formidable in the half-shadow cast by the hot sun.

Quarrel cooked lunch on a primus stove so that no smoke would betray them and in the afternoon Bond slept and then went over the gear from London that had been sent across from Kingston by Strangways. He tried on the thin black rubber frogman's suit that covered him from the skull-tight helmet with the perspex window to the long black flippers over his feet. It fitted like a glove and Bond blessed the efficiency of M's 'Q' Branch.

They tested the twin cylinders each containing a thousand litres of free air compressed to two hundred atmospheres and Bond found the manipulation of the demand valve and the reserve mechanism simple and foolproof. At the depth he would be working the supply of air would last him for nearly two hours under water.

There was a new and powerful Champion harpoon gun and a commando dagger of the type devised by Wilkinsons during the war. Finally, in a box covered with danger-labels, there was the heavy limpet mine, a flat cone of explosive on a base, studded with wide copper bosses, so powerfully magnetized that the mine would stick like a clam to any metal hull. There were a dozen pencil-shaped metal and glass fuses set for ten minutes to eight hours and a careful memorandum of instructions that were as simple as the rest of the gear. There was even a box of benzedrine tablets to give endurance and heightened perception during the operation and an assortment of underwater torches including one that threw only a tiny pencil-thin beam.

Bond and Quarrel went through everything, testing joints and contacts until they were satisfied that nothing further remained to be done, then Bond went down among the trees and gazed and gazed at the waters of the bay, guessing at depths, tracing routes through the broken reef and estimating the path of the moon which would be his only point of reckoning on the tortuous journey.

At five o'clock, Strangways arrived with news of the *Secatur*.

'They've cleared Port Maria,' he said. 'They'll be here in ten minutes at the outside. Mr Big had a passport in the name of Gallia and the girl in the name of Latrelle, Simone Latrelle. She was in her cabin, prostrate with what the negro captain of the *Secatur* described as seasickness. It may have been. Scores of empty fish-tanks on board. More than a hundred. Otherwise nothing suspicious and they were given a clean bill. I wanted to go on board as one of the Customs team but I thought it best that the show should be absolutely normal. Mr Big stuck to his cabin. He was reading when they went to see his papers. How's the gear?'

'Perfect,' said Bond. 'Guess we'll operate tomorrow night. Hope there's a bit of a wind. If the air-bubbles are spotted we shall be in a mess.'

Quarrel came in. 'She's coming through the reef now, Cap'n.'

They went down as close to the shore as they dared and put their glasses on her.

She was a handsome craft, black with a grey superstructure, seventy feet long and built for speed — at least twenty knots, Bond guessed. He knew her history, built for a millionaire in 1947 and powered with twin General Motors Diesels, steel hull and all the latest wireless gadgets including ship-to-shore telephone and Decca navigator. She was wearing the Red Ensign at her cross-trees and the Stars and Stripes aft and she was making about three knots through the twenty-foot opening of the reef.

She turned sharply inside the reef and came down to seaward of the island. When she was below it, she put her helm hard over and came up with the island to port. At the same time three negroes in white ducks came running down the cliff steps to the narrow jetty and stood by to catch lines. There was a minimum of backing and filling before she was made fast just opposite to the watchers ashore and the two anchors roared down among the rocks and coral scattered round the island's foundations in the sand. She lay well secured even against a 'Norther'. Bond estimated there would be about twenty feet of water below her keel.

As they watched, the huge figure of Mr Big appeared on deck. He stepped on to the jetty and started slowly to climb the steep cliff steps. He paused often, and Bond thought of the diseased heart pumping laboriously in the great grey-black body.

He was followed by two negro members of the crew hauling up a light stretcher on which a body was strapped. Through his glasses Bond could see Solitaire's black hair. Bond was worried and puzzled and he felt a tightening of the heart at her nearness. He prayed the stretcher was only a precaution to prevent Solitaire from being recognized from the shore.

Then a chain of twelve men was established up the steps and the fish-tanks were handed up one by one. Quarrel counted a hundred and twenty of them.

Then some stores went up by the same method.

'Not taking much up this time,' commented Strangways when the operation ceased. 'Only half a dozen cases gone up. Generally about fifty. Can't be staying long.'

He had hardly finished speaking before a fish-tank, which their glasses showed was half full of water and sand, was being gingerly passed back to the ship, down the human ladder of hands. Then another and another, at about five-minute intervals.

'My God,' said Strangways. 'They're loading her up already. That means they'll be sailing in the morning. Wonder if it means they've decided to clean the place out and that this is the last cargo.'

Bond watched carefully for a while and then they walked quietly up through the trees, leaving Quarrel to report developments.

They sat down in the living-room and while Strangways mixed himself a whisky-and-soda, Bond gazed out of the window and marshalled his thoughts.

It was six o'clock and the fireflies were beginning to show in the shadows. The pale primrose moon was already high up in the eastern sky and the day was dying swiftly at their backs. A light breeze was ruffling the bay and the scrolls of small waves were unfurling on the white beach across the lawn. A few small clouds, pink and orange in the sunset, were meandering by overhead and the palm trees clashed softly in the cool Undertaker's Wind.

Undertaker's Wind, thought Bond and smiled wryly. So it would have to be tonight. The only chance and the conditions were so nearly perfect. Except that the shark repellent stuff would not arrive in time. And that was only a refinement. There was no excuse. This was what he had travelled two thousand miles and five deaths to do. And yet he shivered at the prospect of the dark adventure under the sea that he had already put off in his mind until tomorrow. Suddenly he loathed and feared the sea and everything in it. The millions of tiny antennae that would stir and point as he went by that night, the eyes that would wake and watch him, the pulses that would miss for the hundredth of a second and then go beating quietly on, the jelly tendrils that would grope and reach for him, as blind in the light as in the dark.

He would be walking through thousands of millions of secrets. In three hundred yards, alone and cold, he would be blundering through a forest of mystery towards a deadly citadel whose guardians had already killed three men. He, Bond, after a week's paddling with his nanny beside him in the sunshine, was going out tonight, in a few hours, to walk alone under that black sheet of water. It was crazy, unthinkable. Bond's flesh cringed and his fingers dug into his wet palms.

There was a knock on the door and Quarrel came in. Bond was glad to get up and move away from the window to where Strangways was enjoying his drink under a shaded reading light.

'They're working with lights now, Cap'n,' Quarrel said with a grin. 'Still a tank every five minutes. I figure that'll be ten hours' work. Be through about four in the morning. Won't sail before six. Too dangerous to try the passage without plenty light.'

Quarrel's warm grey eyes in the splendid mahogany face were looking into Bond's, waiting for orders.

'I'll start at ten sharp,' Bond found himself saying. 'From the rocks to the left of the beach. Can you get us some dinner and then get the gear out on to the lawn? Conditions are perfect. I'll be over there in half an hour.' He counted on his fingers. 'Give me fuses for five to eight hours. And the quarter-hour one in reserve in case anything goes wrong. Okay?'

'Aye aye, Cap'n,' said Quarrel. 'You jes leave 'em all to me.'

He went out.

Bond looked at the whisky bottle, then he made up his mind and poured half a glass on top of three ice cubes. He took the box of benzedrine tablets out of his pocket and slipped a tablet between his teeth.

'Here's luck,' he said to Strangways and took a deep swallow. He sat down and enjoyed the tough hot taste of his first drink for more than a week. 'Now,' he said, 'tell me exactly what they do when they're ready to sail. How long it takes them to clear the island and get through the reef. If it's the last time, don't forget they'll be taking off an extra six men and some stores. Let's try to work it out as closely as we can.'

In a moment Bond was immersed in a sea of practical details and the shadow of fear had fled back to the dark pools under the palm trees.

Exactly at ten o'clock, with nothing but anticipation and excitement in him, the shimmering black bat-like figure slipped off the rocks into ten feet of water and vanished under the sea.

'Go safely,' said Quarrel to the spot where Bond had disappeared. He crossed himself. Then he and Strangways moved back through the shadows to the house to sleep uneasily in watches and wait fearfully for what might come.

19

VALLEY OF SHADOWS

BOND WAS CARRIED straight to the bottom by the weight of the limpet mine that he had secured to his chest with tapes and by the leaded belt which he wore round his waist to correct the buoyancy of the compressed air cylinders.

He didn't pause for an instant but immediately streaked across the first fifty yards of open sand in a fast crawl, his face just above the sand. The long webbed feet would almost have doubled his normal speed if he had not been hampered by the weight he was carrying and by the light harpoon gun in his left hand, but he travelled fast and in under a minute he came to rest in the shadow of a mass of sprawling coral.

He paused and examined his sensations.

He was warm in the rubber suit, warmer than he would have been swimming in the sunshine. He found his movements very easy and breathing perfectly simple so long as his breath was even and relaxed. He watched the tell-tale bubbles streaming up against the coral in a fountain of silver pearls and prayed that the small waves were hiding them.

In the open he had been able to see perfectly. The light was soft and milky but not strong enough to melt the mackerel shadows of the surface waves that chequered the sand. Now, up against the reef, there was no reflection from the bottom, and the shadows under the rocks were black and impenetrable.

He risked a quick glance with his pencil torch and immediately the underbelly of the mass of brown tree-coral came alive. Anemones with crimson centres waved their velvet tentacles at him, a colony of black sea-eggs moved their toledo-steel spines in sudden alarm and a hairy sea-centipede halted in its hundred strides and questioned with its eyeless head. In the sand at the base of the tree a toad-fish softly drew its hideous warty head back into its funnel and a number of flower-like sea-worms whisked out of sight down their gelatinous tubes. A covey of bejewelled butterfly and angel fish flirted into the light and he marked the flat spiral of a long-spined star shell.

Bond tucked the light back in his belt.

Above him the surface of the sea was a canopy of quicksilver. It crackled softly like fat frying in a saucepan. Ahead the moonlight glinted down into the deep crooked valley that sloped down and away on the route he had to follow. He left his sheltering tree of coral and walked softly forward. Now it was not so easy. The light was tricky and bad and the petrified forest of the coral reef was full of culs-de-sac and tempting but misleading avenues.

Sometimes he had to climb almost to the surface to get over a tangled scrub of tree- and antler-coral and when this happened he profited by it to check his position with the moon that glowed like a huge pale rocket-burst through the broken water. Sometimes the hourglass waist of a niggerhead gave him shelter and he rested for a few moments knowing that the small froth of his air-bubbles would be hidden by the jagged knob protruding above the surface. Then he would focus his eyes on the phosphorescent scribbles of the minute underwater night-life and perceive whole colonies and populations about their microscopic business.

There were no big fish about, but many lobsters were out of their holes looking huge and prehistoric in the magnifying lens of the water. Their stalk-like eyes glared redly at him and their foot-long spined antennae asked him for the password. Occasionally they scuttled nervously backwards into their shelters, their powerful tails kicking up the sand, and crouched on the tips of their eight hairy feet, waiting for the danger to pass. Once the great streamers of a Portuguese man-of-war floated slowly by. They almost reached his head from the surface, fifteen feet away, and he remembered the whiplash of a sting from the contact of one of their tendrils that had burned for three of his days at Manatee Bay. If they caught a man across the heart they could kill him. He saw several green and speckled moray eels, the latter moving like big yellow and black snakes along patches of sand, the green ones baring their teeth from some hole in the rock, and several West Indian blowfish, like brown owls with huge soft green eyes. He poked at one with the end of his gun and it swelled out to the size of a football and became a mass of dangerous white spines. Wide sea fans swayed and beckoned in the eddies, and in the grey valleys they caught the light of the moon and waved spectrally, like fragments of the shrouds of men buried at sea. Often in the shadows there were unexplained, heavy movements and swirls in the water and the sudden glare of large eyes at once extinguished. Then Bond would whirl round, thumbing up the safety-catch on his harpoon gun, and stare back into the darkness. But he shot at nothing and nothing attacked him as he scrambled and slithered through the reef.

The hundred yards of coral took him a quarter of an hour. When he got through and rested on a round lump of brain-coral under the shelter of a last niggerhead, he was glad that nothing but a hundred yards of grey-white water lay in front of him. He still felt perfectly fresh and the elation and clarity of mind produced by the benzedrine were still with him, but the gauntlet of hazards through the reef had been a constant fret, with the risk of tearing his rubber skin always on his mind. Now the forest of razor-blade coral was behind, to be exchanged for shark and barracuda or perhaps a sudden stick of dynamite dropped into the centre of the little flower of his bubbles on the surface.

It was while he was measuring the dangers ahead that the octopus got him. Round both ankles.

He had been sitting with his feet on the sand and suddenly they were manacled to the base of the round toadstool of coral on which he was resting. Even as he realized what had happened a tentacle began to snake up his leg and another one, purple in the dim light, wandered down his webbed left foot.

He gave a start of fear and disgust and at once he was on his feet, shuffling and straining to get away. But there was no inch of yield and his movements only gave the octopus an opportunity to pull his heels tighter under the overhang of the round rock. The strength of the brute was prodigious and Bond could feel his balance going fast. In a moment he would be pulled down flat on his face and then, hampered by the mine on his chest and the cylinders on his back, it might be almost impossible to get at the beast.

Bond snatched his dagger out of his belt and jabbed down between his legs. But the overhang of the rock impeded him and he was terrified of cutting his rubber skin. Suddenly he was toppled over, lying on the sand. At once his feet began to be drawn into a wide lateral cleft under the rock. He scrabbled at the sand and tried to curl round to get within range with the dagger. But the thick hump of the mine protruding from his chest prevented him. On the edge of panic, he remembered the harpoon gun. Before, he had dismissed it as being a hopeless weapon at that short range, but now it was the only chance. It lay on the sand where he had left it. He reached for it and put up the safety-catch. The mine prevented him from aiming. He slid the barrel along his legs and probed each of his feet with the tip of the harpoon to find the gap between them. At once a tentacle seized the steel tip and began tugging. The gun slipped between his manacled feet and he pulled the trigger blindly.

Immediately a great cloud of viscous, stringy ink rolled out of the cleft towards his face. But one leg was free and then the other and he whipped them round and under him and seized the haft of the three-foot harpoon where it disappeared under the rock. He pulled and strained until, with a rending of flesh, it came away from the black fog that hung over the hole. Panting, he got up and stood away from the rock, the sweat pouring down his face under the mask. Above him, the tell-tale stream of silver bubbles rose straight to the surface and he cursed the wounded 'pus-feller' in its lair.

But there was no time to worry further with it and he reloaded his gun and struck out with the moon over his right shoulder.

Now he made good going through the misty grey water and he concentrated only on keeping his face a few inches above the sand and his head well down to streamline his body. Once, out of the corner of his eye, he saw a stingray as big as a ping-pong table shuffle out of his path, the tips of its great speckled wings beating like a bird's, its long horned tail streaming out behind it. But he paid it no attention, remembering that Quarrel had said that rays never attack except in self-defence. He reflected that it had probably come in over the outer reef to lay its eggs, or 'Mermaids' Purses' as the fishermen call them, because they are shaped like a pillow with a stiff black string at each corner, on the sheltered sandy bottom.

Many shadows of big fish lazed across the moonlit sand, some as long as himself. When one followed beside him for at least a minute he looked up to see the white belly of a shark ten feet above him like a glaucous tapering airship. Its blunt nose was buried inquisitively in his stream of air-bubbles. The wide sickle slit of its mouth looked like a puckered scar. It leant sideways and glanced down at him out of one hard pink naked eye, then it wobbled its great scythe-shaped tail and moved slowly into the wall of grey mist.

He frightened a family of squids, ranging from about six pounds down to an infant of six ounces, frail and luminous in the half-light, hanging almost vertical in a diminishing chorus-line. They righted themselves and shot off with streamlined jet propulsion.

Bond rested for a moment about half way and then went on. Now there were barracuda about, big ones of up to twenty pounds. They looked just as deadly as he had remembered them. They glided above him like silver submarines, looking down out of their angry tigers' eyes. They were curious about him and about his bubbles and they followed him, around and above him, like a pack of silent wolves. By the time Bond met the first bit of coral that meant he was coming up with the island there must have been twenty of them moving quietly, watchfully, in and out of the opaque wall that enclosed him.

Bond's skin cringed under the black rubber but he could do nothing about them and he concentrated on his objective.

Suddenly there was a long metallic shape hanging in the water above him. Behind it there was a jumble of broken rock leading steeply upwards.

It was the keel of the *Secatur* and Bond's heart thumped in his chest.

He looked at the Rolex watch on his wrist. It was three minutes past eleven o'clock. He selected the seven-hour fuse from the handful he extracted from a zipped side-pocket and inserted it in the fuse pocket of the mine and pushed it home. The rest of the fuses he buried in the sand so that if he was captured the mine would not be betrayed.

As he swam up, carrying the mine between his hands, bottom upwards, he was aware of a commotion in the water behind him. A barracuda flashed by, its jaws half open, almost hitting him, its eyes fixed on something at his back. But Bond was intent only on the centre of the ship's keel and on a point about three feet above it.

The mine almost dragged him the last few feet, its huge magnets straining for the metallic kiss with the hull. Bond had to pull hard against it to prevent the clang of contact. Then it was silently in place and with its weight removed Bond had to swim strongly to counter his new buoyancy and get down again and away from the surface.

It was as he turned to swim towards the twin propellers on his way to the shelter of the rocks that he suddenly saw the terrible things that had been going on behind him.

The great pack of barracudas seemed to have gone mad. They were whirling and snapping in the water like hysterical dogs. Three sharks that had joined them were charging through the water with a clumsier frenzy. The water was boiling with the dreadful fish and Bond was slammed in the face and buffeted again and again within a few yards. At any moment he knew his rubber skin would be torn with the flesh below it and then the pack would be on him.

'Extreme mob behaviour conditions.' The Navy Department's phrase flashed into his mind. This was just when he might have saved himself with the shark repellent stuff. Without it he might only have a few more minutes to live.

In desperation he threshed through the water along the ship's keel, the safety-catch up on the harpoon gun that was now only a toy in the face of this drove of maddened cannibal fish.

He reached the two big copper screws and clung to one of them, panting, his lips drawn back from his teeth in a snarl of fear, his eyes distended as he faced the frenzy of the boiling sea around him.

He at once saw that the mouths of the hurtling, darting fish were half open and that they were plunging in and out of a brownish cloud, spreading downwards from the surface. Close to him a barracuda hung for an instant, something brown and glittering in its jaws. It gave a great swallow and then swirled back into the mêlée.

At the same time he noticed that it was getting darker. He looked up and saw with dawning comprehension that the quicksilver surface of the sea had turned red, a horrible glinting crimson.

Threads of the stuff drifted within his reach. He hooked some towards him with the end of his gun. Held the end close up against his glass mask.

There was no doubt about it.

Up above, someone was spraying the surface of the sea with blood and offal.

20

BLOODY MORGAN'S CAVE

IMMEDIATELY BOND UNDERSTOOD why all these barracuda and shark were lurking round the island, how they were kept frenzied with bloodlust by this nightly banquet, why, against all reason, the three men had been washed up half-eaten by the fish.

Mr Big had just harnessed the forces of the sea for his protection. It was a typical invention — imaginative, technically foolproof and very easy to operate.

Even as Bond's mind grasped it all, something hit him a terrific blow in the shoulder and a twenty-pound barracuda backed away, black rubber and flesh hanging from its jaws. Bond felt no pain as he let go of the bronze propeller and threshed wildly for the rocks, only a horrible sickness in the pit of his stomach at the thought of part of himself between those hundred razor-sharp teeth. Water started to ooze between the close-fitting rubber and his skin. It would not be long before it penetrated up his neck and into the mask.

He was just going to give up and shoot the twenty feet to the surface when he saw a wide fissure in the rocks in front of him. Beside it a great boulder lay on its side and somehow he got behind it. He turned from the partial shelter it gave just in time to see the same barracuda coming at him again, its upper jaw held at right angles to the lower for its infamous gaping strike.

Bond fired almost blind with the harpoon gun. The rubber thongs whammed down the barrel and the barbed harpoon caught the big fish in the centre of its raised upper jaw, pierced it and stuck with half the shaft and the line still free.

The barracuda stopped dead in its tracks, three feet from Bond's stomach. It tried to get its jaws together and then gave a mighty shake of its long reptile's head. Then it shot away, zigzagging madly, the gun and line, jerked from Bond's hand, streaming behind it. Bond knew that the other fish would be on to it, tearing it to bits, before it had gone a hundred yards.

Bond thanked God for the diversion. His shoulder was now surrounded by a cloud of blood. In a matter of seconds the other fish would catch the scent. He slipped round the boulder with the thought that he would scramble up under the shelter of the jetty and somehow hide himself above the level of the sea until he had made a fresh plan.

Then he saw the cave that the boulder had hidden.

It was really almost a door into the base of the island. If Bond had not been swimming for his life he could have walked in. As it was, he dived straight through the opening and only stopped when several yards separated him from the glimmering entrance.

Then he stood upright on the soft sand and switched on his torch. A shark might conceivably come in after him but in the confined space it would be almost impossible for it to bring its underslung mouth to bear on him. It would certainly not come in with a rush for even the shark is frightened of hazarding its tough skin among rocks, and he would have plenty of chance of going for its eyes with his dagger.

Bond shone his torch on the ceiling and sides of the cave. It had certainly been fashioned or finished by man. Bond guessed that it had been dug outwards from somewhere in the centre of the island.

'At least another twenty yards to go, men,' Bloody Morgan must have said to the slave overseers. And then the picks would have burst suddenly through to the sea and a welter of arms and legs and screaming mouths, gagged for ever with water, would have hurtled back into the rock to join the bodies of other witnesses.

The great boulder at the entrance would have been put in position to seal the seaward exit. The Shark Bay fisherman who suddenly disappeared six months before must have one day found it rolled away by a storm or by the tidal wave following a hurricane. Then he had found the treasure and had known he would need help to dispose of it. A white man would cheat him. Better go to the great negro gangster in Harlem and make the best terms he could. The gold belonged to the black men who had died to hide it. It should go back to the black men.

Standing there, swaying in the slight current in the tunnel, Bond guessed that one more barrel of cement had splashed into the mud of the Harlem River.

It was then that he heard the drums.

Out amongst the big fish he had heard a soft thunder in the water that had grown as he entered the cave. But he had thought it was only the waves against the base of the island, and anyway he had had other things to think about.

But now he could distinguish a definite rhythm and the sound boomed and swelled around him in a muffled roar as if he himself was imprisoned inside a vast kettle-drum. The water seemed to tremble with it. He guessed its double purpose. It was a great fish-call used, when intruders were about, to attract and excite the fish still further. Quarrel had told him how the fishermen at night beat the sides of their canoes with the paddle to wake and bring the fish. This must be the same idea. And at the same time it would be a sinister Voodoo warning to the people on shore, made doubly effective when the dead body was washed up on the following day.

Another of Mr Big's refinements, thought Bond. Another spark thrown off by that extraordinary mind.

Well, at least he knew where he was now. The drums meant that he had been spotted. What would Strangways and Quarrel think as they heard them? They would just have to sit and sweat it out. Bond had guessed the drums were some sort of trick and he had made them promise not to interfere unless the *Secatur* got safely away. That would mean that all Bond's plans had failed. He had told Strangways where the gold was hidden and the ship would have to be intercepted on the high seas.

Now the enemy was alerted, but they would not know who he was nor that he was still alive. He would have to go on if only to stop Solitaire at all costs from sailing in the doomed ship.

Bond looked at his watch. It was half an hour after midnight. So far as Bond was concerned, it might have been a week since he started his lonely voyage through the sea of dangers.

He felt the Beretta under his rubber skin and wondered if it was already ruined by the water that had got in through the rent made by the barracuda's teeth.

Then, the roar of the drums getting louder every moment, he moved on into the cave, his torch throwing a tiny pinpoint of light ahead of him.

He had gone about ten yards when a faint glimmer showed in the water ahead of him. He dowsed the torch and went cautiously towards it. The sandy floor of the cave started to move upwards and with every yard the light grew brighter. Now he could see dozens of small fish playing around him and ahead the water seemed full of them, attracted into the cave by the light. Crabs peered from the small crevices in the rocks and a baby octopus flattened itself into a phosphorescent star against the ceiling.

Then he could make out the end of the cave and a wide shining pool beyond it, the white sandy bottom as bright as day. The throb of the drums was very loud. He stopped in the shadow of the entrance and saw that the surface was only a few inches away and that lights were shining down into the pool.

Bond was in a quandary. Any further step and he would be in full view of anyone looking at the pool. As he stood, debating with himself, he was horrified to see a thin red cloud of blood spreading beyond the entrance from his shoulder. He had forgotten the wound, but now it began to throb, and when he moved his arm the pain shot through it. There was also the thin stream of bubbles from the cylinders, but he hoped these were just creeping up to burst unnoticed at the lip of the entrance.

Even as he drew back a few inches into his hole, his future was settled for him.

Above his head there was a single huge splash and two negroes, naked except for the glass masks over their faces, were on to him, long daggers held like lances in their left hands.

Before his hand reached the knife at his belt they had seized both his arms and were hauling him to the surface.

Hopelessly, helplessly, Bond let himself be man-handled out of the pool on to flat sand. He was pulled to his feet and the zips of his rubber suit were torn open. His helmet was snatched off his head and his holster from his shoulder and suddenly he was standing among the debris of his black skin, like a flayed snake, naked except for his brief swimming trunks. Blood oozed down from the jagged hole in his left shoulder.

When his helmet came off Bond was almost deafened by the shattering boom and stutter of the drums. The noise was in him and all around him. The hastening syncopated rhythm galloped and throbbed in his blood. It seemed enough to wake all Jamaica. Bond grimaced and clenched his senses against the buffeting tempest of noise. Then his guards turned him round and he was faced with a scene so extraordinary that the sound of the drums receded and all his consciousness was focused through his eyes.

In the foreground, at a green baize card-table, littered with papers, in a folding chair, sat Mr Big, a pen in his hand, looking incuriously at him. A Mr Big in a well-cut fawn tropical suit, with a white shirt and black knitted silk tie. His broad chin rested on his left hand and he looked up at Bond as if he had been disturbed in his office by a member of the staff asking for a raise in salary. He looked polite but faintly bored.

A few steps away from him, sinister and incongruous, the scarecrow effigy of Baron Samedi, erect on a rock, gaped at Bond from under its bowler hat.

Mr Big took his hand off his chin, and his great golden eyes looked Bond over from top to toe.

'Good morning, Mister James Bond,' he said at last, throwing his flat voice against the dying crescendo of the drums. 'The fly has indeed been a long time coming to the spider, or perhaps I should say "the minnow to the whale". You left a pretty wake of bubbles after the reef.'

He leant back in his chair and was silent. The drums softly thudded and boomed.

So it was the fight with the octopus that had betrayed him. Bond's mind automatically registered the fact as his eyes moved on past the man at the table.

He was in a rock chamber as big as a church. Half the floor was taken up with the clear white pool from which he had come and which verged into aquamarine and then blue near the black hole of the underwater entrance. Then there was the narrow strip of sand on which he was standing and the rest of the floor was smooth flat rock dotted with a few grey and white stalagmites.

Some way behind Mr Big, steep steps mounted towards a vaulted ceiling from which short limestone stalactites hung down. From their white nipples water dripped intermittently into the pool or on to the points of the young stalagmites that rose towards them from the floor.

A dozen bright arc lights were fixed high up on the walls and reflected golden highlights from the naked chests of a group of negroes standing to his left on the stone floor rolling their eyes and watching Bond, their teeth showing in delighted cruel grins.

Round their black and pink feet, in a debris of broken timber and rusty iron hoops, mildewed strips of leather and disintegrating canvas, was a blazing sea of gold coin — yards, piles, cascades of round golden specie from which the black legs rose as if they had been halted in the middle of a walk through flame.

Beside them were piled row upon row of shallow wooden trays. There were some on the floor partly filled with gold coin, and at the bottom of the steps a single negro had stopped on his way up and he was holding one of the trays in his hands and it was full of gold coin, four cylindrical rows of it, held out as if for sale between his hands.

Further to the left, in a corner of the chamber, two negroes stood by a bellying iron cauldron suspended over three hissing blow lamps, its base glowing red. They held iron skimmers in their hands and these were splashed with gold half way up the long handles. Beside them was a towering jumble of gold objects, plate, altar pieces, drinking vessels, crosses, and a stack of gold ingots of various sizes. Along the wall near them were ranged rows of metal cooling trays, their segmented surfaces gleaming yellow, and there was an empty tray on the floor near the cauldron and a long gold-spattered ladle, its handle bound with cloth.

Squatting on the floor not far from Mr Big, a single negro had a knife in one hand and a jewelled goblet in the other. Beside him on a tin plate was a pile of gems that winked dully, red and blue and green, in the glare of the arcs.

It was warm and airless in the great rock chamber and yet Bond shivered as his eyes took in the whole splendid scene, the blazing violet-white lights, the shimmering bronze of the sweating bodies, the bright glare of the gold, the rainbow pool of jewels and the milk and aquamarine of the pool. He shivered at the beauty of it all, at this fabulous petrified ballet in the great treasure-house of Bloody Morgan.

His eyes came back to the square of green baize and the great zombie face and he looked at the face and into the wide yellow eyes with awe, almost with reverence.

'Stop the drums,' said The Big Man to no one in particular. They had died almost to a whisper, a lisping beat right on the pulse of the blood. One of the negroes took two softly clanging steps amongst the gold coin and bent down. There was a portable phonograph on the floor and a powerful amplifier leant beside it against the rock wall. There was a click and the drums stopped. The negro shut the lid of the machine and went back to his place.

'Get on with the work,' said Mr Big, and at once all the figures started moving as if a penny had been put in a slot. The cauldron was stirred, the gold was picked up and clinked into the boxes, the man picked busily at his jewelled goblet and the negro with the tray of gold moved on up the stairs.

Bond stood and dripped sweat and blood.

The Big Man bent over the lists on his table and wrote one or two figures with his pen.

Bond stirred and felt the prick of a dagger over his kidneys.

The Big Man put down his pen and got slowly to his feet. He moved away from the table.

'Take over,' he said to one of Bond's guards and the naked man walked round the table and sat down in Mr Big's chair and picked up the pen.

'Bring him up.' Mr Big walked over to the steps in the rock and started to climb them slowly.

Bond felt a prick in his side. He stepped out of the debris of his black skin and followed the slowly climbing figure.

No one looked up from his work. No one would slacken when Mr Big was out of sight. No one would put a jewel or a coin in his mouth.

Baron Samedi was left in charge.

Only his Zombie had gone from the cave.

21

'GOOD NIGHT TO YOU BOTH'

THEY CLIMBED SLOWLY up, past an open door near the ceiling, for about forty feet and then paused on a wide landing in the rock. Here a single negro with an acetylene light beside him was fitting trays full of gold coin into the centre of the fish-tanks, scores of which were stacked against the wall.

As they waited, two negroes came down the steps from the surface, picked up one of the prepared tanks and went back up the steps with it.

Bond guessed the tanks were stocked with sand and weed and fish somewhere up above and then passed to the human chain that stretched down the cliff face.

Bond noticed that some of the waiting tanks had gold ingots fitted in the centre, and others a gravel of jewels, and he revised his estimate of the treasure, quadrupling it to around four million sterling.

Mr Big stood for a few moments with his eyes on the stone floor. His breathing was deep but controlled. Then they went on up.

Twenty steps higher there was another landing, smaller and with a door leading off it. The door had a new chain and padlock on it. The door itself was made of platted iron slats, brown and corroded with rust.

Mr Big paused again and they stood side by side on the small platform of rock.

For a moment Bond thought of escape, but, as if reading his mind, the negro guard crowded him up against the stone wall away from The Big Man. And Bond knew his first duty was to stay alive and get to Solitaire and somehow keep her away from the doomed ship where the acid was slowly eating through the copper of the time-fuse.

From above, a strong draught of cold air was coming down the shaft and Bond felt the sweat drying on him. He put his right hand up to the wound in his shoulder, undeterred by the prick of the guard's dagger in his side. The blood was dry and caked and most of the arm was numb. It ached viciously.

Mr Big spoke.

'That wind, Mister Bond,' he pointed up the shaft, 'is known in Jamaica as "The Undertaker's Wind".'

Bond shrugged his right shoulder and saved his breath.

Mr Big turned to the iron door, took a key from his pocket and unlocked it. He went through and Bond and his guard followed.

It was a long narrow passage of a room with rusty shackles low down in the walls at less than yard intervals.

At the far end, where a hurricane light hung from the stone roof, there was a motionless figure under a blanket on the floor. There was one more hurricane light over their heads near the door, otherwise nothing but a smell of damp rock, and ancient torture, and death.

'Solitaire,' said Mr Big, softly.

Bond's heart leapt and he started forward. At once a huge hand grasped him by the arm.

'Hold it, white man,' snapped his guard and twisted his wrist up between his shoulder blades, hefting it higher until Bond lashed out with his left heel. It hit the other man's shin, and hurt Bond more than the guard.

Mr Big turned round. He had a small gun almost covered by his huge hand.

'Let him go,' he said, quietly. 'If you want an extra navel, Mister Bond, you can have one. I have six of them in this gun.'

Bond brushed past The Big Man. Solitaire was on her feet, coming towards him. When she saw his face she broke into a run holding out her two hands.

'James,' she sobbed. 'James.'

She almost fell at his feet. Their hands clutched at each other.

'Get me some rope,' said Mr Big in the doorway.

'It's all right, Solitaire,' said Bond, knowing that it wasn't. 'It's all right. I'm here now.'

He picked her up and held her at arm's length. It hurt his left arm. She was pale and dishevelled. There was a bruise on her forehead and black circles under her eyes. Her face was grimy and tears had made streaks down the pale skin. She had no make-up. She wore a dirty white linen suit and sandals. She looked thin.

'What's the bastard been doing to you?' said Bond. He suddenly held her tightly to him. She clung to him, her face buried in his neck.

Then she drew away and looked at her hand.

'But you're bleeding,' she said. 'What is it?'

She turned him half round and saw the black blood on his shoulder and down his arm.

'Oh my darling, what is it?'

She started to cry again, forlornly, hopelessly, realizing suddenly that they were both lost.

'Tie them up,' said The Big Man from the door. 'Here under the light. I have things to say to them.'

The negro came towards them and Bond turned. Was it worth a gamble? The negro had nothing but rope in his hands. But The Big Man had stepped sideways and was watching him, the gun held loosely, half pointing at the floor.

'No, Mister Bond,' he said simply.

Bond eyed the big negro and thought of Solitaire and his own wounded arm.

The negro came up and Bond allowed his arms to be tied behind his back. They were good knots. There was no play in them. They hurt.

Bond smiled at Solitaire. He half closed one eye. It was nothing but bravado, but he saw a hopeful awareness dawn through her tears.

The negro led him back to the doorway.

'There,' said The Big Man, pointing at one of the shackles.

The negro cut Bond's legs from under him with a sudden sweep of his shin. Bond fell on his wounded shoulder. The negro pulled him by the rope up to the shackle, tested it, and put the rope through and then down to Bond's ankles which he bound securely. He had stuck his dagger in a crevice in the rock. He pulled it out and cut the rope and went back to where Solitaire was standing.

Bond was left sitting on the stone floor, his legs straight out in front, his arms hoisted up and secured behind him. Blood dripped down from his freshly opened wound. Only the remains of the benzedrine in his system kept him from fainting.

Solitaire was bound and placed almost opposite him. There was a yard between their feet.

When it was done, The Big Man looked at his watch.

'Go,' he said to the guard. He closed the iron door behind the man and leant against it.

Bond and the girl looked at each other and The Big Man gazed down on both of them.

After one of his long silences he addressed Bond. Bond looked up at him. The great grey football of a head under the hurricane lamp looked like an elemental, a malignant spectre from the centre of the earth, as it hung in mid air, the golden eyes blazing steadily, the great body in shadow. Bond had to remind himself that he had heard its heart pumping in its chest, had heard it breathe, had seen sweat on the grey skin. It was only a man, of the same species as himself, a big man, with a brilliant brain, but still a man who walked and defecated, a mortal man with a diseased heart.

The wide rubbery mouth split open and the flat slightly everted lips drew back from the big white teeth.

'You are the best of those that have been sent against me,' said Mr Big. His quiet flat voice was thoughtful, measured. 'And you have achieved the death of four of my assistants. My followers find this incredible. It was fully time that accounts should be squared. What happened to the American was not sufficient. The treachery of this girl,' he still looked at Bond, 'whom I found in the gutter and whom I was prepared to put on my right hand, has also brought my infallibility in question. I was wondering how she should die, when providence, or Baron Samedi as my followers will believe, brought you also to the altar with your head bowed ready for the axe.'

The mouth paused, with the lips parted. Bond saw the teeth come together to form the next word.

'So it is convenient that you should die together. That will happen, in an appropriate fashion,' The Big Man looked at his watch, 'in two and a half hours' time. At six o'clock, give or take,' he added, 'a few minutes.'

'Let's give those minutes,' said Bond. 'I enjoy my life.'

'In the history of negro emancipation,' Mr Big continued in an easy conversational tone, 'there have already appeared great athletes, great musicians, great writers, great doctors and scientists. In due course, as in the developing history of other races, there will appear negroes great and famous in every other walk of life.' He paused. 'It is unfortunate for you, Mister Bond, and for this girl, that you have encountered the first of the great negro criminals. I use a vulgar word, Mister Bond, because it is the one you, as a form of policeman, would yourself use. But I prefer to regard myself as one who has the ability and the mental and nervous equipment to make his own laws and act according to them rather than accept the laws that suit the lowest common denominator of the people. You have doubtless read Trotter's *Instincts of the Herd in War and Peace*, Mister Bond. Well, I am by nature and predilection a wolf and I live by a wolf's laws. Naturally the sheep describe such a person as a "criminal".

'The fact, Mister Bond,' The Big Man continued after a pause, 'that I survive and indeed enjoy limitless success, although I am alone against countless millions of sheep, is attributable to the modern techniques I described to you on the occasion of our last talk, and to an infinite capacity for taking pains. Not dull, plodding pains, but artistic, subtle pains. And I find, Mister Bond, that it is not difficult to outwit sheep, however many of them there may be, if one is dedicated to the task and if one is by nature an extremely well-equipped wolf.

'Let me illustrate to you, by an example, how my mind works. We will take the method I have decided upon by which you are both to die. It is a modern variation on the method used in the time of my kind patron, Sir Henry Morgan. In those days it was known as "keel-hauling".'

'Pray continue,' said Bond, not looking at Solitaire.

'We have a paravane on board the yacht,' continued Mr Big as if he was a surgeon describing a delicate operation to a body of students, 'which we use for trawling for shark and other big fish. This paravane, as you know, is a large buoyant torpedo-shaped device, which rides on the end of a cable, away from the side of a ship, and which can be used for sustaining the end of a net and drawing it through the water when the ship is in motion, or if fitted with a cutting device, for severing the cables of moored mines in time of war.

'I intend,' said Mr Big, in a matter-of-fact discursive tone of voice, 'to bind you together to a line streamed from this paravane and to tow you through the sea until you are eaten by sharks.'

He paused, and his eyes looked from one to the other. Solitaire was gazing wide-eyed at Bond and Bond was thinking hard, his eyes blank and his mind boring into the future. He felt he ought to say something.

'You are a big man,' he said, 'and one day you will die a big, horrible death. If you kill us, that death will come soon. I have arranged for it. You are going mad very fast or you would see what our murder will bring down on you.'

Even as he spoke Bond's mind was working fast, counting hours and minutes, knowing that The Big Man's own death was creeping, with the acid in the fuse, round the minute hand towards his personal hour of final rendezvous. But would he and Solitaire be dead before that hour struck? There would not be more than minutes, perhaps seconds in it. The sweat poured off his face on to his chest. He smiled across at Solitaire. She looked back at him opaquely, her eyes not seeing him.

Suddenly she gave an agonized cry that made Bond's nerves jerk.

'I don't know,' she cried. 'I can't see. It's so near, so close. There is much death. But . . . '

'Solitaire,' shouted Bond, terrified that whatever strange things she saw in the future might give a warning to The Big Man. 'Pull yourself together.'

There was an angry bite in his voice.

Her eyes cleared. She looked dumbly at him, without comprehension.

The Big Man spoke again.

'I am not going mad, Mister Bond,' he said evenly, 'and nothing you have arranged will affect me. You will die beyond the reef and there will be no evidence. I shall tow the remains of your bodies until there is nothing left. That is part of the dexterity of my intentions. You may also know that shark and barracuda play a role in Voodooism. They will have their sacrifice and Baron Samedi will be appeased. That will satisfy my followers. I wish also to continue my experiments with carnivorous fish. I believe they only attack when there is blood in the water. So your bodies will be towed from the island. The paravane will take them over the reef. I believe you will not be harmed inside the reef. The blood and offal that is thrown into these waters every night will have dispersed or been consumed. But when your bodies have been dragged over the reef, then I'm afraid you will bleed, your bodies will be very raw. And then we will see if my theories are correct.'

The Big Man put his hand behind him and pulled the door open.

'I will leave you now,' he said, 'to reflect on the excellence of the method I have invented for your death together. Two necessary deaths are achieved. No evidence is left behind. Superstition is satisfied. My followers pleased. The bodies are used for scientific research.

'That is what I meant, Mister James Bond, by an infinite capacity for taking artistic pains.'

He stood in the doorway and looked at them.

'A short, but very good night to you both.'

22

TERROR BY SEA

IT WAS NOT yet light when their guards came for them. Their leg ropes were cut and with their arms still pinioned they were led up the remaining stone stairs to the surface.

They stood amongst the sparse trees and Bond sniffed the cool morning air. He gazed through the trees towards the east and saw that there the stars were paler and the horizon luminous with the breaking dawn. The night-song of the crickets was almost done and somewhere on the island a mocking bird bubbled its first notes.

He guessed that it was either side of half past five.

They stood there for several minutes. Negroes brushed past them carrying bundles and jippa-jappa holdalls, talking in cheerful whispers. The doors of the handful of thatched huts among the trees had been left swinging open. The men filed to the edge of the cliff to the right of where Bond and Solitaire were standing and disappeared over the edge. They didn't come back. It was evacuation. The whole garrison of the island was decamping.

Bond rubbed his naked shoulder against Solitaire and she pressed against him. It was cold after the stuffy dungeon and Bond shivered. But it was better to be on the move than for the suspense down below to be prolonged.

They both knew what had to be done, the nature of the gamble.

When The Big Man had left them, Bond had wasted no time. In a whisper, he had told the girl of the limpet mine against the side of the ship timed to explode a few minutes after six o'clock and he had explained the factors that would decide who would die that morning.

First, he gambled on Mr Big's mania for exactitude and efficiency. The *Secatur* must sail on the dot of six o'clock. Then there must be no cloud, or visibility in the half-light of dawn would not be sufficient for the ship to make the passage through the reef and Mr Big would postpone the sailing. If Bond and Solitaire were on the jetty alongside the ship, they would then be killed with Mr Big.

Supposing the ship sailed dead on time, how far behind and to one side of her would their bodies be towed? It would have to be on the port side for the paravane to clear the island. Bond guessed the cable to the paravane would be fifty yards and that they would be towed twenty or thirty yards behind the paravane.

If he was right, they would be hauled over the outer reef about fifty yards after the *Secatur* had cleared the passage. She would probably approach the passage at about three knots and then put on speed to ten or even twenty. At first their bodies would be swept away from the island in a slow arc, twisting and turning at the end of the tow-rope. Then the paravane would straighten out and when the ship had got through the reef, they would still be approaching it. The paravane would then cross the reef when the ship was about forty yards outside it and they would follow.

Bond shuddered to think of the mauling their bodies would suffer being dragged at any speed over the razor-sharp ten yards of coral rocks and trees. The skin on their backs and legs would be flayed off.

Once over the reef they would be just a huge bleeding bait and it would be only a matter of minutes before the first shark or barracuda was on to them.

And Mr Big would sit comfortably in the stern sheets, watching the bloody show, perhaps with glasses, and ticking off the seconds and minutes as the living bait got smaller and smaller and finally the fish snapped at the bloodstained rope.

Until there was nothing left.

Then the paravane would be hoisted inboard and the yacht would plough gracefully on towards the distant Florida Keys, Cape Sable and the sun-soaked wharf in St Petersburg Harbour.

And if the mine exploded while they were still in the water, only fifty yards away from the ship? What would be the effect of the shock-wave on their bodies? It might not be deadly. The hull of the ship should absorb most of it. The reef might protect them.

Bond could only guess and hope.

Above all they must stay alive to the last possible second. They must keep breathing as they were hauled, a living bundle, through the sea. Much depended on how they would be bound together. Mr Big would want them to stay alive. He would not be interested in dead bait.

If they were still alive when the first shark's fin showed on the surface behind them Bond had coldly decided to drown Solitaire. Drown her by twisting her body under his and holding her there. Then he would try and drown himself by twisting her dead body back over his to keep him under.

There was nightmare at every turn of his thoughts, sickening horror in every grisly aspect of the monstrous torture and death this man had invented for them. But Bond knew he must remain cold and absolutely resolved to fight for their lives to the end. There was at least warmth in the knowledge that Mr Big and most of his men would also die. And there was a glimmer of hope that he and Solitaire would survive. Unless the mine failed, there was no such hope for the enemy.

All this, and a hundred other details and plans went through Bond's mind in the last hour before they were brought up the shaft to the surface. He shared all his hopes with Solitaire. None of his fears.

She had lain opposite him, her tired blue eyes fixed on him, obedient, trusting, drinking in his face and his words, pliant, loving.

'Don't worry about me, my darling,' she had said when the men came for them. 'I am happy to be with you again. My heart is full of it. For some reason I am not afraid although there is much death very close. Do you love me a little?'

'Yes,' said Bond. 'And we shall have our love.'

'Giddap,' said one of the men.

And now, on the surface, it was getting lighter, and from below the cliff Bond heard the great twin Diesels stutter and roar. There was a light flutter of breeze to windward, but to leeward, where the ship lay, the bay was a gunmetal mirror.

Mr Big appeared up the shaft, a businessman's leather briefcase in his hand. He stood for a moment looking round, gaining his breath. He paid no attention to Bond and Solitaire nor to the two guards standing beside them with revolvers in their hands.

He looked up at the sky, and suddenly called out, in a loud clear voice, towards the rim of the sun:

'Thank you, Sir Henry Morgan. Your treasure will be well spent. Give us a fair wind.'

The negro guards showed the whites of their eyes.

'The Undertaker's Wind it is,' said Bond.

The Big Man looked at him.

'All down?' he asked the guards.

'Yassuh, Boss,' answered one of them.

'Take them along,' said The Big Man.

They went to the edge of the cliff and down the steep steps, one guard in front, one behind. Mr Big followed.

The engines of the long graceful yacht were turning over quietly, the exhaust bubbling glutinously, a thread of blue vapour rising astern.

There were two men on the jetty at the guide ropes. There were only three men on deck besides the Captain and the navigator on the grey streamlined bridge. There was no room for more. All the available deckspace, save for a fishing chair rigged right aft, was covered with fish-tanks. The Red Ensign had been struck and only the Stars and Stripes hung motionless at the stern.

A few yards clear of the ship the red torpedo-shaped paravane, about six feet long, lay quietly on the water, now aquamarine in the early dawn. It was attached to a thick pile of wire cable, coiled up on the deck aft. To Bond there looked to be a good fifty yards of it. The water was crystal clear and there were no fish about.

The Undertaker's Wind was almost dead. Soon the Doctor's Wind would start to breathe in from the sea. How soon? wondered Bond. Was it an omen?

Away beyond the ship he could see the roof of Beau Desert among the trees, but the jetty and the ship and the cliff path were still in deep shadow. Bond wondered if night-glasses would be able to pick them out. And if they could, what Strangways would be thinking.

Mr Big stood on the jetty and supervised the process of binding them together.

'Strip her,' he said to Solitaire's guard.

Bond flinched. He stole a glance at Mr Big's wrist watch. It said ten minutes to six. Bond kept silence. There must not be even a minute's delay.

'Throw the clothes on board,' said Mr Big. 'Tie some strips round his shoulder. I don't want any blood in the water, yet.'

Solitaire's clothes were cut off her with a knife. She stood pale and naked. She hung her head and the heavy black hair fell forward over her face. Bond's shoulder was roughly bound with strips of her linen skirt.

'You bastard,' said Bond through his teeth.

Under Mr Big's direction, their hands were freed. Their bodies were pressed together, face to face, and their arms held round each other's waists and then bound tightly again.

Bond felt Solitaire's soft breasts pressed against him. She leant her chin on his right shoulder.

'I didn't want it to be like this,' she whispered tremulously.

Bond didn't answer. He hardly felt her body. He was counting seconds.

On the jetty there was a pile of rope to the paravane. It hung down off the jetty and Bond could see it lying along the sand until it rose to meet the belly of the red torpedo.

The free end was tied under their armpits and knotted tightly between them in the space between their necks. It was all very carefully done. There was no possible escape.

Bond was counting the seconds. He made it five minutes to six.

Mr Big had a last look at them.

'Their legs can stay free,' he said. 'They'll make appetizing bait.' He stepped off the jetty on to the deck of the yacht.

The two guards went aboard. The two men on the jetty unhitched their lines and followed. The screws churned up the still water and with the engines at half speed ahead the *Secatur* slid swiftly away from the island.

Mr Big went aft and sat down in the fishing chair. They could see his eyes fixed on them. He said nothing. Made no gesture. He just watched.

The *Secatur* cut through the water towards the reef. Bond could see the cable to the paravane snaking over the side. The paravane started to move softly after the ship. Suddenly it put its nose down, then righted itself and sped away, its rudder pulling out and away from the wake of the ship.

The coil of rope beside them leapt into life.

'Look out,' said Bond urgently, holding tighter to the girl.

Their arms were pulled almost out of their sockets as they were jerked together off the jetty into the sea.

For a second they both went under, then they were on the surface, their joined bodies smashing through the water.

Bond gasped for breath amongst the waves and spray that dashed past his twisted mouth. He could hear the rasping of Solitaire's breath next to his ear.

'Breathe, breathe,' he shouted through the rushing of the water. 'Lock your legs against mine.'

She heard him and he felt her knee pressing between his thighs. She had a paroxysm of coughing, then her breath became more even against his ear and the thumping of her heart eased against his breast. At the same time their speed slackened.

'Hold your breath,' shouted Bond. 'I've got to have a look. Ready?'

A pressure of her arms answered him. He felt her chest heave as she filled her lungs.

With the weight of his body he swung her round so that his head was now quite out of the water.

They were ploughing along at about three knots. He twisted his head above the small bow-wave they were throwing up.

The *Secatur* was entering the passage through the reef, about eighty yards away, he guessed. The paravane was skimming slowly along almost at right angles to her. Another thirty yards and the red torpedo would be crossing the broken water over the reef. A further thirty yards behind, they were riding slowly across the surface of the bay.

Sixty yards to go to the reef.

Bond twisted his body and Solitaire came up, gasping.

Still they moved slowly along through the water.

Five yards, ten, fifteen, twenty.

Only forty yards to go before they hit the coral.

The *Secatur* would be just through. Bond gathered his breath. It must be past six now. What had happened to the blasted mine? Bond thought a quick fervent prayer. God save us, he said into the water.

Suddenly he felt the rope tighten under his arms.

'Breathe, Solitaire, breathe,' he shouted as they got under way and the water started to hiss past them.

Now they were flying over the sea towards the crouching reef.

There was a slight check. Bond guessed that the paravane had fouled a niggerhead or a piece of surface coral. Then their bodies hurtled on again in their deadly embrace.

Thirty yards to go, twenty, ten.

Jesus Christ, thought Bond. We're for it. He braced his muscles to take the crashing, searing pain, edged Solitaire further above him to protect her from the worst of it.

Suddenly the breath whistled out of his body and a giant fist thumped him into Solitaire so that she rose right out of the sea above him and then fell back. A split second later lightning flashed across the sky and there was the thunder of an explosion.

They stopped dead in the water and Bond felt the weight of the slack rope pulling them under.

His legs sank down beneath his stunned body and water rushed into his mouth.

It was this that brought him back to consciousness. His legs pounded under him and brought their mouths to the surface. The girl was a dead weight in his arms. He trod water desperately and looked round him, holding Solitaire's lolling head on his shoulder above the surface.

The first thing he saw was the swirling waters of the reef not five yards away. Without its protection they would both have been crushed by the shock-wave of the explosion. He felt the tug and eddy of its currents round his legs. He backed desperately towards it, catching gulps of air when he could. His chest was bursting with the strain and he saw the sky through a red film. The rope dragged him down and the girl's hair filled his mouth and tried to choke him.

Suddenly he felt the sharp scrape of the coral against the back of his legs. He kicked and felt frantically with his feet for a foothold, flaying the skin off with every movement.

He hardly felt the pain.

Now his back was being scraped and his arms. He floundered clumsily, his lungs burning in his chest. Then there was a bed of needles under his feet. He put all his weight on it, leaning back against the strong eddies that tried to dislodge him. His feet held and there was rock at his back. He leant back panting, blood streaming up around him in the water, holding the girl's cold, scarcely breathing body against him.

For a minute he rested, blessedly, his eyes shut and the blood pounding through his limbs, coughing painfully, waiting for his senses to focus again. His first thought was for the blood in the water around him. But he guessed the big fish would not venture into the reef. Anyway there was nothing he could do about it.

Then he looked out to sea.

There was no sign of the *Secatur*.

High up in the still sky there was a mushroom of smoke, beginning to trail, with the Doctor's Wind, in towards the land.

There were things strewn all over the water and a few heads bobbing up and down and the whole sea was glinting with the white stomachs of fish stunned or killed by the explosion. There was a strong smell of explosive in the air. On the fringe of the debris, the red paravane lay quietly, hull down, anchored by the cable whose other end must lie somewhere on the bottom. Fountains of bubbles were erupting on the glassy surface of the sea.

On the edge of the circle of bobbing heads and dead fish a few triangular fins were cutting fast through the water. More appeared as Bond watched. Once he saw a great snout come out of the water and smash down on something. The fins threw up spray as they flashed among the tidbits. Two black arms suddenly stuck up in the air and then disappeared. There were screams. Two or three pairs of arms started to flail the water towards the reef. One man stopped to bang the water in front of him with the flat of his hand. Then his hands disappeared under the surface. Then he too began to scream and his body jerked to and fro in the water. Barracuda hitting into him, said Bond's dazed mind.

But one of the heads was getting nearer, making for the bit of reef where Bond stood, the small waves breaking under his armpits, the girl's black hair hanging down his back.

It was a large head and a veil of blood streamed down over the face from a wound in the great bald skull.

Bond watched it come on.

The Big Man was executing a blundering breast-stroke, making enough flurry in the water to attract any fish that wasn't already occupied.

Bond wondered whether he would make it. Bond's eyes narrowed and his breath became calmer as he watched the cruel sea for its decision.

The surging head came nearer. Bond could see the teeth showing in a rictus of agony and frenzied endeavour. Blood half veiled the eyes that Bond knew would be bulging in their sockets. He could almost hear the great diseased heart thumping under the grey-black skin. Would it give out before the bait was taken?

The Big Man came on. His shoulders were naked, his clothes stripped off him by the explosion, Bond supposed, but the black silk tie had remained and it showed round the thick neck and streamed behind the head like a Chinaman's pigtail.

A splash of water cleared some blood away from the eyes. They were wide open, staring madly towards Bond. They held no appeal for help, only a fixed glare of physical exertion.

Even as Bond looked into them, now only ten yards away, they suddenly shut and the great face contorted in a grimace of pain.

'Aarrh,' said the distorted mouth.

Both arms stopped flailing the water and the head went under and came up again. A cloud of blood welled up and darkened the sea. Two six-foot thin brown shadows backed out of the cloud and then dashed back into it. The body in the water jerked sideways. Half of The Big Man's left arm came out of the water. It had no hand, no wrist, no wrist watch.

But the great turnip head, the drawn-back mouth full of white teeth almost splitting it in half, was still alive. And now it was screaming, a long gurgling scream that only broke each time a barracuda hit into the dangling body.

There was a distant shout from the bay behind Bond. He paid no attention. All his senses were focused on the horror in the water in front of him.

A fin split the surface a few yards away and stopped.

Bond could feel the shark pointing like a dog, the short-sighted pink button eyes trying to pierce the cloud of blood and weigh up the prey. Then it shot in towards the chest and the screaming head went under as sharply as a fisherman's float.

Some bubbles burst on the surface.

There was the swirl of a sharp brown-spotted tail as the huge leopard shark backed out to swallow and attack again.

The head floated back to the surface. The mouth was closed. The yellow eyes seemed still to look at Bond.

Then the shark's snout came right out of the water and it drove in towards the head, the lower curved jaw open so that light glinted on the teeth. There was a horrible grunting scrunch and a great swirl of water. Then silence.

Bond's dilated eyes went on staring at the brown stain that spread wider and wider across the sea.

Then the girl moaned and Bond came to his senses.

There was another shout from behind him and he turned his head towards the bay.

It was Quarrel, his brown gleaming chest towering above the slim hull of a canoe, his arms flailing at the paddle, and a long way behind him all the other canoes of Shark Bay skimming like water-boatmen across the small waves that had started to ripple the surface.

The fresh north-east trade winds had started to blow and the sun was shining down on the blue water and on the soft green flanks of Jamaica.

The first tears since his childhood came into James Bond's blue-grey eyes and ran down his drawn cheeks into the blood-stained sea.

23

PASSIONATE LEAVE

LIKE DANGLING EMERALD pendants the two humming-birds were making their last rounds of the hibiscus and a mocking bird had started on its evening song, sweeter than a nightingale's, from the summit of a bush of night-scented jasmine.

The jagged shadow of a man-of-war bird floated across the green Bahama grass of the lawn as it sailed on the air currents up the coast to some distant colony, and a slate-blue kingfisher chattered angrily as it saw the man sitting in the chair in the garden. It changed its flight and swerved off across the sea to the island. A brimstone butterfly flirted among the purple shadows under the palms.

The graded blue waters of the bay were quite still. The cliffs of the island were a deep rose in the light of the setting sun behind the house.

There was a smell of evening and of coolness after a hot day and a slight scent of peat-smoke that came from cassava being roasted in one of the fisherman's huts in the village away to the right.

Solitaire came out of the house and walked on naked feet across the lawn. She was carrying a tray with a cocktail shaker and two glasses. She put it down on a bamboo table beside Bond's chair.

'I hope I've made it right,' she said. 'Six to one sounds terribly strong. I've never had Vodka Martinis before.'

Bond looked up at her. She was wearing a pair of his white silk pyjamas. They were far too large for her. She looked absurdly childish.

She laughed. 'How do you like my Port Maria lipstick?' she asked, 'and the eyebrows made up with an HB pencil. I couldn't do anything with the rest of me except wash it.'

'You look wonderful,' said Bond. 'You're far the prettiest girl in the whole of Shark Bay. If I had some legs and arms I'd get up and kiss you.'

Solitaire bent down and kissed him long on the lips, one arm tightly round his neck. She stood up and smoothed back the comma of black hair that had fallen down over his forehead.

They looked at each other for a moment then she turned to the table and poured him out a cocktail. She poured half a glass for herself and sat down on the warm grass and put her head against his knee. He played with her hair with his right hand and they sat for a while looking out between the trunks of the palm trees at the sea and the light fading on the island.

The day had been given over to licking wounds and cleaning up the remains of the mess.

When Quarrel had landed them on the little beach at Beau Desert, Bond had half carried Solitaire across the lawn and into the bathroom. He had filled the bath full of warm water. Without her knowing what was happening he had soaped and washed her whole body and her hair. When he had cleaned away all the salt and coral slime he helped her out, dried her and put merthiolate on the coral cuts that striped her back and thighs. Then he gave her a sleeping draught and put her naked between the sheets in his own bed. He kissed her. Before he had finished closing the jalousies she was asleep.

Then he got into the bath and Strangways soaped him down and almost bathed his body in merthiolate. He was raw and bleeding in a hundred places and his left arm was numb from the barracuda bite. He had lost a mouthful of muscle at the shoulder. The sting of the merthiolate made him grind his teeth.

He put on a dressing-gown and Quarrel drove him to the hospital at Port Maria. Before he left he had a Lucullian breakfast and a blessed first cigarette. He fell asleep in the car and he slept on the operating table and in the cot where they finally put him, a mass of bandages and surgical tape.

Quarrel brought him back in the early afternoon. By that time Strangways had acted on the information Bond had given him. There was a police detachment on the Isle of Surprise, the wreck of the *Secatur*, lying in about twenty fathoms, was buoyed and the position being patrolled by the Customs launch from Port Maria. The salvage tug and divers were on their way from Kingston. Reporters from the local press had been given a brief statement and there was a police guard on the entrance to Beau Desert prepared to repel the flood of newspapermen who would arrive in Jamaica when the full story got out to the world. Meanwhile a detailed report had gone to M, and to Washington, so that The Big Man's team in Harlem and St Petersburg could be rounded up and provisionally held on a blanket gold-smuggling charge.

There were no survivors from the *Secatur*, but the local fishermen had brought in nearly a ton of dead fish that morning.

Jamaica was aflame with rumours. There were serried ranks of cars on the cliffs above the bay and along the beach below. Word had got out about Bloody Morgan's treasure, but also about the packs of shark and barracuda that had defended it, and because of them there was not a swimmer who was planning to get out to the scene of the wreck under cover of darkness.

A doctor had been to visit Solitaire but had found her chiefly concerned about getting some clothes and the right shade of lipstick. Strangways had arranged for a selection to be sent over from Kingston next day. For the time being she was experimenting with the contents of Bond's suitcase and a bowl of hibiscus.

Strangways got back from Kingston shortly after Bond's return from hospital. He had a signal for Bond from M. It read:

PRESUME YOU HAVE FILED CLAIM TO TREASURE IN YOUR NAME BEHALF UNIVERSAL EXPORT STOP PROCEED IMMEDIATELY WITH SALVAGE STOP HAVE ENGAGED COUNSEL TO PRESS OUR RIGHTS WITH TREASURY AND COLONIAL OFFICE STOP MEANWHILE VERY WELL DONE STOP FORTNIGHT'S PASSIONATE LEAVE GRANTED ENDIT

'I suppose he means "Compassionate",' said Bond.

Strangways looked solemn. 'I expect so,' he said. 'I made a full report of the damage to you. And to the girl,' he added.

'Hm,' said Bond. 'M's cipherenes don't often pick a wrong group. However.'

Strangways looked carefully out of the window with his one eye.

'It's so like the old devil to think of the gold first,' said Bond. 'Suppose he thinks he can get away with it and somehow dodge a reduction in the Secret Fund when the next parliamentary estimates come round. I expect half his life is taken up with arguing with the Treasury. But still he's been pretty quick off the mark.'

'I filed your claim at Government House directly I got the signal,' said Strangways. 'But it's going to be tricky. The Crown will be after it and America will come in somewhere as he was an American citizen. It'll be a long business.'

They had talked some more and then Strangways had left and Bond had walked painfully out into the garden to sit for a while in the sunshine with his thoughts.

In his mind he ran once more the gauntlet of dangers he had entered on his long chase after The Big Man and the fabulous treasure, and he lived again through the searing flashes of time when he had looked various deaths in the face.

And now it was over and he sat in the sunshine among the flowers with the prize at his feet and his hand in her long black hair. He clasped the moment to him and thought of the fourteen tomorrows that would be theirs between them.

There was a crash of broken crockery from the kitchen at the back of the house and the sound of Quarrel's voice thundering at someone.

'Poor Quarrel,' said Solitaire. 'He's borrowed the best cook in the village and ransacked the markets for surprises for us. He's even found some black crabs, the first of the season. Then he's roasting a pitiful little sucking pig and making an avocado pear salad and we're to finish up with guavas and coconut cream. And Commander Strangways has left a case of the best champagne in Jamaica. My mouth's watering already. But don't forget it's supposed to be a secret. I wandered into the kitchen and found he had almost reduced the cook to tears.'

'He's coming with us on our passionate holiday,' said Bond. He told her of M's cable. 'We're going to a house on stilts with palm trees and five miles of golden sand. And you'll have to look after me very well because I shan't be able to make love with only one arm.'

There was open sensuality in Solitaire's eyes as she looked up at him. She smiled innocently.

'What about my back?' she said.

MOONRAKER

It was Monday and a routine day for James Bond in the quiet office at the headquarters of the Secret Service. Idly he ticked off his number — 007 — on the charge sheets of the Top Secret files that had come in over the week-end. He was bored. Mondays were hell.

Then, suddenly, the red telephone screamed in the quiet room: 'M. wants you.' . . . and Bond walked out of his office and into the assignment that was to put even his adventures in France (*Casino Royale*) and Harlem and Jamaica (*Live and Let Die*) in the shade.

And yet what was to happen to him was to happen out of the clear blue skies of early summer, here, in England. As it might have been yesterday. Or, as it might be, some dreadful tomorrow.

Part One

MONDAY

I

SECRET PAPER-WORK

THE TWO THIRTY-EIGHTS roared simultaneously. The walls of the underground room took the crash of sound and batted it to and fro between them until there was silence. James Bond watched the smoke being sucked from each end of the room towards the central Ventaxia fan. The memory in his right hand of how he had drawn and fired with one sweep from the left made him confident. He broke the chamber sideways out of the Colt Detective Special and waited, his gun pointing at the floor, while the Instructor walked the twenty yards towards him through the half-light of the gallery.

Bond saw that the Instructor was grinning. 'I don't believe it,' he said. 'I got you that time.'

The Instructor came up with him. 'I'm in hospital, but you're dead, sir,' he said. In one hand he held the silhouette target of the upper body of a man. In the other a polaroid film, postcard size. He handed this to Bond and they turned to a table behind them on which there was a green-shaded desk-light and a large magnifying glass.

Bond picked up the glass and bent over the photograph. It was a flash-light photograph of him. Around his right hand there was a blurred burst of white flame. He focused the glass carefully on the left side of his dark jacket. In the centre of his heart there was a tiny pinpoint of light.

Without speaking, the Instructor laid the big white man-shaped target under the lamp. Its heart was a black bullseye, about three inches across. Just below and half an inch to the right was the rent made by Bond's bullet.

'Through the left wall of the stomach and out at the back,' said the Instructor, with satisfaction. He took out a pencil and scribbled an addition on the side of the target. 'Twenty rounds and I make it you owe me seven-and-six, sir,' he said impassively.

Bond laughed. He counted out some silver. 'Double the stakes next Monday,' he said.

'That's all right with me,' said the Instructor. 'But you can't beat the machine, sir. And if you want to get into the team for the Dewar Trophy we ought to give the thirty-eights a rest and spend some time on the Remington. That new long twenty-two cartridge they've just brought out is going to mean at least 7,900 out of a possible 8,000 to win. Most of your bullets have got to be in the X-ring and that's only as big as a shilling when it's under your nose. At a hundred yards it isn't there at all.'

'To hell with the Dewar Trophy,' said Bond. 'It's your money I'm after.' He shook the unfired bullets in the chamber of his gun into his cupped hand and laid them and the gun on the table. 'See you Monday. Same time?'

'Ten o'clock'll be fine, sir,' said the Instructor, jerking down the two handles on the iron door. He smiled at Bond's back as it disappeared up the steep concrete stairs leading to the ground floor. He was pleased with Bond's shooting, but he wouldn't have thought of telling him that he was the best shot in the Service. Only M. was allowed to know that, and his Chief of Staff, who would be told to enter the scores of that day's shoot on Bond's Confidential Record.

Bond pushed through the green baize door at the top of the basement steps and walked over to the lift that would take him up to the eighth floor of the tall, grey building near Regent's Park that is the headquarters of the Secret Service. He was satisfied with his score but not proud of it. His trigger finger twitched in his pocket as he wondered how to conjure up that little extra flash of speed that would beat the machine, the complicated box of tricks that sprung the target for just three seconds, fired back at him with a blank .38, and shot a pencil of light at him and photographed it as he stood and fired from the circle of chalk on the floor.

The lift doors sighed open and Bond got in. The liftman could smell the cordite on him. They always smelled like that when they came up from the shooting gallery. He liked it. It reminded him of the Army. He pressed the button for the eighth and rested the stump of his left arm against the control handle.

If only the light was better thought Bond. But M. insisted that all shooting should be done in averagely bad conditions. A dim light and a target that shot back at you was as close as he could get to copying the real thing. 'Shooting hell out of a piece of cardboard doesn't prove anything' was his single-line introduction to the Small-arms Defence Manual.

The lift eased to a stop and as Bond stepped out into the drab Ministry-of-Works-green corridor and into the bustling world of girls carrying files, doors opening and shutting, and muted telephone bells, he emptied his mind of all thoughts of his shoot and prepared himself for the normal business of a routine day at Headquarters.

He walked along to the end door on the right. It was as anonymous as all the others he had passed. No numbers. If you had any business on the eighth floor, and your office was not on that floor, someone would come and fetch you to the room you needed and see you back into the lift when you were through.

Bond knocked and waited. He looked at his watch. Eleven o'clock. Mondays were hell. Two days of dockets and files to plough through. And week-ends were generally busy times abroad. Empty flats got burgled. People were photographed in compromising positions. Motor-car 'accidents' looked better, got more cursory handling, amidst the week-end slaughter on the roads. The weekly bags from Washington, Istanbul, and Tokyo would have come in and been sorted. They might hold something for him.

The door opened and he had his daily moment of pleasure at having a beautiful secretary. 'Morning Lil,' he said.

The careful warmth of her smile of welcome dropped about ten degrees.

'Give me that coat,' she said. 'It stinks of cordite. And don't call me Lil. You know I hate it.'

Bond took off his coat and handed it to her. 'Anyone who gets christened Loelia Ponsonby ought to get used to pet names.'

He stood beside her desk in the little anteroom which she had somehow made to seem a little more human than an office and watched her hang his coat on the iron frame of the open window.

She was tall and dark with a reserved, unbroken beauty to which the war and five years in the Service had lent a touch of sternness. Unless she married soon, Bond thought for the hundredth time, or had a lover, her cool air of authority might easily become spinsterish and she would join the army of women who had married a career.

Bond had told her as much, often, and he and the two other members of the OO Section had at various times made determined assaults on her virtue. She had handled them all with the same cool motherliness (which, to salve their egos, they privately defined as frigidity) and, the day after, she treated them with small attentions and kindnesses to show that it was really all her fault and that she forgave them.

What they didn't know was that she worried herself almost to death when they were in danger and that she loved them equally; but that she had no intention of becoming emotionally involved with any man who might be dead next week. And it was true that an appointment in the Secret Service was a form of peonage. If you were a woman there wasn't much of you left for other relationships. It was easier for the men. They had an excuse for fragmentary affairs. For them marriage and children and a home were out of the question if they were to be of any use 'in the field' as it was cosily termed. But, for the women, an affair outside the Service automatically made you a 'security risk' and in the last analysis you had a choice of resignation from the Service and a normal life, or of perpetual concubinage to your King and Country.

Loelia Ponsonby knew that she had almost reached the time for decision and all her instincts told her to get out. But every day the drama and romance of her Cavell-Nightingale world locked her more securely into the company of the other girls at Headquarters and every day it seemed more difficult to betray by resignation the father-figure which the Service had become.

Meanwhile she was one of the most envied girls in the building and a member of the small company of Principal Secretaries who had access to the innermost secrets of the Service — 'The Pearls and Twin-set' as they were called behind their backs by the other girls, with ironical reference to their supposedly 'Country' and 'Kensington' backgrounds — and, so far as the Personnel Branch was concerned, her destiny in twenty years' time would be that single golden line right at the end of a New Year's Honours List, among the medals for officials of the Fishery Board, of the Post Office, of the Women's Institute, towards the bottom of the O.B.E.s: 'Miss Loelia Ponsonby, Principal Secretary in the Ministry of Defence.'

She turned away from the window. She was dressed in a sugar-pink and white striped shirt and a plain dark blue skirt.

Bond smiled into her grey eyes. 'I only call you Lil on Mondays,' he said. 'Miss Ponsonby the rest of the week. But I'll never call you Loelia. It sounds like somebody in an indecent limerick. Any messages?'

'No,' she said shortly. She relented. 'But there's piles of stuff on your desk. Nothing urgent. But there's an awful lot of it. Oh, and the powder-vine says that 008's got out. He's in Berlin, resting. Isn't it wonderful!'

Bond looked quickly at her. 'When did you hear that?'

'About half an hour ago,' she said.

Bond opened the inner door to the big office with the three desks and shut it behind him. He went and stood by the window, looking out at the late spring green of the trees in Regent's Park. So Bill had made it after all. Peenemunde and back. Resting in Berlin sounded bad. Must be in pretty poor shape. Well, he'd just have to wait for news from the only leak in the building — the girls' rest-room, known to the impotent fury of the Security staff as 'the powder-vine'.

Bond sighed and sat down at his desk, pulling towards him the tray of brown folders bearing the top-secret red star. And what about 0011? It was two months since he had vanished into the 'Dirty Half-mile' in Singapore. Not a word since. While he, Bond, No. 007, the senior of the three men in the Service who had earned the double 0 number, sat at his comfortable desk doing paper-work and flirting with their secretary.

He shrugged his shoulders and resolutely opened the top folder. Inside there was a detailed map of southern Poland and north-eastern Germany. Its feature was a straggling red line connecting Warsaw and Berlin. There was also a long typewritten memorandum headed *Mainline: A well-established Escape Route from East to West.*

Bond took out his black gunmetal cigarette-box and his black-oxidized Ronson lighter and put them on the desk beside him. He lit a cigarette, one of the Macedonian blend with the three gold rings round the butt that Morlands of Grosvenor

Street made for him, then he settled himself forward in the padded swivel chair and began to read.

It was the beginning of a typical routine day for Bond. It was only two or three times a year that an assignment came along requiring his particular abilities. For the rest of the year he had the duties of an easy-going senior civil servant — elastic office hours from around ten to six; lunch, generally in the canteen; evenings spent playing cards in the company of a few close friends, or at Crockford's; or making love, with rather cold passion, to one of three similarly disposed married women; weekends playing golf for high stakes at one of the clubs near London.

He took no holidays, but was generally given a fortnight's leave at the end of each assignment — in addition to any sick-leave that might be necessary. He earned £1,500 a year, the salary of a Principal Officer in the Civil Service, and he had a thousand a year free of tax of his own. When he was on a job he could spend as much as he liked, so for the other months of the year he could live very well on his £2,000 a year net.

He had a small but comfortable flat off the King's Road, an elderly Scottish housekeeper — a treasure called May — and a 1930 4½-litre Bentley coupé, supercharged, which he kept expertly tuned so that he could do a hundred when he wanted to.

On these things he spent all his money and it was his ambition to have as little as possible in his banking account when he was killed, as, when he was depressed he knew he would be, before the statutory age of forty-five.

Eight years to go before he was automatically taken off the OO list and given a staff job at Headquarters. At least eight tough assignments. Probably sixteen. Perhaps twenty-four. Too many.

There were five cigarette-ends in the big glass ashtray by the time Bond had finished memorizing the details of 'Mainline'. He picked up a red pencil and ran his eye down the distribution list on the cover. The list started with 'M.', then 'C.o.S.', then a dozen or so letters and numbers and then, at the end, 'oo'. Against this he put a neat tick, signed it with the figure 7, and tossed the file into his out-tray.

It was twelve o'clock. Bond took the next folder off the pile and opened it. It was from the Radio Intelligence Division of

N.A.T.O., 'For Information Only' and it was headed 'Radio Signatures'.

Bond pulled the rest of the pile towards him and glanced at the first page of each. These were their titles:

The Inspectoscope — a machine for the detection of contraband.

Philopon — A Japanese murder-drug.

Possible points of concealment on trains. No. II. Germany.

The methods of Smersh. No. 6. Kidnapping.

Route Five to Pekin.

Vladivostock. A Photographic Reconnaissance by U.S. Thunderjet.

Bond was not surprised by the curious mixture he was supposed to digest. The OO Section of the Secret Service was not concerned with the current operations of other sections and stations, only with background information which might be useful or instructive to the only three men in the Service whose duties included assassination — who might be ordered to kill. There was no urgency about these files. No action was required by him or by his two colleagues except that each of them jotted down the numbers of dockets which he considered the other two should also read when they were next attached to Headquarters. When the OO Section had finished with this lot they would go down to their final destination in 'Records'.

Bond turned back to the N.A.T.O. paper.

'The almost inevitable manner', he read, 'in which individuality is revealed by minute patterns of behaviour is demonstrated by the indelible characteristics of the "fist" of each radio operator. This "fist", or manner of tapping out messages, is distinctive and recognizable by those who are practised in receiving messages. It can also be measured by very sensitive mechanisms. To illustrate, in 1943 the United States Radio Intelligence Bureau made use of this fact in tracing an enemy station in Chile operated by "Pedro", a young German. When the Chilean police closed in on the station, "Pedro" escaped. A year later, expert listeners spotted a new illegal transmitter and were able to recognize "Pedro" as the operator. In order to disguise his "fist" he was transmitting left-handed, but the disguise was not effective and he was captured.

'N.A.T.O. Radio Research has recently been experimenting with a form of "scrambler" which can be attached to the wrist of operators with the object of interfering minutely with the nerve centres which control the muscles of the hand. However . . . '

There were three telephones on Bond's desk. A black one for outside calls, a green office telephone, and a red one which went only to M. and his Chief of Staff. It was the familiar burr of the red one that broke the silence of the room.

It was M.'s Chief of Staff.

'Can you come up?' asked the pleasant voice.

'M.?' asked Bond.

'Yes.'

'Any clue?'

'Simply said if you were about he'd like to see you.'

'Right,' said Bond, and put down the receiver.

He collected his coat, told his secretary he would be with M. and not to wait for him, left his office and walked along the corridor to the lift.

While he waited for it, he thought of those other times, when, in the middle of an empty day, the red telephone had suddenly broken the silence and taken him out of one world and set him down in another. He shrugged his shoulders — Monday! He might have expected trouble.

The lift came. 'Ninth,' said Bond, and stepped in.

2

THE COLUMBITE KING

THE NINTH WAS the top floor of the building. Most of it was occupied by Communications, the hand-picked inter-services team of operators whose only interest was the world of microwaves, sunspots, and the Heaviside Layer. Above them, on the flat roof, were the three squat masts of one of the most powerful transmitters in England, explained on the bold bronze list of occupants in the entrance hall of the building by the words 'Radio Tests Ltd.' The other tenants were declared to be 'Universal Export Co.', 'Delaney Bros. (1940) Ltd.', 'The Omnium Corporation', and 'Enquiries (Miss E. Twining, O.B.E.)'.

Miss Twining was a real person. Forty years earlier she had been a Loelia Ponsonby. Now, in retirement, she sat in a small office on the ground floor and spent her days tearing up circulars, paying the rates and taxes of her ghostly tenants, and politely brushing off salesmen and people who wanted to export something or have their radios mended.

It was always very quiet on the ninth floor. As Bond turned to the left outside the lift and walked along the softly carpeted corridor to the green baize door that led to the offices of M. and his personal staff, the only sound he heard was a thin high-pitched whine that was so faint that you almost had to listen for it.

Without knocking he pushed through the green door and walked into the last room but one along the passage.

Miss Moneypenny, M.'s private secretary, looked up from her typewriter and smiled at him. They liked each other and she knew that Bond admired her looks. She was wearing the same model shirt as his own secretary, but with blue stripes.

'New uniform, Penny?' said Bond.

She laughed. 'Loelia and I share the same little woman,' she said. 'We tossed and I got blue.'

A snort came through the open door of the adjoining room.

The Chief of Staff, a man of about Bond's age, came out, a sardonic grin on his pale, overworked face.

'Break it up,' he said. 'M.'s waiting. Lunch afterwards?'

'Fine,' said Bond. He turned to the door beside Miss Moneypenny, walked through and shut it after him. Above it, a green light went on. Miss Moneypenny raised her eyebrows at the Chief of Staff. He shook his head.

'I don't think it's business, Penny,' he said. 'Just sent for him out of the blue.' He went back into his own room and got on with the day's work.

When Bond came through the door, M. was sitting at his broad desk, lighting a pipe. He made a vague gesture with the lighted match towards the chair on the other side of the desk and Bond walked over and sat down. M. glanced at him sharply through the smoke and then threw the box of matches on to the empty expanse of red leather in front of him.

'Have a good leave?' he asked abruptly.

'Yes, thank you, sir,' said Bond.

'Still sunburned, I see.' M. looked his disapproval. He didn't really begrudge Bond a holiday which had been partly convalescence. The hint of criticism came from the puritan and the jesuit who live in all leaders of men.

'Yes, sir,' said Bond non-committally. 'It's very hot near the equator.'

'Quite,' said M. 'Well-deserved rest.' He screwed up his eyes without humour. 'Hope the colour won't last too long. Always suspicious of sunburned men in England. Either they've not got a job of work to do or they put it on with a sun-lamp.' He dismissed the subject with a short sideways jerk of his pipe.

He put the pipe back in his mouth and pulled at it absentmindedly. It had gone out. He reached for the matches and wasted some time getting it going again.

'Looks as if we'll get that gold after all,' he said finally. 'There's been some talk of the Hague Court, but Ashenheim's a fine lawyer.'[1]

'Good,' said Bond.

There was silence for a moment. M. gazed into the bowl of his pipe. Through the open windows came the distant roar of

[1] This refers to Bond's previous assignment; described in *Live and Let Die* by the same author.

London's traffic. A pigeon landed on one of the window-sills with a clatter of wings and quickly took off again.

Bond tried to read something in the weatherbeaten face he knew so well and which held so much of his loyalty. But the grey eyes were quiet and the little pulse that always beat high up on the right temple when M. was tense showed no sign of life.

Suddenly Bond suspected that M. was embarrassed. He had the feeling that M. didn't know where to begin. Bond wanted to help. He shifted in his chair and took his eyes off M. He looked down at his hands and idly picked at a rough nail.

M. lifted his eyes from his pipe and cleared his throat.

'Got anything particular on at the moment, James?' he asked in a neutral voice.

'James.' That was unusual. It was rare for M. to use a Christian name in this room.

'Only paper-work and the usual courses,' said Bond. 'Anything you want me for, sir?'

'As a matter of fact there is,' said M. He frowned at Bond. 'But it's really got nothing to do with the Service. Almost a personal matter. Thought you might give me a hand.'

'Of course, sir,' said Bond. He was relieved for M.'s sake that the ice had been broken. Probably one of the old man's relations had got into trouble and M. didn't want to ask a favour of Scotland Yard. Blackmail, perhaps. Or drugs. He was pleased that M. should have chosen him. Of course he would take care of it. M. was such a desperate stickler about Government property and personnel. Using Bond on a personal matter must have seemed to him like stealing the Government's money.

'Thought you'd say so,' said M., gruffly. 'Won't take up much of your time. An evening ought to be enough.' He paused. 'Well now, you've heard of this man Sir Hugo Drax?'

'Of course, sir,' said Bond, surprised at the name. 'You can't open a paper without reading something about him. *Sunday Express* is running his life. Extraordinary story.'

'I know,' said M. shortly. 'Just give me the facts as you see them. I'd like to know if your version tallies with mine.'

Bond gazed out of the window for a moment to marshal his thoughts. M. didn't like haphazard talk. He liked a fully detailed story with no um-ing and er-ing. No afterthoughts or hedging.

'Well, sir,' said Bond finally. 'For one thing the man's a national hero. The public have taken to him. I suppose he's in much the same class as Jack Hobbs or Gordon Richards. They've got a real feeling for him. They consider he's one of them, but a glorified version. A sort of superman. He's not much to look at, with all those scars from his war injuries, and he's a bit loud-mouthed and ostentatious. But they rather like that. Makes him a sort of Lonsdale figure, but more in their class. They like his friends calling him "Hugger" Drax. It makes him a bit of a card and I expect it gives the women a thrill. And then when you think what he's doing for the country, out of his own pocket and far beyond what any government seems to be able to do, it's really extraordinary that they don't insist on making him Prime Minister.'

Bond saw the cold eyes getting chillier, but he was determined not to let his admiration for Drax's achievements be dampened by the older man. 'After all, sir,' he continued reasonably, 'it looks as if he's made this country safe from war for years. And he can't be much over forty. I feel the same as most people about him. And then there's all this mystery about his real identity. I'm not surprised people feel rather sorry for him, although he is a multi-millionaire. He seems to be a lonely sort of man in spite of his gay life.'

M. smiled drily. 'All that sounds rather like a trailer for the *Express* story. He's certainly an extraordinary man. But what's your version of the facts? I don't expect I know much more than you do. Probably less. Don't read the papers very carefully, and there are no files on him except at the War Office and they're not very illuminating. Now then. What's the gist of this *Express* story?'

'Sorry, sir,' said Bond. 'But the facts are pretty slim. Well,' he looked out of the window again and concentrated, 'in the German break-through in the Ardennes in the winter of '44, the Germans made a lot of use of guerrillas and saboteurs. Gave them the rather spooky name of Werewolves. They did quite a lot of damage of one sort or another. Very good at camouflage and stay-behind tricks of all sorts and some of them went on operating long after Ardennes had failed and we had crossed the Rhine. They were supposed to carry on even when we had overrun the country. But they packed up pretty quickly when things got really bad.

'One of their best coups was to blow up one of the rear liaison H.Q.s between the American and British armies. Reinforcement Holding Units I think they're called. It was a mixed affair, all kinds of Allied personnel — American signals, British ambulance drivers — a rather shifting group from every sort of unit. The Werewolves somehow managed to mine the mess-hall and, when it blew, it took with it quite a lot of the field hospital as well. Killed or wounded over a hundred. Sorting out all the bodies was the hell of a business. One of the English bodies was Drax. Half his face blown away. Total amnesia that lasted a year and at the end of that time they didn't know who he was and nor did he. There were about twenty-five other unidentified bodies that neither we nor the Americans could sort out. Either not enough bits, or perhaps people in transit, or there without authorization. It was that sort of a unit. Two commanding officers, of course. Sloppy staff work. Lousy records. So after a year in various hospitals they took Drax through the War Office file of Missing Men. When they came to the papers of a no-next-of-kin called Hugo Drax, an orphan who had been working in the Liverpool docks before the war, he showed signs of interest, and the photograph and physical description seemed to tally more or less with what our man must have looked like before he was blown up. From that time he began to mend. He started to talk a bit about simple things he remembered, and the doctors got very proud of him. The War Office found a man who had served in the same Pioneer unit as this "Hugo Drax" and he came along to the hospital and said he was sure the man was Drax. That settled it. Advertising didn't produce another Hugo Drax and he was finally discharged late in 1945 in that name with back pay and a full disability pension.'

'But he still says he doesn't really know who he is,' interrupted M. 'He's a member of Blades. I've often played cards with him and talked to him afterwards at dinner. He says he sometimes gets a strong feeling of "having been there before". Often goes to Liverpool to try and hunt up his past. Anyway, what else?'

Bond's eyes were turned inwards, remembering. 'He seems to have disappeared for about three years after the war,' he said. 'Then the City started to hear about him from all over the world. The Metal Market heard about him first. Seems he'd cornered a very valuable ore called Columbite. Everybody was wanting the stuff. It's got an extraordinarily high melting point. Jet engines can't be made without it. There's very little of it in the world, only a few thousand tons are produced every year, mostly as a by-product of the Nigerian tin mines. Drax must have looked at the Jet Age and somehow put his finger on its main scarcity. He must have got hold of about £10,000 from somewhere because the *Express* says that in 1946 he'd bought three tons of Columbite, which cost him around £3,000 a ton. He got a £5,000 premium on this lot from an American aircraft firm who wanted it in a hurry. Then he started buying futures in the stuff, six months, nine months, a year forward. In three years he'd made a corner. Anyone who wanted Columbite went to Drax Metals for it. All this time he'd been playing about with futures in other small commodities — Shellac, Sisal, Black Pepper — anything where you could build up a big position on margin. Of course he gambled on a rising commodity market but he had the guts to keep his foot right down on the pedal even when the pace got hot as hell. And whenever he took a profit he ploughed the money back again. For instance, he was one of the first men to buy up used ore-dumps in South Africa. Now they're being re-mined for their uranium content. Another fortune there.'

M.'s quiet eyes were fixed on Bond. He puffed at his pipe, listening.

'Of course,' continued Bond, lost in his story, 'all this made the City wonder what the hell was going on. The commodity brokers kept on coming across the name of Drax. Whatever they wanted Drax had got it and was holding out for a much higher price than they were prepared to pay. He operated from Tangier — free port, no taxes, no currency restrictions. By 1950 he was a multi-millionaire. Then he came back to England and started spending it. He simply threw it about. Best houses, best cars, best women. Boxes at the Opera, at Goodwood. Prize-winning Jersey herds. Prize-winning carnations. Prize-winning two-year-olds. Two yachts; money for the Walker Cup team; £100,000 for the Flood Disaster Fund; Coronation Ball for Nurses at the Albert Hall — there wasn't a week when he wasn't hitting the headlines with some splash or other. And all the time he went on getting richer and the people simply loved it. It was the Arabian Nights. It lit up their lives. If a wounded soldier from Liverpool could get there in five years, why shouldn't they or their sons? It sounded almost as easy as winning a gigantic football pool.

'And then came his astonishing letter to the Queen: "Your Majesty, may I have the temerity . . . " and the typical genius of the single banner-line across the *Express* next day: "TEMERITY DRAX", and the story of how he had given to Britain his entire holding in Columbite to build a super atomic rocket with a range that would cover nearly every capital in Europe — the immediate answer to anyone who tried to atom-bomb London. £10,000,000 he was going to put up out of his own pocket, and he had the design of the thing and was prepared to find the staff to build it.

'And then there were months of delay and everyone got impatient. Questions in the House. The Opposition nearly forced a vote of Confidence. And then the announcement by the Prime Minister that the design had been approved by the Woomera Range experts of the Ministry of Supply, and that the Queen had been graciously pleased to accept the gift on behalf of the people of Britain and had conferred a knighthood on the donor.'

Bond paused, almost carried away by the story of this extraordinary man.

'Yes,' said M. ' "Peace in Our Time — This Time". I remember the headline. A year ago. And now the rocket's nearly ready. "The Moonraker". And from all I hear it really should do what he says. It's very odd.' He relapsed into silence, gazing out of the window.

He turned back and faced Bond across the desk.

'That's about it,' he said slowly. 'I don't know much more than you do. A wonderful story. Extraordinary man.' He paused, reflecting. 'There's only one thing . . . ' M. tapped the stem of his pipe against his teeth.

'What's that, sir?' asked Bond.

M. seemed to make up his mind. He looked mildly across at Bond.

'Sir Hugo Drax cheats at cards.'

3

'BELLY STRIPPERS', ETC.

'CHEATS AT CARDS?'

M. frowned. 'That's what I said,' he commented drily. 'It doesn't seem to you odd that a multi-millionaire should cheat at cards?'

Bond grinned apologetically. 'Not as odd as all that, sir,' he said. 'I've known very rich people cheat themselves at patience. But it just didn't fit in with my picture of Drax. Bit of an anti-climax.'

'That's the point,' said M. 'Why does he do it? And don't forget that cheating at cards can still smash a man. In so-called "Society", it's about the only crime that can still finish you, whoever you are. Drax does it so well that nobody's caught him yet. As a matter of fact I doubt if anyone has begun to suspect him except Basildon. He's the Chairman of Blades. He came to me. He's got a vague idea I've got something to do with Intelligence and I've given him a hand over one or two little troubles in the past. Asked my advice. Said he didn't want a fuss at the club, of course, but above all he wants to save Drax from making a fool of himself. He admires him as much as we all do and he's terrified of an incident. You couldn't stop a scandal like that getting out. A lot of M.P.s are members and it would soon get talked about in the Lobby. Then the gossip-writers would get hold of it. Drax would have to resign from Blades and the next thing there'd be a libel action brought in his defence by one of his friends. Tranby Croft all over again. At least, that's how Basildon's mind is working and I must say I can see it that way too. Anyway,' said M. with finality, 'I've agreed to help and,' he looked levelly at Bond, 'that's where you come in. You're the best card-player in the Service, or,' he smiled ironically, 'you should be after the casino jobs you've been on, and I remembered that we'd spent quite a lot of money putting you through a course in card-sharping before you went after those Roumanians in Monte Carlo before the war.'

Bond smiled grimly. 'Steffi Esposito,' he said softly. 'That was the chap. American. Made me work ten hours a day for a week learning a thing called the Riffle Stack and how to deal Seconds and Bottoms and Middles. I wrote a long report about it at the time. Must be buried in Records. He knew every trick in the game. How to wax the aces so that the pack will break at them; Edge Work and Line Work with a razor on the backs of the high cards; Trimming; Arm Pressure Holdouts — mechanical gadgets up your sleeve that feed you cards. Belly Strippers — trimming a whole pack less than a millimetre down both sides, but leaving a slight belly on the cards you're interested in — the aces, for instance. Shiners, tiny mirrors built into rings, or fitted into the bottom of a pipe-bowl. Actually,' Bond admitted, 'it was his tip about "Luminous Readers" that helped me on the Monte Carlo job. A croupier was using an invisible ink the team could pick out with special glasses. But Steffi was a wonderful chap. Scotland Yard found him for us. He could shuffle the pack once and then cut the four aces out of it. Absolute magic.'

'Sounds a bit too professional for our man,' commented M. 'That sort of work needs hours of practice every day, or an accomplice, and I can't believe he'd find that at Blades. No, there's nothing sensational about his cheating and for all I know it might be a fantastic run of luck. It's odd. He's not a particularly good player — he only plays bridge by the way — but quite often he brings off bids or doubles or finesses that are absolutely phenomenal — quite against the odds. Or the conventions. But they come off. He's always a big winner and they play high at Blades. He hasn't lost on a weekly settlement since he joined a year ago. We've got two or three of the finest players in the world in the club and none of them has ever had a record like that over twelve months. It's getting talked about in a sort of joking way and I think Basildon's right to do something about it. What system do you suppose Drax has got?'

Bond was longing for his lunch. The Chief of Staff must have given him up half an hour ago. He could have talked to M. about cheating for hours, and M., who never seemed to be interested in food or sleep, would have listened to everything and remembered it afterwards. But Bond was hungry.

'Assuming he's not a professional, sir, and can't doctor the cards in any way, there are only two answers. He's either looking, or else he's got a system of signals with his partner. Does he often play with the same man?'

'We always cut for partners after each rubber,' said M. 'Unless there's a challenge. And on guest nights, Mondays and Thursdays, you stick to your guest. Drax nearly always brings a man called Meyer, his metal broker. Nice chap. Jew. Very fine player.'

'I might be able to tell if I watched,' said Bond.

'That's what I was going to say,' said M. 'How about coming along tonight? At any rate you'll get a good dinner. Meet me there about six. I'll take some money off you at piquet and we'll watch the bridge for a little. After dinner we'll have a rubber or two with Drax and his friend. They're always there on Monday. All right? Sure I'm not taking you away from your work?'

'No, sir,' said Bond with a grin. 'And I'd like to come very much. Bit of a busman's holiday. And if Drax is cheating, I'll show him I've spotted it and that should be enough to warn him off. I wouldn't like to see him get into a mess. That all, sir?'

'Yes, James,' said M. 'And thank you for your help. Drax must be a bloody fool. Obviously a bit of a crank. But it isn't the man I'm worried about. I wouldn't like to chance anything going wrong with this rocket of his. And Drax more or less *is* the Moonraker. Well, see you at six. Don't bother about dressing. Some of us do for dinner and some of us don't. Tonight we won't. Better go along now and sandpaper your fingertips or whatever you sharpers do.'

Bond smiled back at M. and got to his feet. It sounded a promising evening. As he walked over to the door and let himself out he reflected that here at last was an interview with M. that didn't cast a shadow.

M.'s secretary was still at her desk. There was a plate of sandwiches and a glass of milk beside her typewriter. She looked sharply at Bond, but there was nothing to be read in his expression.

'I suppose he gave up,' said Bond.

'Nearly an hour ago,' said Miss Moneypenny reproachfully. 'It's half-past two. He'll be back any minute now.'

'I'll go down to the canteen before it closes,' he said. 'Tell him I'll pay for his lunch next time.' He smiled at her and walked out into the corridor and along to the lift.

There were only a few people left in the officers' canteen. Bond sat by himself and ate a grilled sole, a large mixed salad with his own dressing laced with mustard, some Brie cheese and toast, and half a carafe of white Bordeaux. He had two cups of black coffee and was back in his office by three. With half his mind preoccupied with M.'s problem, he hurried through the rest of the N.A.T.O. file, said goodbye to his secretary after telling her where he would be that evening, and at four-thirty was collecting his car from the staff garage at the back of the building.

'Supercharger's whining a bit, sir,' said the ex-R.A.F. mechanic who regarded Bond's Bentley as his own property. 'Take it down tomorrow if you won't be needing her at lunch-time.'

'Thanks,' said Bond, 'that'll be fine.' He took the car quietly out into the park and over to Baker Street, the two-inch exhaust bubbling fatly in his wake.

He was home in fifteen minutes. He left the car under the plane trees in the little square and let himself into the ground-floor flat of the converted Regency house, went into the book-lined sitting-room and, after a moment's search, pulled *Scarne on Cards* out of its shelf and dropped it on the ornate Empire desk near the broad window.

He walked through into the smallish bedroom with the white and gold Cole wallpaper and the deep red curtains, undressed and threw his clothes, more or less tidily, on the dark blue counterpane of the double bed. Then he went into the bathroom and had a quick shower. Before leaving the bathroom he examined his face in the glass and decided that he had no intention of sacrificing a lifetime prejudice by shaving twice in one day.

In the glass, the grey-blue eyes looked back at him with the extra light they held when his mind was focused on a problem that interested him. The lean, hard face had a hungry, competitive edge to it. There was something swift and intent in the way he ran his fingers along his jaw and in the impatient stroke of the hairbrush to put back the comma of black hair that fell down an inch above his right eyebrow. It crossed his mind that, with the fading of his sunburn, the scar down the right cheek that had shown so white was beginning to be less prominent, and automatically he glanced down his naked body and registered that the almost indecent white area left by his bathing trunks was less sharply defined. He smiled at some memory and went through into the bedroom.

Ten minutes later, in a heavy white silk shirt, dark blue trousers of navy serge, dark blue socks, and well-polished black moccasin shoes, he was sitting at his desk with a pack of cards in one hand and Scarne's wonderful guide to cheating open in front of him.

For half an hour, as he ran quickly through the section on Methods, he practised the vital Mechanic's Grip (three fingers curled round the long edge of the cards, and the index finger at the short upper edge away from him), Palming, and Nullifying the Cut. His hands worked automatically at these basic manoeuvres while his eyes read, and he was glad to find that his fingers were supple and assured and that there was no noise from the cards even with the very difficult single-handed Annulment.

At five-thirty he slapped the cards on the table and shut the book.

He went into his bedroom, filled the wide black case with cigarettes and slipped it into his hip pocket, put on a black knitted silk tie and his coat and verified that his cheque book was in his notecase.

He stood for a moment, thinking. Then he selected two white silk handkerchiefs, carefully rumpled them, and put one into each side-pocket of his coat.

He lit a cigarette and walked back into the sitting-room and sat down at his desk again and relaxed for ten minutes, gazing out of the window at the empty square and thinking about the evening that was just going to begin and about Blades, probably the most famous private card club in the world.

The exact date of the foundation of Blades is uncertain. The second half of the eighteenth century saw the opening of many coffee houses and gaming rooms, and premises and proprietors shifted often with changing fashions and fortunes. Whites was founded in 1755, Almacks in 1764, and Brooks's in 1774, and it was in that year that the Scavoir Vivre, which was to be the cradle of Blades, opened its doors on to Park Street, a quiet backwater off St. James's.

The Scavoir Vivre was too exclusive to live and it blackballed itself to death within a year. Then, in 1776, Horace Walpole wrote: 'A new club is opened off St. James's Street that piques itself in surpassing all its predecessors' and in 1778 'Blades' first occurs in a letter from Gibbon, the historian, who coupled it with the name of its founder, a German called Longchamp at that time conducting the Jockey Club at Newmarket.

From the outset Blades seems to have been a success, and in 1782 we find the Duke of Wirtemberg writing excitedly home to his younger brother: 'This is indeed the "Ace of Clubs"! There have been four or five quinze tables going in the room at the same time, with whist and piquet, after which a full Hazard table. I have known two at the same time. Two chests each containing 4000 guinea rouleaus were scarce sufficient for the night's circulation.'

Mention of Hazard perhaps provides a clue to the club's prosperity. Permission to play this dangerous but popular game must have been given by the Committee in contravention of its own rules which laid down that 'No game is to be admitted to the House of the Society but Chess, Whist, Picket, Cribbage, Quadrille, Ombre and Tredville'.

In any event the club continued to flourish and remains to this day the home of some of the highest 'polite' gambling in the world. It is not as aristocratic as it was, the redistribution of wealth has seen to that, but it is still the most exclusive club in London. The membership is restricted to two hundred and each candidate must have two qualifications for election: he must behave like a gentleman and he must be able to 'show' £100,000 in cash or gilt-edged securities.

The amenities of Blades, apart from the gambling, are so desirable that the Committee has had to rule that every member is required to win or lose £500 a year on the club premises, or pay an annual fine of £250. The food and wine are the best in London and no bills are presented, the cost of all meals being deducted at the end of each week *pro rata* from the profits of the winners. Seeing that about £5,000 changes hands each week at the tables the impost is not too painful and the losers have the satisfaction of saving something from the wreck; and the custom explains the fairness of the levy on infrequent gamblers.

Club servants are the making or breaking of any club and the servants of Blades have no equal. The half-dozen waitresses in the dining-room are of such a high standard of beauty that some of the younger members have been known to smuggle them undetected into débutante balls, and if, at night, one or another of the girls is persuaded to stray into one of the twelve members' bedrooms at the back of the club, that is regarded as the member's private concern.

There are one or two other small refinements which contribute to the luxury of the place. Only brand-new currency notes and silver are paid out on the premises and, if a member is staying overnight, his notes and small change are taken away by the valet who brings the early morning tea and *The Times* and are replaced with new money. No newspaper comes to the reading room before it has been ironed. Floris provides the soaps and lotions in the lavatories and bedrooms; there is a direct wire to Ladbroke's from the porter's lodge; the club has the finest tents and boxes at the principal race-meetings, at Lords, Henley, and Wimbledon, and members travelling abroad have automatic membership of the leading club in every foreign capital.

In short, membership of Blades, in return for the £100 entrance fee and the £50 a year subscription, provides the standard of luxury of the Victorian age together with the opportunity to win or lose, in great comfort, anything up to £20,000 a year.

Bond, reflecting on all this, decided that he was going to enjoy his evening. He had played at Blades only a dozen times in his life, and on the last occasion he had burnt his fingers badly in a high poker game, but the prospect of some expensive bridge and of the swing of a few, to him, not unimportant hundred pounds made his muscles taut with anticipation.

And then, of course, there was the little business of Sir Hugo Drax, which might bring an additional touch of drama to the evening.

He was not even disturbed by a curious portent he encountered while he was driving along King's Road into Sloane Square with half his mind on the traffic and the other half exploring the evening ahead.

It was a few minutes to six and there was thunder about. The sky threatened rain and it had become suddenly dark. Across the square from him, high up in the air, a bold electric sign started to flash on and off. The fading light-waves had caused the cathode tube to start the mechanism which would keep the sign flashing through the dark hours until, around six in the morning, the early light of day would again sensitize the tube and cause the circuit to close.

Startled at the great crimson words, Bond pulled in to the kerb, got out of the car and crossed to the other side of the street to get a better view of the big skysign.

Ah! That was it. Some of the letters had been hidden by a neighbouring building. It was only one of those Shell advertisements. 'SUMMER SHELL IS HERE' was what it said.

Bond smiled to himself and walked back to his car and drove on.

When he had first seen the sign, half-hidden by the building, the great crimson letters across the evening sky had flashed a different message.

They had said: 'HELL IS HERE . . . HELL IS HERE . . . HELL IS HERE.'

4

THE 'SHINER'

BOND LEFT THE Bentley outside Brooks's and walked round the corner into Park Street.

The Adam frontage of Blades, recessed a yard or so back from its neighbours, was elegant in the soft dusk. The dark red curtains had been drawn across the ground-floor bow windows on either side of the entrance and a liveried servant showed for a moment as he drew them across the three windows of the floor above. In the centre of the three, Bond could see the heads and shoulders of two men bent over a game, probably backgammon he thought, and he caught a glimpse of the spangled fire of one of the three great chandeliers that illuminate the famous gambling room.

Bond pushed through the swing doors and walked up to the old-fashioned porter's lodge ruled over by Brevett, the guardian of Blades and the counsellor and family friend of half the members.

'Evening, Brevett. Is the Admiral in?'

'Good evening, sir,' said Brevett, who knew Bond as an occasional guest at the club. 'The Admiral's waiting for you in the card-room. Page, take Commander Bond up to the Admiral. Lively now!'

As Bond followed the liveried page boy across the worn black and white marble floor of the hall and up the wide staircase with its fine mahogany balustrade, he remembered the story of how, at one election, nine blackballs had been found in the box when there were only eight members of the Committee present. Brevett, who had handed the box from member to member, was said to have confessed to the Chairman that he was so afraid the candidate would be elected that he put in a blackball himself. No one had objected. The Committee would rather have lost its chairman than the porter whose family had held the same post at Blades for a hundred years.

The page pushed open one wing of the tall doors at the top of the stairs and held it for Bond to go through. The long room was not crowded and Bond saw M. sitting by himself playing patience in the alcove formed by the left hand of the three bow windows. He dismissed the page and walked across the heavy carpet, noticing the rich background smell of cigar-smoke, the quiet voices that came from the three tables of bridge, and the sharp rattle of dice across an unseen backgammon board.

'There you are,' said M. as Bond came up. He waved to the chair that faced him across the card-table. 'Just let me finish this. I haven't cracked this man Canfield for months. Drink?'

'No, thanks,' said Bond. He sat down and lit a cigarette and watched with amusement the concentration M. was putting into his game.

'Admiral Sir M**** M******* — something at the Ministry of Defence.' M. looked like any member of any of the clubs in St. James's Street. Dark grey suit, stiff white collar, the favourite dark blue bow-tie with white spots, rather loosely tied, the thin black cord of the rimless eyeglass that M. seemed only to use to read menus, the keen sailor's face, with the clear, sharp sailor's eyes. It was difficult to believe that an hour before he had been playing with a thousand live chessmen against the enemies of England; that there might be, this evening, fresh blood on his hands, or a successful burglary, or the hideous knowledge of a disgusting blackmail case.

And what could the casual observer think of him, 'Commander James Bond, C.M.G., R.N.V.S.R.', also 'something at the Ministry of Defence', the rather saturnine young man in his middle thirties sitting opposite the Admiral? Something a bit cold and dangerous in that face. Looks pretty fit. May have been attached to Templer in Malaya. Or Nairobi. Mau Mau work. Tough-looking customer. Doesn't look the sort of chap one usually sees in Blades.

Bond knew that there was something alien and un-English about himself. He knew that he was a difficult man to cover up. Particularly in England. He shrugged his shoulders. Abroad was what mattered. He would never have a job to do in England. Outside the jurisdiction of the Service. Anyway, he didn't need a cover this evening. This was recreation.

M. snorted and threw his cards down. Bond automatically gathered in the pack and as automatically gave it the Scarne shuffle, marrying the two halves with the quick downward riffle that never brings the cards off the table. He squared off the pack and pushed it away.

M. beckoned to a passing waiter. 'Piquet cards, please, Tanner,' he said.

The waiter went away and came back a moment later with the two thin packs. He stripped off the wrapping and placed them, with two markers, on the table. He stood waiting.

'Bring me a whisky and soda,' said M. 'Sure you won't have anything?'

Bond looked at his watch. It was half-past six. 'Could I have a dry martini?' he said. 'Made with vodka. Large slice of lemon peel.'

'Rot-gut,' commented M. briefly as the waiter went away. 'Now I'll just take a pound or two off you and then we'll go and have a look at the bridge. Our friend hasn't turned up yet.'

For half an hour they played the game at which the expert player can nearly always win even with the cards running slightly against him. At the end of the game Bond laughed and counted out three pound-notes.

'One of these days I'm going to take some trouble and really learn piquet,' he said. 'I've never won against you yet.'

'It's all memory and knowing the odds,' said M. with satisfaction. He finished his whisky and soda. 'Let's go over and see what's going on at the bridge. Our man's playing at Basildon's table. Came in about ten minutes ago. If you notice anything, just give me a nod and we'll go downstairs and talk about it.'

He stood up and Bond followed suit.

The far end of the room had begun to fill up and half a dozen tables of bridge were going. At the round poker table under the centre chandelier three players were counting out chips into five stacks, waiting for two more players to come in. The kidney-shaped baccarat table was still shrouded and would probably remain so until after dinner, when it would be used for chemin-de-fer.

Bond followed M. out of their alcove, relishing the scene down the long room, the oases of green, the tinkle of glasses as the waiters moved amongst the tables, the hum of talk punctuated by sudden exclamations and warm laughter, the haze of blue smoke rising up through the dark red lamp-shades that hung over the centre of each table. His pulses quickened with the smell of it all and his nostrils flared slightly as the two men came down the long room and joined the company.

M., with Bond beside him, wandered casually from table to table, exchanging greetings with the players until they reached the last table beneath the fine Lawrence of Beau Brummel over the wide Adam fireplace.

'Double, damn you,' said the loud, cheerful voice of the player with his back to Bond. Bond thoughtfully noted the head of tight reddish hair that was all he could see of the speaker, then he looked to the left at the rather studious profile of Lord Basildon. The Chairman of Blades was leaning back, looking critically down his nose at the hand of cards which was held out and away from him as if it were a rare object.

'My hand is so exquisite that I am forced to redouble, my dear Drax,' he said. He looked across at his partner. 'Tommy,' he said. 'Charge this to me if it goes wrong.'

'Rot,' said his partner. 'Meyer? Better take Drax out.'

'Too frightened,' said the middle-aged florid man who was playing with Drax. 'No bid.' He picked up his cigar from the brass ashtray and put it carefully into the middle of his mouth.

'No bid here,' said Basildon's partner.

'And nothing here,' came Drax's voice.

'Five clubs redoubled,' said Basildon. 'Your lead, Meyer.'

Bond looked over Drax's shoulder. Drax had the ace of spades and the ace of hearts. He promptly made them both and led another heart which Basildon took on the table with the king.

'Well,' said Basildon. 'There are four trumps against me including the queen. I shall play Drax to have her.' He finessed against Drax. Meyer took the trick with the queen.

'Hell and damnation,' said Basildon. 'What's the queen doing in Meyer's hand? Well I'm damned. Anyway the rest are mine.' He fanned his cards down on the table. He looked defensively at his partner. 'Can you beat it, Tommy? Drax doubles and Meyer has the queen.' There was not more than a natural exasperation in his voice.

Drax chuckled. 'Didn't expect my partner to have a Yarborough did you?' he said cheerfully to Basildon. 'Well that's just the four hundred above the line. Your deal.' He cut the cards to Basildon and the game went on.

So it had been Drax's deal the hand before. That might be important. Bond lit a cigarette and reflectively examined the back of Drax's head.

M.'s voice cut in on Bond's thoughts. 'You remember my friend Commander Bond, Basil? Thought we'd come along and play some cards this evening.'

Basildon smiled up at Bond. 'Evening,' he said. He waved a hand round the table from left to right. 'Meyer, Dangerfield, Drax.' The three men looked up briefly and Bond nodded a greeting to the table in general. 'You all know the Admiral,' added the Chairman, starting to deal.

Drax half turned in his chair. 'Ah, the Admiral,' he said boisterously. 'Glad to have you aboard, Admiral. Drink?'

'No, thanks,' said M. with a thin smile. 'Just had one.'

Drax turned and glanced up at Bond, who caught a glimpse of a tuft of reddish moustache and a rather chilly blue eye. 'What about you?' asked Drax perfunctorily.

'No, thanks,' said Bond.

Drax swivelled back to the table and picked up his cards. Bond watched the big blunt hands sort them.

Then he moved round the table with a second clue to ponder.

Drax didn't sort his cards into suits as most players do, but only into reds and blacks, ungraded, making his hand very difficult to kibitz and almost impossible for one of his neighbours, if they were so inclined, to decipher.

Bond knew it for the way people hold their hands who are very careful card-players indeed.

Bond went and stood beside the chimneypiece. He took out a cigarette and lit it at the flame from a small gas-jet enclosed in a silver grille — a relic of the days before the use of matches — that protruded from the wall beside him.

From where he stood he could see the hand of Meyer, and by moving a pace to the right, of Basildon. His view of Sir Hugo Drax was uninterrupted and he inspected him carefully while appearing to interest himself only in the game.

Drax gave the impression of being a little larger than life. He was physically big — about six foot tall, Bond guessed — and his shoulders were exceptionally broad. He had a big square head and the tight reddish hair was parted in the middle. On either side of the parting the hair dipped down in a curve towards the temples with the object, Bond assumed, of hiding as much as possible of the tissue of shining puckered skin that covered most of the right half of his face. Other relics of plastic surgery could be detected in the man's right ear, which was not a perfect match with its companion on the left, and the right eye, which had been a surgical failure. It was considerably larger than the left eye, because of a contraction of the borrowed skin used to rebuild the upper and lower eyelids, and it looked painfully bloodshot. Bond doubted if it was capable of closing completely and he guessed that Drax covered it with a patch at night.

To conceal as much as possible of the unsightly taut skin that covered half his face, Drax had grown a bushy reddish moustache and had allowed his whiskers to grow down to the level of the lobes of his ears. He also had patches of hair on his cheek-bones.

The heavy moustache served another purpose. It helped to hide a naturally prognathous upper jaw and a marked protrusion of the upper row of teeth. Bond reflected that this was probably due to sucking his thumb as a child, and it had resulted in an ugly splaying, or diastema, of what Bond had heard his dentist call 'the centrals'. The moustache helped to hide these 'ogre's teeth' and it was only when Drax uttered, as he frequently did, his short braying laugh that the splay could be seen.

The general effect of the face — the riot of red-brown hair, the powerful nose and jaw, the florid skin — was flamboyant. It put Bond in mind of a ring-master at a circus. The contrasting sharpness and coldness of the left eye supported the likeness.

A bullying, boorish, loud-mouthed vulgarian. That would have been Bond's verdict if he had not known something of Drax's abilities. As it was, it crossed his mind that much of the effect might be Drax's idea of a latter-day Regency buck — the harmless disguise of a man with a smashed face who was also a snob.

Looking for further clues, Bond noticed that Drax was sweating rather freely. Despite the occasional growl of thunder outside it was a cool evening, and yet Drax was constantly mopping his face and neck with a huge bandana handkerchief. He smoked incessantly, stubbing out the cork-tipped Virginian cigarettes after a dozen lungfuls of smoke and almost immediately lighting another from a box of fifty in his coat pocket. His big hands, their backs thickly covered with reddish hair, were always on the move, fiddling with his cards, handling the cigarette lighter that stood beside a plain flat silver cigarette-case in front of him, twisting a lock of hair on the side of his head, using the handkerchief on his face and neck. Occasionally he put a finger greedily to his mouth and worried a nail. Even at a distance Bond could see that every finger-nail was bitten down to the quick.

The hands themselves were strong and capable but the thumbs had something ungainly about them which it took Bond a moment or two to define. He finally detected that they were unnaturally long and reached level with the top joint of the index finger.

Bond concluded his inspection with Drax's clothes which were expensive and in excellent taste — a dark blue pinstripe in lightweight flannel, double-breasted with turn-back cuffs, a heavy white silk shirt with a stiff collar, an unobtrusive tie with a small grey and white check, modest cuff-links, which looked like Cartier, and a plain gold Patek Phillipe watch with a black leather strap.

Bond lit another cigarette and concentrated on the game, leaving his subconscious to digest the details of Drax's appearance and manner that had seemed to him significant and that might help to explain the riddle of his cheating, the nature of which had still to be discovered.

Half an hour later the cards had completed the circle.

'My deal,' said Drax with authority. 'Game all and we have a satisfactory inflation above the line. Now then, Max, see if you can't pick up a few aces. I'm tired of doing all the work.' He dealt smoothly and slowly round the table, keeping up a running fire of rather heavy-handed banter with the company. 'Long rubber,' he said to M. who was sitting smoking his pipe between Drax and Basildon. 'Sorry to have kept you out so long. How about a challenge after dinner? Max and I'll take on you and Commander Thingummy. What did you say his name was? Good player?'

'Bond,' said M. 'James Bond. Yes, I think we'd like that very much. What do you say, James?'

Bond's eyes were glued to the bent head and slowly moving hands of the dealer. Yes, that was it! Got you, you bastard. A Shiner. A simple, bloody Shiner that wouldn't have lasted five minutes in a pro's game. M. saw the glint of assurance in Bond's eyes as they met his across the table.

'Fine,' said Bond cheerfully. 'Couldn't be better.'

He made an imperceptible movement of the head. 'How about showing me the Betting Book before dinner? You always say it'll amuse me.'

M. nodded. 'Yes. Come along. It's in the Secretary's office. Then Basildon can come down and give us a cocktail and tell us the result of this death-struggle.' He got up.

'Order what you want,' said Basildon with a sharp glance at M. 'I'll be down directly we've polished them off.'

'Around nine then,' said Drax, glancing from M. to Bond. 'Show him the bet about the girl in the balloon.' He picked up his hand. 'Looks like I shall have the Casino's money to play with,' he said after a rapid glance at his cards. 'Three No Trumps.' He shot a triumphant glance at Basildon. 'Put that in your pipe and smoke it.'

Bond, following M. out of the room, missed Basildon's reply.

They walked down the stairs and along to the Secretary's office in silence. The room was in darkness. M. switched on the light and went and sat down in the swivel chair in front of the busy-looking desk. He turned the chair to face Bond who had walked over to the empty fireplace and was taking out a cigarette.

'Any luck?' he asked looking up at him.

'Yes,' said Bond. 'He cheats all right.'

'Ah,' said M. unemotionally. 'How does he do it?'

'Only on the deal,' said Bond. 'You know that silver cigarette-case he has in front of him, with his lighter? He never takes cigarettes from it. Doesn't want to get finger-marks on the surface. It's plain silver and very highly polished. When he deals, it's almost concealed by the cards and his big hands. And he doesn't move his hands away from it. Deals four piles quite close to him. Every card is reflected in the top of the case. It's just as good as a mirror although it looks perfectly innocent lying there. As he's such a good businessman it would be normal for him to have a first-class memory. You remember I told you about "Shiners"? Well, that's just a version of one. No wonder he brings off these miraculous finesses every once in a while. That double we watched was easy. He knew his partner had the guarded queen. With his two aces the double was a certainty. The rest of the time he just plays his average game. But knowing all the cards on every fourth deal is a terrific edge. It's not surprising he always shows a profit.'

'But one doesn't notice him doing it,' protested M.

'It's quite natural to look down when one's dealing,' said Bond. 'Everybody does. And he covers up with a lot of banter, much more than he produces when someone else is dealing. I expect he's got very good peripheral vision — the thing they mark us so highly for when we take our medical for the Service. Very wide angle of sight.'

The door opened and Basildon came in. He was bristling. He shut the door behind him. 'That dam' shut-out bid of Drax's,' he exploded. 'Tommy and I could have made four hearts if we could have got around to bidding it. Between them they had the ace of hearts, six club tricks, and the ace, king of diamonds and a bare guard in spades. Made nine tricks straight off. How he had the face to open Three No Trumps I can't imagine.' He calmed down a little. 'Well, Miles,' he said, 'has your friend got the answer?'

M. gestured to Bond, who repeated what he had told M.

Lord Basildon's face got angrier as Bond talked.

'Damn the man,' he exploded when Bond had finished. 'What the hell does he want to do that for? Bloody millionaire. Rolling in money. Fine scandal we're in for. I'll simply have to tell the Committee. Haven't had a cheating case since the 'fourteen-eighteen war.' He paced up and down the room. The club was quickly forgotten as he remembered the significance of Drax himself. 'And they say this rocket of his is going to be ready before long. Only comes up here once or twice a week for a bit of relaxation. Why, the man's a public hero! This is terrible.'

Basildon's anger was chilled by the thought of his responsibility. He turned to M. for help. 'Now, Miles, what am I to do?

He's won thousands of pounds in this club and others have lost it. Take this evening. It doesn't matter about my losses, of course. But what about Dangerfield? I happen to know he's been having a bad time on the stock market lately. I don't see how I can avoid telling the Committee. Can't shirk it — whoever Drax is. And you know what that'll mean. There are ten on the Committee. Bound to be a leak. And then look at the scandal. They tell me the Moonraker can't exist without Drax and the papers say the whole future of the country depends on the thing. This is a damned serious business.' He paused and shot a hopeful glance at M. and then at Bond. 'Is there any alternative?'

Bond stubbed out his cigarette. 'He could be stopped,' he said quietly. 'That is,' he added with a thin smile, 'if you don't mind paying him out in his own coin.'

'Do anything you bloody well like,' said Basildon emphatically. 'What are you thinking of?' Hope dawned in his eyes at Bond's assurance.

'Well,' said Bond. 'I could show him I'd spotted him and at the same time flay the hide off him at his own game. Of course Meyer'd get hurt in the process. Might lose a lot of money as Drax's partner. Would that matter?'

'Serve him right,' said Basildon, overcome with relief and ready to grasp at any solution. 'He's been riding along on Drax's back. Making plenty of money playing with him. You don't think . . . '

'No,' said Bond. 'I'm sure he doesn't know what's going on. Although some of Drax's bids must come as a bit of a shock. Well,' he turned to M., 'is it all right with you, sir?'

M. reflected. He looked at Basildon. There was no doubt of his view.

He looked at Bond. 'All right,' he said. 'What must be, must be. Don't like the idea, but I can see Basildon's point. So long as you can bring it off and,' he smiled, 'as long as you don't want me to palm any cards or anything of that sort. No talent for it.'

'No,' said Bond. He put his hands in his coat pockets and touched the two silk handkerchiefs. 'And I think it should work. All I need is a couple of packs of used cards, one of each colour, and ten minutes in here alone.'

5

DINNER AT BLADES

IT WAS EIGHT o'clock as Bond followed M. through the tall doors, across the well of the staircase from the card-room, that opened into the beautiful white and gold Regency dining-room of Blades.

M. chose not to hear a call from Basildon who was presiding over the big centre table where there were still two places vacant. Instead, he walked firmly across the room to the end one of a row of six smaller tables, waved Bond into the comfortable armed chair that faced outwards into the room, and himself took the one on Bond's left so that his back was to the company.

The head steward was already behind Bond's chair. He placed a broad menu card beside his plate and handed another to M. 'Blades' was written in fine gold script across the top. Below there was a forest of print.

'Don't bother to read through all that,' said M., 'unless you've got no ideas. One of the first rules of the club, and one of the best, was that any member may speak for any dish, cheap or dear, but he must pay for it. The same's true today, only the odds are one doesn't have to pay for it. Just order what you feel like.' He looked up at the steward. 'Any of that Beluga caviar left, Porterfield?'

'Yes, sir. There was a new delivery last week.'

'Well,' said M. 'Caviar for me. Devilled kidney and a slice of your excellent bacon. Peas and new potatoes. Strawberries in kirsch. What about you, James?'

'I've got a mania for really good smoked salmon,' said Bond. Then he pointed down the menu. 'Lamb cutlets. The same vegetables as you, as it's May. Asparagus with Hollandaise sauce sounds wonderful. And perhaps a slice of pineapple.' He sat back and pushed the menu away.

'Thank heavens for a man who makes up his mind,' said M.

He looked up at the steward. 'Have you got all that, Porterfield?'

'Yes, sir.' The steward smiled. 'You wouldn't care for a marrow bone after the strawberries, sir? We got half a dozen in today from the country, and I'd specially kept one in case you came in.'

'Of course. You know I can't resist them. Bad for me but it can't be helped. God knows what I'm celebrating this evening. But it doesn't often happen. Ask Grimley to come over, would you.'

'He's here now, sir,' said the steward, making way for the wine-waiter.

'Ah, Grimley, some vodka please.' He turned to Bond. 'Not the stuff you had in your cocktail. This is real pre-war Wolfschmidt from Riga. Like some with your smoked salmon?'

'Very much,' said Bond.

'Then what?' asked M. 'Champagne? Personally I'm going to have a half-bottle of claret. The Mouton Rothschild '34, please, Grimley. But don't pay any attention to me, James. I'm an old man. Champagne's no good for me. We've got some good champagnes, haven't we, Grimley? None of that stuff you're always telling me about, I'm afraid, James. Don't often see it in England. Taittinger, wasn't it?'

Bond smiled at M.'s memory. 'Yes,' he said, 'but it's only a fad of mine. As a matter of fact, for various reasons I believe I would like to drink champagne this evening. Perhaps I could leave it to Grimley.

The wine-waiter was pleased. 'If I may suggest it, sir, the Dom Perignon '46. I understand that France only sells it for dollars, sir, so you don't often see it in London. I believe it was a gift from the Regency Club in New York, sir. I have some on ice at the moment. It's the Chairman's favourite and he's told me to have it ready every evening in case he needs it.'

Bond smiled his agreement.

'So be it, Grimley,' said M. 'The Dom Perignon. Bring it straight away, would you?'

A waitress appeared and put racks of fresh toast on the table and a silver dish of Jersey butter. As she bent over the table her black skirt brushed Bond's arm and he looked up into two pert, sparkling eyes under a soft fringe of hair. The eyes held his for a fraction of a second and then she whisked away. Bond's eyes followed the white bow at her waist and the starched collar and cuffs of her uniform as she went down the long room. His eyes narrowed. He recalled a pre-war establishment in Paris where the girls were dressed with the same exciting severity. Until they turned round and showed their backs.

He smiled to himself. The *Marthe Richards* law had changed all that.

M. turned from studying their neighbours behind him. 'Why were you so cryptic about drinking champagne?'

'Well, if you don't mind, sir,' Bond explained, 'I've got to get a bit tight tonight. I'll have to seem very drunk when the time comes. It's not an easy thing to act unless you do it with a good deal of conviction. I hope you won't get worried if I seem to get frayed at the edges later on.'

M. shrugged his shoulders. 'You've got a head like a rock, James,' he said. 'Drink as much as you like if it's going to help. Ah, here's the vodka.'

When M. poured him three fingers from the frosted carafe Bond took a pinch of black pepper and dropped it on the surface of the vodka. The pepper slowly settled to the bottom of the glass leaving a few grains on the surface which Bond dabbed up with the tip of a finger. Then he tossed the cold liquor well to the back of his throat and put his glass, with the dregs of the pepper at the bottom, back on the table.

M. gave him a glance of rather ironical inquiry.

'It's a trick the Russians taught me that time you attached me to the Embassy in Moscow,' apologized Bond. 'There's often quite a lot of fusel oil on the surface of this stuff — at least there used to be when it was badly distilled. Poisonous. In Russia, where you get a lot of bath-tub liquor, it's an understood thing to sprinkle a little pepper in your glass. It takes the fusel oil to the bottom. I got to like the taste and now it's a habit. But I shouldn't have insulted the club Wolfschmidt,' he added with a grin.

M. grunted. 'So long as you don't put pepper in Basildon's favourite champagne,' he said drily.

A harsh bray of laughter came from a table at the far end of the room. M. looked over his shoulder and then turned back to his caviar.

'What do you think of this man Drax?' he said through a mouthful of buttered toast.

Bond helped himself to another slice of smoked salmon from the silver dish beside him. It had the delicate glutinous texture only achieved by the Highland curers — very different from the desiccated products of Scandinavia. He rolled a wafer-thin slice of brown bread-and-butter into a cylinder and contemplated it thoughtfully.

'One can't like his manner much. At first I was rather surprised that you tolerate him here.' He glanced at M., who shrugged his shoulders. 'But that's none of my business and anyway clubs would be very dull without a sprinkling of eccentrics. And in any case he's a national hero and a millionaire and obviously an adequate card-player. Even when he isn't helping himself to the odds,' he added. 'But I can see he's the sort of man I always imagined. Full-blooded, ruthless, shrewd. Plenty of guts. I'm not surprised he's managed to get where he is. What I don't understand is why he should be quite happy to throw it all away. This cheating of his. It's really beyond belief. What's he trying to prove with it? That he can beat everyone at everything? He seems to put so much passion into his cards — as if it wasn't a game at all, but some sort of trial of strength. You've only got to look at his finger-nails. Bitten to the quick. And he sweats too much. There's a lot of tension there somewhere. It comes out in those ghastly jokes of his. They're harsh. There's no light touch about them. He seemed to want to squash Basildon like a fly. Hope I shall be able to keep my temper. That manner of his is pretty riling. He even treats his partner as if he was muck. He hasn't quite got under my skin, but I shan't at all mind sticking a very sharp pin into him tonight.' He smiled at M. 'If it comes off, that is.'

'I know what you mean,' said M. 'But you may be being a bit hard on the man. After all, it's a big step from the Liverpool docks, or wherever he came from, to where he is now. And he's one of those people who was born with naturally hairy heels. Nothing to do with snobbery. I expect his mates in Liverpool found him just as loud-mouthed as Blades does. As for his cheating, there's probably a crooked streak in him somewhere. I daresay he took plenty of short cuts on his way up. Somebody said that to become very rich you have to be helped by a combination of remarkable circumstances and an unbroken run of luck. It certainly isn't only the qualities of people that make them rich. At least that's my experience. At the beginning, getting together the first ten thousand, things have got to go damn right. And in that commodity business after the war, with all the regulations and restrictions, I expect it was often a case of being able to drop a thousand pounds in the right pocket. Officials. The ones who understood nothing but addition, division — and silence. The useful ones.'

M. paused while the next course came. With it arrived the champagne in a silver ice-bucket, and the small Waterford decanter containing M.'s half-bottle of claret.

The wine-steward waited until they had delivered a favourable judgment on the wines and then moved away. As he did so a page came up to their table. 'Commander Bond?' he asked.

Bond took the envelope that was handed to him and slit it open. He took out a thin paper packet and carefully opened it under the level of the table. It contained a white powder. He took a silver fruit knife off the table and dipped the tip of the blade into the packet so that about half its contents were transferred to the knife. He reached for his glass of champagne and tipped the powder into it.

'Now what?' said M. with a trace of impatience.

There was no hint of apology in Bond's face. It wasn't M. who was going to have to do the work that evening. Bond knew what he was doing. Whenever he had a job of work to do he would take infinite pains beforehand and leave as little as possible to chance. Then if something went wrong it was the unforeseeable. For that he accepted no responsibility.

'Benzedrine,' he said. 'I rang up my secretary before dinner and asked her to wangle some out of the surgery at Headquarters. It's what I shall need if I'm going to keep my wits about me tonight. It's apt to make one a bit over-confident, but that'll be a help too.' He stirred the champagne with a scrap of toast so that the white powder whirled among the bubbles. Then he drank the mixture down with one long swallow. 'It doesn't taste,' said Bond, 'and the champagne is quite excellent.'

M. smiled at him indulgently. 'It's your funeral,' he said. 'Now we'd better get on with our dinner. How were the cutlets?'

'Superb,' said Bond. 'I could cut them with a fork. The best English cooking is the best in the world — particularly at this time of the year. By the way, what stakes will we be playing for this evening? I don't mind very much. We ought to end up the winners. But I'd like to know how much it will cost Drax.'

'Drax likes to play for what he calls "One and One",' said M., helping himself from the strawberries that had just been put on the table. 'Modest-sounding stake, if you don't know what it stands for. In fact it's one tenner a hundred and one hundred pounds on the rubber.'

'Oh,' said Bond, respectfully. 'I see.'

'But he's perfectly happy to play for Two and Two or even Three and Three. Mounts up at those figures. The average rubber of bridge at Blades is about ten points. That's £200 at One and One. And the bridge here makes for big rubbers. There are no conventions so there's plenty of gambling and bluffing. Sometimes it's more like poker. They're a mixed lot of players. Some of them are the best in England, but others are terribly wild. Don't seem to mind how much they lose. General Bealey, just behind us,' M. made a gesture with his head, 'doesn't know the reds from the blacks. Nearly always a few hundred down at the end of the week. Doesn't seem to care. Bad heart. No dependants. Stacks of money from jute. But Duff Sutherland, the scruffy-looking chap next to the Chairman, is an absolute killer. Makes a regular ten thousand a year out of the club. Nice chap. Wonderful card manners. Used to play chess for England.'

M. was interrupted by the arrival of his marrow bone. It was placed upright in a spotless lace napkin on the silver plate. An ornate silver marrow-scoop was laid beside it.

After the asparagus, Bond had little appetite for the thin slivers of pineapple. He tipped the last of the ice-cold champagne into his glass. He felt wonderful. The effects of the benzedrine and champagne had more than offset the splendour of the food. For the first time he took his mind away from the dinner and his conversation with M. and glanced round the room.

It was a sparkling scene. There were perhaps fifty men in the room, the majority in dinner jackets, all at ease with themselves and their surroundings, all stimulated by the peerless food and drink, all animated by a common interest — the prospect of high gambling, the grand slam, the ace pot, the key-throw in a 64 game at backgammon. There might be cheats or possible cheats amongst them, men who beat their wives, men with perverse instincts, greedy men, cowardly men, lying men; but the elegance of the room invested each one with a kind of aristocracy.

At the far end, above the cold table, laden with lobsters, pies, joints, and delicacies in aspic, Romney's unfinished full-length portrait of Mrs. Fitzherbert gazed provocatively across at Fragonard's *Jeu de Cartes*, the broad conversation-piece which half-filled the opposite wall above the Adam fireplace. Along the lateral walls, in the centre of each gilt-edged panel, was one of the rare engravings of the Hell-Fire Club in which each figure is shown making a minute gesture of scatological or magical significance. Above, marrying the walls into the ceiling, ran a frieze in plaster relief of carved urns and swags interrupted at intervals by the capitals of the fluted pilasters which framed the windows and the tall double doors, the latter delicately carved with a design showing the Tudor Rose interwoven with a ribbon effect.

The central chandelier, a cascade of crystal ropes terminating in a broad basket of strung quartz, sparkled warmly above the white damask tablecloths and George IV silver. Below, in the centre of each table, branched candlesticks distributed the golden light of three candles, each surmounted by a red silk shade, so that the faces of the diners shone with a convivial warmth which glossed over the occasional chill of an eye or cruel twist of a mouth.

Even as Bond drank in the warm elegance of the scene, some of the groups began to break up. There was a drift towards the door accompanied by an exchange of challenges, side-bets, and exhortations to hurry up and get down to business. Sir Hugo Drax, his hairy red face shining with cheerful anticipation, came towards them with Meyer in his wake.

'Well, gentlemen,' he said jovially as he reached their table. 'Are the lambs ready for the slaughter and the geese for the plucking?' He grinned and in wolfish pantomime drew a finger across his throat. 'We'll go ahead and lay out the axe and the basket. Made your wills?'

'Be with you in a moment,' said M. edgily. 'You go along and stack the cards.'

Drax laughed. 'We shan't need any artificial aids,' he said. 'Don't be long.' He turned and made for the door. Meyer enveloped them in an uncertain smile and followed him.

M. grunted. 'We'll have coffee and brandy in the card-room,' he said to Bond. 'Can't smoke here. Now then. Any final plans?'

'I'll have to fatten him up for the kill, so please don't worry if I seem to be betting high,' said Bond. 'We'll just have to play our normal game till the time comes. When it's his deal, we'll have to be careful. Of course, he can't alter the cards and there's no reason why he shouldn't deal us good hands, but he's bound to bring off some pretty remarkable coups. Do you mind if I sit on his left?'

'No,' said M. 'Anything else?'

Bond reflected for a moment. 'Only one thing, sir,' he said. 'When the time comes, I shall take a white handkerchief out of my coat pocket. That will mean that you are about to be dealt a Yarborough. Would you please leave the bidding of that hand to me?'

6

CARDS WITH A STRANGER

DRAX AND MEYER were waiting for them. They were leaning back in their chairs, smoking Cabinet Havanas.

On the small tables beside them there was coffee and large balloons of brandy. As M. and Bond came up, Drax was tearing the paper cover off a new pack of cards. The other pack was fanned out across the green baize in front of him.

'Ah, there you are,' said Drax. He leant forward and cut a card. They all followed suit. Drax won the cut and elected to stay where he was and take the red cards.

Bond sat down on Drax's left.

M. beckoned to a passing waiter. 'Coffee and the club brandy,' he said. He took out a thin black cheroot and offered one to Bond who accepted it. Then he picked up the red cards and started to shuffle them.

'Stakes?' asked Drax, looking at M. 'One and One? Or more? I'll be glad to accommodate you up to Five and Five.'

'One and One'll be enough for me,' said M. 'James?'

Drax cut in, 'I suppose your guest knows what he's in for?' he asked sharply.

Bond answered for M. 'Yes,' he said briefly. He smiled at Drax. 'And I feel rather generous tonight. What would you like to take off me?'

'Every penny you've got,' said Drax cheerfully. 'How much can you afford?'

'I'll tell you when there's none left,' said Bond. He suddenly decided to be ruthless. 'I'm told that Five and Five is your limit. Let's play for that.'

Almost before the words were out of his mouth he regretted them. £50 a hundred! £500 side-bets! Four bad rubbers would be double his income for a year. If something went wrong he'd look pretty stupid. Have to borrow from M. And M. wasn't a particularly rich man. Suddenly he saw that this ridiculous game might end in a very nasty mess. He felt the prickle of sweat on his forehead. That damned benzedrine. And for him of all people to allow himself to be needled by a blustering loud-mouthed bastard like Drax. And he wasn't even on a job. The whole evening was a bit of social pantomime that meant less than nothing to him. Even M. had only been dragged into it by chance. And all of a sudden he'd let himself be swept up into a duel with this multi-millionaire, into a gamble for literally all Bond possessed, for the simple reason that the man had got filthy manners and he'd wanted to teach him a lesson. And supposing the lesson didn't come off? Bond cursed himself for an impulse that earlier in the day would have seemed unthinkable. Champagne and benzedrine! Never again.

Drax was looking at him in sarcastic disbelief. He turned to M. who was still unconcernedly shuffling the cards. 'I suppose your guest is good for his commitments,' he said. Unforgivably.

Bond saw the blood rush up M.'s neck and into his face. M. paused for an instant in his shuffling. When he continued Bond noticed that his hands were quite calm. M. looked up and took the cheroot very deliberately out from between his teeth. His voice was perfectly controlled. 'If you mean "Am I good for my guest's commitments",' he said coldly, 'the answer is yes.'

He cut the cards to Drax with his left hand and with his right knocked the ash off his cheroot into the copper ashtray in the corner of the table. Bond heard the faint hiss as the burning ash hit the water.

Drax squinted sideways at M. He picked up the cards. 'Of course, of course,' he said hastily. 'I didn't mean . . . ' He left the sentence unfinished and turned to Bond. 'Right, then,' he said, looking rather curiously at Bond. 'Five and Five it is. Meyer,' he turned to his partner, 'how much would you like to take? There's Six and Six to cut up.'

'One and One's enough for me, Hugger,' said Meyer apologetically. 'Unless you'd like me to take some more.' He looked anxiously at his partner.

'Of course not,' said Drax. 'I like a high game. Never get enough on generally. Now then,' he started to deal, 'off we go.'

And suddenly Bond didn't care about the high stakes. Suddenly all he wanted to do was to give this hairy ape the lesson of his life, give him a shock which would make him remember this evening for ever, remember Bond, remember M., remember the last time he would cheat at Blades, remember the time of day, the weather outside, what he had had for dinner.

For all its importance, Bond had forgotten the Moonraker. This was a private affair between two men.

As he watched the casual downward glance at the cigarette-case between the two hands and felt the cool memory ticking up the card values as they passed over its surface, Bond cleared his mind of all regrets, absolved himself of all blame for what was about to happen, and focused his attention on the game. He settled himself more comfortably into his chair and rested his hands on the padded leather arms. Then he took the thin cheroot from between his teeth, laid it on the burnished copper surround of the ashtray beside him and reached for his coffee. It was very black and strong. He emptied the cup and picked up the ballon glass with its fat measure of pale brandy. As he sipped it and then drank again, more deeply, he looked over the rim at M. M. met his eye and smiled briefly.

'Hope you like it,' he said. 'Comes from one of the Rothschild estates at Cognac. About a hundred years ago one of the family bequeathed us a barrel of it every year in perpetuity. During the war they hid a barrel for us every year and then sent us over the whole lot in 1945. Ever since then we've been drinking doubles. And,' he gathered up his cards, 'now we shall have to concentrate.'

Bond picked up his hand. It was average. A bare two and a half quick tricks, the suits evenly distributed. He reached for his cheroot and gave it a final draw then killed it in the ashtray.

'Three clubs,' said Drax.

No bid from Bond.

Four clubs from Meyer.

No bid from M.

Hm, thought Bond. He's not quite got the cards for a game call this time. Shut-out call — knows that his partner has got a bare raise. M. may have got a perfectly good bid. We may have all the hearts between us, for instance. But M. never gets a bid. Presumably they'll make four clubs.

They did, with the help of one finesse through Bond. M. turned out not to have had hearts, but a long string of diamonds, missing only the king, which was in Meyer's hand and would have been caught. Drax didn't have nearly enough length for a three call. Meyer had the rest of the clubs.

Anyway, thought Bond as he dealt the next hand, we were lucky to escape without a game call.

Their good luck continued. Bond opened a No Trump, was put up to three by M., and they made it with an overtrick. On Meyer's deal they went one down in five diamonds, but on the next hand M. opened four spades and Bond's three small trumps and an outside king, queen were all M. needed for the contract.

First rubber to M. and Bond. Drax looked annoyed. He had lost £900 on the rubber and the cards seemed to be running against them.

'Shall we go straight on?' he asked. 'No point in cutting.'

M. smiled across at Bond. The same thought was in both their minds. So Drax wanted to keep the deal. Bond shrugged his shoulders.

'No objection,' said M. 'These seats seem to be doing their best for us.'

'Up to now,' said Drax, looking more cheerful.

And with reason. On the next hand he and Meyer bid and made a small slam in spades that required two hair-raising finesses, both of which Drax, after a good deal of pantomime and hemming and hawing, negotiated smoothly, each time commenting loudly on his good fortune.

'Hugger, you're wonderful,' said Meyer fulsomely. 'How the devil do you do it?'

Bond thought it time to sow a tiny seed. 'Memory,' he said.

Drax looked at him, sharply. 'What do you mean, memory?' he said. 'What's that got to do with taking a finesse?'

'I was going to add "and card sense",' said Bond smoothly. 'They're the two qualities that make great card-players.'

'Oh,' said Drax slowly. 'Yes, I see.' He cut the cards to Bond and as Bond dealt he felt the other man's eyes examining him carefully.

The game proceeded at an even pace. The cards refused to get hot and no one seemed inclined to take chances. M. doubled Meyer in an incautious four-spade bid and got him two down vulnerable, but on the next hand Drax went out with a lay-down three No Trumps. Bond's win on the first rubber was wiped out and a bit more besides.

'Anyone care for a drink?' asked M. as he cut the cards to Drax for the third rubber. 'James. A little more champagne? The second bottle always tastes better.'

'I'd like that very much,' said Bond.

The waiter came. The others ordered whiskies and sodas.

Drax turned to Bond. 'This game needs livening up,' he said. 'A hundred we win this hand.' He had completed the deal and the cards lay in neat piles in the centre of the table.

Bond looked at him. The damaged eye glared at him redly. The other was cold and hard and scornful. There were beads of sweat on either side of the large, beaky nose.

Bond wondered if he was having a fly thrown over him to see if he was suspicious of the deal. He decided to leave the man in doubt. It was a hundred down the drain, but it would give him an excuse for increasing the stakes later.

'On your deal?' he said with a smile. 'Well,' he weighed imaginary chances, 'yes. All right.' An idea seemed to come to him. 'And the same on the next hand. If you like,' he added.

'All right, all right,' said Drax impatiently. 'If you want to throw good money after bad.'

'You seem very certain about this hand,' said Bond indifferently, picking up his cards. They were a poor lot and he had no answer to Drax's opening No Trump except to double it. The bluff had no effect on Drax's partner. Meyer said 'Two No Trumps' and Bond was relieved when M., with no long suit, said 'No bid'. Drax left it in two No Trumps and made the contract.

'Thanks,' he said with relish, and wrote carefully on his score. 'Now let's see if you can get it back.'

Much to his annoyance, Bond couldn't. The cards still ran for Meyer and Drax and they made three hearts and the game.

Drax was pleased with himself. He took a long swallow at his whisky and soda and wiped down his face with his bandana handkerchief.

'God is with the big battalions,' he said jovially. 'Got to have the cards as well as play them. Coming back for more or had enough?'

Bond's champagne had come and was standing beside him in its silver bucket. There was a glass goblet three-quarters full beside it on the side table. Bond picked it up and drained it, as if to give himself Dutch courage. Then he filled it again.

'All right,' he said thickly, 'a hundred on the next two hands.'

And promptly lost them both, and the rubber.

Bond suddenly realized that he was nearly £1,500 down. He drank another glass of champagne. 'Save trouble if we just double the stakes on this rubber,' he said rather wildly. 'All right with you?'

Drax had dealt and was looking at his cards. His lips were wet with anticipation. He looked at Bond who seemed to be having difficulty lighting his cigarette. 'Taken,' he said quickly. 'A hundred pounds a hundred and a thousand on the rubber.' Then he felt he could risk a touch of sportsmanship. Bond could hardly cancel the bet now. 'But I seem to have got some good tickets here,' he added. 'Are you still on?'

'Of course, of course,' said Bond, clumsily picking up his hand. 'I made the bet, didn't I?'

'All right then,' said Drax with satisfaction. 'Three No Trumps here.'

7
THE QUICKNESS OF THE HAND

THERE WAS A moment's silence at the table. It was broken by the agitated voice of Meyer.

'Here I say,' he said anxiously. 'Don't include me in on this, Hugger.' He knew it was a private bet with Bond, but he wanted to show Drax that he was thoroughly nervous about the whole affair. He saw himself making some ghastly mistake that would cost his partner a lot of money.

'Don't be ridiculous, Max,' said Drax harshly. 'You play your hand. This is nothing to do with you. Just an enjoyable little bet with our rash friend here. Come along, come along. My deal, Admiral.'

M. cut the cards and the game began.

Bond lit a cigarette with hands that had suddenly become quite steady. His mind was clear. He knew exactly what he had to do, and when, and he was glad that the moment of decision had come.

He sat back in his chair and for a moment he had the impression that there was a crowd behind him at each elbow, and that faces were peering over his shoulder, waiting to see his cards. He somehow felt that the ghosts were friendly, that they approved of the rough justice that was about to be done.

He smiled as he caught himself sending this company of dead gamblers a message, that they should see that all went well.

The background noise of the famous gaming room broke in on his thoughts. He looked round. In the middle of the long room, under the central chandelier, there were several onlookers round the poker game. 'Raise you a hundred.' 'And a hundred.' 'And a hundred.' 'Damn you. I'll look,' and a shout of triumph followed by a hubbub of comment. In the distance he could hear the rattle of a croupier's rake against the counters at the Shemmy game. Nearer at hand, at his end of the room, there were three other tables of bridge over which the smoke of cigars and cigarettes rose towards the barrelled ceiling.

Nearly every night for more than a hundred and fifty years there had been just such a scene, he reflected, in this famous room. The same cries of victory and defeat, the same dedicated faces, the same smell of tobacco and drama. For Bond, who loved gambling, it was the most exciting spectacle in the world. He gave it a last glance to fix it all in his mind and then he turned back to his table.

He picked up his cards and his eyes glittered. For once, on Drax's deal, he had a cast-iron game hand; seven spades with the four top honours, the ace of hearts, and the ace, king of diamonds. He looked at Drax. Had he and Meyer got the clubs? Even so Bond could overbid. Would Drax try and force him too high and risk a double? Bond waited.

'No bid,' said Drax, unable to keep the bitterness of his private knowledge of Bond's hand out of his voice.

'Four spades,' said Bond.

No bid from Meyer; from M.; reluctantly from Drax.

M. provided some help, and they made five.

One hundred and fifty points below the line. A hundred above for honours.

'Humph,' said a voice at Bond's elbow. He looked up. It was Basildon. His game had finished and he had strolled over to see what was happening on this separate battlefield.

He picked up Bond's score-sheet and looked at it.

'That was a bit of a beetle-crusher,' he said cheerfully. 'Seems you're holding the champions. What are the stakes?'

Bond left the answer to Drax. He was glad of the diversion. It could not have been better timed. Drax had cut the blue cards to him. He married the two halves and put the pack just in front of him, near the edge of the table.

'Fifteen and fifteen. On my left,' said Drax.

Bond heard Basildon draw in his breath.

'Chap seemed to want to gamble, so I accommodated him. Now he goes and gets all the cards . . . '

Drax grumbled on.

Across the table, M. saw a white handkerchief materialize in Bond's right hand. M.'s eyes narrowed. Bond seemed to wipe his face with it. M. saw him glance sharply at Drax and Meyer then the handkerchief was back in his pocket.

A blue pack was in Bond's hands and he had started to deal.

'That's the hell of a stake,' said Basildon. 'We once had a thousand-pound side-bet on a game of bridge. But that was in the rubber boom before the 'fourteen-eighteen war. Hope nobody's going to get hurt.' He meant it. Very high stakes in a private game generally led to trouble. He walked round and stood between M. and Drax.

Bond completed the deal. With a touch of anxiety he picked up his cards.

He had nothing but five clubs to the ace, queen, ten, and eight small diamonds to the queen.

It was all right. The trap was set.

He almost felt Drax stiffen as the big man thumbed through his cards, and then, unbelieving, thumbed them through again. Bond knew that Drax had an incredibly good hand. Ten certain tricks, the ace, king of diamonds, the four top honours in spades, the four top honours in hearts, and the king, knave, nine of clubs.

Bond had dealt them to him — in the Secretary's room before dinner.

Bond waited, wondering how Drax would react to the huge hand. He took an almost cruel interest in watching the greedy fish come to the lure.

Drax exceeded his expectations.

Casually he folded his hand and laid it on the table. Nonchalantly he took the flat carton out of his pocket, selected a cigarette and lit it. He didn't look at Bond. He glanced up at Basildon.

Yes,' he said, continuing the conversation about their stakes. 'It's a high game, but not the highest I've ever played. Once played for two thousand a rubber in Cairo. At the Mahomet Ali as a matter of fact. They've really got guts there. Often bet on every trick as well as on the game and rubber. Now,' he picked up his hand and looked slyly at Bond, 'I've got some good tickets here. I'll admit it. But then you may have too, for all I know.' (Unlikely, you old shark, thought Bond, with three of the ace-kings in your own hand.) 'Care to have something extra just on this hand?'

Bond made a show of studying his cards with the minuteness of someone who is nearly very drunk. 'I've got a promising lot too,' he said thickly. 'If my partner fits and the cards lie right I might make a lot of tricks myself. What are you suggesting?'

'Sounds as if we're pretty evenly matched,' lied Drax. 'What do you say to a hundred a trick on the side? From what you say that shouldn't be too painful.'

Bond looked thoughtful and rather fuddled. He took another careful look at his hand, running through the cards one by one. 'All right,' he said. 'You're on. And frankly you've made me gamble. You've obviously got a big hand, so I must shut you out and chance it.'

Bond looked blearily across at M. 'Pay your losses on this one, partner,' he said. 'Here we go. Er — seven clubs.'

In the dead silence that followed, Basildon, who had seen Drax's hand, was so startled that he dropped his whisky and soda on the floor. He looked dazedly down at the broken glass and let it lie.

Drax said 'What?' in a startled voice and hastily ran through his cards again for reassurance.

'Did you say grand slam in clubs?' he asked, looking curiously at his obviously drunken opponent. 'Well, it's your funeral. What do you say, Max?'

'No bid,' said Meyer, feeling in the air the electricity of just that crisis he had hoped to avoid. Why the hell hadn't he gone home before this last rubber? He groaned inwardly.

'No bid,' said M., apparently unperturbed.

'Double.' The word came viciously out of Drax's mouth. He put down his hand and looked cruelly, scornfully at this tipsy oaf who had at last, inexplicably, fallen into his hands.

'That mean you double the side-bets too?' asked Bond.

'Yes,' said Drax greedily. 'Yes. That's what I meant.'

'All right,' said Bond. He paused. He looked at Drax and not at his hand. 'Redouble. The contract and the side-bets. £400 a trick on the side.'

It was at that moment that the first hint of a dreadful, incredible doubt entered Drax's mind. But again he looked at his hand, and again he was reassured. At the very worst he couldn't fail to make two tricks.

A muttered 'No bid' from Meyer. A rather strangled 'No bid' from M. An impatient shake of the head from Drax.

Basildon stood, his face very pale, looking intently across the table at Bond.

Then he walked slowly round the table, scrutinizing all the hands. What he saw was this:

BOND
♢ Queen, 8, 7, 6, 5, 4, 3, 2
♣ Ace, queen, 10, 8, 4

DRAX	MEYER
♠ Ace, king, queen, knave	♠ 6, 5, 4, 3, 2
♡ Ace, king, queen, knave	♡ 10, 9, 8, 7, 2
♢ Ace, king	♢ Knave, 10, 9
♣ King, knave, 9	

M.
♠ 10, 9, 8, 7
♡ 6, 5, 4, 3
♣ 7, 6, 5, 3, 2

And suddenly Basildon understood. It was a laydown grand slam for Bond against any defence. Whatever Meyer led, Bond must get in with a trump in his own hand or on the table. Then, in between clearing trumps, finessing of course against Drax, he would play two rounds of diamonds, trumping them in dummy and catching Drax's ace and king in the process. After five plays he would be left with the remaining trumps and six winning diamonds. Drax's aces and kings would be totally valueless.

It was sheer murder.

Basildon, almost in a trance, continued round the table and stood between M. and Meyer so that he could watch Drax's face, and Bond's. His own face was impassive, but his hands, which he had stuffed into his trouser pockets so that they would not betray him, were sweating. He waited, almost fearfully, for the terrible punishment that Drax was about to receive — thirteen separate lashes whose scars no card-player would ever lose.

'Come along, come along,' said Drax impatiently. 'Lead something, Max. Can't be here all night.'

You poor fool, thought Basildon. In ten minutes you'll wish that Meyer had died in his chair before he could pull out that first card.

In fact, Meyer looked as if at any moment he might have a stroke. He was deathly pale, and the perspiration was dropping off his chin on to his shirt front. For all he knew, his first card might be a disaster.

At last, reasoning that Bond might be void in his own long suits, spades and hearts, he led the knave of diamonds.

It made no difference what he led, but when M.'s hand went down showing chicane in diamonds, Drax snarled across at his partner. 'Haven't you got anything else, you dam' fool? Want to hand it to him on a plate? Whose side are you on, anyway?'

Meyer cringed into his clothes. 'Best I could do, Hugger,' he said miserably, wiping his face with his handkerchief.

But by this time Drax had got his own worries.

Bond trumped on the table, catching Drax's king of diamonds, and promptly led a club. Drax put up his nine. Bond took it with his ten and led a diamond, trumping it on the table. Drax's ace fell. Another club from the table, catching Drax's knave.

Then the ace of clubs.

As Drax surrendered his king, for the first time he saw what might be happening. His eyes squinted anxiously at Bond, waiting fearfully for the next card. Had Bond got the diamonds? Hadn't Meyer got them guarded? After all, he had opened with them. Drax waited, his cards slippery with sweat.

Morphy, the great chess player, had a terrible habit. He would never raise his eyes from the game until he knew his opponent could not escape defeat. Then he would slowly lift his great head and gaze curiously at the man across the board. His opponent would feel the gaze and would slowly, humbly raise his eyes to meet Morphy's. At that moment he would know that it was no good continuing the game. The eyes of Morphy said so. There was nothing left but surrender.

Now, like Morphy, Bond lifted his head and looked straight into Drax's eyes. Then he slowly drew out the queen of diamonds and placed it on the table. Without waiting for Meyer to play he followed it, deliberately, with the 8, 7, 6, 5, 4, and the two winning clubs.

Then he spoke. 'That's all, Drax,' he said quietly, and sat slowly back in his chair.

Drax's first reaction was to lurch forward and tear Meyer's cards out of his hand. He faced them on the table, scrabbling feverishly among them for a possible winner.

Then he flung them back across the baize.

His face was dead white, but his eyes blazed redly at Bond. Suddenly he raised one clenched fist and crashed it on the table among the pile of impotent aces and kings and queens in front of him.

Very low, he spat the words at Bond. 'You're a che . . . '

'That's enough, Drax.' Basildon's voice came across the table like a whiplash. 'None of that talk here. I've been watching the whole game. Settle up. If you've got any complaints, put them in writing to the Committee.'

Drax got slowly to his feet. He stood away from his chair and ran a hand through his wet red hair. The colour came slowly back into his face and with it an expression of cunning. He glanced down at Bond and there was in his good eye a contemptuous triumph which Bond found curiously disturbing.

He turned to the table. 'Good night, gentlemen,' he said, looking at each of them with the same oddly scornful expression. 'I owe about £15,000. I will accept Meyer's addition.'

He leant forward and picked up his cigarette-case and lighter.

Then he looked again at Bond and spoke very quietly, the red moustache lifting slowly from the splayed upper teeth.

'I should spend the money quickly, Commander Bond,' he said.

Then he turned away from the table and walked swiftly out of the room.

Part Two

TUESDAY, WEDNESDAY

8

THE RED TELEPHONE

ALTHOUGH HE HAD not got to bed until two, Bond walked into his headquarters punctually at ten the next morning. He was feeling dreadful. As well as acidity and liver as a result of drinking nearly two whole bottles of champagne, he had a touch of the melancholy, and the spiritual deflation that were partly the after-effects of the benzedrine and partly reaction to the drama of the night before.

When he went up in the lift towards another routine day, the bitter taste of the midnight hours was still with him.

After Meyer had scuttled thankfully off to bed, Bond had taken the two packs of cards out of the pockets of his coat and had put them on the table in front of Basildon and M. One was the blue pack that Drax had cut to him and that he had pocketed, substituting instead, under cover of his handkerchief, the stacked blue pack in his right-hand pocket. The other was the stacked red pack in his left-hand pocket which had not been needed.

He fanned the red pack out on the table and showed M. and Basildon that it would have produced the same freak grand slam that had defeated Drax.

'It's a famous Culbertson hand,' he explained. 'He used it to spoof his own quick-trick conventions. I had to doctor a red and a blue pack. Couldn't know which colour I would be dealing with.'

'Well, it certainly went with a bang,' said Basildon gratefully. 'I expect he'll put two and two together and either stay away or play straight in future. Expensive evening for him. Don't let's have any argument about your winnings,' he added. 'You've done everyone — and particularly Drax — a good turn tonight. Things might have gone wrong. Then it would have been your fingers that would have got burned. Cheque will reach you on Saturday.'

They had said good-night and Bond, in a mood of anticlimax, had gone off to bed. He had taken a mild sleeping pill to try and clear his mind of the bizarre events of the evening and prepare himself for the morning and the office. Before he slept he reflected, as he had often reflected in other moments of triumph at the card table, that the gain to the winner is, in some odd way, always less than the loss to the loser.

When he closed the door behind him Loelia Ponsonby looked curiously at the dark shadows under his eyes. He noticed the glance, as she had intended.

He grinned. 'Partly work and partly play,' he explained. 'In strictly masculine company,' he added. 'And thanks very much for the benzedrine. It really was badly needed. Hope I didn't interfere with your evening?'

'Of course not,' she said, thinking of the dinner and the library book she had abandoned when Bond telephoned. She looked down at her shorthand pad. 'The Chief of Staff telephoned half an hour ago. He said that M. would be wanting you today. He couldn't say when. I told him that you've got Unarmed Combat at three and he said to cancel it. That's all, except the dockets left over from yesterday.'

'Thank heavens,' said Bond. 'I couldn't have stood being thrown about by that dam' Commando chap today. Any news of 008?'

'Yes,' she said. 'They say he's all right. He's been moved to the military hospital at Wahnerheide. Apparently it's only shock.'

Bond knew what 'shock' might mean in his profession. 'Good,' he said without conviction. He smiled at her and went into his office and closed the door.

He walked decisively round his desk to the chair, sat down, and pulled the top file towards him. Monday was gone. This was Tuesday. A new day. Closing his mind to his headache and to thoughts about the night, he lit a cigarette and opened the brown folder with the Top Secret red star on it. It was a memorandum from the Office of the Chief Preventive Officer of the United States Customs Branch and it was headed *The Inspectoscope.*

He focused his eyes. 'The Inspectoscope,' he read, 'is an instrument using fluoroscopic principles for the detection of contraband. It is manufactured by the Sicular Inspectoscope

Company of San Francisco and is widely used in American prisons for the secret detection of metal objects concealed in the clothing or on the person of criminals and prison visitors. It is also used in the detection of I.D.B. (Illicit Diamond Buying) and diamond smuggling in the diamond fields of Africa and Brazil. The instrument costs seven thousand dollars, is approximately eight feet long by seven feet high and weighs nearly three tons. It requires two trained operators. Experiments have been made with this instrument in the customs hall of the International Airport at Idlewild with the following results . . . '

Bond skipped two pages containing details of a number of petty smuggling cases and studied the 'Summary of Conclusions' from which he deduced, with some irritation, that he would have to think of some place other than his armpit for carrying his .25 Beretta the next time he travelled abroad. He made a mental note to discuss the problem with the Technical Devices Section.

He ticked and initialled the distribution slip and automatically reached for the next folder entitled *Philopon. A Japanese murder-drug.*

'Philopon,' his mind was trying to wander and he dragged it sharply back to the typewritten pages, 'Philopon is the chief factor in the increase in crime in Japan. According to the Welfare Ministry there are now 1,500,000 addicts in the country, of whom one million are under the age of 20, and the Tokyo Metropolitan Police attribute 70% of juvenile crime to the influences of the drug.

'Addiction, as in the case of marijuana in the United States, begins with one "shot". The effect is "stimulating" and the drug is habit-forming. It is also cheap — about ten yen (sixpence) a shot — and the addict rapidly increases his shots to the neighbourhood of one hundred a day. In these quantities the addiction becomes expensive and the victim automatically turns to crime to pay for the drug. That the crime often includes physical assault and murder is due to a peculiar property of the drug. It induces an acute persecution complex in the addict who becomes prey to the illusion that people want to kill him and that he is always being followed with harmful intent. He will turn with his feet and fists, or with a razor, on a stranger in the streets who he thinks has scrutinized him offensively. Less advanced addicts tend to avoid an old friend who has reached the one hundred shots a day dosage, and this of course merely increases his feeling of persecution.

'In this way murder becomes an act of self-defence, virtuous and justified, and it will readily be seen what a dangerous weapon it can become in the handling and direction of organized crime by a "master-mind".

'Philopon has been traced as the motive power behind the notorious Bar Mecca murder case and as a result of that unpleasant affair the police rounded up more than 5,000 *purveyors* of the drug in a matter of weeks.

'As usual Korean nationals are being blamed . . . '

Suddenly Bond rebelled. What the hell was he doing reading all this stuff? When would he conceivably require to know about a Japanese murder-drug called Philopon?

Inattentively he skimmed through the remaining pages, ticked himself off the distribution slip, and threw the docket into his out-tray.

His headache was still sitting over his right eye as if it had been nailed there. He opened one of the drawers of his desk and took out a bottle of Phensic. He considered asking his secretary for a glass of water, but he disliked being cosseted. With distaste he crunched two tablets between his teeth and swallowed down the harsh powder.

Then he lit a cigarette and got up and stood by the window. He looked across the green panorama far below him and, without seeing it, let his eyes wander aimlessly along the jagged horizon of London while his mind focused on the strange events of the night before.

And the more he thought about it, the stranger it all seemed.

Why should Drax, a millionaire, a public hero, a man with a unique position in the country, why should this remarkable man cheat at cards? What could he achieve by it? What could he prove to himself? Did he think that he was so much a law unto himself, so far above the common herd and their puny canons of behaviour that he could spit in the face of public opinion?

Bond's mind paused. Spit in their faces. That just about described his manner at Blades. The combination of superiority and scorn. As if he was dealing with human muck so far beneath contempt that there was no need to put up even a pretence of decent behaviour in its company.

Presumably Drax enjoyed gambling. Perhaps it eased the tensions in him, the tensions that showed in his harsh voice, his nail-biting, the constant sweating. But he mustn't lose. It would be contemptible to lose to these inferior people. So, at whatever risk, he must cheat his way to victory. As for the possibility of detection, presumably he thought that he could bluster his way out of any corner. If he thought about it at all. And people with obsessions, reflected Bond, were blind to danger. They even courted it in a perverse way. Kleptomaniacs would try to steal more and more difficult objects. Sex maniacs would parade their importunities as if they were longing to be arrested. Pyromaniacs often made no attempt to avoid being linked with their fire-raising.

But what obsession was it that was consuming this man? What was the origin of the compulsive urge that was driving him down the steep hill into the sea?

All the signs pointed to paranoia. Delusions of grandeur and, behind that, of persecution. The contempt in his face. The bullying voice. The expression of secret triumph with which he had met defeat after a moment of bitter collapse. The triumph of the maniac who knows that whatever the facts may say he is right. Whoever may try to thwart him he can overcome. For him there is no defeat because of his secret power. He knows how to make gold. He can fly like a bird. He is almighty — the man in the padded cell who is God.

Yes, thought Bond, gazing blindly out over Regent's Park. That is the solution. Sir Hugo Drax is a raving paranoiac. That is the power which has driven him on, by devious routes, to make his millions. That is the mainspring of the gift to England of this giant rocket that will annihilate our enemies. Thanks to the all-powerful Drax.

But who can tell how near to breaking-point this man is? Who has penetrated behind that bluster, behind all that red hair on his face, who has read the signs as more than the effect of his humble origins or of sensitivity about his war wounds?

Apparently no one. Then was he, Bond, right in his analysis? What was it based on? Was this glimpse through a shuttered window into a man's soul sufficient evidence? Perhaps others had caught such a glimpse. Perhaps there had been other moments of supreme tension in Singapore, Hong Kong, Nigeria, Tangier, when some merchant sitting across a table from Drax had noticed the sweat and the bitten nails and the red blaze of the eyes in the face from which all the blood had suddenly been drained.

If one had time, thought Bond, one ought to seek those people out, if they existed, and really find out about this man, perhaps get him in the killing-bottle before it was too late.

Too late? Bond smiled to himself. What was he being so dramatic about? What had this man done to him? Made him a present of £15,000. Bond shrugged. It was none of his business anyway. But that last remark of his, 'Spend it quickly, Commander Bond'. What had he meant by that? It must be those words, Bond reflected, that had stayed in the back of his mind and made him ponder so carefully over the problem of Drax.

Bond turned brusquely away from the window. To hell with it, he thought. I'm getting obsessed myself. Now then. Fifteen thousand pounds. A miraculous windfall. All right then, he *would* spend it quickly. He sat down at his desk and picked up a pencil. He thought for a moment and then wrote carefully on a memorandum pad headed 'Top Secret':

(1) Rolls-Bentley Convertible, say £5,000.

(2) Three diamond clips at £250 each, £750.

He paused. That still left nearly £ 10,000. Some clothes, paint the flat, a set of the new Henry Cotton irons, a few dozen of the Taittinger champagne. But those could wait. He would go that afternoon and buy the clips and talk to Bentley's. Put all the rest into gold shares. Make a fortune. Retire.

In angry protest the red telephone splintered the silence.

'Can you come up? M. wants you.' It was the Chief of Staff, speaking urgently.

'Coming,' said Bond, suddenly alert. 'Any clue?'

'Search me,' said the Chief of Staff. 'Hasn't touched his signals yet. Been over at the Yard and the Ministry of Supply all the morning.'

He rang off.

9
TAKE IT FROM HERE

A FEW MINUTES LATER Bond was walking through the familiar door and the green light had gone on over the entrance.

M. looked sharply at him. 'You look pretty dreadful, 007,' he said. 'Sit down.'

It's business, thought Bond, his pulse quickening. No Christian names today. He sat down. M. was studying some pencilled notes on a scratch-pad. He looked up. His eyes were no longer interested in Bond.

'Trouble down at Drax's plant last night,' he said. 'Double killing. Police tried to get hold of Drax. Didn't think of Blades apparently. Caught up with him when he got back to the Ritz about half-past one this morning. Two men from the Moonraker got shot in a public house near the plant. Both dead. Drax told the police he couldn't care less and then hung up. Typical of the man. He's down there now. Taking the thing a bit more seriously, I gather.'

'Curious coincidence,' said Bond thoughtfully. 'But where do we come in, sir? Isn't it a police job?'

'Partly,' said M., 'but it happens that we're responsible for a lot of the key personnel down there. Germans,' he added. 'I'd better explain.' He looked down at his pad. 'It's an R.A.F. establishment and the cover-plan is that it's part of the big radar network along the east coast. The R.A.F. are responsible for guarding the perimeter and the Ministry of Supply only has authority at the centre where the work is going on. It's on the edge of the cliffs between Dover and Deal. The whole area covers about a thousand acres, but the site itself is about two hundred. On the site there are only Drax and fifty-two others left. All the construction team have gone.'

Pack of cards and a joker, reflected Bond.

'Fifty of these are Germans,' continued M., 'more or less all the guided missile experts the Russians didn't get. Drax paid for them to come over here and work on the Moonraker. Nobody was very happy with the arrangement but there was no alternative. The Ministry of Supply couldn't spare any of their experts from Woomera. Drax had to find his men where he could. To strengthen the R.A.F. security people, the Ministry appointed their own security officer to live on the site. Man called Major Tallon.'

M. paused and looked up at the ceiling.

'He was one of the two who got killed last night. Shot by one of the Germans, who then shot himself.'

M. lowered his eyes and looked at Bond. Bond said nothing, waiting for the rest of the story.

'It happened in a public house near the site. Plenty of witnesses. Apparently it's an inn on the edge of the site that is in bounds to the men. Must have somewhere to go to, I suppose.' M. paused. He kept his eyes on Bond. 'Now you asked where we come in on all this. We come in because we cleared this particular German, and all the others, before they were allowed to come over here. We've got the dossiers of all of them. So when this happened the first thing R.A.F. Security and Scotland Yard wanted was the dossier of the dead man. They got on to the Duty Officer last night and he dug the papers out of Records and sent them over to the Yard. Routine job. He noted it in the log. When I got here this morning and saw this entry in the log I suddenly got interested.' M. spoke quietly. 'After spending the evening with Drax, it was, as you remarked, a curious coincidence.'

'Very curious, sir,' said Bond, still waiting.

'And there's one more thing,' concluded M. 'And this is the real reason why I've let myself get involved instead of keeping clear of the whole business. This has got to take priority over everything.' M.'s voice was very quiet. 'They're going to fire the Moonraker on Friday. Less than four days' time. Practice shoot.'

M. paused and reached for his pipe and busied himself lighting it.

Bond said nothing. He still couldn't see what all this had to do with the Secret Service whose jurisdiction runs only outside the United Kingdom. It seemed a job for the Special Branch of Scotland Yard, or conceivably for M.I.5. He waited. He looked at his watch. It was noon.

M. got his pipe going and continued.

'But quite apart from that,' said M., 'I got interested because last night I got interested in Drax.'

'So did I, sir,' said Bond.

'So when I read the log,' said M., ignoring Bond's comment, 'I telephoned Vallance at the Yard and asked him what it was all about. He was rather worried and asked me to come over. I said I didn't want to tread on Five's corns but he said he had already spoken to them. They maintained it was a matter between my department and the police since it was we who had cleared the German who did the killing. So I went along.'

M. paused and looked down at his notes.

'The place is on the coast about three miles north of Dover,' he said. 'There's this inn near by on the main coast-road, the World Without Want, and the men from the site go there in the evening. Last night, about seven-thirty, the Security man from the Ministry, this man Tallon, went along there and was having a whisky and soda and chatting away with some of the Germans when the murderer, if you like to call him that, came in and walked straight up to Tallon. He pulled a Luger — no serial numbers by the way — out of his shirt and said,' M. looked up, ' "I love Gala Brand. You shall not have her." Then he shot Tallon through the heart and put the smoking gun in his own mouth and pulled the trigger.'

'What a ghastly business,' said Bond. He could see every detail of the shambles in the crowded taproom of a typical English public house. 'Who's the girl?'

'That's another complication,' said M. 'She's an agent of the Special Branch. Bilingual in German. One of Vallance's best girls. She and Tallon were the only two non-Germans Drax had with him on the site. Vallance is a suspicious chap. Has to be. This Moonraker plan is obviously the most important thing happening in England. Without telling anyone and acting more or less on instinct, he planted this Brand girl on Drax and somehow fixed for her to be taken on as his private secretary. Been on the site since the beginning. She's had absolutely nothing to report. Says that Drax is an excellent chief, except for his manners, and drives his men like hell. Apparently he started by making passes at her, even after she'd spun the usual yarn about being engaged, but after she'd shown she could defend herself, which of course she can, he gave up and she says they're perfectly good friends. Naturally she knew Tallon, but he was old enough to be her father, besides being happily married with four children, and she told Vallance's man who got a word with her this morning that he's taken her to the cinema in a paternal sort of way twice in eighteen months. As for the killer, man called Egon Bartsch, he was an electronics expert whom she barely knew by sight.'

'What do his friends say about all this?' asked Bond.

'The man who shared his room with him backs up Bartsch. Says he was madly in love with the Brand woman and put his whole lack of success down to "The Englishman". He says Bartsch had been getting very moody and reserved lately and that he wasn't a bit surprised to hear of the shooting.'

'Sounds pretty corroborative,' said Bond. 'Somehow one can see the picture. One of those highly strung nervous chaps with the usual German chip on the shoulder. What does Vallance think?'

'He's not sure,' said M. 'He's mainly concerned with protecting his girl from the Press and seeing that her cover doesn't get blown. All the papers are on to it of course. It'll be in the midday editions. And they're all howling for a picture of the girl. Vallance is having one cooked up and got down to her that'll look more or less like any girl, but just sufficiently like her. She'll send it out this evening. Fortunately the reporters can't get near the place. She's refusing to talk and Vallance is praying that some friend or relation won't blow the gaff. They're holding the inquest today and Vallance is hoping that the case will be officially closed by this evening and that the papers will have to let it die for lack of material.'

'What about this practice shoot?' asked Bond.

'They're sticking to the schedule,' said M. 'Noon on Friday. They're using a dummy warhead and firing her vertically with only three-quarter tanks. They're clearing about a hundred square miles of the North Sea from about Latitude 52 up. That's north of a line joining The Hague and the Wash. Full details are going to be given out by the P.M. on Thursday night.'

M. stopped talking. He swivelled his chair round so that he could look out of the window. Bond heard a distant clock chime the four quarters. One o'clock. Was he going to miss his lunch again? If M. would stop ferreting about in the business of other Departments he could have a quick lunch and get round to Bentley's. Bond shifted slightly in his chair.

M. turned back and faced him again across the desk.

'The people who are most worried about all this,' he said, 'are the Ministry of Supply. Tallon was one of their best men. His reports had been completely negative all along. Then he suddenly rang up the Assistant Under-Secretary yesterday afternoon and said he thought something fishy was going on at the site and he asked to see the Minister personally at ten o'clock this morning. Wouldn't say anything more on the telephone. And a few hours later he gets shot. Another funny coincidence, wasn't it?'

'Very funny,' said Bond. 'But why don't they close down the site and have a wholesale inquiry? After all, this thing's too big to take a chance on.'

'The Cabinet met early this morning,' said M., 'and the Prime Minister asked the obvious question. What evidence was there of any attempt, or even of any intention, to sabotage the Moonraker? The answer was none. There were only fears which had been brought to the surface in the last twenty-four hours by Tallon's vague message and the double murder. Everyone agreed that unless there was a grain of evidence, which so far hasn't turned up, both these incidents could be put down to the terrific nervous tension on the site. The way things are in the world at the moment it was decided that the sooner the Moonraker could give us an independent say in world affairs the better for us and,' M. shrugged his shoulders, 'quite possibly for the world. And it was agreed that for a thousand reasons why the Moonraker should be fired the reasons against didn't stand up. The Minister of Supply had to agree, but he knows as well as you or I that, whatever the facts, it would be a colossal victory for the Russians to sabotage the Moonraker on the eve of her practice shoot. If they did it well enough they might easily get the whole project shelved. There are fifty Germans working on the thing. Any one of them could have relatives still being held in Russia whose lives could be used as a lever.' M. paused. He looked up at the ceiling. Then his eyes came down and rested thoughtfully on Bond.

'The Minister asked me to go and see him after the Cabinet. He said that the least he could do was replace Tallon at once. The new man must be bilingual in German, a sabotage expert, and have had plenty of experience of our Russian friends. M.I.5 have put up three candidates. They're all on cases at the moment, but they could be extricated in a few hours. But then the Minister asked my opinion. I gave it. He talked to the Prime Minister and a lot of red tape got cut very quickly.'

Bond looked sharply, resentfully, into the grey, uncompromising eyes.

'So,' said M. flatly, 'Sir Hugo Drax has been notified of your appointment and he expects you down at his headquarters in time for dinner this evening.'

10

SPECIAL BRANCH AGENT

AT SIX O'CLOCK that Tuesday evening towards the end of May, James Bond was thrashing the big Bentley down the Dover road along the straight stretch that runs into Maidstone.

Although he was driving fast and with concentration, part of his mind was going back over his movements since he had left M.'s office four and a half hours earlier.

After giving a brief outline of the case to his secretary and eating a quick lunch at a table to himself in the canteen, he had told the garage for God's sake to hurry up with his car and deliver it, filled up, to his flat not later than four o'clock. Then he had taken a taxi down to Scotland Yard where he had an appointment with Assistant Commissioner Vallance at a quarter to three.

The courtyards and cul-de-sacs of the Yard had reminded him as usual of a prison without roofs. The overhead strip lighting in the cold corridor took the colour out of the cheeks of the police sergeant who asked his business and watched him sign the apple-green chit. It did the same for the face of the constable who led him up the short steps and along the bleak passage between the rows of anonymous doors to the waiting-room.

A quiet, middle-aged woman with the resigned eyes of someone who had seen everything came in and said the Assistant Commissioner would be free in five minutes. Bond had gone to the window and had looked out into the grey courtyard below. A constable, looking naked without his helmet, had come out of a building and walked across the yard munching a split roll with something pink between the two halves. It had been very quiet and the noise of the traffic on Whitehall and on the Embankment had sounded far away. Bond had felt dispirited. He was getting tangled up with strange departments. He would be out of touch with his own people and his own Service routines. Already, in this waiting-room, he felt out of his element. Only criminals or informers came and waited here, or influential people vainly trying to get out of a dangerous driving charge or desperately hoping to persuade Vallance that their sons were not really homosexuals. You could not be in the waiting-room of the Special Branch for any innocent purpose. You were either prosecuting or defending.

At last the woman came for him. He stubbed out his cigarette in the top of the Player's cigarette tin that serves as an ashtray in the waiting-rooms of government departments, and followed her across the corridor.

After the gloom of the waiting-room the unseasonable fire on the hearth of the large cheerful room had seemed like a trick, like the cigarette offered you by the Gestapo.

It had taken Bond a full five minutes to shake off his depression and realize that Ronnie Vallance was relieved to see him, that he was not interested in inter-departmental jealousies and that he was only looking to Bond to protect the Moonraker and get one of his best officers out of what might be a bad mess.

Vallance was a man of great tact. For the first few minutes he had spoken only of M. And he had spoken with inside knowledge and with sincerity. Without even mentioning the case he had gained Bond's friendship and co-operation.

As Bond swung the Bentley through the crowded streets of Maidstone he reflected that Vallance's gift had come from twenty years of avoiding the corns of M.I.5, of working in with the uniformed branch of the police, and of handling ignorant politicians and affronted foreign diplomats.

When Bond had left him after a quarter of an hour's hard talking, each man knew that he had acquired an ally. Vallance had sized up Bond and knew that Gala Brand would get all Bond's help and whatever protection she needed. He also respected Bond's professional approach to the assignment and his absence of departmental rivalry with the Special Branch. As for Bond, he was full of admiration for what he had learned about Vallance's agent, and he felt that he was no longer naked and that he had Vallance and the whole of Vallance's department behind him.

Bond had left Scotland Yard with the feeling that he had achieved Clausewitz's first principle. He had made his base secure.

His visit to the Ministry of Supply had added nothing to his knowledge of the case. He had studied Tallon's record and his reports. The former was quite straightforward — a lifetime in Army Intelligence and Field Security — and the latter painted a picture of a very lively and well-managed technical establishment — one or two cases of drunkenness, one of petty theft, several personal vendettas leading to fights and mild bloodshed, but otherwise a loyal and hardworking team of men.

Then he had had an inadequate half-hour in the Operations Room of the Ministry with Professor Train, a fat, scruffy, undistinguished-looking man who had been runner-up for the Physics Division of the Nobel Prize the year before and who was one of the greatest experts on guided missiles in the world.

Professor Train had walked up to a row of huge wall maps and had pulled down the cord of one of them. Bond was faced with a ten-foot horizontal scale diagram of something that looked like a V2 with big fins.

'Now,' said Professor Train, 'you know nothing about rockets so I'm going to put this in simple terms and not fill you up with a lot of stuff about Nozzle Expansion Ratios, Exhaust Velocity, and the Keplerian Ellipse. The Moonraker, as Drax chooses to call it, is a single-stage rocket. It uses up all its fuel shooting itself into the air and then it homes on to the objective. The V2's trajectory was more like a shell fired from a gun. At the top of its 200-mile flight it had climbed to about 70 miles. It was fuelled with a very combustible mixture of alcohol and liquid oxygen which was watered down so as not to burn out the mild steel which was all they were allocated for the engine. There are far more powerful fuels available but until now we hadn't been able to achieve very much with them for the same reason, their combustion temperature is so high that they would burn out the toughest engine.'

The Professor paused and stuck a finger in Bond's chest. 'All you, my dear sir, have to remember about this rocket is that, thanks to Drax's Columbite which has a melting point of about 3,500 degrees Centigrade, compared with 1,300 in the V2 engines, we can use one of the super fuels without burning out the engine. In fact,' he looked at Bond as if Bond should be impressed, 'we are using fluorine and hydrogen.'

'Oh, really,' said Bond reverently.

The Professor looked at him sharply. 'So we hope to achieve a speed in the neighbourhood of 15,000 miles an hour and a vertical range of about 1,000 miles. This should produce an operational range of about 4,000 miles, bringing every European capital within reach of England. Very useful,' he added drily, 'in certain circumstances. But, for the scientists, chiefly desirable as a step towards escape from the earth. Any questions?'

'How does it work?' asked Bond dutifully.

The Professor gestured brusquely towards the diagram. 'Let's start from the nose,' he said. 'First comes the warhead. For the practice shoot this will contain upper-atmosphere instruments, radar and suchlike. Then the gyro compasses to make it fly straight — pitch-and-yaw gyro and roll gyro. Then various minor instruments, servo motors, power supply. And then the big fuel tanks — 30,000 pounds of the stuff.

'At the stern you get two small tanks to drive the turbine. Four hundred pounds of hydrogen peroxide mixes with forty pounds of potassium permanganate and makes steam which drives the turbines underneath them. These drive a set of centrifugal pumps which force the main fuel into the rocket motor. Under terrific pressure. Do you follow me?' He cocked a dubious eyebrow at Bond.

'Sounds much the same principle as a jet plane,' said Bond.

The Professor seemed pleased. 'More or less,' he said, 'but the rocket carries all its fuel inside it, instead of sucking in oxygen from outside like the Comet. Well then,' he continued, 'the fuel gets ignited in the motor and squirts out at the end in a continuous blast. Rather like a continuous recoil from a gun. And this blast forces the rocket into the air like any other firework. Of course it's at the stern that the Columbite comes in. It's allowed us to make a motor that won't be melted by the fantastic heat. And then,' he pointed, 'those are the tail fins to keep it steady at the beginning of its flight. Also made of Columbite alloy or they'd break away with the colossal air pressure. Anything else?'

'How can you be certain it'll come down where you mean it to?' asked Bond. 'What's to prevent it falling on The Hague next Monday?'

'The gyros will see to that. But as a matter of fact we're taking no chances on Monday and we're using a radar homing device on a raft in the middle of the sea. There'll be a radar transmitter in the nose of the rocket which will pick up an echo from our gadget in the sea and home on to it automatically. Of course,' the Professor grinned, 'if we ever had to use the thing in wartime it would be a great help to have a homing device transmitting energy from the middle of Moscow or Warsaw or Prague or Monte Carlo or wherever we might be shooting at. It'll probably be up to you chaps to get one there. Good luck to you.'

Bond smiled non-committally. 'One more question,' he said. 'If you wanted to sabotage the rocket what would be the easiest way?'

'Any number,' said the Professor cheerfully. 'Sand in the fuel. Grit in the pumps. A small hole anywhere on the fuselage or the fins. With that power and at those speeds the smallest fault would finish it.'

'Thanks very much,' said Bond. 'It seems you've got fewer worries about the Moonraker than I have.'

'It's a wonderful machine,' said the Professor. 'She'll fly all right if nobody interferes with her. Drax has done a sound job. Wonderful organizer. That's a brilliant team he put together. And they'll do anything for him. We've got a lot to thank him for.'

Bond did a racing change and swung the big car left at the Charing fork, preferring the clear road by Chilham and Canterbury to the bottlenecks of Ashford and Folkestone. The car howled up to eighty in third and he held it in the same gear to negotiate the hairpin at the top of the long gradient leading up to the Molash road.

And, he wondered, going back into top and listening with satisfaction to the relaxed thunder of the exhaust, and what about Drax? What sort of a reception was Drax going to give him this evening? According to M., when his name had been suggested over the telephone, Drax had paused for a moment and then said, 'Oh yes. I know the fellow. Didn't know he was mixed up in that racket. I'd be interested to have another look at him. Send him along. I'll expect him in time for dinner.' Then he had rung off.

The people at the Ministry had their own view of Drax. In their dealings with him they had found him a dedicated man, completely bound up in the Moonraker, living for nothing but its success, driving his men to the limit, fighting for priorities in material with other departments, goading the Ministry of Supply into clearing his requirements at Cabinet level. They disliked his hectoring manners but they respected him for his know-how and his drive and his dedication. And, like the rest of England, they considered him a possible saviour of the country.

Well, thought Bond, accelerating down the straight stretch of road past Chilham Castle, he could see that picture too and if he was going to work with the man he must adjust himself to the heroic version. If Drax was willing, he would put the whole affair at Blades out of his mind and concentrate on protecting Drax and his wonderful project from their country's enemies. There were only about three days to go. The security precautions were already minute and Drax might resent suggestions for increasing them. It was not going to be easy and a great deal of tact would have to be used. Tact. Not Bond's long suit and not, he reflected, connected in any way with what he knew of Drax's character.

Bond took the short cut out of Canterbury by the old Dover road and looked at his watch. It was six-thirty. Another fifteen minutes to Dover and then another ten minutes along the Deal road. Were there any other plans to be made? The double killing was out of his hands, thank heaven. 'Murder and suicide while of unsound mind' had been the coroner's verdict. The girl had not even been called. He would stop for a drink at the World Without Want and have a quick word with the innkeeper. The next day he would have to try and smell out the 'something fishy' that Tallon had wanted to see the Minister about. No clue about that. Nothing had been found in Tallon's room, which presumably he would now be taking over. Well, at any rate that would give him plenty of leisure to go through Tallon's papers.

Bond concentrated on his driving as he coasted down into Dover. He kept left and was soon climbing out of the town again past the wonderful cardboard castle.

There was a patch of low cloud on top of the hill and a spit of rain on his windshield. There was a cold breeze coming in from the sea. The visibility was bad and he switched on his lights as he motored slowly along the coast-road, the ruby-spangled masts of the Swingate radar station rising like petrified Roman candles on his right.

The girl? He would have to be careful how he contacted her and careful not to upset her. He wondered if she would be any use to him. After a year on the site she would have had all the opportunities of a private secretary to 'The Chief' to get under the skin of the whole project — and of Drax. And she had a mind trained to his own particular craft. But he would have to be prepared for her to be suspicious of the new broom and perhaps resentful. He wondered what she was really like. The photograph on her record-sheet at the Yard had shown an attractive but rather severe girl and any hint of seductiveness had been abstracted by the cheerless jacket of her policewoman's uniform.

Hair: Auburn. Eyes: Blue. Height: 5 ft. 7. Weight: 9 stone. Hips: 38. Waist: 26. Bust: 38. Distinguishing marks: Mole on upper curvature of right breast.

Hm! thought Bond.

He put the statistics out of his mind as he came to the turning to the right. There was a signpost that said Kingsdown, and the lights of a small inn.

He pulled up and switched off the engine. Above his head a sign which said 'World Without Want' in faded gold lettering groaned in the salt breeze that came over the cliffs half a mile away. He got out, stretched and walked over to the door of the public bar. It was locked. Closed for cleaning? He tried the next door, which opened and gave access to the small private bar. Behind the bar a stolid-looking man in shirt-sleeves was reading an evening paper.

He looked up as Bond entered, and put his paper down. 'Evening, sir,' he said, evidently relieved to see a customer.

'Evening,' said Bond. 'Large whisky and soda, please.' He sat up at the bar and waited while the man poured two measures of Black and White and put the glass in front of him with a syphon of soda.

Bond filled the glass with soda and drank. 'Bad business you had here last night,' he said, putting the glass down.

'Terrible, sir,' said the man. 'And bad for trade. Would you be from the Press, sir? Had nothing but reporters and policemen in and out of the house all day long.'

'No,' said Bond. 'I've come to take over the job of the fellow who got shot. Major Tallon. Was he one of your regular customers?'

'Never came here but the once, sir, and that was the end of him. Now I've been put out of bounds for a week and the public has got to be painted from top to bottom. But I will say that Sir Hugo has been very decent about it. Sent me fifty quid this afternoon to pay for the damage. He must be a fine gentleman that. Made himself well liked in these parts. Always very generous and a cheery word for one and all.'

'Yes. Fine man,' said Bond. 'Did you see it all happen?'

'Didn't see the first shot, sir. Serving a pint at the time. Then of course I looked up. Dropped the ruddy pint on the floor.'

'What happened then?'

'Well, everybody's standing back of course. Nothing but Germans in the place. About a dozen of them. There's the body on the floor and the chap with the gun looking down at him. Then suddenly he stands to attention and sticks his left arm up in the air. "Eil!" he shouts like the silly bastards used to do during the war. Then he puts the end of the gun in his mouth. Next thing,' the man made a grimace, 'he's all over my ruddy ceiling.'

'That was all he said after the shot?' asked Bond. 'Just "Heil"?'

'That's all, sir. Don't seem to be able to forget the bloody word, do they?'

'No,' said Bond thoughtfully, 'they certainly don't.'

11

POLICEWOMAN BRAND

FIVE MINUTES LATER Bond was showing his Ministry pass to the uniformed guard on duty at the gate in the high wire fence.

The R.A.F. sergeant handed it back to him and saluted. 'Sir Hugo's expecting you, sir. It's the big house up in the woods there.' He pointed to some lights a hundred yards further on towards the cliffs.

Bond heard him telephoning to the next guard point. He motored slowly along the new tarmac road that had been laid across the fields behind Kingsdown. He could hear the distant boom of the sea at the foot of the tall cliffs and from somewhere closer at hand there was a high-pitched whine of machinery which grew louder as he approached the trees.

He was stopped again by a plain-clothes guard at a second wire fence through which a five-bar gate gave access to the interior of the wood, and as he was waved through he heard the distant baying of police dogs which suggested some form of night patrol. All these precautions seemed efficient. Bond decided that he wouldn't have to worry himself with problems of external security.

Once through the trees the car was running over a flat concrete apron the limits of which, in the bad light, were out of range even of the huge twin beams of his Marchal headlamps. A hundred yards to his left, on the edge of the trees, there were the lights of a large house half-hidden behind a wall six feet thick, that rose straight up off the surface of the concrete almost to the height of the house. Bond slowed the car down to walking pace and turned its bonnet away from the house towards the sea and towards a dark shape that suddenly glinted white in the revolving beams of the South Goodwin Lightship far out in the Channel. His lights cut a path down the apron to where, almost on the edge of the cliff and at least half a mile away, a squat dome surged up about fifty feet out of the concrete. It looked like the top of an observatory and Bond could distinguish the flange of a joint running east and west across the surface of the dome.

He turned the car back and slowly ran it up between what he now assumed to be a blast-wall and the front of the house. As he pulled up outside the house the door opened and a manservant in a white jacket came out. He smartly opened the door of the car.

'Good evening, sir. This way please.'

He spoke woodenly and with a trace of accent. Bond followed him into the house and across a comfortable hall to a door on which the butler knocked.

'In.'

Bond smiled to himself at the harsh tone of the well-remembered voice and at the note of command in the single monosyllable.

At the far end of the long, bright, chintzy living-room Drax was standing with his back to an empty grate, a huge figure in a plum-coloured velvet smoking-jacket that clashed with the reddish hair on his face. There were three other people standing near him, two men and a woman.

'Ah, my dear fellow,' said Drax boisterously, striding forward to meet him and shaking him cordially by the hand. 'So we meet again. And so soon. Didn't realize you were a ruddy spy for my Ministry or I'd have been more careful about playing cards against you. Spent that money yet?' he asked, leading him towards the fire.

'Not yet,' smiled Bond. 'Haven't seen the colour of it.'

'Of course. Settlement on Saturday. Probably get the cheque just in time to celebrate our little firework display, what? Now let's see.' He led Bond up to the woman. 'This is my secretary, Miss Brand.'

Bond looked into a pair of very level blue eyes.

'Good evening.' He gave her a friendly smile.

There was no answering smile in the eyes which looked calmly into his. No answering pressure of her hand. 'How do you do,' she said indifferently, almost, Bond sensed, with hostility.

It crossed Bond's mind that she had been well-chosen. Another Loelia Ponsonby. Reserved, efficient, loyal, virginal. Thank heavens, he thought. A professional.

'My right-hand man, Dr. Walter.' The thin elderly man with a pair of angry eyes under a shock of black hair seemed not to notice Bond's outstretched hand. He sprang to attention and gave a quick nod of the head. 'Valter,' said the thin mouth above the black imperial, correcting Drax's pronunciation.

'And my — what shall I say — my dogsbody. What you might call my A.D.C., Willy Krebs.' There was the touch of a slightly damp hand. 'Ferry pleased to meet you,' said an ingratiating voice and Bond looked into a pale round unhealthy face now split in a stage smile which died almost as Bond noticed it. Bond looked into his eyes. They were like two restless black buttons and they twisted away from Bond's gaze.

Both men wore spotless white overalls with plastic zip fasteners at the sleeves and ankles and down the back. Their hair was close-cropped so that the skin shone through and they would have looked like people from another planet but for the untidy black moustache and imperial of Dr. Walter and the pale wispy moustache of Krebs. They were both caricatures — a mad scientist and a youthful version of Peter Lorre.

The colourful ogreish figure of Drax was a pleasant contrast in this chilly company and Bond was grateful to him for the cheerful roughness of his welcome and for his apparent wish to bury the hatchet and make the best of his new security officer.

Drax was very much the host. He rubbed his hands together. 'Now, Willy,' he said, 'how about making one of your excellent dry martinis for us? Except, of course, for the Doctor. Doesn't drink or smoke,' he explained to Bond, returning to his place by the mantelpiece. 'Hardly breathes.' He barked out a short laugh. 'Thinks of nothing but the rocket. Do you, my friend?'

The Doctor looked stonily in front of him. 'You are pleased to joke,' he said.

'Now, now,' said Drax, as if to a child. 'We will go back to those leading edges later. Everybody's quite happy about them except you.' He turned to Bond. 'The good Doctor is always frightening us,' he explained indulgently. 'He's always having nightmares about something. Now it's the leading edges of the fins. They're already as sharp as razor blades — hardly any wind resistance at all. And he suddenly gets it into his head that they're going to melt. Friction of the air. Of course everything's possible, but they've been tested at over 3,000 degrees and, as I tell him, if they're going to melt then the whole rocket will melt. And that's just not going to happen,' he added with a grim smile.

Krebs came up with a silver tray with four full glasses and a frosted shaker. The martini was excellent and Bond said so.

'You are ferry kind,' said Krebs with a smirk of satisfaction. 'Sir Hugo is ferry exacting.'

'Fill up his glass,' said Drax, 'and then perhaps our friend would like to wash. We dine at eight sharp.'

As he spoke, there came the muffled wail of a siren and almost immediately the sound of a body of men running in strict unison across the concrete apron outside.

'That's the first night shift,' explained Drax. 'Barracks are just behind the house. Must be eight o'clock. We do everything at the double here,' he added with a gleam of satisfaction in his eye. 'Precision. Lot of scientists about, but we try to run the place like a military establishment. Willy, look after the Commander. We'll go ahead. Come along, my dear.'

As Bond followed Krebs to the door through which he had entered, he saw the other two with Drax in the lead make for the double doors at the end of the room which had opened as Drax finished speaking. The manservant in the white coat stood in the entrance. As Bond went out into the hall it crossed his mind that Drax would certainly go into the dining-room ahead of Miss Brand. Forceful personality. Treated his staff like children. Obviously a born leader. Where had he got it from? The Army? Or did it grow on one with millions of money? Bond followed the slug-like neck of Krebs and wondered.

The dinner was excellent. Drax was a genial host and at his own table his manners were faultless. Most of his conversation consisted in drawing out Dr. Walter for the benefit of Bond, and it covered a wide range of technical matters which Drax took pains to explain briefly after each topic had been exhausted. Bond was impressed by the confidence with which Drax handled each abstruse problem as it was raised, and by his immense grasp of detail. A genuine admiration for the man gradually developed in him and overshadowed much of his previous dislike. He felt more than ever inclined to forget the Blades affair now that he was faced with the other Drax, the creator and inspired leader of a remarkable enterprise.

Bond sat between his host and Miss Brand. He made several attempts to engage her in conversation. He failed completely. She answered with polite monosyllables and would hardly meet his eye. Bond became mildly irritated. He found her physically very attractive and it annoyed him to be unable to extract the smallest response. He felt that her frigid indifference was overacted and that security would have been far better met with an easy, friendly approach instead of this exaggerated reticence. He felt a strong urge to give her a sharp kick on the ankle. The idea entertained him and he found himself observing her with a fresh eye — as a girl and not as an official colleague. As a start, and under cover of a long argument between Drax and Walter, in which she was required to join, about the collation of weather reports from the Air Ministry and from Europe, he began to add up his impressions of her.

She was far more attractive than her photograph had suggested and it was difficult to see traces of the severe competence of a policewoman in the seductive girl beside him. There was authority in the definite line of the profile, but the long black eyelashes over the dark blue eyes and the rather wide mouth might have been painted by Marie Laurencin. Yet the lips were too full for a Laurencin and the dark brown hair that curved inwards at the base of the neck was of a different fashion. There was a hint of northern blood in the high cheek-bones and in the very slight upward slant of the eyes, but the warmth of her skin was entirely English. There was too much poise and authority in her gestures and in the carriage of her head for her to be a very convincing portrait of a secretary. In fact she seemed almost a member of Drax's team, and Bond noticed that the men listened with attention as she answered Drax's questions.

Her rather severe evening dress was in charcoal black grosgrain with full sleeves that came below the elbow. The wrap-over bodice just showed the swell of her breasts, which were as splendid as Bond had guessed from the measurements on her record sheet. At the point of the vee there was a bright blue cameo brooch, a Tassie intaglio, Bond guessed, cheap but imaginative. She wore no other jewellery except a half-hoop of small diamonds on her engagement finger. Apart from the warm rouge on her lips, she wore no make-up and her nails were square cut with a natural polish.

Altogether, Bond decided, she was a very lovely girl and, beneath her reserve, a very passionate one. And, he reflected, she might be a policewoman and an expert at jujitsu, but she also had a mole on her right breast.

With this comforting thought Bond turned the whole of his attention to the conversation between Drax and Walter and made no further attempts to make friends with the girl.

Dinner ended at nine. 'Now we will go over and introduce you to the Moonraker,' said Drax, rising abruptly from the table. 'Walter will accompany us. He has much to do. Come along, my dear Bond.'

Without a word to Krebs or the girl he strode out of the room. Bond and Walter followed him.

They left the house and walked across the concrete towards the distant shape on the edge of the cliff. The moon had risen and in the distance the squat dome shone palely in its light.

A hundred yards from the site Drax stopped. 'I will explain the geography,' he said. 'Walter, you go ahead. They will be waiting for you to have another look at those fins. Don't worry about them, my dear fellow. Those people at High Duty Alloys know what they're doing. Now,' he turned to Bond and gestured towards the milk-white dome, 'in there is the Moonraker. What you see is the lid of a wide shaft that has been cut about forty foot down into the chalk. The two halves of the dome are opened hydraulically and fold back flush with that twenty-foot wall. If they were open now, you would see the nose of the Moonraker just protruding above the level of the wall. Over there,' he pointed to a square shape that was almost out of sight in the direction of Deal, 'is the firing point. Concrete blockhouse. Full of radar tracking gadgets — Doppler velocity radar and flight-path radar, for instance. Information is fed to them by twenty telemetering channels in the nose of the rocket. There's a big television screen in there too so that you can watch the behaviour of the rocket inside the shaft after the pumps have been started. Another television set to follow the beginning of its climb. Alongside the blockhouse there's a hoist down the face of the cliff. Quite a lot of gear has been brought to the site by sea and then sent up on the hoist. That whine you hear is from the power house over there.' He gestured vaguely in the direction of Dover. 'The men's barracks and the house are protected by the blast-wall, but when we fire there won't be anyone within a mile of the site, except the Ministry experts and the B.B.C. team who are going to be in the firing point. Hope it'll stand up to the blast. Walter says that the site and a lot of the concrete apron will be melted by the heat. That's all. Nothing else you need to know about until we get inside. Come along.'

Bond noted again the abrupt tone of command. He followed in silence across the moonlit expanse until they came to the supporting wall of the dome. A naked red bulb glowed over a steel-plated door in the wall. It illuminated a bold sign which said in English and German: MORTAL DANGER. ENTRY FORBIDDEN WHEN RED LAMP SHOWS. RING AND WAIT.

Drax pressed a button beneath the notice and there was the muffled clang of an alarm bell. 'Might be somebody working with oxy-acetylene or doing some other delicate job,' he explained. 'Take his mind off his job for a split second as someone comes in and you could have an expensive mistake. Everybody downs tools when the bell rings and then starts up again when they see what it is.' Drax stood away from the door and pointed upwards to a row of four-foot-wide gratings just below the top of the wall. 'Ventilator shafts,' he explained. 'Air-conditioned inside to 70 degrees.'

The door was opened by a man with a truncheon in his hand and a revolver at his hip. Bond followed Drax through into a small anteroom. It contained nothing but a bench and a neat row of felt slippers.

'Have to put these on,' said Drax sitting down and kicking off his shoes. 'Might slip and knock into someone. Better leave your coat here too. Seventy degrees is quite warm.'

'Thanks,' said Bond remembering the Beretta at his armpit. 'As a matter of fact I don't feel the heat.'

Feeling like a visitor to an operating theatre, Bond followed Drax through a communicating door out on to an iron catwalk and into a blaze of spotlights that made him automatically put a hand up to his eyes as he grasped the guard-rail in front of him.

When he took his hand away he was greeted by a scene of such splendour that for several minutes he stood speechless, his eyes dazzled by the terrible beauty of the greatest weapon on earth.

12

THE MOONRAKER

IT WAS LIKE being inside the polished barrel of a huge gun. From the floor, forty feet below, rose circular walls of polished metal near the top of which he and Drax clung like two flies. Up through the centre of the shaft, which was about thirty feet wide, soared a pencil of glistening chromium, whose point, tapering to a needle-sharp antenna, seemed to graze the roof twenty feet above their heads.

The shimmering projectile rested on a blunt cone of latticed steel which rose from the floor between the tips of three severely back-swept delta fins that looked as sharp as surgeons' scalpels. But otherwise nothing marred the silken sheen of the fifty feet of polished chrome steel except the spidery fingers of two light gantries which stood out from the walls and clasped the waist of the rocket between thick pads of foam-rubber.

Where they touched the rocket, small access doors stood open in the steel skin and, as Bond looked down, a man crawled out of one door on to the narrow platform of the gantry and closed the door behind him with a gloved hand. He walked gingerly along the narrow bridge to the wall and turned a handle. There was the sharp whine of machinery and the gantry took its padded hand off the rocket and held it poised in the air, like the forelegs of a praying mantis. The whine altered to a deeper tone and the gantry slowly telescoped in on itself. Then it reached out again and seized the rocket ten feet lower down. Its operator crawled out along its arm and opened another small access door and disappeared inside.

'Probably checking the fuel-feed from the after tanks,' said Drax. 'Gravity feed. Tricky bit of design. What do you think of her?' He looked with pleasure at Bond's rapt expression.

'One of the most beautiful things I've ever seen,' said Bond. It was easy to talk. There was hardly a sound in the great steel shaft and the voices of the men clustered below under the tail of the rocket were no more than a murmur.

Drax pointed upwards. 'Warhead,' he explained. 'Experimental one now. Full of instruments. Telemeters and so forth. Then the gyros just opposite us here. Then mostly fuel tanks all the way down until you get to the turbines near the tail. Driven by superheated steam, made by decomposing hydrogen peroxide. The fuel, fluorine and hydrogen' (he glanced sharply at Bond. 'That's top-secret by the way') 'falls down the feed tubes and gets ignited as soon as it's forced into the motor. Sort of controlled explosion which shoots the rocket into the air. That steel floor under the rocket slides away. There's a big exhaust pit underneath. Comes out at the base of the cliff. You'll see it tomorrow. Looks like a huge cave. When we ran a static test the other day the chalk melted and ran out into the sea like water. Hope we don't burn down the famous white cliffs when we come to the real thing. Like to come and have a look at the works?'

Bond followed silently as Drax led the way down the steep iron ladder that curved down the side of the steel wall. He felt a glow of admiration and almost of reverence for this man and his majestic achievement. How could he ever have been put off by Drax's childish behaviour at the card-table? Even the greatest men have their weaknesses. Drax must need an outlet for the tension of the fantastic responsibility he was carrying. It was clear from the conversation at dinner that he couldn't shed much on to the shoulders of his highly strung deputy. From him alone had to spring the vitality and confidence to buoy up his whole team. Even in such a small thing as winning at cards it must be important to him to be constantly reassuring himself, constantly searching out omens of good fortune and success, even to the point of creating these omens for himself. Who, Bond asked himself, wouldn't sweat and bite his nails when so much had been dared, when so much was at stake?

As they filed down the long curve of the stairway, their figures grotesquely reflected back at them by the mirror of the rocket's chromium skin, Bond almost felt the man-in-the-street's affection for the man whom, only a few hours previously, he had been dissecting without pity, almost with loathing.

When they reached the steel-plated floor of the shaft, Drax paused and looked up. Bond followed his eyes. Seen from that angle it seemed as if they were gazing up a thin straight shaft of light into the blazing heaven of the arcs, a shaft of light that was not pure white but a shot mother-of-pearl satin. There were shimmers of red in it picked up from the crimson canisters of a giant foam fire-extinguisher that stood near them, a man in an asbestos suit beside it aiming its nozzle at the base of the rocket. There was a streak of violet whose origin was a violet bulb on the board of an instrument panel in the wall, which controlled the steel cover over the exhaust pit. And there was a whisper of emerald green from the shaded light over a plain deal table at which a man sat and wrote down figures as they were called to him from the group gathered directly beneath the Moonraker's tail.

Gazing up this pastel column, so incredibly slim and graceful, it seemed unthinkable that anything so delicate could withstand the pressures which it had been designed to meet on Friday — the howling stream of the most powerful controlled explosion that had ever been attempted; the impact of the sound barrier; the unknown pressures of the atmosphere at 15,000 miles an hour; the terrible shock as it plunged back from a thousand miles up and hit the atmospheric envelope of the earth.

Drax seemed to read his thoughts. He turned to Bond. 'It will be like committing murder,' he said. Then surprisingly, he burst into a braying laugh. 'Walter,' he called to the group of men. 'Come here.' Walter detached himself and came over. 'Walter. I was saying to our friend the Commander that when we fire the Moonraker it will be like committing murder.'

Bond was not surprised to see a look of puzzled incredulity come over the Doctor's face.

Drax said irritably, 'Child murder. Murder of our child.' He gestured at the rocket. 'Wake up. Wake up. What's the matter with you?'

Walter's faced cleared. Frostily he beamed his appreciation of the simile. 'Murder. Yes, that is good. Ha! ha! And now, Sir Hugo. The graphite slats in the exhaust vent. The Ministry is quite happy about their melting-point? They do not feel that . . . ' Still talking, Walter led Drax under the tail of the rocket. Bond followed.

The faces of the ten men were turned towards them as they came up. Drax introduced him with a wave of the hand. 'Commander Bond, our new security officer,' he said briefly.

The group eyed Bond in silence. There was no move to greet him and the ten pairs of eyes were incurious.

'Now then, what's all this fuss about the graphite? . . . ' The group closed round Drax and Walter. Bond was left standing alone.

He was not surprised by the coolness of his reception. He would have regarded the intrusion of an amateur into the secrets of his own department with much the same indifference mixed with resentment. And he sympathized with these hand-picked technicians who had lived for months among the highest realms of astronautics and were now on the threshold of the final arbitration. And yet, he reminded himself, the innocent among them must know that Bond had his own duty to perform, his own vital part in this project. Supposing one pair of those uncommunicative eyes concealed a man within a man, an enemy, perhaps at this very moment exulting in his knowledge that the graphite which Walter seemed to mistrust was indeed under-strength. It was true that they had the look of a well-knit team, almost of a brotherhood, as they stood round Drax and Walter, hanging on their words, their eyes intent on the mouths of the two men. But was part of one brain moving within the privacy of some secret orbit, ticking off its hidden calculus like the stealthy mechanism of an infernal machine?

Bond moved casually up and down the triangle made by the three points of the fins as they rested in their rubber-lined cavities in the steel floor, interesting himself in whatever met his eyes, but every now and then focusing the group of men from a new angle.

With the exception of Drax they all wore the same tight nylon overalls fastened with plastic zips. There was nowhere a hint of metal and none wore spectacles. As in the case of Walter and Krebs their heads were close-shaved, presumably, Bond would have thought, to prevent a loose hair falling into the mechanism. And yet, and this struck Bond as a most bizarre characteristic of the team, each man sported a luxuriant moustache to whose culture it was clear that a great deal of attention had been devoted. They were in all shapes and tints: fair or mousy or dark; handlebar, walrus, Kaiser, Hitler — each face bore its own hairy badge amongst which the rank, reddish growth of Drax's facial hair blazed like the official stamp of their paramount chief.

Why, wondered Bond, should every man on the site wear a moustache? He had never liked the things, but combined with these shaven heads, there was something positively obscene about this crop of hairy tufts. It would have been just bearable if they had all been cut to the same pattern, but this range of individual fashions, this riot of personalized growth, had something particularly horrible about it against the background of the naked round heads.

There was nothing else to notice; the men were of average height and they were all on the slim side — tailored, Bond supposed, more or less to the requirements of their work. Agility would be needed on the gantries, and compactness for manoeuvring through the access doors and around the tiny compartments in the rocket. Their hands looked relaxed and spotlessly clean, and their feet in the felt slippers were motionless with concentration. He never once caught any of them glancing in his direction and, as for penetrating their minds or weighing up their loyalties, he admitted to himself that the task of unmasking the thoughts of fifty of these robot-like Germans in three days was quite hopeless. Then he remembered. It was fifty no longer. Only forty-nine. One of these robots had blown his top (apt expression, reflected Bond). And what had come out of Bartsch's secret thoughts? Lust for a woman and a Heil Hitler. Would he be far wrong, wondered Bond, if he guessed that, forgetting the Moonraker, those were also the dominant thoughts inside the other forty-nine heads?

'Dr. Walter! That is an order.' Drax's voice of controlled anger broke in on Bond's thoughts as he stood fingering the sharp leading edge of the tail of one of the Columbite fins. 'Back to work. We have wasted enough time.'

The men scattered smartly about their duties and Drax came up to where Bond was standing, leaving Walter hanging about indecisively beneath the exhaust vent of the rocket.

Drax's face was thunderous. 'Damn fool. Always seeing trouble,' he muttered. And then abruptly, as if he wanted to clear his deputy out of his mind, 'Come along to my office. Show you the flight plan. Then we'll go off to bed.'

Bond followed him across the floor. Drax turned a small handle flush with the steel wall and a narrow door opened with a soft hiss. Three feet inside there was another steel door and

Bond noticed that they were both edged with rubber. Air-lock. Before closing the outer door Drax paused on the threshold and pointed along the circular wall to a number of similar inconspicuous flat knobs in the wall. 'Workshops,' he said. 'Electricians, generators, fuelling control, washrooms, stores.' He pointed to the adjoining door. 'My secretary's room.' He closed the outer door before he opened the second and walked into his office and shut the inner door behind Bond.

It was a severe room painted pale grey, containing a broad desk and several chairs of tubular metal and dark blue canvas. The floor was carpeted in grey. There were two green filing cabinets and a large metal radio set. A half-open door showed part of a tiled bathroom. The desk faced a wide blank wall which seemed to be made of opaque glass. Drax walked up to the wall and snapped down two switches on its extreme right. The whole wall lit up and Bond was faced with two maps each about six feet square traced on the back of the glass.

The left-hand map showed the eastern quarter of England from Portsmouth to Hull and the adjoining waters from Latitude 50 to 55. From the red dot near Dover which was the site of the Moonraker, arcs showing the range in ten-mile intervals had been drawn up the map. At a point eighty miles from the site, between the Friesian Islands and Hull, there was a red diamond in the middle of the ocean.

Drax waved towards the dense mathematical tables and columns of compass readings which filled the right-hand side of the map. 'Wind velocities, atmospheric pressure, ready-reckoner for the gyro settings,' he said. 'All worked out using the rocket's velocity and range as constants. We get the weather every day from the Air Ministry and readings from the upper atmosphere every time the R.A.F. jet can get up there. When he's at maximum altitude he releases helium balloons that can get up still further. The earth's atmosphere reaches about fifty miles up. After twenty there's hardly any density to affect the Moonraker. It'll coast up almost in a vacuum. Getting through the first twenty miles is the problem. The gravity pull's another worry. Walter can explain all those things if you're interested. There'll be continuous weather reports during the last few hours on Friday. And we'll set the gyros just before the take-off. For the time being, Miss

Brand gets together the data every morning and keeps a table of gyro settings in case they're wanted.'

Drax pointed at the second of the two maps. This was a diagram of the rocket's flight ellipse from firing point to target. There were more columns of figures. 'Speed of the earth and its effect on the rocket's trajectory,' explained Drax. 'The earth will be turning to the east while the rocket's in flight. That factor has to be married in with the figures on the other map. Complicated business. Fortunately you don't have to understand it. Leave it to Miss Brand. Now then,' he switched off the lights and the wall went blank, 'any particular questions about your job? Don't think there'll be much for you to do. You can see that the place is already riddled with security. The Ministry's insisted on it from the beginning.'

'Everything looks all right,' said Bond. He examined Drax's face. The good eye was looking at him sharply. Bond paused. 'Do you think there was anything between your secretary and Major Tallon?' he asked. It was an obvious question and he might just as well ask it now.

'Could have been,' said Drax easily. 'Attractive girl. They were thrown together a lot down here. At any rate she seems to have got under Bartsch's skin.'

'I hear Bartsch saluted and shouted "Heil Hitler" before he put the gun in his mouth,' said Bond.

'So they tell me,' said Drax evenly. 'What of it?'

'Why do all the men wear moustaches?' asked Bond, ignoring Drax's question. Again he had the impression that his question had nettled the other man.

Drax gave one of his short barking laughs. 'My idea,' he said. 'They're difficult to recognize in those white overalls and with their heads shaved. So I told them all to grow moustaches. The thing's become quite a fetish with them. Like in the R.A.F. during the war. See anything wrong with it?'

'Of course not,' said Bond. 'Rather startling at first. I would have thought that large numbers on their suits with a different colour for each shift would have been more effective.'

'Well,' said Drax, turning away towards the door as if to end the conversation, 'I decided on moustaches.'

13

DEAD RECKONING

ON WEDNESDAY MORNING Bond woke early in the dead man's bed.

He had slept little. Drax had said nothing on their way back to the house and had bidden him a curt good-night at the foot of the stairs. Bond had walked along the carpeted corridor to where light shone from an open door and had found his things neatly laid out in a comfortable bedroom. The room was furnished in the same expensive taste as the ground floor and there were biscuits and a bottle of Vichy (not a Vichy bottle of tap-water, Bond established) beside the Heal bed.

There were no signs of the previous occupant except a leather case containing binoculars on the dressing-table and a metal filing cabinet which was locked. Bond knew about filing cabinets. He tilted it against the wall, reached underneath, and found the bottom end of the bar-lock which protrudes downwards when the top section has been locked. Upwards pressure released the drawers one by one and he softly lowered the edge of the cabinet back on to the floor with the unkind reflection that Major Tallon would not have survived very long in the Secret Service.

The top drawer contained scale maps of the site and its component buildings and Admiralty Chart No. 1895 of the Straits of Dover. Bond laid each sheet on the bed and examined them minutely. There were traces of cigarette ash in the folds of the Admiralty chart.

Bond fetched his tool-box — a square leather case that stood beside the dressing-table. He examined the numbers on the wheels of the combination lock and, satisfied that they had not been disturbed, turned them to the code number. The box was closely fitted with instruments. Bond selected a fingerprint powder-spray and a large magnifying glass. He puffed the fine greyish powder foot by foot over the whole expanse of the chart. A forest of fingerprints showed. By going over these with the magnifying glass he established that they belonged to two people. He isolated two of the best sets, took a Leica with a flashbulb attachment out of the leather case and photographed them. Then he carefully examined through his glass two minute furrows in the paper which the powder had brought to light.

These appeared to be two lines drawn out from the coast to form a cross-bearing in the sea. It was a very narrow bearing, and both lines seemed to originate from the house where Bond was. In fact, thought Bond, they might indicate observations of some object in the sea made from each wing of the house.

The two lines were drawn not with a pencil, but, presumably to avoid detection, with a stylus which had barely furrowed the paper.

At the point where they met there was the trace of a question mark, and this point was on the twelve-fathom line about fifty yards from the cliff on a direct bearing from the house to the South Goodwin Lightship.

There was nothing else to be gathered from the chart. Bond glanced at his watch. Twenty minutes to one. He heard distant footsteps in the hall and the click of a light being extinguished. On an impulse he rose and softly switched off the lights in his room, leaving only the shaded reading-light beside the bed.

He heard the heavy footsteps of Drax approaching up the stairs. There was the click of another switch and then silence. Bond could imagine the great hairy face turned down the corridor, looking, listening. Then there was a creak and the sound of a door being softly opened and as softly closed. Bond waited, visualizing the motions of the man as he prepared for bed. There was the muffled sound of a window being thrown open and the distant trumpet of a nose being blown. Then silence.

Bond gave Drax another five minutes then he went over to the filing cabinet and softly pulled out the other drawers. There was nothing in the second and third, but the bottom one was solid with files arranged under index letters. They were the dossiers of all the men working on the site. Bond pulled out the 'A' section and went back to the bed and started to read.

In each case the formula was the same: full name, address, date of birth, description, distinguishing marks, profession or trade since the war, war record, political record and present sympathies, criminal record, health, next of kin. Some of the men had wives and children whose particulars were noted, and with each dossier there were photographs, full face and profile, and the fingerprints of both hands.

Two hours and ten cigarettes later he had worked through all of them and had discovered two points of general interest. First, that every one of the fifty men appeared to have led a blameless life without a breath of political or criminal odium. This seemed so unlikely that he decided to refer every single dossier back to Station D for a thorough recheck at the first opportunity.

The second point was that none of the faces in the photographs bore a moustache. Despite Drax's explanation, this fact raised a second tiny question mark in Bond's mind.

Bond got up from the bed and locked everything away, putting the Admiralty Chart and one of the files in his leather case. He turned the wheels of the combination lock and thrust the case far under his bed so that it rested directly beneath his pillow at the inside angle of the wall. Then he quietly washed and cleaned his teeth in the adjoining bathroom and eased the window wide open.

The moon was still shining: as it must have shone, Bond thought, when, aroused perhaps by some unusual noise, Tallon had climbed up to the roof, maybe only a couple of nights before, and had seen, out at sea, what he had seen. He would have had his glasses with him and Bond, remembering, turned back from the window and picked them up. They were a very powerful German pair, booty perhaps from the war, and the 7 × 50 on the top plates told Bond that they were night glasses. And then the careful Tallon must have walked softly (but not softly enough?) to the other end of the roof and raised his glasses again, estimating the distance from the edge of the cliff to the object in the sea, and from the object to the Goodwin Lightship. Then he would have come back the way he had gone and softly re-entered his room.

Bond saw Tallon, perhaps for the first time since he had been in the house, carefully lock the door and walk over to the filing cabinet and take out the chart which he had hardly glanced at till then and on it softly mark the lines of his rough bearing. Perhaps he looked at it for a long while before putting the minute question mark beside it.

And what had the unknown object been? Impossible to say. A boat? A light? A noise?

Whatever it was Tallon had not been supposed to see it. And somebody had heard him. Somebody had guessed he had seen it and had waited until Tallon had left his room next morning. Then that man had come into his room and had searched it. Probably the chart had revealed nothing, but there were the night glasses by the window.

That had been enough. And that night Tallon had died.

Bond pulled himself up. He was going too fast, building up a case on the flimsiest evidence. Bartsch had killed Tallon and Bartsch was not the man who had heard the noise, the man who had left his fingerprints on the chart, the man whose dossier Bond had put away in his leather case.

That man had been the oily A.D.C., Krebs, the man with the neck like a white slug. They were his prints on the chart. For a quarter of an hour Bond had compared the impressions on the chart with the prints on Krebs's dossier. But who said Krebs had heard a noise or done anything about it if he had? Well, to begin with, he looked like a natural snooper. He had the eyes of a petty thief. And those prints of his had definitely been made on the chart after Tallon had studied it. Krebs's fingers overlaid Tallon's at several points.

But how could Krebs possibly be involved, with Drax's eye constantly on him? The confidential assistant. But what about Cicero, the trusted valet of the British Ambassador in Ankara during the war? The hand in the pocket of the striped trousers hanging over the back of the chair. The Ambassador's keys. The safe. The secrets. This picture looked very much the same.

Bond shivered. He suddenly realized that he had been standing for a long time in front of the open windows and that it was time to get some sleep.

Before he got into bed he took his shoulder-holster from the chair where it hung beside his discarded clothes and removed the Beretta with the skeleton grip and slipped it under his pillow. As a defence against whom? Bond didn't know, but his intuition told him quite definitely that there was danger about. The smell of it was insistent although it was still imprecise and lingered only on the threshold of his subconscious. In fact he knew his feelings were based on a number of tiny question marks which had materialized during the past twenty-four hours — the riddle of Drax; Bartsch's 'Heil Hitler'; the bizarre moustaches; the fifty worthy Germans; the chart; the night glasses; Krebs.

First he must pass on his suspicions to Vallance. Then explore the possibilities of Krebs. Then look to the defences of the Moonraker — the seaward side for instance. And then get together with this Brand girl and agree on a plan for the next two days. There wasn't much time to lose.

While he forced sleep to come into his teeming mind, Bond visualized the figure seven on the dial of a clock and left it to the hidden cells of his memory to wake him. He wanted to be out of the house and on the telephone to Vallance as early as possible. If his actions aroused suspicion he would not be dismayed. One of his objects was to attract into his orbit the same forces that had concerned themselves with Tallon, for of one thing he felt reasonably certain, Major Tallon had not died because he loved Gala Brand.

The extra-sensory alarm clock did not fail him. Punctually at seven, his mouth dry with too many cigarettes the night before, he forced himself out of bed and into a cold bath. He had shaved, gargled with a sharp mouthwash, and now, in a battered black and white dogtooth suit, dark blue Sea Island cotton shirt and black silk knitted tie, he was walking softly, but not surreptitiously, along the corridor to the head of the stairs, the square leather case in his left hand.

He found the garage at the back of the house and the big engine of the Bentley answered with the first pressure on the starter. He motored slowly across the concrete apron beneath the indifferent gaze of the curtained windows of the house and pulled up, the engine idling in neutral, at the edge of the trees. His eyes travelled back to the house and confirmed his calculation that a man standing on its roof would be able to see over the top of the blast-wall and get a view of the edge of the cliff and of the sea beyond.

There was no sign of life round the domed emplacement of the Moonraker, and the concrete, already beginning to shimmer in the early morning sun, stretched emptily away towards Deal. It looked like a newly laid aerodrome or rather, he thought, with its three disparate concrete 'things', the beehive dome, the flat-iron blast-wall, and the distant cube of the firing point, each casting black pools of shadow towards him in the early sun, like a Dali desert landscape on which three *objets trouvés* reposed at carefully calculated random.

Out at sea, in the early mist that promised a hot day, the South Goodwin Lightship could just be seen, a dim red barque married for ever to the same compass point and condemned, like a property ship on the stage of Drury Lane, to watch the diorama of the waves and clouds sail busily into the wings while, without papers or passengers or cargo, it lay anchored for ever to the departure point which was also its destination.

At thirty seconds' intervals it blared its sad complaint into the mist, a long double trumpet note on a falling cadence. A siren song, Bond reflected, to repel instead of to seduce. He wondered how the seven men of its crew were now supporting the noise as they munched their pork and beans. Did they flinch as it punctuated the Housewife's Choice coming at full strength from the radio in the narrow mess? But a secure life,* Bond decided, although anchored to the gates of a graveyard.

He made a mental note to find out if those seven men had seen or heard the thing that Tallon had marked on the chart, then he drove quickly on through the guard posts.

In Dover, Bond pulled up at the Café Royal, a modest little restaurant with a modest kitchen but capable, as he knew of old, of turning out excellent fish and egg dishes. The Italian-Swiss mother and son who ran it welcomed him as an old friend and he asked for a plate of scrambled eggs and bacon and plenty of coffee to be ready in half an hour. Then he drove on to the police station and put in a call to Vallance through the Scotland Yard switchboard. Vallance was at home having breakfast. He listened without comment to Bond's guarded talk, but he expressed surprise that Bond had not had an opportunity to have a talk with Gala Brand. 'She's a bright girl, that,' he said. 'If Mr K. is up to something she's sure to have an idea what it is. And if T. heard a noise on Sunday night, she may have heard it too. Though I'll admit she's said nothing about it.'

Bond said nothing about the reception he had had from Vallance's agent. 'Going to talk to her this morning,' he said, 'and

* Bond was wrong: Friday, November 26th 1954. R.I.P.

I'll send up the chart and the Leica film for you to have a look at. I'll give them to the Inspector. Perhaps one of his road patrols could bring them up. By the way, where did T. telephone from when he rang up his employer on Monday?'

'I'll have the call traced and let you know,' said Vallance. 'And I'll have Trinity House ask the South Goodwins and the Coastguards if they can help. Anything else?'

'No,' said Bond. The line went through too many switchboards. Perhaps if it had been M. he would have hinted more. It seemed ridiculous to talk to Vallance about moustaches and the creep of danger he had felt the night before and which the daylight had dissipated. These policemen wanted hard facts. They were better, he decided, at solving crimes than at anticipating them. 'No. That's all.' He hung up.

He felt more cheerful after an excellent breakfast. He read the *Express* and *The Times* and found a bare report of the inquest on Tallon. The *Express* had made a big play with the girl's photograph and he was amused to see what a neutral likeness Vallance had managed to produce. He decided that he must try and work with her. He would take her completely into his confidence whether she was receptive or not. Perhaps she also had her suspicions and intuitions which were so vague that she was keeping them to herself.

Bond drove back fast to the house. It was just nine o'clock and as he came through the trees on to the concrete there was the wail of a siren and from the woods behind the house a double file of twelve men appeared running, in purposeful unison, towards the launching dome. They marked time while one of their number rang the bell, then the door opened and they filed through and out of sight.

Scratch a German and you find precision, thought Bond.

15

ITCHING FINGERS

HALF AN HOUR before, Gala Brand had stubbed out her breakfast cigarette, swallowed the remains of her coffee, left her bedroom and walked across to the site, looking very much the private secretary in a spotless white shirt and dark blue pleated skirt.

Punctually at eight-thirty she was in her office. There was a sheaf of Air Ministry teleprints on her desk and her first action was to transfer a digest of their contents on to a weather map and walk through the communicating door into Drax's office and pin the map to the board that hung in the angle of the wall beside the blank glass wall. Then she pressed the switch that illuminated the wall map, made some calculations based on the columns of figures revealed by the light, and entered the results on the diagram she had pinned to the board.

She had done this, with Air Ministry figures that became more and more precise as the practice shoot drew nearer, every day since the site was completed and the building of the rocket had begun inside it, and she had become so expert that she now carried in her head the gyro settings for almost every variation in the weather at the different altitudes.

So it irritated her all the more that Drax did not seem to accept her figures. Every day when, punctually at nine, the warning bells clanged and he came down the steep iron stairway and into his office, his first action was to call for the insufferable Dr. Walter and together they would work out all her figures afresh and transfer the results to the thin black notebook that Drax always carried in the hip pocket of his trousers. She knew that this was an invariable routine and she had become tired of watching it through an inconspicuous hole she had drilled, so as to be able to send Vallance a weekly record of Drax's visitors, in the thin wall between the two offices. The method was amateurish but effective and she had slowly built up a complete picture of the daily routine she came to find so irritating. It was irritating for two reasons. It meant that Drax didn't trust her figures, and it undermined her chance of having some part, however modest, in the final launching of the rocket.

It was natural that over the months she should have become as immersed in her disguise as she was in her real profession. It was fundamental to the thoroughness of her cover that her personality should be as truly split as possible. And now, while she spied and probed and sniffed the wind around Drax for her Chief in London, she was passionately concerned with the success of the Moonraker and had become as dedicated to its service as anyone else on the site.

And the rest of her duties as Drax's private secretary were insufferably dull. Every day there was a big post addressed to Drax in London and forwarded down by the Ministry, and that morning she had found the usual batch of about fifty letters waiting on her desk. They would be of three kinds. Begging letters, letters from rocket cranks, and business letters from Drax's stockbroker and from other commercial agents. To these Drax would dictate brief replies and the rest of her day would be occupied with typing and filing.

So it was natural that her one duty connected with the operation of the rocket should bulk very large in the dull round, and that morning, as she checked and rechecked her flight plan, she was more than ever determined that her figures should be accepted on The Day. And yet, as she often reminded herself, perhaps there was no question but that they would be. Perhaps the daily calculations of Drax and Walter for entry in the little black book were nothing but a recheck of her own figures. Certainly Drax had never queried either her weather plan or the gyro settings she calculated from them. And when one day she had asked straight out whether her figures were correct he had replied with evident sincerity, 'Excellent, my dear. Most valuable. Couldn't manage without them.'

Gala Brand walked back into her own office and started slitting open the letters. Only two more flight plans, for Thursday and Friday and then, on her figures or on a different set, the set in Drax's pocket, the gyros would be finally adjusted and the switch would be pulled in the firing point.

She absentmindedly looked at her finger-nails and then stretched her two hands out with their backs towards her. How often in the course of her training at the Police College had she been sent out among the other pupils and told not to come back without a pocketbook, a vanity case, a fountain pen, even a wristwatch? How often during the courses had the hand of her instructor whipped round and caught her wrist with a 'Now, now, Miss. That won't do at all. Might have been an elephant looking for sugar in the keeper's pocket. Try again?'

Coolly she flexed her fingers and then, her mind made up, turned back to the pile of letters.

At a few minutes to nine the alarm bells rang and she heard Drax arrive in the office. A moment later she heard him open the double doors again and call for Walter. Then came the usual mumble of voices whose words were drowned by the soft whirr of the ventilators.

She arranged the letters in their three piles and sat forward relaxed, her elbows resting on the desk and her chin in her left hand.

Commander Bond. James Bond. Clearly a conceited young man like so many of them in the Secret Service. And why had he been sent down instead of somebody she could work with, one of her friends from the Special Branch, or even somebody from M.I.5? The message from the Assistant Commissioner had said that there was no one else available at short notice, that this was one of the stars of the Secret Service who had the complete confidence of the Special Branch and the blessings of M.I.5. Even the Prime Minister had had to give permission for him to operate, for just this one assignment, inside England. But what use could he be in the short time that was left? He could probably shoot all right and talk foreign languages and do a lot of tricks that might be useful abroad. But what good could he do down here without any beautiful spies to make love to? Because he was certainly good-looking. (Gala Brand automatically reached into her bag for her vanity case. She examined herself in the little mirror and dabbed at her nose with a powder puff.) Rather like Hoagy Carmichael in a way. That black hair falling down over the right eyebrow. Much the same bones. But there was something a bit cruel in the mouth, and the eyes were cold. Were they grey or blue? It had been difficult to say last night. Well, at any rate she had put him in his place and shown him that she wasn't impressed by dashing young men from the Secret Service, however romantic they might look.

There were just as good-looking men in the Special Branch, and they were real detectives, not just people that Phillips Oppenheim had dreamed up with fast cars and special cigarettes with gold bands on them and shoulder-holsters. Oh, she had spotted that all right and had even brushed against him to make sure. Ah well, she supposed she would have to make some sort of show of working along with him, though in what direction heaven only knew. If she had been down there ever since the place had been built without spotting anything, what could this Bond man hope to discover in a couple of days? And what was there to find out? Of course there were one or two things she couldn't understand. Should she tell him about Krebs for instance? The first thing was to see that he didn't blow her cover by doing something stupid. She would have to be cool and firm and extremely careful. But that didn't mean, she decided, as the buzzer went and she collected the letters and her shorthand book, that she couldn't be friendly. Entirely on her own terms, of course.

Her second decision made, she opened the communicating door and walked into the office of Sir Hugo Drax.

When she came back into her room half an hour later she found Bond sitting back in her chair with Whitaker's *Almanack* open on the desk in front of him. She pursed her lips as Bond got up and wished her a cheerful good morning. She nodded briefly and walked round her desk and sat down. She moved the Whitaker's carefully aside and put her letters and notebook in its place.

'You might have a spare chair for visitors,' said Bond with a grin which she defined as impertinent, 'and something better to read than reference books.'

She ignored him. 'Sir Hugo wants you,' she said. 'I was just going to see if you had got up yet.'

'Liar,' said Bond. 'You heard me go by at half-past seven. I saw you peering out between the curtains.'

'I did nothing of the sort,' she said indignantly. 'Why should I be interested in a car going by?'

'I told you you heard the car,' said Bond. He pressed home his advantage. 'And by the way,' he said, 'you shouldn't scratch your head with the blunt end of the pencil when you're taking dictation. None of the best private secretaries do.'

Bond glanced significantly at a point against the jamb of the communicating door. He shrugged his shoulders.

Gala's defences dropped. Damn the man, she thought. She gave him a reluctant smile. 'Oh, well,' she said. 'Come on. I can't spend all the morning playing guessing games. He wants both of us and he doesn't like being kept waiting.' She rose and walked over to the communicating door and opened it. Bond followed her through and shut the door behind him.

Drax was standing looking at the illuminated wall map. He turned as they came in. 'Ah, there you are,' he said with a sharp glance at Bond. 'Thought you might have left us. Guards reported you out at seven-thirty this morning.'

'I had to make a telephone call,' said Bond. 'I hope I didn't disturb anyone.'

'There's a telephone in my study,' Drax said curtly. 'Tallon found it good enough.'

'Ah, poor Tallon,' said Bond non-committally. There was a hectoring note in Drax's voice that he particularly disliked and that made him instinctively want to deflate the man. On this occasion he was successful.

Drax shot him a hard glance which he covered up with a short barking laugh and a shrug of the shoulders. 'Do as you please,' he said. 'You've got your job to do. So long as you don't upset the routines down here. You must remember,' he added more reasonably, 'all my men are nervous as kittens just now and I can't have them upset by mysterious goings-on. I hope you're not wanting to ask them a lot of questions today. I'd rather they didn't have anything more to worry about. They haven't recovered from Monday yet. Miss Brand here can tell you all about them, and I believe all their files are in Tallon's room. Have you had a look at them yet?'

'No key to the filing cabinet,' said Bond truthfully.

'Sorry, my fault,' said Drax. He went to his desk and opened a drawer from which he took a small bunch of keys and handed them to Bond. 'Should have given you these last night. The Inspector chap on the case asked me to hand them over to you. Sorry.'

'Thanks very much,' said Bond. He paused. 'By the way, how long have you had Krebs?' He asked the question on an impulse. There was a moment's quiet in the room.

'Krebs?' repeated Drax thoughtfully. He walked over to his desk and sat down. He reached into his trouser pocket and pulled out a packet of his cork-tipped cigarettes. His blunt fingers scrabbled with its cellophane wrapping. He extracted a cigarette and stuffed it into his mouth under the fringe of his reddish moustache and lit it.

Bond was surprised. 'I didn't realize one could smoke down here,' he said, taking out his own case.

Drax's cigarette, a tiny white faggot in the middle of the big red face, waggled up and down as he answered without taking it out of his mouth. 'Quite all right in here,' he said. 'These rooms are air-tight. Doors lined with rubber. Separate ventilation. Have to keep the workshops and generators separate from the shaft and anyway,' his lips grinned round the cigarette, 'I have to be able to smoke.'

Drax took the cigarette out of his mouth and looked at it. He seemed to make up his mind. 'You were asking about Krebs,' he said. 'Well,' he looked meaningly up at Bond, 'just between ourselves I don't entirely trust the fellow.' He held up an admonitory hand. 'Nothing definite, of course, or I'd have had him put away, but I've found him snooping about the house and once I caught him in my study going through my private papers. He had a perfectly good explanation and I let him off with a warning. But quite honestly I have my suspicions of the man. Of course, he can't do any harm. He's part of the household staff and none of them is allowed in here but,' he looked candidly into Bond's eyes, 'I would have said you ought to concentrate on him. Bright of you to have bowled him out so quickly,' he added with respect. 'What put you on to him?'

'Oh, nothing much,' said Bond. 'He's got a shifty look. But what you say's interesting and I'll certainly keep an eye on him.'

He turned to Gala Brand who had remained silent ever since they had entered the room.

'And what do you think of Krebs, Miss Brand?' he asked politely.

The girl spoke to Drax. 'I don't know much about these things, Sir Hugo,' she said with a modesty and a touch of impulsiveness which Bond admired. 'But I don't trust the man at all. I hadn't meant to tell you, but he's been poking around my room, opening letters and so forth. I know he has.'

Drax was shocked. 'Has he indeed?' he said. He bashed his cigarette out in the ashtray and killed the glowing fragments one by one. 'So much for Krebs,' he said, without looking up.

15

ROUGH JUSTICE

THERE WAS A moment's silence in the room during which Bond reflected how odd it was that suspicions should have fallen so suddenly and so unanimously on one man. And did that automatically clear all the others? Might not Krebs be the inside man of a gang? Or was he working on his own and, if so, with what object? And what did his snooping have to do with the death of Tallon and Bartsch?

Drax broke the silence. 'Well, that seems to settle it,' he said, looking to Bond for confirmation. Bond gave a non-committal nod. 'Just have to leave him to you. At all events, we must see he is kept well away from the site. As a matter of fact I shall be taking him to London tomorrow. Last-minute details to be settled with the Ministry and Walter can't be spared. Krebs is the only man I've got who can do the work of an A.D.C. That'll keep him out of trouble. We'll all have to keep an eye on him until then. Unless of course you want to put him under lock and key straight away. I'd prefer not,' he said candidly. 'Don't want to upset the team any more.'

'It shouldn't be necessary,' said Bond. 'Has he got any particular friends among the other men?'

'Never seen him speak to any of them except Walter and the household,' said Drax. 'Daresay he considers himself a cut above the others. Personally I don't believe there's much harm in the chap or I wouldn't have kept him. He's left alone in that house all day long and I expect he's one of those people who like playing the detective and prying into other people's affairs. What do you say? Perhaps we could leave it like that?'

Bond nodded, keeping his thoughts to himself.

'Well, then,' said Drax, obviously glad to leave a distasteful subject and get back to business, 'we've got other things to talk about. Two more days to go and I'd better tell you the programme.' He got up from his chair and paced heavily up and down the room behind his desk. 'Today is Wednesday,' he said. 'At one o'clock the site will be closed for fuelling. This will be supervised by Dr. Walter and myself and two men from the Ministry. Just in case anything goes wrong a television camera will record everything we do. Then, if there is an explosion, our successors will know better next time.' He barked a short laugh. 'Weather permitting, the roof will be opened tonight to allow the fumes to clear. My men will stand guard in watches at ten-yard intervals a hundred yards from the site. There will be three armed men on the beach opposite the exhaust hole in the cliff. Tomorrow morning the site will be opened again until midday for a final check and from that moment, except for the gyro settings, the Moonraker will be ready to go. The guards will be permanently on duty round the site. On Friday morning I shall personally supervise the gyro settings. The men from the Ministry will take over the firing point and the R.A.F. will man the radar. The B.B.C. will set up their vans behind the firing point and will begin their running commentary at eleven-forty-five. At midday exactly I shall press the plunger, a radio beam will break an electric circuit and,' he smiled broadly, 'we shall see what we shall see.' He paused, fingering his chin. 'Now what else? Well now. Shipping will be cleared from the target area from midnight on Thursday. The Navy will provide a patrol of the boundaries of the area all through the morning. There will be a B.B.C. commentator in one of the ships. The Ministry of Supply experts will be in a salvage ship with deep-sea television and after the rocket has landed they will try to bring up the remains. You may be interested to know,' continued Drax, rubbing his hands with almost childish pleasure, 'that a messenger from the Prime Minister has brought me the very welcome news that not only will there be a special Cabinet Meeting to listen to the broadcast, but the Palace will also be listening in to the launching.'

'Splendid,' said Bond, pleased for the man's sake.

'Thank you,' said Drax. 'Now I want to be quite certain that you are satisfied with my security arrangements on the site itself. I don't think we need worry about what goes on outside. The R.A.F. and the police seem to be doing a very thorough job.'

'Everything seems to have been taken care of,' said Bond. 'There doesn't seem to be very much for me to do in the time that's left.'

'Nothing that I can think of,' agreed Drax, 'except our friend Krebs. This afternoon he will be in the television van taking notes, so he will be out of trouble. Why don't you have a look at the beach and the bottom of the cliff while he's out of action? That's the only weak spot I can think of. I've often thought that if someone wanted to get into the site he would try the exhaust pit. Take Miss Brand with you. Two pairs of eyes, and so forth, and she won't be able to use her office until tomorrow morning.'

'Good,' said Bond. 'I'd certainly like to have a look at the seaward side after lunch, and if Miss Brand's got nothing better to do . . . ' He turned towards her with his eyebrows raised.

Gala Brand looked down her nose. 'Certainly, if Sir Hugo wishes,' she said without enthusiasm.

Drax rubbed his hands together. 'Then that's settled,' he said. 'And now I must get down to work. Miss Brand, would you ask Dr. Walter to come along if he's free. See you at lunch,' he said to Bond, on a note of dismissal.

Bond nodded. 'I think I'll walk over and have a look at the firing point,' he said, not quite knowing why he lied. He turned and followed Gala Brand out through the double doors into the base of the shaft.

A huge black snake of rubber piping meandered over the shining steel floor and Bond watched the girl pick her way among its coils to where Walter was standing alone. He was gazing up at the mouth of the fuel pipe being hoist to where a gantry, outstretched to the threshold of an access door halfway up the rocket, indicated the main fuel tanks.

She said something to Walter and then stood beside him looking upwards as the pipe was delicately manhandled through into the interior of the rocket.

Bond thought she looked very innocent standing there with her brown hair falling back from her head and the curve of her ivory throat sweeping down into the plain white shirt. With her hands clasped behind her back, gazing raptly upwards at the glittering fifty feet of the Moonraker, she might have been a schoolgirl looking at a Christmas tree — except for the impudent pride of the jutting breasts, swept up by the thrown-back head and shoulders.

Bond smiled to himself as he walked to the foot of the iron stairway and started to climb. That innocent, desirable girl, he reminded himself, is an extremely efficient policewoman. She knows how to kick, and where; she can break my arm probably more easily and quickly than I can break hers, and at least half of her belongs to the Special Branch of Scotland Yard. Of course, he reflected, looking down just in time to see her follow Dr. Walter into Drax's office, there is always the other half.

Outside, the brilliant May sunshine seemed particularly golden after the blue-white of the arcs and Bond could feel it hot on his back as he walked purposefully across the concrete towards the house. The foghorn from the Goodwins was silent and the morning was so quiet that he could hear the rhythmic thump of a ship's engines as a coaster negotiated the Inner Leads, between the Goodwins and the shore, on its way northwards.

He approached the house under cover of the wide blast-wall and then quickly crossed the few yards to the front door, the crepe rubber soles of his shoes making no noise. He eased open the door and left it ajar and walked softly into the hall and stood listening. There was the early summer noise of a bumblebee fussing against the pane of one of the windows and a distant clatter from the barracks behind the house. Otherwise the silence was deep and warm and reassuring.

Bond walked carefully across the hall and up the stairs, placing his feet flat on the ground and using the extreme edges of the steps where the boards would be less likely to creak. There was no noise in the corridor but Bond saw that his door at the far end was wide open. He took his gun from under his armpit and walked swiftly down the carpeted passage.

Krebs had his back to him. He was kneeling forward in the middle of the floor with his elbows on the ground. His hands were at the wheels of the combination lock of Bond's leather case. His whole attention was focused on the click of the tumblers in the lock.

The target was tempting and Bond didn't hesitate. His teeth showing in a hard smile, he took two quick paces into the room and his foot lashed out.

All his force was behind the point of his shoe and his balance and timing were perfect.

The scream of a jay was driven out of Krebs as, like the caricature of a leaping frog, he hurtled over Bond's case, across a yard or so of carpet, and into the front of the mahogany dressing-table. His head hit the middle of it so hard that the heavy piece of furniture rocked on its base. The scream was abruptly cut off and he crashed in an inert spreadeagle on the floor and lay still.

Bond stood looking at him and listening for the sound of hurrying footsteps, but there was still silence in the house. He walked over to the sprawling figure and bent down and heaved it over on its back. The face around the smudge of yellow moustache was pale and some blood had oozed down over the forehead from a cut in the top of the skull. The eyes were closed and the breathing was laboured.

Bond knelt down on one knee and went carefully through every pocket of Krebs's neat grey pinstripe suit, laying the disappointingly meagre contents on the carpet beside the body. There was no pocketbook and no papers. The only objects of interest were a bunch of skeleton keys, a spring knife with a well-sharpened stiletto blade, and an obscene little truss-shaped black leather cosh. Bond pocketed these and then went to his bedside table and fetched the untouched bottle of Vichy water.

It took five minutes to revive Krebs and get him into a sitting position with his back to the dressing-table and another five for him to be capable of speaking. Gradually the colour came back to his face and the craftiness to his eyes.

'I answer no questions except to Sir Hugo,' he said as Bond started the interrogation. 'You have no right to question me. I was doing my duty.' His voice was surly and assured.

Bond took the empty Vichy bottle by the neck. 'Think again,' he said. 'Or I'll beat the daylights out of you until this breaks and then use the neck for some plastic surgery. Who told you to go over my room?'

'*Leck mich am Arsch.*' Krebs spat the obscene insult at him.

Bond bent down and cracked him sharply across the shins.

Krebs's body cringed, but, as Bond raised his arm again, he suddenly shot up from the floor and dived under the descending bottle. The blow caught him hard on the shoulder, but it didn't check his momentum and he was out of the door and halfway down the corridor before Bond started in pursuit.

Bond stopped outside the door and watched the flying figure swerve down the stairs and out of sight. Then, as he heard the scurrying squeak of the rubber-soled shoes as they fled down the stairs and across the hall, he laughed abruptly to himself and went back into his room and locked the door. Short of beating the man's brains out it hadn't looked as if he would get much out of Krebs. He had given him something to think about. Crafty little brute. His injuries couldn't have been so bad after all. Well, it would be up to Drax to punish him.

Unless, of course, Krebs had been carrying out Drax's orders.

Bond cleaned up the mess in his room and sat down on his bed and gazed at the opposite wall with unseeing eyes.

It had not been only instinct that had made him tell Drax he was going to the firing point instead of to the house. It had seriously crossed his mind that the snooping of Krebs was on Drax's orders, and that Drax ran his own security system. And yet how did that tally with the deaths of Tallon and Bartsch? Or had the double killing been a coincidence unrelated to the marks on the chart and the fingerprints of Krebs?

As if summoned by his thoughts, there came a knock on the door and the butler came in. He was followed by a police sergeant in road patrol uniform who saluted and handed Bond a telegram. Bond took it over to the window. It was signed Baxter, which meant Vallance, and it read:

FIRSTLY CALL WAS FROM HOUSE SECONDLY FOG REQUIRED OPERATION OF FOGHORN SO SHIP HEARD COMMA OBSERVED NOTHING THIRDLY YOUR COMPASS RECKONING TOO NEAR SHORE THUS OUT OF SIGHT OF SAINT MARGARETS OR DEAL COASTGUARDS ENDS.

'Thank you,' said Bond. 'No answer.'

When the door was closed Bond put his lighter to the telegram and dropped it in the fireplace, scuffing the charred remains into powder with the sole of his shoe.

Nothing much there except that Tallon's call to the Ministry might indeed have been heard by someone in the house, which might have resulted in the search of his room, which might have resulted in his death. But what about Bartsch? If all this was part of something much bigger how could it be linked up with an attempt to sabotage the rocket? Wasn't it much simpler to conclude that Krebs was a natural snooper, or more likely that he was operating for Drax, who seemed to be meticulously security-conscious and who might want to be sure of the loyalty of his secretary, of Tallon, and certainly, after their encounter at

Blades, of Bond? Wasn't he just acting like the chief (and Bond had known many of them who would fit the picture) of some super-secret project during the war who had reinforced official security with his own private spy system?

If that theory was correct there only remained the double killing. Now that Bond had caught the magic and the tension of the Moonraker the facts of the hysterical shooting seemed more reasonable. As for the mark on the chart, that might have been made any day in the past year; the night glasses were just night glasses and the moustaches on the men were just a lot of moustaches.

Bond sat on in the silent room, shifting the pieces in the jigsaw so that two entirely different pictures alternated in his mind. In one the sun shone and all was clear and innocent as the day outside. The other was a dark confusion of guilty motives, obscure suspicions, and nightmare queries.

When the gong sounded for lunch he still did not know which picture to choose. To shelve a decision he cleared his mind of everything but the prospect of his afternoon alone with Gala Brand.

16

A GOLDEN DAY

IT WAS A wonderful afternoon of blue and green and gold. When they left the concrete apron through the guard-gate near the empty firing point, now connected by a thick cable with the launching site, they stopped for a moment on the edge of the great chalk cliff and stood gazing over the whole corner of England where Caesar had first landed two thousand years before.

To their left the carpet of green turf, bright with small wild-flowers, sloped gradually down to the long pebble beaches of Walmer and Deal which curved off towards Sandwich and the Bay. Beyond, the cliffs of Ramsgate, showing white through the distant haze that hid the North Foreland, guarded the grey scar of Manston aerodrome above which American Thunderjets wrote their white scribbles in the sky. Then came the Isle of Thanet and, out of sight, the mouth of the Thames.

It was low tide and the Goodwins were golden and tender in the sparkling blue of the Straits with only the smattering of masts and spars that stretched along their length to tell the true story. The white lettering on the South Goodwins Lightship was easy to read and even the name of her sister ship to the north showed white against the red of her hull.

Between the sands and the coast, along the twelve-fathom channel of the Inner Leads, there were half a dozen ships beating up through the Downs, the thud of their engines coming clearly off the quiet sea, and between the evil sands and the sharp outline of the French coast there were ships of all registries going about their business — liners, merchantmen, ungainly Dutch schuyts, and even a slim corvette hastening down south, perhaps to Portsmouth. As far as the eye could reach the Eastern Approaches of England were dotted with traffic plying towards near or distant horizons, towards a home port, or towards the other side of the world. It was a panorama full of colour and excitement and romance and the two people on the edge of the cliff were silent as they stood for a time and watched it all.

The peace was broken by two blasts on the siren from the house and they turned to gaze back at the ugly concrete world that had been cleaned out of their minds. As they watched, a red flag was broken out above the dome of the launching site and two R.A.F. crash-wagons with red crosses on their sides rolled out of the trees to the edge of the blast-wall and pulled up.

'Fuelling's going to begin,' said Bond. 'Let's get on with our walk. There'll be nothing to see and if there happened to be something we probably wouldn't survive it at this range.'

She smiled at him. 'Yes,' she said. 'And I'm sick of the sight of all this concrete.'

They walked on down the gentle slope and were soon out of sight of the firing point and the high wire fence.

The ice of Gala's reserve melted quickly in the sunshine.

The exotic gaiety of her clothes, a black and white striped cotton shirt tucked into a wide hand-stitched black leather belt above a medium-length skirt in shocking pink, seemed to have infected her, and it was impossible for Bond to recognize the chill woman of the night before in the girl who now walked beside him and laughed happily at his ignorance of the names of the wildflowers, the samphire, viper's bugloss, and fumitory round their feet.

Triumphantly she found a bee orchis and picked it.

'You wouldn't do that if you knew that flowers scream when they are picked,' said Bond.

Gala looked at him. 'What do you mean?' she asked, suspecting a joke.

'Didn't you know?' He smiled at her reaction. 'There's an Indian called Professor Bhose, who's written a treatise on the nervous system of flowers. He measured their reaction to pain. He even recorded the scream of a rose being picked. It must be one of the most heartrending sounds in the world. I heard something like it as you picked that flower.'

'I don't believe it,' she said, looking suspiciously at the torn root. 'Anyway,' she said maliciously, 'I wouldn't have thought you were a person to get sentimental. Don't people in your section of the Service make a business of killing? And not just flowers either. People.'

'Flowers can't shoot back,' said Bond.

She looked at the orchis. 'Now you've made me feel like a murderer. It's very unkind of you. But,' she admitted reluctantly, 'I shall have to find out about this Indian and if you're right I shall never pick a flower again as long as I live. What am I going to do with this one? You make me feel it's bleeding all over my hands.'

'Give it to me,' said Bond. 'According to you, my hands are dripping with blood already. A little more won't hurt.'

She handed it to him and their hands touched. 'You can stick it in the muzzle of your revolver,' she said to cover the flash of contact.

Bond laughed. 'So the eyes aren't only for decoration,' he said. 'Anyway it's an automatic and I left it in my room.' He drew the stalk of the flower through one of the button-holes in his blue cotton shirt. 'I thought a shoulder-holster would look a bit conspicuous without a coat to cover it. And I don't think anyone will be going over my room this afternoon.'

By tacit agreement they edged away from the moment of warmth. Bond told her of his discovery of Krebs and of the scene in his bedroom.

'Serves him right,' she said. 'I've never trusted him. But what did Sir Hugo say?'

'I had a word with him before lunch,' said Bond. 'Gave him Krebs's knife and keys as proof. He was furious and went straight off to see the man, muttering with rage. When he came back he said that Krebs seemed to be in a pretty bad way and was I satisfied that he'd been punished enough? All that business about not wanting to upset the team at the last moment and so forth. So I agreed that he'd be sent back to Germany next week and that meanwhile he would consider himself under open arrest — only allowed out of his room under surveillance.'

They scrambled down a steep cliff-path to the beach and turned to the right beside the deserted small-arms range of the Royal Marine Garrison at Deal. They walked along in silence until they came to the two-mile stretch of shingle that runs at low tide beneath the towering white cliffs to St. Margaret's Bay.

As they trudged slowly through the deep smooth pebbles Bond told her of all that had gone through his mind since the previous day. He held nothing back and he showed each false hare as it had been started and finally run to earth, leaving nothing but a thin scent of ill-founded suspicions and a muddle of clues that all ended in the same question mark . . . where was a pattern? Where was a plan into which the clues would fit? And always the same answer, that nothing Bond knew or suspected seemed to have any conceivable bearing on the security from sabotage of the Moonraker. And that, when all was said and done, was the only matter with which he and the girl were concerned. Not with the death of Tallon and Bartsch, not with the egregious Krebs, but only with the protection of the whole Moonraker project from its possible enemies.

'Isn't that so?' Bond concluded.

Gala stopped and stood for a moment looking out across the tumbled rocks and seaweed towards the quiet glimmering swell of the sea. She was hot and out of breath from the hard going through the shingle and she thought how wonderful it would be to bathe — to step back for a moment into those childish days beside the sea before her life had been caught up in this strange cold profession with its tensions and hollow thrills. She glanced at the ruthless brown face of the man beside her. Did he have moments of longing for the peaceful simple things of life? Of course not. He liked Paris and Berlin and New York and trains and aeroplanes and expensive food, and, yes certainly, expensive women.

'Well?' said Bond, wondering if she was going to come out with some piece of evidence that he had overlooked. 'What do you think?'

'I'm sorry,' said Gala. 'I was dreaming. No,' she answered his question, 'I think you're right. I've been down here since the beginning and although there've been odd little things from time to time, and of course the shooting, I've seen absolutely nothing wrong. Every one of the team, from Sir Hugo down, is heart and soul behind the rocket. It's all they live for and it's been wonderful to see the whole thing grow. The Germans are terrific workers — and I can quite believe that Bartsch broke under the strain — and they love being driven by Sir Hugo and he loves driving them. They worship him. And as for security, the place is solid with it and I'm sure that anyone who tried to get near the Moonraker would be torn to pieces. I agree with you about Krebs and that he was probably working under Drax's orders. It was because I believed that, that I didn't bother to report him when he went through my things. There was nothing for him to find, of course. Just private letters and so on. It would be typical of Sir Hugo to make absolutely sure. And I must say,' she said candidly, 'that I admire him for it. He's a ruthless man with deplorable manners and not a very nice face under all that red hair, but I love working for him and I'm longing for the Moonraker to be a success. Living with it for so long has made me feel just like his men do about it.'

She looked up to see his reactions.

He nodded. 'After only a day I can understand that,' he said. 'And I suppose I agree with you. There's nothing to go on except my intuition and that will have to look after itself. The main thing is that the Moonraker looks as safe as the Crown Jewels, and probably safer.' He shrugged his shoulders impatiently, dissatisfied with himself for disowning the intuitions that were so much of his trade. 'Come on,' he said, almost roughly. 'We're wasting time.'

Understanding, she smiled to herself and followed.

Round the next bend of the cliff they came up with the base of the hoist, encrusted with seaweed and barnacles. Fifty yards further on they reached the jetty, a strong tubular iron frame paved with latticed iron strips that ran out over the rocks and beyond.

Between the two, and perhaps twenty feet up the cliff face, yawned the wide black mouth of the exhaust tunnel which slanted up inside the cliff to the steel floor beneath the stern of the rocket. From the under-lip of the cave melted chalk drooled down like lava and there were splashes of the stuff all over the pebbles and rocks below. In his mind's eye Bond could see the blazing white shaft of flame come howling out of the face of the cliff and he could hear the sea hiss and bubble as the liquid chalk poured into the water.

He looked up at the narrow section of the launching dome that showed above the edge of the cliff two hundred feet up in the sky, and imagined the four men in their gas-masks and asbestos suits watching the gauges as the terrible liquid explosive pulsed down the black rubber tube into the stomach of the rocket. He suddenly realized that they were in range if anything went wrong with the fuelling.

'Let's get away from here,' he said to the girl.

When they had put a hundred yards between themselves and the cave Bond stopped and looked back. He imagined himself with six tough men and all the right gear, and he wondered how he would set about attacking the site from the sea — kayaks to the jetty at low tide; a ladder to the lip of the cave — and then what? Impossible to climb the polished steel walls of the exhaust tunnel. It would be a question of firing an anti-tank weapon through the steel floor beneath the rocket, following up with some phosphorous shells and hoping that something would catch fire. Untidy business, but it might be effective. Getting away afterwards would be nasty. Sitting targets from the top of the cliff. But that wouldn't worry a Russian suicide squad. It was all quite feasible.

Gala had been standing beside him watching the eyes that measured and speculated. 'It's not as easy as you might think,' she said, seeing the frown on his face. 'Even when it's high tide and very rough they have guards along the top of the cliff at night. And they've got searchlights and Brens and grenades. Their orders are to shoot and ask questions afterwards. Of course it would be better to floodlight the cliff at night. But that would only pinpoint the site. I really believe they've thought of everything.'

Bond was still frowning. 'If they had covering fire from a submarine or an X-craft a good team could still do it,' he said. 'It'll be hell, but I'm going for a swim. The Admiralty chart says there's a twelve-fathom channel out there, but I'd like to have a look. There must be plenty of water at the end of the jetty but I'll be happier when I've seen for myself.' He smiled at her. 'Why don't you have a bathe too? It's going to be dam' cold, but it would do you good after stewing inside that concrete dome all the morning.'

Gala's eyes lit up. 'Do you think I could?' she asked doubtfully. 'I'm frightfully hot. But what are we going to wear?' She blushed at the thought of her brief and almost transparent nylon pants and brassière.

'To hell with that,' said Bond airily. 'You must have got some bits and pieces on underneath and I've got pants on. We shall be perfectly respectable and there's no one to see, and I promise not to look,' he lied cheerfully, leading the way round the next bend in the cliff. 'You undress behind that rock and I'll use this one,' he said. 'Come on. Don't be a goose. It's all in the line of duty.'

Without waiting for her to answer he moved behind the tall rock, taking off his shirt as he did so.

'Oh, well,' said Gala, relieved to have the decision taken out of her hands. She went behind her rock and slowly unbuttoned her skirt.

When she peered nervously out, Bond was already halfway down the strip of coarse brown sand that led out among the pools to where the incoming tide eddied through the green and black moraine of the rocks. He looked lithe and brown. The blue pants were reassuring.

Gingerly she followed him, and then suddenly she was in the water. At once nothing else mattered but the velvet ice of the sea and the beauty of the patches of sand between the waving hair of the seaweed that she could see in the clear green depths below her as she buried her head and swam along parallel with the shore in a fast crawl.

When she was level with the jetty she stopped for a moment to get her breath. There was no sign of Bond whom she had last seen streaking along a hundred yards ahead of her. She trod water hard to keep up her circulation and then started back again, unwillingly thinking of him, thinking of the hard brown body that must be somewhere near her, among the rocks, perhaps, or diving to the sand to gauge the depth of water that would be available to an enemy.

She turned back to look for him again and it was then that he suddenly surged up from the sea beneath her. She felt the quick tight clasp of his arms round her and the swift hard impact of his lips on hers.

'Damn you,' she said furiously, but already he had dived again and by the time she had spat out a mouthful of sea-water and got her bearings he was swimming blithely twenty yards away.

She turned and swam aloofly out to sea, feeling rather ridiculous but determined to snub him. It was just as she had thought. These Secret Service people always seemed to have time for sex however important their jobs might be.

But her body obstinately tingled with the shock of the kiss and the golden day seemed to have taken on a new beauty. As she swam further out to sea and then turned back and looked along the snarling milk-white teeth of England to the distant arm of Dover and at the black and white confetti of the ravens and gulls tossed against the vivid backcloth of green fields, she decided that anything was permissible on such a day and that, just this once, she would forgive him.

Half an hour later they were lying, waiting for the sun to dry them, separated by a respectable yard of sand at the foot of the cliff.

The kiss had not been mentioned, but Gala's efforts to preserve an atmosphere of aloofness had collapsed under the excitement of examining a lobster that Bond had dived for and caught with his hands. Reluctantly they put it back into one of the rockpools and watched it scuttle backwards into the shelter of the seaweed. And now they lay, tired and exhilarated by their icy swim, and prayed that the sun would not slip behind the clifftop high above their heads before they were warm and dry enough to get back into their clothes.

But those were not Bond's only thoughts. The beautiful strapping body of the girl beside him, incredibly erotic in the tight emphasis of the clinging brassière and pants, came between him and his concern about the Moonraker. And anyway there was nothing he could do about the Moonraker for another hour. It was not yet five o'clock and the fuelling would not be finished until after six. It would only be then that he could get hold of Drax and make certain that for the next two nights the guards were strengthened on the cliff and that they had the right weapons. For he had seen for himself that there was plenty of water, even at low tide, for a submarine.

So there was at least a quarter of an hour to spare before they would have to start back.

Meanwhile this girl. The half-stripped body splayed above him on the surface as he swam up from below; the soft-hard quick kiss with his arms about her; the pointed hillocks of her breasts, so close to him, and the soft flat stomach descending into the mystery of her tightly closed thighs.

To hell with it.

He wrenched his mind out of its fever and gazed straight up into the endless blue of the sky, forcing himself to watch the soaring beauty of the herring gulls as they ranged effortlessly among the air currents that fountained up over the high clifftop above them. But the soft down of the birds' white underbellies seduced his thoughts back to her and gave him no rest.

'Why are you called Gala?' he said to break his hot, crouching thoughts.

She laughed. 'I was teased about it all through school,' she said, and Bond was impatient at the easy, clear voice, 'and then through the Wrens and then by half the police force of London. But my real name's even worse. It's Galatea. She was a cruiser my father was serving in when I was born. I suppose Gala's not too bad. I've almost forgotten what I'm called. I'm always having to change my name now that I'm in the Special Branch.'

'In the Special Branch.' 'In the Special Branch.' 'In the . . . '

When the bomb falls. When the pilot miscalculates and the plane hits short of the runway. When the blood leaves the heart and consciousness goes, there are thoughts in the mind, or words, or perhaps a phrase of music, which ring on for the few seconds before death like the dying clang of a bell.

Bond wasn't killed, but the words were still in his mind, several seconds later, after it had all happened.

Ever since they had lain down on the sand up against the cliff, while his thoughts had been of Gala, his eyes had been carelessly watching two gulls playing around a wisp of straw that was the edge of their nest on a small ledge about ten feet below the distant top of the cliff. They would crane and bow in their loveplay, with only their heads visible to Bond against the dazzling white of the chalk, and then the male would soar out and away and at once back to the ledge to take up his lovemaking again.

Bond was dreamily watching them as he listened to the girl, when suddenly both gulls dashed away from the ledge with a single shrill scream of fear. At the same moment there was a puff of black smoke and a soft boom from the top of the cliff and a great section of the white chalk directly above Bond and Gala seemed to sway outwards, zigzag cracks snaking down its face.

The next thing Bond knew was that he was lying on top of Gala, his face pressed into her cheek, that the air was full of thunder, that his breath was stifled and that the sun had gone out. His back was numb and aching under a great weight and in his left ear, besides the echo of the thunder, there was the end of a choking scream.

He was barely conscious and he had to wait until his senses came halfway back to life.

The Special Branch. What was it she had said about the Special Branch?

He made frantic efforts to move. Only in his right arm, the arm nearest to the cliff, was there any play at all, but as he jerked his shoulder the arm became freer until at last, with a great backward heave, light and air reached down to them.

Retching in the fog of chalk dust, he widened the hole until his head could take its crushing weight off Gala. He felt the feeble movement as she turned her head sideways towards the light and air. A growing trickle of dust and stones into the hole he had cleared made him dig fiercely again. Gradually he enlarged the space until he could get a purchase on his right elbow and then, coughing so that he thought his lungs would burst, he heaved his right shoulder up until suddenly it and his head were free.

His first thought was that there had been an explosion in the Moonraker. He looked up at the cliff and then along the shore. No. They were a hundred yards from the site. It was only in the skyline directly above them that a great mouthful had been bitten out of the cliff.

Then he thought of their immediate danger. Gala moaned and he could feel the frantic thud of her heart against his chest, but the ghastly white mask of her face was now free to the air and he wrenched his body from side to side on top of her to try and ease the pressure on her lungs and stomach. Slowly, inch by inch, his muscles cracking under the strain, he worked his way under the pile of dust and rubble towards the cliff face where he knew the weight would be less.

And then at last his chest was free and he could snake his body into a kneeling position beside her. Blood dripped from his cut back and arms and mingled with the chalk dust that continually poured down the sides of the hole he had made, but he could feel that no bones were broken and, in the rage of the rescue work, he felt no pain.

Grunting and coughing and without a pause to take breath he heaved her up into a sitting position and with a bleeding hand wiped some of the chalk dust from her face. Then, freeing his legs from the tomb of chalk, he somehow manhandled her up on to the top of the mound with her back against the cliff.

He knelt and looked at her, at the terrible white scarecrow that minutes before had been one of the most beautiful girls he had ever seen, and as he looked at her and at the streaks of his blood down her face he prayed that her eyes would open.

When, seconds later, they did, the relief was so great that Bond turned away and was rackingly sick.

17

WILD SURMISES

WHEN THE PAROXYSM was over he felt Gala's hand in his hair. He looked round and saw her wince at the sight of him. She tugged at his hair and pointed up the cliffs. As she did so a shower of small pieces of chalk rattled down beside them.

Weakly he got to his knees and then to his feet and together they scrambled and slid down off the mountain of chalk and away from the crater against the cliff from which they had escaped.

The harsh sand under their feet was like velvet. They both collapsed full length and lay clutching at it with their horrible white hands as if its rough gold would wash the filthy whiteness away. Then Gala too was mercifully sick and Bond crawled a few paces away to leave her alone. He hauled himself to his feet against a single lump of chalk as big as a small motor-car, and at last his bloodshot eyes took in the hell that had almost engulfed them.

Down to the beginning of the rocks, now lapped by the incoming tide, sprawled the debris of the cliff face, an avalanche of chalk blocks and shapes. The white dust of its collapse covered nearly an acre. Above it a jagged rent had appeared in the cliff and a wedge of blue sky had been bitten out of the distant top where before the line of the horizon had been almost straight. There were no longer any seabirds near them and Bond guessed that the smell of disaster would keep them away from the place for days.

The nearness of their bodies to the cliff was what had saved them, that and the slight protection of the overhang below which the sea had bitten into the base of the cliff. They had been buried by the deluge of smaller stuff. The heavier chunks, any one of which would have crushed them, had fallen outwards, the nearest missing them by a few feet. And their nearness to the cliff was the reason for Bond's right arm having been comparatively free so that they had been able to burrow out of the mound before they were stifled. Bond realized that if some reflex had not hurled him on top of Gala at the moment of the avalanche they would now both be dead.

He felt her hand on his shoulder. Without looking at her he put his arm round her waist and together they got down to the blessed sea and let their bodies fall weakly, thankfully, into the shallows.

Ten minutes later it was two comparatively human beings who walked back up the sand to the rocks where their clothes lay, a few yards away from the cliff-fall. They were both completely naked. The rags of their underclothing lay somewhere under the pile of chalk dust, torn off in their struggle to escape. But, like survivors from a shipwreck, their nakedness meant nothing. Washed clean of the cloying gritty chalk dust and with their hair and mouths scoured with the salt water, they felt weak and bedraggled, but by the time they had got their clothes on and had shared Gala's comb there was little to show what they had been through.

They sat with their backs to a rock and Bond lit a first delicious cigarette, drinking the smoke deeply into his lungs and expelling it slowly through his nostrils. When Gala had done the best she could with her powder and lipstick he lit a cigarette for her and, as he handed it to her, for the first time they looked into each other's eyes and smiled. Then they sat and looked silently out to sea, at the golden panorama that was the same and yet entirely new.

Bond broke the silence.

'Well, by God,' he said. 'That was close.'

'I still don't know what happened,' said Gala. 'Except that you saved my life.' She put her hand on his and then took it away.

'If you hadn't been there I should be dead,' said Bond. 'If I'd stayed where I was — ' He shrugged his shoulders.

Then he turned and looked at her. 'I suppose you realize,' he said flatly, 'that someone pushed the cliff down on us?' She looked back at him with wide eyes. 'If we searched around in all that,' he gestured towards the avalanche of chalk, 'we would find the marks of two or three drill-holes and traces of dynamite. I saw the smoke and I heard the bang of the explosion a split second before the cliff came down. And so did the gulls,' he added.

'And what's more,' continued Bond after a pause, 'it can't have been only Krebs. It was done in full view of the site. And it was done by several people, well organized, with spies on us from the moment we went down the cliff path to the beach.'

There was comprehension in Gala's eyes and a flash of fear. 'What are we to do?' she asked anxiously. 'What's it all about?'

'They want us dead,' said Bond calmly. 'So we have to stay alive. As to what it's all about, we'll just have to find that out.'

'You see,' he went on, 'I'm afraid even Vallance isn't going to be much help. When they made up their minds we were properly buried, they'll have got away from the top of the cliff as fast as they could. They'd know that even if someone saw the cliff-fall, or heard it, they wouldn't get very excited. There are twenty miles of these cliffs and not many people come here until the summer. If the coastguards heard it they may have made a note in the log. But in the spring I expect they get plenty of falls. The winter frosts thaw out in cracks that may be hundreds of years old. So our friends would wait until we didn't turn up tonight and then get the police and coastguards to search for us. They'd keep quiet until the high tide had made porridge out of a good deal of this.' He gestured towards the shambles of fallen chalk. 'The whole scheme is admirable. And even if Vallance believes us, there's not enough evidence to make the Prime Minister interfere with the Moonraker. The damn thing's so infernally important. All the world's waiting to see if it'll work or not. And anyway, what's our story? What the hell's it all about? Some of those bloody Germans up there seem to want us dead before Friday. But what for?' He paused. 'It's up to us, Gala. It's a lousy business but we've simply got to solve it ourselves.'

He looked into her eyes. 'What about it?'

Gala laughed abruptly. 'Don't be ridiculous,' she said. 'It's what we're paid for. Of course we'll take them on. And I agree we'd get nowhere with London. We'd look absolutely ridiculous telephoning reports about cliffs falling on our heads. What are we doing down here anyway, fooling around without any clothes on instead of getting on with our jobs?'

Bond grinned. 'We only lay down for ten minutes to get dry,' he protested mildly. 'How do you think we ought to have spent the afternoon? Taking everybody's fingerprints all over again? That's about all you police think about.' He felt ashamed when he saw her stiffen. He held his hand up. 'I didn't really mean that,' he said. 'But can't you see what we've done this afternoon? Just what had to be done. We've made the enemy show his hand. Now we've got to take the next step and find out who the enemy is and why he wanted us out of the way. And then if we've got enough evidence that someone's trying to sabotage the Moonraker we'll have the whole place turned inside out, the practice shoot postponed, and to hell with politics.'

She jumped to her feet. 'Oh, of course you're right,' she said impatiently. 'It's just that I want to do something about it in a hurry.' She looked for a moment out to sea, away from Bond. 'You've only just come into the picture. I've been living with this rocket for more than a year and I can't bear the idea that something may happen to it. So much seems to depend on it. For all of us. I want to get back there quickly and find out who wanted to kill us. It may be nothing to do with the Moonraker, but I want to make sure.'

Bond stood up, showing nothing of the pain from the cuts and bruises on his back and legs. 'Come on,' he said, 'it's nearly six o'clock. The tide's coming in fast but we can get to St. Margaret's before it catches us. We'll clean up at the Granville there and have a drink and some food and then we'll go back to the house in the middle of dinner. I shall be interested to see what sort of a reception we get. After that we'll have to concentrate on staying alive and seeing what we can see. Can you make it to St. Margaret's?'

'Don't be silly,' said Gala. 'Policewomen aren't made of gossamer.' She gave a reluctant smile at Bond's ironically respectful 'Of course not', and they turned towards the distant tower of the South Foreland lighthouse and set off through the shingle.

At half-past eight the taxi from St. Margaret's dropped them at the second guard-gate and they showed their passes and walked quietly up through the trees on to the expanse of concrete. They both felt keyed up and in high spirits. A hot bath and an hour's rest at the accommodating Granville had been followed by two stiff brandies-and-sodas for Gala and three for

Bond followed by delicious fried soles and Welsh rarebits and coffee. And now, as they confidently approached the house, it would have needed second sight to tell that they were both dead tired and that they were naked and bruised under their walking clothes.

They let themselves quietly in through the front door and stood for a moment in the lighted hall. A cheerful mumble of voices came from the dining-room. There was a pause followed by a burst of laughter which was dominated by the harsh bark of Sir Hugo Drax.

Bond's mouth twisted wryly as he led the way across the hall to the door of the dining-room. Then he fixed a cheerful smile on his face and opened the door for Gala to pass through.

Drax sat at the head of the table, festive in his plum-coloured smoking-jacket. A forkful of food, halfway to his open mouth, had stopped in mid-air as they appeared in the doorway. Unnoticed, the food slid off the fork and fell with a soft, distinct 'plep' on to the edge of the table.

Krebs had been in the act of drinking a glass of red wine and the glass, frozen against his mouth, poured a thin trickle down his chin and thence on to his brown satin tie and yellow shirt.

Dr. Walter had had his back to the door and it was not until he observed the unusual behaviour of the others, the bulging eyes, the gape of the mouths, and the blood-drained faces, that he whipped his head round towards the door. His reactions, thought Bond, were slower than the others, or else his nerves were steadier. '*Ach so*,' he said softly. '*Die Engländer*.'

Drax was on his feet. 'My dear chap,' he said thickly. 'My dear chap. We were really very worried. Just wondering whether to send out a search party. Few minutes ago one of the guards came in and reported there seemed to have been a cliff-fall.' He came round towards them, his napkin in one hand and the fork still erect in the other.

With the movement the blood surged back into his face, which became first mottled and then its usual red. 'You really might have let me know.' He spoke to the girl, anger rising in his voice. 'Most extraordinary behaviour.'

'It was my fault,' said Bond, moving forward into the room so that he could keep them all in view. 'The walk was longer than I expected. I thought we might get caught by the tide so we went on to St. Margaret's and had something to eat there and took a taxi. Miss Brand wanted to telephone but I thought we would be back before eight. You must put the blame on me. But please go ahead with your dinner. Perhaps I might join you for coffee and dessert. I expect Miss Brand would prefer to go to her room. She must be tired after her long day.'

Bond walked deliberately round the table and took the chair next to Krebs. Those pale eyes, he noticed, after the first shock, had been fixed firmly on his plate. As Bond came up behind him he was delighted to see a large mound of Elastoplast on the crown of Krebs's head.

'Yes, go to bed, Miss Brand. I will talk to you in the morning,' said Drax testily. Gala obediently left the room and Drax went to his chair and sat heavily down.

'Most remarkable those cliffs,' said Bond blithely. 'Quite awe-inspiring walking along wondering if they're going to choose just that moment to collapse on one. Reminded me of Russian roulette. And yet one never reads of people being killed by cliffs falling on them. The odds against getting hurt must be terrific.' He paused. 'By the way, what was that you were saying about a cliff-fall just now?'

There was a faint groan on Bond's right, followed by a crash of glass and china as Krebs's head fell forward on to the table.

Bond looked at him with polite curiosity.

'Walter,' said Drax sharply. 'Can't you see that Krebs is ill? Take the man out and put him to bed. And don't be too soft with him. The man drinks too much. Hurry up.'

Walter, his face crumpled and angry, strode round the table and jerked Krebs's head out of the debris. He took him by his coat collar and hauled him to his feet and away from his chair.

'*Du Scheisskerl*,' hissed Walter at the mottled, vacant face. '*Marsch!*' He turned him round and hustled him to the swing door into the pantry and rammed him through. There were muffled sounds of stumbling and cursing and then a door banged and there was silence.

'He must have had a heavy day,' said Bond looking at Drax.

The big man was sweating freely. He wiped his face with a circular sweep of his napkin. 'Nonsense,' he said shortly. 'He drinks.'

The butler, erect and unperturbed by the apparition of Krebs and Walter in his pantry, brought in the coffee. Bond took some and sipped it. He waited for the pantry door to close again. Another German, he thought. He'll already have passed the news back to the barracks. Or perhaps all the team weren't involved. Perhaps there was a team within a team. And if so, did Drax know about it? His behaviour when Bond and Gala had come through the door had been inconclusive. Had part of his astonishment been affronted dignity, the shock of a vain man whose programme has been upset by a chit of a secretary? He had certainly covered up well. And all the afternoon he had been down the shaft supervising the fuelling. Bond decided to probe a little.

'How did the fuelling go?' he asked, his eyes fixed on the other man.

Drax was lighting a long cigar. He glanced up at Bond through the smoke and the flame of his match.

'Excellently.' He puffed at the cigar to get it going. 'Everything is ready now. The guards are out. An hour or two clearing up down there in the morning and then the site will be closed. By the way,' he added. 'I shall be taking Miss Brand up to London in the car tomorrow afternoon. I shall need a secretary as well as Krebs. Have you got any plans?'

'I have to go to London too,' said Bond on an impulse. 'I have my final report to make to the Ministry.'

'Oh, really?' said Drax casually. 'What about? I thought you were satisfied with the arrangements.'

'Yes,' said Bond non-committally.

'That's all right then,' said Drax breezily. 'And now if you don't mind,' he got up from the table, 'I've got some papers waiting for me in my study. So I'll say good-night.'

'Good-night,' said Bond to the already retreating back.

Bond finished his coffee and went out into the hall and up to his bedroom. It was obvious that it had been searched again. He shrugged his shoulders. There was only the leather case. Its contents would show nothing except that he had come equipped with the tools of his trade.

His Beretta in its shoulder-holster was still where he had hidden it, in the empty leather case that belonged to Tallon's night glasses. He took the gun out and slipped it under his pillow.

He took a hot bath and used half a bottle of iodine on the cuts and bruises he could reach. Then he got into bed and turned out the light. His body hurt and he was exhausted.

For a moment he thought of Gala. He had told her to take a sleeping pill and lock her door, but otherwise not to worry about anything until the morning.

Before he emptied his mind for sleep he wondered uneasily about her trip with Drax the next day to London.

Uneasily, but not desperately. In due course many questions would have to be answered and many mysteries probed, but the basic facts seemed solid and unanswerable. This extraordinary millionaire had built this great weapon. The Ministry of Supply were pleased with it and considered it sound. The Prime Minister and Parliament thought so too. The rocket was to be fired in less than thirty-six hours under full supervision and the security arrangements were as strict as they could possibly be. Somebody, and probably several people, wanted him and the girl out of the way. Nerves were stretched down here. There was a lot of tension about. Perhaps there was jealousy. Perhaps some people actually suspected them of being saboteurs. But what would that matter so long as he and Gala kept their eyes open? Not much more than a day to go. They were right out in the open here, in May, in England, in peacetime. It was crazy to worry about a few lunatics so long as the Moonraker was out of danger.

And as for tomorrow, reflected Bond as sleep reached out for him, he would arrange to meet Gala in London and bring her back with him. Or she could even stay up in London for the night. Either way he would look after her until the Moonraker was safely fired and then, before work began on the Mark II weapon, there would have to be a very thorough clean-up indeed.

But these were treacherously comforting thoughts. There was danger about and Bond knew it.

He finally drifted into sleep with one small scene firmly fixed in his mind.

There had been something very disquieting about the dinner-table downstairs. It had been laid for only three people.

Part Three

THURSDAY, FRIDAY —

18

BENEATH THE FLAT STONE

THE MERCEDES WAS a beautiful thing. Bond pulled his battered grey Bentley up alongside it and inspected it.

It was a Type 300S, the sports model with a disappearing hood — one of only half a dozen in England, he reflected. Left-hand drive. Probably bought in Germany. He had seen a few of them over there. One had hissed by him on the Munich Autobahn the year before when he was doing a solid ninety in the Bentley. The body, too short and heavy to be graceful, was painted white, with red leather upholstery. Garish for England, but Bond guessed that Drax had chosen white in honour of the famous Mercedes-Benz racing colours that had already swept the board again since the war at Le Mans and the Nurburgring.

Typical of Drax to buy a Mercedes. There was something ruthless and majestic about the cars, he decided, remembering the years from 1934 to 1939 when they had completely dominated the Grand Prix scene, children of the famous Blitzen Benz that had captured the world's speed record at 142 m.p.h. back in 1911. Bond recalled some of their famous drivers, Caracciola, Lang, Seaman, Brauschitz, and the days when he had seen them drifting the fast sweeping bends of Tripoli at 190, or screaming along the tree-lined straight at Berne with the Auto Unions on their tails.

And yet, Bond looked across at his supercharged Bentley, nearly twenty-five years older than Drax's car and still capable of beating 100, and yet when Bentleys were racing, before Rolls had tamed them into sedate town carriages, they had whipped the blown SS-Ks almost as they wished.

Bond had once dabbled on the fringe of the racing world and he was lost in his memories, hearing again the harsh scream of Caracciola's great white beast of a car as it howled past the grandstands at Le Mans, when Drax came out of the house followed by Gala Brand and Krebs.

'Fast car,' said Drax, pleased with Bond's look of admiration. He gestured towards the Bentley. 'They used to be good in the old days,' he added with a touch of patronage. 'Now they're only built for going to the theatre. Too well-mannered. Even the Continental. Now then you, get in the back.'

Krebs obediently climbed into the narrow back seat behind the driver. He sat sideways, his mackintosh up round his ears, his eyes fixed enigmatically on Bond.

Gala Brand, smart in a dark grey tailor-made and black beret and carrying a lightweight black raincoat and gloves, climbed into the right half of the divided front seat. The wide door closed with the rich double click of a Fabergé box.

No sign passed between Bond and Gala. They had made their plans at a whispered meeting in his room before lunch — dinner in London at half-past seven and then back to the house in Bond's car. She sat demurely, her hands in her lap and her eyes to the front, as Drax climbed in, pressed the starter, and pulled the gleaming lever on the steering wheel back into third. The car surged away with hardly a purr from the exhaust and Bond watched it disappear into the trees before he climbed into the Bentley and moved off in leisurely pursuit.

In the hastening Mercedes, Gala busied herself with her thoughts. The night had been uneventful and the morning had been devoted to clearing the launching site of everything that might possibly burn when the Moonraker was fired. Drax had not referred to the events of the previous day and there had been no change in his usual manner. She had prepared her last firing plan (Drax himself was to do it on the morrow) and as usual Walter had been sent for and through her spy-hole she had seen the figures being entered in Drax's black book.

It was a hot, sunny day and Drax was driving in his shirt-sleeves. She glanced down and to the left at the top of the little book protruding from his hip pocket. This drive might be her last chance. Since the evening before she had felt a different person. Perhaps Bond had aroused her competitive spirit, perhaps it was revulsion from playing the secretary too long, perhaps it was the shock of the cliff-fall and the zest of realizing after so many quiet months that she was playing a dangerous game. But now she felt the time had come to take risks. Discovery of the

Moonraker's flight plan was a routine affair and it would give her personal satisfaction to find out the secret of the black notebook. It would be easy.

Casually she laid her folded coat over the space between herself and Drax. At the same time she made a show of arranging herself comfortably, during the course of which she drew an inch or two nearer Drax and her hand came to rest in the folds of the coat between them. Then she settled herself to wait.

Her chance came, as she had thought it might, in the congested traffic of Maidstone. Drax, intent, was trying to beat the traffic lights at the corner of King Street and Gabriel's Hill, but the line of traffic was too slow and he was checked behind a battered family saloon. Gala could see that when the lights changed he was determined to cut in front of the car in front and teach it a lesson. He was a brilliant driver, but a vindictive and impatient one who was always anxious for any car that held him up to be given something to remember.

As the lights went green he gave a blast on his triple horns, pulled out to the right at the intersection, accelerated brutally and got by, shaking his head angrily at the driver of the saloon as he passed it.

In the middle of this harsh manoeuvre it was natural for Gala to allow herself to be thrown towards him. At the same time her left hand dived under the coat and her fingers touched, felt, and extracted the book in one flow of motion. Then the hand was back in the folds of the coat again and Drax, all his feeling in his feet and his hands, was seeing nothing but the traffic ahead and the chances of getting across the zebra outside the Royal Star without hitting two women and a boy who were nearly halfway across it.

Now it was a question of facing Drax's growl of rage as with a maidenly but urgent voice she asked if she could possibly stop for a moment to powder her nose.

A garage would be dangerous. He might decide to fill up with petrol. And perhaps he also carried his money in his hip pocket. But was there an hotel? Yes, she remembered, the Thomas Wyatt just outside Maidstone. And it had no petrol pumps. She started to fidget slightly. She pulled the coat back on to her lap. She cleared her throat.

'Oh, excuse me, Sir Hugo,' she said in a strangled voice.

'Yes. What is it?'

'I'm terribly sorry, Sir Hugo. But could you possibly stop for just a moment. I want, I mean, I'm terribly sorry but I'd like to powder my nose. It's terribly stupid of me. I'm so sorry.'

'Christ,' said Drax. 'Why the hell didn't you . . . Oh, yes. Well, all right. Find a place.' He grumbled on into his moustache, but brought the big car down into the fifties.

'There's a hotel just around this bend,' said Gala nervously. 'Thank you so much, Sir Hugo. It was stupid of me. I won't be a moment. Yes, here it is.'

The car swerved up to the front of the inn and stopped with a jerk. 'Hurry up. Hurry up,' said Drax as Gala, leaving the door of the car open, sped obediently across the gravel, her coat with its precious secret held tightly in front of her body.

She locked the door of the lavatory and snatched open the notebook.

There they were, just as she had thought. On each page, under the date, the neat columns of figures, the atmospheric pressure, the wind velocity, the temperature, just as she had recorded them from the Air Ministry figures. And at the foot of each page the estimated settings for the gyro compasses.

Gala frowned. At a glance she could see that they were entirely different from hers. Drax's figures simply bore no relation to hers whatsoever.

She turned to the last completed page containing the figures for that day. Why, she was wrong by nearly ninety degrees on the estimated course. If the rocket were fired on her flight plan it would land somewhere in France. She looked wildly at her face in the mirror over the washbasin. How could she have gone so monstrously wrong? And why hadn't Drax ever told her? Why, she ran quickly through the book again, every day she had been ninety degrees out, firing the Moonraker at right angles to its true course. And yet she simply couldn't have made such a mistake. Did the Ministry know these secret figures? And why should they be secret?

Suddenly her bewilderment turned to fright. She must somehow get safely, quietly to London and tell somebody. Even though she might be called a fool and a meddler.

Coldly she turned back several pages in the book, took her nail file out of her bag and, as neatly as she could, cut out a specimen page, rolled it up into a tight ball and stuffed it into the tip of a finger of one of her gloves.

She glanced at her face in the mirror. It was pale and she quickly rubbed her cheeks to bring back the colour. Then she put back the look of an apologetic secretary and hurried out and ran across the gravel to the car, clutching the notebook among the folds of her coat.

The engine of the Mercedes was turning over. Drax glowered at her impatiently as she scrambled back into her seat.

'Come on. Come on,' he said, putting the car into third and taking his foot off the clutch so that she nearly caught her ankle in the heavy door. The tyres churned up the gravel as he accelerated out of the parking place and dry-skidded into the London road.

Gala was jerked back, but she remembered to let the coat with her guilty hand in its folds fall on the seat between her and the driver.

And now the book back into the hip pocket.

She watched the speedometer hovering in the seventies as Drax flung the heavy car along the crown of the road.

She tried to remember her lessons. Distracting pressure on to some other part of the body. Distracting the attention. Distraction. The victim must not be at ease. His senses must be focused away. He must be unaware of the touch on his body. Anaesthetized by a stronger stimulus.

Like now, for instance. Drax, bent forward over the wheel, was fighting for a chance to get past a sixty-foot R.A.F. trailer, but the oncoming traffic was leaving no room on the crown of the road. There was a gap and Drax rammed the lever into second and took it, his horns braying imperiously.

Gala's hand reached to the left under the coat.

But another hand struck like a snake.

'Got you.'

Krebs was leaning half over the back of the driving seat. His hand was crushing hers into the slippery cover of the notebook under the folds of the coat.

Gala sat frozen into black ice. With all her strength she wrenched at her hand. It was no good. Krebs had all his weight on it now.

Drax had got past the trailer and the road was empty. Krebs said urgently in German, 'Please stop the car, *mein Kapitän*. Miss Brand is a spy.'

Drax gave a startled glance to his right. What he saw was enough. He put his hand quickly down to his hip pocket, and then, slowly, deliberately, put it back on the wheel. The sharp turning to Mereworth was just coming up on his left. 'Hold her,' said Drax. He braked so that the tyres screamed, changed down and wrenched the car into the side-road. A few hundred yards down it he pulled the car into the side and stopped.

Drax looked up and down the road. It was empty. He reached over one gloved hand and wrenched Gala's face towards him.

'What is this?'

'I can explain it, Sir Hugo.' Gala tried to bluff against the horror and desperation she knew was in her face. 'It's a mistake. I didn't mean . . . '

Under cover of an angry shrug of the shoulders, her right hand moved softly behind her and the guilty pair of gloves were thrust behind the leather cushion.

'*Sehen sie her, mein Kapitän*. I saw her edging up close to you. It seemed to me strange.'

With his other hand Krebs had whipped the coat away and there were the bent white fingers of her left hand crushed into the cover of the notebook still a foot away from Drax's hip pocket.

'So.'

The word was deadly cold and with a shivering finality.

Drax let go her chin, but her horrified eyes remained locked into his.

A kind of frozen cruelty was showing through the jolly façade of red skin and whiskers. It was a different man. The man behind the mask. The creature beneath the flat stone that Gala Brand had lifted.

Drax glanced again up and down the empty road.

Then, looking carefully into the suddenly aware blue eyes, he drew the leather driving gauntlet off his left hand and with his right whipped her as hard as he could across the face with it.

Only a short cry was forced out of Gala's constricted throat, but tears of pain ran down her cheeks. Suddenly she began to fight like a mad woman.

With all her strength she heaved and fought against the two iron arms that held her. With her free right hand she tried to reach the face that leant over her and get at the eyes. But Krebs easily moved his head out of her reach and quietly increased the pressure across her throat, hissing murderously to himself as her nails tore strips of skin off the backs of his hands, but noting with a scientist's eye as her struggles became weaker.

Drax watched carefully, with one eye on the road, as Krebs brought her under control and then he started the car and drove cautiously on along the wooded road. He grunted with satisfaction as he came upon a cart-track into the woods and he turned up it and only stopped when he was well out of sight of the road.

Gala had just realized that there was no noise from the engine when she heard Drax say 'there'. A finger touched her skull behind the left ear. Krebs's arm came away from her throat and she slumped gratefully forward, gasping for air. Then something crashed into the back of her head where the finger had touched it and there was a flash of wonderfully releasing pain and blackness.

An hour later passers-by saw a white Mercedes draw up outside a small house at the Buckingham Palace end of Ebury Street and two kind gentlemen help a sick girl out and through the front door. Those who were near could see that the poor girl's face was very pale and that her eyes were shut and that the kind gentlemen almost had to carry her up the steps. The big gentleman with the red face and whiskers was heard to say quite distinctly to the other man that poor Mildred had promised she wouldn't go out until she was quite well again. Very sad.

Gala came to herself in a large top-floor room that seemed to be full of machinery. She was tied very securely to a chair and apart from the searing pain in her head she could feel that her lips and cheek were bruised and swollen.

Heavy curtains were drawn across the window and there was a musty smell in the room as if it was rarely used. There was dust on the few pieces of conventional furniture and only the chromium and ebonite dials on the machines looked clean and new. She thought that she was probably in hospital. She closed her eyes and wondered. It was not long before she remembered. She spent several minutes controlling herself and then she opened her eyes again.

Drax, his back to her, was watching the dials on a machine that looked like a very large radio set. There were three more similar machines in her line of sight and from one of them a thin steel aerial reached up to a rough hole that had been cut for it in the plaster of the ceiling. The room was brightly lit by several tall standard lamps, each of which held a naked high-wattage bulb.

To her left there was a noise of tinkering and by swivelling her half-closed eyes in their sockets, which made the pain in her head much worse, she saw the figure of Krebs bent over an electric generator on the floor. Beside it there was a small petrol engine and it was this that was giving trouble. Every now and then Krebs would grasp the starting-handle and crank it hard and a feeble stutter would come from the engine before he went back to his tinkering.

'You dam' fool,' said Drax in German, 'hurry up. I've got to go and see those bloody oafs at the Ministry.'

'At once, *mein Kapitän*,' said Krebs dutifully. He seized the handle again. This time after two or three coughs the engine started up and began to purr.

'It won't make too much noise?' asked Drax.

'No, *mein Kapitän*. The room has been soundproofed,' answered Krebs. 'Dr. Walter assures me that nothing will be heard outside.'

Gala closed her eyes and decided that her only hope was to feign unconsciousness for as long as possible. Did they intend to kill her? Here in this room? And what was all this machinery? It looked like wireless, or perhaps radar. That curved glass screen above Drax's head that had given an occasional flicker as Drax fiddled with the knobs below the dials.

Slowly her mind started to work again. Why, for instance, was Drax suddenly talking perfect German? And why did Krebs address him as *mein Kapitän*? And the figures in the black book. Why did they nearly kill her because she had seen them? What did they mean?

Ninety degrees, ninety degrees.

Lazily her mind turned the problem over.

Ninety degrees difference. Supposing her figures had been right all the time for the target eighty miles away in the North Sea. Just supposing she had been right. Then she wouldn't have been aiming the rocket into the middle of France after all. But Drax's figures? Ninety degrees to the left of her North Sea target? Somewhere in England presumably. Eighty miles from Dover. Yes, of course. That was it. Drax's figures. The firing plan in the little black book. They would drop the Moonraker just about in the middle of London.

But on London! On London!!

So one's heart really does go into one's throat. How extraordinary. Such a commonplace and yet there it is and it really does almost stop one breathing.

And now, let me see, so this is a radar homing device. How ingenious. The same as there would be on the raft in the North Sea. This would bring the rocket down within a hundred yards of Buckingham Palace. But would that matter with a warhead full of instruments?

It was probably the cruelty of Drax's blow across her face that settled it, but suddenly she knew, she KNEW that somehow it would be a real warhead, an atomic warhead, and that Drax was an enemy of England and that tomorrow at noon he was going to destroy London.

Gala made a last effort to understand.

Through this ceiling, through this chair, into the ground. The thin needle of the rocket. Dropping fast as light out of a clear sky. The crowds in the streets. The Palace. The nursemaids in the park. The birds in the trees. The great bloom of flame a mile wide. And then the mushroom cloud. And nothing left. Nothing. Nothing. Nothing.

'No. Oh, NO!'

But the scream was only in her mind and Gala, her body a twisted black potato crisp amongst a million others, had already fainted.

19

MISSING PERSON

BOND SAT AT his favourite restaurant table in London, the right-hand corner table for two on the first floor, and watched the people and the traffic in Piccadilly and down the Haymarket.

It was 7.45 and his second vodka dry martini with a large slice of lemon peel had just been brought to him by Baker, the head waiter. He sipped it, wondering idly why Gala was late. It was not like her. She was the sort of girl who would telephone if she had been kept at the Yard. Vallance, whom he had visited at five, had said that Gala was due with him at six.

Vallance had been very anxious to see her. He was a worried man and when Bond reported briefly on the security of the Moonraker, Vallance seemed to be listening with only half his mind.

It appeared that all that day there had been heavy selling of sterling. It had started in Tangier and quickly spread to Zürich and New York. The pound had been fluctuating wildly in the money markets of the world and the arbitrage dealers had made a killing. The net result was that the pound was a whole three cents down on the day and the forward rates were still weaker. It was front-page news in the evening papers and at the close of business the Treasury had got on to Vallance and told him the extraordinary news that the selling wave had been started by Drax Metals Ltd. in Tangier. The operation had begun that morning and by close of business the firm had managed to sell British currency short to the tune of twenty million pounds. This had been too much for the markets, and the Bank of England had had to step in and buy in order to stop a still sharper run. It was then that Drax Metals had come to light as the seller.

Now the Treasury wanted to know what it was all about — whether it was Drax himself selling or one of the big commodity interests who were clients of his firm. The first thing they did was to tackle Vallance. Vallance could only think that in some way the Moonraker was to be a failure and that Drax knew it and wanted to profit by his knowledge. He at once spoke to the Ministry of Supply, but they pooh-poohed the idea. There was no reason to think the Moonraker would be a failure and even if its practice flight was not successful the fact would be covered up with talk of technical hitches and so forth. In any case, whether the rocket was a success or not, there could be no possible reaction on British financial credit. No, they certainly wouldn't think of mentioning the matter to the Prime Minister. Drax Metals was a big trading organization. They were probably acting for some foreign government. The Argentine. Perhaps even Russia. Someone with big sterling balances. Anyway it was nothing to do with the Ministry, or with the Moonraker, which would be launched punctually at noon the next day.

This had made sense to Vallance, but he was still worried. He didn't like mysteries and he was glad to share his concern with Bond. Above all he wanted to ask Gala if she had seen any Tangier cables and if so whether Drax had made any comment on them.

Bond was sure Gala would have mentioned anything of the sort to him, and he said so to Vallance. They had talked some more and then Bond had left for his headquarters where M. was expecting him.

M. had been interested in everything, even the shaven heads and moustaches of the men. He questioned Bond minutely and when Bond finished his story with the gist of his last conversation with Vallance M. sat for a long time lost in thought.

'007,' he said at last, 'I don't like any part of this. There's something going on down there but I can't for the life of me make any sense out of it. And I don't see where I can possibly interfere. All the facts are known to the Special Branch and to the Ministry and, God knows, I've got nothing to add to them. Even if I had a word with the P.M., which would be damned unfair on Vallance, what am I to tell him? What facts? What's it all about? There's nothing but the smell of it all. And it's a bad smell. And,' he added, 'a very big one, if I'm not mistaken.'

'No.' He looked across at Bond and his eyes held an unusual note of urgency. 'It looks as if it's all up to you. And that girl. You're lucky she's a good one. Anything you want? Anything I can do to help?'

'No, thank you, sir,' Bond had said and he had walked out through the familiar corridors and down in the lift to his own office where he had terrified Loelia Ponsonby by giving her a kiss as he said good-night. The only times he ever did that were at Christmas, on her birthday, and just before there was something dangerous to be done.

Bond drank down the rest of his martini and looked at his watch. Now it was eight o'clock and suddenly he shivered.

He got straight up from his table and walked out to the telephone.

The switchboard at the Yard said that the Assistant Commissioner had been trying to reach him. He had had to go to a dinner at the Mansion House. Could Commander Bond please stay by the telephone? Bond waited impatiently. All his fears surged up at him from the chunk of black bakelite. He could see the rows of polite faces. The uniformed waiter slowly edging his way round to Vallance. The quickly pulled-back chair. The unobtrusive exit. Those echoing stone lobbies. The discreet booth.

The telephone screamed at him. 'That you, Bond? Vallance here. Seen anything of Miss Brand?'

Bond's heart went cold. 'No,' he said sharply. 'She's half an hour late for dinner. Didn't she turn up at six?'

'No, and I've had a "trace" sent out and there's no sign of her at the usual address she stays at when she comes to London. None of her friends has seen her. If she left in Drax's car at two-thirty she should have been in London by half-past four. There's been no crash on the Dover road during the afternoon and the A.A. and the R.A.C. are negative.' There was a pause. 'Now listen.' There was urgent appeal in Vallance's voice. 'She's a good girl that, and I don't want anything to happen to her. Can you handle it for me? I can't put out a general call for her. The killing down there has made her news and we'd have the whole Press round our ears. It will be even worse after ten tonight. Downing Street are issuing a communiqué about the practice shoot and tomorrow's papers are going to be nothing but

Moonraker. The P.M.'s going to broadcast. Her disappearance would turn the whole thing into a crime story. Tomorrow's too important for that and anyway the girl may have had a fainting fit or something. But I want her found. Well? What do you say? Can you handle it? You can have all the help you want. I'll tell the Duty Officer that he's to accept your orders.'

'Don't worry,' said Bond. 'Of course I'll look after it.' He paused, his mind racing. 'Just tell me something. What do you know about Drax's movements?'

'He wasn't expected at the Ministry until seven,' said Vallance. 'I left word . . .' There was a confused noise on the line and Bond heard Vallance say 'Thanks'. He came back on the line. 'Just got a report passed on by the City police,' he said. 'The Yard couldn't get me on the 'phone. Talking to you. Let's see,' he read, ' "Sir Hugo Drax arrived Ministry 1900 left at 2000. Left message dining at Blades if wanted. Back at site 2300." ' Vallance commented: 'That means he'll be leaving London about nine. Just a moment.' He read on: ' "Sir Hugo stated Miss Brand felt unwell on arrival in London and at her request he left her at Victoria Station bus terminal at 16.45. Miss Brand stated she would rest with some friends, address unknown, and contact Sir Hugo at Ministry at 1900. She had not done so." And that's all,' said Vallance. 'Oh, by the way, we made the inquiry about Miss Brand on your behalf. Said you had arranged to meet her at six and she hadn't turned up.'

'Yes,' said Bond, his thoughts elsewhere. 'That doesn't seem to get us anywhere. I'll have to get busy. Just one more thing. Has Drax got a place in London, flat or anything like that?'

'He always stays at the Ritz nowadays,' said Vallance. 'Sold his house in Grosvenor Square when he moved down to Dover. But we happen to know he's got some sort of an establishment in Ebury Street. We checked there. But there was no answer to the bell and my man said the house looked unoccupied. Just behind Buckingham Palace. Some sort of hideout of his. Keeps it very quiet. Probably takes his women there. Anything else? I ought to be getting back or all this big brass will think the Crown Jewels have been stolen.'

'You go ahead,' said Bond. 'I'll do my best and if I get stuck I'll call on your men to help. Don't worry if you don't hear from me. So long.'

'So long,' said Vallance with a note of relief in his voice. 'And thanks. Best of luck.'

Bond rang off.

He picked up the receiver again and called Blades.

'This is the Ministry of Supply,' he said. 'Is Sir Hugo Drax in the club?'

'Yes, sir.' It was the friendly voice of Brevett. 'He's in the dining-room. Do you wish to speak to him?'

'No, it's all right,' said Bond. 'I just wanted to make certain he hadn't left yet.'

Without noticing what he was eating Bond wolfed down some food and left the restaurant at 8.45. His car was outside waiting for him and he said good-night to the driver from Headquarters and drove to St. James's Street. He parked under cover of the central row of taxis opposite Boodle's and settled himself behind an evening paper over which he could keep his eyes on a section of Drax's Mercedes which he was relieved to see standing in Park Street, unattended.

He had not long to wait. Suddenly a broad shaft of yellow light shone out from the doorway of Blades and the big figure of Drax appeared. He wore a heavy ulster up round his ears and a cap pulled down over his eyes. He walked quickly to the white Mercedes, slammed the door, and was away across to the left-hand side of St. James's Street and braking to turn opposite St. James's Palace while Bond was still in third.

God the man moves quickly, thought Bond, doing a racing change round the island in the Mall with Drax already passing the statue in front of the Palace. He kept the Bentley in third and thundered in pursuit. Buckingham Palace Gate. So it looked like Ebury Street. Keeping the white car just in view, Bond made hurried plans. The lights at the corner of Lower Grosvenor Place were green for Drax and red for Bond. Bond jumped them and was just in time to see Drax swing left into the beginning of Ebury Street. Gambling on Drax making a stop at his house, Bond accelerated to the corner and pulled up just short of it. As he jumped out of the Bentley, leaving the engine ticking over, and took the few steps towards Ebury Street, he heard two short blasts on the Mercedes' horn and as he carefully edged round the corner he was in time to see Krebs helping the muffled figure of a girl across the pavement.

Then the door of the Mercedes slammed and Drax was off again.

Bond ran back to his car, whipped into third, and went after him.

Thank God the Mercedes was white. There it went, its stop-lights blazing briefly at the intersections, the headlamps full on and the horn blaring at any hint of a check in the sparse traffic.

Bond set his teeth and rode his car as if she was a Lipizaner at the Spanish Riding School in Vienna. He could not use head-lights or horn for fear of betraying his presence to the car in front. He just had to play on his brakes and gears and hope for the best.

The deep note of his two-inch exhaust thundered back at him from the houses on either side and his tyres screamed on the tarmac. He thanked heavens for the new set of racing Michelins that were only a week old. If only the lights would be kind. He seemed to be getting nothing but amber and red while Drax was always being swept on by the green. Chelsea Bridge. So it did look like the Dover road by the South Circular! Could he hope to keep up with the Mercedes on A20? Drax had two passen-gers. His car might not be tuned. But with that independent springing he could corner better than Bond. The old Bentley was a bit high off the ground for this sort of work. Bond stamped on his brakes and risked a howl on his triple klaxons as a homeward-bound taxi started to weave over to the right. It jerked back to the left and Bond heard a four-letter yell as he shot past.

Clapham Common and the flicker of the white car through the trees. Bond ran the Bentley up to eighty along the safe bit of road and saw the lights go red just in time to stop Drax at the end of it. He put the Bentley into neutral and coasted up silent-ly. Fifty yards away. Forty, thirty, twenty. The lights changed and Drax was over the crossing and away again, but not before Bond had seen that Krebs was beside the driver and that there was no sign of Gala except the hump of a rug over the narrow back seat.

So there was no question. You don't take a sick girl for a drive like a sack of potatoes. Nor at that speed for the matter of that. So she was a prisoner. Why? What had she done? What had she discovered? What the hell, in fact, was all this about?

Each dark conjecture came and for a moment settled like a vulture on Bond's shoulder and croaked into his ear that he had been a blind fool. Blind, blind, blind. From the moment he had sat in his office after the night at Blades and made his mind up about Drax being a dangerous man he should have been on his toes. At the first smell of trouble, the marks on the chart for instance, he should have taken action. But what action? He had passed on each clue, each fear. What could he have done except kill Drax? And get hanged for his pains? Well, then. What about the present? Should he stop and telephone the Yard? And let the car get away? For all he knew Gala was being taken for a ride and Drax planned to get rid of her on the way to Dover. And that Bond might conceivably prevent if only his car could take it.

As if to echo his thoughts the tortured rubber screamed as he left the South Circular road into A20 and took the round-about at forty. No. He had told M. that he would stay with it. He had told Vallance the same. The case had been dumped firmly into his lap and he must do what he could. At least if he kept up with the Mercedes he might shoot up its tyres and apologize afterwards. To let it get away would be criminal.

So be it, said Bond to himself.

He had to slow for some lights and he used the pause to pull a pair of goggles out of the dashboard compartment and cover his eyes with them. Then he leant over to the left and twisted the big screw on the windscreen and then eased the one beside his right hand. He pressed the narrow screen flat down on the bonnet and tightened the screws again.

Then he accelerated away from Swanley Junction and was soon doing ninety astride the cats' eyes down the Farningham by-pass, the wind howling past his ears and the shrill scream of his supercharger riding with him for company.

A mile ahead the great eyes of the Mercedes hooded themselves as they went over the crest of Wrotham Hill and disappeared down into the moonlit panorama of the Weald of Kent.

20

DRAX'S GAMBIT

THERE WERE THREE separate sources of pain in Gala's body. The throbbing ache behind her left ear, the bite of the flex at her wrists, and the chafing of the strap round her ankles.

Every bump in the road, every swerve, every sudden pressure of Drax's foot on the brakes or the accelerator awoke one or another of these pains and rasped at her nerves. If only she had been wedged into the back seat more tightly. But there was just room enough for her body to roll a few inches on the occasional seat so that she was constantly having to twist her bruised face away from contact with the walls of shiny pig-skin.

The air she breathed was stuffy with the smell of new leather upholstery, exhaust fumes, and the occasional sharp stench of burning rubber as Drax flayed the tyres on a sharp corner.

And yet the discomfort and pain were nothing.

Krebs! Curiously enough her fear and loathing of Krebs tormented her most. The other things were too big. The mystery of Drax and his hatred of England. The riddle of his perfect command of German. The Moonraker. The secret of the atomic warhead. How to save London. These were matters which she had long ago put away in the back of her mind as insoluble.

But the afternoon alone with Krebs was present and dreadful and her mind went back and back to the details of it like a tongue to an aching tooth.

Long after Drax had gone she had kept up her pretence of unconsciousness. At first Krebs had occupied himself with the machines, talking to them in German in a cooing baby-talk. 'There, my *Liebchen*. That's better now, isn't it? A drop of oil for you, my *Pupperl?* But certainly. Coming up at once. No, no, lazybones. I said a thousand revolutions. Not nine hundred. Come along now. We can do better than that, can't we? Yes, my *Schatz*. That's it. Round and round we go. Up and down. Round and round. Let me wipe your pretty face for you so that we can see what the little dial is saying. *Jesu Maria, bist du ein braves Kind!'*

And so it had gone on with intervals of standing in front of Gala, picking his nose and sucking at his teeth in a horribly ruminative way. Until he stayed longer and longer in front of her, forgetting the machines, wondering, making up his mind.

And then she had felt his hand undo the top button of her dress and the automatic recoil of her body had had to be covered by a realistic groan and a pantomime of consciousness returning.

She had asked for water and he had gone into a bathroom and fetched some for her in a toothglass. Then he had pulled a kitchen chair up in front of her and had sat down astride it, his chin resting on the top rail of its back, and had gazed at her speculatively from under his pale drooping lids.

She had been the first to break the silence. 'Why have I been brought here?' she asked. 'What are all those machines?'

He licked his lips and the little pouting red mouth opened under the smudge of yellow moustache and formed itself slowly into a rhomboid-shaped smile. 'That is a lure for little birds,' he said. 'Soon it will lure a little bird into this warm nest. Then the little bird will lay an egg. Oh, such a big round egg! Such a beautiful fat egg.' The lower half of his face giggled with delight while his eyes mooned. 'And the pretty girl is here because otherwise she might frighten the little bird away. And that would be so sad, wouldn't it,' he spat out the next three words, 'filthy English bitch?'

His eyes became intent and purposeful. He hitched his chair nearer so that his face was only a foot away from hers and she was enveloped in the miasma of his breath. 'Now English bitch. Who are you working for?' He waited. 'You must answer me, you know,' he said softly. 'We are all alone here. There is no one to hear you scream.'

'Don't be stupid,' said Gala desperately. 'How could I be working for anyone except Sir Hugo?' (Krebs smiled at the name.) 'I was just curious about the flight plan . . . ' She went into a rambling explanation about her figures and Drax's figures and how she had wanted to share in the success of the Moonraker.

'Try again,' whispered Krebs when she had finished. 'You must do better than that,' and suddenly his eyes had turned hot with cruelty and his hands had reached towards her from behind the back of his chair . . .

In the rear of the hurtling Mercedes Gala ground her teeth together and whimpered at the memory of the soft crawling fingers on her body, probing, pinching, pulling, while all the time the hot vacant eyes gazed curiously into hers until finally she gathered the saliva in her mouth and spat full in his face.

He hadn't even paused to wipe his face, but suddenly he had really hurt her and she had screamed once and then mercifully fainted.

And then she had found herself being pushed into the back of the car, a rug was thrown over her, and they were hurtling through the streets of London and she could hear other cars near them, the frantic ringing of a bicycle bell, an occasional shout, the animal growl of an old klaxon, the whirring putter of a motor-scooter, a scream of brakes, and she had realized that she was back in the real world, that English people, friends, were all around her. She had struggled to get to her knees and scream but Krebs must have felt her movement because his hands were suddenly at her ankles, strapping them to the foot-rail along the floor, and she knew that she was lost and suddenly the tears were pouring down her cheeks and she was praying that somehow, somebody would be in time.

That had been less than an hour ago and now she could tell from the slow pace of the car and the noise of other traffic that they had reached a large town — Maidstone if she was being taken back to the site.

In the comparative silence of their progress through the town she suddenly heard Krebs's voice. There was a note of urgency in it.

'*Mein Kapitän*,' he said. 'I have been watching a car for some time. It is certainly following us. It has seldom been using its lights. It is only a hundred metres behind us now. I think it is the car of Commander Bond.'

Drax grunted with surprise and she could hear his big body shift round to get a quick look.

He swore sharply and then there was silence and she could feel the big car weaving and straining in the thin traffic. '*Ja*, *sowas!*' said Drax finally. His voice was thoughtful. 'So that old museum-piece of his can still move. So much the better, my dear Krebs. He seems to be alone.' He laughed harshly. 'So we will give him a run for his money and if he survives it we will get him in the bag with the woman. Turn on the radio. Home Service. We will soon find out if there is a hitch.'

There was a short crackle of static and then Gala could hear the voice of the Prime Minister, the voice of all the great occasions in her life, coming through in broken fragments as Drax put the car into third and accelerated out of the town '. . . weapon devised by the ingenuity of Man . . . a thousand miles into the firmament . . . area patrolled by Her Majesty's ships . . . designed exclusively for the defence of our beloved island . . . a long era of peace . . . development for Man's great journey away from the confines of this planet . . . Sir Hugo Drax, that great patriot and benefactor of our country . . .'

Gala heard Drax's roar of laughter above the howling of the wind, a great scornful bray of triumph, and then the set was switched off.

'James,' whispered Gala to herself. 'There's only you left. Be careful. But make haste.'

Bond's face was a mask of dust and filthy with the blood of flies and moths that had smashed against it. Often he had had to take a cramped hand off the wheel to clear his goggles, but the Bentley was going beautifully and he felt sure of holding the Mercedes.

He was touching ninety-five on the straight just before the entrance to Leeds Castle when great lights were suddenly switched on behind him and a four-tone windhorn sounded its impudent 'pom-pim-pom-pam' almost in his ear.

The apparition of a third car in the race was almost unbelievable. Bond had hardly troubled to look in his driving-mirror since he left London. No one but a racing-driver or a desperate man could have kept up with them, and his mind was in a turmoil as he automatically pulled over to the left and saw out of the corner of his eye a low, fire-engine-red car come up level with him and draw away with a good ten miles an hour extra on its clock.

He caught a glimpse of the famous Alfa radiator and along the edge of the bonnet in bold white script the words 'Attaboy

II'. Then there was the grinning face of a youth in shirt-sleeves who stuck two rude fingers in the air before he pulled away in the welter of sound which an Alfa at speed compounds from the whine of its supercharger, the Gatling crackle of its exhaust, and the thunderous howl of its transmission.

Bond grinned in admiration as he raised a hand to the driver. Alfa-Romeo supercharged straight-eight, he thought to himself. Must be nearly as old as mine. 'Thirty-two or '33 probably. And only half my c.c. Targa Florio in 1931 and did well everywhere after that. Probably a hot-rod type from one of the R.A.F. stations round here. Trying to get back from a party in time to sign in before he's put on the report. He watched affectionately as the Alfa wagged its tail in the S-bend abreast of Leeds Castle and then howled off on the long wide road towards the distant Charing fork.

Bond could imagine the grin of delight as the boy came up with Drax. 'Oh, boy. It's a Merc!' And the rage of Drax at the impudent music of the windhorn. Must be doing 105, reflected Bond. Hope the damn fool doesn't run out of road. He watched the two sets of tail lights closing up, the boy in the Alfa preparing for his trick of coming up behind and suddenly switching everything on when he could see a chance to get by.

There. Four hundred yards away the Mercedes showed white in the sudden twin shafts from the Alfa. There was a mile of clear road ahead, straight as a die. Bond could almost feel the boy's feet stamping the pedal still further into the floorboards. Attaboy!

Up front in the Mercedes Krebs had his mouth close to Drax's ear. 'Another of them,' he shouted urgently. 'Can't see his face. Coming up to pass now.'

Drax let out a harsh obscenity. His bared teeth showed white in the pale glimmer from the dashboard. 'Teach the swine a lesson,' he said, setting his shoulders and gripping the wheel tightly in the great leather gauntlets. Out of the corner of his eye he watched the nose of the Alfa creep up to starboard. 'Pom-pim-pom-pam' chirped the windhorn. Softly, delicately, Drax inched the wheel of the Mercedes to the right and, at the horrible crash of metal, whipped it back again to correct the slew of his tail.

'Bravo! Bravo!' screamed Krebs, beside himself with excitement as he knelt on the seat and looked back. 'Double somersault. Jumped the hedge upside down. I think he's burning already. Yes. There are flames.'

'That'll give our fine Mister Bond something to think about,' snarled Drax, breathing heavily.

But Bond, his face a tight mask, had hardly checked his speed and there was nothing but revenge in his mind as he hurtled on after the flying Mercedes.

He had seen it all. The grotesque flight of the red car as it turned over and over, the flying figure of the driver, his arms and legs spreadeagled as he soared out of the driving seat, and the final thunder as the car hurdled the hedge upside down and crashed into the field.

As he flashed by, noting the horrible graffiti of the black skid-marks across the tarmac, his mind recorded one final macabre touch. Somehow undamaged in the holocaust, the windhorn was still making contact and its ululations were going on up to the sky, stridently clearing imaginary roads for the passage of Attaboy II — 'Pom-pim-pom-pam.' 'Pom-pim-pom-pam . . . '

So a murder had taken place in front of his eyes. Or at any rate an attempted murder. So, whatever his motives, Sir Hugo Drax had declared war and didn't mind Bond knowing it. This made a lot of things easier. It meant that Drax was a criminal and probably a maniac. Above all it meant certain danger for the Moonraker. That was enough for Bond. He reached under the dashboard and from its concealed holster drew out the long-barrelled .45 Colt Army Special and laid it on the seat beside him. The battle was now in the open and somehow the Mercedes must be stopped.

Using the road as if it was Donnington, Bond rammed his foot down and kept it there. Gradually, with the needle twitching either side of the hundred mark, he began to narrow the gap.

Drax took the left-hand fork at Charing and hissed up the long hill. Ahead, in the giant beam of his headlights, one of Bowaters' huge eight-wheeled A.E.C. Diesel carriers was just grinding into the first bend of the hairpin, labouring under the fourteen tons of newsprint it was taking on a night run to one of the East Kent newspapers.

Drax cursed under his breath as he saw the long carrier with the twenty gigantic rolls, each containing five miles of newsprint, roped to its platform. Right in the middle of the tricky S-bend at the top of the hill.

He looked in the driving-mirror and saw the Bentley coming into the fork.

And then Drax had his idea.

'Krebs.' The word was a pistol shot. 'Get out your knife.'

There was a sharp click and the stiletto was in Krebs's hand. One didn't dawdle when there was that note in the master's voice.

'I am going to slow down behind this lorry. Take your shoes and socks off and climb out on to the bonnet and when I come up behind the lorry jump on to it. I shall be going at walking-pace. It will be safe. Cut the ropes that hold the rolls of paper. The left ones first. Then the right. I shall have pulled up level with the lorry and when you have cut the second lot jump into the car. Be careful you are not swept off with the paper. *Verstanden? Also. Hals und Beinbruch!*'

Drax dowsed his headlights and swept round the bend at eighty. The lorry was twenty yards ahead and Drax had to brake hard to avoid crashing into its tail. The Mercedes executed a dry skid until its radiator was almost underneath the platform of the carrier.

Drax changed down to second. 'Now!' He held the car steady as a rock as Krebs, with bare feet, went over the windscreen and scrambled along the shining bonnet, his knife in his hand.

With a leap he was up and hacking at the left-hand ropes. Drax pulled away to the right and crawled up level with the rear wheels of the Diesel, the oily smoke from its exhaust in his eyes and nostrils.

Bond's lights were just showing round the bend.

There was a series of huge thuds as the left-hand rolls poured off the back of the lorry into the road and went hurtling off into the darkness. And more thuds as the right-hand ropes parted. One roll burst as it landed and Drax heard a tearing rattle as the unwinding paper crashed back down the one-in-ten gradient.

Released of its load the lorry almost bounded forward and Drax had to accelerate a little to catch the flying figure of Krebs who landed half across Gala's back and half in the front seat.

Drax stamped his foot into the floor and sped off up the hill, ignoring a shout from the lorry-driver above the clatter of the Diesel pistons as he shot ahead.

As he hurtled round the next bend he saw the shaft of two headlights curve up into the sky over the tops of the trees until they were almost vertical. They wavered there for an instant and then the beams whirled away across the sky and went out.

A great barking laugh broke out of Drax as for a split second he took his eyes off the road and raised his face triumphantly towards the stars.

21

'THE PERSUADER'

KREBS ECHOED THE maniac laugh with a high giggle. 'A master-stroke, *mein Kapitän.* You should have seen them charge off down the hill. The one that burst. *Wunderschön!* Like the lavatory paper of a giant. That one will have made a pretty parcel of him. He was just coming round the bend. And the second salvo was as good as the first. Did you see the driver's face? *Zum Kotzen!* And the *Firma* Bowater! A fine paperchase they have got on their hands.'

'You did well,' said Drax briefly, his mind elsewhere.

Suddenly he pulled into the side of the road with a scream of protest from the tyres.

'*Donnerwetter*,' he said angrily, as he started to turn the car. 'But we can't leave the man there. We must get him.' The car was already hissing back down the road. 'Gun,' ordered Drax briefly.

They passed the lorry at the top of the hill. It was stopped and there was no sign of the driver. Probably telephoning to the company, thought Drax, slowing up as they went round the first bend. There were lights on in the two or three houses and a group of people were standing round one of the rolls of newsprint that lay amongst the ruins of their front gate. There were more rolls in the hedge on the right of the road. On the left a telegraph pole leant drunkenly, snapped in the middle. Then at the next bend was the beginning of a great confusion of paper stretching away down the long hill, festooning the hedges and the road like the sweepings of some elephantine fancy-dress ball.

The Bentley had nearly broken through the railings that fenced off the right of the bend from a steep bank. Amidst a puzzle of twisted iron stanchions it hung, nose down, with one wheel, still attached to the broken back axle, poised crookedly over its rump like a surrealist umbrella.

Drax pulled up and he and Krebs got out and stood quietly, listening.

There was no sound except the distant rumination of a car travelling fast on the Ashford road and the chirrup of a sleepless cricket.

With their guns out they walked cautiously over to the remains of the Bentley, their feet crunching the broken glass on the road. Deep furrows had been cut across the grass verge and there was a strong smell of petrol and burnt rubber in the air. The hot metal of the car ticked and crackled softly and steam was still fountaining from the shattered radiator.

Bond was lying face downwards at the bottom of the bank twenty feet away from the car. Krebs turned him over. His face was covered with blood but he was breathing. They searched him thoroughly and Drax pocketed the slim Beretta. Then together they hauled him across the road and wedged him into the back seat of the Mercedes, half on top of Gala.

When she realized who it was she gave a cry of horror.

'*Halt's Maul*,' snarled Drax. He got into the front seat and while he turned the car Krebs leant over from the front seat and busied himself with a long piece of flex. 'Make a good job of it,' said Drax. 'I don't want any mistakes.' He had an afterthought. 'And then go back to the wreck and get the number plates. Hurry. I will watch the road.'

Krebs pulled the rug over the two inert bodies and jumped out of the car. Using his knife as a screwdriver he was soon back with the plates, and the big car started to move just as a group of the local residents appeared walking nervously down the hill shining their torches over the scene of devastation.

Krebs grinned happily to himself at the thought of the stupid English having to clean up all this mess. He settled himself back to enjoy the part of the drive he had always liked best, the spring woods full of bluebells and celandines on the way to Chilham.

They made him particularly happy at night. Lit up amongst the green torches of the young trees by the great headlamps of the Mercedes, they made him think of the beautiful forests of the Ardennes and of the devoted little band with which he had served, and of driving along in a captured American jeep with, just like tonight, his adored leader at the wheel. *Der Tag* had been a long time coming, but now it was here. With young

Krebs in the van. At last the cheering crowds, the medals, the women, the flowers. He gazed out at the fleeting hosts of bluebells and felt warm and happy.

Gala could taste Bond's blood. His face was beside hers on the leather seat and she shifted to give him more room. His breathing was heavy and irregular and she wondered how badly he was hurt. Tentatively she whispered into his ear. And then louder. He groaned and his breath came faster.

'James,' she whispered urgently. 'James.'

He mumbled something and she pushed hard against him.

He uttered a string of obscenities and his body heaved.

He lay still again and she could almost feel him exploring his sensations.

'It's me, Gala.' She felt him stiffen.

'Christ,' he said. 'Hell of a mess.'

'Are you all right? Is anything broken?'

She felt him tense his arms and legs. 'Seems all right,' he said. 'Crack on the head. Am I talking sense?'

'Of course,' said Gala. 'Now listen.'

Hurriedly she told him all she knew, beginning with the notebook.

His body was as rigid as a board against her, and he hardly breathed as he listened to the incredible story.

Then they were running into Canterbury and Bond put his mouth to her ear. 'Going to try and chuck myself over the back,' he whispered. 'Get to a telephone. Only hope.'

He started to heave himself up on his knees, his weight almost grinding the breath out of the girl.

There was a sharp crack and he fell back on top of her.

'Another move out of you and you're dead,' said the voice of Krebs coming softly between the front seats.

Only another twenty minutes to the site! Gala gritted her teeth and set about bringing Bond back to consciousness again.

She had only just succeeded when the car drew up at the door of the launching-dome and Krebs, a gun in his hand, was undoing the bonds round their ankles.

They had a glimpse of the familiar moonlit cement and of the semi-circle of guards some distance away before they were hustled through the door and, when their shoes had been torn off by Krebs, out on to the iron catwalk inside the launching-dome.

There the gleaming rocket stood, beautiful, innocent, like a new toy for Cyclops.

But there was a horrible smell of chemicals in the air and to Bond the Moonraker was a giant hypodermic needle ready to be plunged into the heart of England. Despite a growl from Krebs he paused on the stairway and looked up at its glittering nose. A million deaths. A million. A million. A million.

On his hands? For God's sake! On HIS hands?

With Krebs's gun prodding him, he went slowly down the steps on the heels of Gala.

As he turned through the doors of Drax's office, he pulled himself together. Suddenly his mind was clear and all the lethargy and pain had left his body. Something, anything, must be done. Somehow he would find a way. His whole body and mind became focused and sharp as a blade. His eyes were alive again and defeat sloughed off him like the skin of a snake.

Drax had gone ahead and was sitting at his desk. He had a Luger in his hand. It was pointing at a spot halfway between Bond and Gala and it was steady as a rock.

Behind him, Bond heard the double doors thud shut.

'I was one of the best shots in the Brandenburg Division,' said Drax conversationally. 'Tie her to that chair, Krebs. Then the man.'

Gala looked desperately at Bond.

'You won't shoot,' said Bond. 'You'd be afraid of touching off the fuel.' He walked slowly towards the desk.

Drax smiled cheerfully and looked along the barrel at Bond's stomach. 'Your memory is bad, Englishman,' he said flatly. 'I told you this room is cut off from the shaft by the double doors. Another step and you will have no stomach.'

Bond looked at the confident, narrowed eyes and stopped.

'Go ahead, Krebs.'

When they were both tied securely and painfully to the arms and legs of two tubular steel chairs a few feet apart beneath the glass wall map, Krebs left the room. He came back in a moment with a mechanic's blowtorch.

He set the ugly machine on the desk, pumped air into it with a few brisk strokes of the plunger, and set a match to it. A blue flame hissed out a couple of inches into the room. He picked up the instrument and walked towards Gala. He stopped a few feet to one side of her.

'Now then,' said Drax grimly. 'Let's get this over without any fuss. The good Krebs is an artist with one of those things. We used to call him "*Der Zwangsman* — The Persuader". I shall never forget the way he went over the last spy we caught together. Just south of the Rhine, wasn't it, Krebs?'

Bond pricked up his ears.

'Yes, *mein Kapitän*,' Krebs chuckled reminiscently. 'It was a pig of a Belgian.'

'All right then,' said Drax. 'Just remember, you two. There's no fair play down here. No jolly good sports and all that. This is business.' The voice cracked like a whip on the word. 'You,' he looked at Gala Brand, 'who are you working for?'

Gala was silent.

'Anywhere you like, Krebs.'

Krebs's mouth was half open. His tongue ran up and down his lower lip. He seemed to be having difficulty with his breathing as he took a step towards the girl.

The little flame roared greedily.

'Stop,' said Bond coldly. 'She works for Scotland Yard. So do I.' These things were pointless now. They were of no conceivable use to Drax. In any case, by tomorrow afternoon there might be no Scotland Yard.

'That's better,' said Drax. 'Now, does anybody know you are prisoners? Did you stop and telephone anyone?'

If I say yes, thought Bond, he will shoot us both and get rid of the bodies and the last chance of stopping the Moonraker will be gone. And if the Yard knows, why aren't they here already? No. Our chance may come. The Bentley will be found. Vallance may get worried when he doesn't hear from me.

'No,' he said. 'If I had, they'd be here by now.'

'True,' said Drax reflectively. 'In that case I am no longer interested in you and I congratulate you on making the interview so harmonious. It might have been more difficult if you had been alone. A girl is always useful on these occasions. Krebs, put that down. You may go. Tell the others what is necessary. They will be wondering. I shall entertain our guests for a while and then I shall come up to the house. See the car gets properly washed down. The back seat. And get rid of the marks on the right-hand side. Tell them to take the whole panel off if necessary. Or they can set fire to the dam' thing. We shan't be needing it any more.' He laughed abruptly. '*Verstanden?*'

'Yes, *mein Kapitän*.' Krebs reluctantly placed the softly roaring blowtorch on the desk beside Drax. 'In case you need it,' he said, looking hopefully at Gala and Bond. He went out through the double doors.

Drax put the Luger down on the desk in front of him. He opened a drawer and took out a cigar and lit it from a Ronson desk lighter. Then he settled himself comfortably. There was silence in the room for several minutes while Drax puffed contentedly at his cigar. Then he seemed to make up his mind. He looked benevolently at Bond.

'You don't know how I have longed for an English audience,' he said as if he was addressing a Press conference. 'You don't know how I have longed to tell my story. As a matter of fact, a full account of my operations is now in the hands of a very respectable firm of Edinburgh solicitors. I beg their pardon — Writers to the Signet. Well out of danger.' He beamed from one to the other. 'And these good folk have instructions to open the envelope on the completion of the first successful flight of the Moonraker. But you lucky people shall have a preview of what I have written and then, when tomorrow at noon you see through those open doors,' he gestured to his right, 'the first wisp of steam from the turbines and know that you are to be burnt alive in about half a second, you will have the momentary satisfaction of knowing what it is all in aid of, as,' he grinned wolfishly, 'we Englishmen say.'

'You can spare us the jokes,' said Bond roughly. 'Get on with your story, Kraut.'

Drax's eyes blazed momentarily. 'A Kraut. Yes, I am indeed a *Reichsdeutscher*' — the mouth beneath the red moustache savoured the fine word — 'and even England will soon agree that they have been licked by just one single German. And then perhaps they'll stop calling us Krauts — BY ORDER!' The words were yelled out and the whole of Prussian militarism was in the parade-ground bellow.

Drax glowered across the desk at Bond, the great splayed teeth under the red moustache tearing nervously at one fingernail after another. Then, with an effort, he crammed his right hand into his trouser pocket, as if to put it out of temptation, and picked up his cigar with his left. He puffed at it for a moment and then, his voice still taut, he began.

22

PANDORA'S BOX

'MY REAL NAME,' said Drax, addressing himself to Bond, 'is Graf Hugo von der Drache. My mother was English and because of her I was educated in England until I was twelve. Then I could stand this filthy country no longer and I completed my education in Berlin and Leipzig.'

Bond could imagine that the hulking bully with the ogre's teeth had not been very welcome at an English private school. And being a foreign count with a mouthful of names would not have helped much.

'When I was twenty,' Drax's eyes glowed reminiscently, 'I went to work in the family business. It was a subsidiary of the great steel combine *Rheinmetal Börsig*. Never heard of it, I suppose. Well, if you'd been hit by an 88 mm. shell during the war it would probably have been one of theirs. Our subsidiary were experts in special steels and I learned all about them and a lot about the aircraft industry. Our most exacting customers. That's when I first heard about Columbite. Worth diamonds in those days. Then I joined the party and almost immediately we were at war. A wonderful time. I was twenty-eight and a lieutenant in the 140th Panzer Regiment. And we ran through the British Army and France like a knife through butter. Intoxicating.'

For a moment Drax puffed luxuriously at his cigar and Bond guessed that he was seeing the burning villages of Belgium in the smoke.

'Those were great days, my dear Bond.' Drax reached out a long arm and tapped the ash of his cigar off on to the floor. 'But then I was picked out for the Brandenburg Division and I had to leave the girls and the champagne and go back to Germany and start training for the big water-jump to England. My English was needed in the Division. We were all going to be in English uniforms. It would have been fun, but the damned generals said it couldn't be done and I was transferred to the Foreign Intelligence Service of the S.S. The R.S.H.A. it was called, and SS *Obergruppenführer* Kaltenbrunner had just taken over the command after Heydrich was assassinated in '42. He was a good man and I was under the direct orders of a still better one, *Obersturmbannführer*,' he rolled out the delicious title with relish, 'Otto Skorzeny. His job in the R.S.H.A. was terrorism and sabotage. A pleasant interlude, my dear Bond, during which I was able to bring many an Englishman to book which,' Drax beamed coldly at Bond, 'gave me much pleasure. But then,' Drax's fist crashed down on the desk, 'Hitler was betrayed again by those swinish generals and the English and Americans were allowed to land in France.'

'Too bad,' said Bond drily.

'Yes, my dear Bond, it was indeed too bad.' Drax chose to ignore the irony. 'But for me it was the high-spot of the whole war. Skorzeny turned all his saboteurs and terrorists into SS *Jagdverbände* for use behind the enemy lines. Each *Jagdverbänd* was divided into *Streifkorps* and then into *Kommandos*, each carrying the name of its commanding officer. With the rank of *Oberleutnant*,' Drax swelled visibly, 'at the head of *Kommando* "Drache" I went right through the American lines with the famous 150 Panzer Brigade in the Ardennes break-through in December '44. No doubt you will remember the effect of this Brigade in its American uniforms and with its captured American tanks and vehicles. *Kolossal!* When the Brigade had to withdraw I stayed where I was and went to ground in the Forests of Ardennes, fifty miles behind the Allied lines. There were twenty of us, ten good men and ten Hitlerjugend Werewolves. In their teens, but good lads all of them. And, by a coincidence, in charge of them was a young man called Krebs who turned out to have certain gifts which qualified him for the post of executioner and "persuader" to our merry little band.' Drax chuckled pleasantly.

Bond licked his lips as he remembered the crack Krebs's head had made against the dressing-table. Had he kicked him as hard as he possibly could? Yes, his memory reassured him, with every ounce of strength he could put into his shoe.

'We stayed in those woods for six months,' continued Drax proudly, 'and all the time we reported back to the Fatherland by radio. The location vans never spotted us. Then one day disaster came.' Drax shook his head at the memory. 'There was a big farmhouse a mile away from our hideout in the forest. A lot of Nissen huts had been built round it and it was used as a rear headquarters for some sort of liaison group, English and Americans. A hopeless place. No discipline, no security, and full of hangers-on and shirkers from all over the place. We had kept an eye on it for some time and one day I decided to blow it up. It was a simple plan. In the evening, two of my men, one in American uniform and one in British, were to drive up in a captured scout car containing two tons of explosive. There was a car park — no sentries of course — near the mess hall and they were to run the car in as close to the mess hall as possible, time the fuse for the seven o'clock dinner hour, and then get away. All quite easy and I went off that morning on my own business and left the job to my second in command. I was dressed in the uniform of your Signal Corps and I set off on a captured British motor-cycle to shoot a dispatch rider from the same unit who made a daily run along a near-by road. Sure enough he came along dead on time and I went after him out of a side road. I caught up with him,' said Drax conversationally, 'and shot him in the back, took his papers and put him on top of his machine in the woods and set fire to him.'

Drax saw the fury in Bond's eyes and held up his hand. 'Not very sporting? My dear chap, the man was already dead. However, to continue. I went on my way and then what should happen? One of our own planes coming back from a reconnaissance came after me down the road with his cannon. One of our own planes! Blasted me right off the road. God knows how long I lay in the ditch. Some time in the afternoon I came to for a bit and had the sense to hide my cap and jacket and the dispatches. In the hedge. They're probably still there. I must go and collect them one day. Interesting souvenirs. Then I set fire to the remains of the motor-cycle and I must have fainted again because the next thing I knew I had been picked up by a British vehicle and we were driving into that damned liaison headquarters! Believe it or not! And there was the scout car, right up alongside the mess hall! It was too much for me. I was full of shell splinters and my leg was broken. Well, I fainted and when I came round there was half the hospital on top of me and I only had half a face.' He put up his hand and stroked the shiny skin on his left temple and cheek. 'After that it was just a question of acting a part. They had no idea who I was. The car that had picked me up had gone or been blown to pieces. I was just an Englishman in an English shirt and trousers who was nearly dead.'

Drax paused and took out another cigar and lit it. There was silence in the room save for the soft, diminished roar of the blowtorch. Its threatening voice was quieter. Pressure running out, reflected Bond.

He turned his head and looked at Gala. For the first time he saw the ugly bruise behind her left ear. He gave her a smile of encouragement and she smiled wryly back.

Drax spoke through the cigar smoke: 'There is not much more to tell,' he said. 'During the year that I was being pushed from one hospital to the next I made my plans down to the smallest detail. They consisted quite simply of revenge on England for what she had done to me and to my country. It gradually became an obsession. I admit it. Every day during that year of the rape and destruction of my country, my hatred and scorn for the English grew more bitter.' The veins on Drax's face started to swell and suddenly he pounded on the desk and shouted across at them, looking with bulging eyes from one to the other. 'I loathe and despise you all. You swine! Useless, idle, decadent fools, hiding behind your bloody white cliffs while other people fight your battles. Too weak to defend your colonies, toadying to America with your hats in your hands. Stinking snobs who'll do anything for money. Hah!' he was triumphant, 'I knew that all I needed was money and the façade of a gentleman. Gentleman! *Pfui Teufel!* To me a gentleman is just someone I can take advantage of. Those bloody fools in Blades for instance. Moneyed oafs. For months I took thousands of pounds off them, swindled them right under their noses until you came along and upset the apple-cart.'

Drax's eyes narrowed. 'What put you on to the cigarette-case?' he asked sharply.

Bond shrugged his shoulders. 'My eyes,' he said indifferently.

'Ah well,' said Drax, 'perhaps I was a bit careless that night. But where was I? Ah yes, in hospital. And the good doctors were so anxious to help me find out who I really was.' He let out a roar of laughter. 'It was easy. So easy.' His eyes became cunning. 'From the identities they offered me so helpfully I came upon the name of Hugo Drax. What a coincidence! From Drache to Drax! Tentatively I thought it *might* be me. They were very proud. Yes, they said, *of course* it is you. The doctors triumphantly forced me into his shoes. I put them on and walked out of the hospital in them and I walked round London looking for someone to kill and rob. And one day, in a little office high above Piccadilly, a Jewish moneylender.' (Now Drax was talking faster. The words poured excitedly from his lips. Bond watched a fleck of foam gather at one corner of his mouth and grow.) 'Ha. It was easy. Crack on his bald skull. £15,000 in the safe. And then away and out of the country. Tangier — where you could do anything, buy anything, fix anything. Columbite. Rarer than platinum and everyone would want it. The Jet Age. I knew about these things. I had not forgotten my own profession. And then by God I worked. For five years I lived for money. And I was brave as a lion. I took terrible risks. And suddenly the first million was there. Then the second. Then the fifth. Then the twentieth. I came back to England. I spent a million of it and London was in my pocket. And then I went back to Germany. I found Krebs. I found fifty of them. Loyal Germans. Brilliant technicians. All living under false names like so many others of my old comrades. I gave them their orders and they waited, peacefully, innocently. And where was I?' Drax stared across at Bond, his eyes wide. 'I was in Moscow. Moscow! A man with Columbite to sell can go anywhere. I got to the right people. They listened to my plans. They gave me Walter, the new genius of their guided missile station at Peenemunde, and the good Russians started to build the atomic warhead,' he gestured up to the ceiling, 'that is now waiting up there. Then I came back to London.' A pause. 'The Coronation. My letter to the Palace. Triumph. Hooray for Drax.' He burst into a roar of laughter. 'England at my feet. Every bloody fool in the country! And then my men come over and we start. Under the very skirts of Britannia. On top of her famous cliffs. We work like devils. We built a jetty into your English Channel. For supplies! For supplies from my good friends the Russians that came in dead on time last Monday night. But then Tallon has to hear something. The old fool. He talks to the Ministry.

But Krebs is listening. There were fifty volunteers to kill the man. Lots are drawn and Bartsch dies a hero's death.' Drax paused. 'He will not be forgotten.' Then he went on. 'The new warhead is hoisted into place. It fits. A perfect piece of design. The same weight. Everything perfect, and the old one, the tin can full of the Ministry's cherished instruments, is now in Stettin — behind the Iron Curtain. And the faithful submarine is on her way back here and will soon,' he looked at his watch, 'be creeping under the waters of the English Channel to take us all off at one minute past midday tomorrow.'

Drax wiped his mouth with the back of his hand and lay back in his chair and gazed up at the ceiling, his eyes full of visions. Suddenly he chuckled and squinted quizzically down his nose at Bond.

'And do you know what we shall do first when we go on board? We shall shave off those famous moustaches you were so interested in. You smelt a mouse, my dear Bond, where you ought to have smelt a rat. Those shaven heads and those moustaches we all cultivated so assiduously. Just a precaution, my dear fellow. Try shaving your own head and growing a big black moustache. Even your mother wouldn't recognize you. It's the combination that counts. Just a tiny refinement. Precision, my dear fellow. Precision in every detail. That has been my watchword.' He chuckled fatly and puffed away at his cigar.

Suddenly he looked sharply, suspiciously up at Bond. 'Well. Say something. Don't sit there like a dummy. What do you think of my story? Don't you think it's extraordinary, remarkable? For one man to have done all that? Come on, come on.' A hand came up to his mouth and he started tearing furiously at his nails. Then it was plunged back into his pocket and his eyes became cruel and cold. 'Or do you want me to have to send for Krebs?' He made a gesture towards the house telephone on his desk. 'The Persuader. Poor Krebs. He's like a child who's had his toys taken away from him. Or perhaps Walter. He would give you both something to remember. There's no softness in that one. Well?'

'Yes,' said Bond. He looked levelly at the great red face across the desk. 'It's a remarkable case-history. Galloping paranoia. Delusions of jealousy and persecution. Megalomaniac hatred and desire for revenge. Curiously enough,' he went on conversationally, 'it may have something to do with your teeth. Diastema, they call it. Comes from sucking your thumb when you're a child. Yes. I expect that's what the psychologists will say when they get you into the lunatic asylum. "Ogre's teeth." Being bullied at school and so on. Extraordinary the effect it has on a child. Then Nazism helped to fan the flames and then came the crack on your ugly head. The crack you engineered yourself. I expect that settled it. From then on you were really mad. Same sort of thing as people who think they're God. Extraordinary what tenacity they have. Absolute fanatics. You're almost a genius. Lombroso would have been delighted with you. As it is you're just a mad dog that'll have to be shot. Or else you'll commit suicide. Paranoiacs generally do. Too bad. Sad business.'

Bond paused and put all the scorn he could summon into his voice. 'And now let's get on with this farce, you great hairy-faced lunatic.'

It worked. With every word Drax's face had become more contorted with rage, his eyes were red with it, the sweat of fury was dripping off his jowls on to his shirt, the lips were drawn back from the gaping teeth and a string of saliva had crept out of his mouth and was hanging down from his chin. Now, at the last private-school insult that must have awoken God knows what stinging memories, he leapt up from his chair and lunged round the desk at Bond, his hairy fists flailing.

Bond gritted his teeth and took it.

When Drax had twice had to pick the chair up with Bond in it, the tornado of rage suddenly passed. He took out his silk handkerchief and wiped his face and hands. Then he walked quietly to the door and spoke across the lolling head of Bond to the girl.

'I don't think you two will give me any more trouble,' he said, and his voice was quite calm and certain. 'Krebs never makes a mistake with his knots.' He gesticulated towards the bloody figure in the other chair. 'When he wakes up,' he said, 'you can tell him that these doors will open once more, just before noon tomorrow. A few minutes later there will be nothing left of either of you. Not even,' he added as he wrenched open the inner door, 'the stoppings in your teeth.'

The outer door slammed.

Bond slowly raised his head and grinned painfully at the girl with his bloodstained lips.

'Had to get him mad,' he said with difficulty. 'Didn't want to give him time to think. Had to work up a brainstorm.'

Gala looked at him uncomprehendingly, her eyes wide at the terrible mask of his face.

''S'all right,' said Bond thickly. 'Don't worry. London's okay. Got a plan.'

Over on the desk the blowtorch gave a quiet 'plop' and went out.

23

ZERO MINUS

THROUGH HALF-CLOSED EYES Bond looked intently at the torch while for a few precious seconds he sat and let life creep back into his body. His head felt as if it had been used as a football, but there was nothing broken. Drax had hit him unscientifically and with the welter of blows of a drunken man.

Gala watched him anxiously. The eyes in the bloody face were almost shut, but the line of the jaw was taut with concentration and she could feel the effort of will he was making.

He gave his head a shake and when he turned towards her she could see that his eyes were feverish with triumph.

He nodded towards the desk. 'The lighter,' he said urgently. 'I had to try and make him forget it. Follow me. I'll show you.' He started to rock the light steel chair inch by inch towards the desk. 'For God's sake don't tip over or we've had it. But make it fast or the blowlamp'll get cold.'

Uncomprehendingly, and feeling almost as if they were playing some ghastly children's game, Gala carefully rocked her way across the floor in his wake.

Seconds later Bond told her to stop beside the desk while he went rocking on round to Drax's chair. Then he manoeuvred himself into position opposite his target and with a sudden lurch heaved himself and the chair forward so that his head came down.

There was a painful crack as the Ronson desk lighter connected with his teeth, but his lips held it and the top of it was in his mouth as he heaved the chair back with just enough force to prevent it spilling over. Then he started his patient journey back to where Gala was sitting at the corner of the desk on which Krebs had left the blowlamp.

He rested until his breath was steady again. 'Now we come to the difficult part,' he said grimly. 'While I try to get this torch going, you get your chair round so that your right arm is as close in front of me as possible.'

Obediently she edged herself round while Bond swayed his chair so that it leant against the edge of the desk and allowed his mouth to reach forward and grip the handle of the blowtorch between his teeth.

Then he eased the torch towards him and after minutes of patient work he had the torch and the lighter arranged to his liking at the edge of the desk.

After another rest he bent down, closed the valve of the torch with his teeth, and proceeded to get pressure back by slowly and repeatedly pulling up the plunger with his lips and pressing it back with his chin. His face could feel the warmth in the preheater and he could smell the remnants of gas in it. If only it hadn't cooled off too much.

He straightened up.

'Last lap, Gala,' he said, smiling crookedly at her. 'I may have to hurt you a bit. All right?'

'Of course,' said Gala.

'Then here goes,' said Bond, and he bent forward and released the safety valve on the left of the canister.

Then he quickly bent forward over the Ronson, which was standing at right angles and just below the neck of the torch, and with his two front teeth pressed down sharply on the ignition lever.

It was a horrible manoeuvre and though he whipped back his head with the speed of a snake he let out a gasp of pain as the jet of blue fire from the torch seared across his bruised cheek and the bridge of his nose.

But the vaporized paraffin was hissing out its vital tongue of flame and he shook the water out of his streaming eyes and bent his head almost at right angles and again got his teeth to the handle of the blowtorch.

He thought his jaw would break with the weight of the thing and the nerves of his front teeth screamed at him, but he swayed his chair carefully upright away from the desk and then strained his bent neck forward until the tip of blue fire from the torch was biting into the flex that bound Gala's right wrist to the arm of her chair.

He tried desperately to keep the flame steady but the breath rasped through the girl's teeth as the handle shifted between his jaws and the flame of the torch brushed her forearm.

But then it was over. Melted by the fierce heat, the copper strands parted one by one and suddenly Gala's right arm was free and she was reaching to take the torch out of Bond's mouth.

Bond's head fell back on to his shoulders and he twisted his neck luxuriously to get the blood moving in the aching muscles.

Almost before he knew it, Gala was bending over his arms and legs and he too was free.

As he sat still for a moment, his eyes closed, waiting for the life to come back into his body, he suddenly, delightedly felt Gala's soft lips on his mouth.

He opened his eyes. She was standing in front of him, her eyes shining. 'That's for what you did,' she said seriously.

'You're a wonderful girl,' he said simply.

But then, knowing what he was going to have to do, knowing that while she might conceivably survive, he had only another few minutes to live, he closed his eyes so that she should not see the hopelessness in them.

Gala saw the expression on his face and she turned away. She thought it was only exhaustion and the cumulative effect of what his body had suffered, and she suddenly remembered the peroxide in the washroom next to her office.

She went through the communicating door. How extraordinary it was to see her familiar things again. It must be someone else who had sat at that desk and typed letters and powdered her nose. She shrugged her shoulders and went into the little washroom. God what a sight and God how tired she felt! But first she took a wet towel and some peroxide and went back and spent ten minutes attending to the battlefield which was Bond's face.

He sat silent, a hand resting on her waist, and watched her gratefully. Then when she had gone back into her room and he heard her shut the door of the washroom behind her he got up, turned off the still hissing blowtorch, and walked into Drax's shower, stripped and stood for five minutes under the icy water. 'Preparing the corpse!' he reflected ruefully as he surveyed his battered face in the mirror.

He put on his clothes and went back to Drax's desk which he searched methodically. It yielded only one prize, the 'office bottle', a half-full bottle of Haig and Haig. He fetched two glasses and some water and called to Gala.

He heard the door of the washroom open. 'What is it?'

'Whisky.'

'You drink. I'll be ready in a minute.'

Bond looked at the bottle and poured himself three-quarters of a toothglass and drank it straight down in two gulps. Then he gingerly lit a blessed cigarette and sat on the edge of the desk and felt the liquor burn down through his stomach into his legs.

He picked up the bottle again and looked at it. Plenty for Gala and a whole full glass for himself before he walked out through the door. Better than nothing. It wouldn't be too bad with that inside him so long as he walked quickly out and shut the doors behind him. No looking back.

Gala came in, a transformed Gala, looking as beautiful as the night he had first seen her, except for the lines of exhaustion under the eyes that the powder could not quite conceal and the angry welts at her wrists and ankles.

Bond gave her a drink and took another one himself and their eyes smiled at each other over the rims of their glasses.

Then Bond stood up.

'Listen, Gala,' he said in a matter-of-fact voice. 'We've got to face it and get it over so I'll make it short and then we'll have another drink.' He heard her catch her breath, but he went on. 'In ten minutes or so I'm going to shut you into Drax's bathroom and put you under the shower and turn it full on.'

'James,' she cried. She stepped close to him. 'Don't go on. I know you're going to say something dreadful. Please stop, James.'

'Come on, Gala,' said Bond roughly. 'What the hell does it matter. It's a bloody miracle we've got the chance.' He moved away from her. He walked to the doors leading out into the shaft.

'And then,' he said, and he held up the precious lighter in his right hand, 'I shall walk out of here and shut the doors and go and light a last cigarette under the tail of the Moonraker.'

'God,' she whispered. 'What are you saying? You're mad.' She looked at him through eyes wide with horror.

'Don't be ridiculous,' said Bond impatiently. 'What the hell else is there to do? The explosion will be so terrific that one won't feel anything. And it's bound to work with all that fuel vapour hanging around. It's me or a million people in London. The warhead won't go off. Atom bombs don't explode like that. It'll be melted probably. There's just a chance you may get away. Most of the explosion will take the line of least resistance through the roof — and down the exhaust pit, if I can work the machinery that opens up the floor.' He smiled. 'Cheer up,' he said, walking over to her and taking one of her hands. 'The boy stood on the burning deck. I've wanted to copy him since I was five.'

Gala pulled her hand away. 'I don't care what you say,' she said angrily. 'We've got to think of something else. You don't trust me to have any ideas. You just tell me what you think we've got to do.' She walked over to the wall map and pressed down the switch. 'Of course if we have to use the lighter we have to.' She gazed at the map of the false flight plan, barely seeing it. 'But the idea of you walking in there alone and standing in the middle of all those ghastly fumes from the fuel and calmly flicking that thing and then being blown to dust . . . And anyway, if we have to do it, we'll do it together. I'd rather that than be burnt to death in here. And anyway,' she paused, 'I'd like to go with you. We're in this together.'

Bond's eyes were tender as he walked towards her and put an arm round her waist and hugged her to him. 'Gala, you're a darling,' he said simply. 'And if there's any other way we'll take it. But,' he looked at his watch, 'it's past midnight and we've got to decide quickly. At any moment it may occur to Drax to send guards down to see that we're all right, and God knows what time he'll be coming down to set the gyros.'

Gala twisted her body round like a cat. She gazed at him with her mouth open, her face taut with excitement. 'The gyros,' she whispered, 'to set the gyros.' She leant weakly back against the wall, her eyes searching Bond's face. 'Don't you SEE?' Her voice was on the edge of hysteria. 'After he's gone, we could alter the gyros back, back to the old flight plan, then the rocket will simply fall into the North Sea where it's supposed to go.'

She stepped away from the wall and seized his shirt in both hands and looked imploringly at him. 'Can't we?' she said. 'Can't we?'

'Do you know the other settings?' asked Bond sharply.

'Of course I do,' she said urgently. 'I've been living with them for a year. We won't have a weather report but we'll just have to chance that. The forecast this morning said we would have the same conditions as today.'

'By God,' said Bond. 'We might do it. If only we can hide somewhere and make Drax think we've escaped. What about the exhaust pit? If I can work the machine to open the floor.'

'It's a straight hundred-foot drop,' said Gala, shaking her head. 'And the walls are polished steel. Just like glass. And there's no rope or anything down here. They cleared everything out of the workshop yesterday. And anyway there are guards on the beach.'

Bond reflected. Then his eyes brightened. 'I've got an idea,' he said. 'But first of all what about the radar, the homing device in London. Won't that pull the rocket off its course and back on to London?'

Gala shook her head. 'It's only got a range of about a hundred miles,' she said. 'The rocket won't even pick up its signal. If it's aimed into the North Sea it will get into the orbit of the transmitter on the raft. There's absolutely nothing wrong with my plan. But where can we hide?'

'One of the ventilator shafts,' said Bond. 'Come on.'

He gave a last look round the room. The lighter was in his pocket. That would still be the last resort. There was nothing else they would want. He followed Gala out into the gleaming shaft and made for the instrument panel which controlled the steel cover to the exhaust pit.

After a quick examination he threw over a heavy lever from '*Zu*' to '*Auf*'. There was a soft hiss from the hydraulic machinery behind the wall and the two semi-circles of steel opened beneath the tail of the rocket and slid back into their grooves. He walked over and looked down.

The arcs in the roof above glinted back at him from the polished walls of the wide steel funnel until they curved away out of sight towards the distant hollow boom of the sea.

Bond went back into Drax's office and pulled down the shower curtain in the bathroom. Then Gala and he tore it into strips and tied them together. He made a jagged rent at the end of the last strip so as to give an impression that the escape rope had broken. Then he tied the other end firmly round the pointed tip of one of the Moonraker's three fins and dropped the rest so that it hung down the shaft.

It was not much of a false scent, but it might gain some time.

The big round mouths of the ventilator shafts were spaced about ten yards apart and about four feet off the floor. Bond counted. There were fifty of them. He carefully opened the hinged grating that covered one of them and looked up. Forty feet away there was a faint glimmer from the moonlight outside. He decided that they were tunnelled straight up inside the wall of the site until they turned at right angles towards the gratings in the outside walls.

Bond reached up and ran his hand along the surface. It was unfinished roughcast concrete and he grunted with satisfaction as he felt first one sharp protuberance and then another. They were the jagged ends of the steel rods reinforcing the walls, cut off where the shafts had been bored.

It was going to be a painful business, but there was no doubt they could inch their way up one of these shafts, like mountaineers up a rock chimney, and, in the turn at the top, lie hidden from anything but the sort of painstaking search that would be difficult in the morning with all the officials from London round the site.

Bond knelt down and the girl climbed on to his back and started up.

An hour later, their feet and shoulders bruised and cut, they lay exhausted, squeezed tight in each other's arms, their heads inches away from the circular grating directly above the outside door, and listened to the guards restlessly shifting their feet in the darkness a hundred yards away.

Five o'clock, six, seven.

Slowly the sun came up behind the dome and the seagulls started to call in the cliffs and then suddenly there were the three figures walking towards them in the distance, passed by a fresh platoon of guards doubling, chins up, knees up, to relieve the night watch.

The figures came nearer and the squinting, exhausted eyes of the hidden couple could see every detail of Drax's blood-orange face, the lean, pale foxiness of Dr. Walter, the suety, overslept puffiness of Krebs.

The three men walked like executioners, saying nothing. Drax took out his key and they silently filed through the door a few feet below the taut bodies of Bond and Gala.

Then for ten minutes there was silence except for the occasional boom of voices up the ventilator shaft as the three men moved about down on the steel floor round the exhaust pit. Bond smiled to himself at the thought of the rage and consternation on Drax's face; the miserable Krebs wilting under the lash of Drax's tongue; the bitter accusation in Walter's eyes. Then the door burst open beneath him and Krebs was calling urgently to the leader of the guards. A man detached himself from the semi-circle and ran up.

'*Die Engländer.*' Krebs's voice was almost hysterical. 'Escaped. The *Herr Kapitän* thinks they may be in one of the ventilator shafts. We are going to take a chance. The dome will be opened again and we will clear out the fumes from the fuel. And then the *Herr Doktor* will put the steam hose up each shaft. If they're there it will finish them. Choose four men. The rubber gloves and firesuits are down there. We'll take the pressure off the heating. Tell the others to listen for the screams. *Verstanden?* '

'*Zu Befehl.*' The man doubled smartly back to his troop and Krebs, the sweat of anxiety on his face, turned and disappeared back through the door.

For a moment Bond lay motionless.

There was a heavy rumble above their heads as the dome divided and swung open.

The steam hose!

He had heard of mutinies in ships being fought with it. Rioters in factories. Would it reach forty feet? Would the pressure last? How many boilers fed the heating? Among the fifty ventilator shafts, where would they choose to begin? Had Bond or Gala left any clue to the one they had climbed?

He felt that Gala was waiting for him to explain. To do something. To protect them.

Five men came doubling from the semi-circle of guards. They passed underneath and disappeared.

Bond put his mouth to Gala's ear. 'This may hurt,' he said. 'Can't say how much. Can't be helped. Just have to take it. No noise.' He felt the answering tentative pressure from her arms.

'Bring your knees up. Don't be shy. This is no time to be maidenly.'

'Shut up,' whispered Gala angrily. He felt one knee creep up until it was locked between his thighs. His own knee followed suit until it would go no further. She squirmed furiously. 'Don't be a bloody fool,' whispered Bond, pulling her head in close to his chest so that it was half covered by his open shirt.

He overlay her as much as possible. There was nothing to be done about their ankles or his hands. He pulled his shirt collar up as far over their heads as possible. They held tightly to each other.

Hot, cramped, breathless. Waiting, it suddenly occurred to Bond, like two lovers in the undergrowth. Waiting for the footsteps to go by so that they could start again. He smiled grimly to himself and listened.

There was silence down the shaft. They must be in the engine room. Walter would be watching the hose being coupled to the outlet valve. Now there were distant noises. Where would they start?

Somewhere, not far away, there was a soft, long-drawn-out whisper, like the inefficient whistle of a distant train.

He drew his shirt collar back and stole a look out through the grating at the guards. Those he could see were looking straight at the launching-dome, somewhere to his left.

Again the long harsh whisper. And again.

It was getting louder. He could see the heads of the guards pivoting towards the grating in the wall which hid him and Gala. They must be watching, fascinated, as the thick white jets of steam shot out through the gratings high up in the cement wall, wondering if this one, or that one, or that one, would be accompanied by a double scream.

He could feel Gala's heart beating against his. She didn't know what was coming. She trusted him.

'It may hurt,' he whispered to her again. 'It may burn. It won't kill us. Be brave. Don't make a sound.'

'I'm all right,' she whispered angrily. But he could feel her body press closer in to his.

Whoosh. It was getting closer.

Whoosh! Two away.

WHOOSH!! Next door. A suspicion of the wet smell of steam came to him.

Hold tight, Bond said to himself. He smothered her in towards him and held his breath.

Now. Quick. Get it over, damn you.

And suddenly there was a great pressure and heat and a roaring in the ears and a moment of blazing pain.

Then dead silence, a mixture of sharp cold and fire on the ankles and hands, a feeling of soaking wet and a desperate, choking effort to get pure air into the lungs.

Their bodies automatically fought to withdraw from each other, to capture some inches of space and air for the areas of skin that were already blistering. The breath rattled in their throats and the water poured off the cement into their open mouths until they bent sideways and choked the water out to join the trickle that was oozing under their soaking bodies and along past their scalded ankles and then down the vertical walls of the shaft up which they had come.

And the howl of the steam pipe drew away from them until it became a whisper and finally stopped, and there was silence in their narrow cement prison except for their stubborn breathing and the ticking of Bond's watch.

And the two bodies lay and waited, nursing their pain.

Half an hour — half a year — later, Walter and Krebs and Drax filed out below them.

But, as a precaution, the guards had been left behind in the launching-dome.

24

ZERO

'THEN WE'RE ALL agreed?'

'Yes, Sir Hugo.' It was the Minister of Supply speaking. Bond recognized the dapper, assured figure. 'Those are the settings. My people have checked them independently with the Air Ministry this morning.'

'Then if you'll allow me the privilege.' Drax held up the slip of paper and made to turn towards the launching-dome.

'Hold it, Sir Hugo. Just like that, please. Arm in the air.' The bulbs flashed and the bank of cameras whirred and clicked for the last time and Drax turned and walked the few yards towards the dome, almost, it seemed to Bond, looking him straight in the eye through the grating above the door of the site.

The small crowd of reporters and cameramen dissolved and straggled off across the concrete apron, leaving only a nervously chatting group of officials to wait for Drax to emerge.

Bond looked at his watch. 11.45. Hurry up, damn you, he thought.

For the hundredth time he repeated to himself the figures Gala had taught him during the hours of cramped pain that had followed their ordeal by steam, and for the hundredth time he shifted his limbs to keep the circulation going.

'Get ready,' he whispered into Gala's ear. 'Are you all right?'

He could feel the girl smile. 'Fine.' She shut her mind to the thought of her blistered legs and the quick rasping descent back down the ventilator shaft.

The door clanged shut beneath them followed by the click of the lock and, preceded by the five guards, the figure of Drax appeared below striding masterfully towards the group of officials, the slip of lying figures in his hand.

Bond looked at his watch. 11.47. 'Now,' he whispered.

'Good luck,' she whispered back.

Slither, scrape, rip. His shoulders carefully expanding and contracting; blistered, bloodstained feet scrabbling for the sharp knobs of iron, Bond, his lacerated body tearing its way down the forty feet of shaft, prayed that the girl would have strength to stand it when she followed.

A last ten-foot drop that jarred his spine, a kick at the grating and he was out on the steel floor and running for the stairs, leaving a trail of red footprints and a spray of blood-drops from his raw shoulders.

The arcs had been extinguished, but the daylight streamed down through the open roof and the blue from the sky mingling with the fierce glitter of the sunshine gave Bond the impression that he was running up inside a huge sapphire.

The great deadly needle in the centre might have been made of glass. Looking above him as he sweated and panted up the endless sweep of the iron stairway, it was difficult for him to see where its tapering nose ended and the sky began.

Behind the crouching silence that enveloped the shimmering bullet, Bond could hear a quick, deadly ticking, the hasty tripping of tiny metal feet somewhere in the body of the Moonraker. It filled the great steel chamber like the beating heart in Poe's story and Bond knew that directly Drax at the firing point pressed the switch that sent the radio beam zinging over the two hundred yards to the waiting rocket, the ticking would suddenly cease, there would be the soft whine of the lighted pinwheel, a wisp of steam from the turbines, and then the howling jet of flame on which the rocket would slowly rise and sweep majestically out on the start of its gigantic acceleration curve.

And then in front of him there was the spidery arm of the gantry folded back against the wall and Bond's hand was at the lever and the arm was slowly stretching down and out towards the square hairline on the glittering skin of the rocket that was the door of the gyro chamber.

Bond, on hands and knees, was along it even before the rubber pads came to rest against the polished chrome. There was the flush disc the size of a shilling, just as Gala had described. Press, click, and the tiny door had flicked open on its hard spring. Inside. Careful not to cut your head. The gleaming handles beneath the staring compass-roses. Turn. Twist. Steady.

That's for the roll. Now the pitch and yaw. Turn. Twist, ever so gently. And steady. A last look. A glance at his watch. Four minutes to go. Don't panic. Back out. Door click. A cat-like scurry. Don't look down. Gantry up. Clang against the wall. And now for the stairs.

Tick-tick-tick-tick.

As Bond shot down he caught a glimpse of Gala's tense, white face as she stood holding open the outer door of Drax's office. God, how his body hurt! A final leap and a clumsy swerve to the right. Clang as Gala slammed the outer door. Another clang and they were across the room and into the shower and the water was hissing down on their clinging, panting bodies.

Through the noise of it, above the beating of his heart, Bond heard a sudden crackle of static and then the voice of the B.B.C. announcer coming from the big set in Drax's room a few inches away through the thin wall of the bathroom. It had been Gala again who had remembered Drax's wireless and who had found time to throw the switches while Bond was working on the gyros.

' . . . be five minutes delay,' said the breezy, excited voice. 'Sir Hugo has been persuaded to say a few words into the microphone.' Bond turned off the shower and the voice came to them more clearly. 'He looks very confident. Just saying something into the Minister's ear. They're both laughing. Wonder what it was? Ah, here's my colleague with the latest weather report from the Air Ministry. What's that? Perfect at all altitudes. Good show. It certainly is a wonderful day down below here. Haha. Those crowds in the distance by the coastguard station will be getting quite a sunburn. There must be thousands. What's that you say? Twenty thousand? Well, it certainly looks like it. And Walmer Beach is black with them too. The whole of Kent seems to be out. Terrible crick in the neck we're all going to get, I'm afraid. Worse than Wimbledon. Haha. Hullo, what's going on down there by the jetty? By jove, there's a submarine just surfaced alongside. I say, what a sight. One of our biggest I should say. And Sir Hugo's team is down there too. Lined up on the jetty as if they were on parade. Magnificent body of men. Now they're filing on board. Perfect discipline. Must be an idea of the Admiralty's. Give them a special grandstand out in the Channel. Splendid show. Wish you could be here to see it. Now

Sir Hugo is coming towards us. In a moment he'll be speaking to you. Fine figure of a man. Everyone in the firing point is giving him a cheer. I'm sure we all feel like cheering him today. He's coming into the firing point. I can see the sun glinting on the nose of the Moonraker way over there behind him. Just showing out of the top of the launching-dome. Hope somebody's got a camera. Now here he is.' A pause. 'Sir Hugo Drax.'

Bond looked into Gala's dripping face. Soaked and bleeding they stood in each other's arms, speechless and trembling slightly with the storm of their emotions. Their eyes were blank and fathomless as they met and held each other's gaze.

'Your Majesty, men and women of England.' The voice was a velvet snarl. 'I am about to change the course of England's history.' A pause. 'In a few minutes' time the lives of all of you will be altered, in some cases, ahem, drastically, by the, er, impact of the Moonraker. I am very proud and pleased that fate has singled me out, from amongst all my fellow countrymen, to fire this great arrow of vengeance into the skies and thus to proclaim for all time, and for all the world to witness, the might of my fatherland. I hope that this occasion will be forever a warning that the fate of my country's enemies will be written in dust, in ashes, in tears, and,' a pause, 'in blood. And now thank you all for listening and I sincerely hope that those of you who are able will repeat my words to your children, if you have any, tonight.'

A rattle of rather hesitant applause sounded out of the machine and then came the breezy voice of the announcer. 'And that was Sir Hugo Drax saying a few words to you before he walks across the floor of the firing point to the switch on the wall which will fire the Moonraker. The first time he has spoken in public. Very, ahem, forthright. Doesn't mince his words. However, a lot of us will say there's no harm in that. And now it's time for me to hand over to the expert, Group Captain Tandy of the Ministry of Supply, who will describe to you the actual firing of the Moonraker. After that you will hear Peter Trimble in one of the naval security patrols, H.M.S. *Merganzer*, describe the scene in the target area. Group Captain Tandy.'

Bond glanced at his watch. 'Only a minute more,' he said to Gala. 'God, I'd like to get my hands on Drax. Here,' he reached for the cake of soap and gouged some pieces off it, 'stuff this in your ears when the time comes. The noise is going to be terrific. I don't know about the heat. It won't last long and the steel walls may stand up to it.'

Gala looked at him. She smiled. 'If you hold me it won't be too bad,' she said.

'. . . and now Sir Hugo has his hand on the switch and he's watching the chronometer.'

'TEN,' broke in another voice, heavy and sonorous as the toll of a bell.

Bond turned on the shower and the water hissed down on their clinging bodies.

'NINE,' tolled the voice of the time-keeper.

'. . . the radar operators are watching the screens. Nothing but a mass of wavy lines . . . '

'EIGHT.'

'. . . all wearing ear-plugs. Blockhouse should be indestructible. Concrete walls are twelve feet thick. Pyramid roof, twenty-seven feet thick at the point . . . '

'SEVEN.'

'. . . first the radio beam will stop the time mechanism alongside the turbines. Set the pinwheel going. Flaming thing like a catherine wheel . . . '

'SIX.'

'. . . Valves will open. Liquid fuel. Secret formula. Terrific stuff. Dynamite. Pours down from the fuel tanks . . . '

'FIVE.'

'. . . ignited by the pinwheel when the fuel gets to the rocket motor . . . '

'FOUR.'

'. . . meanwhile the peroxide and permanganate have mixed, made steam and the turbine pumps begin to turn . . . '

'THREE.'

'. . . pumping the flaming fuel through the motor out of the stern of the rocket into the exhaust pit. Gigantic heat . . . 3,500 degrees . . . '

'TWO.'

'. . . Sir Hugo is about to press the switch. He's staring out through the slit. Perspiration on his forehead. Absolute silence in here. Terrific tension.'

'ONE.'

Nothing but the noise of the water, steadily pouring down on the two clinging bodies.

FIRE!

Bond's heart jumped into his throat at the shout. He felt Gala shudder. Silence. Nothing but the hissing of the water . . .

' . . . Sir Hugo's left the firing point. Walking calmly over to the edge of the cliff. So confident. He's stepped on to the hoist. He's going down. Of course. He must be going out to the submarine. Television screen shows a little steam coming out of the tail of the rocket. A few more seconds. Yes, he's out on the jetty. He looked back and raised his arm in the air. Good old Sir Hu . . . '

A soft thunder came to Bond and Gala. Louder. Louder. The tiled floor began to tremble under their feet. A hurricane scream. They were being pulverized by it. The walls were quaking, steaming. Their legs began going out of control under their teetering bodies. Hold her up. Hold her up. Stop it! Stop it!! STOP THAT NOISE!!!

Christ, he was going to faint. The water was boiling. Must turn it off. Got it. No. Pipe's burst. Steam, smell, iron, paint.

Get her out! Get her out!! Get her out!!!

And then there was silence. Silence you could feel, hold, squeeze. And they were on the floor of Drax's office. Only the light in the bathroom still shining out. And the smoke's clearing. And the filthy smell of burning iron and paint. Being sucked out by the air-conditioner. And the steel wall is bent towards them like a huge blister. Gala's eyes are open and she's smiling. But the rocket. What happened? London? North Sea? The radio. Looks all right. He shook his head and the deafness slowly cleared. He remembered the soap. Gouged it out.

' . . . through the sound barrier. Travelling perfectly, right in the centre of the radar screen. A perfect launching. Afraid you couldn't hear anything because of the noise. Terrific. First of all the great sheet of flame coming out of the cliff from the exhaust pit and then you should have seen the nose slowly creep up out of the dome. And there she was like a great silver pencil. Standing upright on this huge column of flame and slowly climbing into the air and the flame splashing for hundreds of yards over the concrete. The howl of the thing must have nearly burst our microphones. Great bits have fallen off the cliff and the concrete looks like a spider's web. Terrible vibration. And then she was climbing faster and faster. A hundred miles an hour. A thousand. And,' he broke off, 'what's that you say? Really! And now she's travelling at over ten thousand miles an hour! She's three hundred miles up. Can't hear her any more, of course. We could only see her flame for a few seconds. Like a star. Sir Hugo must be a proud man. He's out there in the Channel now. The submarine went off like a rocket, haha, must be doing more than thirty knots. Throwing up a huge wake. Off the East Goodwins now. Travelling north. She'll soon be up with the patrol ships. They'll have a view of the launching and of the landing. Quite a surprise trip that. No one here had an inkling. Even the Naval authorities seem a bit mystified. C.-in-C. Nore has been on the telephone. But now that's all I can tell you from here and I'll hand you over to Peter Trimble on board H.M.S. *Merganzer* somewhere off the east coast.'

Nothing but the pumping lungs showed that the two limp bodies in the creeping pool of water on the floor were still alive, but their battered ear-drums were desperately clinging to the crackle of static that came briefly from the blistered metal cabinet. Now for the verdict on their work.

'And this is Peter Trimble speaking. It's a beautiful morning, I mean — er — afternoon here. Just north of the Goodwin Sands. Calm as a millpond. No wind. Bright sunshine. And the target area is reported clear of shipping. Is that right, Commander Edwards? Yes, the Captain says it's quite clear. Nothing on the radar screens yet. I'm not allowed to tell you the range we shall pick her up at. Security and all that. But we shall only catch the rocket for a split second. Isn't that right, Captain? But the target's just showing on the screen. Out of sight from the bridge, of course. Must be seventy miles north of here. We could see the Moonraker going up. Terrific sight. Noise like thunder. Long flame coming out of the tail. Must have been ten miles away but you couldn't miss the light. Yes, Captain? Oh yes, I see. Well, that's very interesting. Big submarine coming up fast. Only about a mile away. Suppose it's the one they say Sir Hugo's aboard with his men. None of us here were told anything about her. Captain Edwards says she doesn't answer the Aldis lamp. Not flying colours. Very mysterious. I've got her now. Quite clear in my glasses. We've changed course to intercept her. The Captain says she isn't one of ours. Thinks she must be a foreigner. Hullo! She's broken out her colours. WHAT'S that? Good heavens. The Captain says she's a Russian. I say! And now she's hauled down her colours and she's submerging. Bang. Did you hear that? We fired a shot across her bows. But she's disappeared. What's that? The asdic operator says she's going even faster under water. Twenty-five knots. Terrific. Well, she can't see much under water. But she's right in the target area now. Twelve minutes past noon. The Moonraker must have turned and be on her way down. A thousand miles up. Coming down at ten thousand miles an hour. She'll be here any second now. Hope there's not going to be a tragedy. The Russian's well inside the danger zone. The radar operator's holding up his hand. That means she's due. She's coming. She's COMING. . . . Whew! Not even a whisper. GOD! What's that? Look out! Look out! Terrific explosion. Black cloud going up into the air. There's a tidal wave coming at us. Great wall of water tearing down. There goes the submarine. God! Thrown out of the water upside down. It's coming. It's COMING . . . '

25

ZERO PLUS

'... TWO HUNDRED DEAD so far and about the same number missing,' said M. 'Reports still coming in from the east coast and there's bad news from Holland. Breached miles of their sea defences. Most of our losses were among the patrol craft. Two of them capsized, including the *Merganzer*. Commanding Officer missing. And that B.B.C. chap. Goodwin Lightships broke their moorings. No news from Belgium or France yet. There are going to be some pretty heavy bills to pay when everything gets sorted out.'

It was the next afternoon and Bond, a rubber-tipped stick beside his chair, was back where he had started — across the desk from the quiet man with the cold grey eyes who had invited him to dinner and a game of cards a hundred years ago.

Under his clothes Bond was latticed with surgical tape. Pain burned up his legs whenever he moved his feet. There was a vivid red streak across his left cheek and the bridge of his nose, and the tannic ointment dressing glinted in the light from the window. He held a cigarette clumsily in one gloved hand. Incredibly M. had invited him to smoke.

'Any news of the submarine, sir?' he asked.

'They've located her,' said M. with satisfaction. 'Lying on her side in about thirty fathoms. The salvage ship that was to look after the remains of the rocket is over her now. The divers have been down and there's no answer to signals against her hull. The Soviet Ambassador has been round at the Foreign Office this morning. I gather he says a salvage ship is on her way down from the Baltic, but we've said that we can't wait as the wreck's a danger to navigation.' M. chuckled. 'So she would be I dare say if anyone happened to be navigating at thirty fathoms in the Channel. But I'm glad I'm not a member of the Cabinet,' he added drily. 'They've been in session on and off since the end of the broadcast. Vallance got hold of those Edinburgh solicitors before they'd opened Drax's message to the world. I gather it's a terrific document. Reads as if it had been written by Jehovah. Vallance took it to the Cabinet last night and stayed at No. 10 to fill in the blanks.'

'I know,' said Bond. 'He kept on telephoning me at the hospital for details until after midnight. I could hardly think straight for all the dope they'd pushed into me. What's going to happen?'

'They're going to try the biggest cover-up job in history,' said M. 'A lot of scientific twaddle about the fuel having been only half used up. Unexpectedly powerful explosion on impact. Full compensation to be paid. Tragic loss of Sir Hugo Drax and his team. Great patriot. Tragic loss of one of H.M. submarines. Latest experimental model. Orders misunderstood. Very sad. Fortunately only a skeleton crew. Next of kin will be informed. Tragic loss of B.B.C. man. Unaccountable error in mistaking White Ensign for Soviet naval colours. Very similar design. White Ensign recovered from the wreck.'

'But what about the atomic explosion?' asked Bond. 'Radiation and atomic dust and all that. The famous mushroom-shaped cloud. Surely that's going to be a bit of a problem.'

'Apparently it's not worrying them too much,' said M. 'The cloud is going to be passed off as the normal formation after an explosion of that size. The Ministry of Supply know the whole story. Had to be told. Their men were down on the east coast all last night with Geiger counters and there's not been a positive report yet.' M. smiled coldly. 'The cloud's got to come down somewhere, of course, but by a happy chance such wind as there is is drifting it up north. Back home, as you might say.'

Bond smiled painfully. 'I see,' he said. 'How very appropriate.'

'Of course,' continued M., picking up his pipe and starting to fill it, 'there are going to be some nasty rumours. They've begun already. A lot of people saw you and Miss Brand being brought out of the site on stretchers. Then there's Bowaters' case against Drax for the loss of all that newsprint. There'll be the inquest on the young man who was killed in the Alfa Romeo. And somebody's got to explain away the remains of your car, amongst which,' he looked accusingly at Bond, 'a long-barrel

Colt was found. And then there's the Ministry of Supply. Vallance had to call some more of their men yesterday to help clean out that house in Ebury Street. But those people are trained to keep secrets. You won't get a leak there. Naturally it's going to be a risky business. The big lie always is. But what's the alternative? Trouble with Germany? War with Russia? Lots of people on both sides of the Atlantic would be only too glad of an excuse.'

M. paused and put a match to his pipe. 'If the story holds,' he continued reflectively, 'we shan't come out of this too badly. We've wanted one of their high-speed U-boats and we'll be glad of the clues we can pick up about their atom bombs. The Russians know that we know that their gamble failed. Malenkov's none too firmly in the saddle and this may mean another Kremlin revolt. As for the Germans. Well, we all knew there was plenty of Nazism left and this will make the Cabinet go just a bit more carefully on German rearmament. And, as a very minor consequence,' he gave a wry smile, 'it will make Vallance's security job, and mine for the matter of that, just a little bit easier in the future. These politicians can't see that the atomic age has created the most deadly saboteur in the history of the world — the little man with the heavy suitcase.'

'Will the Press wear the story?' asked Bond dubiously.

M. shrugged his shoulders. 'The Prime Minister saw the editors this morning,' he said, putting another match to his pipe, 'and I gather he's got away with it so far. If the rumours get bad later on, he'll probably have to see them again and tell them some of the truth. Then they'll play all right. They always do when it's important enough. The main thing is to gain time and stave off the firebrands. For the moment everyone's so proud of the Moonraker that they're not inquiring too closely into what went wrong.'

There was a soft burr from the intercom on M.'s desk and a ruby light winked on and off. M. picked up the single earphone and leant towards it. 'Yes?' he said. There was a pause. 'I'll take it on the Cabinet line.' He picked up the white receiver from the bank of four telephones.

'Yes,' said M. 'Speaking.' There was a pause. 'Yes, sir? Over.' M. pressed down the button of his scrambler. He held the receiver close to his ear and not a sound from it reached Bond.

There was a long pause during which M. puffed occasionally at the pipe in his left hand. He took it out of his mouth. 'I agree, sir.' Another pause. 'I know my man would have been very proud, sir. But of course it's a rule here.' M. frowned. 'If you will allow me to say so, sir, I think it would be very unwise.' A pause, then M.'s face cleared. 'Thank you, sir. And of course Vallance has not got the same problem. And it would be the least she deserves.' Another pause. 'I understand. That will be done.' Another pause. 'That's very kind of you, sir.'

M. put the white receiver back on its cradle and the scrambler button clicked back to the *en clair* position.

For a moment M. continued to look at the telephone as if in doubt about what had been said. Then he twisted his chair round away from the desk and gazed thoughtfully out of the window.

There was silence in the room and Bond shifted in his chair to ease the pain that was creeping back into his body.

The same pigeon as on Monday, or perhaps another one, came to rest on the window-sill with the same clatter of wings. It walked up and down, nodding and cooing, and then planed off towards the trees in the park. The traffic murmured sleepily in the distance.

How nearly it had come, thought Bond, to being stilled. How nearly there might be nothing now but the distant clang of the ambulance bells underneath a lurid black and orange sky, the stench of burning, the screams of people still trapped in the buildings. The softly beating heart of London silenced for a generation. And a whole generation of her people dead in the streets amongst the ruins of a civilization that might not rise again for centuries.

All that would have come about but for a man who scornfully cheated at cards to feed the fires of his maniac ego; but for the stuffy chairman of Blades who detected him; but for M. who agreed to help an old friend; but for Bond's half-remembered lessons from a card-sharper; but for Vallance's precautions; but for Gala's head for figures; but for a whole pattern of tiny circumstances, a whole pattern of chance.

Whose pattern?

There was a shrill squeak as M.'s chair swivelled round. Bond carefully focused again on the grey eyes across the desk.

'That was the Prime Minister,' M. said gruffly. 'Says he wants you and Miss Brand out of the country.' M. lowered his eyes and looked stolidly into the bowl of his pipe. 'You're both to be out by tomorrow afternoon. There are too many people in this case who know your faces. Might put two and two together when they see the shape you're both in. Go anywhere you like. Unlimited expenses for both of you. Any currency you like. I'll tell the Paymaster. Stay away a month. But keep out of circulation. You'd both be gone this afternoon only the girl's got an appointment at eleven tomorrow morning. At the Palace. Immediate award of the George Cross. Won't be gazetted until the New Year of course. Like to meet her one day. Must be a good girl. As a matter of fact,' M.'s expression as he looked up was unreadable, 'the Prime Minister had something in mind for you. Forgotten that we don't go in for those sort of things here. So he asked me to thank you for him. Said some nice things about the Service. Very kind of him.'

M. gave one of the rare smiles that lit up his face with quick brightness and warmth. Bond smiled back. They understood the things that had been left unsaid.

Bond knew it was time to go. He got up. 'Thank you very much, sir,' he said. 'And I'm glad about the girl.'

'All right then,' said M. on a note of dismissal. 'Well, that's the lot. See you in a month. Oh and by the way,' he added casually. 'Call in at your office. You'll find something there from me. Little memento.'

James Bond went down in the lift and limped along the familiar corridor to his office. When he walked through the inner door he found his secretary arranging some papers on the next desk to his.

'008 coming back?' he asked.

'Yes,' she smiled happily. 'He's being flown out tonight.'

'Well I'm glad you'll have company,' said Bond. 'I'm going off again.'

'Oh,' she said. She looked quickly at his face and then away. 'You look as if you needed a bit of a rest.'

'I'm going to get one,' said Bond. 'A month's exile.' He thought of Gala. 'It's going to be pure holiday. Anything for me?'

'Your new car's downstairs. I've inspected it. The man said you'd ordered it on trial this morning. It looks lovely. Oh, and there's a parcel from M.'s office. Shall I unpack it?'

'Yes, do,' said Bond.

He sat down at his desk and looked at his watch. Five o'clock. He was feeling tired. He knew he was going to feel tired for several days. He always got these reactions at the end of an ugly assignment, the aftermath of days of taut nerves, tension, fear.

His secretary came back into the room with two heavy-looking cardboard boxes. She put them on his desk and he opened the top one. When he saw the grease-paper he knew what to expect.

There was a card in the box. He took it out and read it. In M.'s green ink it said: 'You may be needing these.' There was no signature.

Bond unwrapped the grease-paper and cradled the shining new Beretta in his hand. A memento. No. A reminder. He shrugged his shoulders and slipped the gun under his coat into the empty holster. He got clumsily to his feet.

'There'll be a long-barrel Colt in the other box,' he said to his secretary. 'Keep it until I get back. Then I'll take it down to the range and fire it in.'

He walked to the door. 'So long, Lil,' he said, 'regards to 008 and tell him to be careful of you. I'll be in France. Station F will have the address. But only in an emergency.'

She smiled at him. 'How much of an emergency?' she asked.

Bond gave a short laugh. 'Any invitation to a quiet game of bridge,' he said.

He limped out and shut the door behind him.

The 1953 Mark VI had an open touring body. It was battleship grey like the old 4½ litre that had gone to its grave in a Maidstone garage, and the dark blue leather upholstery gave a luxurious hiss as he climbed awkwardly in beside the test driver.

Half an hour later the driver helped him out at the corner of Birdcage Walk and Queen Anne's Gate. 'We could get more speed out of her if you want it, sir,' he said. 'If we could have her back for a fortnight we could tune her to do well over the hundred.'

'Later,' said Bond. 'She's sold. On one condition. That you get her over to the ferry terminal at Calais by tomorrow evening.'

The test driver grinned. 'Roger,' he said. 'I'll take her over myself. See you on the pier, sir.'

'Fine,' said Bond. 'Go easy on A20. The Dover road's a dangerous place these days.'

'Don't worry, sir,' said the driver, thinking that this man must be a bit of a cissy for all that he seemed to know plenty about motor-cars. 'Piece of cake.'

'Not every day,' said Bond with a smile. 'See you at Calais.'

Without waiting for a reply, he limped off with his stick through the dusty bars of evening sunlight that filtered down through the trees in the park.

Bond sat down on one of the seats opposite the island in the lake and took out his cigarette-case and lit a cigarette. He looked at his watch. Five minutes to six. He reminded himself that she was the sort of girl who would be punctual. He had reserved the corner table for dinner. And then? But first there would be the long luxurious planning. What would she like? Where would she like to go? Where had she ever been? Germany, of course. France? Miss out Paris. They could do that on their way back. Get as far as they could the first night, away from the Pas de Calais. There was that farmhouse with the wonderful food between Montreuil and Etaples. Then the fast sweep down to the Loire. The little places near the river for a few days. Not the chateau towns. Places like Beaugency, for instance. Then slowly south, always keeping to the western roads, avoiding the five-star life. Slowly exploring. Bond pulled himself up. Exploring what? Each other? Was he getting serious about this girl?

'James.'

It was a clear, high, rather nervous voice. Not the voice he had expected.

He looked up. She was standing a few feet away from him. He noticed that she was wearing a black beret at a rakish angle and that she looked exciting and mysterious like someone you see driving by abroad, alone in an open car, someone unattainable and more desirable than anyone you have ever known. Someone who is on her way to make love to somebody else. Someone who is not for you.

He got up and they took each other's hands.

It was she who released herself. She didn't sit down.

'I wish you were going to be there tomorrow, James.' Her eyes were soft as she looked at him. Soft, but, he thought, somehow evasive.

He smiled. 'Tomorrow morning or tomorrow night?'

'Don't be ridiculous,' she laughed, blushing, 'I meant at the Palace.'

'What are you going to do afterwards?' asked Bond.

She looked at him carefully. What did the look remind him of? The Morphy look? The look he had given Drax on that last hand at Blades? No. Not quite. There was something else there. Tenderness? Regret?

She looked over his shoulder.

Bond turned round. A hundred yards away there was the tall figure of a young man with fair hair trimmed short. His back was towards them and he was idling along, killing time.

Bond turned back and Gala's eyes met his squarely.

'I'm going to marry that man,' she said quietly. 'Tomorrow afternoon.' And then, as if no other explanation was needed, 'His name's Detective-Inspector Vivian.'

'Oh,' said Bond. He smiled stiffly. 'I see.'

There was a moment of silence during which their eyes slid away from each other.

And yet why should he have expected anything else? A kiss. The contact of two frightened bodies clinging together in the midst of danger. There had been nothing more. And there had been the engagement ring to tell him. Why had he automatically assumed that it had only been worn to keep Drax at bay? Why had he imagined that she shared his desires, his plans?

And now what? wondered Bond. He shrugged his shoulders to shift the pain of failure — the pain of failure that is so much greater than the pleasure of success. An exit line. He must get out of these two young lives and take his cold heart elsewhere. There must be no regrets. No false sentiment. He must play the role which she expected of him. The tough man of the world. The Secret Agent. The man who was only a silhouette.

She was looking at him rather nervously, waiting to be relieved of the stranger who had tried to get his foot in the door of her heart.

Bond smiled warmly at her. 'I'm jealous,' he said. 'I had other plans for you tomorrow night.'

She smiled back at him, grateful that the silence had been broken. 'What were they?' she asked.

'I was going to take you off to a farmhouse in France,' he said. 'And after a wonderful dinner I was going to see if it's true what they say about the scream of a rose.'

She laughed. 'I'm sorry I can't oblige. But there are plenty of others waiting to be picked.'

'Yes, I suppose so,' said Bond. 'Well, goodbye, Gala.' He held out his hand.

'Goodbye, James.'

He touched her for the last time and then they turned away from each other and walked off into their different lives.

FROM RUSSIA, WITH LOVE

SMERSH is the Soviet organ of vengeance — of interrogation, torture and death — and James Bond is dedicated to the destruction of its tentacles wherever he finds them.

But, in its turn, the baleful eye of SMERSH focuses on James Bond and far away in Moscow a trap is laid for him — a death-trap baited with an enticing lure.

Ian Fleming takes us into the headquarters of SMERSH. We watch Bond's assassination being minutely devised. We sit in at the planning, we inspect the lure, we meet the executioner.

And then the button is pressed in Moscow, and in London, Istanbul and Paris the wheels begin to turn.

Will James Bond fall into the trap? Will he take the lure — the beautiful lure called Tania, first proffered to Bond wearing nothing but a black velvet ribbon round her throat?

Ian Fleming's other Secret Service thrillers — *Casino Royale, Live and Let Die, Moonraker* and *Diamonds Are Forever* — may have made your pulse race.

Be careful of *From Russia, With Love.* Weak nerves will be shredded by it.

AUTHOR'S NOTE

NOT that it matters, but a great deal of the background to this story is accurate.

SMERSH, a contraction of Smiert Spionam — Death to Spies — exists and remains today the most secret department of the Soviet government.

At the beginning of 1956, when this book was written, the strength of SMERSH at home and abroad was about 40,000 and General Grubozaboyschikov was its chief. My description of his appearance is correct.

Today, the headquarters of SMERSH are where, in Chapter 4, I have placed them — at No. 13 Sretenka Ulitsa, Moscow. The Conference Room is faithfully described and the Intelligence chiefs who meet round the table are real officials who are frequently summoned to that room for purposes similar to those I have recounted.

I. F.
March 1956

Part One

THE PLAN

I

ROSELAND

THE NAKED MAN who lay splayed out on his face beside the swimming pool might have been dead.

He might have been drowned and fished out of the pool and laid out on the grass to dry while the police or the next-of-kin were summoned. Even the little pile of objects in the grass beside his head might have been his personal effects, meticulously assembled in full view so that no one should think that something had been stolen by his rescuers.

To judge by the glittering pile, this had been, or was, a rich man. It contained the typical membership badges of the rich man's club — a money clip, made of a Mexican fifty-dollar piece and holding a substantial wad of banknotes, a well-used gold Dunhill lighter, an oval gold cigarette case with the wavy ridges and discreet turquoise button that means Fabergé, and the sort of novel a rich man pulls out of the bookcase to take into the garden — *The Little Nugget* — an old P. G. Wodehouse. There was also a bulky gold wrist-watch on a well-used brown crocodile strap. It was a Girard-Perregaux model designed for people who like gadgets, and it had a sweep second-hand and two little windows in the face to tell the day of the month, and the month, and the phase of the moon. The story it now told was 2.30 on June 10th with the moon three-quarters full.

A blue and green dragon-fly flashed out from among the rose bushes at the end of the garden and hovered in mid-air a few inches above the base of the man's spine. It had been attracted by the golden shimmer of the June sunshine on the ridge of fine blond hairs above the coccyx. A puff of breeze came off the sea. The tiny field of hairs bent gently. The dragon-fly darted nervously sideways and hung above the man's left shoulder, looking down. The young grass below the man's open mouth stirred. A large drop of sweat rolled down the side of the fleshy nose and dropped glittering into the grass. That was enough. The dragon-fly flashed away through the roses and over the jagged glass on top of the high garden wall. It might be good food, but it moved.

The garden in which the man lay was about an acre of well-kept lawn surrounded on three sides by thickly banked rose bushes from which came the steady murmur of bees. Behind the drowsy noise of the bees the sea boomed softly at the bottom of the cliff at the end of the garden.

There was no view of the sea from the garden — no view of anything except of the sky and the clouds above the twelve-foot wall. In fact you could only see out of the property from the two upstairs bedrooms of the villa that formed the fourth side of this very private enclosure. From them you could see a great expanse of blue water in front of you and, on either side, the upper windows of neighbouring villas and the tops of the trees in their gardens — Mediterranean-type evergreen oaks, stone pines, casuarinas and an occasional palm tree.

The villa was modern — a squat elongated box without ornament. On the garden side the flat pink-washed façade was pierced by four iron-framed windows and by a central glass door leading on to a small square of pale green glazed tiles. The tiles merged into the lawn. The other side of the villa, standing back a few yards from a dusty road, was almost identical. But on this side the four windows were barred, and the central door was of oak.

The villa had two medium-sized bedrooms on the upper floor and on the ground floor a sitting-room and a kitchen, part of which was walled off into a lavatory. There was no bathroom.

The drowsy luxurious silence of early afternoon was broken by the sound of a car coming down the road. It stopped in front of the villa. There was the tinny clang of a car door being slammed and the car drove on. The door bell rang twice. The naked man beside the swimming pool did not move, but, at the noise of the bell and of the departing car, his eyes had for an instant opened very wide. It was as if the eyelids had pricked up like an animal's ears. The man immediately remembered where he was and the day of the week and the time of the day. The noises were identified. The eyelids with their fringe of short sandy eyelashes drooped drowsily back over the very pale blue, opaque, inward-looking eyes. The small cruel lips opened in a wide jaw-breaking yawn which brought saliva into the mouth. The man spat the saliva into the grass and waited.

A young woman carrying a small string bag and dressed in a white cotton shirt and a short, unalluring blue skirt came through the glass door and strode mannishly across the glazed tiles and the stretch of lawn towards the naked man. A few yards away from him, she dropped her string bag on the grass and sat down and took off her cheap and rather dusty shoes. Then she stood up and unbuttoned her shirt and took it off and put it, neatly folded, beside the string bag.

The girl had nothing on under the shirt. Her skin was pleasantly sunburned and her shoulders and fine breasts shone with health. When she bent her arms to undo the side-buttons of her skirt, small tufts of fair hair showed in her armpits. The impression of a healthy animal peasant girl was heightened by the chunky hips in faded blue stockinet bathing trunks and the thick short thighs and legs that were revealed when she had stripped.

The girl put the skirt neatly beside her shirt, opened the string bag, took out an old soda-water bottle containing some heavy colourless liquid and went over to the man and knelt on the grass beside him. She poured some of the liquid, a light olive oil, scented, as was everything in that part of the world, with roses, between his shoulder blades and, after flexing her fingers like a pianist, began massaging the sterno-mastoid and the trapezius muscles at the back of the man's neck.

It was hard work. The man was immensely strong and the bulging muscles at the base of the neck hardly yielded to the girl's thumbs even when the downward weight of her shoulders was behind them. By the time she was finished with the man she would be soaked in perspiration and so utterly exhausted that she would fall into the swimming pool and then lie down in the shade and sleep until the car came for her. But that wasn't what she minded as her hands worked automatically on across the man's back. It was her instinctive horror for the finest body she had ever seen.

None of this horror showed in the flat, impassive face of the masseuse, and the upward-slanting black eyes under the fringe of short coarse black hair were as empty as oil slicks, but inside her the animal whimpered and cringed and her pulse-rate, if it had occurred to her to take it, would have been high.

Once again, as so often over the past two years, she wondered why she loathed this splendid body, and once again she vaguely tried to analyse her revulsion. Perhaps this time she would get rid of feelings which she felt guiltily certain were much more unprofessional than the sexual desire some of her patients awoke in her.

To take the small things first: his hair. She looked down at the round, smallish head on the sinewy neck. It was covered with tight red-gold curls that should have reminded her pleasantly of the formalized hair in the pictures she had seen of classical statues. But the curls were somehow too tight, too thickly pressed against each other and against the skull. They set her teeth on edge like finger-nails against pile carpet. And the golden curls came down so low into the back of the neck — almost (she thought in professional terms) to the fifth cervical vertebra. And there they stopped abruptly in a straight line of small stiff golden hairs.

The girl paused to give her hands a rest and sat back on her haunches. The beautiful upper half of her body was already shining with sweat. She wiped the back of her forearm across her forehead and reached for the bottle of oil. She poured about a tablespoonful on to the small furry plateau at the base of the man's spine, flexed her fingers and bent forward again.

This embryo tail of golden down above the cleft of the buttocks — in a lover it would have been gay, exciting, but on this man it was somehow bestial. No, reptilian. But snakes had no hair. Well, she couldn't help that. It seemed reptilian to her. She shifted her hands on down to the two mounds of the gluteal muscles. Now was the time when many of her patients, particularly the young ones on the football team, would start joking with her. Then, if she was not very careful, the suggestions would come. Sometimes she could silence these by digging sharply down towards the sciatic nerve. At other times, and particularly if she found the man attractive, there would be giggling arguments, a brief wrestling-match and a quick, delicious surrender.

With this man it was different, almost uncannily different. From the very first he had been like a lump of inanimate meat. In two years he had never said a word to her. When she had done his back and it was time for him to turn over, neither his eyes nor his body had once shown the smallest interest in her. When she tapped his shoulder, he would just roll over and gaze at the sky through half-closed lids and occasionally let out one of the long shuddering yawns that were the only sign that he had human reactions at all.

The girl shifted her position and slowly worked down the right leg towards the Achilles tendon. When she came to it, she looked back up the fine body. Was her revulsion *only* physical? Was it the reddish colour of the sunburn on the naturally milk-white skin, the sort of roast meat look? Was it the texture of the skin itself, the deep, widely spaced pores in the satiny surface? The thickly scattered orange freckles on the shoulders? Or was it the asexuality of the man? The indifference of these splendid, insolently bulging muscles? Or was it spiritual — an animal instinct telling her that inside this wonderful body there was an evil person?

The masseuse got to her feet and stood, twisting her head slowly from side to side and flexing her shoulders. She stretched her arms out sideways and then upwards and held them for a moment to get the blood down out of them. She went to her string bag and took out a hand-towel and wiped the perspiration off her face and body.

When she turned back to the man, he had already rolled over and now lay, his head resting on one open hand, gazing blankly at the sky. The disengaged arm was flung out on the grass, waiting for her. She walked over and knelt on the grass behind his head. She rubbed some oil into her palms, picked up the limp half-open hand and started kneading the short thick fingers.

The girl glanced nervously sideways at the red-brown face below the crown of tight golden curls. Superficially it was all right — handsome in a butcher's-boyish way, with its full pink cheeks, upturned nose and rounded chin. But, looked at closer, there was something cruel about the thin-lipped rather pursed mouth, a pigginess about the wide nostrils in the upturned nose, and the blankness that veiled the very pale blue eyes communicated itself over the whole face and made it look drowned and morgue-like. It was, she reflected, as if someone had taken a china doll and painted its face to frighten.

The masseuse worked up the arm to the huge biceps. Where had the man got these fantastic muscles from? Was he a boxer?

What did he do with his formidable body? Rumour said this was a police villa. The two men-servants were obviously guards of some sort, although they did the cooking and the housework. Regularly every month the man went away for a few days and she would be told not to come. And from time to time she would be told to stay away for a week, or two weeks, or a month. Once, after one of these absences, the man's neck and the upper part of his body had been a mass of bruises. On another occasion the red corner of a half-healed wound had shown under a foot of surgical plaster down the ribs over his heart. She had never dared to ask about him at the hospital or in the town. When she had first been sent to the house, one of the men-servants had told her that if she spoke about what she saw she would go to prison. Back at the hospital, the Chief Superintendent, who had never recognized her existence before, had sent for her and had said the same thing. She would go to prison. The girl's strong fingers gouged nervously into the big deltoid muscle on the point of the shoulder. She had always known it was a matter of State Security. Perhaps that was what revolted her about this splendid body. Perhaps it was just fear of the organization that had the body in custody. She squeezed her eyes shut at the thought of who he might be, of what he could order to be done to her. Quickly she opened them again. He might have noticed. But the eyes gazed blankly up at the sky.

Now — she reached for the oil — to do the face.

The girl's thumbs had scarcely pressed into the sockets of the man's closed eyes when the telephone in the house started ringing. The sound reached impatiently out into the quiet garden. At once the man was up on one knee like a runner waiting for the gun. But he didn't move forward. The ringing stopped. There was the mutter of a voice. The girl could not hear what it was saying, but it sounded humble, noting instructions. The voice stopped and one of the men-servants showed briefly at the door, made a gesture of summons, and went back into the house. Half way through the gesture, the naked man was already running. She watched the brown back flash through the open glass door. Better not let him find her there when he came out again — doing nothing, perhaps listening. She got to her feet, took two steps to the concrete edge of the pool and dived gracefully in.

Although it would have explained her instincts about the man whose body she massaged, it was as well for the girl's peace of mind that she did not know who he was.

His real name was Donovan Grant, or 'Red' Grant. But, for the past ten years, it had been Krassno Granitsky, with the code-name of 'Granit'.

He was the Chief Executioner of SMERSH, the murder *apparat* of the M.G.B., and at this moment he was receiving his instructions on the M.G.B. direct line with Moscow.

2

THE SLAUGHTERER

GRANT PUT THE telephone softly back on its cradle and sat looking at it.

The bullet-headed guard standing over him said, 'You had better start moving.'

'Did they give you any idea of the task?' Grant spoke Russian excellently but with a thick accent. He could have passed for a national of any of the Soviet Baltic provinces. The voice was high and flat as if it was reciting something dull from a book.

'No. Only that you are wanted in Moscow. The plane is on its way. It will be here in about an hour. Half an hour for refuelling and then three or four hours, depending on whether you come down at Kharkov. You will be in Moscow by midnight. You had better pack. I will order the car.'

Grant got nervously to his feet. 'Yes. You are right. But they didn't even say if it was an operation? One likes to know. It was a secure line. They could have given a hint. They generally do.'

'This time they didn't.'

Grant walked slowly out through the glass door on to the lawn. If he noticed the girl sitting on the far edge of the pool he made no sign. He bent and picked up his book, and the golden trophies of his profession, and walked back into the house and up the few stairs to his bedroom.

The room was bleak and furnished only with an iron bedstead, from which the rumpled sheets hung down on one side to the floor, a cane chair, an unpainted clothes cupboard and a cheap washstand with a tin basin. The floor was strewn with English and American magazines. Garish paper-backs and hard-cover thrillers were stacked against the wall below the window.

Grant bent down and pulled a battered Italian fibre suitcase from under the bed. He packed into it a selection of well-laundered cheap respectable clothes from the cupboard. Then he washed his body hurriedly with cold water, and the inevitably rose-scented soap, and dried himself on one of the sheets from the bed.

There was the noise of a car outside. Grant hastily dressed in clothes as drab and nondescript as those he had packed, put on his wrist-watch, pocketed his other belongings and picked up his suitcase and went down the stairs.

The front door was open. He could see his two guards talking to the driver of a battered Zil saloon. Bloody fools, he thought. (He still did most of his thinking in English.) Probably telling him to see I get on the plane all right. Probably can't imagine that a foreigner would want to live in their blasted country. The cold eyes sneered as Grant put down his suitcase on the door-step and hunted among the bunch of coats that hung from pegs on the kitchen door. He found his 'uniform', the drab raincoat and black cloth cap of Soviet officialdom, put them on, picked up his suitcase and went out and climbed in beside the plain-clothes driver, roughly shouldering aside one of the guards as he did so.

The two men stood back, saying nothing, but looking at him with hard eyes. The driver took his foot off the clutch, and the car, already in gear, accelerated fast away down the dusty road.

The villa was on the south-eastern coast of the Crimea, about half way between Feodosiya and Yalta. It was one of many official holiday *dachas* along the favourite stretch of mountainous coastline that is part of the Russian Riviera. Red Grant knew that he was immensely privileged to be housed there instead of in some dreary villa on the outskirts of Moscow. As the car climbed up into the mountains, he thought that they certainly treated him as well as they knew how, even if their concern for his welfare had two faces.

The forty-mile drive to the airport at Simferopol took an hour. There were no other cars on the road and the occasional cart from the vineyards quickly pulled into the ditch at the sound of their horn. As everywhere in Russia, a car meant an official, and an official could only mean danger.

There were roses all the way, fields of them alternating with the vineyards, hedges of them along the road and, at the approach to the airport, a vast circular bed planted with red and white varieties to make a red star against a white background. Grant was sick of them and he longed to get to Moscow and away from their sweet stench.

They drove past the entrance to the Civil Airport and followed a high wall for about a mile to the military side of the aerodrome. At a tall wire gate the driver showed his pass to two tommy-gunned sentries and drove through on to the tarmac. Several planes stood about, big camouflaged military transports, small twin-engined trainers and two Navy helicopters. The driver stopped to ask a man in overalls where to find Grant's plane. At once a metallic twanging came from the observant control tower and a loudspeaker barked at them: 'To the left. Far down to the left. Number V-BO.'

The driver was obediently motoring on across the tarmac when the iron voice barked again. 'Stop!'

As the driver jammed on his brakes, there sounded a deafening scream above their heads. Both men instinctively ducked as a flight of four MIG 17s came out of the setting sun and skimmed over them, their squat wind-brakes right down for the landing. The planes hit the huge runway one after the other, puffs of blue smoke spurting from their nose-tyres, and, with jets howling, taxied to the distant boundary line and turned to come back to the control tower and the hangars.

'Proceed!'

A hundred yards further on they came to a plane with the recognition letters V-BO. It was a two-engined Ilyushin 12. A small aluminium ladder hung down from the cabin door and the car stopped beside it. One of the crew appeared at the door. He came down the ladder and carefully examined the driver's pass and Grant's identity papers and then waved the driver away and gestured Grant to follow him up the ladder. He didn't offer to help with the suitcase, but Grant carried it up the ladder as if it had been no heavier than a book. The crewman pulled the ladder up after him, banged the wide hatch shut and went forward to the cockpit.

There were twenty empty seats to choose from. Grant settled into the one nearest the hatch and fastened his seat-belt. A short crackle of talk with the control tower came through the open door to the cockpit, the two engines whined and coughed and fired and the plane turned quickly as if it had been a motor car, rolled out to the start of the north-south runway, and, without any further preliminaries, hurtled down it and up into the air.

Grant unbuckled his seat-belt, lit a gold-tipped Troika cigarette and settled back to reflect comfortably on his past career and to consider the immediate future.

Donovan Grant was the result of a midnight union between a German professional weight-lifter and a Southern Irish waitress. The union lasted for a quarter of an hour on the damp grass behind a circus tent outside Belfast. Afterwards the father gave the mother half-a-crown and the mother walked happily home to her bed in the kitchen of a café near the railway station. When the baby was expected, she went to live with an aunt in the small village of Aughmacloy that straddles the border, and there, six months later, she died of puerperal fever shortly after giving birth to a twelve-pound boy. Before she died, she said that the boy was to be called Donovan (the weight-lifter had styled himself 'The Mighty O'Donovan) and Grant, which was her own name.

The boy was reluctantly cared for by the aunt and grew up healthy and extremely strong, but very quiet. He had no friends. He refused to communicate with other children and when he wanted anything from them he took it with his fists. In the local school he continued to be feared and disliked, but he made a name for himself boxing and wrestling at local fairs where the bloodthirsty fury of his attack, combined with guile, gave him victory over much older and bigger boys.

It was through his fighting that he came to the notice of the Sinn-Feiners who used Aughmacloy as a principal pipeline for their comings and goings with the north, and also of the local smugglers who used the village for the same purpose. When he left school he became a strong-arm man for both these groups. They paid him well for his work but saw as little of him as they could.

It was about this time that his body began to feel strange and violent compulsions around the time of the full moon. When, in October of his sixteenth year, he first got 'The Feelings' as he called them to himself, he went out and strangled a cat. This made him 'feel better' for a whole month. In November, it was a big sheep-dog, and, for Christmas, he slit the throat of a cow, at midnight in a neighbour's shed. These actions made him 'feel good'. He had enough sense to see that the village would soon start wondering about the mysterious deaths, so he bought a bicycle and on one night every month he rode off into the countryside. Often he had to go very far to find what he wanted and, after two months of having to satisfy himself with geese and chickens, he took a chance and cut the throat of a sleeping tramp.

There were so few people abroad at night that soon he took to the roads earlier, bicycling far and wide so that he came to distant villages in the dusk when solitary people were coming home from the fields and girls were going out to their trysts.

When he killed the occasional girl he did not 'interfere' with her in any way. That side of things, which he had heard talked about, was quite incomprehensible to him. It was only the wonderful act of killing that made him 'feel better'. Nothing else.

By the end of his seventeenth year, ghastly rumours were spreading round the whole of Fermanagh, Tyrone and Armagh. When a woman was killed in broad daylight, strangled and thrust carelessly into a haystack, the rumours flared into panic. Groups of vigilantes were formed in the villages, police reinforcements were brought in with police dogs, and stories about the 'Moon Killer' brought journalists to the area. Several times Grant on his bicycle was stopped and questioned, but he had powerful protection in Aughmacloy and his story of training-spins to keep him fit for his boxing were always backed up, for he was now the pride of the village and contender for the North of Ireland light-heavyweight championship.

Again, before it was too late, instinct saved him from discovery and he left Aughmacloy and went to Belfast and put himself in the hands of a broken-down boxing promoter who wanted him to turn professional. Discipline in the sleazy gymnasium was strict. It was almost a prison and, when the blood first boiled again in Grant's veins, there was nothing for it but to half kill one of his sparring partners. After twice having to be pulled off a man in the ring, it was only by winning the championship that he was saved from being thrown out by the promoter.

Grant won the championship in 1945, on his eighteenth birthday, then they took him for National Service and he became a driver in the Royal Corps of Signals. The training period in

England sobered him, or at least made him more careful when he had 'The Feelings'. Now, at the full moon, he took to drink instead. He would take a bottle of whisky into the woods round Aldershot and drink it all down as he watched his sensations, coldly, until unconsciousness came. Then, in the early hours of the morning, he would stagger back to camp, only half satisfied, but not dangerous any more. If a sentry caught him, it was only a day's C.B., because his commanding officer wanted to keep him happy for the Army championships.

But Grant's transport section was rushed to Berlin about the time of the Corridor trouble with the Russians and he missed the championships. In Berlin, the constant smell of danger intrigued him and made him even more careful and cunning. He still got dead drunk at the full moon, but all the rest of the time he was watching and plotting. He liked all he heard about the Russians, their brutality, their carelessness of human life, and their guile, and he decided to go over to them. But how? What could he bring them as a gift? What did they want?

It was the B.A.O.R. championships that finally told him to go over. By chance they took place on a night of the full moon. Grant, fighting for the Royal Corps, was warned for holding and hitting low and was disqualified in the third round for persistent foul fighting. The whole stadium hissed him as he left the ring — the loudest demonstration came from his own regiment — and the next morning the commanding officer sent for him and coldly said he was a disgrace to the Royal Corps and would be sent home with the next draft. His fellow drivers sent him to Coventry and, since no one would drive transport with him, he had to be transferred to the coveted motor cycle dispatch service.

The transfer could not have suited Grant better. He waited a few days and then, one evening when he had collected the day's outgoing mail from the Military Intelligence Headquarters on the Reichskanzlerplatz, he made straight for the Russian Sector, waited with his engine running until the British control gate was opened to allow a taxi through, and then tore through the closing gate at forty and skidded to a stop beside the concrete pillbox of the Russian Frontier post.

They hauled him roughly into the guardroom. A wooden-faced officer behind a desk asked him what he wanted.

'I want the Soviet Secret Service,' said Grant flatly. 'The Head of it.'

The officer stared coldly at him. He said something in Russian. The soldiers who had brought Grant in started to drag him out again. Grant easily shook them off. One of them lifted his tommy gun.

Grant said, speaking patiently and distinctly, 'I have a lot of secret papers. Outside. In the leather bags on the motor cycle.' He had a brainwave. 'You will get into bad trouble if they don't get to your Secret Service.'

The officer said something to the soldiers and they stood back. 'We have no Secret Service,' he said in stilted English. 'Sit down and complete this form.'

Grant sat down at the desk and filled in a long form which asked questions about anyone who wanted to visit the Eastern zone — name, address, nature of business and so forth. Meanwhile the officer spoke softly and briefly into a telephone.

By the time Grant had finished, two more soldiers, non-commissioned officers wearing drab green forage caps and with green badges of rank on their khaki uniforms, had come into the room. The frontier officer handed the form, without looking at it, to one of them and they took Grant out and put him and his motor cycle into the back of a closed van and locked the door on him. After a fast drive lasting a quarter of an hour the van stopped, and when Grant got out he found himself in the courtyard behind a large new building. He was taken into the building and up in a lift and left alone in a cell without windows. It contained nothing but one iron bench. After an hour, during which, he supposed, they went through the secret papers, he was led into a comfortable office in which an officer with three rows of decorations and the gold tabs of a full colonel was sitting behind a desk.

The desk was bare except for a bowl of roses.

Ten years later, Grant, looking out of the window of the plane at a wide cluster of lights twenty thousand feet below, which he guessed was Kharkov, grinned mirthlessly at his reflection in the Perspex window.

Roses. From that moment his life had been nothing but roses. Roses, roses, all the way.

3

POST-GRADUATE STUDIES

'SO YOU WOULD like to work in the Soviet Union, Mister Grant?' It was half an hour later and the M.G.B. colonel was bored with the interview. He thought that he had extracted from this rather unpleasant British soldier every military detail that could possibly be of interest. A few polite phrases to repay the man for the rich haul of secrets his dispatch bags had yielded, and then the man could go down to the cells and in due course be shipped off to Vorkuta or some other labour camp.

'Yes, I would like to work for you.'

'And what work could you do, Mister Grant? We have plenty of unskilled labour. We do not need truck-drivers and,' the colonel smiled fleetingly, 'if there is any boxing to be done we have plenty of men who can box. Two possible Olympic champions amongst them, incidentally.'

'I am an expert at killing people. I do it very well. I like it.'

The colonel saw the red flame that flickered for an instant behind the very pale blue eyes under the sandy lashes. He thought, the man means it. He's mad as well as unpleasant. He looked coldly at Grant, wondering if it was worth while wasting food on him at Vorkuta. Better perhaps have him shot. Or throw him back into the British Sector and let his own people worry about him.

'You don't believe me,' said Grant impatiently. This was the wrong man, the wrong department. 'Who does the rough stuff for you here?' He was certain the Russians had some sort of a murder squad. Everybody said so. 'Let me talk to them. I'll kill somebody for them. Anybody they like. Now.'

The colonel looked at him sourly. Perhaps he had better report the matter. 'Wait here.' He got up and went out of the room, leaving the door open. A guard came and stood in the doorway and watched Grant's back, his hand on his pistol.

The colonel went into the next room. It was empty. There were three telephones on the desk. He picked up the receiver of the M.G.B. direct line to Moscow. When the military operator answered he said, 'SMERSH.' When SMERSH answered he asked for the Chief of Operations.

Ten minutes later he put the receiver back. What luck! A simple, constructive solution. Whichever way it went it would turn out well. If the Englishman succeeded, it would be splendid. If he failed, it would still cause a lot of trouble in the Western Sector — trouble for the British because Grant was their man, trouble with the Germans because the attempt would frighten a lot of their spies, trouble with the Americans because they were supplying most of the funds for the Baumgarten ring and would now think Baumgarten's security was no good. Pleased with himself, the colonel walked back into his office and sat down again opposite Grant.

'You mean what you say?'

'Of course I do.'

'Have you a good memory?'

'Yes.'

'In the British Sector there is a German called Dr. Baumgarten. He lives in Flat 5 at No. 22 Kurfürstendamm. Do you know where that is?'

'Yes.'

'Tonight, with your motor cycle, you will be put back into the British Sector. Your number plates will be changed. Your people will be on the lookout for you. You will take an envelope to Dr. Baumgarten. It will be marked to be delivered by hand. In your uniform, and with this envelope, you will have no difficulty. You will say that the message is so private that you must see Dr. Baumgarten alone. Then you will kill him.' The colonel paused. His eyebrows lifted. 'Yes?'

'Yes,' said Grant stolidly. 'And if I do, will you give me more of this work?'

'It is possible,' said the colonel indifferently. 'First you must show what you can do. When you have completed your task and returned to the Soviet Sector, you may ask for Colonel Boris.' He rang a bell and a man in plain clothes came in. The colonel gestured towards him. 'This man will give you food. Later he will give you the envelope and a sharp knife of American manufacture. It is an excellent weapon. Good luck.'

The colonel reached and picked a rose out of the bowl and sniffed it luxuriously.

Grant got to his feet. 'Thank you, sir,' he said warmly.

The colonel did not answer or look up from the rose. Grant followed the man in plain clothes out of the room.

The plane roared on across the Heartland of Russia. They had left behind them the blast furnaces flaming far away to the east around Stalino and, to the west, the silver thread of the Dnieper branching away at Dnepropetrovsk. The splash of light around Kharkov had marked the frontier of the Ukraine, and the smaller blaze of the phosphate town of Kursk had come and gone. Now Grant knew that the solid unbroken blackness below hid the great central Steppe where the billions of tons of Russia's grain were whispering and ripening in the darkness. There would be no more oases of light until, in another hour, they would have covered the last three hundred miles to Moscow.

For by now Grant knew a lot about Russia. After the quick, neat, sensational murder of a vital West German spy, Grant had no sooner slipped back over the frontier and somehow fumbled his way to 'Colonel Boris' than he was put into plain clothes, with a flying helmet to cover his hair, hustled into an empty M.G.B. plane and flown straight to Moscow.

Then began a year of semi-prison which Grant had devoted to keeping fit and to learning Russian while people came and went around him — interrogators, stool-pigeons, doctors. Meanwhile, Soviet spies in England and Northern Ireland had painstakingly investigated his past.

At the end of the year Grant was given as clean a bill of political health as any foreigner can get in Russia. The spies had confirmed his story. The English and American stool-pigeons reported that he was totally uninterested in the politics or social customs of any country in the world, and the doctors and psychologists agreed that he was an advanced manic depressive whose periods coincided with the full moon. They added that Grant was also a narcissist and asexual and that his tolerance of pain was high. These peculiarities apart, his physical health was superb and, though his educational standards were hopelessly low, he was as naturally cunning as a fox. Everyone agreed that Grant was an exceedingly dangerous member of society and that he should be put away.

When the dossier came before the Head of Personnel of the M.G.B., he was about to write 'Kill him' in the margin when he had second thoughts.

A great deal of killing has to be done in the U.S.S.R., not because the average Russian is a cruel man, although some of their races are among the cruellest peoples in the world, but as an instrument of policy. People who act against the State are enemies of the State, and the State has no room for enemies. There is too much to do for precious time to be allotted to them, and, if they are a persistent nuisance, they get killed. In a country with a population of 200,000,000, you can kill many thousands a year without missing them. If, as happened in the two biggest purges, a million people have to be killed in one year, that is also not a grave loss. The serious problem is the shortage of executioners. Executioners have a short 'life'. They get tired of the work. The soul sickens of it. After ten, twenty, a hundred death-rattles, the human being, however sub-human he may be, acquires, perhaps by a process of osmosis with death itself, a germ of death which enters his body and eats into him like a canker. Melancholy and drink take him, and a dreadful lassitude which brings a glaze to the eyes and slows up the movements and destroys accuracy. When the employer sees these signs he has no alternative but to execute the executioner and find another one.

The Head of Personnel of the M.G.B. was aware of the problem and of the constant search not only for the refined assassin, but also for the common butcher. And here at last was a man who appeared to be expert at both forms of killing, dedicated to his craft and indeed, if the doctors were to be believed, destined for it.

Head of Personnel wrote a short, pungent minute on Grant's papers, marked them 'SMERSH Otdyel II' and tossed them into his OUT tray.

Department 2 of SMERSH, in charge of Operations and Executions, took over the body of Donovan Grant, changed his name to Granitsky and put him on their books.

The next two years were hard for Grant. He had to go back to school, and to a school that made him long for the chipped deal desks in the corrugated iron shed, full of the smell of little boys and the hum of drowsy blue-bottles, that had been his only conception of what a school was like. Now, in the Intelligence School for Foreigners outside Leningrad, squashed tightly among the ranks of Germans, Czechs, Poles, Balts, Chinese and Negroes, all with serious dedicated faces and pens that raced across their notebooks, he struggled with subjects that were pure double-dutch to him.

There were courses in 'General Political Knowledge', which included the history of Labour movements, of the Communist Party and the Industrial Forces of the world, and the teachings of Marx, Lenin and Stalin, all dotted with foreign names which he could barely spell. There were lessons on 'The Class-enemy we are fighting', with lectures on Capitalism and Fascism; weeks spent on 'Tactics, Agitation and Propaganda' and more weeks on the problems of minority peoples, Colonial races, the Negroes, the Jews. Every month ended with examinations during which Grant sat and wrote illiterate nonsense, interspersed with scraps of half-forgotten English history and mis-spelled Communist slogans, and inevitably had his papers torn up, on one occasion, in front of the whole class.

But he stuck it out, and when they came to 'Technical Subjects' he did better. He was quick to understand the rudiments of Codes and Ciphers, because he wanted to understand them. He was good at Communications, and immediately grasped the maze of contacts, cut-outs, couriers and post-boxes, and he got excellent marks for Fieldwork in which each student had to plan and operate dummy assignments in the suburbs and countryside around Leningrad. Finally, when it came to tests of Vigilance, Discretion, 'Safety First', Presence of Mind, Courage and Coolness, he got top marks out of the whole school.

At the end of the year, the report that went back to SMERSH concluded 'Political value Nil. Operational value Excellent' — which was just what Otdyel II wanted to hear.

The next year was spent, with only two other foreign students among several hundred Russians, at the School for Terror and Diversion at Kuchino, outside Moscow. Here Grant went triumphantly through courses in judo, boxing, athletics, photography and radio under the general supervision of the famous Colonel Arkady Fotoyev, father of the modern Soviet spy, and completed his small-arms instruction at the hands of Lieutenant-Colonel Nikolai Godlovsky, the Soviet Rifle Champion.

Twice during this year, without warning, an M.G.B. car came for him on the night of the full moon and took him to one of the Moscow jails. There, with a black hood over his head, he was allowed to carry out executions with various weapons — the rope, the axe, the sub-machine gun. Electro-cardiograms, blood-pressure and various other medical tests were applied to him before, during and after these occasions, but their purpose and findings were not revealed to him.

It was a good year and he felt, and rightly, that he was giving satisfaction.

In 1949 and '50 Grant was allowed to go on minor operations with Mobile Groups, or *Avanposts*, in the satellite countries. These were beatings-up and simple assassinations of Russian spies and intelligence workers suspected of treachery or other aberrations. Grant carried out these duties neatly, exactly and inconspicuously, and though he was carefully and constantly watched he never showed the smallest deviation from the standards required of him, and no weaknesses of character or technical skill. It might have been different if he had been required to kill when doing a solo task at the full-moon period, but his superiors, realizing that at that period he would be outside their control, or his own, chose safe dates for his operations. The moon period was reserved exclusively for butchery in the prisons, and from time to time this was arranged for him as a reward for a successful operation in cold blood.

In 1951 and '52 Grant's usefulness became more fully and more officially recognized. As a result of excellent work, notably in the Eastern Sector of Berlin, he was granted Soviet citizenship and increases in pay which by 1953 amounted to a handsome 5000 roubles a month. In 1953 he was given the rank of Major, with pension rights back-dated to the day of his first contact with 'Colonel Boris', and the villa in the Crimea was allotted to him. Two bodyguards were attached to him, partly to protect him and partly to guard against the outside chance of his 'going private', as defection is called in M.G.B. jargon, and, once a month, he was transported to the nearest jail and allowed as many executions as there were candidates available.

Naturally Grant had no friends. He was hated or feared or envied by everyone who came in contact with him. He did not even have any of those professional acquaintanceships that pass for friendship in the discreet and careful world of Soviet officialdom. But, if he noticed the fact, he didn't care. The only individuals he was interested in were his victims. The rest of his life was inside him. And it was richly and excitingly populated with his thoughts.

Then, of course, he had SMERSH. No one in the Soviet Union who has SMERSH on his side need worry about friends, or indeed about anything whatever except keeping the black wings of SMERSH over his head.

Grant was still thinking vaguely of how he stood with his employers when the plane started to lose altitude as it picked up the radar beam of Tushino Airport just south of the red glow that was Moscow.

He was at the top of his tree, the chief executioner of SMERSH, and therefore of the whole of the Soviet Union. What could he aim for now? Further promotion? More money? More gold nicknacks? More important targets? Better techniques?

There really didn't seem to be anything more to go for. Or was there perhaps some other man whom he had never heard of, in some other country, who would have to be set aside before absolute supremacy was his?

4
THE MOGULS OF DEATH

SMERSH IS THE official murder organization of the Soviet government. It operates both at home and abroad and, in 1955, it employed a total of 40,000 men and women. SMERSH is a contraction of 'Smiert Spionam', which means 'Death to Spies'. It is a name used only among its staff and among Soviet officials. No sane member of the public would dream of allowing the word to pass his lips.

The headquarters of SMERSH is a very large and ugly modern building on the Sretenka Ulitsa. It is No. 13 on this wide, dull street, and pedestrians keep their eyes to the ground as they pass the two sentries with sub-machine guns who stand on either side of the broad steps leading up to the big iron double door. If they remember in time, or can do so inconspicuously, they cross the street and pass by on the other side.

The direction of SMERSH is carried out from the second floor. The most important room on the second floor is a very large light room painted in the pale olive green that is the common denominator of government offices all over the world. Opposite the sound-proofed door, two wide windows look over the courtyard at the back of the building. The floor is close-fitted with a colourful Caucasian carpet of the finest quality. Across the far left-hand corner of the room stands a massive oak desk. The top of the desk is covered with red velvet under a thick sheet of plate glass.

On the left side of the desk are IN and OUT baskets and on the right four telephones.

From the centre of the desk, to form a T with it, a conference table stretches diagonally out across the room. Eight straight-backed red leather chairs are drawn up to it. This table is also covered with red velvet, but without protective glass. Ash-trays are on the table, and two heavy carafes of water with glasses.

On the walls are four large pictures in gold frames. In 1955, these were a portrait of Stalin over the door, one of Lenin between the two windows and, facing each other on the other two walls, portraits of Bulganin and, where until January 13th, 1954, a portrait of Beria had hung, a portrait of Army General Ivan Aleksandrovitch Serov, Chief of the Committee of State Security.

On the left-hand wall, under the portrait of Bulganin, stands a large *Televisor*, or TV set, in a handsome polished oak cabinet. Concealed in this is a tape-recorder which can be switched on from the desk. The microphone for the recorder stretches under the whole area of the conference table and its leads are concealed in the legs of the table. Next to the *Televisor* is a small door leading into a personal lavatory and wash-room and into a small projection room for showing secret films.

Under the portrait of General Serov is a bookcase containing, on the top shelves, the works of Marx, Engels, Lenin and Stalin, and more accessibly, books in all languages on espionage, counter-espionage, police methods and criminology. Next to the bookcase, against the wall, stands a long narrow table on which are a dozen large leather-bound albums with dates stamped in gold on the covers. These contain photographs of Soviet citizens and foreigners who have been assassinated by SMERSH.

About the time Grant was coming in to land at Tushino Airport, just before 11.30 at night, a tough-looking, thick-set man of about fifty was standing at this table leafing through the volume for 1954.

The Head of SMERSH, Colonel General Grubozaboyschikov, known in the building as 'G.', was dressed in a neat khaki tunic with a high collar, and dark blue cavalry trousers with two thin red stripes down the sides. The trousers ended in riding boots of soft, highly polished black leather. On the breast of the tunic were three rows of medal ribbons — two Orders of Lenin, Order of Suvorov, Order of Alexander Nevsky, Order of the Red Banner, two Orders of the Red Star, the Twenty Years Service medal and medals for the Defence of Moscow and the Capture of Berlin. At the tail of these came the rose-pink and grey ribbon of the British C.B.E. and the claret and white ribbon of the American Medal for Merit. Above the ribbons hung the gold star of a Hero of the Soviet Union.

Above the high collar of the tunic the face was narrow and sharp. There were flabby pouches under the eyes, which were round and brown and protruded like polished marbles below thick black brows. The skull was shaven clean and the tight white skin glittered in the light of the central chandelier. The mouth was broad and grim above a deeply cleft chin. It was a hard, unyielding face of formidable authority.

One of the telephones on the desk buzzed softly. The man walked with tight and precise steps to his tall chair behind the desk. He sat down and picked up the receiver of the telephone marked in white with the letters V.Ch. These letters are short for *Vysokochastoty*, or High Frequency. Only some fifty supreme officials are connected to the V.Ch. switchboard, and all are Ministers of State or Heads of selected Departments. It is served by a small exchange in the Kremlin operated by professional security officers. Even they cannot overhear conversations on it, but every word spoken over its lines is automatically recorded.

'Yes?'

'Serov speaking. What action has been taken since the meeting of the Praesidium this morning?'

'I have a meeting here in a few minutes' time, Comrade General — R.U.M.I.D., G.R.U. and of course M.G.B. After that, if action is agreed, I shall have a meeting with my Head of Operations and Head of Plans. In case liquidation is decided upon, I have taken the precaution of bringing the necessary operative to Moscow. This time I shall myself supervise the preparations. We do not want another Khoklov affair.'

'The devil knows we don't. Telephone me after the first meeting. I wish to report to the Praesidium tomorrow morning.'

'Certainly, Comrade General.'

General G. put back the receiver and pressed a bell under his desk. At the same time he switched on the wire-recorder. His A.D.C., an M.G.B. captain, came in.

'Have they arrived?'

'Yes, Comrade General.'

'Bring them in.'

In a few minutes six men, five of them in uniform, filed in through the door and, with hardly a glance at the man behind the desk, took their places at the conference table. They were three senior officers, heads of their departments, and each was accompanied by an A.D.C. In the Soviet Union, no man goes alone to a conference. For his own protection, and for the reassurance of his department, he invariably takes a witness so that his department can have independent versions of what went on at the conference and, above all, of what was said on its behalf. This is important in case there is a subsequent investigation. No notes are taken at the conference and decisions are passed back to departments by word of mouth.

On the far side of the table sat Lieutenant-General Slavin, head of the G.R.U., the intelligence department of the General Staff of the Army, with a full colonel beside him. At the end of the table sat Lieutenant-General Vozdvishensky of R.U.M.I.D., the Intelligence Department of the Ministry of Foreign Affairs, with a middle-aged man in plain clothes. With his back to the door, sat Colonel of State Security Nikitin, Head of Intelligence for the M.G.B., the Soviet Secret Service, with a major at his side.

'Good evening, Comrades.'

A polite, careful murmur came from the three senior officers. Each one knew, and thought he was the only one to know, that the room was wired for sound, and each one, without telling his A.D.C., had decided to utter the bare minimum of words consonant with good discipline and the needs of the State.

'Let us smoke.' General G. took out a packet of Moskwa-Volga cigarettes and lit one with an American Zippo lighter. There was a clicking of lighters round the table. General G. pinched the long cardboard tube of his cigarette so that it was almost flat and put it between his teeth on the right side of his mouth. He stretched his lips back from his teeth and started talking in short clipped sentences that came out with something of a hiss from between the teeth and the uptilted cigarette.

'Comrades, we meet under instructions from Comrade General Serov. General Serov, on behalf of the Praesidium, has ordered me to make known to you certain matters of State Policy. We are then to confer and recommend a course of action which will be in line with this Policy and assist it. We have to reach our decision quickly. But our decision will be of supreme importance to the State. It will therefore have to be a correct decision.'

General G. paused to allow the significance of his words time to sink in. One by one, he slowly examined the faces of the three senior officers at the table. Their eyes looked stolidly back at him. Inside, these extremely important men were perturbed. They were about to look through the furnace door. They were about to learn a State secret, the knowledge of which might one day have most dangerous consequences for them. Sitting in the quiet room, they felt bathed in the dreadful incandescence that shines out from the centre of all power in the Soviet Union — the High Praesidium.

The final ash fell off the end of General G.'s cigarette on to his tunic. He brushed it off and threw the cardboard butt into the basket for secret waste beside his desk. He lit another cigarette and spoke through it.

'Our recommendation concerns a conspicuous act of terrorism to be carried out in enemy territory within three months.'

Six pairs of expressionless eyes stared at the head of SMERSH, waiting.

'Comrades,' General G. leant back in his chair and his voice became expository, 'the foreign policy of the U.S.S.R. has entered a new phase. Formerly, it was a "Hard" policy — a policy [he allowed himself the joke on Stalin's name] of steel. This policy, effective as it was, built up tensions in the West, notably in America, which were becoming dangerous. The Americans are unpredictable people. They are hysterical. The reports of our Intelligence began to indicate that we were pushing America to the brink of an undeclared atomic attack on the U.S.S.R. You have read these reports and you know what I say is true. We do not want such a war. If there is to be a war, it is we who will choose the time. Certain powerful Americans, notably the Pentagon Group led by Admiral Radford, were helped in their firebrand schemes by the very successes of our "Hard" policy. So it was decided that the time had come to change our methods, while maintaining our aims. A new policy was created — the "Hard-Soft" policy. Geneva was the beginning of this policy. We were "soft". China threatens Quemoy and Matsu. We are "hard". We open our frontiers to a lot of newspaper men and actors and artists although we know many of them to be spies. Our leaders laugh and make jokes at receptions in Moscow. In the middle of the jokes we drop the biggest test bomb of all time. Comrades Bulganin and Khrushchev and Comrade General Serov [General G. carefully included the names for the ears of the tape-recorder] visit India and the East and blackguard the English. When they get back, they have friendly discussions with the British Ambassador about their forthcoming goodwill visit to London. And so it goes on — the stick and then the carrot, the smile and then the frown. And the West is confused. Tensions are relaxed before they have time to harden. The reactions of our enemies are clumsy, their strategy disorganized. Meanwhile the common people laugh at our jokes, cheer our football teams and slobber with delight when we release a few prisoners of war whom we wish to feed no longer!'

There were smiles of pleasure and pride round the table. What a brilliant policy! What fools we are making of them in the West!

'At the same time,' continued General G., himself smiling thinly at the pleasure he had caused, 'we continue to forge everywhere stealthily ahead — revolution in Morocco, arms to Egypt, friendship with Yugoslavia, trouble in Cyprus, riots in Turkey, strikes in England, great political gains in France — there is no front in the world on which we are not quietly advancing.'

General G. saw the eyes shining greedily round the table. The men were softened up. Now it was time to be hard. Now it was time for them to feel the new policy on themselves. The Intelligence services would also have to pull their weight in this great game that was being played on their behalf. Smoothly General G. leaned forward. He planted his right elbow on the desk and raised his fist in the air.

'But Comrades,' his voice was soft, 'where has there been failure in carrying out the State Policy of the U.S.S.R.? Who has all along been soft when we wished to be hard? Who has suffered defeats while victory was going to all other departments of the State? Who, with their stupid blunders, has made the Soviet Union look foolish and weak throughout the world? WHO?'

The voice had risen almost to a scream. General G. thought how well he was delivering the denunciation demanded by the

Praesidium. How splendid it would sound when the tape was played back to Serov!

He glared down the conference table at the pale, expectant faces. General G.'s fist crashed forward on to the desk.

'The whole Intelligence *apparat* of the Soviet Union, Comrades.' The voice was now a furious bellow. 'It is we who are the sluggards, the saboteurs, the traitors! It is we who are failing the Soviet Union in its great and glorious struggle! We!' His arm swept round the room. 'All of us!' The voice came back to normal, became more reasonable. 'Comrades, look at the record. *Sookin Sin* [he allowed himself the peasant obscenity], son-of-a-bitch, look at the record! First we lose Gouzenko and the whole of the Canadian *apparat* and the scientist Fuchs, then the American *apparat* is cleaned up, then we lose men like Tokaev, then comes the scandalous Khoklov affair which did great damage to our country, then Petrov and his wife in Australia — a bungled business if ever there was one! The list is endless — defeat after defeat, and the devil knows I have not mentioned the half of it.'

General G. paused. He continued in his softest voice. 'Comrades, I have to tell you that unless tonight we make a recommendation for a great Intelligence victory, and unless we act correctly on that recommendation, if it is approved, there will be trouble.'

General G. sought for a final phrase to convey the threat without defining it. He found it. 'There will be,' he paused and looked, with artificial mildness, down the table, 'displeasure.'

5

KONSPIRATSIA

THE MOUJIKS HAD received the knout. General G. gave them a few minutes to lick their wounds and recover from the shock of the official lashing that had been meted out.

No one said a word for the defence. No one spoke up for his department or mentioned the countless victories of Soviet Intelligence that could be set against the few mistakes. And no one questioned the right of the Head of SMERSH, who shared the guilt with them, to deliver this terrible denunciation. The Word had gone out from the Throne, and General G. had been chosen as the mouthpiece for the Word. It was a great compliment to General G. that he had been thus chosen, a sign of grace, a sign of coming preferment, and everyone present made a careful note of the fact that, in the Intelligence hierarchy, General G., with SMERSH behind him, had come to the top of the pile.

At the end of the table, the representative of the Foreign Ministry, Lieutenant-General Vozdvishensky of R.U.M.I.D., watched the smoke curl up from the tip of his long Kazbek cigarette and remembered how Molotov had privately told him, when Beria was dead, that General G. would go far. There had been no great foresight in this prophecy, reflected Vozdvishensky. Beria had disliked G. and had constantly hindered his advancement, side-tracking him away from the main ladder of power into one of the minor departments of the then Ministry of State Security, which, on the death of Stalin, Beria had quickly abolished as a Ministry. Until 1952, G. had been deputy to one of the heads of this Ministry. When the post was abolished, he devoted his energies to plotting the downfall of Beria, working under the secret orders of the formidable General Serov, whose record put him out of even Beria's reach.

Serov, a Hero of the Soviet Union and a veteran of the famous predecessors of the M.G.B. — the Cheka, the Ogpu, the N.K.V.D. and the M.V.D. — was in every respect a bigger man than Beria. He had been directly behind the mass executions of the 1930s when a million died, he had been *metteur en scène* of most of the great Moscow show trials, he had organized the bloody genocide in the Central Caucasus in February 1944, and it was he who had inspired the mass deportations from the Baltic States and the kidnapping of the German atom and other scientists who had given Russia her great technical leap forward after the war.

And Beria and all his court had gone to the gallows, while General G. had been given SMERSH as his reward. As for Army General Ivan Serov, he, with Bulganin and Khrushchev, now ruled Russia. One day, he might even stand on the peak, alone. But, guessed General Vozdvishensky, glancing up the table at the gleaming billiard-ball skull, probably with General G. not far behind him.

The skull lifted and the hard bulging brown eyes looked straight down the table into the eyes of General Vozdvishensky. General Vozdvishensky managed to look back calmly and even with a hint of appraisal.

That is a deep one, thought General G. Let us put the spotlight on him and see how he shows up on the sound-track.

'Comrades,' gold flashed from both corners of his mouth as he stretched his lips in a chairman's smile, 'let us not be too dismayed. Even the highest tree has an axe waiting at its foot. We have never thought that our departments were so successful as to be beyond criticism. What I have been instructed to say to you will not have come as a surprise to any of us. So let us take up the challenge with a good heart and get down to business.'

Round the table there was no answering smile to these platitudes. General G. had not expected that there would be. He lit a cigarette and continued.

'I said that we have at once to recommend an act of terrorism in the Intelligence field, and one of our departments — no doubt my own — will be called upon to carry out this act.'

An inaudible sigh of relief went round the table. So at least SMERSH would be the responsible department! That was something.

'But the choice of a target will not be an easy matter, and our collective responsibility for the correct choice will be a heavy one.'

Soft-hard, hard-soft. The ball was now back with the conference.

'It is not just a question of blowing up a building or shooting a prime minister. Such bourgeois horseplay is not contemplated. Our operation must be delicate, refined and aimed at the heart of the Intelligence *apparat* of the West. It must do grave damage to the enemy *apparat* — hidden damage which the public will hear perhaps nothing of, but which will be the secret talk of government circles. But it must also cause a public scandal so devastating that the world will lick its lips and sneer at the shame and stupidity of our enemies. Naturally governments will know that it is a Soviet *konspiratsia*. That is good. It will be a piece of "hard" policy. And the agents and spies of the West will know it, too, and they will marvel at our cleverness and they will tremble. Traitors and possible defectors will change their minds. Our own operatives will be stimulated. They will be encouraged to greater efforts by our display of strength and genius. But of course we shall deny any knowledge of the deed, whatever it may be, and it is desirable that the common people of the Soviet Union should remain in complete ignorance of our complicity.'

General G. paused and looked down the table at the representative of R.U.M.I.D., who again held his gaze impassively.

'And now to choose the organization at which we will strike, and then to decide on the specific target within that organization. Comrade Lieutenant-General Vozdvishensky, since you observe the foreign Intelligence scene from a neutral standpoint [this was a jibe at the notorious jealousies that exist between the military intelligence of the G.R.U. and the Secret Service of the M.G.B.], perhaps you would survey the field for us. We wish to have your opinion of the relative importance of the Western Intelligence Services. We will then choose the one which is the most dangerous and which we would most wish to damage.'

General G. sat back in his tall chair. He rested his elbows on the arms and supported his chin on the interlaced fingers of his joined hands, like a teacher preparing to listen to a long construe.

General Vozdvishensky was not dismayed by his task. He had been in Intelligence, mostly abroad, for thirty years. He had served as a 'doorman' at the Soviet Embassy in London under Litvinoff. He had worked with the Tass Agency in New York and had then gone back to London, to Amtorg, the Soviet Trade Organization. For five years he had been Military Attaché under the brilliant Madame Kollontai in the Stockholm Embassy. He had helped train Sorge, the Soviet master spy, before Sorge went to Tokyo. During the war, he had been for a while Resident Director in Switzerland, or 'Schmidtland', as it had been known in the spy-jargon, and there he had helped sow the seeds of the sensationally successful but tragically misused 'Lucy' network. He had even gone several times into Germany as a courier to the 'Rote Kapelle', and had narrowly escaped being cleaned up with it. And after the war, on transfer to the Foreign Ministry, he had been on the inside of the Burgess and Maclean operation and on countless other plots to penetrate the Foreign Ministries of the West. He was a professional spy to his finger-tips and he was perfectly prepared to put on record his opinions of the rivals with whom he had been crossing swords all his life.

The A.D.C. at his side was less comfortable. He was nervous at R.U.M.I.D. being pinned down in this way, and without a full departmental briefing. He scoured his brain clear and sharpened his ears to catch every word.

'In this matter,' said General Vozdvishensky carefully, 'one must not confuse the man with the office. Every country has good spies and it is not always the biggest countries that have the most or the best. But Secret Services are expensive, and small countries cannot afford the co-ordinated effort which produces good intelligence — the forgery departments, the radio network, the record department, the digestive apparatus that evaluates and compares the reports of the agents. There are individual agents serving Norway, Holland, Belgium and even Portugal who could be a great nuisance to us if these countries knew the value of their reports or made good use of them. But they do not. Instead of passing their information on to the larger powers, they prefer to sit on it and feel important. So we need not worry with these smaller countries,' he paused, 'until we come to Sweden. There they have been spying on us for centuries. They have always had better information on the Baltic than even Finland or Germany. They are dangerous. I would like to put a stop to their activities.'

General G. interrupted. 'Comrade, they are always having spy scandals in Sweden. One more scandal would not make the world look up. Please continue.'

'Italy can be dismissed,' went on General Vozdvishensky, without appearing to notice the interruption. 'They are clever and active, but they do us no harm. They are only interested in their own backyard, the Mediterranean. The same can be said of Spain, except that their counter-intelligence is a great hindrance to the Party. We have lost many good men to these Fascists. But to mount an operation against them would probably cost us more men. And little would be achieved. They are not yet ripe for revolution. In France, while we have penetrated most of their Services, the Deuxième Bureau is still clever and dangerous. There is a man called Mathis at the head of it. A Mendès-France appointment. He would be a tempting target and it would be easy to operate in France.'

'France is looking after herself,' commented General G.

'England is another matter altogether. I think we all have respect for her Intelligence Service.' General Vozdvishensky looked round the table. There were grudging nods from everyone present, including General G. 'Their Security Service is excellent. England, being an island, has great security advantages and their so-called M.I.5 employs men with good education and good brains. Their Secret Service is still better. They have notable successes. In certain types of operation, we are constantly finding that they have been there before us. Their agents are good. They pay them little money — only a thousand or two thousand roubles a month — but they serve with devotion. Yet these agents have no special privileges in England, no relief from taxation and no special shops such as we have, from which they can buy cheap goods. Their social standing abroad is not high, and their wives have to pass as the wives of secretaries. They are rarely awarded a decoration until they retire. And yet these men and women continue to do this dangerous work. It is curious. It is perhaps the Public School and University tradition. The love of adventure. But still it is odd that they play this game so well, for they are not natural conspirators.' General Vozdvishensky felt that his remarks might be taken as too laudatory. He hastily qualified them. 'Of course, most of their strength lies in the myth — in the myth of Scotland Yard, of Sherlock Holmes, of the Secret Service. We certainly have nothing to fear from these gentlemen. But this myth is a hindrance which it would be good to set aside.'

'And the Americans?' General G. wanted to put a stop to Vozdvishensky's attempts to qualify his praise of British Intelligence. One day that bit about the Public School and University tradition would sound well in court. Next, hoped General G., he will be saying that the Pentagon is stronger than the Kremlin.

'The Americans have the biggest and richest service among our enemies. Technically, in such matters as radio and weapons and equipment, they are the best. But they have no understanding for the work. They get enthusiastic about some Balkan spy who says he has a secret army in the Ukraine. They load him with money with which to buy boots for this army. Of course he goes at once to Paris and spends the money on women. Americans try to do everything with money. Good spies will not work for money alone — only bad ones, of which the Americans have several divisions.'

'They have successes, Comrade,' said General G. silkily. 'Perhaps you underestimate them.'

General Vozdvishensky shrugged. 'They must have successes, Comrade General. You cannot sow a million seeds without reaping one potato. Personally I do not think the Americans need engage the attention of this conference.' The head of R.U.M.I.D. sat back in his chair and stolidly took out his cigarette case.

'A very interesting exposition,' said General G. coldly. 'Comrade General Slavin?'

General Slavin of the G.R.U. had no intention of committing himself on behalf of the General Staff of the Army. 'I have listened with interest to the words of Comrade General Vozdvishensky. I have nothing to add.'

Colonel of State Security Nikitin of the M.G.B. felt it would do no great harm to show up the G.R.U. as being too stupid to have any ideas at all, and at the same time to make a modest recommendation that would probably tally with the inner thoughts of those present — and what was certainly on the tip of General G.'s tongue. Colonel Nikitin also knew that, given the proposition that had been posed by the Praesidium, the Soviet Secret Service would back him up.

'I recommend the English Secret Service as the object of terrorist action,' he said decisively. 'The devil knows my department hardly finds them a worthy adversary, but they are the best of an indifferent lot.'

General G. was annoyed by the authority in the man's voice, and by having his thunder stolen, for he also had intended to sum up in favour of an operation against the British. He tapped his lighter softly on the desk to reimpose his chairmanship. 'Is it agreed then, Comrades? An act of terrorism against the British Secret Service?'

There were careful, slow nods all round the table.

'I agree. And now for the target within that organization. I remember Comrade General Vozdvishensky saying something about a myth upon which much of the alleged strength of this Secret Service depends. How can we help to destroy the myth and thus strike at the very motive force of this organization? Where does this myth reside? We cannot destroy all its personnel at one blow. Does it reside in the Head? Who is the Head of the British Secret Service?'

Colonel Nikitin's aide whispered in his ear. Colonel Nikitin decided that this was a question he could and perhaps should answer.

'He is an Admiral. He is known by the letter M. We have a *zapiska* on him, but it contains little. He does not drink very much. He is too old for women. The public does not know of his existence. It would be difficult to create a scandal round his death. And he would not be easy to kill. He rarely goes abroad. To shoot him in a London street would not be very refined.'

'There is much in what you say, Comrade,' said General G. 'But we are here to find a target who *will* fulfil our requirements. Have they no one who is a hero to the organization? Someone who is admired and whose ignominious destruction would cause dismay? Myths are built on heroic deeds and heroic people. Have they no such men?'

There was silence round the table while everyone searched his memory. So many names to remember, so many dossiers, so many operations going on every day all over the world. Who was there in the British Secret Service? Who was that man who . . . ?

It was Colonel Nikitin of the M.G.B. who broke the embarrassed silence.

He said hesitantly, 'There is a man called Bond.'

6

DEATH WARRANT

'Y*B**NNA MAT!' The gross obscenity was a favourite with General G. His hand slapped down on the desk. 'Comrade, there certainly is "a man called Bond" as you put it.' His voice was sarcastic. 'James Bond. [He pronounced it 'Shems'.] And nobody, myself included, could think of this spy's name! We are indeed forgetful. No wonder the Intelligence *apparat* is under criticism.'

General Vozdvishensky felt he should defend himself and his department. 'There are countless enemies of the Soviet Union, Comrade General,' he protested. 'If I want their names, I send to the Central Index for them. Certainly I know the name of this Bond. He has been a great trouble to us at different times. But today my mind is full of other names — names of people who are causing us trouble today, this week. I am interested in football, but I cannot remember the name of every foreigner who has scored a goal against the Dynamos.'

'You are pleased to joke, Comrade,' said General G. to underline this out-of-place comment. 'This is a serious matter. I for one admit my fault in not remembering the name of this notorious agent. Comrade Colonel Nikitin will no doubt refresh our memories further, but I recall that this Bond has at least twice frustrated the operations of SMERSH. That is,' he added, 'before I assumed control of the department. There was this affair in France, at that Casino town. The man Le Chiffre. An excellent leader of the Party in France. He foolishly got into some money troubles. But he would have got out of them if this Bond had not interfered. I recall that the department had to act quickly and liquidate the Frenchman. The executioner should have dealt with the Englishman at the same time, but he did not. Then there was this negro of ours in Harlem. A great man — one of the greatest foreign agents we have ever employed, and with a vast network behind him. There was some business about a treasure in the Caribbean. I forget the details. This Englishman was sent out by the Secret Service and smashed the whole organization and killed our man. It was a great reverse. Once again my predecessor should have proceeded ruthlessly against this English spy.'

Colonel Nikitin broke in. 'We had a similar experience in the case of the German, Drax, and the rocket. You will recall the matter, Comrade General. A most important *konspiratsia*. The General Staff were deeply involved. It was a matter of High Policy which could have borne decisive fruit. But again it was this Bond who frustrated the operation. The German was killed. There were grave consequences for the State. There followed a period of serious embarrassment which was only solved with difficulty.'

General Slavin of G.R.U. felt that he should say something. The rocket had been an Army operation and its failure had been laid at the door of G.R.U. Nikitin knew this perfectly well. As usual M.G.B. was trying to make trouble for G.R.U. —raking up old history in this manner. 'We asked for this man to be dealt with by your department, Comrade Colonel,' he said icily. 'I cannot recall that any action followed our request. If it had, we should not now be having to bother with him.'

Colonel Nikitin's temples throbbed with rage. He controlled himself. 'With due respect, Comrade General,' he said in a loud, sarcastic voice, 'the request of G.R.U. was not confirmed by Higher Authority. Further embarrassment with England was not desired. Perhaps that detail has slipped your memory. In any case, if such a request had reached M.G.B., it would have been referred to SMERSH for action.'

'My department received no such request,' said General G. sharply. 'Or the execution of this man would have rapidly followed. However, this is no time for historical researches. The rocket affair was three years ago. Perhaps the M.G.B. could tell us of the more recent activities of this man.'

Colonel Nikitin whispered hurriedly with his aide. He turned back to the table. 'We have very little further information, Comrade General,' he said defensively. 'We believe that he was involved in some diamond smuggling affair. That was last year. Between Africa and America. The case did not concern us.

Since then we have no further news of him. Perhaps there is more recent information on his file.'

General G. nodded. He picked up the receiver of the telephone nearest to him. This was the so-called *Kommandant Telefon* of the M.G.B. All lines were direct and there was no central switchboard. He dialled a number. 'Central Index? Here General Grubozaboyschikov. The *zapiska* of "Bond" — English spy. Emergency.' He listened for the immediate 'At once, Comrade General,' and put back the receiver. He looked down the table with authority. 'Comrades, from many points of view this spy sounds an appropriate target. He appears to be a dangerous enemy of the State. His liquidation will be of benefit to all departments of our Intelligence *apparat*. Is that so?'

The conference grunted.

'Also his loss will be felt by the Secret Service. But will it do more? Will it seriously wound them? Will it help to destroy this myth about which we have been speaking? Is this man a hero to his organization and his country?'

General Vozdvishensky decided that this question was intended for him. He spoke up. 'The English are not interested in heroes unless they are footballers or cricketers or jockeys. If a man climbs a mountain or runs very fast he also is a hero to some people, but not to the masses. The Queen of England is also a hero, and Churchill. But the English are not greatly interested in military heroes. This man Bond is unknown to the public. If he was known, he would still not be a hero. In England, neither open war nor secret war is a heroic matter. They do not like to think about war, and after a war the names of their war heroes are forgotten as quickly as possible. Within the Secret Service, this man may be a local hero or he may not. It will depend on his appearance and personal characteristics. Of these I know nothing. He may be fat and greasy and unpleasant. No one makes a hero out of such a man, however successful he is.'

Nikitin broke in. 'English spies we have captured speak highly of this man. He is certainly much admired in his Service. He is said to be a lone wolf, but a good-looking one.'

The internal office telephone purred softly. General G. lifted the receiver, listened briefly and said, 'Bring it in.' There was a knock on the door. The A.D.C. came in carrying a bulky file in cardboard covers. He crossed the room and placed the file on the desk in front of the General and walked out, closing the door softly behind him.

The file had a shiny black cover. A thick white stripe ran diagonally across it from top right-hand corner to bottom left. In the top left-hand space there were the letters 'S.S.' in white, and under them 'SOVERSHENNOE SEKRETNO', the equivalent of 'Top Secret'. Across the centre was neatly painted in white letters 'JAMES BOND', and underneath '*Angliski Spion*'.

General G. opened the file and took out a large envelope containing photographs which he emptied on to the glass surface of the desk. He picked them up one by one. He looked closely at them, sometimes through a magnifying glass which he took out of a drawer, and passed them across the desk to Nikitin who glanced at them and handed them on.

The first was dated 1946. It showed a dark young man sitting at a table outside a sunlit café. There was a tall glass beside him on the table and a soda-water siphon. The right forearm rested on the table and there was a cigarette between the fingers of the right hand that hung negligently down from the edge of the table. The legs were crossed in that attitude that only an Englishman adopts — with the right ankle resting on the left knee and the left hand grasping the ankle. It was a careless pose. The man didn't know that he was being photographed from a point about twenty feet away.

The next was dated 1950. It was a face and shoulders, blurred, but of the same man. It was a close-up and Bond was looking with careful, narrowed eyes at something, probably the photographer's face, just above the lens. A miniature buttonhole camera, guessed General G.

The third was from 1951. Taken from the left flank, quite close, it showed the same man in a dark suit, without a hat, walking down a wide empty street. He was passing a shuttered shop whose sign said 'Charcuterie'. He looked as if he was going somewhere urgently. The clean-cut profile was pointing straight ahead and the crook of the right elbow suggested that his right hand was in the pocket of his coat. General G. reflected that it was probably taken from a car. He thought that the decisive look of the man, and the purposeful slant of his striding figure, looked dangerous, as if he was making quickly for something bad that was happening further down the street.

The fourth and last photograph was marked *Passe. 1953*. The corner of the Royal Seal and the letters '. . . REIGN OFFICE' in the segment of a circle showed in the bottom right-hand corner. The photograph, which had been blown up to cabinet size, must have been made at a frontier, or by the concierge of an hotel when Bond had surrendered his passport. General G. carefully went over the face with his magnifying glass.

It was a dark, clean-cut face, with a three-inch scar showing whitely down the sunburned skin of the right cheek. The eyes were wide and level under straight, rather long black brows. The hair was black, parted on the left, and carelessly brushed so that a thick black comma fell down over the right eyebrow. The longish straight nose ran down to a short upper lip below which was a wide and finely drawn but cruel mouth. The line of the jaw was straight and firm. A section of dark suit, white shirt and black knitted tie completed the picture.

General G. held the photograph out at arm's length. Decision, authority, ruthlessness — these qualities he could see. He didn't care what else went on inside the man. He passed the photograph down the table and turned to the file, glancing rapidly down each page and flipping brusquely on to the next.

The photographs came back to him. He kept his place with a finger and looked briefly up. 'He looks a nasty customer,' he said grimly. 'His story confirms it. I will read out some extracts. Then we must decide. It is getting late.' He turned back to the first page and began to rattle off the points that struck him.

'First name: JAMES. Height: 183 centimetres; weight: 76 kilograms; slim build; eyes: blue; hair: black; scar down right cheek and on left shoulder; signs of plastic surgery on back of right hand (see Appendix "A"); all-round athlete; expert pistol shot, boxer, knife-thrower; does not use disguises. Languages: French and German. Smokes heavily (N.B.: special cigarettes with three gold bands); vices: drink, but not to excess, and women. Not thought to accept bribes.'

General G. skipped a page and went on:

'This man is invariably armed with a .25 Beretta automatic carried in a holster under his left arm. Magazine holds eight rounds. Has been known to carry a knife strapped to his left forearm; has used steel-capped shoes; knows the basic holds of judo. In general, fights with tenacity and has a high tolerance of pain (see Appendix "B").'

General G. riffled through more pages giving extracts from agents' reports from which this data was drawn. He came to the last page before the Appendices which gave details of the cases on which Bond had been encountered. He ran his eye to the bottom and read out: 'Conclusion. This man is a dangerous professional terrorist and spy. He has worked for the British Secret Service since 1938 and now (see Highsmith file of December 1950) holds the secret number "007" in that Service. The double o numerals signify an agent who has killed and who is privileged to kill on active service. There are believed to be only two other British agents with this authority. The fact that this spy was decorated with the C.M.G. in 1953, an award usually given only on retirement from the Secret Service, is a measure of his worth. If encountered in the field, the fact and full details to be reported to headquarters (see SMERSH, M.G.B. and G.R.U. Standing Orders 1951 onwards).'

General G. shut the file and slapped his hand decisively on the cover. 'Well, Comrades. Are we agreed?'

'Yes,' said Colonel Nikitin, loudly.

'Yes,' said General Slavin in a bored voice.

General Vozdvishensky was looking down at his fingernails. He was sick of murder. He had enjoyed his time in England. 'Yes,' he said. 'I suppose so.'

General G.'s hand went to the internal office telephone. He spoke to his A.D.C. 'Death Warrant,' he said harshly. 'Made out in the name of "James Bond".' He spelled the names out. 'Description: *Angliski Spion*. Crime: Enemy of the State.' He put the receiver back and leant forward in his chair. 'And now it will be a question of devising an appropriate *konspiratsia*. And one that cannot fail!' He smiled grimly. 'We cannot have another of those Khoklov affairs.'

The door opened and the A.D.C. came in carrying a bright yellow sheet of paper. He put it in front of General G. and went out. General G. ran his eyes down the paper and wrote the words 'To be killed. Grubozaboyschikov' at the head of the large empty space at the bottom. He passed the paper to the M.G.B. man who read it and wrote 'Kill him. Nikitin' and handed it across to the head of G.R.U. who wrote 'Kill him.

Slavin'. One of the A.D.C.s passed the paper to the plain-clothes man sitting beside the representative of R.U.M.I.D. The man put it in front of General Vozdvishensky and handed him a pen.

General Vozdvishensky read the paper carefully. He raised his eyes slowly to those of General G. who was watching him and, without looking down, scribbled the 'Kill him' more or less under the other signatures and scrawled his name after it. Then he took his hands away from the paper and got to his feet.

'If that is all, Comrade General?' He pushed his chair back.

General G. was pleased. His instincts about this man had been right. He would have to put a watch on him and pass on his suspicions to General Serov. 'One moment, Comrade General,' he said. 'I have something to add to the warrant.'

The paper was handed up to him. He took out his pen and scratched out what he had written. He wrote again, speaking the words slowly as he did so.

'To be killed WITH IGNOMINY. Grubozaboyschikov.'

He looked up and smiled pleasantly to the company. 'Thank you, Comrades. That is all. I shall advise you of the decision of the Praesidium on our recommendation. Good night.'

When the conference had filed out, General G. rose to his feet and stretched and gave a loud controlled yawn. He sat down again at his desk, switched off the wire-recorder and rang for his A.D.C. The man came in and stood beside his desk.

General G. handed him the yellow paper. 'Send this over to General Serov at once. Find out where Kronsteen is and have him fetched by car. I don't care if he's in bed. He will have to come. Otdyel II will know where to find him. And I will see Colonel Klebb in ten minutes.'

'Yes, Comrade General.' The man left the room.

General G. picked up the V.Ch. receiver and asked for General Serov. He spoke quietly for five minutes. At the end he concluded: 'And I am now about to give the task to Colonel Klebb and the Planner, Kronsteen. We will discuss the outlines of a suitable *konspiratsia* and they will give me detailed proposals tomorrow. Is that in order, Comrade General?'

'Yes,' came the quiet voice of General Serov of the High Praesidium. 'Kill him. But let it be excellently accomplished. The Praesidium will ratify the decision in the morning.'

The line went dead. The inter-office telephone rang. General G. said 'Yes' into the receiver and put it back.

A moment later the A.D.C. opened the big door and stood in the entrance. 'Comrade Colonel Klebb,' he announced.

A toad-like figure in an olive green uniform which bore the single red ribbon of the Order of Lenin came into the room and walked with quick short steps over to the desk.

General G. looked up and waved to the nearest chair at the conference table. 'Good evening, Comrade.'

The squat face split into a sugary smile. 'Good evening, Comrade General.'

The Head of Otdyel II, the department of SMERSH in charge of Operations and Executions, hitched up her skirts and sat down.

7
THE WIZARD OF ICE

THE TWO FACES of the double clock in the shiny, domed case looked out across the chess-board like the eyes of some huge sea monster that had peered over the edge of the table to watch the game.

The two faces of the chess clock showed different times. Kronsteen's showed twenty minutes to one. The long red pendulum that ticked off the seconds was moving in its staccato sweep across the bottom half of his clock's face, while the enemy clock was silent and its pendulum motionless down the face. But Makharov's clock said five minutes to one. He had wasted time in the middle of the game and he now had only five minutes to go. He was in bad 'time-trouble' and unless Kronsteen made some lunatic mistake, which was unthinkable, he was beaten.

Kronsteen sat motionless and erect, as malevolently inscrutable as a parrot. His elbows were on the table and his big head rested on clenched fists that pressed into his cheeks, squashing the pursed lips into a pout of hauteur and disdain. Under the wide, bulging brow the rather slanting black eyes looked down with deadly calm on his winning board. But, behind the mask, the blood was throbbing in the dynamo of his brain, and a thick worm-like vein in his right temple pulsed at a beat of over ninety. He had sweated away a pound of weight in the last two hours and ten minutes, and the spectre of a false move still had one hand at his throat. But to Makharov, and to the spectators, he was still 'The Wizard of Ice' whose game had been compared to a man eating fish. First he stripped off the skin, then he picked out the bones, then he ate the fish. Kronsteen had been Champion of Moscow two years running, was now in the final for the third time and, if he won this game, would be a contender for Grand Mastership.

In the pool of silence round the roped-off top table there was no sound except the loud tripping feet of Kronsteen's clock. The two umpires sat motionless in their raised chairs. They knew, as did Makharov, that this was certainly the kill. Kronsteen had introduced a brilliant twist into the Meran Variation of the Queen's Gambit Declined. Makharov had kept up with him until the 28th move. He had lost time on that move. Perhaps he had made a mistake there, and perhaps again on the 31st and 33rd moves. Who could say? It would be a game to be debated all over Russia for weeks to come.

There came a sigh from the crowded tiers opposite the Championship game. Kronsteen had slowly removed the right hand from his cheek and had stretched it across the board. Like the pincers of a pink crab, his thumb and forefinger had opened, then they had descended. The hand, holding a piece, moved up and sideways and down. Then the hand was slowly brought back to the face.

The spectators buzzed and whispered as they saw, on the great wall map, the 41st move duplicated with a shift of one of the three-foot placards. R-Kt8. That must be the kill!

Kronsteen reached deliberately over and pressed down the lever at the bottom of his clock. His red pendulum went dead. His clock showed a quarter to one. At the same instant, Makharov's pendulum came to life and started its loud, inexorable beat.

Kronsteen sat back. He placed his hands flat on the table and looked coldly across at the glistening, lowered face of the man whose guts he knew, for he too had suffered defeat in his time, would be writhing in agony like an eel pierced with a spear. Makharov, Champion of Georgia. Well, tomorrow Comrade Makharov could go back to Georgia and stay there. At any rate this year he would not be moving with his family up to Moscow.

A man in plain clothes slipped under the ropes and whispered to one of the umpires. He handed him a white envelope. The umpire shook his head, pointing at Makharov's clock, which now said three minutes to one. The man in plain clothes whispered one short sentence which made the umpire sullenly bow his head. He pinged a handbell.

'There is an urgent personal message for Comrade Kronsteen,' he announced into the microphone. 'There will be a three minutes' pause.'

A mutter went round the hall. Even though Makharov now courteously raised his eyes from the board and sat immobile, gazing up into the recesses of the high, vaulted ceiling, the spectators knew that the position of the game was engraved on his brain. A three minutes' pause simply meant three extra minutes for Makharov.

Kronsteen felt the same stab of annoyance, but his face was expressionless as the umpire stepped down from his chair and handed him a plain, unaddressed envelope. Kronsteen ripped it open with his thumb and extracted the anonymous sheet of paper. It said, in the large typewritten characters he knew so well, 'YOU ARE REQUIRED THIS INSTANT'. No signature and no address.

Kronsteen folded the paper and carefully placed it in his inside breast pocket. Later it would be recovered from him and destroyed. He looked up at the face of the plain-clothes man standing beside the umpire. The eyes were watching him impatiently, commandingly. To hell with these people, thought Kronsteen. He would *not* resign with only three minutes to go. It was unthinkable. It was an insult to the People's Sport. But, as he made a gesture to the umpire that the game could continue, he trembled inside, and he avoided the eyes of the plain-clothes man who remained standing, in coiled immobility, inside the ropes.

The bell pinged. 'The game proceeds.'

Makharov slowly bent down his head. The hand of his clock slipped past the hour and he was still alive.

Kronsteen continued to tremble inside. What he had done was unheard of in an employee of SMERSH, or of any other State agency. He would certainly be reported. Gross disobedience. Dereliction of duty. What might be the consequences? At the best a tongue-lashing from General G., and a black mark on his *zapiska*. At the worst? Kronsteen couldn't imagine. He didn't like to think. Whatever happened, the sweets of victory had turned bitter in his mouth.

But now it was the end. With five seconds to go on his clock, Makharov raised his whipped eyes no higher than the pouting lips of his opponent and bent his head in the brief, formal bow of surrender. At the double ping of the umpire's bell, the crowded hall rose to its feet with a thunder of applause.

Kronsteen stood up and bowed to his opponent, to the umpires, and finally, deeply, to the spectators. Then, with the plain-clothes man in his wake, he ducked under the ropes and fought his way coldly and rudely through the mass of his clamouring admirers towards the main exit.

Outside the Tournament Hall, in the middle of the wide Pushkin Ulitza, with its engine running, stood the usual anonymous black Zil saloon. Kronsteen climbed into the back and shut the door. As the plain-clothes man jumped on to the running-board and squeezed into the front seat, the driver crashed his gears and the car tore off down the street.

Kronsteen knew it would be a waste of breath to apologize to the plain-clothes guard. It would also be contrary to discipline. After all, he was Head of the Planning Department of SMERSH, with the honorary rank of full Colonel. And his brain was worth diamonds to the organization. Perhaps he could argue his way out of the mess. He gazed out of the window at the dark streets, already wet with the work of the night cleaning squad, and bent his mind to his defence. Then there came a straight street at the end of which the moon rode fast between the onion spires of the Kremlin, and they were there.

When the guard handed Kronsteen over to the A.D.C., he also handed the A.D.C. a slip of paper. The A.D.C. glanced at it and looked coldly up at Kronsteen with half-raised eyebrows. Kronsteen looked calmly back without saying anything. The A.D.C. shrugged his shoulders and picked up the office telephone and announced him.

When they went into the big room and Kronsteen had been waved to a chair and had nodded acknowledgment of the brief pursed smile of Colonel Klebb, the A.D.C. went up to General G. and handed him the piece of paper. The General read it and looked hard across at Kronsteen. While the A.D.C. walked to the door and went out, the General went on looking at Kronsteen. When the door was shut, General G. opened his mouth and said softly, 'Well, Comrade?'

Kronsteen was calm. He knew the story that would appeal. He spoke quietly and with authority. 'To the public, Comrade General, I am a professional chess player. Tonight I became Champion of Moscow for the third year in succession. If, with only three minutes to go, I had received a message that my wife was being murdered outside the door of the Tournament Hall, I would not have raised a finger to save her. My public know that. They are as dedicated to the game as myself. Tonight, if I had resigned the game and had come immediately on receipt of that message, five thousand people would have known that it could only be on the orders of such a department as this. There would have been a storm of gossip. My future goings and comings would have been watched for clues. It would have been the end of my cover. In the interests of State Security, I waited three minutes before obeying the order. Even so, my hurried departure will be the subject of much comment. I shall have to say that one of my children is gravely ill. I shall have to put a child into hospital for a week to support the story. I deeply apologize for the delay in carrying out the order. But the decision was a difficult one. I did what I thought best in the interests of the department.'

General G. looked thoughtfully into the dark slanting eyes. The man was guilty, but the defence was good. He read the paper again as if weighing up the size of the offence, then he took out his lighter and burned it. He dropped the last burning corner on to the glass top of his desk and blew the ashes sideways on to the floor. He said nothing to reveal his thoughts, but the burning of the evidence was all that mattered to Kronsteen. Now nothing could go on his *zapiska*. He was deeply relieved and grateful. He would bend all his ingenuity to the matter on hand. The General had performed an act of great clemency. Kronsteen would repay him with the full coin of his mind.

'Pass over the photographs, Comrade Colonel,' said General G., as if the brief court-martial had not occurred. 'The matter is as follows . . . '

So it is another death, thought Kronsteen, as the General talked and he examined the dark ruthless face that gazed levelly at him from the blown-up passport photograph. While Kronsteen listened with half his mind to what the General was saying, he picked out the salient facts — English spy. Great scandal desired. No Soviet involvement. Expert killer. Weakness for women (therefore not homosexual, thought Kronsteen). Drinks (but nothing is said about drugs). Unbribable (who knows? There is a price for every man). No expense would be spared. All equipment and personnel available from all Intelligence departments. Success to be achieved within three months. Broad ideas required now. Details to be worked out later.

General G. fastened his sharp eyes on Colonel Klebb. 'What are your immediate reactions, Comrade Colonel?'

The square-cut rimless glass of the spectacles flashed in the light of the chandelier as the woman straightened from her position of bowed concentration and looked across the desk at the General. The pale moist lips below the sheen of nicotine-stained fur over the mouth parted and started moving rapidly up and down as the woman gave her views. To Kronsteen, watching the face across the table, the square, expressionless opening and shutting of the lips reminded him of the boxlike jabber of a puppet.

The voice was hoarse and flat and without emotion, '. . . resembles in some respects the case of Stolzenberg. If you remember, Comrade General, this also was a matter of destroying a reputation as well as a life. On that occasion the matter was simple. The spy was also a pervert. If you recall . . . '

Kronsteen stopped listening. He knew all these cases. He had handled the planning of most of them and they were filed away in his memory like so many chess gambits. Instead, with closed ears, he examined the face of this dreadful woman and wondered casually how much longer she would last in her job — how much longer he would have to work with her.

Dreadful? Kronsteen was not interested in human beings — not even in his own children. Nor did the categories of 'good' and 'bad' have a place in his vocabulary. To him all people were chess pieces. He was only interested in their reactions to the movements of other pieces. To foretell their reactions, which was the greater part of his job, one had to understand their individual characteristics. Their basic instincts were immutable. Self-preservation, sex and the instinct of the herd — in that order. Their temperaments could be sanguine, phlegmatic, choleric or melancholic. The temperament of an individual would largely decide the comparative strength of his emotions and his sentiments. Character would greatly depend on upbringing and, whatever Pavlov and the Behaviourists might say, to a certain extent on the character of the parents. And, of course, people's lives and behaviour would be partly conditioned by physical strengths and weaknesses.

It was with these basic classifications at the back of his mind that Kronsteen's cold brain considered the woman across the table. It was the hundredth time he had summed her up, but now they had weeks of joint work in front of them and it was as well to refresh the memory so that a sudden intrusion of the human element in their partnership should not come as a surprise.

Of course Rosa Klebb had a strong will to survive, or she would not have become one of the most powerful women in the State, and certainly the most feared. Her rise, Kronsteen remembered, had begun with the Spanish Civil War. Then, as a double agent inside P.O.U.M. — that is, working for the O.G.P.U. in Moscow as well as for Communist Intelligence in Spain — she had been the right hand, and some sort of a mistress, they said, of her chief, the famous Andreas Nin. She had worked with him from 1935 to 37. Then, on the orders of Moscow, he was murdered and, it was rumoured, murdered by her. Whether this was true or not, from then on she had progressed slowly but straight up the ladder of power, surviving setbacks, surviving wars, surviving, because she forged no allegiances and joined no factions, all the purges, until, in 1953, with the death of Beria, the bloodstained hands grasped the rung, so few from the very top, that was Head of the Operations Department of SMERSH.

And, reflected Kronsteen, much of her success was due to the peculiar nature of her next most important instinct, the Sex Instinct. For Rosa Klebb undoubtedly belonged to the rarest of all sexual types. She was a Neuter. Kronsteen was certain of it. The stories of men and, yes, of women, were too circumstantial to be doubted. She might enjoy the act physically, but the instrument was of no importance. For her, sex was nothing more than an itch. And this psychological and physiological neutrality of hers at once relieved her of so many human emotions and sentiments and desires. Sexual neutrality was the essence of coldness in an individual. It was a great and wonderful thing to be born with.

In her, the Herd Instinct would also be dead. Her urge for power demanded that she should be a wolf and not a sheep. She was a lone operator, but never a lonely one, because the warmth of company was unnecessary to her. And, of course, temperamentally, she would be a phlegmatic — imperturbable, tolerant of pain, sluggish. Laziness would be her besetting vice, thought Kronsteen. She would be difficult to get out of her warm, hoggish bed in the morning. Her private habits would be slovenly, even dirty. It would not be pleasant, thought Kronsteen, to look into the intimate side of her life, when she relaxed, out of uniform. Kronsteen's pouting lips curled away from the thought and his mind hastened on, skipping her character, which was certainly cunning and strong, to her appearance.

Rosa Klebb would be in her late forties, he assumed, placing her by the date of the Spanish War. She was short, about five foot four, and squat, and her dumpy arms and short neck, and the calves of the thick legs in the drab khaki stockings, were very strong for a woman. The devil knows, thought Kronsteen, what her breasts were like, but the bulge of uniform that rested on the table-top looked like a badly packed sandbag, and in general her figure, with its big pear-shaped hips, could only be likened to a 'cello.

The *tricoteuses* of the French Revolution must have had faces like hers, decided Kronsteen, sitting back in his chair and tilting his head slightly to one side. The thinning orange hair scraped back to the tight, obscene bun; the shiny yellow-brown eyes that stared so coldly at General G. through the sharp-edged squares of glass, the wedge of thickly powdered, large-pored nose; the wet trap of a mouth, that went on opening and shutting as if it was operated by wires under the chin. Those French women, as they sat and knitted and chatted while the guillotine clanged down, must have had the same pale, thick chicken's skin that scragged in little folds under the eyes and at the corners of the mouth and below the jaws, the same big peasant's ears, the same tight, hard dimpled fists, like knobkerries, that, in the case of the Russian woman, now lay tightly clenched on the red velvet table-top on either side of the big bundle of bosom. And their faces must have conveyed the same impression, concluded Kronsteen, of coldness and cruelty and strength as this, yes, he had to allow himself the emotive word, *dreadful* woman of SMERSH.

'Thank you, Comrade Colonel. Your review of the position is of value. And now, Comrade Kronsteen, have you anything to add? Please be short. It is two o'clock and we all have a heavy day before us.' General G.'s eyes, bloodshot with strain and lack of sleep, stared fixedly across the desk into the fathomless brown pools below the bulging forehead. There had been no need to tell this man to be brief. Kronsteen never had much to say, but each of his words was worth speeches from the rest of the staff.

Kronsteen had already made up his mind, or he would not have allowed his thoughts to concentrate for so long on the woman.

He slowly tilted back his head and gazed into the nothingness of the ceiling. His voice was extremely mild, but it had the authority that commands close attention.

'Comrade General, it was a Frenchman, in some respects a predecessor of yours, Fouché, who observed that it is no good killing a man unless you also destroy his reputation. It will, of course, be easy to kill this man Bond. Any paid Bulgarian assassin would do it, if properly instructed. The second part of the operation, the destruction of this man's character, is more important and more difficult. At this stage it is only clear to me that the deed must be done away from England, and in a country over whose press and radio we have influence. If you ask me how the man is to be got there, I can only say that if the bait is important enough, and its capture is open to this man alone, he will be sent to seize it from wherever he may happen to be. To avoid the appearance of a trap, I would consider giving the bait a touch of eccentricity, of the unusual. The English pride themselves on their eccentricity. They treat the eccentric proposition as a challenge. I would rely partly on this reading of their psychology to have them send this important operator after the bait.'

Kronsteen paused. He lowered his head so that he was looking just over General G.'s shoulder.

'I shall proceed to devise such a trap,' he said indifferently. 'For the present, I can only say that if the bait is successful in attracting its prey, we are then likely to require an assassin with a perfect command of the English language.'

Kronsteen's eyes moved to the red velvet table-top in front of him. Thoughtfully, as if this was the kernel of the problem, he added: 'We shall also require a reliable and extremely beautiful girl.'

8

THE BEAUTIFUL LURE

SITTING BY THE window of her one room and looking out at the serene June evening, at the first pink of the sunset reflected in the windows across the street, at the distant onion spire of a church that flamed like a torch above the ragged horizon of Moscow roofs, Corporal of State Security Tatiana Romanova thought that she was happier than she had ever been before.

Her happiness was not romantic. It had nothing to do with the rapturous start to a love affair — those days and weeks before the first tiny tear-clouds appear on the horizon. It was the quiet, settled happiness of security, of being able to look forward with confidence to the future, heightened by the immediate things, a word of praise she had had that afternoon from Professor Denikin, the smell of a good supper cooking on the electric stove, her favourite prelude to *Boris Godonov* being played by the Moscow State Orchestra on the radio, and, over all, the beauty of the fact that the long winter and short spring were past and it was June.

The room was a tiny box in the huge modern apartment building on the Sadovaya-Chernogriazskay Ulitsa that is the women's barracks of the State Security Departments. Built by prison labour, and finished in 1939, the fine eight-storey building contains two thousand rooms, some, like hers on the third floor, nothing but square boxes with a telephone, hot and cold water, a single electric light and a share of the central bathrooms and lavatories, others, on the two top floors, consisting of two- and three-room flats with bathrooms. These were for high-ranking women. Graduation up the building was strictly by rank, and Corporal Romanova had to rise through Sergeant, Lieutenant, Captain, Major and Lieutenant-Colonel before she would reach the paradise of the eighth and Colonels' floor.

But heaven knew she was content enough with her present lot. A salary of 1200 roubles a month (thirty per cent more than she could have earned in any other Ministry), a room to herself; cheap food and clothes from the 'closed shops' on the ground floor of the building; a monthly allocation of at least two Ministry tickets to the Ballet or the Opera; a full two weeks' paid holiday a year. And, above all, a steady job with good prospects in Moscow — not in one of those dreary provincial towns where nothing happened month after month, and where the arrival of a new film or the visit of a travelling circus was the only thing to keep one out of bed in the evening.

Of course, you had to pay for being in the M.G.B. The uniform put you apart from the world. People were afraid, which didn't suit the nature of most girls, and you were confined to the society of other M.G.B. girls and men, one of whom, when the time came, you would have to marry in order to stay with the Ministry. And they worked like the devil — eight to six, five and a half days a week, and only forty minutes off for lunch in the canteen. But it was a good lunch, a real meal, and you could do with little supper and save up for the sable coat that would one day take the place of the well-worn Siberian fox.

At the thought of her supper, Corporal Romanova left the chair by the window and went to examine the pot of thick soup, with a few shreds of meat and some powdered mushroom, that was to be her supper. It was nearly done and smelled delicious. She turned off the electricity and let the pot simmer while she washed and tidied, as, years before, she had been taught to do before meals.

While she dried her hands, she examined herself in the big oval looking-glass over the washstand.

One of her early boy-friends had said she looked like the young Greta Garbo. What nonsense! And yet tonight she did look rather well. Fine dark brown silken hair brushed straight back from a tall brow and falling heavily down almost to the shoulders, there to curl slightly up at the ends (Garbo had once done her hair like that and Corporal Romanova admitted to herself that she had copied it), a good, soft pale skin with an ivory sheen at the cheek-bones; wide apart, level eyes of the deepest blue under straight natural brows (she closed one eye after the other. Yes, her lashes were certainly long enough!), a straight, rather imperious nose — and then the mouth. What about the mouth? Was it too broad? It must look terribly wide when she smiled. She smiled at herself in the mirror. Yes, it was wide; but then so had Garbo's been. At least the lips were full and finely etched. There was the hint of a smile at the corners. No one could say it was a cold mouth! And the oval of her face. Was that too long? Was her chin a shade too sharp? She swung her head sideways to see it in profile. The heavy curtain of hair swung forward and across her right eye so that she had to brush it back. Well, the chin was pointed, but at least it wasn't sharp. She faced the mirror again and picked up a brush and started on the long, heavy hair. Greta Garbo! She was all right, or so many men wouldn't tell her that she was — let alone the girls who were always coming to her for advice about their faces. But a film star — a famous one! She made a face at herself in the glass and went to eat her supper.

In fact Corporal Tatiana Romanova was a very beautiful girl indeed. Apart from her face, the tall, firm body moved particularly well. She had been a year in the ballet school in Leningrad and had abandoned dancing as a career only when she grew an inch over the prescribed limit of five feet six. The school had taught her to hold herself well and to walk well. And she looked wonderfully healthy, thanks to her passion for figure-skating, which she practised all through the year at the Dynamo ice-stadium and which had already earned her a place on the first Dynamo women's team. Her arms and breasts were faultless. A purist would have disapproved of her behind. Its muscles were so hardened with exercise that it had lost the smooth downward feminine sweep, and now, round at the back and flat and hard at the sides, it jutted like a man's.

Corporal Romanova was admired far beyond the confines of the English translation section of the M.G.B. Central Index. Everyone agreed that it would not be long before one of the senior officers came across her and peremptorily hauled her out of her modest section to make her his mistress, or if absolutely necessary, his wife.

The girl poured the thick soup into a small china bowl, decorated with wolves chasing a galloping sleigh round the rim, broke some black bread into it and went and sat in her chair by the window and ate it slowly with a nice shiny spoon she had slipped into her bag not many weeks before after a gay evening at the Hotel Moskwa.

When she had finished, she washed up and went back to her chair and lit the first cigarette of the day (no respectable girl in Russia smokes in public, except in a restaurant, and it would have meant instant dismissal if she had smoked at her work) and listened impatiently to the whimpering discords of an orchestra from Turkmenistan. This dreadful oriental stuff they were always putting on to please the kulaks of one of those barbaric outlying states! Why couldn't they play something *kulturny*? Some of that modern jazz music, or something classical. This stuff was hideous. Worse, it was old-fashioned.

The telephone rang harshly. She walked over and turned down the radio and picked up the receiver.

'Corporal Romanova?'

It was the voice of her dear Professor Denikin. But out of office hours he always called her Tatiana or even Tania. What did this mean?

The girl was wide-eyed and tense. 'Yes, Comrade Professor.'

The voice at the other end sounded strange and cold. 'In fifteen minutes, at 8.30, you are required for interview by Comrade Colonel Klebb, of Otdyel II. You will call on her in her apartment, No. 1875, on the eighth floor of your building. Is that clear?'

'But, Comrade, why? What is . . . What is . . . ?'

The odd, strained voice of her beloved Professor cut her short.

'That is all, Comrade Corporal.'

The girl held the receiver away from her face. She stared at it with frenzied eyes as if she could wring more words out of the circles of little holes in the black ear-piece. 'Hullo! Hullo!' The empty mouthpiece yawned at her. She realized that her hand and her forearm were aching with the strength of her grip. She bent slowly forward and put the receiver down on the cradle.

She stood for a moment, frozen, gazing blindly at the black machine. Should she call him back? No, that was out of the question. He had spoken as he had because he knew, and she knew, that every call, in and out of the building, was listened to or recorded. That was why he had not wasted a word. This was a State matter. With a message of this sort, you got rid of it as quickly as you could, in as few words as possible, and wiped your hands of it. You had got the dreadful card out of your hand. You had passed the Queen of Spades to someone else. Your hands were clean again.

The girl put her knuckles up to her open mouth and bit on them, staring at the telephone. What did they want her for? What had she done? Desperately she cast her mind back, scrabbling through the days, the months, the years. Had she made some terrible mistake in her work and they had just discovered it? Had she made some remark against the State, some joke that had been reported back? That was always possible. But which remark? When? If it had been a bad remark, she would have felt a twinge of guilt or fear at the time. Her conscience was clear. Or was it? Suddenly she remembered. What about the spoon she had stolen? Was it that? Government property! She would throw it out of the window, now, far to one side or the other. But no, it couldn't be that. That was too small. She shrugged her shoulders resignedly and her hand dropped to her side. She got up and moved towards the clothes cupboard to get out her best uniform, and her eyes were misty with the tears of fright and bewilderment of a child. It could be none of those things. SMERSH didn't send for one for that sort of thing. It must be something much, much worse.

The girl glanced through her wet eyes at the cheap watch on her wrist. Only seven minutes to go! A new panic seized her. She brushed her forearm across her eyes and grabbed down her parade uniform. On top of it all, whatever it was, to be late! She tore at the buttons of her white cotton blouse.

As she dressed and washed her face and brushed her hair, her mind went on probing at the evil mystery like an inquisitive child poking into a snake's hole with a stick. From whatever angle she explored the hole, there came an angry hiss.

Leaving out the nature of her guilt, contact with any tentacle of SMERSH was unspeakable. The very name of the organization was abhorred and avoided. SMERSH, 'Smiert Spionam', 'Death to Spies'. It was an obscene word, a word from the tomb, the very whisper of death, a word never mentioned even in secret office gossip among friends. Worst of all, within this horrible organization, Otdyel II, the Department of Torture and Death, was the central horror.

And the Head of Otdyel II, the woman, Rosa Klebb! Unbelievable things were whispered about this woman, things that came to Tatiana in her nightmares, things she forgot again during the day, but that she now paraded.

It was said that Rosa Klebb would let no torturing take place without her. There was a blood-spattered smock in her office, and a low camp-stool, and they said that when she was seen scurrying through the basement passages dressed in the smock and with the stool in her hand, the word would go round, and even the workers in SMERSH would hush their words and bend low over their papers — perhaps even cross their fingers in their pockets — until she was reported back in her room.

For, or so they whispered, she would take the camp-stool and draw it up close below the face of the man or woman that hung down over the edge of the interrogation table. Then she would squat down on the stool and look into the face and quietly say 'No. 1' or 'No. 10' or 'No. 25' and the inquisitors would know what she meant and they would begin. And she would watch the eyes in the face a few inches away from hers and breathe in the screams as if they were perfume. And, depending on the eyes, she would quietly change the torture, and say 'Now No. 36' or 'Now No. 64' and the inquisitors would do something else. As the courage and resistance seeped out of the eyes, and they began to weaken and beseech, she would start cooing softly. 'There, there my dove. Talk to me, my pretty one, and it will stop. It hurts. Ah me, it hurts so, my child. And one is so tired of the pain. One would like it to stop, and to be able to lie down in peace, and for it never to begin again. Your mother is here beside you, only waiting to stop the pain. She has a nice soft cosy bed all ready for you to sleep on and forget, forget, forget. Speak,' she would whisper lovingly. 'You have only to speak and you will have peace and no more pain.' If the eyes still resisted, the cooing would start again. 'But you are foolish, my pretty one. Oh so foolish. This pain is nothing. Nothing! You don't believe me, my little dove? Well then, your mother must try a little, but only a very little, of No. 87.' And the interrogators would hear and change their instruments and their aim, and she would squat there and watch the life slowly ebbing from the eyes until she had to speak loudly into the ear of the person or the words would not reach the brain.

But it was seldom, so they said, that the person had the will to travel far along SMERSH'S road of pain, let alone to the end, and, when the soft voice promised peace, it nearly always won, for somehow Rosa Klebb knew from the eyes the moment when the adult had been broken down into a child crying for its mother. And she provided the image of the mother and melted the spirit where the harsh words of a man would have toughened it.

Then, after yet another suspect had been broken, Rosa Klebb would go back down the passage with her camp-stool and take off her newly soiled smock and get back to her work and the word would go round that all was over and normal activity would come back to the basement.

Tatiana, frozen by her thoughts, looked again at her watch. Four minutes to go. She ran her hands down her uniform and gazed once more at her white face in the glass. She turned and said farewell to the dear, familiar little room. Would she ever see it again?

She walked straight down the long corridor and rang for the lift.

When it came, she squared her shoulders and lifted her chin and walked into the lift as if it was the platform of the guillotine.

'Eighth,' she said to the girl operator. She stood facing the doors. Inside her, remembering a word she had not used since childhood, she repeated over and over 'My God — My God — My God.'

9

A LABOUR OF LOVE

OUTSIDE THE ANONYMOUS, cream-painted door, Tatiana already smelled the inside of the room. When the voice told her curtly to come in, and she opened the door, it was the smell that filled her mind while she stood and stared into the eyes of the woman who sat behind the round table under the centre light.

It was the smell of the Metro on a hot evening — cheap scent concealing animal odours. People in Russia soak themselves in scent, whether they have had a bath or not, but mostly when they have not, and healthy, clean girls like Tatiana always walk home from the office, unless the rain or the snow is too bad, so as to avoid the stench in the trains and the Metro.

Now Tatiana was in a bath of the smell. Her nostrils twitched with disgust.

It was her disgust and her contempt for a person who could live in the middle of such a smell that helped her to look down into the yellowish eyes that stared at her through the square glass panes. Nothing could be read in them. They were receiving eyes, not giving eyes. They slowly moved all over her, like camera lenses, taking her in.

Colonel Klebb spoke:

'You are a fine-looking girl, Comrade Corporal. Walk across the room and back.'

What were these honeyed words? Taut with a new fear, fear of the notorious personal habits of the woman, Tatiana did as she was told.

'Take your jacket off. Put it down on the chair. Raise your hands above your head. Higher. Now bend and touch your toes. Upright. Good. Sit down.' The woman spoke like a doctor. She gestured to the chair across the table from her. Her staring, probing eyes hooded themselves as they bent over the file on the table.

It must be my *zapiska*, thought Tatiana. How interesting to see the actual instrument that ordered the whole of one's life. How thick it was — nearly two inches thick. What could be on all those pages? She looked across at the open folder with wide, fascinated eyes.

Colonel Klebb riffled through the last pages and shut down the cover. The cover was orange with a diagonal black stripe. What did those colours signify?

The woman looked up. Somehow Tatiana managed to look bravely back.

'Comrade Corporal Romanova.' It was the voice of authority, of the senior officer. 'I have good reports of your work. Your record is excellent, both in your duties and in sport. The State is pleased with you.'

Tatiana could not believe her ears. She felt faint with reaction. She blushed to the roots of her hair and then turned pale. She put out a hand to the table edge. She stammered in a weak voice, 'I am g-grateful, Comrade Colonel.'

'Because of your excellent services you have been singled out for a most important assignment. This is a great honour for you. Do you understand?'

Whatever it was, it was better than what might have been. 'Yes, indeed, Comrade Colonel.'

'This assignment carries much responsibility. It bears a higher rank. I congratulate you on your promotion, Comrade Corporal, on completion of the assignment, to the rank of Captain of State Security.'

This was unheard of for a girl of twenty-four! Tatiana sensed danger. She stiffened like an animal who sees the steel jaws beneath the meat. 'I am deeply honoured, Comrade Colonel.' She was unable to keep the wariness out of her voice.

Rosa Klebb grunted non-committally. She knew exactly what the girl must have thought when she got the summons. The effect of her kindly reception, her shock of relief at the good news, her reawakening fears, had been transparent. This was a beautiful, guileless, innocent girl. Just what the *konspiratsia* demanded. Now she must be loosened up. 'My dear,' she said smoothly. 'How remiss of me. This promotion should be celebrated in a glass of wine. You must not think we senior officers are inhuman. We will drink together. It will be a good excuse to open a bottle of French champagne.'

Rosa Klebb got up and went over to the sideboard where her batman had laid out what she had ordered.

'Try one of these chocolates while I wrestle with the cork. It is never easy getting out champagne corks. We girls really need a man to help us with that sort of work, don't we?'

The ghastly prattle went on as she put a spectacular box of chocolates in front of Tatiana. She went back to the sideboard. 'They're from Switzerland. The very best. The soft centres are the round ones. The hard ones are square.'

Tatiana murmured her thanks. She reached out and chose a round one. It would be easier to swallow. Her mouth was dry with fear of the moment when she would finally see the trap and feel it snap round her neck. It must be something dreadful to need to be concealed under all this play-acting. The bit of chocolate stuck in her mouth like chewing-gum. Mercifully the glass of champagne was thrust into her hand.

Rosa Klebb stood over her. She lifted her glass merrily. '*Za vashe zdarovie*, Comrade Tatiana. And my warmest congratulations!'

Tatiana stitched a ghastly smile on her face. She picked up her glass and gave a little bow. '*Za vashe zdarovie*, Comrade Colonel.' She drained the glass, as is the custom in Russian drinking, and put it down in front of her.

Rosa Klebb immediately filled it again, slopping some over the table-top. 'And now to the health of your new department, Comrade.' She raised her glass. The sugary smile tightened as she watched the girl's reactions.

'To SMERSH!'

Numbly, Tatiana got to her feet. She picked up the full glass. 'To SMERSH.' The word scarcely came out. She choked on the champagne and had to take two gulps. She sat heavily down.

Rosa Klebb gave her no time for reflection. She sat down opposite and laid her hands flat on the table. 'And now to business, Comrade.' Authority was back in the voice. 'There is much work to be done.' She leant forward. 'Have you ever wished to live abroad, Comrade? In a foreign country?'

The champagne was having its effect on Tatiana. Probably worse was to come, but now let it come quickly.

'No, Comrade. I am happy in Moscow.'

'You have never thought what it might be like living in the West — all those beautiful clothes, the jazz, the modern things?'

'No, Comrade.' She was truthful. She had never thought about it.

'And if the State required you to live in the West?'

'I would obey.'

'Willingly?'

Tatiana shrugged her shoulders with a hint of impatience. 'One does what one is told.'

The woman paused. There was girlish conspiracy in the next question.

'Are you a virgin, Comrade?'

Oh, my God, thought Tatiana. 'No, Comrade Colonel.'

The wet lips glinted in the light.

'How many men?'

Tatiana coloured to the roots of her hair. Russian girls are reticent and prudish about sex. In Russia the sexual climate is mid-Victorian. These questions from the Klebb woman were all the more revolting for being asked in this cold inquisitorial tone by a State official she had never met before in her life. Tatiana screwed up her courage. She stared defensively into the yellow eyes. 'What is the purpose of these intimate questions please, Comrade Colonel?'

Rosa Klebb straightened. Her voice cut back like a whip. 'Remember yourself, Comrade. You are not here to ask questions. You forget to whom you are speaking. Answer me!'

Tatiana shrank back. 'Three men, Comrade Colonel.'

'When. How old were you?' The hard yellow eyes looked across the table into the hunted blue eyes of the girl and held them and commanded.

Tatiana was on the edge of tears. 'At school. When I was seventeen. Then at the Institute of Foreign Languages. I was twenty-two. Then last year. I was twenty-three. It was a friend I met skating.'

'Their names, please, Comrade.' Rosa Klebb picked up a pencil and pulled a scribbling pad towards her.

Tatiana covered her face with her hands and burst into tears. 'No,' she cried between her sobs. 'No, never, whatever you do to me. You have no right.'

'Stop that nonsense.' The voice was a hiss. 'In five minutes I could have those names from you, or anything else I wish to know. You are playing a dangerous game with me, Comrade. My patience will not last for ever.' Rosa Klebb paused. She was being too rough. 'For the moment we will pass on. Tomorrow you will give me the names. No harm will come to these men. They will be asked one or two questions about you — simple technical questions, that is all. Now sit up and dry your tears. We cannot have any more of this foolishness.'

Rosa Klebb got up and came round the table. She stood looking down at Tatiana. The voice became oily and smooth. 'Come, come, my dear. You must trust me. Your little secrets are safe with me. Here, drink some more champagne and forget this little unpleasantness. We must be friends. We have work to do together. You must learn, my dear Tatiana, to treat me as you would your mother. Here, drink this down.'

Tatiana pulled a handkerchief out of the waistband of her skirt and dabbed at her eyes. She reached out a trembling hand for the glass of champagne and sipped at it with bowed head.

'Drink it down, my dear.'

Rosa Klebb stood over the girl like some dreadful mother duck, clucking encouragement.

Obediently Tatiana emptied the glass. She felt drained of resistance, tired, willing to do anything to finish with this interview and get away somewhere and sleep. She thought, so this is what it is like on the interrogation table, and that is the voice the Klebb uses. Well, it was working. She was docile now. She would co-operate.

Rosa Klebb sat down. She observed the girl appraisingly from behind the motherly mask.

'And now, my dear, just one more intimate little question. As between girls. Do you enjoy making love? Does it give you pleasure? Much pleasure?'

Tatiana's hands came up again and covered her face. From behind them, in a muffled voice, she said, 'Well yes, Comrade Colonel. Naturally, when one is in love . . . ' Her voice trailed away. What else could she say? What answer did this woman want?

'And supposing, my dear, you were not in love. Then would love-making with a man still give you pleasure?'

Tatiana shook her head indecisively. She took her hands down from her face and bowed her head. The hair fell down on either side in a heavy curtain. She was trying to think, to be helpful, but she couldn't imagine such a situation. She supposed . . . 'I suppose it would depend on the man, Comrade Colonel.'

'That is a sensible answer, my dear.' Rosa Klebb opened a drawer in the table. She took out a photograph and slipped it across to the girl. 'What about this man, for instance?'

Tatiana drew the photograph cautiously towards her as if it might catch fire. She looked down warily at the handsome, ruthless face. She tried to think, to imagine . . . 'I cannot tell, Comrade Colonel. He is good-looking. Perhaps if he was gentle . . . ' She pushed the photograph anxiously away from her.

'No, keep it, my dear. Put it up beside your bed and think of this man. You will learn more about him later in your new work. And now,' the eyes glittered behind the square panes of glass, 'would you like to know what your new work is to be? The task for which you have been chosen from all the girls in Russia?'

'Yes, indeed, Comrade Colonel.' Tatiana looked obediently across at the intent face that was now pointing at her like a gun-dog.

The wet, rubbery lips parted enticingly. 'It is a simple, delightful duty you have been chosen for, Comrade Corporal — a real labour of love, as we say. It is a matter of falling in love. That is all. Nothing else. Just falling in love with this man.'

'But who is he? I don't even know him.'

Rosa Klebb's mouth revelled. This would give the silly chit of a girl something to think about.

'He is an English spy.'

'*Bozhi moi!*' Tatiana clapped a hand over her mouth as much to stifle the use of God's name as from terror. She sat, tense with the shock, and gazed at Rosa Klebb through wide, slightly drunk eyes.

'Yes,' said Rosa Klebb, pleased with the effect of her words. 'He is an English spy. Perhaps the most famous of them all. And from now on you are in love with him. So you had better get used to the idea. And no silliness, Comrade. We must be serious. This is an important State matter for which you have been chosen as the instrument. So no nonsense, please. Now for some practical details.' Rosa Klebb stopped. She said sharply, 'And take your hand away from your silly face. And stop looking like a frightened cow. Sit up in your chair and pay attention. Or it will be the worse for you. Understood?'

'Yes, Comrade Colonel.' Tatiana quickly straightened her back and sat up with her hands in her lap as if she was back at the Security Officers' School. Her mind was in a ferment, but this was no time for personal things. Her whole training told her that this was an operation for the State. She was now working for her country. Somehow she had come to be chosen for an important *konspiratsia*. As an officer in the M.G.B., she must do her duty and do it well. She listened carefully and with her whole professional attention.

'For the moment,' Rosa Klebb put on her official voice, 'I will be brief. You will hear more later. For the next few weeks you will be most carefully trained for this operation until you know exactly what to do in all contingencies. You will be taught certain foreign customs. You will be equipped with beautiful clothes. You will be instructed in all the arts of allurement. Then you will be sent to a foreign country, somewhere in Europe. There you will meet this man. You will seduce him. In this matter you will have no silly compunctions. Your body belongs to the State. Since your birth, the State has nourished it. Now your body must work for the State. Is that understood?'

'Yes, Comrade Colonel.' The logic was inescapable.

'You will accompany this man to England. There, you will no doubt be questioned. The questioning will be easy. The English do not use harsh methods. You will give such answers as you can without endangering the State. We will supply you with certain answers which we would like to be given. You will probably be sent to Canada. That is where the English send a certain category of foreign prisoner. You will be rescued and brought back to Moscow.' Rosa Klebb peered at the girl. She seemed to be accepting all this without question. 'You see, it is a comparatively simple matter. Have you any questions at this stage?'

'What will happen to the man, Comrade Colonel?'

'That is a matter of indifference to us. We shall simply use him as a means to introduce you into England. The object of the operation is to give false information to the British. We shall, of course, Comrade, be very glad to have your own impressions of life in England. The reports of a highly trained and intelligent girl such as yourself will be of great value to the State.'

'Really, Comrade Colonel!' Tatiana felt important. Suddenly it all sounded exciting. If only she could do it well. She would assuredly do her very best. But supposing she could not make the English spy love her. She looked again at the photograph. She put her head on one side. It was an attractive face. What were these 'arts of allurement' that the woman had talked about? What could they be? Perhaps they would help.

Satisfied, Rosa Klebb got up from the table. 'And now we can relax, my dear. Work is over for the night. I will go and tidy up and we will have a friendly chat together. I shan't be a moment. Eat up those chocolates or they will go to waste.' Rosa Klebb made a vague gesture of the hand and disappeared with a preoccupied look into the next room.

Tatiana sat back in her chair. So that was what it was all about! It really wasn't so bad after all. What a relief! And what an honour to have been chosen. How silly to have been so frightened! Naturally the great leaders of the State would not allow harm to come to an innocent citizen who worked hard and had no black marks on her *zapiska*. Suddenly she felt immensely grateful to the father-figure that was the State, and proud that she would now have a chance to repay some of her debt. Even the Klebb woman wasn't really so bad after all.

Tatiana was still cheerfully reviewing the situation when the bedroom door opened and 'the Klebb woman' appeared in the opening. 'What do you think of this my dear?' Colonel Klebb opened her dumpy arms and twirled on her toes like a mannequin. She struck a pose with one arm outstretched and the other arm crooked at her waist.

Tatiana's mouth had fallen open. She shut it quickly. She searched for something to say.

Colonel Klebb of SMERSH was wearing a semi-transparent nightgown in orange *crêpe de chine*. It had scallops of the same material round the low square neckline and scallops at the wrists of the broadly flounced sleeves. Underneath could be seen a brassière consisting of two large pink satin roses. Below, she wore old-fashioned knickers of pink satin with elastic above the knees. One dimpled knee, like a yellowish coconut, appeared thrust forward between the half-open folds of the nightgown in the classic stance of the modeller. The feet were enclosed in pink satin slippers with pompoms of ostrich feathers. Rosa Klebb had taken off her spectacles and her naked face was now thick with mascara and rouge and lipstick.

She looked like the oldest and ugliest whore in the world.

Tatiana stammered, 'It is very pretty.'

'Isn't it,' twittered the woman. She went over to a broad couch in the corner of the room. It was covered with a garish piece of peasant tapestry. At the back, against the wall, were rather grimy satin cushions in pastel colours.

With a squeak of pleasure, Rosa Klebb threw herself down in the caricature of a Recamier pose. She reached up an arm and turned on a pink shaded table-lamp whose stem was a naked woman in sham Lalique glass. She patted the couch beside her.

'Turn out the top light, my dear. The switch is by the door. Then come and sit beside me. We must get to know each other better.'

Tatiana walked to the door. She switched off the top light. Her hand dropped decisively to the door knob. She turned it and opened the door and stepped coolly out into the corridor. Suddenly her nerve broke. She banged the door shut behind her and ran wildly off down the corridor with her hands over her ears against the pursuing scream that never came.

10

THE FUSE BURNS

IT was the morning of the next day.

Colonel Klebb sat at her desk in the roomy office that was her headquarters in the underground basement of SMERSH. It was more an operations room than an office. One wall was completely papered with a map of the Western Hemisphere. The opposite wall was covered with the Eastern Hemisphere. Behind her desk and within reach of her left hand, a Telekrypton occasionally chattered out a signal *en clair*, duplicating another machine in the Cipher Department under the tall radio masts on the roof of the building. From time to time, when Colonel Klebb thought of it, she tore off the lengthening strip of tape and read through the signals. This was a formality. If anything important happened, her telephone would ring. Every agent of SMERSH throughout the world was controlled from this room, and it was a vigilant and iron control.

The heavy face looked sullen and dissipated. The chicken-skin under the eyes was pouched and the whites of the eyes were veined with red.

One of the three telephones at her side purred softly. She picked up the receiver. 'Send him in.'

She turned to Kronsteen who sat, picking his teeth thoughtfully with an opened paper clip, in an armchair up against the left-hand wall, under the toe of Africa.

'Granitsky.'

Kronsteen slowly turned his head and looked at the door.

Red Grant came in and closed the door softly behind him. He walked up to the desk and stood looking down, obediently, almost hungrily, into the eyes of his Commanding Officer. Kronsteen thought that he looked like a powerful mastiff, waiting to be fed.

Rosa Klebb surveyed him coldly. 'Are you fit and ready for work?'

'Yes, Comrade Colonel.'

'Let's have a look at you. Take off your clothes.'

Red Grant showed no surprise. He took off his coat and, after looking around for somewhere to put it, dropped it on the floor. Then, unselfconsciously, he took off the rest of his clothes and kicked off his shoes. The great red-brown body with its golden hair lit up the drab room. Grant stood relaxed, his hands held loosely at his sides and one knee bent slightly forward, as if he was posing for an art class.

Rosa Klebb got to her feet and came round the desk. She studied the body minutely, prodding here, feeling there, as if she was buying a horse. She went behind the man and continued her minute inspection. Before she came back in front of him, Kronsteen saw her slip something out of her jacket pocket and fit it into her hand. There was a glint of metal.

The woman came round and stood close up to the man's gleaming stomach, her right arm behind her back. She held his eyes in hers.

Suddenly, with terrific speed and the whole weight of her shoulder behind the blow, she whipped her right fist, loaded with a heavy brass knuckle-duster, round and exactly into the solar plexus of the man.

Whuck!

Grant let out a snort of surprise and pain. His knees gave slightly, and then straightened. For a flash the eyes closed tight with agony. Then they opened again and glared redly down into the cold yellow probing eyes behind the square glasses. Apart from an angry flush on the skin just below the breast bone, Grant showed no ill effects from a blow that would have sent any normal man writhing to the ground.

Rosa Klebb smiled grimly. She slipped the knuckle-duster back in her pocket and walked to her desk and sat down. She looked across at Kronsteen with a hint of pride. 'At least he is fit enough,' she said.

Kronsteen grunted.

The naked man grinned with sly satisfaction. He brought up one hand and rubbed his stomach.

Rosa Klebb sat back in her chair and watched him thoughtfully. Finally she said, 'Comrade Granitsky, there is work for you. An important task. More important than anything you have attempted. It is a task that will earn you a medal' — Grant's eyes gleamed — 'for the target is a difficult and dangerous one. You will be in a foreign country, and alone. Is that clear?'

'Yes, Comrade Colonel.' Grant was excited. Here was a chance for that big step forward. What would the medal be? The Order of Lenin? He listened carefully.

'The target is an English spy. You would like to kill an English spy?'

'Very much indeed, Comrade Colonel.' Grant's enthusiasm was genuine. He asked nothing better than to kill an Englishman. He had accounts to settle with the bastards.

'You will need many weeks of training and preparation. On this assignment you will be operating in the guise of an English agent. Your manners and appearance are uncouth. You will have to learn at least some of the tricks,' the voice sneered, 'of a *chentleman*. You will be placed in the hands of a certain Englishman we have here. A former *chentleman* of the Foreign Office in London. It will be his task to make you pass as some sort of an English spy. They employ many different kinds of men. It should not be difficult. And you will have to learn many other things. The operation will be at the end of August, but you will start your training at once. There is much to be done. Put on your clothes and report back to the A.D.C. Understood?'

'Yes, Comrade Colonel.' Grant knew not to ask any questions. He scrambled into his clothes, indifferent to the woman's eyes on him, and walked over to the door, buttoning his jacket. He turned. 'Thank you, Comrade Colonel.'

Rosa Klebb was writing up her notes of the interview. She didn't answer or look up and Grant went out and closed the door softly behind him.

The woman threw down her pen and sat back.

'And now, Comrade Kronsteen. Are there any points to discuss before we put the full machinery in motion? I should mention that the Praesidium has approved the target and ratified the death warrant. I have reported the broad lines of your plan to Comrade General Grubozaboyschikov. He is in agreement. The detailed execution has been left entirely in my hands. The combined planning and operations staff has been selected and is waiting to begin work. Have you any last-minute thoughts, Comrade?'

Kronsteen sat looking up at the ceiling, the tips of his fingers joined in front of him. He was indifferent to the condescension in the woman's voice. The pulse of concentration beat in his temples.

'This man Granitsky. He is reliable? You can trust him in a foreign country? He will not go private?'

'He has been tested for nearly ten years. He has had many opportunities to escape. He has been watched for signs of itching feet. There has never been a breath of suspicion. The man is in the position of a drug addict. He would no more abandon the Soviet Union than a drugger would abandon the source of his cocaine. He is my top executioner. There is no one better.'

'And this girl, Romanova. She was satisfactory?'

The woman said grudgingly, 'She is very beautiful. She will serve our purpose. She is not a virgin, but she is prudish and sexually unawakened. She will receive instruction. Her English is excellent. I have given her a certain version of her task and its object. She is co-operative. If she should show signs of faltering, I have the addresses of certain relatives, including children. I shall also have the names of her previous lovers. If necessary, it would be explained to her that these people will be hostages until her task is completed. She has an affectionate nature. Such a hint would be sufficient. But I do not anticipate any trouble from her.'

'Romanova. That is the name of a *buivshi* — of one of the former people. It seems odd to be using a Romanov for such a delicate task.'

'Her grandparents were distantly related to the Imperial Family. But she does not frequent *buivshi* circles. Anyway, all our grandparents were former people. There is nothing one can do about it.'

'Our grandparents were not called Romanov,' said Kronsteen drily. 'However, so long as you are satisfied.' He reflected a moment. 'And this man Bond. Have we discovered his whereabouts?'

'Yes. The M.G.B. English network reports him in London. During the day, he goes to his headquarters. At night he sleeps in his flat in a district of London called Chelsea.'

'That is good. Let us hope he stays there for the next few weeks. That will mean that he is not engaged on some operation. He will be available to go after our bait when they get the scent. Meanwhile,' Kronsteen's dark, pensive eyes continued to examine a particular point on the ceiling, 'I have been studying the suitability of centres abroad. I have decided on Istanbul for the first contact. We have a good *apparat* there. The Secret Service has only a small station. The head of the station is reported to be a good man. He will be liquidated. The centre is conveniently placed for us, with short lines of communication with Bulgaria and the Black Sea. It is relatively far from London. I am working out details of the point of assassination and the means of getting this Bond there, after he has contacted the girl. It will be either in France or very near it. We have excellent leverage on the French press. They will make the most of this kind of story, with its sensational disclosures of sex and espionage. It also remains to be decided when Granitsky shall enter the picture. These are minor details. We must choose the cameramen and the other operatives and move them quietly into Istanbul. There must be no crowding of our *apparat* there, no congestion, no unusual activity. We will warn all departments that wireless traffic with Turkey is to be kept absolutely normal before and during the operation. We don't want the British interceptors smelling a rat. The Cipher Department has agreed that there is no Security objection to handing over the outer case of a Spektor machine. That will be attractive. The machine will go to the Special Devices section. They will handle its preparation.'

Kronsteen stopped talking. His gaze slowly came down from the ceiling. He rose thoughtfully to his feet. He looked across and into the watchful, intent eyes of the woman.

'I can think of nothing else at the moment, Comrade,' he said. 'Many details will come up and have to be settled from day to day. But I think the operation can safely begin.'

'I agree, Comrade. The matter can now go forward. I will issue the necessary directives.' The harsh, authoritative voice unbent. 'I am grateful for your co-operation.'

Kronsteen lowered his head one inch in acknowledgment. He turned and walked softly out of the room.

In the silence, the Telekrypton gave a warning ping and started up its mechanical chatter. Rosa Klebb stirred in her chair and reached for one of the telephones. She dialled a number.

'Operations Room,' said a man's voice.

Rosa Klebb's pale eyes, gazing out across the room, lit on the pink shape on the wall map that was England. Her wet lips parted.

'Colonel Klebb speaking. The *konspiratsia* against the English spy Bond. The operation will commence forthwith.'

Part Two

THE EXECUTION

11

THE SOFT LIFE

THE BLUBBERY ARMS of the soft life had Bond round the neck and they were slowly strangling him. He was a man of war and when, for a long period, there was no war, his spirit went into a decline.

In his particular line of business, peace had reigned for nearly a year. And peace was killing him.

At 7.30 on the morning of Thursday, August 12th, Bond awoke in his comfortable flat in the plane-tree'd square off the King's Road and was disgusted to find that he was thoroughly bored with the prospect of the day ahead. Just as, in at least one religion, *accidie* is the first of the cardinal sins, so boredom, and particularly the incredible circumstance of waking up bored, was the only vice Bond utterly condemned.

Bond reached out and gave two rings on the bell to show May, his treasured Scottish housekeeper, that he was ready for breakfast. Then he abruptly flung the single sheet off his naked body and swung his feet to the floor.

There was only one way to deal with boredom — kick oneself out of it. Bond went down on his hands and did twenty slow press-ups, lingering over each one so that his muscles had no rest. When his arms could stand the pain no longer, he rolled over on his back and, with his hands at his sides, did the straight leg-lift until his stomach muscles screamed. He got to his feet and, after touching his toes twenty times, went over to arm and chest exercises combined with deep breathing until he was dizzy. Panting with the exertion, he went into the big white-tiled bathroom and stood in the glass shower cabinet under very hot and then cold hissing water for five minutes.

At last, after shaving and putting on a sleeveless dark blue Sea Island cotton shirt and navy blue tropical worsted trousers, he slipped his bare feet into black leather sandals and went through the bedroom into the long big-windowed sitting-room with the satisfaction of having sweated his boredom, at any rate for the time being, out of his body.

May, an elderly Scotswoman with iron grey hair and a handsome closed face, came in with the tray and put it on the table in the bay window together with *The Times*, the only paper Bond ever read.

Bond wished her good morning and sat down to breakfast.

'Good morning-s.' (To Bond, one of May's endearing qualities was that she would call no man 'sir' except — Bond had teased her about it years before — English kings and Winston Churchill. As a mark of exceptional regard, she accorded Bond an occasional hint of an 's' at the end of a word.)

She stood by the table while Bond folded his paper to the centre news page.

'Yon man was here again last night about the televeesion.'

'What man was that?' Bond looked along the headlines.

'Yon man that's always coming. Six times he's been here pestering me since June. After what I said to him the first time about the sinful thing, you'd think he'd give up trying to sell us one. By hire purchase, too, if you please!'

'Persistent chaps these salesmen.' Bond put down his paper and reached for the coffee pot.

'I gave him a right piece of my mind last night. Disturbing folk at their supper. Asked him if he'd got any papers — anything to show who he was.'

'I expect that fixed him.' Bond filled his large coffee cup to the brim with black coffee.

'Not a bit of it. Flourished his union card. Said he had every right to earn his living. Electricians Union it was too. They're the Communist one, aren't they-s?'

'Yes, that's right,' said Bond vaguely. His mind sharpened. Was it possible *They* could be keeping an eye on him? He took a sip of the coffee and put the cup down. 'Exactly what did this man say, May?' he asked, keeping his voice indifferent, but looking up at her.

'He said he's selling televeesion sets on commission in his spare time. And are we sure we don't want one. He says we're one of the only folk in the square that haven't got one. Sees there isn't one of those aerial things on the house, I daresay. He's always asking if you're at home so that he can have a word with you about it. Fancy his cheek! I'm surprised he hasn't thought to catch you coming in or going out. He's always asking if I'm expecting you home. Naturally I don't tell him anything about your movements. Respectable, quiet-spoken body, if he wasn't so persistent.'

Could be, thought Bond. There are many ways of checking up whether the owner's at home or away. A servant's appearance and reactions — a glance through the open door. 'Well, you're wasting your time because he's away,' would be the obvious reception if the flat was empty. Should he tell the Security Section? Bond shrugged his shoulders irritably. What the hell. There was probably nothing in it. Why would *They* be interested in him? And, if there was something in it, Security was quite capable of making him change his flat.

'I expect you've frightened him away this time.' Bond smiled up at May. 'I should think you've heard the last of him.'

'Yes-s,' said May doubtfully. At any rate she had carried out her orders to tell him if she saw anyone 'hanging about the place'. She bustled off with a whisper of the old-fashioned black uniform she persisted in wearing even in the heat of August.

Bond went back to his breakfast. Normally it was little straws in the wind like this that would start a persistent intuitive ticking in his mind, and, on other days, he would not have been happy until he had solved the problem of the man from the Communist union who kept on coming to the house. Now, from months of idleness and disuse, the sword was rusty in the scabbard and Bond's mental guard was down.

Breakfast was Bond's favourite meal of the day. When he was stationed in London it was always the same. It consisted of very strong coffee, from De Bry in New Oxford Street, brewed in an American *Chemex*, of which he drank two large cups, black and without sugar. The single egg, in the dark blue egg cup with a gold ring round the top, was boiled for three and a third minutes.

It was a very fresh, speckled brown egg from French *Marans* hens owned by some friend of May in the country. (Bond disliked white eggs and, faddish as he was in many small things, it amused him to maintain that there was such a thing as the perfect boiled egg.) Then there were two thick slices of whole-wheat toast, a large pat of deep yellow Jersey butter and three squat glass jars containing Tiptree 'Little Scarlet' strawberry jam, Cooper's Vintage Oxford marmalade and Norwegian Heather Honey from Fortnum's. The coffee pot and the silver on the tray were Queen Anne, and the china was Minton, of the same dark blue and gold and white as the egg cup.

That morning, while Bond finished his breakfast with honey, he pinpointed the immediate cause of his lethargy and of his low spirits. To begin with, Tiffany Case, his love for so many happy months, had left him and, after final painful weeks during which she had withdrawn to an hotel, had sailed for America at the end of July. He missed her badly and his mind still sheered away from the thought of her. And it was August, and London was hot and stale. He was due for leave, but he had not the energy or the desire to go off alone, or to try and find some temporary replacement for Tiffany to go with him. So he had stayed on in the half-empty headquarters of the Secret Service grinding away at the old routines, snapping at his secretary and rasping his colleagues.

Even M. had finally got impatient with the surly caged tiger on the floor below, and, on Monday of this particular week, he had sent Bond a sharp note appointing him to a Committee of Inquiry under Paymaster Captain Troop. The note said that it was time Bond, as a senior officer in the Service, took a hand in major administrative problems. Anyway, there was no one else available. Headquarters were short-handed and the 00 Section was quiescent. Bond would pray report that afternoon, at 2.30, to Room 412.

It was Troop, reflected Bond, as he lit his first cigarette of the day, who was the most nagging and immediate cause of his discontent.

In every large business, there is one man who is the office tyrant and bugbear and who is cordially disliked by all the staff. This individual performs an unconsciously important role by acting as a kind of lightning conductor for the usual office hates and fears. In fact, he reduces their disruptive influence by providing them with a common target. The man is usually the general manager, or the Head of Admin. He is that indispensable man who is a watchdog over the small things — petty cash, heat and light, towels and soap in the lavatories, stationery supplies, the canteen, the holiday rota, the punctuality of the staff. He is the one man who has real impact on the office comforts and amenities and whose authority extends into the privacy and personal habits of the men and women of the organization. To want such a job, and to have the necessary qualifications for it, the man must have exactly those qualities which irritate and abrade. He must be parsimonious, observant, prying and meticulous. And he must be a strong disciplinarian and indifferent to opinion. He must be a little dictator. In all well-run businesses there is such a man. In the Secret Service, it is Paymaster Captain Troop, R.N. Retired, Head of Admin., whose job it is, in his own words, 'to keep the place shipshape and Bristol fashion'.

It was inevitable that Captain Troop's duties would bring him into conflict with most of the organization, but it was particularly unfortunate that M. could think of no one but Troop to spare as Chairman for this particular committee.

For this was yet one more of those Committees of Inquiry dealing with the delicate intricacies of the Burgess and Maclean case, and with the lessons that could be learned from it. M. had dreamed it up, five years after he had closed his own particular file on that case, purely as a sop to the Privy Council Inquiry into the Security Services which the Prime Minister had ordered in 1955.

At once Bond had got into a hopeless wrangle with Troop over the employment of 'intellectuals' in the Secret Service.

Perversely, and knowing it would annoy, Bond had put forward the proposition that, if M.I.5 and the Secret Service were to concern themselves seriously with the atom age 'intellectual spy', they must employ a certain number of intellectuals to counter them. 'Retired officers of the Indian Army,' Bond had pronounced, 'can't possibly understand the thought processes of a Burgess or a Maclean. They won't even know such people exist — let alone be in a position to frequent their cliques and get to know their friends and their secrets. Once Burgess and Maclean went to Russia, the only way to make contact with them again and, perhaps, when they got tired of Russia, turn them into double agents against the Russians, would have been to send their closest friends to Moscow and Prague and Budapest with orders to wait until one of these chaps crept out of the masonry and made contact. And one of them, probably Burgess, would have been driven to make contact by his loneliness and by his ache to tell his story to someone.[1] But they certainly wouldn't take the risk of revealing themselves to some man with a trench-coat and a cavalry moustache and a beta minus mind.'

'Oh really,' Troop had said with icy calm. 'So you suggest we should staff the organization with long-haired perverts. That's quite an original notion. I thought we were all agreed that homosexuals were about the worst security risk there is. I can't see the Americans handing over many atom secrets to a lot of pansies soaked in scent.'

'All intellectuals aren't homosexual. And many of them are bald. I'm just saying that . . . ,' and so the argument had gone on intermittently through the hearings of the past three days, and the other committee members had ranged themselves more or less with Troop. Now, today, they had to draw up their recommendations and Bond was wondering whether to take the unpopular step of entering a minority report.

How seriously did he feel about the whole question? Bond wondered as, at nine o'clock, he walked out of his flat and down the steps to his car. Was he just being petty and obstinate? Had he constituted himself into a one-man opposition only to give his teeth something to bite into? Was he so bored that he could find nothing better to do than make a nuisance of himself inside his own organization? Bond couldn't make up his mind. He felt restless and indecisive, and, behind it all, there was a nagging disquiet he couldn't put his finger on.

As he pressed the self-starter and the twin exhausts of the Bentley woke to their fluttering growl, a curious bastard quotation slipped from nowhere into Bond's mind.

'Those whom the Gods wish to destroy, they first make bored.'

[1] Written in March 1956. I .F.

12

A PIECE OF CAKE

AS IT TURNED out, Bond never had to make a decision on the Committee's final report.

He had complimented his secretary on a new summer frock, and was half way through the file of signals that had come in during the night, when the red telephone that could only mean M. or his Chief-of-Staff gave its soft, peremptory burr.

Bond picked up the receiver. '007.'

'Can you come up?' It was the Chief-of-Staff.

'M.?'

'Yes. And it looks like a long session. I've told Troop you won't be able to make the Committee.'

'Any idea what it's about?'

The Chief-of-Staff chuckled. 'Well, I have as a matter of fact. But you'd better hear about it from him. It'll make you sit up. There's quite a swerve on this one.'

As Bond put on his coat and went out into the corridor, banging the door behind him, he had a feeling of certainty that the starter's gun had fired and that the dog days had come to an end. Even the ride up to the top floor in the lift and the walk down the long quiet corridor to the door of M.'s staff office seemed to be charged with the significance of all those other occasions when the bell of the red telephone had been the signal that had fired him, like a loaded projectile, across the world towards some distant target of M.'s choosing. And the eyes of Miss Moneypenny, M.'s private secretary, had that old look of excitement and secret knowledge as she smiled up at him and pressed the switch on the intercom.

'007's here, sir.'

'Send him in,' said the metallic voice, and the red light of privacy went on above the door.

Bond went through the door and closed it softly behind him. The room was cool, or perhaps it was the venetian blinds that gave an impression of coolness. They threw bars of light and shadow across the dark green carpet up to the edge of the big central desk. There the sunshine stopped so that the quiet figure behind the desk sat in a pool of suffused greenish shade. In the ceiling directly above the desk, a big twin-bladed tropical fan, a recent addition to M.'s room, slowly revolved, shifting the thundery August air that, even high up above the Regent's Park, was heavy and stale after a week of heat-wave.

M. gestured to the chair opposite him across the red leather desk. Bond sat down and looked across into the tranquil, lined sailor's face that he loved, honoured and obeyed.

'Do you mind if I ask you a personal question, James?' M. never asked his staff personal questions and Bond couldn't imagine what was coming.

'No, sir.'

M. picked his pipe out of the big copper ash-tray and began to fill it, thoughtfully watching his fingers at work with the tobacco. He said harshly: 'You needn't answer, but it's to do with your, er, friend, Miss Case. As you know, I don't generally interest myself in these matters, but I did hear that you had been, er, seeing a lot of each other since that diamond business. Even some idea you might be going to get married.' M. glanced up at Bond and then down again. He put the loaded pipe into his mouth and set a match to it. Out of the corner of his mouth, as he drew at the jigging flame, he said: 'Care to tell me anything about it?'

Now what? wondered Bond. Damn these office gossips. He said gruffly, 'Well, sir, we did get on well. And there was some idea we might get married. But then she met some chap in the American Embassy. On the Military Attaché's staff. Marine Corps major. And I gather she's going to marry him. They've both gone back to the States, as a matter of fact. Probably better that way. Mixed marriages aren't often a success. I gather he's a nice enough fellow. Probably suit her better than living in London. She couldn't really settle down here. Fine girl, but she's a bit neurotic. We had too many rows. Probably my fault. Anyway it's over now.'

M. gave one of the brief smiles that lit up his eyes more than his mouth. 'I'm sorry if it went wrong, James,' he said. There was no sympathy in M.'s voice. He disapproved of Bond's 'womanizing', as he called it to himself, while recognizing that his prejudice was the relic of a Victorian upbringing. But, as Bond's chief, the last thing he wanted was for Bond to be permanently tied to one woman's skirts. 'Perhaps it's for the best. Doesn't do to get mixed up with neurotic women in this business. They hang on your gun-arm, if you know what I mean. Forgive me for asking about it. Had to know the answer before I told you what's come up. It's a pretty odd business. Be difficult to get you involved if you were on the edge of marrying or anything of that sort.'

Bond shook his head, waiting for the story.

'All right then,' said M. There was a note of relief in his voice. He leant back in his chair and gave several quick pulls on his pipe to get it going. 'This is what's happened. Yesterday there was a long signal in from Istanbul. Seems on Tuesday the Head of Station T got an anonymous typewritten message which told him to take a round ticket on the 8 p.m. ferry steamer from the Galata Bridge to the mouth of the Bosphorus and back. Nothing else. Head of T's an adventurous sort of chap, and of course he took the steamer. He stood up for'ard by the rail and waited. After about a quarter of an hour a girl came and stood beside him, a Russian girl, very good-looking, he says, and after they'd talked a bit about the view and so on, she suddenly switched and in the same sort of conversational voice she told him an extraordinary story.'

M. paused to put another match to his pipe. Bond interjected, 'Who is Head of T, sir? I've never worked in Turkey.'

'Man called Kerim, Darko Kerim. Turkish father and English mother. Remarkable fellow. Been Head of T since before the war. One of the best men we've got anywhere. Does a wonderful job. Loves it. Very intelligent and he knows all that part of the world like the back of his hand.' M. dismissed Kerim with a sideways jerk of his pipe. 'Anyway, the girl's story was that she was a Corporal in the M.G.B. Had been in the show since she left school and had just got transferred to the Istanbul centre as a cipher officer. She'd engineered the transfer because she wanted to get out of Russia and come over.'

'That's good,' said Bond. 'Might be useful to have one of their cipher girls. But why does she want to come over?'

M. looked across the table at Bond. 'Because she's in love.'

He paused and added mildly, 'She says she's in love with you.'

'In love with *me*?'

'Yes, with you. That's what she says. Her name's Tatiana Romanova. Ever heard of her?'

'Good God, no! I mean, no, sir.' M. smiled at the mixture of expressions on Bond's face. 'But what the hell does she mean? Has she ever met me? How does she know I exist?'

'Well,' said M. 'The whole thing sounds absolutely ridiculous. But it's so crazy that it just might be true. This girl is twenty-four. Ever since she joined the M.G.B. she's been working in their Central Index, the same as our Records. And she's been working in the English section of it. She's been there six years. One of the files she had to deal with was yours.'

'I'd like to see that one,' commented Bond.

'Her story is that she first took a fancy to the photographs they've got of you. Admired your looks and so on.' M.'s mouth turned downwards at the corners as if he had just sucked at a lemon. 'She read up all your cases. Decided that you were the hell of a fellow.'

Bond looked down his nose. M.'s face was non-committal.

'She said you particularly appealed to her because you reminded her of the hero of a book by some Russian fellow called Lermontov. Apparently it was her favourite book. This hero chap liked gambling and spent his whole time getting in and out of scraps. Anyway, you reminded her of him. She says she came to think of nothing else, and one day the idea came to her that if only she could transfer to one of their foreign centres she could get in touch with you and you would come and rescue her.'

'I've never heard such a crazy story, sir. Surely Head of T didn't swallow it.'

'Now wait a moment.' M.'s voice was testy. 'Just don't be in too much of a hurry simply because something's turned up you've never come across before. Suppose you happened to be a film star instead of being in this particular trade. You'd get daft letters from girls all over the world stuffed with heaven knows what sort of rot about not being able to live without you and so on. Here's a silly girl doing a secretary's job in Moscow. Probably the whole department is staffed by women, like our Records. Not a man in the room to look at, and here she is, faced with your, er, dashing features on a file that's constantly coming up for review. And she gets what I believe they call a "crush" on these pictures just as secretaries all over the world get crushes on these dreadful faces in the magazines.' M. waved his pipe sideways to indicate his ignorance of these grisly female habits. 'The Lord knows I don't know much about these things, but you must admit that they happen.'

Bond smiled at the appeal for help. 'Well, as a matter of fact, sir, I'm beginning to see there is some sense in it. There's no reason why a Russian girl shouldn't be just as silly as an English one. But she must have got guts to do what she did. Does Head of T say if she realized the consequences if she was found out?'

'He said she was frightened out of her wits,' said M. 'Spent the whole time on the boat looking round to see if anybody was watching her. But it seems they were the usual peasants and commuters that take these boats, and as it was a late boat there weren't many passengers anyway. But wait a minute. You haven't heard half the story.' M. took a long pull at his pipe and blew a cloud of smoke up towards the slowly turning fan above his head. Bond watched the smoke get caught up in the blades and whirled into nothingness. 'She told Kerim that this passion for you gradually developed into a phobia. She got to hate the sight of Russian men. In time this turned into a dislike of the régime and particularly of the work she was doing for them and, so to speak, against you. So she applied for a transfer abroad, and since her languages were very good — English and French — in due course she was offered Istanbul if she would join the Cipher Department, which meant a cut in pay. To cut a long story short, after six months' training, she got to Istanbul about three weeks ago. Then she sniffed about and soon got hold of the name of our man, Kerim. He's been there so long that everybody in Turkey knows what he does by now. He doesn't mind, and it takes people's eyes off the special men we send in from time to time. There's no harm in having a front man in some of these places. Quite a lot of customers would come to us if they knew where to go and who to talk to.'

Bond commented: 'The public agent often does better than the man who has to spend a lot of time and energy keeping under cover.'

'So she sent Kerim the note. Now she wants to know if he can help her.' M. paused and sucked thoughtfully at his pipe. 'Of course Kerim's first reactions were exactly the same as yours, and he fished around looking for a trap. But he simply couldn't see what the Russians could gain from sending this girl over to us. All this time the steamer was getting further and further up the Bosphorus and soon it would be turning to come back to Istanbul. And the girl got more and more desperate as Kerim went on trying to break down her story. Then,' M.'s eyes glittered softly across at Bond, 'came the clincher.'

That glitter in M.'s eyes, thought Bond. How well he knew those moments when M.'s cold grey eyes betrayed their excitement and their greed.

'She had a last card to play. And she knew it was the ace of trumps. If she could come over to us, she would bring her cipher machine with her. It's the brand-new Spektor machine. The thing we'd give our eyes to have.'

'God,' said Bond softly, his mind boggling at the immensity of the prize. The Spektor! The machine that would allow them to decipher the Top Secret traffic of all. To have that, even if its loss was immediately discovered and the settings changed, or the machine taken out of service in Russian embassies and spy centres all over the world, would be a priceless victory. Bond didn't know much about cryptography, and, for security's sake, in case he was ever captured, wished to know as little as possible about its secrets, but at least he knew that, in the Russian Secret Service, loss of the Spektor would be counted a major disaster.

Bond was sold. At once he accepted all M.'s faith in the girl's story, however crazy it might be. For a Russian to bring them this gift, and take the appalling risk of bringing it, could only mean an act of desperation — of desperate infatuation if you liked. Whether the girl's story was true or not, the stakes were too high to turn down the gamble.

'You see, 007?' said M. softly. It was not difficult to read Bond's mind from the excitement in his eyes. 'You see what I mean?'

Bond hedged. 'But did she say how she could do it?'

'Not exactly. But Kerim says she was absolutely definite. Some business about night duty. Apparently she's on duty alone certain nights of the week and sleeps on a camp bed in the office. She seemed to have no doubts about it, although she realized that she would be shot out of hand if anyone even dreamed of her plan. She was even worried about Kerim reporting all this back to me. Made him promise he would encode the signal himself and send it on a one-time-only pad and keep no copy. Naturally he did as she asked. Directly she mentioned the Spektor, Kerim knew he might be on to the most important coup that's come our way since the war.'

'What happened then, sir?'

'The steamer was coming up to a place called Ortakoy. She said she was going to get off there. Kerim promised to get a signal off that night. She refused to make any arrangements for staying in touch. Just said that she would keep her end of the bargain if we would keep ours. She said good night and mixed in the crowd going down the gang-plank and that was the last Kerim saw of her.'

M. suddenly leant forward in his chair and looked hard at Bond. 'But of course he couldn't *guarantee* that we would make the bargain with her.'

Bond said nothing. He thought he could guess what was coming.

'This girl will only do these things on one condition.' M.'s eyes narrowed until they were fierce, significant slits. 'That you go out to Istanbul and bring her and the machine back to England.'

Bond shrugged his shoulders. That presented no difficulties. But . . . He looked candidly back at M. 'Should be a piece of cake, sir. As far as I can see there's only one snag. She's only seen photographs of me and read a lot of exciting stories. Suppose that when she sees me in the flesh, I don't come up to her expectations.'

'That's where the work comes in,' said M. grimly. 'That's why I asked those questions about Miss Case. It's up to you to see that you *do* come up to her expectations.'

13

'B.E.A. TAKES YOU THERE . . . '

THE FOUR SMALL square-ended propellers turned slowly, one by one, and became four whizzing pools. The low hum of the turbo-jets rose to a shrill smooth whine. The quality of the noise, and the complete absence of vibration, were different from the stuttering roar and straining horsepower of all other aircraft Bond had flown in. As the Viscount wheeled easily out to the shimmering east-west runway of London Airport, Bond felt as if he was sitting in an expensive mechanical toy.

There was a pause as the chief pilot gunned up the four turbo-jets into a banshee scream and then, with a jerk of released brakes, the 10.30 B.E.A. Flight 130 to Rome, Athens and Istanbul gathered speed and hurtled down the runway and up into a quick, easy climb.

In ten minutes they had reached 20,000 feet and were heading south along the wide air-channel that takes the Mediterranean traffic from England. The scream of the jets died to a low, drowsy whistle. Bond unfastened his seat-belt and lit a cigarette. He reached for the slim, expensive-looking attaché case on the floor beside him and took out *The Mask of Dimitrios* by Eric Ambler and put the case, which was very heavy in spite of its size, on the seat beside him. He thought how surprised the ticket clerk at London Airport would have been if she had weighed the case instead of letting it go unchecked as an 'over-night bag'. And if, in their turn, Customs had been intrigued by its weight, how interested they would have been when it was slipped under the Inspectoscope.

Q Branch had put together this smart-looking little bag, ripping out the careful handiwork of Swaine and Adeney to pack fifty rounds of .25 ammunition, in two flat rows, between the leather and the lining of the spine. In each of the innocent sides there was a flat throwing knife, built by Wilkinsons, the sword makers, and the tops of their handles were concealed cleverly by the stitching at the corners. Despite Bond's efforts to laugh them out of it, Q's craftsmen had insisted on building a hidden compartment into the handle of the case, which, by pressure at a certain point, would deliver a cyanide death-pill into the palm of his hand. (Directly he had taken delivery of the case, Bond had washed this pill down the lavatory.) More important was the thick tube of Palmolive shaving cream in the otherwise guileless spongebag. The whole top of this unscrewed to reveal the silencer for the Beretta, packed in cotton wool. In case hard cash was needed, the lid of the attaché case contained fifty golden sovereigns. These could be poured out by slipping sideways one ridge of welting.

The complicated bag of tricks amused Bond, but he also had to admit that, despite its eight-pound weight, the bag was a convenient way of carrying the tools of his trade, which otherwise would have had to be concealed about his body.

Only a dozen miscellaneous passengers were on the plane. Bond smiled at the thought of Loelia Ponsonby's horror if she knew that that made the load thirteen. The day before, when he had left M. and had gone back to his office to arrange the details of his flight, his secretary had protested violently at the idea of his travelling on Friday the thirteenth.

'But it's always best to travel on the thirteenth,' Bond had explained patiently. 'There are practically no passengers and it's more comfortable and you get better service. I always choose the thirteenth when I can.'

'Well,' she had said resignedly, 'it's your funeral. But I shall spend the day worrying about you. And for heaven's sake don't go walking under ladders or anything silly this afternoon. You oughtn't to overplay your luck like this. I don't know what you're going to Turkey for, and I don't want to know. But I have a feeling in my bones.'

'Ah, those beautiful bones!' Bond had teased her. 'I'll take them out to dinner the night I get back.'

'You'll do nothing of the sort,' she had said coldly. Later she had kissed him goodbye with a sudden warmth, and for the hundredth time Bond had wondered why he bothered with other women when the most darling of them all was his secretary.

The plane sang steadily on above the endless sea of whipped-cream clouds that looked solid enough to land on if the engines failed. The clouds broke up and a distant blue haze, far away to their left, was Paris. For an hour they flew high over the burned-up fields of France until, after Dijon, the land turned from a pale to a darker green as it sloped up into the Juras.

Lunch came. Bond put aside his book and the thoughts that kept coming between him and the printed page, and, while he ate, he gazed down at the cool mirror of the Lake of Geneva. As the pine forests began to climb towards the snow patches between the beautifully scoured teeth of the Alps, he remembered early skiing holidays. The plane skirted the great eye-tooth of Mont Blanc, a few hundred yards to port, and Bond looked down at the dirty grey elephant's skin of the glaciers and saw himself again, a young man in his teens, with the leading end of the rope round his waist, bracing himself against the top of a rock-chimney on the Aiguilles Rouges as his two companions from the University of Geneva inched up the smooth rock towards him.

And now? Bond smiled wryly at his reflection in the Perspex as the plane swung out of the mountains and over the gros-grained terrazza of Lombardy. If that young James Bond came up to him in the street and talked to him, would he recognize the clean, eager youth that had been him at seventeen? And what would that youth think of him, the secret agent, the older James Bond? Would he recognize himself beneath the surface of this man who was tarnished with years of treachery and ruthlessness and fear — this man with the cold arrogant eyes and the scar down his cheek and the flat bulge beneath his left armpit? If the youth did recognize him what would his judgment be? What would he think of Bond's present assignment? What would he think of the dashing secret agent who was off across the world in a new and most romantic role — to pimp for England?

Bond put the thought of his dead youth out of his mind. Never job backwards. What-might-have-been was a waste of time. Follow your fate, and be satisfied with it, and be glad not to be a second-hand motor salesman, or a yellow-press journalist, pickled in gin and nicotine, or a cripple — or dead.

Gazing down on the sun-baked sprawl of Genoa and the gentle blue waters of the Mediterranean, Bond closed his mind to the past and focused it on the immediate future — on this business, as he sourly described it to himself, of 'pimping for England'.

For that, however else one might like to describe it, was what he was on his way to do — to seduce, and seduce very quickly, a girl whom he had never seen before, whose name he had heard yesterday for the first time. And all the while, however attractive she was — and Head of T had described her as 'very beautiful' — Bond's whole mind would have to be not on what she was, but on what she had — the dowry she was bringing with her. It would be like trying to marry a rich woman for her money. Would he be able to act the part? Perhaps he could make the right faces and say the right things, but would his body dissociate itself from his secret thoughts and effectively make the love he would declare? How did men behave credibly in bed when their whole minds were focused on a woman's bank balance? Perhaps there was an erotic stimulus in the notion that one was ravaging a sack of gold. But a cipher machine?

Elba passed below them and the plane slid into its fifty-mile glide towards Rome. Half an hour among the jabbering loud-speakers of Ciampino Airport, time to drink two excellent Americanos, and they were on their way again, flying steadily down towards the toe of Italy, and Bond's mind went back to sifting the minutest details of the rendezvous that was drawing closer at three hundred miles an hour.

Was it all a complicated M.G.B. plot of which he couldn't find the key? Was he walking into some trap that not even the tortuous mind of M. could fathom? God knew M. was worried about the possibility of such a trap. Every conceivable angle of the evidence, for and against, had been scrutinized — not only by M., but also by a full-dress operations meeting of Heads of Sections that had worked all through the afternoon and evening before. But, whichever way the case had been examined, no one had been able to suggest what the Russians might get out of it. They might want to kidnap Bond and interrogate him. But why Bond? He was an operating agent, unconcerned with the general working of the Service, carrying in his head nothing of use to the Russians except the details of his current duty and a certain amount of background information that could not possibly be vital. Or they might want to kill Bond, as an act of revenge. Yet he had not come up against them for two years. If they wanted to kill him, they had only to shoot him in the streets of London, or in his flat, or put a bomb in his car.

Bond's thoughts were interrupted by the stewardness. 'Fasten your seat-belts, please.' As she spoke the plane dropped sickeningly and soared up again with an ugly note of strain in the scream of the jets. The sky outside was suddenly black. Rain hammered on the windows. There came a blinding flash of blue and white light and a crash as if an anti-aircraft shell had hit them, and the plane heaved and bucketed in the belly of the electric storm that had ambushed them out of the mouth of the Adriatic.

Bond smelt the smell of danger. It is a real smell, something like the mixture of sweat and electricity you get in an amusement arcade. Again the lightning flung its hands across the windows. Crash! It felt as if they were the centre of the thunder clap. Suddenly the plane seemed incredibly small and frail. Thirteen passengers! Friday the Thirteenth! Bond thought of Loelia Ponsonby's words and his hands on the arms of his chair felt wet. How old is this plane? he wondered. How many flying hours has it done? Had the deathwatch beetle of metal fatigue got into the wings? How much of their strength had it eaten away? Perhaps he wouldn't get to Istanbul after all. Perhaps a plummeting crash into the Gulf of Corinth was going to be the destiny he had been scanning philosophically only an hour before.

In the centre of Bond was a hurricane-room, the kind of citadel found in old-fashioned houses in the tropics. These rooms are small, strongly built cells in the heart of the house, in the middle of the ground floor and sometimes dug down into its foundations. To this cell the owner and his family retire if the storm threatens to destroy the house, and they stay there until the danger is past. Bond went to his hurricane-room only when the situation was beyond his control and no other possible action could be taken. Now he retired to this citadel, closed his mind to the hell of noise and violent movement, and focused on a single stitch in the back of the seat in front of him, waiting with slackened nerves for whatever fate had decided for B.E.A. Flight No. 130.

Almost at once it got lighter in the cabin. The rain stopped crashing on the Perspex window and the noise of the jets settled back into their imperturbable whistle. Bond opened the door of his hurricane-room and stepped out. He slowly turned his head and looked curiously out of the window and watched the tiny shadow of the plane hastening far below across the quiet waters of the Gulf of Corinth. He heaved a deep sigh and reached into his hip-pocket for his gunmetal cigarette case. He was pleased to see his hands were dead steady as he took out his lighter and lit one of the Morland cigarettes with the three gold rings. Should he tell Lil that perhaps she had almost been right? He decided that if he could find a rude enough postcard in Istanbul he would.

The day outside faded through the colours of a dying dolphin and Mount Hymettus came at them, blue in the dusk. Down over the twinkling sprawl of Athens and then the Viscount was wheeling across the standard concrete air-strip with its drooping windsock and the notices in the strange dancing letters Bond had hardly seen since school.

Bond climbed out of the plane with the handful of pale, silent passengers and walked across to the transit lounge and up to the bar. He ordered a tumbler of ouzo and drank it down and chased it with a mouthful of ice water. There was a strong bite under the sickly anisette taste and Bond felt the drink light a quick, small fire down his throat and in his stomach. He put down his glass and ordered another.

By the time the loudspeakers called him out again it was dusk and the half moon rode clear and high above the lights of the town. The air was soft with evening and the smell of flowers and there was the steady pulse-beat of the cicadas — zing-a-zing-a-zing — and the distant sound of a man singing. The voice was clear and sad and the song had a note of lament. Near the airport a dog barked excitedly at an unknown human smell. Bond suddenly realized that he had come into the East where the guard-dog howls all night. For some reason the realization sent a pang of pleasure and excitement into his heart.

They had only a ninety-minute flight to Istanbul, across the dark Aegean and the Sea of Marmara. An excellent dinner, with two dry martinis and a half-bottle of Calvet claret, put Bond's reservations about flying on Friday the thirteenth, and his worries about his assignment, out of his mind and substituted a mood of pleased anticipation.

Then they were there and the plane's four propellers wheeled to a stop outside the fine modern airport of Yesilkoy, an hour's drive from Istanbul. Bond said goodbye and thank you for a good flight to the stewardess, carried the heavy little attaché case through the passport check into the customs, and waited for his suitcase to come off the plane.

So these dark, ugly, neat little officials were the modern Turks. He listened to their voices, full of broad vowels and quiet sibilants and modified u-sounds, and he watched the dark eyes that belied the soft, polite voices. They were bright, angry, cruel eyes that had only lately come down from the mountains. Bond thought he knew the history of those eyes. They were eyes that had been trained for centuries to watch over sheep and decipher small movements on far horizons. They were eyes that kept the knife-hand in sight without seeming to, that counted the grains of meal and the small fractions of coin and noted the flicker of the merchant's fingers. They were hard, untrusting, jealous eyes. Bond didn't take to them.

Outside the customs, a tall rangy man with drooping black moustaches stepped out of the shadows. He wore a smart dust-coat and a chauffeur's cap. He saluted and, without asking Bond his name, took his suitcase and led the way over to a gleaming aristocrat of a car — an old black basket-work Rolls-Royce coupé-de-ville that Bond guessed must have been built for some millionaire of the '20s.

When the car was gliding out of the airport, the man turned and said politely over his shoulder, in excellent English, 'Kerim Bey thought you would prefer to rest tonight, sir. I am to call for you at nine tomorrow morning. What hotel are you staying at, sir?'

'The Kristal Palas.'

'Very good, sir.' The car sighed off down the wide modern road.

Behind them, in the dappled shadows of the airport parking place, Bond vaguely heard the crackle of a motor scooter starting up. The sound meant nothing to him and he settled back to enjoy the drive.

14

DARKO KERIM

JAMES BOND AWOKE early in his dingy room at the Kristal Palas on the heights of Pera and absent-mindedly reached down a hand to explore a sharp tickle on the outside of his right thigh. Something had bitten him during the night. Irritably he scratched the spot. He might have expected it.

When he had arrived the night before, to be greeted by a surly night-concierge in trousers and a collarless shirt, and had briefly inspected the entrance hall with the fly-blown palms in copper pots, and the floor and walls of discoloured Moorish tiles, he had known what he was in for. He had half thought of going to another hotel. Inertia, and a perverse liking for the sleazy romance that clings to old-fashioned Continental hotels, had decided him to stay, and he had signed in and followed the man up to the third floor in the old rope-and-gravity lift.

His room, with its few sticks of aged furniture and an iron bedstead, was what he had expected. He only looked to see if there were the blood spots of squashed bugs on the wall-paper behind the bedhead before dismissing the concierge.

He had been premature. When he went into the bathroom and turned on the hot tap it gave a deep sigh, then a deprecating cough, and finally ejected a small centipede into the basin. Bond morosely washed the centipede away with the thin stream of brownish water from the cold tap. So much, he had reflected wryly, for choosing an hotel because its name had amused him and because he had wanted to get away from the soft life of big hotels.

But he had slept well, and now, with the reservation that he must buy some insecticide, he decided to forget about his comforts and get on with the day.

Bond got out of bed, drew back the heavy red plush curtains and leant on the iron balustrade and looked out over one of the most famous views in the world — on his right the still waters of the Golden Horn, on his left the dancing waves of the unsheltered Bosphorus, and, in between, the tumbling roofs, soaring minarets and crouching mosques of Pera. After all, his choice had been good. The view made up for many bedbugs and much discomfort.

For ten minutes Bond stood and gazed out across the sparkling water barrier between Europe and Asia, then he turned back into the room, now bright with sunshine, and telephoned for his breakfast. His English was not understood, but his French at last got through. He turned on a cold bath and shaved patiently with cold water and hoped that the exotic breakfast he had ordered would not be a fiasco.

He was not disappointed. The yoghourt, in a blue china bowl, was deep yellow and with the consistency of thick cream. The green figs, ready peeled, were bursting with ripeness, and the Turkish coffee was jet black and with the burned taste that showed it had been freshly ground. Bond ate the delicious meal on a table drawn up beside the open window. He watched the steamers and the caïques criss-crossing the two seas spread out before him and wondered about Kerim and what fresh news there might be.

Punctually at nine, the elegant Rolls came for him and took him through Taksim Square and down the crowded Istiklal and out of Asia. The thick black smoke of the waiting steamers, badged with the graceful crossed anchors of the Merchant Marine, streamed across the first span of the Galata Bridge and hid the other shore towards which the Rolls nosed forward through the bicycles and trams, the well-bred snort of the ancient bulb horn just keeping the pedestrians from under its wheels. Then the way was clear and the old European section of Istanbul glittered at the end of the broad half-mile of bridge with the slim minarets lancing up into the sky and the domes of the mosques, crouching at their feet, looking like big firm breasts. It should have been the Arabian Nights, but to Bond, seeing it first above the tops of trams and above the great scars of modern advertising along the river frontage, it seemed a once beautiful theatre-set that modern Turkey had thrown aside in favour of the steel and concrete flat-iron of the Istanbul-Hilton Hotel, blankly glittering behind him on the heights of Pera.

Across the bridge, the car nosed to the right down a narrow cobbled street parallel with the waterfront and stopped outside a high wooden porte-cochère.

A tough-looking watchman with a chunky, smiling face, dressed in frayed khaki, came out of a porter's lodge and saluted. He opened the car door and gestured for Bond to follow him. He led the way back into his lodge and through a door into a small courtyard with a neatly raked gravel parterre. In the centre was a gnarled eucalyptus tree at whose foot two white ring-doves were pecking about. The noise of the town was a distant rumble and it was quiet and peaceful.

They walked across the gravel and through another small door and Bond found himself at one end of a great vaulted godown with high circular windows through which dusty bars of sunshine slanted across a vista of bundles and bales of merchandise. There was a cool, musty scent of spices and coffee and, as Bond followed the watchman down the central passageway, a sudden strong wave of mint.

At the end of the long warehouse was a raised platform enclosed by a balustrade. On it half a dozen young men and girls sat on high stools and wrote busily in fat, old-fashioned ledgers. It was like a Dickensian counting-house and Bond noticed that each high desk had a battered abacus beside the inkpot. Not one of the clerks looked up as Bond walked between them, but a tall, swarthy man with a lean face and unexpected blue eyes came forward from the furthest desk and took delivery of him from the watchman. He smiled warmly at Bond, showing a set of extremely white teeth, and led him to the back of the platform. He knocked on a fine mahogany door with a Yale lock and, without waiting for an answer, opened it and let Bond in and closed the door softly behind him.

'Ah, my friend. Come in. Come in.' A very large man in a beautifully cut cream tussore suit got up from a mahogany desk and came to meet him, holding out his hand.

A hint of authority behind the loud friendly voice reminded Bond that this was the Head of Station T, and that Bond was in another man's territory and juridically under his command. It was no more than a point of etiquette, but a point to remember.

Darko Kerim had a wonderfully warm dry handclasp. It was

a strong Western handful of operative fingers — not the banana-skin handshake of the East that makes you want to wipe your fingers on your coat-tails. And the big hand had a coiled power that said it could easily squeeze your hand tighter and tighter until finally it cracked your bones.

Bond was six feet tall, but this man was at least two inches taller and he gave the impression of being twice as broad and twice as thick as Bond. Bond looked up into two wide apart, smiling blue eyes in a large smooth brown face with a broken nose. The eyes were watery and veined with red, like the eyes of a hound who lies too often too close to the fire. Bond recognized them as the eyes of furious dissipation.

The face was vaguely gipsy-like in its fierce pride and in the heavy curling black hair and crooked nose, and the effect of a vagabond soldier of fortune was heightened by the small thin gold ring Kerim wore in the lobe of his right ear. It was a startlingly dramatic face, vital, cruel and debauched, but what one noticed more than its drama was that it radiated life. Bond thought he had never seen so much vitality and warmth in a human face. It was like being close to the sun, and Bond let go the strong dry hand and smiled back at Kerim with a friendliness he rarely felt for a stranger.

'Thanks for sending the car to meet me last night.'

'Ha!' Kerim was delighted. 'You must thank our friends too. You were met by both sides. They always follow my car when it goes to the airport.'

'Was it a Vespa or a Lambretta?'

'You noticed? A Lambretta. They have a whole fleet of them for their little men, the men I call "The Faceless Ones". They look so alike, we have never managed to sort them out. Little gangsters, mostly stinking Bulgars, who do their dirty work for them. But I expect this one kept well back. They don't get up close to the Rolls any more since the day my chauffeur stopped suddenly and then reversed back as hard as he could. Messed up the paintwork and bloodied the bottom of the chassis but it taught the rest of them manners.'

Kerim went to his chair and waved to an identical one across the desk. He pushed over a flat white box of cigarettes and Bond sat down and took a cigarette and lit it. It was the most wonderful cigarette he had ever tasted — the mildest and sweetest of Turkish tobacco in a slim long oval tube with an elegant gold crescent.

While Kerim was fitting one into a long nicotine-stained ivory holder, Bond took the opportunity to glance round the room, which smelled strongly of paint and varnish as if it had just been redecorated.

It was big and square and panelled in polished mahogany, except behind Kerim's chair where a length of Oriental tapestry hung down from the ceiling and gently moved in the breeze as if there was an open window behind it. But this seemed unlikely as light came from three circular windows high up in the walls. Perhaps, behind the tapestry, was a balcony looking out over the Golden Horn, whose waves Bond could hear lapping at the walls below. In the centre of the right-hand wall hung a gold-framed reproduction of Annigoni's portrait of the Queen. Opposite, also imposingly framed, was Cecil Beaton's war-time photograph of Winston Churchill looking up from his desk in the Cabinet Offices like a contemptuous bulldog. A broad bookcase stood against one wall and, opposite, a comfortably padded leather settee. In the centre of the room the big desk winked with polished brass handles. On the littered desk were three silver photograph frames, and Bond caught a sideways view of the copperplate script of two Mentions in Dispatches and the Military Division of the O.B.E.

Kerim lit his cigarette. He jerked his head back at the piece of tapestry. 'Our friends paid me a visit yesterday,' he said casually. 'Fixed a limpet bomb on the wall outside. Timed the fuse to catch me at my desk. By good luck, I had taken a few minutes off to relax on the couch over there with a young Rumanian girl who still believes that a man will tell secrets in exchange for love. The bomb went off at a vital moment. I refused to be disturbed, but I fear the experience was too much for the girl. When I released her, she had hysterics. I'm afraid she had decided that my love-making is altogether too violent.' He waved his cigarette holder apologetically. 'But it was a rush to get the room put to rights in time for your visit. New glass for the windows and my pictures, and the place stinks of paint. However.' Kerim sat back in his chair. There was a slight frown on his face. 'What I cannot understand is this sudden breach of the peace. We live together very amicably in Istanbul. We all have our work to do. It is unheard of that my *chers collègues* should suddenly declare war in this way. It is quite worrying. It can only lead to trouble for our Russian friends. I shall be forced to rebuke the man who did it when I have found out his name.' Kerim shook his head. 'It is most confusing. I am hoping it has nothing to do with this case of ours.'

'But was it necessary to make my arrival so public?' Bond asked mildly. 'The last thing I want is to get you involved in all this. Why send the Rolls to the airport? It only ties you in with me.'

Kerim's laugh was indulgent. 'My friend, I must explain something which you should know. We and the Russians and the Americans have a paid man in all the hotels. And we have all bribed an official of the Secret Police at Headquarters and we receive a carbon copy of the list of all foreigners entering the country every day by air or train or sea. Given a few more days I could have smuggled you in through the Greek frontier. But for what purpose? Your existence here has to be known to the other side so that our friend can contact you. It is a condition she has laid down that she will make her own arrangements for the meeting. Perhaps she does not trust our security. Who knows? But she was definite about it and she said, as if I didn't know it, that her centre would immediately be advised of your arrival.' Kerim shrugged his broad shoulders. 'So why make things difficult for her? I am merely concerned with making things easy and comfortable for you so that you will at least enjoy your stay — even if it is fruitless.'

Bond laughed. 'I take it all back. I'd forgotten the Balkan formula. Anyway I'm under your orders here. You tell me what to do and I'll do it.'

Kerim waved the subject aside. 'And now, since we are talking of your comfort, how is your hotel? I was surprised you chose the Palas. It is little better than a disorderly house — what the French call a *baisodrome*. And it's quite a haunt of the Russians. Not that that matters.'

'It's not too bad. I just didn't want to stay at the Istanbul-Hilton or one of the other smart places.'

'Money?' Kerim reached into a drawer and took out a flat packet of new green notes. 'Here's a thousand Turkish pounds. Their real value, and their rate on the black market, is about twenty to the pound. The official rate is seven. Tell me when you've finished them and I'll give you as many more as you want. We can do our accounts after the game. It's muck, anyway. Ever since Croesus, the first millionaire, invented gold coins, money has depreciated. And the face of the coin has been debased as fast as its value. First the faces of gods were on the coins. Then the faces of kings. Then of presidents. Now there's no face at all. Look at this stuff!' Kerim tossed the money over to Bond. 'Today it's only paper, with a picture of a public building and the signature of a cashier. Muck! The miracle is that you can still buy things with it. However. What else? Cigarettes? Smoke only these. I will have a few hundred sent up to your hotel. They're the best. *Diplomates*. They're not easy to get. Most of them go to the Ministries and the Embassies. Anything else before we get down to business? Don't worry about your meals and your leisure. I will look after both. I shall enjoy it and, if you will forgive me, I wish to stay close to you while you are here.'

'Nothing else,' said Bond. 'Except that you must come over to London one day.'

'Never,' said Kerim definitely. 'The weather and the women are far too cold. And I am proud to have you here. It reminds me of the war. Now,' he rang a bell on his desk, 'do you like your coffee plain or sweet? In Turkey we cannot talk seriously without coffee or raki and it is too early for raki.'

'Plain.'

The door behind Bond opened. Kerim barked an order. When the door was shut, Kerim unlocked a drawer and took out a file and put it in front of him. He smacked his hand down on it.

'My friend,' he said grimly, 'I do not know what to say about this case.' He leant back in his chair and linked his hands behind his neck. 'Has it ever occurred to you that our kind of work is rather like shooting a film? So often I have got everybody on location and I think I can start turning the handle. Then it's the weather, and then it's the actors, and then it's the accidents. And there is something else that also happens in the making of a film. Love appears in some shape or form, at the very worst, as it is now, between the two stars. To me that is the most confusing factor in this case, and the most inscrutable one. Does this girl really love her idea of you? Will she love you when she sees you? Will you be able to love her enough to make her come over?'

Bond made no comment. There was a knock on the door and the head clerk put a china eggshell, enclosed in gold filigree, in front of each of them and went out. Bond sipped his coffee and put it down. It was good, but thick with grains. Kerim swallowed his at a gulp and fitted a cigarette into his holder and lit it.

'But there is nothing we can do about this love matter,' Kerim continued, speaking half to himself. 'We can only wait and see. In the meantime there are other things.' He leant forward against the desk and looked across at Bond, his eyes suddenly very hard and shrewd.

'There is something going on in the enemy camp, my friend. It is not only this attempt to get rid of me. There are comings and goings. I have few facts,' he reached up a big index finger and laid it alongside his nose, 'but I have this.' He tapped the side of his nose as if he was patting a dog. 'But this is a good friend of mine and I trust him.' He brought his hand slowly and significantly down on to the desk and added softly, 'And if the stakes were not so big, I would say to you, "Go home my friend. Go home. There is something here to get away from".'

Kerim sat back. The tension went out of his voice. He barked out a harsh laugh. 'But we are not old women. And this is our work. So let us forget my nose and get on with the job. First of all, is there anything I can tell you that you do not know? The girl has made no sign of life since my signal and I have no other information. But perhaps you would like to ask me some questions about the meeting.'

'There's only one thing I want to know,' said Bond flatly. 'What do you think of this girl? Do you believe her story or not? Her story about me? Nothing else matters. If she hasn't got some sort of a hysterical crush on me, the whole business falls to the ground and it's some complicated M.G.B. plot we can't understand. Now. Did you believe the girl?' Bond's voice was urgent and his eyes searched the other man's face.

'Ah, my friend.' Kerim shook his head. He spread his arms wide. 'That is what I asked myself then, and it is what I ask myself the whole time since. But who can tell if a woman is lying about these things? Her eyes were bright — those beautiful innocent eyes. Her lips were moist and parted in that heavenly mouth. Her voice was urgent and frightened at what she was doing and saying. Her knuckles were white on the guard rail of the ship. But what was in her heart?' Kerim raised his hands. 'God alone knows.' He brought his hands down resignedly. He placed them flat on the desk and looked straight at Bond. 'There is only one way of telling if a woman really loves you, and even that way can only be read by an expert.'

'Yes,' said Bond dubiously. 'I know what you mean. In bed.'

15

BACKGROUND TO A SPY

COFFEE CAME AGAIN, and then more coffee, and the big room grew thick with cigarette smoke as the two men took each shred of evidence, dissected it and put it aside. At the end of an hour they were back where they had started. It was up to Bond to solve the problem of this girl and, if he was satisfied with her story, get her and the machine out of the country.

Kerim undertook to look after the administrative problems. As a first step he picked up the telephone and spoke to his travel agent and reserved two seats on every outgoing plane for the next week — by B.E.A., Air France, S.A.S. and Turkair.

'And now you must have a passport,' he said. 'One will be sufficient. She can travel as your wife. One of my men will take your photograph and he will find a photograph of some girl who looks more or less like her. As a matter of fact, an early picture of Garbo would serve. There is a certain resemblance. He can get one from the newspaper files. I will speak to the Consul General. He's an excellent fellow who likes my little cloak-and-dagger plots. The passport will be ready by this evening. What name would you like to have?'

'Take one out of a hat.'

'Somerset. My mother came from there. David Somerset. Profession, Company Director. That means nothing. And the girl? Let us say Caroline. She looks like a Caroline. A couple of clean-limbed young English people with a taste for travel. Finance Control Form? Leave that to me. It will show eighty pounds in travellers' cheques, let's say, and a receipt from the bank to show you changed fifty while you were in Turkey. Customs? They never look at anything. Only too glad if somebody has bought something in the country. You will declare some Turkish Delight — presents for your friends in London. If you have to get out quickly, leave your hotel bill and luggage to me. They know me well enough at the Palas. Anything else?'

'I can't think of anything.'

Kerim looked at his watch. 'Twelve o'clock. Just time for the car to take you back to your hotel. There might be a message. And have a good look at your things to see if anyone has been inquisitive.'

He rang the bell and fired instructions at the head clerk who stood with his sharp eyes on Kerim's and his lean head straining forward like a whippet's.

Kerim led Bond to the door. There came again the warm powerful handclasp. 'The car will bring you to lunch,' he said. 'A little place in the Spice Bazaar.' His eyes looked happily into Bond's. 'And I am glad to be working with you. We will do well together.' He let go of Bond's hand. 'And now I have a lot of things to do very quickly. They may be the wrong things, but at any rate,' he grinned broadly, '*jouons mal, mais jouons vite!*'

The head clerk, who seemed to be some sort of chief-of-staff to Kerim, led Bond through another door in the wall of the raised platform. The heads were still bowed over the ledgers. There was a short passage with rooms on either side. The man led the way into one of these and Bond found himself in an extremely well-equipped dark-room and laboratory. In ten minutes he was out again on the street. The Rolls edged out of the narrow alley and back again on to the Galata Bridge.

A new concierge was on duty at the Kristal Palas, a small obsequious man with guilty eyes in a yellow face. He came out from behind the desk, his hands spread in apology. 'Effendi, I greatly regret. My colleague showed you to an inadequate room. It was not realized that you are a friend of Kerim Bey. Your things have been moved to No. 12. It is the best room in the hotel. In fact,' the concierge leered, 'it is the room reserved for honeymoon couples. Every comfort. My apologies, Effendi. The other room is not intended for visitors of distinction.' The man executed an oily bow, washing his hands.

If there was one thing Bond couldn't stand it was the sound of his boots being licked. He looked the concierge in the eyes and said, 'Oh.' The eyes slid away. 'Let me see this room. I may not like it. I was quite comfortable where I was.'

'Certainly, Effendi,' the man bowed Bond to the lift, 'but alas the plumbers are in your former room. The water supply . . . '

The voice trailed away. The lift rose about ten feet and stopped at the first floor.

Well, the story of the plumbers makes sense, reflected Bond. And, after all, there was no harm in having the best room in the hotel.

The concierge unlocked a high door and stood back.

Bond had to approve. The sun streamed in through wide double windows that gave on to a small balcony. The motif was pink and grey and the style was mock French Empire, battered by the years, but still with all the elegance of the turn of the century. There were fine Bokhara rugs on the parquet floor. A glittering chandelier hung from the ornate ceiling. The bed against the right-hand wall was huge. A large mirror in a gold frame covered most of the wall behind it. (Bond was amused. The honeymoon room! Surely there should be a mirror on the ceiling as well.) The adjoining bathroom was tiled and fitted with everything, including a bidet and a shower. Bond's shaving things were neatly laid out.

The concierge followed Bond back into the bedroom, and when Bond said he would take the room, bowed himself gratefully out.

Why not? Bond again walked round the room. This time he carefully inspected the walls and the neighbourhood of the bed and the telephone. Why not take the room? Why would there be microphones or secret doors? What would be the point of them?

His suitcase was on a bench near the chest-of-drawers. He knelt down. No scratches round the lock. The bit of fluff he had trapped in the clasp was still there. He unlocked the suitcase and took out the little attaché case. Again no signs of interference. Bond locked the case and got to his feet.

He washed and went out of the room and down the stairs. No, there had been no messages for the Effendi. The concierge bowed as he opened the door of the Rolls. Was there a hint of conspiracy behind the permanent guilt in those eyes? Bond decided not to care if there was. The game, whatever it was, had to be played out. If the change of rooms had been the opening gambit, so much the better. The game had to begin somewhere.

As the car sped back down the hill, Bond's thoughts turned to Darko Kerim. What a man for Head of Station T! His size alone, in this country of furtive, stunted little men, would give him authority, and his giant vitality and love of life would make everyone his friend. Where had this exuberant shrewd pirate come from? And how had he come to work for the Service? He was the rare type of man that Bond loved, and Bond already felt prepared to add Kerim to the half-dozen of those real friends whom Bond, who had no 'acquaintances', would be ready to take to his heart.

The car went back over the Galata Bridge and drew up outside the vaulted arcades of the Spice Bazaar. The chauffeur led the way up the shallow worn steps and into the fog of exotic scents, shouting curses at the beggars and sack-laden porters. Inside the entrance the chauffeur turned left out of the stream of shuffling, jabbering humanity and showed Bond a small arch in the thick wall. Turret-like stone steps curled upwards.

'Effendi, you will find Kerim Bey in the far room on the left. You have only to ask. He is known to all.'

Bond climbed the cool stairs to a small ante-room where a waiter, without asking his name, took charge and led him through a maze of small, colourfully tiled, vaulted rooms to where Kerim was sitting at a corner table over the entrance to the bazaar. Kerim greeted him boisterously, waving a glass of milky liquid in which ice tinkled.

'Here you are, my friend! Now, at once, some raki. You must be exhausted after your sight-seeing.' He fired orders at the waiter.

Bond sat down in a comfortable-armed chair and took the small tumbler the waiter offered him. He lifted it towards Kerim and tasted it. It was identical with ouzo. He drank it down. At once the waiter refilled his glass.

'And now to order your lunch. They eat nothing but offal cooked in rancid olive oil in Turkey. At least the offal at the Misir Carsarsi is the best.'

The grinning waiter made suggestions.

'He says the doner kebab is very good today. I don't believe him, but it can be. It is very young lamb broiled over charcoal with savoury rice. Lots of onions in it. Or is there anything you prefer? A pilaff or some of those damned stuffed peppers they eat here? All right then. And you must start with a few sardines grilled *en papillotte*. They are just edible.' Kerim harangued the waiter. He sat back, smiling at Bond. 'That is the only way to treat these damned people. They love to be cursed and kicked. It is all they understand. It is in the blood. All this pretence of democracy is killing them. They want some sultans and wars and rape and fun. Poor brutes, in their striped suits and bowler hats. They are miserable. You've only got to look at them. However, to hell with them all. Any news?'

Bond shook his head. He told Kerim about the change of room and the untouched suitcase.

Kerim downed a glass of raki and wiped his mouth on the back of his hand. He echoed the thought Bond had had. 'Well, the game must begin some time. I have made certain small moves. Now we can only wait and see. We will make a little foray into enemy territory after lunch. I think it will interest you. Oh, we shan't be seen. We shall move in the shadows, underground.' Kerim laughed delightedly at his cleverness. 'And now let us talk about other things. How do you like Turkey? No, I don't want to know. What else?'

They were interrupted by the arrival of their first course. Bond's sardines *en papillotte* tasted like any other fried sardines. Kerim set about a large plate of what appeared to be strips of raw fish. He saw Bond's look of interest. 'Raw fish,' he said. 'After this I shall have raw meat and lettuce and then I shall have a bowl of yoghourt. I am not a faddist, but I once trained to be a professional strong man. It is a good profession in Turkey. The public loves them. And my trainer insisted that I should eat only raw food. I got the habit. It is good for me, but,' he waved his fork, 'I do not pretend it is good for everyone. I don't care the hell what other people eat so long as they enjoy it. I can't stand sad eaters and sad drinkers.'

'Why did you decide not to be a strong man? How did you get into this racket?'

Kerim forked up a strip of fish and tore at it with his teeth. He drank down half a tumbler of raki. He lit a cigarette and sat back in his chair. 'Well,' he said with a sour grin, 'we might as well talk about me as about anything else. And you must be wondering "How did this big crazy man get into the Service?" I will tell you, but briefly, because it is a long story. You will stop me if you get bored. All right?'

'Fine.' Bond lit a *Diplomate*. He leant forward on his elbows.

'I come from Trebizond.' Kerim watched his cigarette smoke curl upwards. 'We were a huge family with many mothers. My father was the sort of man women can't resist. All women want to be swept off their feet. In their dreams they long to be slung over a man's shoulder and taken into a cave and raped. That was his way with them. My father was a great fisherman and his fame was spread all over the Black Sea. He went after the sword-fish. They are difficult to catch and hard to fight and he would always outdo all others after these fish. Women like their men to be heroes. He was a kind of hero in a corner of Turkey where it is a tradition for the men to be tough. He was a big, romantic sort of fellow. So he could have any woman he wanted. He wanted them all and sometimes killed other men to get them. Naturally he had many children. We all lived on top of each other in a great rambling old ruin of a house that our "aunts" made habitable. The aunts really amounted to a harem. One of them was an English governess from Istanbul my father had seen watching a circus. He took a fancy to her and she to him and that evening he put her on board his fishing boat and sailed up the Bosphorus and back to Trebizond. I don't think she ever regretted it. I think she forgot all the world except him. She died just after the war. She was sixty. The child before me had been by an Italian girl and the girl had called him Bianco. He was fair. I was dark. I got to be called Darko. There were fifteen of us children and we had a wonderful childhood. Our aunts fought often and so did we. It was like a gipsy encampment. It was held together by my father who thrashed us, women or children, when we were a nuisance. But he was good to us when we were peaceful and obedient. You cannot understand such a family?'

'The way you describe it I can.'

'Anyway so it was. I grew up to be nearly as big a man as my father, but better educated. My mother saw to that. My father only taught us to be clean and to go to the lavatory once a day and never to feel shame about anything in the world. My mother also taught me a regard for England, but that is by the way. By the time I was twenty, I had a boat of my own and I was making money. But I was wild. I left the big house and went to live in two small rooms on the waterfront. I wanted to have my women where my mother would not know. There was a stroke of bad luck. I had a little Bessarabian hell-cat. I had won her in a fight with some gipsies, here in the hills behind Istanbul. They came after me, but I got her on board the boat. I had to knock her unconscious first. She was still trying to kill me when we got back to Trebizond, so I got her to my place and took away all her clothes and kept her chained naked under the table. When I ate, I used to throw scraps to her under the table, like a dog. She had to learn who was master. Before that could happen, my mother did an unheard-of thing. She visited my place without warning. She came to tell me that my father wanted to see me immediately. She found the girl. My mother was really angry with me for the first time in my life. Angry? She was beside herself. I was a cruel ne'er-do-well and she was ashamed to call me son. The girl must immediately be taken back to her people. My mother brought her some of her own clothes from the house. The girl put them on, but when the time came, she refused to leave me.' Darko Kerim laughed hugely. 'An interesting lesson in female psychology, my dear friend. However, the problem of the girl is another story. While my mother was fussing over her and getting nothing but gipsy curses for her pains, I was having an interview with my father, who had heard nothing of all this and who never did hear. My mother was like that. There was another man with my father, a tall, quiet Englishman with a black patch over one eye. They were talking about the Russians. The Englishman wanted to know what they were doing along their frontier, about what was going on at Batoum, their big oil and naval base only fifty miles away from Trebizond. He would pay good money for information. I knew English and I knew Russian. I had good eyes and ears. I had a boat. My father had decided that I would work for the Englishman. And that Englishman, my dear friend, was Major Dansey, my predecessor as Head of this Station. And the rest,' Kerim made a wide gesture with his cigarette holder, 'you can imagine.'

'But what about this training to be a professional strong man?'

'Ah,' said Kerim slyly, 'that was only a sideline. Our travelling circuses were almost the only Turks allowed through the frontier The Russians cannot live without circuses. It is as simple as that. I was the man who broke chains and lifted weights by a rope between the teeth. I wrestled against the local strong men in the Russian villages. And some of those Georgians are giants. Fortunately they are stupid giants and I nearly always won. Afterwards, at the drinking, there was always much talk and gossip. I would look foolish and pretend not to understand. Every now and then I would ask an innocent question and they would laugh at my stupidity and tell me the answer.'

The second course came, and with it a bottle of Kavaklidere, a rich coarse burgundy like any other Balkan wine. The kebab was good and tasted of smoked bacon fat and onions. Kerim ate a kind of steak tartare — a large flat hamburger of finely minced raw meat laced with peppers and chives and bound together with yolk of egg. He made Bond try a forkful. It was delicious. Bond said so.

'You ought to eat it every day,' said Kerim earnestly. 'It is good for those who wish to make much love. There are certain exercises you should do for the same purpose. These things are important to men. Or at least they are to me. Like my father, I consume a large quantity of women. But, unlike him, I also drink and smoke too much, and these things do not go well with making love. Nor does this work I do. Too many tensions and too much thinking. It takes the blood to the head instead of to where it should be for making love. But I am greedy for life. I do too much of everything all the time. Suddenly one day my heart will fail. The Iron Crab will get me as it got my father. But I am not afraid of The Crab. At least I shall have died from an honourable disease. Perhaps they will put on my tombstone "This Man Died from Living Too Much".'

Bond laughed. 'Don't go too soon, Darko,' he said. 'M. would be very displeased. He thinks the world of you.'

'He does?' Kerim searched Bond's face to see if he was telling the truth. He laughed delightedly. 'In that case I will not let The Crab have my body yet.' He looked at his watch. 'Come, James,' he said. 'It is good that you reminded me of my duty. We will have coffee in the office. There is not much time to waste. Every day at 2.30 the Russians have their council of war. Today you and I will do them the honour of being present at their deliberations.'

16

THE TUNNEL OF RATS

BACK IN THE cool office, while they waited for the inevitable coffee, Kerim opened a cupboard in the wall and pulled out sets of engineers' blue overalls. Kerim stripped to his shorts and dressed himself in one of the suits and pulled on a pair of rubber boots. Bond picked out a suit and a pair of boots that more or less fitted him and put them on.

With the coffee, the head clerk brought in two powerful flashlights which he put on the desk.

When the clerk had left the room Kerim said, 'He is one of my sons — the eldest one. The others in there are all my children. The chauffeur and the watchman are uncles of mine. Common blood is the best security. And this spice business is good cover for us all. M. set me up in it. He spoke to friends of his in the City of London. I am now the leading spice merchant in Turkey. I have long ago repaid M. the money that was lent me. My children are shareholders in the business. They have a good life. When there is secret work to be done and I need help, I choose the child who will be most suitable. They all have training in different secret things. They are clever and brave. Some have already killed for me. They would all die for me — and for M. I have taught them he is just below God.' Kerim made a deprecating wave. 'But that is just to tell you that you are in good hands.'

'I hadn't imagined anything different.'

'Ha!' said Kerim non-committally. He picked up the torches and handed one to Bond. 'And now to work.'

Kerim walked over to the wide glass-fronted bookcase and put his hand behind it. There was a click and the bookcase rolled silently and easily along the wall to the left. Behind it was a small door, flush with the wall. Kerim pressed one side of the door and it swung inwards to reveal a dark tunnel with stone steps leading straight down. A dank smell, mixed with a faint zoo stench, came out into the room.

'You go first,' said Kerim. 'Go down the steps to the bottom and wait. I must fix the door.'

Bond switched on his torch and stepped through the opening and went carefully down the stairs. The light of the torch showed fresh masonry, and, twenty feet below, a glimmer of water. When Bond got to the bottom he found that the glimmer was a small stream running down a central gutter in the floor of an ancient stone-walled tunnel that sloped steeply up to the right. To the left, the tunnel went on downwards and would, he guessed, come out below the surface of the Golden Horn.

Out of range of Bond's light there was a steady, quiet, scuttling sound, and in the blackness hundreds of pinpoints of red light flickered and moved. It was the same uphill and downhill. Twenty yards away on either side, a thousand rats were looking at Bond. They were sniffing at his scent. Bond imagined the whiskers lifting slightly from their teeth. He had a quick moment of wondering what action they would take if his torch went out.

Kerim was suddenly beside him. 'It is a long climb. A quarter of an hour. I hope you love animals.' Kerim's laugh boomed hugely away up the tunnel. The rats scuffled and stirred. 'Unfortunately there is not much choice. Rats and bats. Squadrons of them, divisions — a whole air force and army. And we have to drive them in front of us. Towards the end of the climb it becomes quite congested. Let's get started. The air is good. It is dry underfoot on both sides of the stream. But in winter the floods come and then we have to use frogmen's suits. Keep your torch on my feet. If a bat gets in your hair, brush him off. It will not be often. Their radar is very good.'

They set off up the steep slope. The smell of the rats and of the droppings of bats was thick — a mixture of monkey house and chicken battery. It occurred to Bond that it would be days before he got rid of it.

Clusters of bats hung like bunches of withered grapes from the roof and when, from time to time, either Kerim's head or Bond's brushed against them, they exploded twittering into the darkness. Ahead of them as they climbed there was the forest of squeaking, scuffling red pinpoints that grew denser on both sides of the central gutter. Occasionally Kerim flashed his torch forward and the light shone on a grey field sown with glittering teeth and glinting whiskers. When this happened, an extra frenzy seized the rats, and those nearest jumped on the backs of the others to get away. All the while, fighting tumbling grey bodies came sweeping down the central gutter and, as the pressure of the mass higher up the tunnel grew heavier, the frothing rear rank came closer.

The two men kept their torches levelled like guns on the rear ranks until, after a good quarter of an hour's climb, they reached their destination.

It was a deep alcove of newly faced brick in the side wall of the tunnel. There were two benches on each side of a thick tarpaulin-wrapped object that came down from the ceiling of the alcove.

They stepped inside. Another few yards' climb, Bond thought, and mass hysteria must have seized the distant thousands of rats further up the tunnel. The horde would have turned. Out of sheer pressure for space, the rats would have braved the lights and hurled themselves down on to the two intruders, in spite of the two glaring eyes and the threatening scent.

'Watch,' said Kerim.

There was a moment of silence. Further up the tunnel the squeaking had stopped, as if at a word of command. Then suddenly the tunnel was a foot deep in a great wave of hurtling, scrambling grey bodies as, with a continuous high-pitched squeal, the rats turned and pelted back down the slope.

For minutes the sleek grey river foamed by outside the alcove until at last the numbers thinned and only a trickle of sick or wounded rats came limping and probing their way down the tunnel floor.

The scream of the horde slowly vanished down towards the river, until there was silence except for the occasional twitter of a fleeing bat.

Kerim gave a non-committal grunt. 'One of these days those rats will start dying. Then we shall have the plague in Istanbul again. Sometimes I feel guilty for not telling the authorities of this tunnel so that they can clean the place up. But I can't so long as the Russians are up here.' He jerked his head at the roof. He looked at his watch. 'Five minutes to go. They will be pulling up their chairs and fiddling with their papers. There will be the three permanent men — M.G.B., or one of them may be from Army Intelligence, G.R.U. And there will probably be three others. Two came in a fortnight ago, one through Greece and another through Persia. Another one arrived on Monday. God knows who they are, or what they are here for. And sometimes the girl, Tatiana, comes in with a signal and goes out again. Let us hope we will see her today. You will be impressed. She is something.'

Kerim reached up and untied the tarpaulin cover and pulled it downwards. Bond understood. The cover protected the shining butt of a submarine periscope, fully withdrawn. The moisture glistened on the thick grease of the exposed bottom joint. Bond chuckled. 'Where the hell did you get that from, Darko?'

'Turkish Navy. War surplus.' Kerim's voice did not invite further questions. 'Now Q Branch in London is trying to fix some way of wiring the damn thing for sound. It's not going to be easy. The lens at the top of this is no bigger than a cigarette-lighter, end on. When I raise it, it comes up to floor level in their room. In the corner of the room where it comes up, we cut a small mousehole. We did it well. Once when I came to have a look, the first thing I saw was a big mousetrap with a piece of cheese on it. At least it looked big through the lens.' Kerim laughed briefly. 'But there's not much room to fit a sensitive pick-up alongside the lens. And there's no hope of getting in again to do any more fiddling about with their architecture. The only way I managed to install this thing was to get my friends in the Public Works Ministry to turn the Russians out for a few days. The story was that the trams going up the hill were shaking the foundations of the houses. There had to be a survey. It cost me a few hundred pounds for the right pockets. The Public Works inspected half a dozen houses on either side of this one and declared the place safe. By that time, I and the family had finished our construction work. The Russians were suspicious as hell. I gather they went over the place with a toothcomb when they got back, looking for microphones and bombs and so on. But we can't work that trick twice. Unless Q Branch can think up something very clever, I shall have to be content with keeping an eye on them. One of these days they'll give away something useful. They'll be interrogating someone we're interested in or something of that sort.'

Alongside the matrix of the periscope in the roof of the alcove there was a pendulous blister of metal, twice the size of a football. 'What's that?' said Bond.

'Bottom half of a bomb — a big bomb. If anything happens to me, or if war breaks out with Russia, that bomb will be set off by radio-control from my office. It is sad [Kerim didn't look sad] but I fear that many innocent people will get killed besides the Russians. When the blood is on the boil, man is as unselective as nature.'

Kerim had been polishing away at the hooded eyepieces between the two handlebars that stuck out on both sides of the base of the periscope. Now he glanced at his watch and bent down and gripped the two handles and slowly brought them up level with his chin. There was a hiss of hydraulics as the glistening stem of the periscope slid up into its steel sheath in the roof of the alcove. Kerim bent his head and gazed into the eyepieces and slowly inched up the handles until he could stand upright. He twisted gently. He centred the lens and beckoned to Bond. 'Just the six of them.'

Bond moved over and took the handles.

'Have a good look at them,' said Kerim. 'I know them, but you'd better get their faces in your mind. Head of the table is their Resident Director. On his left are his two staff. Opposite them are the three new ones. The latest, who looks quite an important chap, is on the Director's right. Tell me if they do anything except talk.'

Bond's first impulse was to tell Kerim not to make so much noise. It was as if he was in the room with the Russians, as if he was sitting in a chair in the corner, a secretary perhaps, taking shorthand of the conference.

The wide, all-round lens, designed for spotting aircraft as well as surface ships, gave him a curious picture — a mouse's eye view of a forest of legs below the fore-edge of the table, and various aspects of the heads belonging to the legs. The Director and his two colleagues were clear — serious dull Russian faces whose characteristics Bond filed away. There was the studious, professorial face of the Director — thick spectacles, lantern jaw, big forehead and thin hair brushed back. On his left was a square wooden face with deep clefts on either side of the nose, fair hair *en brosse* and a nick out of the left ear. The third member of the permanent staff had a shifty Armenian face with clever bright almond eyes. He was talking now. His face wore a falsely humble look. Gold glinted in his mouth.

Bond could see less of the three visitors. Their backs were half towards him and only the profile of the nearest, and presumably most junior, showed clearly. This man's skin also was dark. He too would be from one of the southern republics. The jaw was badly shaved and the eye in profile was bovine and dull under a thick black brow. The nose was fleshy and porous. The upper lip was long over a sullen mouth and the beginning of a double chin. The tough black hair was cut very short so that most of the back of the neck looked blue to the level of the tips of the ears. It was a military haircut, done with mechanical clippers.

The only clues to the next man were an angry boil on the back of a fat bald neck, a shiny blue suit and rather bright brown shoes. The man was motionless during the whole period that Bond kept watch and apparently never spoke.

Now the senior visitor, on the right of the Resident Director, sat back and began talking. It was a strong, crag-like profile with big bones and a jutting chin under a heavy brown moustache of Stalin cut. Bond could see one cold grey eye under a bushy eyebrow and a low forehead topped by wiry grey-brown hair. This man was the only one who was smoking. He puffed busily at a tiny wooden pipe in the bowl of which stood half a cigarette. Every now and then he shook the pipe sideways so that the ash fell on the floor. His profile had more authority than any of the other faces and Bond guessed that he was a senior man sent down from Moscow.

Bond's eyes were getting tired. He twisted the handles gently and looked round the office as far as the blurring jagged edges of the mousehole would allow. He saw nothing of interest — two olive green filing cabinets, a hatstand by the door, on which he counted six more or less identical grey homburgs, and a sideboard with a heavy carafe of water and some glasses. Bond stood away from the eyepiece, rubbing his eyes.

'If only we could hear,' Kerim said, shaking his head sadly. 'It would be worth diamonds.'

'It would solve a lot of problems,' agreed Bond. Then, 'By the way, Darko, how did you come on this tunnel? What was it built for?'

Kerim bent and gave a quick glance into the eyepieces and straightened up.

'It's a lost drain from the Hall of Pillars,' he said. 'The Hall of Pillars is now a thing for tourists. It's up above us on the heights of Istanbul, near St. Sophia. A thousand years ago it was built as a reservoir in case of siege. It's a huge underground palace, a hundred yards long and about half as broad. It was made to hold millions of gallons of water. It was discovered again about four hundred years ago by a man called Gyllius. One day I was reading his account of finding it. He said it was filled in winter from "*a great pipe with a mighty noise* ". It occurred to me that there might be another "*great pipe* " to empty it quickly if the city fell to the enemy. I went up to the Hall of Pillars and bribed the watchman and rowed about among the pillars all one night in a rubber dinghy with one of my boys. We went over the walls with a hammer and an echo-sounder. At one end, in the most likely spot, there was a hollow sound. I handed out more money to the Minister of Public Works and he closed the place for a week — "for cleaning". My little team got busy.' Kerim ducked down again for a look through the eyepieces and went on. 'We dug into the wall above water-level and came on the top of an arch. The arch was the beginning of a tunnel. We got into the tunnel and went down it. Quite exciting, not knowing where we were going to come out. And, of course, it went straight down the hill — under the Street of Books where the Russians have their place, and out into the Golden Horn, by the Galata Bridge, twenty yards away from my warehouse. So we filled in our hole in the Hall of Pillars and started digging from my end. That was two years ago. It took us a year and a lot of survey work to get directly under the Russians.' Kerim laughed. 'And now I suppose one of these days the Russians will decide to change their offices. By then I hope someone else will be Head of T.'

Kerim bent down to the rubber eyepieces. Bond saw him stiffen. Kerim said urgently, 'The door's opening. Quick. Take over. Here she comes.'

17

KILLING TIME

IT WAS SEVEN o'clock on the same evening and James Bond was back in his hotel. He had had a hot bath and a cold shower. He thought that he had at last scoured the zoo smell out of his skin.

He was sitting, naked except for his shorts, at one of the windows of his room, sipping a vodka and tonic and looking out into the heart of the great tragic sunset over the Golden Horn. But his eyes didn't see the torn cloth of gold and blood that hung behind the minaretted stage beneath which he had caught his first glimpse of Tatiana Romanova.

He was thinking of the tall beautiful girl with the dancer's long gait who had walked through the drab door with a piece of paper in her hand. She had stood beside her Chief and handed him the paper. All the men had looked up at her. She had blushed and looked down. What had that expression on the men's faces meant? It was more than just the way some men look at a beautiful girl. They had shown curiosity. That was reasonable. They wanted to know what was in the signal, why they were being disturbed. But what else? There had been slyness and contempt — the way people stare at prostitutes.

It had been an odd, enigmatic scene. This was part of a highly disciplined para-military organization. These were serving officers, each of whom would be wary of the others. And this girl was just one of the staff, with a Corporal's rank, who was now going through a normal routine. Why had they all unguardedly looked at her with this inquisitive contempt — almost as if she was a spy who had been caught and was going to be executed? Did they suspect her? Had she given herself away? But that seemed less likely as the scene played itself out. The Resident Director read the signal and the other men's eyes turned away from the girl and on to him. He said something, presumably repeating the text of the signal, and the men looked glumly back at him as if the matter did not interest them. Then the Resident Director looked up at the girl and the other eyes followed his. He said something with a friendly, inquiring expression. The girl shook her head and answered briefly. The other men now only looked interested. The Director said one word with a question mark on the end. The girl blushed deeply, and nodded, holding his eyes obediently. The other men smiled encouragement, slyly perhaps, but with approval. No suspicion there. No condemnation. The scene ended with a few sentences from the Director to which the girl seemed to say the equivalent of 'Yes, sir' and turned and walked out of the room. When she had gone, the Director said something with an expression of irony on his face and the men laughed heartily and the sly expression was back on their faces, as if what he had said had been obscene. Then they went back to their work.

Ever since, on their way back down the tunnel, and later in Kerim's office while they discussed what Bond had seen, Bond had racked his brains for a solution to this maddening bit of dumb crambo and now, looking without focus at the dying sun, he was still mystified.

Bond finished his drink and lit another cigarette. He put the problem away and turned his mind to the girl.

Tatiana Romanova. A Romanov. Well, she certainly looked like a Russian princess, or the traditional idea of one. The tall, fine-boned body that moved so gracefully and stood so well. The thick sweep of hair down to the shoulders and the quiet authority of the profile. The wonderful Garbo-esque face with its curiously shy serenity. The contrast between the level innocence of the big, deep blue eyes and the passionate promise of the wide mouth. And the way she had blushed and the way the long eyelashes had come down over the lowered eyes. Had that been the prudery of a virgin? Bond thought not. There was the confidence of having been loved in the proud breasts and the insolently lilting behind — the assertion of a body that knows what it can be for.

On what Bond had seen, could he believe that she was the sort of girl to fall in love with a photograph and a file? How could one tell? Such a girl would have a deeply romantic nature. There were dreams in the eyes and in the mouth. At that age, twenty-four, the Soviet machine would not yet have ground the sentiment out of her. The Romanov blood might well have given her a yearning for men other than the type of modern Russian officer she would meet — stern, cold, mechanical, basically hysterical and, because of their Party education, infernally dull.

It could be true. There was nothing to disprove her story in her looks. Bond wanted it to be true.

The telephone rang. It was Kerim. 'Nothing new?'

'No.'

'Then I will pick you up at eight.'

'I'll be ready.'

Bond laid down the receiver and slowly started to put on his clothes.

Kerim had been firm about the evening. Bond had wanted to stay in his hotel room and wait for the first contact to be made — a note, a telephone call, whatever it might be. But Kerim had said no. The girl had been adamant that she would choose her own time and place. It would be wrong for Bond to seem a slave to her convenience. 'That is bad psychology, my friend,' Kerim had insisted. 'No girl likes a man to run when she whistles. She would despise you if you made yourself too available. From your face and your dossier she would expect you to behave with indifference — even with insolence. She would want that. She wishes to court you, to buy a kiss' — Kerim had winked — 'from that cruel mouth. It is with an image she has fallen in love. Behave like the image. Act the part.'

Bond had shrugged his shoulders. 'All right, Darko. I daresay you're right. What do you suggest?'

'Live the life you would normally. Go home now and have a bath and a drink. The local vodka is all right if you drown it with tonic water. If nothing happens, I will pick you up at eight. We will have dinner at the place of a gipsy friend of mine. A man called Vavra. He is head of a tribe. I must anyway see him tonight. He is one of my best sources. He is finding out who tried to blow up my office. Some of his girls will dance for you. I will not suggest that they should entertain you more intimately. You must keep your sword sharp. There is a saying "Once a King, always a King. But once a Knight is enough!" '

Bond was smiling at the memory of Kerim's dictum when the telephone rang again. He picked up the receiver. It was only the car. As he went down the few stairs and out to Kerim in the waiting Rolls, Bond admitted to himself that he was disappointed.

They were climbing up the far hill through the poorer quarters above the Golden Horn when the chauffeur half turned his head and said something in a non-committal voice.

Kerim answered with a monosyllable. 'He says a Lambretta is on our tail. A Faceless One. It is of no importance. When I wish, I can make a secret of my movements. Often they have trailed this car for miles when there has been only a dummy in the back. A conspicuous car has its uses. They know this gipsy is a friend of mine, but I think they do not understand why. It will do no harm for them to know that we are having a night of relaxation. On a Saturday night, with a friend from England, anything else would be unusual.'

Bond looked back through the rear window and watched the crowded streets. From behind a stopped tram a motor scooter showed for a minute and then was hidden by a taxi. Bond turned away. He reflected briefly on the way the Russians ran their centres — with all the money and equipment in the world, while the Secret Service put against them a handful of adventurous, underpaid men, like this one, with his second-hand Rolls and his children to help him. Yet Kerim had the run of Turkey. Perhaps, after all, the right man was better than the right machine.

At half-past eight they stopped half way up a long hill on the outskirts of Istanbul at a dingy-looking open-air café with a few empty tables on the pavement. Behind it were the tops of trees over a high stone wall. They got out and the car drove off. They waited for the Lambretta, but its wasp-like buzz had stopped and at once it was on its way back down the hill. All they saw of the driver was a glimpse of a short squat man wearing goggles.

Kerim led the way through the tables and into the café. It seemed empty, but a man rose up quickly from behind the till. He kept one hand below the counter. When he saw who it was, he gave Kerim a nervous white smile. Something clanged to the floor. He stepped from behind the counter and led them out through the back and across a stretch of gravel to a door in the high wall and, after knocking once, unlocked it and waved them through.

There was an orchard with plank tables dotted about under the trees. In the centre was a circle of terrazza dancing floor. Round it were strung fairy lights, now dead, on poles planted in the ground. On the far side, at a long table, about twenty people of all ages had been sitting eating, but they had put down their knives and now looked towards the door. Some children had been playing in the grass behind the table. They also were now quiet and watching. The three-quarter moon showed everything up brightly and made pools of membraned shadow under the trees.

Kerim and Bond walked forward. The man at the head of the table said something to the others. He got up and came to meet them. The rest returned to their dinner and the children to their games.

The man greeted Kerim with reserve. He stood for a few moments making a long explanation to which Kerim listened attentively, occasionally asking a question.

The gipsy was an imposing, theatrical figure in Macedonian dress — white shirt with full sleeves, baggy trousers and laced soft leather top-boots. His hair was a tangle of black snakes. A large downward-drooping black moustache almost hid the full red lips. The eyes were fierce and cruel on either side of a syphilitic nose. The moon glinted on the sharp line of the jaw and the high cheek-bones. His right hand, which had a gold ring on the thumb, rested on the hilt of a short curved dagger in a leather scabbard tipped with filigree silver.

The gipsy finished talking. Kerim said a few words, forceful and apparently complimentary, about Bond, at the same time stretching his hand out in Bond's direction as if he was a compère in a nightclub commending a new turn. The gipsy stepped up to Bond and scrutinized him. He bowed abruptly. Bond followed suit. The gipsy said a few words through a sardonic smile. Kerim laughed and turned to Bond. 'He says if you are ever out of work you should come to him. He will give you a job — taming his women and killing for him. That is a great compliment to a *gajo* — a foreigner. You should say something in reply.'

'Tell him that I can't imagine he needs any help in these matters.'

Kerim translated. The gipsy politely bared his teeth. He said something and walked back to the table, clapping his hands sharply. Two women got up and came towards him. He spoke to them curtly and they went back to the table and picked up a large earthenware dish and disappeared among the trees.

Kerim took Bond's arm and led him to one side.

'We have come on a bad night,' he said. 'The restaurant is closed. There are family troubles here which have to be solved — drastically, and in private. But I am an old friend and we are invited to share their supper. It will be disgusting but I have sent for raki. Then we may watch — but on condition that we do not interfere. I hope you understand, my friend.' Kerim gave Bond's arm an additional pressure. 'Whatever you see, you must not move or comment. A court has just been held and justice is to be done — their kind of justice. It is an affair of love and jealousy. Two girls of the tribe are in love with one of his sons. There is a lot of death in the air. They both threaten to kill the other to get him. If he chooses one, the unsuccessful one has sworn to kill him and the girl. It is an *impasse*. There is much argument in the tribe. So the son has been sent up into the hills and the two girls are to fight it out here tonight — to the death. The son has agreed to take the winner. The women are locked up in separate caravans. It will not be for the squeamish, but it will be a remarkable affair. It is a great privilege that we may be present. You understand? We are *gajos*. You will forget your sense of the proprieties? You will not interfere? They would kill you, and possibly me, if you did.'

'Darko,' said Bond. 'I have a French friend. A man called Mathis who is Head of the Deuxième. He once said to me: "J'aime les sensations fortes." I am like him. I shall not disgrace you. Men fighting women is one thing. Women fighting women is another. But what about the bomb? The bomb that blew up your office. What did he say about that?'

'It was the leader of the Faceless Ones. He put it there himself. They came down the Golden Horn in a boat and he climbed up a ladder and fixed it to the wall. It was bad luck he didn't get me. The operation was well thought out. The man is a gangster. A Bulgarian "refugee" called Krilencu. I shall have to have a reckoning with him. God knows why they suddenly want to kill me, but I cannot allow such annoyances. I may decide to take action later tonight. I know where he lives. In case Vavra knew the answer, I told my chauffeur to come back with the necessary equipment.'

A fiercely attractive young girl in a thick old-fashioned black frock, with strings of gold coins round her neck and about ten thin gold bracelets on each wrist, came over from the table and swept a low jingling curtsey in front of Kerim. She said something and Kerim replied.

'We are bidden to the table,' said Kerim. 'I hope you are good at eating with your fingers. I see they are all wearing their smartest clothes tonight. That girl would be worth marrying. She has a lot of gold on her. It is her dowry.'

They walked over to the table. Two places had been cleared on either side of the head gipsy. Kerim gave what sounded like a polite greeting to the table. There was a curt nod of acknowledgment. They sat down. In front of each of them was a large plate of some sort of ragout smelling strongly of garlic, a bottle of raki, a pitcher of water and a cheap tumbler. More bottles of raki, untouched, were on the table. When Kerim reached for his and poured himself half a tumblerful, everyone followed suit. Kerim added some water and raised his glass. Bond did the same. Kerim made a short and vehement speech and all raised their glasses and drank. The atmosphere became easier. An old woman next to Bond passed him a long loaf of bread and said something. Bond smiled and said 'thank you'. He broke off a piece and handed the loaf to Kerim who was picking among his ragout with thumb and forefinger. Kerim took the loaf with one hand and at the same time, with the other, he put a large piece of meat in his mouth and began to eat.

Bond was about to do the same when Kerim said sharply and quietly, 'With the right hand, James. The left hand is used for only one purpose among these people.'

Bond halted his left hand in mid-air and moved it on to grasp the nearest raki bottle. He poured himself another half tumblerful and started to eat with his right hand. The ragout was delicious but steaming hot. Bond winced each time he dipped his fingers into it. Everyone watched them eat and from time to time the old woman dipped her fingers into Bond's stew and chose a piece for him.

When they had scoured their plates, a silver bowl of water, in which rose leaves floated, and a clean linen cloth, were put between Bond and Kerim. Bond washed his fingers and his greasy chin and turned to his host and dutifully made a short speech of thanks which Kerim translated. The table murmured its appreciation. The head gipsy bowed towards Bond and said, according to Kerim, that he hated all *gajos* except Bond, whom he was proud to call his friend. Then he clapped his hands sharply and everybody got up from the table and began pulling the benches away and arranging them round the dance floor.

Kerim came round the table to Bond. They walked off together. 'How do you feel? They've gone to get the two girls.'

Bond nodded. He was enjoying the evening. The scene was beautiful and thrilling — the white moon blazing down on the ring of figures now settling on the benches, the glint of gold or jewellery as somebody shifted his position, the glaring pool of terrazza and, all around, the quiet, sentinel trees standing guard in their black skirts of shadow.

Kerim led Bond to a bench where the chief gipsy sat alone. They took their places on his right.

A black cat with green eyes walked slowly across the terrazza and joined a group of children who were sitting quietly as if someone was about to come on to the dance floor and teach them a lesson. It sat down and began licking its chest.

Beyond the high wall, a horse neighed. Two of the gipsies looked over their shoulders towards the sound as if they were reading the cry of the horse. From the road came the silvery spray of a bicycle bell as someone sped down the hill.

The crouching silence was broken by the clang of a bolt being drawn. The door in the wall crashed back and two girls, spitting and fighting like angry cats, hurtled through and across the grass and into the ring.

18

STRONG SENSATIONS

THE HEAD GIPSY'S voice cracked out. The girls separated reluctantly and stood facing him. The gipsy began to speak in a tone of harsh denunciation.

Kerim put his hand up to his mouth and whispered behind it. 'Vavra is telling them that this is a great tribe of gipsies and they have brought dissension among it. He says there is no room for hatred among themselves, only against those outside. The hatred they have created must be purged so that the tribe can live peacefully again. They are to fight. If the loser is not killed she will be banished for ever. That will be the same as death. These people wither and die outside the tribe. They cannot live in our world. It is like wild beasts forced to live in a cage.'

While Kerim spoke, Bond examined the two beautiful, taut, sullen animals in the centre of the ring.

They were both gipsy-dark, with coarse black hair to their shoulders, and they were both dressed in the collection of rags you associate with shanty-town negroes — tattered brown shifts that were mostly darns and patches. One was bigger-boned than the other, and obviously stronger, but she looked sullen and slow-eyed and might not be quick on her feet. She was handsome in a rather leonine way, and there was a slow red glare in her heavy-lidded eyes as she stood and listened impatiently to the head of the tribe. She ought to win, thought Bond. She is half an inch taller, and she is stronger.

Where this girl was a lioness, the other was a panther — lithe and quick and with cunning sharp eyes that were not on the speaker but sliding sideways, measuring inches, and the hands at her sides were curled into claws. The muscles of her fine legs looked hard as a man's. The breasts were small, and, unlike the big breasts of the other girl, hardly swelled the rags of her shift. She looks a dangerous little bitch of a girl, thought Bond. She will certainly get in the first blow. She will be too quick for the other.

At once he was proved wrong. As Vavra spoke his last word, the big girl, who, Kerim whispered, was called Zora, kicked hard sideways, without taking aim, and caught the other girl square in the stomach and, as the smaller girl staggered, followed up with a swinging blow of the fist to the side of the head that knocked her sprawling on to the stone floor.

'Oi, Vida,' lamented a woman in the crowd. She needn't have worried. Even Bond could see that Vida was shamming as she lay on the ground, apparently winded. He could see her eyes glinting under her bent arm as Zora's foot came flashing at her ribs.

Vida's hands flickered out together. They grasped the ankle and her head struck into the instep like a snake's. Zora gave a scream of pain and wrenched furiously at her trapped foot. It was too late. The other girl was up on one knee, and then standing erect, the foot still in her hands. She heaved upwards and Zora's other foot left the ground and she crashed full length.

The thud of the big girl's fall shook the ground. For a moment she lay still. With an animal snarl, Vida dived on top of her, clawing and tearing.

My God, what a hell-cat, thought Bond. Beside him, Kerim's breath hissed tensely through his teeth.

But the big girl protected herself with her elbows and knees and at last she managed to kick Vida off. She staggered to her feet and backed away, her lips bared from her teeth and the shift hanging in tatters from her splendid body. At once she went in to the attack again, her arms groping forward for a hold and, as the smaller girl leapt aside, Zora's hand caught the neck of her shift and split it down to the hem. But immediately Vida twisted in close under the reaching arms and her fists and knees thudded into the attacker's body.

This in-fighting was a mistake. The strong arms clamped shut round the smaller girl, trapping Vida's hands low down so that they could not reach up for Zora's eyes. And, slowly, Zora began to squeeze, while Vida's legs and knees thrashed ineffectually below.

Bond thought that now the big girl must win. All Zora had to do was to fall on the other girl. Vida's head would crack down on the stone and then Zora could do as she liked. But all of a sudden it was the big girl who began to scream. Bond saw that Vida's head was buried deep in the other's breasts. Her teeth were at work. Zora's arms let go as she reached for Vida's hair to pull the head back and away from her. But now Vida's hands were free and they were scrabbling at the big girl's body.

The girls tore apart and backed away like cats, their shining bodies glinting through the last rags of their shifts and blood showing on the exposed breasts of the big girl.

They circled warily, both glad to have escaped, and as they circled they tore off the last of their rags and threw them into the audience.

Bond held his breath at the sight of the two glistening, naked bodies, and he could feel Kerim's body tense beside him. The ring of gipsies seemed to have come closer to the two fighters. The moon shone on glittering eyes and there was the whisper of hot, panting breath.

Still the two girls circled slowly, their teeth bared and their breath coming harshly. The light glinted off their heaving breasts and stomachs and off their hard, boyish flanks. Their feet left dark sweat marks on the white stones.

Again it was the big girl, Zora, who made the first move with a sudden forward leap and arms held out like a wrestler's. But Vida stood her ground. Her right foot lashed out in a furious *coup de savate* that made a slap like a pistol shot. The big girl gave a wounded cry and clutched at herself. At once Vida's other foot kicked up to the stomach and she threw herself in after it.

There was a low growl from the crowd as Zora went down on her knees. Her hands went up to protect her face, but it was too late. The smaller girl was astride her, and her hands grasped Zora's wrists as she bore down on her with all her weight and bent her to the ground, her bared white teeth reaching towards the offered neck.

'BOOM!'

The explosion cracked the tension like a nut. A flash of flame lit the darkness behind the dance floor and a chunk of masonry sang past Bond's ear. Suddenly the orchard was full of running men and the head gipsy was slinking forward across the stone with his curved dagger held out in front of him. Kerim was going after him, a gun in his hand. As the gipsy passed the two girls, now standing wild-eyed and trembling, he shouted a word at them and they took to their heels and disappeared among the trees where the last of the women and children were already vanishing among the shadows.

Bond, the Beretta held uncertainly in his hand, followed slowly in the wake of Kerim towards the wide breach that had been blown out of the garden wall, and wondered what the hell was going on.

The stretch of grass between the hole in the wall and the dance floor was a turmoil of fighting, running figures. It was only as Bond came up with the fight that he distinguished the squat, conventionally dressed Bulgars from the swirling finery of the gipsies. There seemed to be more of the Faceless Ones than of the gipsies, almost two to one. As Bond peered into the struggling mass, a gipsy youth was ejected from it, clutching his stomach. He groped towards Bond, coughing terribly. Two small dark men came after him, their knives held low.

Instinctively Bond stepped to one side so that the crowd was not behind the two men. He aimed at their legs above the knees and the gun in his hand cracked twice. The two men fell, soundlessly, face downwards in the grass.

Two bullets gone. Only six left. Bond edged closer to the fight.

A knife hissed past his head and clanged on to the dance floor.

It had been aimed at Kerim, who came running out of the shadows with two men on his heels. The second man stopped and raised his knife to throw and Bond shot from the hip, blindly, and saw him fall. The other man turned and fled among the trees and Kerim dropped to one knee beside Bond, wrestling with his gun.

'Cover me,' he shouted. 'Jammed on the first shot. It's those bloody Bulgars. God knows what they think they're doing.'

A hand caught Bond round the mouth and yanked him backwards. On his way to the ground he smelled carbolic soap and nicotine. He felt a boot thud into the back of his neck. As he whirled over sideways in the grass he expected to feel the searing flame of a knife. But the men, and there were three of them, were after Kerim, and as Bond scrambled to one knee he saw the squat black figures pile down on the crouching man, who gave one lash upwards with his useless gun and then went down under them.

At the same moment as Bond leaped forward and brought his gun butt down on a round shaven head, something flashed past his eyes and the curved dagger of the head gipsy was growing out of a heaving back. Then Kerim was on his feet and the third man was running and a man was standing in the breach in the wall shouting one word, again and again, and one by one the attackers broke off their fights and doubled over to the man and past him and out on to the road.

'Shoot, James, shoot!' roared Kerim. 'That's Krilencu.' He started to run forward. Bond's gun spat once. But the man had dodged round the wall, and thirty yards is too far for night shooting with an automatic. As Bond lowered his hot gun, there came the staccato firing of a squadron of Lambrettas, and Bond stood and listened to the swarm of wasps flying down the hill.

There was silence except for the groans of the wounded. Bond listlessly watched Kerim and Vavra come back through the breach in the wall and walk among the bodies, occasionally turning one over with a foot. The other gipsies seeped back from the road and the older women came hurrying out of the shadows to tend their men.

Bond shook himself. What the hell had it all been about? Ten or a dozen men had been killed. What for? Whom had they been trying to get? Not him, Bond. When he was down and ready for the killing they had passed him by and made for Kerim. This was the second attempt on Kerim's life. Was it anything to do with the Romanova business? How could it possibly tie in?

Bond tensed. His gun spoke twice from the hip. The knife clattered harmlessly off Kerim's back. The figure that had risen from the dead twirled slowly round like a ballet dancer and toppled forward on his face. Bond ran forward. He had been just in time. The moon had caught the blade and he had had a clear field of fire. Kerim looked down at the twitching body. He turned to meet Bond.

Bond stopped in his tracks. 'You bloody fool,' he said angrily. 'Why the hell can't you take more care! You ought to have a nurse.' Most of Bond's anger came from knowing that it was he who had brought a cloud of death around Kerim.

Darko Kerim grinned shamefacedly. 'Now it is not good, James. You have saved my life too often. We might have been friends. Now the distance between us is too great. Forgive me, for I can never pay you back.' He held out his hand.

Bond brushed it aside. 'Don't be a damn fool, Darko,' he said roughly. 'My gun worked, that's all. Yours didn't. You'd better get one that does. For Christ's sake tell me what the hell this is all about. There's been too much blood splashing about tonight. I'm sick of it. I want a drink. Come and finish that raki.' He took the big man's arm.

As they reached the table, littered with the remains of the supper, a piercing, terrible scream came out of the depths of the orchard. Bond put his hand on his gun. Kerim shook his head. 'We shall soon know what the Faceless Ones were after,' he said gloomily. 'My friends are finding out. I can guess what they will discover. I think they will never forgive me for having been here tonight. Five of their men are dead.'

'There might have been a dead woman too,' said Bond unsympathetically. 'At least you've saved her life. Don't be stupid, Darko. These gipsies knew the risks when they started spying for you against the Bulgars. It was gang warfare.' He added a dash of water to two tumblers of raki.

They both emptied the glasses at one swallow. The head gipsy came up, wiping the tip of his curved dagger on a handful of grass. He sat down and accepted a glass of raki from Bond. He seemed quite cheerful. Bond had the impression that the fight had been too short for him. The gipsy said something, slyly.

Kerim chuckled. 'He said that his judgment was right. You killed well. Now he wants you to take on those two women.'

'Tell him even one of them would be too much for me. But tell him I think they are fine women. I would be glad if he would do me a favour and call the fight a draw. Enough of his people have been killed tonight. He will need these two girls to bear children for the tribe.'

Kerim translated. The gipsy looked sourly at Bond and said a few bitter words.

'He says that you should not have asked him such a difficult favour. He says that your heart is too soft for a good fighter. But he says he will do what you ask.'

The gipsy ignored Bond's smile of thanks. He started talking fast to Kerim, who listened attentively, occasionally interrupting the flow with a question. Krilencu's name was often mentioned. Kerim talked back. There was deep contrition in his voice and he refused to allow himself to be stopped by protests from the other. There came a last reference to Krilencu. Kerim turned to Bond.

'My friend,' he said drily. 'It is a curious affair. It seems the Bulgars were ordered to kill Vavra and as many of his men as possible. That is a simple matter. They knew the gipsy had been working for me. Perhaps, rather drastic. But in killing, the Russians have not much finesse. They like mass death. Vavra was a main target. I was another. The declaration of war against me personally I can also understand. But it seems that you were not to be harmed. You were exactly described so that there should be no mistake. That is odd. Perhaps it was desired that there should be no diplomatic repercussions. Who can tell? The attack was well planned. They came to the top of the hill by a roundabout route and free-wheeled down so that we should hear nothing. This is a lonely place and there is not a policeman for miles. I blame myself for having treated these people too lightly.' Kerim looked puzzled and unhappy. He seemed to make up his mind. He said, 'But now it is midnight. The Rolls will be here. There remains a small piece of work to be done before we go home to bed. And it is time we left these people. They have much to do before it is light. There are many bodies to go into the Bosphorus and there is the wall to be repaired. By daylight there must be no trace of these troubles. Our friend wishes you very well. He says you must return, and that Zora and Vida are yours until their breasts fall. He refuses to blame me for what has happened. He says that I am to continue sending him Bulgars. Ten were killed tonight. He would like some more. And now we will shake him by the hand and go. That is all he asks of us. We are good friends, but we are also *gajos*. And I expect he does not want us to see his women weeping over their dead.'

Kerim stretched out his huge hand. Vavra took it and held it and looked into Kerim's eyes. For a moment his own fierce eyes seemed to go opaque. Then the gipsy let the hand drop and turned to Bond. The hand was dry and rough and padded like the paw of a big animal. Again the eyes went opaque. He let go of Bond's hand. He spoke rapidly and urgently to Kerim and turned his back on them and walked away towards the trees.

Nobody looked up from his work as Kerim and Bond climbed through the breach in the wall. The Rolls stood, glittering in the moonlight, a few yards down the road opposite the café entrance. A young man was sitting beside the chauffeur. Kerim gestured with his hand. 'That is my tenth son. He is called Boris. I thought I might need him. I shall.'

The youth turned and said, 'Good evening, sir.' Bond recognized him as one of the clerks in the warehouse. He was as dark and lean as the head clerk, and his eyes also were blue.

The car moved down the hill. Kerim spoke to the chauffeur in English. 'It is a small street off the Hippodrome Square. When we get there we will proceed softly. I will tell you when to stop. Have you got the uniforms and the equipment?'

'Yes, Kerim Bey.'

'All right. Make good speed. It is time we were all in bed.'

Kerim sank back in his seat. He took out a cigarette. They sat and smoked. Bond gazed out at the drab streets and reflected that sparse street-lighting is the sure sign of a poor town.

It was some time before Kerim spoke. Then he said, 'The gipsy said we both have the wings of death over us. He said that I am to beware of a son of the snows and you must beware of a man who is owned by the moon.' He laughed harshly. 'That is the sort of rigmarole they talk. But he says that Krilencu isn't either of these men. That is good.'

'Why?'

'Because I cannot sleep until I have killed that man. I do not know if what happened tonight has any connection with you and your assignment. I do not care. For some reason, war has been declared on me. If I do not kill Krilencu, at the third attempt he will certainly kill me. So we are now on our way to keep an appointment with him in Samarra.'

19

THE MOUTH OF MARILYN MONROE

THE CAR SPED through the deserted streets, past shadowy mosques from which dazzling minarets lanced up towards the three-quarter moon, under the ruined Aqueduct and across the Ataturk Boulevard and north of the barred entrances to the Grand Bazaar. At the Column of Constantine the car turned right, through mean twisting streets that smelled of garbage, and finally debouched into a long ornamental square in which three stone columns fired themselves like a battery of space-rockets into the spangled sky.

'Slow,' said Kerim softly. They crept round the square under the shadow of the lime trees. Down a street on the east side, the lighthouse below the Seraglio Palace gave them a great yellow wink.

'Stop.'

The car pulled up in the darkness under the limes. Kerim reached for the door handle. 'We shan't be long, James. You sit up front in the driver's seat and if a policeman comes along just say "*Ben Bey Kerim'in ortagiyim*". Can you remember that? It means "I am Kerim Bey's partner". They'll leave you alone.'

Bond snorted. 'Thanks very much. But you'll be surprised to hear I'm coming with you. You're bound to get into trouble without me. Anyway I'm damned if I'm going to sit here trying to bluff policemen. The worst of learning one good phrase is that it sounds as if one knew the language. The policeman will come back with a barrage of Turkish and when I can't answer he'll smell a rat. Don't argue, Darko.'

'Well, don't blame me if you don't like this.' Kerim's voice was embarrassed. 'It's going to be a straight killing in cold blood. In my country you let sleeping dogs lie, but when they wake up and bite, you shoot them. You don't offer them a duel. All right?'

'Whatever you say,' said Bond. 'I've got one bullet left in case you miss.'

'Come on then,' said Kerim reluctantly. 'We've got quite a walk. The other two will be going another way.'

Kerim took a long walking-stick from the chauffeur, and a leather case. He slung them over his shoulder and they started off down the street into the yellow wink of the lighthouse. Their footsteps echoed hollowly back at them from the iron-shuttered shop frontages. There was not a soul in sight, not a cat, and Bond was glad he was not walking alone down this long street towards the distant baleful eye.

From the first, Istanbul had given him the impression of a town where, with the night, horror creeps out of the stones. It seemed to him a town the centuries had so drenched in blood and violence that, when daylight went out, the ghosts of its dead were its only population. His instinct told him, as it has told other travellers, that Istanbul was a town he would be glad to get out of alive.

They came to a narrow stinking alley that dived steeply down the hill to their right. Kerim turned into it and started gingerly down its cobbled surface. 'Watch your feet,' he said softly. 'Garbage is a polite word for what my charming people throw into their streets.'

The moon shone whitely down the moist river of cobbles. Bond kept his mouth shut and breathed through his nose. He put his feet down one after the other, flat-footedly, and with his knees bent, as if he was walking down a snow-slope. He thought of his bed in the hotel and of the comfortable cushions of the car under the sweetly smelling lime trees, and he wondered how many more kinds of dreadful stench he was going to run into during his present assignment.

They stopped at the bottom of the alley. Kerim turned to him with a broad white grin. He pointed upwards at a towering block of black shadow. 'Mosque of Sultan Ahmet. Famous Byzantine frescoes. Sorry I haven't got time to show you more of the beauties of my country.' Without waiting for Bond's reply, he cut off to the right and along a dusty boulevard, lined with cheap shops, that sloped down towards the distant glint that was the Sea of Marmara. For ten minutes they walked in silence. Then Kerim slowed and beckoned Bond into the shadows.

'This will be a simple operation,' he said softly. 'Krilencu lives down there, beside the railway line.' He gestured vaguely towards a cluster of red and green lights at the end of the boulevard. 'He hides out in a shack behind a bill-hoarding. There is a front door to the shack. Also a trapdoor to the street through the hoarding. He thinks no one knows of this. My two men will go in at the front door. He will slip out through the hoarding. Then I shoot him. All right?'

'If you say so.'

They walked on down the boulevard, keeping close to the wall. After ten minutes, they came in sight of the twenty-foot-high hoarding that formed a facing wall to the T intersection at the bottom of the street. The moon was behind the hoarding and its face was in shadow. Now Kerim walked even more carefully, putting each foot softly in front of him. About a hundred yards from the hoarding the shadows ended and the moon blazed whitely down on the intersection. Kerim stopped in the last dark doorway and stationed Bond in front of him, up against his chest. 'Now we must wait,' he whispered. Bond heard Kerim fiddling behind him. There came a soft plop as the lid of the leather case came off. A thin, heavy steel tube, about two feet long, with a bulge at each end, was pressed into Bond's hand. 'Sniperscope. German model,' whispered Kerim. 'Infra-red lens. Sees in the dark. Have a look at that big film advertisement over there. That face. Just below the nose. You'll see the outline of a trapdoor. In direct line down from the signal box.'

Bond rested his forearm against the door jamb and raised the tube to his right eye. He focused it on the patch of black shadow opposite. Slowly the black dissolved into grey. The outline of a huge woman's face and some lettering appeared. Now Bond could read the lettering. It said: 'NIYAGARA. MARILYN MONROE VE JOSEPH COTTEN' and underneath, the cartoon feature, 'BONZO FUTBOLOU'. Bond inched the glass down the vast pile of Marilyn Monroe's hair, and the cliff of forehead, and down the two feet of nose to the cavernous nostrils. A faint square showed in the poster. It ran from below the nose into the great alluring curve of the lips. It was about three feet deep. From it, there would be a longish drop to the ground.

Behind Bond there sounded a series of soft clicks. Kerim held forward his walking-stick. As Bond had supposed, it was a gun, a rifle, with a skeleton butt which was also a twist breech. The squat bulge of a silencer had taken the place of the rubber tip.

'Barrel from the new 88 Winchester,' whispered Kerim proudly. 'Put together for me by a man in Ankara. Takes the .308 cartridge. The short one. Three of them. Give me the glass. I want to get that trapdoor lined up before my men go in at the front. Mind if I use your shoulder as a rest?'

'All right.' Bond handed Kerim the Sniperscope. Kerim clipped it to the top of the barrel and slid the gun along Bond's shoulder.

'Got it,' whispered Kerim. 'Where Vavra said. He's a good man that.' He lowered his gun just as two policemen appeared at the right-hand corner of the intersection. Bond stiffened.

'It's all right,' whispered Kerim. 'That's my boy and the chauffeur.' He put two fingers in his mouth. A very quick, very low-pitched whistle sounded for a fraction of a second. One of the policemen lifted his hand to the back of his neck. The two policemen turned and walked away, their boots ringing loudly on the paving stones.

'Few minutes more,' whispered Kerim. 'They've got to get round the back of that hoarding.' Bond felt the heavy barrel of the gun slip into place along his right shoulder.

The moonstruck silence was broken by a loud iron clang from the signal box behind the hoarding. One of the signal arms dropped. A green pinpoint of light showed among the cluster of reds. There was a soft slow rumble in the distance, away to the left by Seraglio Point. It came closer and sorted itself into the heavy pant of an engine and the grinding clangour of a string of badly coupled goods trucks. A faint yellow glimmer shone along the embankment to the left. The engine came labouring into view above the hoarding.

The train slowly clanked by on its hundred-mile journey to the Greek frontier, a broken black silhouette against the silver sea, and the heavy cloud of smoke from its cheap fuel drifted towards them on the still air. As the red light on the brake van glimmered briefly and disappeared, there came the deeper rumble as the engine entered a cutting, and then two harsh, mournful whoops as it whistled its approach to the little station of Buyuk, a mile further down the line.

The rumble of the train died away. Bond felt the gun press deeper into his shoulder. He strained his eyes into the target of shadow. In the centre of it, a deeper square of blackness showed.

Bond cautiously lifted his left hand to shade his eyes from the moon. There came a hiss of breath from behind his right ear. 'He's coming.'

Out of the mouth of the huge, shadowed poster, between the great violet lips, half-open in ecstasy, the dark shape of a man emerged and hung down like a worm from the mouth of a corpse.

The man dropped. A ship going up towards the Bosphorus growled in the night like a sleepless animal in a zoo. Bond felt a prickle of sweat on his forehead. The barrel of the rifle depressed as the man stepped softly off the pavement towards them.

When he's at the edge of the shadow, he'll start to run, thought Bond. You damn fool, get the sights further down.

Now. The man bent for a quick sprint across the dazzling white street. He was coming out of the shadow. His right leg was bent forward and his shoulder was twisted to give him momentum.

At Bond's ear there was the clunk of an axe hitting into a tree-trunk. The man dived forward, his arms outstretched. There was a sharp 'tok' as his chin or his forehead hit the ground.

An empty cartridge tinkled down at Bond's feet. He heard the click of the next round going into the chamber.

The man's fingers scrabbled briefly at the cobbles. His shoes knocked on the road. Then he lay absolutely still.

Kerim grunted. The rifle came down off Bond's shoulder, Bond listened to the noises of Kerim folding up the gun and putting away the Sniperscope in its leather case.

Bond looked away from the sprawling figure in the road, the figure of the man who had been, but was no more. He had a moment of resentment against the life that made him witness these things. The resentment was not against Kerim. Kerim had twice been this man's target. In a way it had been a long duel, in which the man had fired twice to Kerim's once. But Kerim was the cleverer, cooler man, and the luckier, and that had been that. But Bond had never killed in cold blood, and he hadn't liked watching, and helping, someone else do it.

Kerim silently took his arm. They walked slowly away from the scene and back the way they had come.

Kerim seemed to sense Bond's thoughts. 'Life is full of death, my friend,' he said philosophically. 'And sometimes one is made the instrument of death. I do not regret killing that man. Nor would I regret killing any of those Russians we saw in that office today. They are hard people. With them, what you don't get from strength, you won't get from mercy. They are all the same, the Russians. I wish your government would realize it and be strong with them. Just an occasional little lesson in manners like I have taught them tonight.'

'In power politics, one doesn't often have the chance of being as quick and neat as you were tonight, Darko. And don't forget it's only one of their satellites you've punished, one of the men they always find to do their dirty work. Mark you,' said Bond, 'I quite agree about the Russians. They simply don't understand the carrot. Only the stick has any effect. Basically they're masochists. They love the knout. That's why they were so happy under Stalin. He gave it them. I'm not sure how they're going to react to the scraps of carrot they're being fed by Khrushchev and Co. As for England, the trouble today is that carrots for all are the fashion. At home and abroad. We don't show teeth any more — only gums.'

Kerim laughed harshly, but made no comment. They were climbing back up the stinking alley and there was no breath for talk. They rested at the top and then walked slowly towards the trees of the Hippodrome Square.

'So you forgive me for today?' It was odd to hear the longing for reassurance in the big man's usually boisterous voice.

'Forgive you? Forgive what? Don't be ridiculous.' There was affection in Bond's voice. 'You've got a job to do and you're doing it. I've been very impressed. You've got a wonderful set-up here. I'm the one who ought to apologize. I seem to have brought a great deal of trouble down on your head. And you've dealt with it. I've just tagged along behind. And I've got absolutely nowhere with my main job. M. will be getting pretty impatient. Perhaps there'll be some sort of message at the hotel.'

But when Kerim took Bond back to the hotel and went with him to the desk there was nothing for Bond. Kerim clapped him on the back. 'Don't worry, my friend,' he said cheerfully. 'Hope makes a good breakfast. Eat plenty of it. I will send the car in the morning and if nothing has happened I will think of some more little adventures to pass the time. Clean your gun and sleep on it. You both deserve a rest.'

Bond climbed the few stairs and unlocked his door and locked and bolted it behind him. Moonlight filtered through the curtains. He walked across and turned on the pink-shaded lights on the dressing-table. He stripped off his clothes and went into the bathroom and stood for a few minutes under the shower. He thought how much more eventful Saturday the fourteenth had been than Friday the thirteenth. He cleaned his teeth and gargled with a sharp mouthwash to get rid of the taste of the day and turned off the bathroom light and went back into the bedroom.

Bond drew aside one curtain and opened wide the tall windows and stood, holding the curtains open and looking out across the great boomerang curve of water under the riding moon. The night breeze felt wonderfully cool on his naked body. He looked at his watch. It said two o'clock.

Bond gave a shuddering yawn. He let the curtains drop back into place. He bent to switch off the lights on the dressing-table. Suddenly he stiffened and his heart missed a beat.

There had been a nervous giggle from the shadows at the back of the room. A girl's voice said, 'Poor Mister Bond. You must be tired. Come to bed.'

20

BLACK ON PINK

BOND WHIRLED ROUND. He looked over to the bed, but his eyes were blind from gazing at the moon. He crossed the room and turned on the pink-shaded light by the bed. There was a long body under the single sheet. Brown hair was spread out on the pillow. The tips of fingers showed, holding the sheet up over the face. Lower down the breasts stood up like hills under snow.

Bond laughed shortly. He leaned forward and gave the hair a soft tug. There was a squeak of protest from under the sheet. Bond sat down on the edge of the bed. After a moment's silence a corner of the sheet was cautiously lowered and one large blue eye inspected him.

'You look very improper.' The voice was muffled by the sheet.

'What about you! And how did you get here?'

'I walked down two floors. I live here too.' The voice was deep and provocative. There was very little accent.

'Well, I'm going to get into bed.'

The sheet came quickly down to the chin and the girl pulled herself up on the pillows. She was blushing. 'Oh no. You mustn't.'

'But it's my bed. And anyway you told me to.' The face was incredibly beautiful. Bond examined it coolly. The blush deepened.

'That was only a phrase. To introduce myself.'

'Well I'm very glad to meet you. My name's James Bond.'

'Mine's Tatiana Romanova.' She sounded the second A of Tatiana and the first A of Romanova very long. 'My friends call me Tania.'

There was a pause while they looked at each other, the girl with curiosity, and with what might have been relief. Bond with cool surmise.

She was the first to break the silence. 'You look just like your photographs.' She blushed again. 'But you must put something on. It upsets me.'

'You upset me just as much. That's called sex. If I got into bed with you it wouldn't matter. Anyway, what have *you* got on?'

She pulled the sheet a fraction lower to show a quarter-inch black velvet ribbon round her neck. 'This.'

Bond looked down into the teasing blue eyes, now wide as if asking if the ribbon was inadequate. He felt his body getting out of control.

'Damn you, Tania. Where are the rest of your things? Or did you come down in the lift like that?'

'Oh no. That would not have been *kulturny*. They are under the bed.'

'Well, if you think you are going to get out of this room without . . . '

Bond left the sentence unfinished. He got up from the bed and went to put on one of the dark blue silk pyjama coats he wore instead of pyjamas.

'What you are suggesting is not *kulturny*.'

'Oh isn't it,' said Bond sarcastically. He came back to the bed and pulled up a chair beside it. He smiled down at her. 'Well I'll tell you something *kulturny*. You're one of the most beautiful women in the world.'

The girl blushed again. She looked at him seriously. 'Are you speaking the truth? I think my mouth is too big. Am I as beautiful as Western girls? I was once told I look like Greta Garbo. Is that so?'

'More beautiful,' said Bond. 'There is more light in your face. And your mouth isn't too big. It's just the right size. For me, anyway.'

'What is that — "light in the face"? What do you mean?'

Bond meant that she didn't look to him like a Russian spy. She seemed to show none of the reserve of a spy. None of the coldness, none of the calculation. She gave the impression of warmth of heart and gaiety. These things shone out through the eyes. He searched for a non-committal phrase. 'There is a lot of gaiety and fun in your eyes,' he said lamely.

Tatiana looked serious. 'That is curious,' she said. 'There is not much fun and gaiety in Russia. No one speaks of these things. I have never been told that before.'

Gaiety? she thought, after the last two months? How could she be looking gay? And yet, yes, there was a lightness in her heart. Was she a loose woman by nature? Or was it something to do with this man she had never seen before? Relief about him after the agony of thinking about what she had to do? It was certainly much easier than she had expected. He made it easy — made it fun, with a spice of danger. He was terribly handsome. And he looked very clean. Would he forgive her when they got to London and she told him? Told him that she had been sent to seduce him? Even the night on which she must do it and the number of the room? Surely he wouldn't mind very much. It was doing him no harm. It was only a way for her to get to England and make those reports. 'Gaiety and fun in her eyes'. Well, why not? It was possible. There was a wonderful sense of freedom being alone with a man like this and knowing that she would not be punished for it. It was really terribly exciting.

'You are very handsome,' she said. She searched for a comparison that would give him pleasure. 'You are like an American film star.'

She was startled by his reaction. 'For God's sake! That's the worst insult you can pay a man!'

She hurried to make good her mistake. How curious that the compliment didn't please him. Didn't everyone in the West want to look like a film star? 'I was lying,' she said. 'I wanted to give you pleasure. In fact you are like my favourite hero. He's in a book by a Russian called Lermontov. I will tell you about him one day.'

One day? Bond thought it was time to get down to business.

'Now listen, Tania.' He tried not to look at the beautiful face on the pillow. He fixed his eyes on the point of her chin. 'We've got to stop fooling and be serious. What *is* all this about? Are you really going to come back to England with me?' He raised his eyes to hers. It was fatal. She had opened them wide again in that damnable guilelessness.

'But of course!'

'Oh!' Bond was taken aback by the directness of her answer. He looked at her suspiciously. 'You're sure?'

'Yes.' Her eyes were truthful now. She had stopped flirting.

'You're not afraid?'

He saw a shadow cross her eyes. But it was not what he

thought. She had remembered that she had a part to play. She was to be frightened of what she was doing. Terrified. It had sounded so easy, this acting, but now it was difficult. How odd! She decided to compromise.

'Yes. I am afraid. But not so much now. You will protect me. I thought you would.'

'Well, yes, of course I will.' Bond thought of her relatives in Russia. He quickly put the thought out of his mind. What was he doing? Trying to dissuade her from coming? He closed his mind to the consequences he imagined for her. 'There's nothing to worry about. I'll look after you.' And now for the question he had been shirking. He felt a ridiculous embarrassment. This girl wasn't in the least what he had expected. It was spoiling everything to ask the question. It had to be done.

'What about the machine?'

Yes. It was as if he had cuffed her across the face. Pain showed in her eyes, and the edge of tears.

She pulled the sheet over her mouth and spoke from behind it. Her eyes above the sheet were cold.

'So that's what you want.'

'Now listen.' Bond put nonchalance in his voice. 'This machine's got nothing to do with you and me. But my people in London want it.' He remembered security. He added blandly, 'It's not all that important. They know all about the machine and they think it's a wonderful Russian invention. They just want one to copy. Like your people copy foreign cameras and things.' God, how lame it sounded!

'Now you're lying.' A big tear rolled out of one wide blue eye and down the soft cheek and on to the pillow. She pulled the sheet up over her eyes.

Bond reached out and put his hand on her arm under the sheet. The arm flinched angrily away.

'Damn the bloody machine,' he said impatiently. 'But for God's sake, Tania, you must know that I've got a job to do. Just say one way or the other and we'll forget about it. There are lots more things to talk about. We've got to arrange our journey and so on. Of course my people want it or they wouldn't have sent me out to bring you home with it.'

Tatiana dabbed her eyes with the sheet. Brusquely she pulled the sheet down to her shoulders again. She knew that she had been forgetting her job. It had just been that . . . Oh well. If only he had said that the machine didn't matter to him so long as she would come. But that was too much to hope for. He was right. He had a job to do. So had she.

She looked up at him calmly. 'I will bring it. Have no fear. But do not let us mention it again. And now listen.' She sat up straighter on the pillows. 'We must go tonight.' She remembered her lesson. 'It is the only chance. This evening I am on night duty from six o'clock. I shall be alone in the office and I will take the Spektor.'

Bond's eyes narrowed. His mind raced as he thought of the problems that would have to be faced. Where to hide her. How to get her out to the first plane after the loss had been discovered. It was going to be a risky business. They would stop at nothing to get her and the Spektor back. Roadblock on the way to the airport. Bomb in the plane. Anything.

'That's wonderful, Tania.' Bond's voice was casual. 'We'll keep you hidden and then we'll take the first plane tomorrow morning.'

'Don't be foolish.' Tatiana had been warned that there would be some difficult lines in her part. 'We will take the train. This Orient Express. It leaves at nine tonight. Do you think I haven't been thinking this thing out? I won't stay a minute longer in Istanbul than I have to. We will be over the frontier at dawn. You must get the tickets and a passport. I will travel with you as your wife.' She looked happily up at him. 'I shall like that. In one of those coupés I have read about. They must be very comfortable. Like a tiny house on wheels. During the day we will talk and read and at night you will stand in the corridor outside our house and guard it.'

'Like hell I will,' said Bond. 'But look here, Tania. That's crazy. They're bound to catch up with us somewhere. It's four days and five nights to London on that train. We've got to think of something else.'

'I won't,' said the girl flatly. 'That's the only way I'll go. If you are clever, how can they find out?'

Oh God, she thought. Why had they insisted on this train? But they had been definite. It was a good place for love, they had said. She would have four days to get him to love her. Then, when they got to London, life would be easy for her. He would protect her. Otherwise, if they flew to London, she would be put straight into prison. The four days were essential. And, they had warned her, we will have men on the train to see you don't get off. So be careful and obey your orders. Oh God. Oh God. Yet now she longed for those four days with him in the little house on wheels How curious! It had been her duty to force him. Now it was her passionate desire.

She watched Bond's thoughtful face. She longed to stretch out a hand to him and reassure him that it would be all right; that this was a harmless *konspiratsia* to get her to England: that no harm could come to either of them, because that was not the object of the plot.

'Well, I still think it's crazy,' said Bond, wondering what M.'s reaction would be. 'But I suppose it may work. I've got the passport. It will need a Yugoslav visa.' He looked at her sternly. 'Don't think I'm going to take you on the part of the train that goes through Bulgaria, or I shall think you want to kidnap me.'

'I do.' Tatiana giggled. 'That's exactly what I want to do.'

'Now shut up, Tania. We've got to work this out. I'll get the tickets and I'll have one of our men come along. Just in case. He's a good man. You'll like him. Your name's Caroline Somerset. Don't forget it. How are you going to get to the train?'

'Karolin Siomerset.' The girl turned the name over in her mind. 'It is a pretty name. And you are Mister Siomerset.' She laughed happily. 'That is fun. Do not worry about me. I will come to the train just before it leaves. It is the Sirkeci Station. I know where it is. So that is all. And we do not worry any more. Yes?'

'Suppose you lose your nerve? Suppose they catch you?' Suddenly Bond was worried at the girl's confidence. How could she be so certain? A sharp tingle of suspicion ran down his spine.

'Before I saw you, I was frightened. Now I am not.' Tatiana tried to tell herself that this was the truth. Somehow it nearly was. 'Now I shall not lose my nerve, as you call it. And they cannot catch me. I shall leave my things in the hotel and take my usual bag to the office. I cannot leave my fur coat behind. I love it too dearly. But today is Sunday and that will be an excuse to come to the office in it. Tonight at half-past eight I shall walk out and take a taxi to the station. And now you must stop looking so worried.' Impulsively, because she had to, she stretched out a hand towards him. 'Say that you are pleased.'

Bond moved to the edge of the bed. He took her hand and looked down into her eyes. God, he thought. I hope it's all right. I hope this crazy plan will work. Is this wonderful girl a cheat? Is she true? Is she real? The eyes told him nothing except that the girl was happy, and that she wanted him to love her, and that she was surprised at what was happening to her. Tatiana's other hand came up and round his neck and pulled him fiercely down to her. At first the mouth trembled under his and then, as passion took her, the mouth yielded into a kiss without end.

Bond lifted his legs on to the bed. While his mouth went on kissing her, his hand went to her left breast and held it, feeling the peak hard with desire under his fingers. His hand strayed on down across her flat stomach. Her legs shifted languidly. She moaned softly and her mouth slid away from his. Below the closed eyes the long lashes quivered like humming birds' wings.

Bond reached up and took the edge of the sheet and pulled it right down and threw it off the end of the huge bed. She was wearing nothing but the black ribbon round her neck and black silk stockings rolled above her knees. Her arms groped up for him.

Above them, and unknown to both of them, behind the gold-framed false mirror on the wall over the bed, the two photographers from SMERSH sat close together in the cramped *cabinet de voyeur*, as, before them, so many friends of the proprietor had sat on a honeymoon night in the stateroom of the Kristal Palas.

And the view-finders gazed coldly down on the passionate arabesques the two bodies formed and broke and formed again, and the clockwork mechanism of the cine-cameras whirred softly on and on as the breath rasped out of the open mouths of the two men and the sweat of excitement trickled down their bulging faces into their cheap collars.

21

ORIENT EXPRESS

THE GREAT TRAINS are going out all over Europe, one by one, but still, three times a week, the Orient Express thunders superbly over the 1400 miles of glittering steel track between Istanbul and Paris.

Under the arc-lights, the long-chassised German locomotive panted quietly with the laboured breath of a dragon dying of asthma. Each heavy breath seemed certain to be the last. Then came another. Wisps of steam rose from the couplings between the carriages and died quickly in the warm August air. The Orient Express was the only live train in the ugly, cheaply architectured burrow that is Istanbul's main station. The trains on the other lines were engineless and unattended — waiting for tomorrow. Only Track No. 3, and its platform, throbbed with the tragic poetry of departure.

The heavy bronze cipher on the side of the dark blue coach said, 'COMPAGNIE INTERNATIONALE DES WAGON-LITS ET DES GRANDS EXPRESS EUROPÉENS'. Above the cipher, fitted into metal slots, was a flat iron sign that announced, in black capitals on white, ORIENT EXPRESS, and underneath, in three lines:

ISTANBUL THESSALONIKI BEOGRAD
VENEZIA MILAN
LAUSANNE PARIS

James Bond gazed vaguely at one of the most romantic signs in the world. For the tenth time he looked at his watch. 8.51. His eyes went back to the sign. All the towns were spelled in the language of the country except MILAN. Why not MILANO? Bond took out his handkerchief and wiped his face. Where the hell was the girl? Had she been caught? Had she had second thoughts? Had he been too rough with her last night, or rather this morning, in the great bed?

8.55. The quiet pant of the engine had stopped. There came an echoing whoosh as the automatic safety-valve let off the excess steam. A hundred yards away, through the milling crowd, Bond watched the station-master raise a hand to the engine driver and fireman and start walking slowly back down the train, banging the doors of the third-class carriages up front. Passengers, mostly peasants going back into Greece after a week-end with their relatives in Turkey, hung out of the windows and jabbered at the grinning crowd below.

Beyond, where the faded arc-lights stopped and the dark blue night and the stars showed through the crescent mouth of the station, Bond saw a red pinpoint turn to green.

The station-master came nearer. The brown-uniformed wagon-lit attendant tapped Bond on the arm. '*En voiture, s'il vous plaît.*' The two rich-looking Turks kissed their mistresses — they were too pretty to be wives — and, with a barrage of laughing injunctions, stepped on to the little iron pedestal and up the two tall steps into the carriage. There were no other wagon-lit travellers on the platform. The conductor, with an impatient glance at the tall Englishman, picked up the iron pedestal and climbed with it into the train.

The station-master strode purposefully by. Two more compartments, the first- and second-class carriages, and then, when he reached the guard's van, he would lift the dirty green flag.

There was no hurrying figure coming up the platform from the *guichet*. High up above the *guichet*, near the ceiling of the station, the minute-hand of the big illuminated clock jumped forward an inch and said 'Nine'.

A window banged down above Bond's head. Bond looked up. His immediate reaction was that the black veil was too wide-meshed. The intention to disguise the luxurious mouth and the excited blue eyes was amateurish.

'Quick.'

The train had begun to move. Bond reached for the passing hand-rail and swung up on to the step. The attendant was still holding open the door. Bond stepped unhurriedly through.

'Madam was late,' said the attendant. 'She came along the corridor. She must have entered by the last carriage.'

Bond went down the carpeted corridor to the centre coupé. A black 7 stood above a black 8 on the white metal lozenge. The door was ajar. Bond walked in and shut it behind him. The girl had taken off her veil and her black straw hat. She was sitting in the corner by the window. A long sleek sable coat was thrown open to show a natural-coloured shantung dress with a pleated skirt, honey-coloured nylons and a black crocodile belt and shoes. She looked composed.

'You have no faith, James.'

Bond sat down beside her. 'Tania,' he said, 'if there was a bit more room I'd put you across my knee and spank you. You nearly gave me heart failure. What happened?'

'Nothing,' said Tatiana innocently. 'What could happen? I said I would be here, and I am here. You have no faith. Since I am sure you are more interested in my dowry than in me, it is up there.'

Bond looked casually up. Two small cases were on the rack beside his suitcase. He took her hand. He said, 'Thank God you're safe.'

Something in his eyes, perhaps the flash of guilt, as he admitted to himself that he had been more interested in the girl than the machine, reassured her. She kept his hand in hers and sank contentedly back in her corner.

The train screeched slowly round Seraglio Point. The lighthouse lit up the roofs of the dreary shacks along the railway line. With his free hand Bond took out a cigarette and lit it. He reflected that they would soon be passing the back of the great bill-board where Krilencu had lived — until less than twenty-four hours ago. Bond saw again the scene in every detail. The white crossroads, the two men in the shadows, the doomed man slipping out through the purple lips.

The girl watched his face with tenderness. What was this man thinking? What was going on behind those cold level grey-blue eyes that sometimes turned soft and sometimes, as they had done last night before his passion had burned out in her arms, blazed like diamonds? Now they were veiled in thought. Was he worrying about them both? Worrying about their safety? If only she could tell him that there was nothing to fear, that he was only her passport to England — him and the heavy case the Resident Director had given her that evening in the office. The Director had said the same thing. 'Here is your passport to England, Corporal,' he had said cheerfully. 'Look.' He had unzipped the bag: 'A brand-new Spektor. Be certain not to open the bag again or let it out of your compartment until you get to the other end. Or this Englishman will take it away from you and throw you on the dust-heap. It is this machine they want. Do not let them take it from you, or you will have failed in your duty. Understood?'

A signal box loomed up in the blue dusk outside the window. Tatiana watched Bond get up and pull down the window and crane out into the darkness. His body was close to her. She moved her knee so that it touched him. How extraordinary, this passionate tenderness that had filled her ever since she had seen him last night standing naked at the window, his arms up to hold the curtains back, his profile, under the tousled black hair, intent and pale in the moonlight. And then the extraordinary fusing of their eyes and their bodies. The flame that had suddenly lit between them — between the two secret agents, thrown together from enemy camps a whole world apart, each involved in his own plot against the country of the other, antagonists by profession, yet turned, and by the orders of their governments, into lovers.

Tatiana stretched out a hand and caught hold of the edge of the coat and tugged at it. Bond pulled up the window and turned. He smiled down at her. He read her eyes. He bent and put his hands on the fur over her breasts and kissed her hard on the lips. Tatiana leant back, dragging him with her.

There came a soft double knock on the door. Bond stood up. He pulled out his handkerchief and brusquely scrubbed the rouge off his lips. 'That'll be my friend Kerim,' he said. 'I must talk to him. I will tell the conductor to make up the beds. Stay here while he does it. I won't be long. I shall be outside the door.' He leant forward and touched her hand and looked at her wide eyes and at her rueful, half-open lips. 'We shall have all the night to ourselves. First I must see that you are safe.' He unlocked the door and slipped out.

Darko Kerim's huge bulk was blocking the corridor. He was leaning on the brass guard rail, smoking and gazing moodily out towards the Sea of Marmara that receded as the long train snaked away from the coast and turned inland and northwards. Bond leaned on the rail beside him. Kerim looked into the reflection of Bond's face in the dark window. He said softly, 'The news is not good. There are three of them on the train.'

'Ah!' An electric tingle ran up Bond's spine.

'It's the three strangers we saw in that room. Obviously they're on to you and the girl.' Kerim glanced sharply sideways. 'That makes her a double. Or doesn't it?'

Bond's mind was cool. So the girl had been bait. And yet, and yet. No, damn it. She couldn't be acting. It wasn't possible. The cipher machine? Perhaps after all it wasn't in that bag. 'Wait a minute,' he said. He turned and knocked softly on the door. He heard her unlock it and slip the chain. He went in and shut the door. She looked surprised. She had thought it was the conductor come to make up the beds.

She smiled radiantly. 'You have finished?'

'Sit down, Tatiana. I've got to talk to you.'

Now she saw the coldness in his face and her smile went out. She sat down obediently with her hands in her lap.

Bond stood over her. Was there guilt in her face, or fear? No, only surprise and a coolness to match his own expression.

'Now listen, Tatiana,' Bond's voice was deadly, 'something's come up. I must look into that bag and see if the machine is there.'

She said indifferently, 'Take it down and look.' She examined the hands in her lap. So now it was going to come. What the Director had said. They were going to take the machine and throw her aside, perhaps have her put off the train. Oh God! This man was going to do that to her.

Bond reached up and hauled down the heavy case and put it on the seat. He tore the zip sideways and looked in. Yes, a grey japanned metal case with three rows of squat keys, rather like a typewriter. He held the bag open towards her. 'Is that a Spektor?'

She glanced casually into the gaping bag. 'Yes.'

Bond zipped the bag shut and put it back on the rack. He sat down beside the girl. 'There are three M.G.B. men on the train. We know they are the ones who arrived at your centre on Monday. What are they doing here, Tatiana?' Bond's voice was soft. He watched her, searched her with all his senses.

She looked up. There were tears in her eyes. Were they the tears of a child found out? But there was no trace of guilt in her face. She only looked terrified of something.

She reached out a hand and then drew it back. 'You aren't going to throw me off the train now you've got the machine?'

'Of course not,' Bond said impatiently. 'Don't be idiotic. But we must know what these men are doing. What's it all about? Did you know they were going to be on the train?' He tried to read some clue in her expression. He could only see a great relief. And what else? A look of calculation? Of reserve? Yes, she was hiding something. But what?

Tatiana seemed to make up her mind. Brusquely she wiped the back of her hand across her eyes. She reached forward and put the hand on his knee. The streak of tears showed on the back of the hand. She looked into Bond's eyes, forcing him to believe her.

'James,' she said. 'I did not know these men were on the train. I was told they were leaving today. For Germany. I assumed they would fly. That is all I can tell you. Until we arrive in England, out of reach of my people, you must not ask me more. I have done what I said I would. I am here with the machine. Have faith in me. Do not be afraid for us. I am certain these men do not mean us harm. Absolutely certain. Have faith.' (Was she so certain? wondered Tatiana. Had the Klebb woman told her all the truth? But she also must have faith — faith in the orders she had been given. These men must be the guards to see that she didn't get off the train. They could mean no harm. Later, when they got to London, this man would hide her away out of reach of SMERSH and she would tell him everything he wanted to know. She had already decided this in the back of her mind. But God knew what would happen if she betrayed *Them* now. *They* would somehow get her, and him. She knew it. There were no secrets from these people. And *They* would have no mercy. So long as she played out her role, all would be well.) Tatiana watched Bond's face for a sign that he believed her.

Bond shrugged his shoulders. He stood up. 'I don't know what to think, Tatiana,' he said. 'You are keeping something from me, but I think it's something you don't know is important. And I believe you think we are safe. We may be. It may be a coincidence that these men are on the train. I must talk to Kerim and decide what to do. Don't worry. We will look after you. But now we must be very careful.'

Bond looked round the compartment. He tried the communicating door with the next coupé. It was locked. He decided to wedge it when the conductor had gone. He would do the same for the door into the passage. And he would have to stay awake. So much for the honeymoon on wheels! Bond smiled grimly to himself and rang for the conductor. Tatiana was looking anxiously up at him. 'Don't worry, Tania,' he said again. 'Don't worry about anything. Go to bed when the man has gone. Don't open the door unless you know it's me. I will sit up tonight and watch. Perhaps tomorrow it will be easier. I will make a plan with Kerim. He is a good man.'

The conductor knocked. Bond let him in and went out into the corridor. Kerim was still there gazing out. The train had picked up speed and was hurtling through the night, its harsh melancholy whistle echoing back at them from the walls of a deep cutting against the sides of which the lighted carriage windows flickered and danced. Kerim didn't move, but his eyes in the mirror of the window were watchful.

Bond told him of the conversation. It was not easy to explain to Kerim why he trusted the girl as he did. He watched the mouth in the window curl ironically as he tried to describe what he had read in her eyes and what his intuition told him.

Kerim sighed resignedly. 'James,' he said, 'you are now in charge. This is your part of the operation. We have already argued most of this out today — the danger of the train, the possibility of getting the machine home in the diplomatic bag, the integrity, or otherwise, of this girl. It certainly appears that she has surrendered unconditionally to you. At the same time you admit that you have surrendered to her. Perhaps only partially. But you have decided to trust her. In this morning's telephone talk with M. he said that he would back your decision. He left it to you. So be it. But he didn't know we were to have an escort of three M.G.B. men. Nor did we. And I think that would have changed all our views. Yes?'

'Yes.'

'Then the only thing to do is eliminate these three men. Get them off the train. God knows what they're here for. I don't believe in coincidences any more than you. But one thing is certain. We are not going to share the train with these men. Right?'

'Of course.'

'Then leave it to me. At least for tonight. This is still my country and I have certain powers in it. And plenty of money. I cannot afford to kill them. The train would be delayed. You and the girl might get involved. But I shall arrange something. Two of them have sleeping berths. The senior man with the moustache and the little pipe is next door to you — here, in No. 6.' He gestured backwards with his head. 'He is travelling on a German passport under the name of "Melchior Benz, salesman". The dark one, the Armenian, is in No. 12. He, too, has a German passport — "Kurt Goldfarb, construction engineer". They have through tickets to Paris. I have seen their documents. I have a police card. The conductor made no trouble. He has all the tickets and passports in his cabin. The third man, the man with a boil on the back of his neck, turns out also to have boils on his face. A stupid, ugly-looking brute. I have not seen his passport. He is travelling sitting up in the first-class, in the next compartment to me. He does not have to surrender his passport until the frontier. But he has surrendered his ticket.' Like a conjuror, Kerim flicked a yellow first-class ticket out of his coat pocket. He slipped it back. He grinned proudly at Bond.

'How the hell?'

Kerim chuckled. 'Before he settled down for the night, this dumb ox went to the lavatory. I was standing in the corridor and I suddenly remembered how we used to steal rides on the train when I was a boy. I gave him a minute. Then I walked up and rattled the lavatory door. I hung on to the handle very tight. "Ticket collector," I said in a loud voice. "Tickets please." I said it in French and again in German. There was a mumble from inside. I felt him try to open the door. I hung on tight so that he would think the door had stuck. "Do not derange yourself, *Monsieur*," I said politely. "Push the ticket under the door." There was more fiddling with the door handle and I could hear heavy breathing. Then there was a pause and a rustle under the door. There was the ticket. I said, "*Merci, Monsieur*" very politely. I picked up the ticket and stepped across the coupling into the next carriage.' Kerim airily waved a hand. 'The stupid oaf will be sleeping peacefully by now. He will think that his ticket will be given back to him at the frontier. He is mistaken. The ticket will be in ashes and the ashes will be on the four winds.' Kerim gestured towards the darkness outside. 'I will see that the man is put off the train, however much money he has got. He will be told that the circumstances must be investigated, his statements corroborated with the ticket agency. He will be allowed to proceed on a later train.'

Bond smiled at the picture of Kerim playing his private school trick. 'You're a card, Darko. What about the other two?'

Darko Kerim shrugged his massive shoulders. 'Something will occur to me,' he said confidently. 'The way to catch Russians is to make them look foolish. Embarrass them. Laugh at them. They can't stand it. We will somehow make these men sweat. Then we will leave it to the M.G.B. to punish them for failing in their duty. Doubtless they will be shot by their own people.'

While they were talking, the conductor had come out of No. 7. Kerim turned to Bond and put a hand on his shoulder. 'Have no fear, James,' he said cheerfully. 'We will defeat these people. Go to your girl. We will meet again in the morning. We shall not sleep much tonight, but that cannot be helped. Every day is different. Perhaps we shall sleep tomorrow.'

Bond watched the big man move off easily down the swaying corridor. He noticed that, despite the movement of the train, Kerim's shoulders never touched the walls of the corridor. Bond felt a wave of affection for the tough, cheerful professional spy.

Kerim disappeared into the conductor's cabin. Bond turned and knocked softly on the door of No. 7.

22

OUT OF TURKEY

THE TRAIN HOWLED on through the night. Bond sat and watched the hurrying moonlit landscape and concentrated on keeping awake.

Everything conspired to make him sleep — the hasty metal gallop of the wheels, the hypnotic swoop of the silver telegraph wires, the occasional melancholy, reassuring moan of the steam whistle clearing their way, the drowsy metallic chatter of the couplings at each end of the corridor, the lullaby creak of the woodwork in the little room. Even the deep violet glimmer of the nightlight above the door seemed to say, 'I will watch for you. Nothing can happen while I am burning. Close your eyes and sleep, sleep.'

The girl's head was warm and heavy on his lap. There was so obviously just room for him to slip under the single sheet and fit close up against her, the front of his thighs against the backs of hers, his head in the spread curtain of her hair on the pillow.

Bond screwed up his eyes and opened them again. He cautiously lifted his wrist. Four o'clock. Only one more hour to the Turkish frontier. Perhaps he would be able to sleep during the day. He would give her the gun and wedge the doors again and she could watch.

He looked down at the beautiful sleeping profile. How innocent she looked, this girl from the Russian Secret Service — the lashes fringing the soft swell of the cheek, the lips parted and unaware, the long strand of hair that had strayed untidily across her forehead and that he wanted to brush back neatly to join the rest, the steady slow throb of the pulse in the offered neck. He felt a surge of tenderness and the impulse to gather her up in his arms and strain her tight against him. He wanted her to wake, from a dream perhaps, so that he could kiss her and tell her that everything was all right, and see her settle happily back to sleep.

The girl had insisted on sleeping like this. 'I won't go to sleep unless you hold me,' she had said. 'I must know you're there all the time. It would be terrible to wake up and not be touching you. Please, James. Please, *duschka*.'

Bond had taken off his coat and tie and had arranged himself in the corner with his feet up on his suitcase and the Beretta under the pillow within reach of his hand. She had made no comment about the gun. She had taken off all her clothes, except the black ribbon round her throat, and had pretended not to be provocative as she scrambled impudently into bed and wriggled herself into a comfortable position. She had held up her arms to him. Bond had pulled her head back by her hair and had kissed her once, long and cruelly. Then he had told her to go to sleep and had leant back and waited icily for his body to leave him alone. Grumbling sleepily, she had settled herself, with one arm flung across his thighs. At first she had held him tightly, but her arm had gradually relaxed and then she was asleep.

Brusquely Bond closed his mind to the thought of her and focused on the journey ahead.

Soon they would be out of Turkey. But would Greece be any easier? No love lost between Greece and England. And Yugoslavia? Whose side was Tito on? Probably both. Whatever the orders of the three M.G.B. men, either they already knew Bond and Tatiana were on the train or they would soon find out. He and the girl couldn't sit for four days in this coupé with the blinds drawn. Their presence would be reported back to Istanbul, telephoned from some station, and by the morning the loss of the Spektor would have been discovered. Then what? A hasty démarche through the Russian Embassy in Athens or Belgrade? Have the girl taken off the train as a thief? Or was that all too simple? And if it was more complicated — if all this was part of some mysterious plot, some tortuous Russian conspiracy — should he dodge it? Should he and the girl leave the train at a wayside station, on the wrong side of the track, and hire a car and somehow get a plane to London?

Outside, the luminous dawn had begun to edge the racing trees and rocks with blue. Bond looked at his watch. Five o'clock. They would soon be at Uzunkopru. What was going on down the train behind him? What had Kerim achieved?

Bond sat back, relaxed. After all there was a simple, common-sense answer to his problem. If, between them, they could quickly get rid of the three M.G.B. agents, they would stick to the train and to their original plan. If not, Bond would get the girl and the machine off the train, somewhere in Greece, and take another route home. But, if the odds improved, Bond was for going on. He and Kerim were resourceful men. Kerim had an agent in Belgrade who was going to meet the train. There was always the Embassy.

Bond's mind raced on, adding up the pros, dismissing the cons. Behind his reasoning, Bond calmly admitted to himself that he had an insane desire to play the game out and see what it was all about. He wanted to take these people on and solve the mystery and, if it was some sort of a plot, defeat it. M. had left him in charge. He had the girl and the machine under his hand. Why panic? What was there to panic about? It would be mad to run away and perhaps only escape one trap in order to fall into another one.

The train gave a long whistle and began to slacken speed.

Now for the first round. If Kerim failed. If the three men stayed on the train . . .

Some goods trucks, led by a straining engine, filed by. The silhouette of sheds showed briefly. With a jolt and a screech of couplings, the Orient Express took the points and swerved away from the through line. Four sets of rails with grass growing between them showed outside the window, and the empty length of the down platform. A cock crowed. The express slowed to walking speed and finally, with a sigh of vacuum brakes and a noisy whoosh of let-off steam, ground to a stop. The girl stirred in her sleep. Bond softly shifted her head on to the pillow and got up and slipped out of the door.

It was a typical Balkan wayside station — a façade of dour buildings in over-pointed stone, a dusty expanse of platform, not raised, but level with the ground so that there was a long step down from the train, some chickens pecking about and a few drab officials standing idly, unshaven, not even trying to look important. Up towards the cheap half of the train, a chattering horde of peasants with bundles and wicker baskets waited for the customs and passport control so that they could clamber aboard and join the swarm inside.

Across the platform from Bond was a closed door with a sign over it which said POLIS. Through the dirty window beside the door Bond thought he caught a glimpse of the head and shoulders of Kerim.

'*Passeports. Douanes!*'

A plain-clothes man and two policemen in dark green uniforms with pistol holsters at their black belts entered the corridor. The wagon-lit conductor preceded them, knocking on the doors.

At the door of No. 12 the conductor made an indignant speech in Turkish, holding out the stack of tickets and passports and fanning through them as if they were a pack of cards. When he had finished, the plain-clothes man, beckoning forward the two policemen, knocked smartly on the door and, when it was opened, stepped inside. The two policemen stood guard behind him.

Bond edged down the corridor. He could hear a jumble of bad German. One voice was cold, the other was frightened and hot. The passport and ticket of Herr Kurt Goldfarb were missing. Had Herr Goldfarb removed them from the conductor's cabin? Certainly not. Had Herr Goldfarb in truth ever surrendered his papers to the conductor? Naturally. Then the matter was unfortunate. An inquiry would have to be held. No doubt the German Legation in Istanbul would put the matter right (Bond smiled at this suggestion). Meanwhile, it was regretted that Herr Goldfarb could not continue his journey. No doubt he would be able to proceed tomorrow. Herr Goldfarb would get dressed. His luggage would be transported to the waiting-room.

The M.G.B. man who erupted into the corridor was the dark Caucasian-type man, the junior of the 'visitors'. His sallow face was grey with fear. His hair was awry and he was dressed only in the bottom half of his pyjamas. But there was nothing comical about his desperate flurry down the corridor. He brushed past Bond. At the door of No. 6 he paused and pulled himself together. He knocked with tense control. The door opened on the chain and Bond glimpsed a thick nose and part of a moustache. The chain was slipped and Goldfarb went in. There was silence, during which the plain-clothes man dealt with the papers of two elderly French women in 9 and 10, and then with Bond's.

The officer barely glanced at Bond's passport. He snapped it shut and handed it to the conductor. 'You are travelling with Kerim Bey?' he asked in French. His eyes were remote.

'Yes.'

'*Merci, Monsieur. Bon voyage.*' The man saluted. He turned and rapped sharply on the door of No. 6. The door opened and he went in.

Five minutes later the door was flung back. The plain-clothes man, now erect with authority, beckoned forward the policemen. He spoke to them harshly in Turkish. He turned back to the coupé. 'Consider yourself under arrest, *mein Herr*. Attempted bribery of officials is a grave crime in Turkey.' There was an angry clamour in Goldfarb's bad German. It was cut short by one hard sentence in Russian. A different Goldfarb, a Goldfarb with madman's eyes, emerged and walked blindly down the corridor and went into No. 12. A policeman stood outside the door and waited.

'And *your* papers, *mein Herr*. Please step forward. I must verify this photograph.' The plain-clothes man held the green-backed German passport up to the light. 'Forward please.'

Reluctantly, his heavy face pale with anger, the M.G.B. man who called himself Benz stepped out into the corridor in a brilliant blue silk dressing-gown. The hard brown eyes looked straight into Bond's, ignoring him.

The plain-clothes man slapped the passport shut and handed it to the conductor. 'Your papers are in order, *mein Herr*. And now, if you please, the baggage.' He went in, followed by the second policeman. The M.G.B. man turned his blue back on Bond and watched the search.

Bond noticed the bulge under the left arm of the dressing-gown, and the ridge of a belt round the waist. He wondered if he should tip off the plain-clothes man. He decided it would be better to keep quiet. He might be hauled in as a witness.

The search was over. The plain-clothes man saluted coldly and moved on down the corridor. The M.G.B. man went back into No. 6 and slammed the door behind him.

Pity, thought Bond. One had got away.

Bond turned back to the window. A bulky man, wearing a grey homburg, and with an angry boil on the back of his neck, was being escorted through the door marked POLIS. Down the corridor a door slammed. Goldfarb, escorted by the policeman, stepped down off the train. With bent head, he walked across the dusty platform and disappeared through the same door.

The engine whistled, a new kind of whistle, the brave shrill blast of a Greek engine-driver. The door of the wagon-lit carriage clanged shut. The plain-clothes man and the second policeman appeared walking over to the station. The guard at the back of the train looked at his watch and held out his flag. There was a jerk and a diminishing crescendo of explosive puffs from the engine and the front section of the Orient Express began to move. The section that would be taking the northern route through the Iron Curtain — through Svilengrad on the Bulgarian frontier, only fifty miles away — was left beside the dusty platform, waiting.

Bond pulled down the window and took a last look back at the Turkish frontier, where two men would be sitting in a bare room under what amounted to sentence of death. Two birds down, he thought. Two out of three. The odds looked more respectable.

He watched the dead, dusty platform, with its chickens and the small black figure of the guard, until the long train took the points and jerked harshly on to the single main line. He looked away across the ugly, parched countryside towards the golden guinea sun climbing out of the Turkish plain. It was going to be a beautiful day.

Bond drew his head in out of the cool, sweet morning air. He pulled up the window with a bang.

He had made up his mind. He would stay on the train and see the thing through.

23

OUT OF GREECE

HOT COFFEE FROM the meagre little buffet at Pithion (there would be no restaurant car until midday), a painless visit from the Greek customs and passport control, and then the berths were folded away as the train hurried south towards the Gulf of Enez at the head of the Aegean. Outside, there was extra light and colour. The air was drier. The men at the little stations and in the fields were handsome. Sunflowers, maize, vines and racks of tobacco were ripening in the sun. It was, as Darko had said, another day.

Bond washed and shaved under the amused eyes of Tatiana. She approved of the fact that he put no oil on his hair. 'It is a dirty habit,' she said. 'I was told that many Europeans have it. We would not think of doing it in Russia. It dirties the pillows. But it is odd that you in the West do not use perfume. All our men do.'

'We wash,' said Bond drily.

In the heat of her protests, there came a knock on the door. It was Kerim. Bond let him in. Kerim bowed towards the girl. 'What a charming domestic scene,' he commented cheerfully, lowering his bulk into the corner near the door. 'I have rarely seen a handsomer pair of spies.'

Tatiana glowered at him. 'I am not accustomed to Western jokes,' she said coldly.

Kerim's laugh was disarming. 'You'll learn, my dear. In England, they are great people for jokes. There it is considered proper to make a joke of everything. I also have learned to make jokes. They grease the wheels. I have been laughing a lot this morning. Those poor fellows at Uzunkopru. I wish I could be there when the police telephone the German Consulate in Istanbul. That is the worst of forged passports. They are not difficult to make, but it is almost impossible to forge also their birth certificate — the files of the country which is supposed to have issued them. I fear the careers of your two comrades have come to a sad end, Mrs. Somerset.'

'How did you do it?' Bond knotted his tie.

'Money and influence. Five hundred dollars to the conductor. Some big talk to the police. It was lucky our friend tried a bribe. A pity that crafty Benz next door,' he gestured at the wall, 'didn't get involved. I couldn't do the passport trick twice. We will have to get him some other way. The man with the boils was easy. He knew no German and travelling without a ticket is a serious matter. Ah well, the day has started favourably. We have won the first round, but our friend next door will now be very careful. He knows what he has to reckon with. Perhaps that is for the best. It would have been a nuisance having to keep you both under cover all day. Now we can move about — even have lunch together, as long as you bring the family jewels with you. We must watch to see if he makes a telephone call at one of the stations. But I doubt if he could tackle the Greek telephone exchange. He will probably wait until we are in Yugoslavia. But there I have my machine. We can get reinforcements if we need them. It should be a most interesting journey. There is always excitement on the Orient Express,' Kerim got to his feet. He opened the door, 'and romance.' He smiled across the compartment. 'I will call for you at lunchtime! Greek food is worse than Turkish, but even my stomach is in the service of the Queen.'

Bond got up and locked the door. Tatiana snapped, 'Your friend is not *kulturny*! It is disloyal to refer to your Queen in that manner.'

Bond sat down beside her. 'Tania,' he said patiently, 'that is a wonderful man. He is also a good friend. As far as I am concerned he can say anything he likes. He is jealous of me. He would like to have a girl like you. So he teases you. It is a form of flirting. You should take it as a compliment.'

'You think so?' She turned her large blue eyes on his. 'But what he said about his stomach and the head of your State. That was being rude to your Queen. It would be considered very bad manners to say such a thing in Russia.'

They were still arguing when the train ground to a halt in the sunbaked, fly-swarming station of Alexandropolis. Bond opened the door into the corridor and the sun poured in across a pale mirrored sea that married, almost without horizon, into a sky the colour of the Greek flag.

They had lunch, with the heavy bag under the table between Bond's feet. Kerim quickly made friends with the girl. The M.G.B. man called Benz avoided the restaurant car. They saw him on the platform buying sandwiches and beer from a buffet on wheels. Kerim suggested they ask him to make a four at bridge. Bond suddenly felt very tired and his tiredness made him feel that they were turning this dangerous journey into a picnic. Tatiana noticed his silence. She got up and said that she must rest. As they went out of the wagon-restaurant they heard Kerim calling gaily for brandy and cigars.

Back in the compartment, Tatiana said firmly, 'Now it is you who will sleep.' She drew down the blind and shut out the hard afternoon light and the endless baked fields of maize and tobacco and wilting sunflowers. The compartment became a dark green underground cavern. Bond wedged the doors and gave her his gun and stretched out with his head in her lap and was immediately asleep.

The long train snaked along the north of Greece below the foothills of the Rhodope Mountains. Xanthi came, and Drama, and Serrai, and then they were in the Macedonian highlands and the line swerved due south towards Salonica.

It was dusk when Bond awoke in the soft cradle of her lap. At once, as if she had been waiting for the moment, Tatiana took his face between her hands and looked down into his eyes and said urgently, '*Dushka*, how long shall we have this for?'

'For long.' Bond's thoughts were still luxurious with sleep.

'But for how long?'

Bond gazed up into the beautiful, worried eyes. He cleared the sleep out of his mind. It was impossible to see beyond the next three days on the train, beyond their arrival in London. One had to face the fact that this girl was an enemy agent. His feelings would be of no interest to the interrogators from his Service and from the Ministries. Other intelligence services would also want to know what this girl had to tell them about the machine she had worked for. Probably at Dover she would be taken away to 'The Cage', that well-sentried private house near Guildford, where she would be put in a comfortable, but oh so well-wired room. And the efficient men in plain clothes would come one by one and sit and talk with her, and the recorder would spin in the room below and the records would be transcribed and sifted for their grains of new fact — and, of course, for the contradictions they would trap her into. Perhaps they would introduce a stool-pigeon — a nice Russian girl who would commiserate with Tatiana over her treatment and suggest ways of escape, of turning double, of getting 'harmless' information back to her parents. This might go on for weeks or months. Meanwhile Bond would be tactfully kept away from her, unless the interrogators thought he could extract further secrets by using their feelings for each other. Then what? The changed name, the offer of a new life in Canada, the thousand pounds a year she would be given from the secret funds? And where would he be when she came out of it all? Perhaps the other side of the world. Or, if he was still in London, how much of her feeling for him would have survived the grinding of the interrogation machine? How much would she hate or despise the English after going through all this? And, for the matter of that, how much would have survived of his own hot flame?

'*Dushka*,' repeated Tatiana impatiently. 'How long?'

'As long as possible. It will depend on us. Many people will interfere. We shall be separated. It will not always be like this in a little room. In a few days we shall have to step out into the world. It will not be easy. It would be foolish to tell you anything else.'

Tatiana's face cleared. She smiled down at him. 'You are right. I will not ask any more foolish questions. But we must waste no more of these days.' She shifted his head and got up and lay down beside him.

An hour later, when Bond was standing in the corridor, Darko Kerim was suddenly beside him. He examined Bond's face. He said slyly, 'You should not sleep so long. You have been missing the historic landscape of northern Greece. And it is time for the *premier service*.'

'All you think about is food,' said Bond. He gestured back with his head. 'What about our friend?'

'He has not stirred. The conductor has been watching for me. That man will end up the richest conductor in the wagon-lit company. Five hundred dollars for Goldfarb's papers, and now a hundred dollars a day retainer until the end of the journey.'

Kerim chuckled. 'I have told him he may even get a medal for his services to Turkey. He believes we are after a smuggling gang. They're always using this train for running Turkish opium to Paris. He is not surprised, only pleased that he is being paid so well. And now, have you found out anything more from this Russian princess you have in there? I still feel disquiet. Everything is too peaceful. Those two men we left behind may have been quite innocently bound for Berlin as the girl says. This Benz may be keeping to his room because he is frightened of us. All is going well with our journey. And yet, and yet . . . ' Kerim shook his head. 'These Russians are great chess players. When they wish to execute a plot, they execute it brilliantly. The game is planned minutely, the gambits of the enemy are provided for. They are foreseen and countered. At the back of my mind,' Kerim's face in the window was gloomy, 'I have a feeling that you and I and this girl are pawns on a very big board — that we are being allowed our moves because they do not interfere with the Russian game.'

'But what is the object of the plot?' Bond looked out into the darkness. He spoke to his reflection in the window. 'What can they want to achieve? We always get back to that. Of course we have all smelt a conspiracy of some sort. And the girl may not even know that she's involved in it. I know she's hiding something, but I think it's only some small secret she thinks is unimportant. She says she'll tell me everything when we get to London. Everything? What does she mean? She only says that I must have faith — that there is no danger. You must admit, Darko,' Bond looked up for confirmation into the slow crafty eyes, 'that she's lived up to her story.'

There was no enthusiasm in Kerim's eyes. He said nothing.

Bond shrugged. 'I admit I've fallen for her. But I'm not a fool, Darko. I've been watching for any clue, anything that would help. You know one can tell a lot when certain barriers are down. Well they are down, and I know she's telling the truth. At any rate ninety per cent of it. And I know she thinks the rest doesn't matter. If she's cheating, she's also being cheated herself. On your chess analogy, that is possible. But you still get back to the question of what it's all in aid of.' Bond's voice hardened. 'And, if you want to know, all I ask is to go on with the game until we find out.'

Kerim smiled at the obstinate look on Bond's face. He laughed abruptly. 'If it was me, my friend, I would slip off the train at Salonica — with the machine, and, if you like, with the girl also, though that is not so important. I would take a hired car to Athens and get on the next plane for London. But I was not brought up "to be a sport".' Kerim put irony into the words. 'This is not a game to me. It is a business. For you it is different. You are a gambler. M. also is a gambler. He obviously is, or he would not have given you a free hand. He also wants to know the answer to this riddle. So be it. But I like to play safe, to make certain, to leave as little as possible to chance. You think the odds look right, that they are in your favour?' Darko Kerim turned and faced Bond. His voice became insistent. 'Listen, my friend,' he put a huge hand on Bond's shoulder, 'this is a billiard table. An easy, flat, green billiard table. And you have hit your white ball and it is travelling easily and quietly towards the red. The pocket is alongside. Fatally, inevitably, you are going to hit the red and the red is going into that pocket. It is the law of the billiard table, the law of the billard room. But, outside the orbit of these things, a jet pilot has fainted and his plane is diving straight at that billiard room, or a gas main is about to explode, or lightning is about to strike. And the building collapses on top of you and on top of the billiard table. Then what has happened to that white ball that could not miss the red ball, and to the red ball that could not miss the pocket? The white ball could not miss according to the laws of the billiard table. But the laws of the billiard table are not the only laws, and the laws governing the progress of this train, and of you to your destination, are also not the only laws in this particular game.'

Kerim paused. He dismissed his harangue with a shrug of the shoulders. 'You already know these things, my friend,' he said apologetically. 'And I have made myself thirsty talking platitudes. Hurry the girl up and we will go and eat. But watch for surprises, I beg of you.' He made a cross with his finger over the centre of his coat. 'I do not cross my heart. That is being too serious. But I cross my stomach, which is an important oath for me. There are surprises on the way for both of us. The gipsy said to watch out. Now I say the same. We can play the game on the billiard table, but we must both be on guard against the world outside the billiard room. My nose,' he tapped it, 'tells me so.'

Kerim's stomach made an indignant noise like a forgotten telephone receiver with an angry caller on the other end. 'There,' he said solicitously. 'What did I say? We must go and eat.'

They finished their dinner as the train pulled into the hideous modern junction of Thessaloniki. With Bond carrying the heavy little bag, they went back down the train and parted for the night. 'We shall soon be disturbed again,' warned Kerim. 'There is the frontier at one o'clock. The Greeks will be no trouble, but those Yugoslavs like waking up anyone who is travelling soft. If they annoy you, send for me. Even in their country there are some names I can mention. I am in the second compartment in the next carriage. I have it to myself. Tomorrow I will move into our friend Goldfarb's bed in No. 12. For the time being, the first-class is an adequate stable.'

Bond dozed wakefully as the train laboured up the moonlit valley of the Vardar towards the instep of Yugoslavia. Tatiana again slept with her head in his lap. He thought of what Darko had said. He wondered if he should not send the big man back to Istanbul when they had got safely through Belgrade. It was not fair to drag him across Europe on an adventure that was outside his territory and with which he had little sympathy. Darko obviously suspected that Bond had become infatuated with the girl and wasn't seeing the operation straight any more. Well, there was a grain of truth in that. It would certainly be safer to get off the train and take another route home. But, Bond admitted to himself, he couldn't bear the idea of running away from this plot, if it was a plot. If it wasn't, he equally couldn't bear the idea of sacrificing the three more days with Tatiana. And M. had left the decision to him. As Darko had said, M. also was curious to see the game through. Perversely, M. too wanted to see what this whole rigmarole was about. Bond dismissed the problem. The journey was going well. Once again, why panic?

Ten minutes after they had arrived at the Greek frontier station of Idomeni there was a hasty knocking on the door. It woke the girl. Bond slipped from under her head. He put his ear to the door. 'Yes?'

'*Le conducteur, Monsieur*. There has been an accident. Your friend Kerim Bey.'

'Wait,' said Bond fiercely. He fitted the Beretta into its holster and put on his coat. He tore open the door.

'What is it?'

The conductor's face was yellow under the corridor light. 'Come.' He ran down the corridor towards the first-class.

Officials were clustered round the open door of the second compartment. They were standing, staring.

The conductor made a path for Bond. Bond reached the door and looked in.

The hair stirred softly on his head. Along the right-hand seat were two bodies. They were frozen in a ghastly death-struggle that might have been posed for a film.

Underneath was Kerim, his knees up in a last effort to rise. The taped hilt of a dagger protruded from his neck near the jugular vein. His head was thrust back and the empty bloodshot eyes stared up at the light. The mouth was contorted into a snarl. A thin trickle of blood ran down the chin.

Half on top of him sprawled the heavy body of the M.G.B. man called Benz, locked there by Kerim's left arm round his neck. Bond could see a corner of the Stalin moustache and the side of a blackened face. Kerim's right arm lay across the man's back, almost casually. The hand ended in a closed fist and the knob of a knife-hilt, and there was a wide stain on the coat under the hand.

Bond listened to his imagination. It was like watching a film. The sleeping Darko, the man slipping quietly through the door, the two steps forward and the swift stroke at the jugular. Then the last violent spasm of the dying man as he flung up an arm and clutched his murderer to him and plunged the knife down towards the fifth rib.

This wonderful man who had carried the sun with him. Now he was extinguished, totally dead.

Bond turned brusquely and walked out of sight of the man who had died for him.

He began, carefully, non-committally, to answer questions.

24

OUT OF DANGER?

THE ORIENT EXPRESS steamed slowly into Belgrade at three o'clock in the afternoon, half an hour late. There would be an eight hours' delay while the other section of the train came in through the Iron Curtain from Bulgaria.

Bond looked out at the crowds and waited for the knock on the door that would be Kerim's man. Tatiana sat huddled in her sable coat beside the door, watching Bond, wondering if he would come back to her.

She had seen it all from the window — the long wicker baskets being brought out to the train, the flash of the police photographer's bulbs, the gesticulating *chef de train* trying to hurry up the formalities, and the tall figure of James Bond, straight and hard and cold as a butcher's knife, coming and going.

Bond had come back and had sat looking at her. He had asked sharp, brutal questions. She had fought desperately back, sticking coldly to her story, knowing that now, if she told him everything, told him for instance that SMERSH was involved, she would certainly lose him for ever.

Now she sat and was afraid, afraid of the web in which she was caught, afraid of what might have been behind the lies she had been told in Moscow — above all afraid that she might lose this man who had suddenly become the light in her life.

There was a knock on the door. Bond got up and opened it. A tough cheerful india-rubbery man, with Kerim's blue eyes and a mop of tangled fair hair above a brown face, exploded into the compartment.

'Stefan Trempo at your service.' The big smile embraced them both. 'They call me "Tempo". Where is the Chef?'

'Sit down,' said Bond. He thought to himself, I know it. This is another of Darko's sons.

The man looked sharply at them both. He sat down carefully between them. His face was extinguished. Now the bright eyes stared at Bond with a terrible intensity in which there was fear and suspicion. His right hand slipped casually into the pocket of his coat.

When Bond had finished, the man stood up. He didn't ask any questions. He said, 'Thank you, sir. Will you come, please. We will go to my apartment. There is much to be done.' He walked into the corridor and stood with his back to them, looking out across the rails. When the girl came out he walked down the corridor without looking back. Bond followed the girl, carrying the heavy bag and his little attaché case.

They walked down the platform and into the station square. It had started to drizzle. The scene, with its sprinkling of battered taxis and vista of dull modern buildings, was depressing. The man opened the rear door of a shabby Morris Oxford saloon. He got in front and took the wheel. They bumped their way over the cobbles and on to a slippery tarmac boulevard and drove for a quarter of an hour through wide, empty streets. They saw few pedestrians and not more than a handful of other cars.

They stopped half way down a cobbled side-street. Tempo led them through a wide apartment-house door and up two flights of stairs that had the smell of the Balkans — the smell of very old sweat and cigarette smoke and cabbage. He unlocked a door and showed them into a two-roomed flat with nondescript furniture and heavy red plush curtains drawn back to show the blank windows on the other side of the street. On a sideboard stood a tray with several unopened bottles, glasses and plates of fruit and biscuits — the welcome to Darko and to Darko's friends.

Tempo waved vaguely towards the drinks. 'Please, sir, make yourself and Madam at home. There is a bathroom. No doubt you would both like to have a bath. If you will excuse me, I must telephone!' The hard façade of the face was about to crumble. The man went quickly into the bedroom and shut the door behind him.

There followed two empty hours during which Bond sat and looked out of the window at the wall opposite. From time to time he got up and paced to and fro and then sat down again. For the first hour, Tatiana sat and pretended to look through a pile of magazines. Then she abruptly went into the bathroom and Bond vaguely heard water gushing into the bath.

At about 6 o'clock, Tempo came out of the bedroom. He told Bond that he was going out. 'There is food in the kitchen. I will return at nine and take you to the train. Please treat my flat as your own.' Without waiting for Bond's reply, he walked out and softly shut the door. Bond heard his foot on the stairs and the click of the front door and the self-starter of the Morris.

Bond went into the bedroom and sat on the bed and picked up the telephone and talked in German to the long-distance exchange.

Half an hour later there was the quiet voice of M.

Bond spoke as a travelling salesman would speak to the managing director of Universal Export. He said that his partner had gone very sick. Were there any fresh instructions?

'Very sick?'

'Yes, sir, very.'

'How about the other firm?'

'There were three with us, sir. One of them caught the same thing. The other two didn't feel well on the way out of Turkey. They left us at Uzunkopru — that's the frontier.'

'So the other firm's packed up?'

Bond could see M.'s face as he sifted the information. He wondered if the fan was slowly revolving in the ceiling, if M. had a pipe in his hand, if the Chief of Staff was listening on the other wire.

'What are your ideas? Would you and your wife like to take another way home?'

'I'd rather you decided, sir. My wife's all right. The sample's in good condition. I don't see why it should deteriorate. I'm still keen to finish the trip. Otherwise it'll remain virgin territory. We shan't know what the possibilities are.'

'Would you like one of our other salesmen to give you a hand?'

'It shouldn't be necessary, sir. Just as you feel.'

'I'll think about it. So you really want to see this sales campaign through?'

Bond could see M.'s eyes glittering with the same perverse curiosity, the same rage to know, as he himself felt. 'Yes, sir. Now that I'm half way, it seems a pity not to cover the whole route.'

'All right then. I'll think about giving you another salesman to lend a hand.' There was a pause on the end of the line. 'Nothing else on your mind?'

'No, sir.'

'Goodbye, then.'

'Goodbye, sir.'

Bond put down the receiver. He sat and looked at it. He suddenly wished he had agreed with M.'s suggestion to give him reinforcements, just in case. He got up from the bed. At least they would soon be out of these damn Balkans and down into Italy. Then Switzerland, France — among friendly people, away from the furtive lands.

And the girl, what about her? Could he blame her for the death of Kerim? Bond went into the next room and stood again by the window, looking out, wondering, going back over everything, every expression and every gesture she had made since he had first heard her voice on that night in the Kristal Palas. No, he knew he couldn't put the blame on her. If she was an agent, she was an unconscious agent. There wasn't a girl of her age in the world who could have played this role, if it was a role she was playing, without betraying herself. And he liked her. And he had faith in his instincts. Besides, with the death of Kerim, had not the plot, whatever it was, played itself out? One day he would find out what the plot had been. For the moment he was certain. Tatiana was not a conscious part of it.

His mind made up, Bond walked over to the bathroom door and knocked.

She came out and he took her in his arms and held her to him and kissed her. She clung to him. They stood and felt the animal warmth come back between them, feeling it push back the cold memory of Kerim's death.

Tatiana broke away. She looked up at Bond's face. She reached up and brushed the black comma of hair away from his forehead.

Her face was alive. 'I am glad you have come back, James,' she said. And then, matter-of-factly, 'And now we must eat and drink and start our lives again.'

Later, after Slivovic and smoked ham and peaches, Tempo came and took them to the station and to the waiting express under the hard lights of the arcs. He said goodbye, quickly and coldly, and vanished down the platform and back into his dark existence.

Punctually at nine the new engine gave its new kind of noise and took the long train out on its all-night run down the valley of the Sava. Bond went along to the conductor's cabin to give him money and look through the passports of the new passengers.

Bond knew most of the signs to look for in forged passports, the blurred writing, the too exact imprints of the rubber stamps, the trace of old gum round the edges of the photograph, the slight transparencies on the pages where the fibres of the paper had been tampered with to alter a letter or a number, but the five new passports — three American and two Swiss — seemed innocent. The Swiss papers, favourites with the Russian forgers, belonged to a husband and wife, both over seventy, and Bond finally passed them and went back to the compartment and prepared for another night with Tatiana's head on his lap.

Vincovci came and Brod and then, against a flaming dawn, the ugly sprawl of Zagreb. The train came to a stop between lines of rusting locomotives captured from the Germans and still standing forlornly amongst the grass and weeds on the sidings. Bond read the plate on one of them — BERLINER MASCHINENBAU GMBH — as they slid out through the iron cemetery. Its long black barrel had been raked with machine-gun bullets. Bond heard the scream of the dive-bomber and saw the upflung arms of the driver. For a moment he thought nostalgically and unreasonably of the excitement and turmoil of the hot war, compared with his own underground skirmishings since the war had turned cold.

They hammered into the mountains of Slovenia where the apple trees and the chalets were almost Austrian. The train laboured its way through Ljubliana. The girl awoke. They had breakfast of fried eggs and hard brown bread and coffee that was mostly chicory. The restaurant car was full of cheerful English and American tourists from the Adriatic coast, and Bond thought with a lift of the heart that by the afternoon they would be over the frontier into western Europe and that a third dangerous night was gone.

He slept until Sezana. The hard-faced Yugoslav plain-clothes men came on board. Then Yugoslavia was gone and Poggioreale came and the first smell of the soft life with the happy jabbering of Italian officials and the carefree upturned faces of the station crowd. The new diesel-electric engine gave a slap-happy whistle, the meadow of brown hands fluttered, and they were loping easily down into Venezia, towards the distant sparkle of Trieste and the gay blue of the Adriatic.

We've made it, thought Bond. I really think we've made it. He thrust the memory of the last three days away from him. Tatiana saw the tense lines in his face relax. She reached over and took his hand. He moved and sat close beside her. They looked out at the gay villas on the Corniche and at the sailing-boats and the people water-skiing.

The train clanged across some points and slid quietly into the gleaming station of Trieste. Bond got up and pulled down the window and they stood side by side, looking out. Suddenly Bond felt happy. He put an arm around the girl's waist and held her hard against him.

They gazed down at the holiday crowd. The sun shone through the tall clean windows of the station in golden shafts. The sparkling scene emphasized the dark and dirt of the countries the train had come from, and Bond watched with an almost sensuous pleasure the gaily dressed people pass through the patches of sunshine towards the entrance, and the sunburned people, the ones who had had their holidays, hasten up the platform to get their seats on the train.

A shaft of sun lit up the head of one man who seemed typical of this happy, playtime world. The light flashed briefly on golden hair under a cap, and on a young golden moustache. There was plenty of time to catch the train. The man walked unhurriedly. It crossed Bond's mind that he was an Englishman. Perhaps it was the familiar shape of the dark green Kangol cap, or the beige, rather well-used macintosh, that badge of the English tourist, or it may have been the grey-flannelled legs, or the scuffed brown shoes. But Bond's eyes were drawn to him, as if it was someone he knew, as the man approached up the platform.

The man was carrying a battered Revelation suitcase and, under the other arm, a thick book and some newspapers. He looks like an athlete, thought Bond. He has the wide shoulders and the healthy, good-looking bronzed face of a professional tennis player going home after a round of foreign tournaments.

The man came nearer. Now he was looking straight at Bond. With recognition? Bond searched his mind. Did he know this man? No. He would have remembered those eyes that stared out so coldly under the pale lashes. They were opaque, almost dead. The eyes of a drowned man. But they had some message for him. What was it? Recognition? Warning? Or just the defensive reaction to Bond's own stare?

The man came up with the wagon-lit. His eyes were now gazing levelly up the train. He walked past, the crêpe-soled shoes making no sound. Bond watched him reach for the rail and swing himself easily up the steps into the first-class carriage.

Suddenly Bond knew what the glance had meant, who the man was. Of course! This man was from the Service. After all M. had decided to send along an extra hand. That was the message of those queer eyes. Bond would bet anything that the man would soon be along to make contact.

How like M. to make absolutely sure!

25

A TIE WITH A WINDSOR KNOT

TO MAKE THE contact easy, Bond went out and stood in the corridor. He ran over the details of the code of the day, the few harmless phrases, changed on the first of each month, that served as a simple recognition signal between English agents.

The train gave a jerk and moved slowly out into the sunshine. At the end of the corridor the communicating door slammed. There was no sound of steps, but suddenly the red and gold face was mirrored in the window.

'Excuse me. Could I borrow a match?'

'I use a lighter.' Bond produced his battered Ronson and handed it over.

'Better still.'

'Until they go wrong.'

Bond looked up into the man's face, expecting a smile at the completion of the childish 'Who goes there? Pass, Friend' ritual.

The thick lips writhed briefly. There was no light in the very pale blue eyes.

The man had taken off his macintosh. He was wearing an old reddish-brown tweed coat with his flannel trousers, a pale yellow Viyella summer shirt, and the dark blue and maroon zigzagged tie of the Royal Artillery. It was tied with a Windsor knot. Bond mistrusted anyone who tied his tie with a Windsor knot. It showed too much vanity. It was often the mark of a cad. Bond decided to forget his prejudice. A gold signet ring, with an indecipherable crest, glinted on the little finger of the right hand that gripped the guard rail. The corner of a red bandana handkerchief flopped out of the breast pocket of the man's coat. On his left wrist there was a battered silver wrist watch with an old leather strap.

Bond knew the type — a minor public school and then caught up by the war. Field Security perhaps. No idea what to do afterwards so he stayed with the occupation troops. At first he would have been with the military police, then, as the senior men drifted home, there came promotion into one of the security services. Moved to Trieste where he did well enough. Wanted to stay on and avoid the rigours of England. Probably had a girl friend, or had married an Italian. The Secret Service had needed a man for the small post that Trieste had become after the withdrawal. This man was available. They took him on. He would be doing routine jobs — have some low-grade sources in the Italian and Yugoslav police, and in their intelligence networks. A thousand a year. A good life, without much being expected from him. Then, out of the blue, this had come along. Must have been a shock getting one of those Most Immediate signals. He'd probably be a bit shy of Bond. Odd face. The eyes looked rather mad. But so they did in most of these men doing secret work abroad. One had to be a bit mad to take it on. Powerful chap, probably on the stupid side, but useful for this kind of guard work. M. had just taken the nearest man and told him to join the train.

All this went through Bond's mind as he photographed an impression of the man's clothes and general appearance. Now he said, 'Glad to see you. How did it happen?'

'Got a signal. Late last night. Personal from M. Shook me I can tell you, old man.'

Curious accent. What was it? A hint of brogue — cheap brogue. And something else Bond couldn't define. Probably came from living too long abroad and talking foreign languages all the time. And that dreadful 'old man' at the end. Shyness.

'Must have,' said Bond sympathetically. 'What did it say?'

'Just told me to get on the Orient this morning and contact a man and a girl in the through carriage. More or less described what you look like. Then I was to stick by you and see you both through to Gay Paree. That's all, old man.'

Was there defensiveness in the voice? Bond glanced sideways. The pale eyes swivelled to meet his. There was a quick red glare in them. It was as if the safety door of a furnace had swung open. The blaze died. The door to the inside of the man was banged shut. Now the eyes were opaque again — the eyes of an introvert, of a man who rarely looks out into the world but is for ever surveying the scene inside him.

There's madness there all right, thought Bond, startled by the sight of it. Shell-shock perhaps, or schizophrenia. Poor chap, with that magnificent body. One day he would certainly crack. The madness would take control. Bond had better have a word with Personnel. Check up on his medical. By the way, what was his name?

'Well I'm very glad to have you along. Probably not much for you to do. We started off with three Redland men on our tail. They've been got rid of, but there may be others on the train. Or some more may get on. And I've got to get this girl to London without trouble. If you'd just hang about. Tonight we'd better stay together and share watches. It's the last night and I don't want to take any chances. By the way, my name's James Bond. Travelling as David Somerset. And that's Caroline Somerset in there.'

The man fished in his inside pocket and produced a battered notecase which seemed to contain plenty of money. He extracted a visiting card and handed it to Bond. It said 'Captain Norman Nash', and, in the left-hand bottom corner, 'Royal Automobile Club'.

As Bond put the card in his pocket he slipped his finger across it. It was engraved. 'Thanks,' he said. 'Well, Nash, come and meet Mrs. Somerset. No reason why we shouldn't travel more or less together.' He smiled encouragingly.

Again the red glare quickly extinguished. The lips writhed under the young golden moustache. 'Delighted, old man.'

Bond turned to the door and knocked softly and spoke his name.

The door opened. Bond beckoned Nash in and shut the door behind him.

The girl looked surprised.

'This is Captain Nash, Norman Nash. He's been told to keep an eye on us.'

'How do you do.' The hand came out hesitantly. The man touched it briefly. His stare was fixed. He said nothing. The girl gave an embarrassed little laugh. 'Won't you sit down?'

'Er, thank you.' Nash sat stiffly on the edge of the banquette. He seemed to remember something, something one did when one had nothing to say. He groped in the side pocket of his coat and produced a packet of Players. 'Will you have a, er, cigarette?' He prised open the top with a fairly clean thumbnail, stripped down the silver paper and pushed out the cigarettes. The girl took one. Nash's other hand flashed forward a lighter with the obsequious speed of a motor salesman.

Nash looked up. Bond was standing leaning against the door and wondering how to help this clumsy, embarrassed man. Nash held out the cigarettes and the lighter as if he was offering glass beads to a native chief. 'What about you, old man?'

'Thanks,' said Bond. He hated Virginia tobacco, but he was prepared to do anything to help put the man at ease. He took a cigarette and lit it. They certainly had to make do with some queer fish in the Service nowadays. How the devil did this man manage to get along in the semi-diplomatic society he would have to frequent in Trieste?

Bond said lamely. 'You look very fit, Nash. Tennis?'

'Swimming.'

'Been long in Trieste?'

There came the brief red glare. 'About three years.'

'Interesting work?'

'Sometimes. You know how it is, old man.'

Bond wondered how he could stop Nash calling him 'old man'. He couldn't think of a way. Silence fell.

Nash obviously felt it was his turn again. He fished in his pocket and produced a newspaper cutting. It was the front page of the *Corriere della Sera*. He handed it to Bond. 'Seen this, old man?' The eyes blazed and died.

It was the front page lead. The thick black lettering on the cheap newsprint was still wet. The headlines said:

TERRIBILE ESPLOSIONE IN ISTANBUL
UFFICIO SOVIETICO DISTRUTTO
TUTTI I PRESENTI UCCISI

Bond couldn't understand the rest. He folded the cutting and handed it back. How much did this man know? Better treat him as a strong-arm man and nothing else. 'Bad show,' he said. 'Gas main I suppose.' Bond saw again the obscene belly of the bomb hanging down from the roof of the alcove in the tunnel, the wires that started off down the damp wall on their way back to the plunger in the drawer of Kerim's desk. Who had pressed the plunger yesterday afternoon when Tempo had got through? The 'Head Clerk'? Or had they drawn lots and then stood round and watched as the hand went down and the deep roar had gone up in the Street of Books on the hill above. They would all have been there, in the cool room. With eyes that glittered with hate. The tears would be reserved for the night. Revenge would have come first. And the rats? How many thousand had been blasted down the tunnel? What time would it have been? About four o'clock. Had the daily meeting been on? Three dead in the room. How many more in the rest of the building? Friends of Tatiana, perhaps. He would have to keep the story from her. Had Darko been watching? From a window in Valhalla? Bond could hear the great laugh of triumph echoing round its walls. At any rate Kerim had taken plenty with him.

Nash was looking at him. 'Yes, I daresay it was a gas main,' he said without interest.

A handbell tinkled down the corridor, coming nearer. '*Deuxième Service. Deuxième Service. Prenez vos places, s'il vous plaît.*'

Bond looked across at Tatiana. Her face was pale. In her eyes there was an appeal to be saved from any more of this clumsy, non-*kulturny* man. Bond said, 'What about lunch?' She got up at once. 'What about you, Nash?'

Captain Nash was already on his feet. 'Had it, thanks old man. And I'd like to have a look up and down the train. Is the conductor — you know . . . ?' He made a gesture of fingering money.

'Oh yes, he'll co-operate all right,' said Bond. He reached up and pulled down the heavy little bag. He opened the door for Nash. 'See you later.'

Captain Nash stepped into the corridor. He said, 'Yes, I expect so, old man.' He turned left and strode off down the corridor, moving easily with the swaying of the train, his hands in his trouser pockets and the light blazing on the tight golden curls at the back of his head.

Bond followed Tatiana up the train. The carriages were crowded with holiday-makers going home. In the third-class corridors people sat on their bags chattering and munching at oranges and at hard-looking rolls with bits of salami sticking out of them. The men carefully examined Tatiana as she squeezed by. The women looked appraisingly at Bond, wondering whether he made love to her well.

In the restaurant car, Bond ordered Americanos and a bottle of Chianti Broglio. The wonderful European hors d'œuvres came. Tatiana began to look more cheerful.

'Funny sort of man.' Bond watched her pick about among the little dishes. 'But I'm glad he's come along. I'll have a chance to get some sleep. I'm going to sleep for a week when we get home.'

'I do not like him,' the girl said indifferently. 'He is not *kulturny*. I do not trust his eyes.'

Bond laughed. 'Nobody's *kulturny* enough for you.'

'Did you know him before?'

'No. But he belongs to my firm.'

'What did you say his name is?'

'Nash. Norman Nash.'

She spelled it out. 'N.A.S.H.? Like that?'

'Yes.'

The girl's eyes were puzzled. 'I suppose you know what that means in Russian. *Nash* means "ours". In our Services, a man is *nash* when he is one of "our" men. He is *svoi* when he is one of "theirs" — when he belong to the enemy. And this man calls himself Nash. That is not pleasant.'

Bond laughed. 'Really, Tania. You do think of extraordinary reasons for not liking people. Nash is quite a common English name. He's perfectly harmless. At any rate he's tough enough for what we want him for.'

Tatiana made a face. She went on with her lunch.

Some *tagliatelli verdi* came, and the wine, and then a delicious escalope. 'Oh it is so good,' she said. 'Since I came out of Russia I am all stomach.' Her eyes widened. 'You won't let me get too fat, James. You won't let me get so fat that I am no use for making love? You will have to be careful, or I shall just eat all day long and sleep. You will beat me if I eat too much?'

'Certainly I will beat you.'

Tatiana wrinkled her nose. He felt the soft caress of her ankles. The wide eyes looked at him hard. The lashes came down demurely. 'Please pay,' she said. 'I feel sleepy.'

The train was pulling into Maestre. There was the beginning of the canals. A cargo gondola full of vegetables was moving slowly along a straight sheet of water into the town.

'But we shall be coming into Venice in a minute,' protested Bond. 'Don't you want to see it?'

'It will be just another station. And I can see Venice another day. Now I want you to love me. Please, James.' Tatiana leaned forward. She put a hand over his. 'Give me what I want. There is so little time.'

Then it was the little room again and the smell of the sea coming through the half-open window and the drawn blind fluttering with the wind of the train. Again there were the two piles of clothes on the floor, and the two whispering bodies on the banquette, and the slow searching hands. And the love-knot formed, and, as the train jolted over the points into the echoing station of Venice, there came the final lost despairing cry.

Outside the vacuum of the tiny room there sounded a confusion of echoing calls and metallic clanging and shuffling footsteps that slowly faded into sleep.

Padua came, and Vicenza, and a fabulous sunset over Verona flickered gold and red through the cracks of the blind. Again the little bell came tinkling down the corridor. They woke. Bond dressed and went into the corridor and leant against the guard rail. He looked out at the fading pink light over the Lombardy Plain and thought of Tatiana and of the future.

Nash's face slid up alongside his in the dark glass. Nash came very close so that his elbow touched Bond's. 'I think I've spotted one of the oppo, old man,' he said softly.

Bond was not surprised. He had assumed that, if it came, it would come tonight. Almost indifferently he said, 'Who is he?'

'Don't know what his real name is, but he's been through Trieste once or twice. Something to do with Albania. May be the Resident Director there. Now he's on an American passport. "Wilbur Frank". Calls himself a banker. In No. 9, right next to you. I don't think I could be wrong about him, old man.'

Bond glanced at the eyes in the big brown face. Again the furnace door was ajar. The red glare shone out and was extinguished.

'Good thing you spotted him. This may be a tough night. You'd better stick by us from now on. We mustn't leave the girl alone.'

'That's what I thought, old man.'

They had dinner. It was a silent meal. Nash sat beside the girl and kept his eyes on his plate. He held his knife like a fountain pen and frequently wiped it on his fork. He was clumsy in his movements. Half way through the meal, he reached for the salt and knocked over Tatiana's glass of Chianti. He apologized profusely. He made a great show of calling for another glass and filling it.

Coffee came. Now it was Tatiana who was clumsy. She knocked over her cup. She had gone very pale and her breath was coming quickly.

'Tatiana!' Bond half rose to his feet. But it was Captain Nash who jumped up and took charge.

'Lady's come over queer,' he said shortly. 'Allow me.' He reached down and put an arm round the girl and lifted her to her feet. 'I'll take her back to the compartment. You'd better look after the bag. And there's the bill. I can take care of her till you come.'

'Is all right,' protested Tatiana with the slack lips of deepening unconsciousness. 'Don' worry, James, I lie down.' Her head lolled against Nash's shoulder. Nash put one thick arm round her waist and manœuvred her quickly and efficiently down the crowded aisle and out of the restaurant car.

Bond impatiently snapped his fingers for the waiter. Poor darling. She must be dead beat. Why hadn't he thought of the strain she was going through? He cursed himself for his selfishness. Thank heavens for Nash. Efficient sort of chap, for all his uncouthness.

Bond paid the bill. He took up the heavy little bag and walked as quickly as he could down the crowded train.

He tapped softly on the door of No. 7. Nash opened the door. He came out with his finger on his lips. He closed the door behind him. 'Threw a bit of a faint,' he said. 'She's all right now. The beds were made up. She's gone to sleep in the top one. Been a bit much for the girl I expect, old man.'

Bond nodded briefly. He went into the compartment. A hand hung palely down from under the sable coat. Bond stood on the bottom bunk and gently tucked the hand under the corner of the coat. The hand felt very cold. The girl made no sound.

Bond stepped softly down. Better let her sleep. He went into the corridor.

Nash looked at him with empty eyes. 'Well, I suppose we'd better settle in for the night. I've got my book.' He held it up. '*War and Peace*. Been trying to plough through it for years. You take the first sleep, old man. You look pretty flaked out yourself. I'll wake you up when I can't keep my eyes open any longer.' He gestured with his head at the door of No. 9. 'Hasn't shown yet. Don't suppose he will if he's up to any monkey tricks.' He paused. 'By the way, you got a gun, old man?'

'Yes. Why, haven't you?'

Nash looked apologetic. ''Fraid not. Got a Luger at home, but it's too bulky for this sort of job.'

'Oh, well,' said Bond reluctantly. 'You'd better take mine. Come on in.'

They went in and Bond shut the door. He took out the Beretta and handed it over. 'Eight shots,' he said softly. 'Semi-automatic. It's on safe.'

Nash took the gun and weighed it professionally in his hand. He clicked the safe on and off.

Bond hated someone else touching his gun. He felt naked without it. He said gruffly, 'Bit on the light side, but it'll kill if you put the bullets in the right places.'

Nash nodded. He sat down near the window at the end of the bottom bunk. 'I'll take this end,' he whispered. 'Good field of fire.' He put his book down on his lap and settled himself.

Bond took off his coat and tie and laid them on the bunk beside him. He leant back against the pillows and propped his feet on the bag with the Spektor that stood on the floor beside his attaché case. He picked up his Ambler and found his place and tried to read. After a few pages he found that his concentration was going. He was too tired. He laid the book down on his lap and closed his eyes. Could he afford to sleep? Was there any other precaution they could take?

The wedges! Bond felt for them in the pocket of his coat. He slipped off the bunk and knelt and forced them hard under the two doors. Then he settled himself again and switched off the reading light behind his head.

The violet eye of the nightlight shone softly down.

'Thanks, old man,' said Captain Nash softly.

The train gave a moan and crashed into a tunnel.

26

THE KILLING BOTTLE

THE LIGHT NUDGE at his ankle woke Bond. He didn't move. His senses came to life like an animal's.

Nothing had changed. There were the noises of the train — the soft iron stride, pounding out the kilometres, the quiet creak of the woodwork, a tinkle from the cupboard over the washbasin where a toothglass was loose in its holder.

What had woken him? The spectral eye of the nightlight cast its deep velvet sheen over the little room. No sound came from the upper bunk. By the window, Captain Nash sat in his place, his book open on his lap, a flicker of moonlight from the edge of the blind showing white on the double page.

He was looking fixedly at Bond. Bond registered the intentness of the violet eyes. The black lips parted. There was a glint of teeth.

'Sorry to disturb you, old man. I feel in the mood for a talk!'

What was there new in the voice? Bond put his feet softly down to the floor. He sat up straighter. Danger, like a third man, was standing in the room.

'Fine,' said Bond easily. What had there been in those few words that had set his spine tingling? Was it the note of authority in Nash's voice? The idea came to Bond that Nash might have gone mad. Perhaps it was madness in the room, and not danger, that Bond could smell. His instincts about this man had been right. It would be a question of somehow getting rid of him at the next station. Where had they got to? When would the frontier come?

Bond lifted his wrist to look at the time. The violet light defeated the phosphorous numerals. Bond tilted the face towards the strip of moonlight from the window.

From the direction of Nash there came a sharp click. Bond felt a violent blow on his wrist. Splinters of glass hit him in the face. His arm was flung back against the door. He wondered if his wrist had been broken. He let his arm hang and flexed his fingers. They all moved.

The book was still open on Nash's lap, but now a thin wisp of smoke was coming out of the hole at the top of its spine and there was a faint smell of fireworks in the room.

The saliva dried in Bond's mouth as if he had swallowed alum.

So there had been a trap all along. And the trap had closed. Captain Nash had been sent to him by Moscow. Not by M. And the M.G.B. agent in No. 9, the man with an American passport, was a myth. And Bond had given Nash his gun. He had even put wedges under the doors so that Nash would feel more secure.

Bond shivered. Not with fear. With disgust.

Nash spoke. His voice was no longer a whisper, no longer oily. It was loud and confident.

'That will save us a great deal of argument, old man. Just a little demonstration. They think I'm pretty good with this little bag of tricks. There are ten bullets in it — .25 dum-dum, fired by an electric battery. You must admit the Russians are wonderful chaps for dreaming these things up. Too bad that book of yours is only for reading, old man.'

'For God's sake stop calling me "old man".' When there was so much to know, so much to think about, this was Bond's first reaction to utter catastrophe. It was the reaction of someone in a burning house who picks up the most trivial object to save from the flames.

'Sorry, old man. It's got to be a habit. Part of trying to be a bloody gentleman. Like these clothes. All from the wardrobe department. They said I'd get by like this. And I did, didn't I, old man? But let's get down to business. I expect you'd like to know what this is all about. Be glad to tell you. We've got about half an hour before you're due to go. It'll give me an extra kick telling the famous Mister Bond of the Secret Service what a bloody fool he is. You see, old man, you're not so good as you think. You're just a stuffed dummy and I've been given the job of letting the sawdust out of you.' The voice was even and flat, the sentences trailing away on a dead note. It was as if Nash was bored by the act of speaking.

'Yes,' said Bond. 'I'd like to know what it's all about. I can spare you half an hour.' Desperately he wondered: was there any way of putting this man off his stride? Upsetting his balance?

'Don't kid yourself, old man.' The voice was uninterested in Bond, or in the threat of Bond. Bond didn't exist except as a target. 'You're going to die in half an hour. No mistake about it. I've never made a mistake or I wouldn't have my job.'

'What is your job?'

'Chief Executioner of SMERSH.' There was a hint of life in the voice, a hint of pride. The voice went flat again. 'You know the name I believe, old man.'

SMERSH. So that was the answer — the worst answer of all. And this was their chief killer. Bond remembered the red glare that flickered in the opaque eyes. A killer. A psychopath — manic depressive, probably. A man who really enjoyed it. What a useful man for SMERSH to have found! Bond suddenly remembered what Vavra had said. He tried a long shot. 'Does the moon have any effect on you, Nash?'

The black lips writhed. 'Clever aren't you, Mister Secret Service. Think I'm barmy. Don't worry. I wouldn't be where I am if I was barmy.'

The angry sneer in the man's voice told Bond that he had touched a nerve. But what could he achieve by getting the man out of control? Better humour him and gain some time. Perhaps Tatiana . . .

'Where does the girl come into all this?'

'Part of the bait.' The voice was bored again. 'Don't worry. She won't butt in on our talk. Fed her a pinch of chloral hydrate when I poured her that glass of wine. She'll be out for the night. And then for every other night. She's to go with you.'

'Oh really.' Bond slowly lifted his aching hand on to his lap, flexing the fingers to get the blood moving. 'Well, let's hear the story.'

'Careful, old man. No tricks. No Bulldog Drummond stuff'll get you out of this one. If I don't like even the smell of a move, it'll be just one bullet through the heart. Nothing more. That's what you'll be getting in the end. One through the centre of the heart. If you move it'll come a bit quicker. And don't forget who I am. Remember your wrist-watch? I don't miss. Not ever.'

'Good show,' said Bond carelessly. 'But don't be frightened. You've got my gun. Remember? Get on with your story.'

'All right, old man, only don't scratch your ear while I'm talking. Or I'll shoot it off. See? Well, SMERSH decided to kill you — at least I gather it was decided even higher up, right at the top. Seems they want to take one good hard poke at the Secret Service — bring them down a peg or two. Follow me?'

'Why choose *me*?'

'Don't ask me, old man. But they say you've got quite a reputation in your outfit. The way you're going to be killed is going to bust up the whole show. It's been three months cooking, this plan, and it's a beaut. Got to be. SMERSH has made one or two mistakes lately. That Khoklov business for one. Remember the explosive cigarette case and all that? Gave the job to the wrong man. Should have given it to me. I wouldn't have gone over to the Yanks. However, to get back. You see, old man, we've got quite a planner in SMERSH. Man called Kronsteen. Great chess player. He said vanity would get you and greed and a bit of craziness in the plot. He said you'd all fall for the craziness in London. And you did, didn't you, old man?'

Had they? Bond remembered just how much the eccentric angles of the story had aroused their curiosity. And vanity? Yes, he had to admit that the idea of this Russian girl being in love with him had helped. And there had been the Spektor. That had decided the whole thing — plain greed for it. He said non-committally: 'We were interested.'

'Then came the operation. Our Head of Operations is quite a character. I'd say she's killed more people than anyone in the world — or arranged for them to be killed. Yes, it's a woman. Name of Klebb — Rosa Klebb. Real swine of a woman. But she certainly knows all the tricks.'

Rosa Klebb. So at the top of SMERSH there was a woman! If he could somehow survive this and get after her! The fingers of Bond's right hand curled softly.

The flat voice in the corner went on: 'Well, she found this Romanova girl. Trained her for the job. By the way, how was she in bed? Pretty good?'

No! Bond didn't believe it. That first night must have been staged. But afterwards? No. Afterwards had been real. He took the opportunity to shrug his shoulders. It was an exaggerated shrug. To get the man accustomed to movement.

'Oh, well. Not interested in that sort of thing myself. But they got some nice pictures of you two.' Nash tapped his coat pocket. 'Whole reel of 16 millimetre. That's going into her handbag. It'll look fine in the papers.' Nash laughed — a harsh, metallic laugh. 'They'll have to cut some of the juiciest bits, of course.'

The change of rooms at the hotel. The honeymoon suite. The big mirror behind the bed. How well it all fitted! Bond felt his hands wet with perspiration. He wiped them down his trousers.

'Steady, old man. You nearly got it then. I told you not to move, remember?'

Bond put his hands back on the book in his lap. How much could he develop these small movements? How far could he go? 'Get on with the story,' he said. 'Did the girl know these pictures were being taken? Did she know SMERSH was involved in all this?'

Nash snorted. 'Of course she didn't know about the pictures. Rosa didn't trust her a yard. Too emotional. But I don't know much about that side. We all worked in compartments. I'd never seen her until today. I only know what I picked up. Yes, of course the girl knew she was working for SMERSH. She was told she had to get to London and do a bit of spying there.'

The silly idiot, thought Bond. Why the hell hadn't she told him that SMERSH was involved? She must have been frightened even to speak the name. Thought he would have her locked up or something. She had always said she would tell him everything when she got to England. That he must have faith and not be afraid. Faith! When she hadn't the foggiest idea herself what was going on. Oh, well. Poor child. She had been as fooled as he had been. But any hint would have been enough — would have saved the life of Kerim, for instance. And what about hers and his own?

'Then this Turk of yours had to be got rid of. I gather that took a bit of doing. Tough nut. I suppose it was his gang that blew up our Centre in Istanbul yesterday afternoon. That's going to create a bit of a panic.'

'Too bad.'

'Doesn't worry me, old man. My end of the job's going to be easy.' Nash took a quick glance at his wrist-watch. 'In about twenty minutes we go into the Simplon tunnel. That's where they want it done. More drama for the papers. One bullet for you. As we go into the tunnel. Just one in the heart. The noise of the tunnel will help in case you're a noisy dier — rattle and so forth. Then one in the back of the neck for her — with your gun — and out of the window she goes. Then one more for you with *your* gun. With your fingers wrapped round it, of course. Plenty of powder on your shirt. Suicide. That's what it'll look like at first. But there'll be two bullets in your heart. That'll come out later. More mystery! Search the Simplon again. Who was the man with the fair hair? They'll find the film in her bag, and in your pocket there'll be a long love letter from her to you — a bit threatening. It's a good one. SMERSH wrote it. It says that she'll give the film to the newspapers unless you marry her. That you promised to marry her if she stole the Spektor . . .' Nash paused and added in parenthesis, 'As a matter of fact, old man, the Spektor's booby-trapped. When your cipher experts start fiddling with it, it's going to blow them all to glory. Not a bad dividend on the side.' Nash chuckled dully. 'And then the letter says that all she's got to offer you is the machine and her body — and all about her body and what you did with it. Hot stuff, that part! Right? So what's the story in the papers — the Left Wing ones that will be tipped off to meet the train? Old man, the story's got everything. Orient Express. Beautiful Russian spy murdered in Simplon tunnel. Filthy pictures. Secret cipher machine. Handsome British spy with career ruined murders her and commits suicide. Sex, spies, luxury train, Mr. and Mrs. Somerset . . . ! Old man, it'll run for months! Talk of the Khoklov case! This'll knock spots off it. And what a poke in the eye for the famous Intelligence Service! Their best man, the famous James Bond. What a shambles. Then bang goes the cipher machine! What's your chief going to think of you? What's the public going to think? And the Government. And the Americans? Talk about security! No more atom secrets from the Yanks.' Nash paused to let it all sink in. With a touch of pride he said, 'Old man, this is going to be the story of the century!'

Yes, thought Bond. Yes. He was certainly right about that. The French papers would give it such a send-off there'd be no stopping it. They wouldn't mind how far they went with the pictures or anything else. There wasn't a press in the world that wouldn't pick it up. And the Spektor! Would M.'s people or the Deuxième have the sense to guess it was booby-trapped? How many of the best cryptographers in the West would go up with it? God, he must get out of this jam! But how?

The top of Nash's *War and Peace* yawned at him. Let's see. There would be the roar as the train went into the tunnel. Then at once the muffled click and the bullet. Bond's eyes stared into the violet gloom, measuring the depth of the shadow in his corner under the roof of the top bunk, remembering exactly where his attaché case stood on the floor, guessing what Nash would do after he had fired.

Bond said: 'You took a bit of a gamble on my letting you team up at Trieste. And how did you know the code of the month?'

Nash said patiently, 'You don't seem to get the picture, old man. SMERSH is good — really good. There's nothing better. We know your code of the month for every year. If anyone in your show noticed these things, noticed the pattern of them, like my show does, you'd realize that every January you lose one of your small chaps somewhere — maybe Tokyo, maybe Timbuctoo. SMERSH just picks one and takes him. Then they screw the code for the year out of him. Anything else he knows, of course. But it's the code they're after. Then it's passed round to the Centres. Simple as falling off a log, old man.'

Bond dug his nails into the palms of his hands.

'As for picking you up at Trieste, old man, I didn't. Rode down with you — in the front of the train. Got out as we stopped and walked back up the platform. You see, old man, we were waiting for you in Belgrade. Knew you'd call your Chief — or the Embassy or someone. Been listening in on that Yugoslav's telephone for weeks. Pity we didn't understand the codeword he shot through to Istanbul. Might have stopped the firework display, or anyway saved our chaps. But the main target was you, old man, and we certainly had you sewn up all right. You were in the killing bottle from the minute you got off that plane in Turkey. It was only a question of when to stuff the cork in.' Nash took another quick glance at his watch. He looked up. His grinning teeth glistened violet. 'Pretty soon now, old man. It's just cork-hour minus fifteen.'

Bond thought: we knew SMERSH was good, but we never knew they were as good as this. The knowledge was vital. Somehow he must get it back. He MUST. Bond's mind raced round the details of his pitifully thin, pitifully desperate plan.

He said: 'SMERSH seems to have thought things out pretty well. Must have taken a lot of trouble. There's only one thing . . . ' Bond let his voice hang in the air.

'What's that, old man?' Nash, thinking of his report, was alert.

The train began to slow down. Domodossola. The Italian frontier. What about customs? But Bond remembered. There were no formalities for the through carriages until they got to France, to the frontier, Vallorbes. Even then not for the sleeping cars. These expresses cut straight across Switzerland. It was only people who got out at Brigue or Lausanne who had to go through customs in the stations.

'Well, come on, old man.' Nash sounded hooked.

'Not without a cigarette.'

'Okay. Go ahead. But if there's a move I don't like, you'll be dead.'

Bond slipped his right hand into his hip-pocket. He drew out his broad gunmetal cigarette case. Opened it. Took out a cigarette. Took his lighter out of his trouser pocket. Lit the cigarette and put the lighter back. He left the cigarette case on his lap beside the book. He put his left hand casually over the book and the cigarette case as if to prevent them slipping off his lap. He puffed away at his cigarette. If only it had been a trick one — magnesium flare, or anything he could throw in the man's face! If only his Service went in for those explosive toys! But at least he had achieved his objective and hadn't been shot in the process. That was a start.

'You see.' Bond described an airy circle with his cigarette to distract Nash's attention. His left hand slipped the flat cigarette case between the pages of his book. 'You see, it looks all right, but what about you? What are you going to do after we come out of the Simplon? The conductor knows you're mixed up with us. They'll be after you in a flash.'

'Oh that.' Nash's voice was bored again. 'You don't seem to have hoisted in that the Russians think these things out. I get off at Dijon and take a car to Paris. I get lost there. A bit of "Third Man" stuff won't do the story any harm. Anyway it'll come out later when they dig the second bullet out of you and can't find the second gun. They won't catch up with me. Matter of fact, I've got a date at noon tomorrow — Room 204 at the

Ritz Hotel, making my report to Rosa. She wants to get the kudos for this job. Then I turn into her chauffeur and we drive to Berlin. Come to think of it, old man,' the flat voice showed emotion, became greedy, 'I think she may have the Order of Lenin for me in her bag. Lovely grub, as they say.'

The train began to move. Bond tensed. In a few minutes it would come. What a way to die, if he was going to die. Through his own stupidity — blind, lethal stupidity. And lethal for Tatiana. Christ! At any moment he could have done something to dodge this shambles. There had been no lack of opportunity. But conceit and curiosity and four days of love had sucked him along on the easy stream down which it had been planned that he should drift. That was the damnable part of the whole business — the triumph for SMERSH, the one enemy he had always sworn to defeat wherever he met it. We will do this, and he will do that. 'Comrades, it is easy with a vain fool like this Bond. Watch him take the bait. You will see. I tell you he's a fool. All Englishmen are fools.' And Tatiana, the lure — the darling lure. Bond thought of their first night. The black stockings and the velvet ribbon. And all the time SMERSH had been watching, watching him go through his conceited paces, as it had been planned that he would, so that the smear could be built up — the smear on him, the smear on M. who had sent him to Istanbul, the smear on the Service that lived on the myth of its name. God, what a mess! If only . . . if only his tiny grain of a plan might work!

Ahead, the rumble of the train became a deep boom.

A few more seconds. A few more yards.

The oval mouth between the white pages seemed to gape wider. In a second the dark tunnel would switch out the moonlight on the pages and the blue tongue would lick out for him.

'Sweet dreams, you English bastard.'

The rumble became a great swift clanging roar.

The spine of the book bloomed flame.

The bullet, homing on Bond's heart, flashed over its two quiet yards.

Bond pitched forward on to the floor and lay sprawled under the funereal violet light.

27

TEN PINTS OF BLOOD

IT HAD ALL depended on the man's accuracy. Nash had said that Bond would get one bullet through the heart. Bond had taken the gamble that Nash's aim was as good as he said it was. And it had been.

Bond lay like a dead man lies. Before the bullet, he had recalled the corpses he had seen — how their bodies had looked in death. Now he lay totally collapsed, like a broken doll, his arms and legs carefully outflung.

He explored his sensations. Where the bullet had crashed into the book, his ribs were on fire. The bullet must have gone through the cigarette case and then through the other half of the book. He could feel the hot lead over his heart. It felt as if it was burning inside his ribs. It was only a sharp pain in his head where it had hit the woodwork, and the violet sheen on the scuffed toecaps against his nose, that said he wasn't dead.

Like an archaeologist, Bond explored the carefully planned ruin of his body. The position of the sprawled feet. The angle of the half-bent knee that would give purchase when it was needed. The right hand that seemed to be clawing at his pierced heart, was within inches, when he could release the book, of the little attaché case — within inches of the lateral stitching that held the flat-bladed throwing-knives, two-edged and sharp as razors, that he had mocked when Q Branch had demonstrated the catch that held them. And his left hand, outflung in the surrender of death, rested on the floor and would provide upward leverage when the moment came.

Above him there sounded a long, cavernous yawn. The brown toecaps shifted. Bond watched the shoe-leather strain as Nash stood up. In a minute, with Bond's gun in his right hand, Nash would climb on to the bottom bunk and reach up and feel through the curtain of hair for the base of the girl's neck. Then the snout of the Beretta would nuzzle in after the probing fingers, Nash would press the trigger. The roar of the train would cover the muffled boom.

It would be a near thing. Bond desperately tried to remember simple anatomy. Where were the mortal places in the lower body of a man? Where did the main artery run? The femoral. Down the inside of the thigh. And the external iliac, or whatever it was called, that became the femoral? Across the centre of the groin. If he missed both, it would be bad. Bond had no illusions about being able to beat this terrific man in unarmed combat. The first violent stab of his knife had to be decisive.

The brown toecaps moved. They pointed towards the bunk. What was the man doing? There was no sound except the hollow iron clang as the great train tore through the Simplon — through the heart of the Wasenhorn and Monte Leone. The toothglass tinkled. The woodwork creaked comfortably. For a hundred yards on both sides of the little death cell rows of people were sleeping, or lying awake, thinking of their lives and loves, making little plans, wondering who would meet them at the Gare de Lyon. And, all the while, just along the corridor, death was riding with them down the same dark hole, behind the same great Diesel, on the same hot rails.

One brown shoe left the floor. It would have stepped half across Bond. The vulnerable arch would be open above Bond's head.

Bond's muscles coiled like a snake's. His right hand flickered a few centimetres to the hard stitching on the edge of the case. Pressed sideways. Felt the narrow shaft of the knife. Drew it softly half way out without moving his arm.

The brown heel lifted off the ground. The toe bent and took the weight.

Now the second foot had gone.

Softly move the weight here, take the purchase there, grasp the knife hard so that it wouldn't turn on a bone, and then . . .

In one violent corkscrew of motion, Bond's body twisted up from the floor. The knife flashed.

The fist with the long steel finger, and all Bond's arm and shoulder behind it, lunged upwards. Bond's knuckles felt flannel. He held the knife in, forcing it further.

A ghastly wailing cry came down to him. The Beretta clattered to the floor. Then the knife was wrenched from

Bond's hand as the man gave a convulsive twist and crashed down.

Bond had planned for the fall, but, as he sidestepped towards the window, a flailing hand caught him and sent him thudding on to the lower bunk. Before he could recover himself, up from the floor rose the terrible face, its eyes shining violet, the violet teeth bared. Slowly, agonizingly, the two huge hands groped for him.

Bond, half on his back, kicked out blindly. His shoe connected; but then his foot was held and twisted and he felt himself slipping downwards.

Bond's fingers scrabbled for a hold in the stuff of the bunk. Now the other hand had him by the thigh. Nails dug into him.

Bond's body was being twisted and pulled down. Soon the teeth would be at him. Bond hammered out with his free leg. It made no difference. He was going.

Suddenly Bond's scrabbling fingers felt something hard. The book! How did one work the thing? Which way up was it? Would it shoot him or Nash? Desperately Bond held it out towards the great sweating face. He pressed at the base of the cloth spine.

'Click!' Bond felt the recoil. 'Click-click-click-click.' Now Bond felt the heat under his fingers. The hands on his legs were going limp. The glistening face was drawing back. A noise came from the throat, a terrible gurgling noise. Then, with a slither and a crack, the body fell forward on to the floor and the head crashed back against the woodwork.

Bond lay and panted through clenched teeth. He stared up at the violet light above the door. He noticed that the loop of the filament waxed and waned. It crossed his mind that the dynamo under the carriage must be defective. He blinked his eyes to focus the light more closely. The sweat ran into them and stung. He lay still, doing nothing about it.

The galloping boom of the train began to change. It sounded hollower. With a final echoing roar, the Orient Express sped out into the moonlight and slackened speed.

Bond lazily reached up and pulled at the edge of the blind. He saw warehouses and sidings. Lights shone brightly, cleanly on the rails. Good, powerful lights. The lights of Switzerland.

The train slid quietly to a stop.

In the steady, singing silence, a small noise came from the floor. Bond cursed himself for not having made certain. He quickly bent down, listening. He held the book forward at the ready, just in case. No movement. Bond reached and felt for the jugular vein. No pulse. The man was quite dead. The corpse had been settling.

Bond sat back and waited impatiently for the train to move again. There was a lot to be done. Even before he could see to Tatiana, there would have to be the cleaning up.

With a jerk the long express started softly rolling. Soon the train would be slaloming fast down through the foothills of the Alps into the Canton Valais. Already there was a new sound in the wheels — a hurrying lilt, as if they were glad the tunnel was past.

Bond got to his feet and stepped over the sprawling legs of the dead man and turned on the top light.

What a shambles! The place looked like a butcher's shop. How much blood did a body contain? He remembered. Ten pints. Well, it would soon all be there. As long as it didn't spread into the passage! Bond stripped the bedclothes off the bottom bunk and set to work.

At last the job was done — the walls swabbed down around the covered bulk on the floor, the suitcases piled ready for the getaway at Dijon.

Bond drank down a whole carafe of water. Then he stepped up and gently shook the shoulder of fur.

There was no response. Had the man lied? Had he killed her with the poison?

Bond thrust his hand in against her neck. It was warm. Bond felt for the lobe of an ear and pinched it hard. The girl stirred sluggishly and moaned. Again Bond pinched the ear, and again. At last a muffled voice said, 'Don't.'

Bond smiled. He shook her. He went on shaking until Tatiana slowly turned over on her side. Two doped blue eyes gazed into his and closed again. 'What is it?' The voice was sleepily angry.

Bond talked to her and bullied her and cursed her. He shook her more roughly. At last she sat up. She gazed vacantly at him. Bond pulled her legs out so that they hung down over the edge. Somehow he manhandled her down on to the bottom bunk.

Tatiana looked terrible — the slack mouth, the upturned, sleep-drunk eyes, the tangle of damp hair. Bond got to work with a wet towel and her comb.

Lausanne came and, an hour later, the French frontier at Vallorbes. Bond left Tatiana and went out and stood in the corridor, just in case. But the customs and passport men brushed past him to the conductor's cabin, and, after five inscrutable minutes, went on down the train.

Bond stepped back into the compartment. Tatiana was asleep again. Bond looked at Nash's watch, which was now on his own wrist. 4.30. Another hour to Dijon. Bond set to work.

At last Tatiana's eyes opened wide. Her pupils were more or less centred. She said, 'Stop it now, James.' She closed her eyes again. Bond wiped the sweat off his face. He took the bags, one by one, to the end of the corridor and piled them against the exit. Then he went along to the conductor and told him that Madame was not well and that they would be leaving the train at Dijon.

Bond gave the conductor a final tip. 'Do not derange yourself,' he said. 'I have taken the luggage out so as not to disturb Madame. My friend, the one with fair hair, is a doctor. He has been sitting up with us all night. I have put him to sleep in my bunk. The man was exhausted. It would be kind not to waken him until ten minutes before Paris.'

'*Certainement, Monsieur.*' The conductor had not been showered with money like this since the good days of travelling millionaires. He handed over Bond's passport and tickets. The train began to slacken speed. '*Voilà que nous y sommes.*'

Bond went back to the compartment. He dragged Tatiana to her feet and out into the corridor and shut the door on the white pile of death beside the bunk.

At last they were down the steps and on to the hard, wonderful, motionless platform. A blue-smocked porter took their luggage.

The sun was beginning to rise. At that hour of the morning there were very few passengers awake. Only a handful in the third class, who had ridden 'hard' through the night, saw a young man help a young girl away from the dusty carriage with the romantic names on its side towards the drab door that said 'SORTIE'.

28

LA TRICOTEUSE

THE TAXI DREW up at the rue Cambon entrance to the Ritz Hotel.

Bond looked at Nash's watch. 11.45. He must be dead punctual. He knew that if a Russian spy was even a few minutes early or late for a rendezvous the rendezvous was automatically cancelled. He paid off the taxi and went through the door on the left that leads into the Ritz bar.

Bond ordered a double vodka martini. He drank it half down. He felt wonderful. Suddenly the last four days, and particularly last night, were washed off the calendar. Now he was on his own, having his private adventure. All his duties had been taken care of. The girl was sleeping in a bedroom at the Embassy. The Spektor, still pregnant with explosive, had been taken away by the bomb-disposal squad of the Deuxième Bureau. He had spoken to his old friend René Mathis, now head of the Deuxième, and the concierge at the Cambon entrance to the Ritz had been told to give him a pass-key and to ask no questions.

René had been delighted to find himself again involved with Bond in *une affaire noire*. 'Have confidence, *cher* James,' he had said. 'I will execute your mysteries. You can tell me the story afterwards. Two laundry-men with a large laundry basket will come to Room 204 at 12.15. I shall accompany them dressed as the driver of their camion. We are to fill the laundry basket and take it to Orly and await an R.A.F. Canberra which will arrive at two o'clock. We hand over the basket. Some dirty washing which was in France will be in England. Yes?'

Head of Station F had spoken to M. on the scrambler. He had passed over a short written report from Bond. He had asked for the Canberra. No, he had no idea what it was for. Bond had only shown up to deliver the girl and the Spektor. He had eaten a huge breakfast and had left the Embassy saying he would be back after lunch.

Bond looked again at the time. He finished his martini. He paid for it and walked out of the bar and up the steps to the concierge's lodge.

The concierge looked sharply at him and handed over a key. Bond walked over to the lift and got in and went up to the third floor.

The lift door clanged behind him. Bond walked softly down the corridor, looking at the numbers.

204. Bond put his right hand inside his coat and on to the taped butt of the Beretta. It was tucked into the waistband of his trousers. He could feel the metal of the silencer warm across his stomach.

He knocked once with his left hand.

'Come in.'

It was a quavering voice. An old woman's voice.

Bond tried the handle of the door. It was unlocked. He slipped the pass-key into his coat-pocket. He pushed the door open with one swift motion and stepped in and shut it behind him.

It was a typical Ritz sitting-room, extremely elegant, with good Empire furniture. The walls were white and the curtains and chair covers were of a small patterned chintz of red roses on white. The carpet was wine-red and close-fitted.

In a pool of sunshine, in a low armed chair beside a Directoire writing desk, a little old woman sat knitting.

The tinkle of the steel needles continued. The eyes behind light-blue tinted bi-focals examined Bond with polite curiosity.

'*Oui, Monsieur?*' The voice was deep and hoarse. The thickly powdered, rather puffy face under the white hair showed nothing but well-bred interest.

Bond's hand on the gun under his coat was taut as a steel spring. His half-closed eyes flickered round the room and back to the little old woman in the chair.

Had he made a mistake? Was this the wrong room? Should he apologize and get out? Could this woman possibly belong to SMERSH? She looked so exactly like the sort of respectable rich widow one would expect to find sitting by herself in the Ritz, whiling the time away with her knitting. The sort of woman who would have her own table, and her favourite waiter, in a corner of the restaurant downstairs — not, of course, the grill room. The sort of woman who would doze after lunch and then be fetched by an elegant black limousine with white side-walled tyres and be driven to the tea-room in the rue de Berri to meet some other rich crone. The old-fashioned black dress with the touch of lace at the throat and wrists, the thin gold chain that hung down over the shapeless bosom and ended in a folding lorgnette, the neat little feet in the sensible black-buttoned boots that barely touched the floor. It couldn't be Klebb! Bond had got the number of the room wrong. He could feel the perpiration under his arms. But now he would have to play the scene through.

'My name is Bond, James Bond.'

'And I, Monsieur, am Comtesse Metterstein. What can I do for you?' The French was rather thick. She might be German Swiss. The needles tinkled busily.

'I am afraid Captain Nash has met with an accident. He won't be coming today. So I came instead.'

Did the eyes narrow a fraction behind the pale blue spectacles?

'I have not the pleasure of the Captain's acquaintance, Monsieur. Nor of yours. Please sit down and state your business.' The woman inclined her head an inch towards the high-backed chair beside the writing desk.

One couldn't fault her. The graciousness of it all was devastating. Bond walked across the room and sat down. Now he was about six feet away from her. The desk held nothing but a tall old-fashioned telephone with a receiver on a hook, and, within reach of her hand, an ivory-buttoned bellpush. The black mouth of the telephone yawned at Bond politely.

Bond stared rudely into the woman's face, examining it. It was an ugly face, toadlike, under the powder and under the tight cottage-loaf of white hair. The eyes were so light brown as to be almost yellow. The pale lips were wet and blubbery below the fringe of nicotine-stained moustache. Nicotine? Where were her cigarettes? There was no ash-tray — no smell of smoke in the room.

Bond's hand tightened again on his gun. He glanced down at the bag of knitting, at the shapeless length of small-denier beige wool the woman was working on. The steel needles. What was there odd about them? The ends were discoloured as if they had been held in fire. Did knitting needles ever look like that?

'*Eh bien, Monsieur?*' Was there an edge to the voice? Had she read something in his face?

Bond smiled. His muscles were tense, waiting for any movement, any trick. 'It's no use,' he said cheerfully, gambling. 'You are Rosa Klebb. And you are Head of Otdyel II of SMERSH. You are a torturer and a murderer. You wanted to kill me and the Romanov girl. I am very glad to meet you at last.'

The eyes had not changed. The harsh voice was patient and polite. The woman reached out her left hand towards the bellpush. 'Monsieur, I am afraid you are deranged. I must ring for the *valet de chambre* and have you shown to the door.'

Bond never knew what saved his life. Perhaps it was the flash of realization that no wires led from the bellpush to the wall or into the carpet. Perhaps it was the sudden memory of the English 'Come in' when the expected knock came on the door. But, as her finger reached the ivory knob, he hurled himself sideways out of the chair.

As Bond hit the ground there was a sharp noise of tearing calico. Splinters from the back of his chair sprayed around him. The chair crashed to the floor.

Bond twisted over, tugging at his gun. Out of the corner of his eye he noticed a curl of blue smoke coming from the mouth of the 'telephone'. Then the woman was on him, the knitting needles glinting in her clenched fists.

She stabbed downwards at his legs. Bond lashed out with his feet and hurled her sideways. She had aimed at his legs! As he got to one knee, Bond knew what the coloured tips of the needles meant. It was poison. Probably one of those German nerve poisons. All she had to do was scratch him, even through his clothes.

Bond was on his feet. She was coming at him again. He tugged furiously at his gun. The silencer had caught. There was a flash of light. Bond dodged. One of the needles rattled against the wall behind him and the dreadful chunk of woman, the white bun of wig askew on her head, the slimy lips drawn back from her teeth, was on top of him.

Bond, not daring to use his naked fists against the needles, vaulted sideways over the desk.

Panting and talking to herself in Russian, Rosa Klebb scuttled round the desk, the remaining needle held forward like a rapier. Bond backed away, working at the stuck gun. The back of his legs came against a small chair. He let go the gun and reached behind him and snatched it up. Holding it by the back, with its legs pointing like horns, he went round the desk to meet her. But she was beside the bogus telephone. She swept it up and aimed it. Her hand went to the button. Bond leapt forward. He crashed the chair down. Bullets sprayed into the ceiling and plaster pattered down on his head.

Bond lunged again. The legs of the chair clutched the woman round the waist and over her shoulders. God she was strong! She gave way, but only to the wall. There she held her ground, spitting at Bond over the top of the chair, while the knitting needle quested towards him like a long scorpion's sting.

Bond stood back a little, holding the chair at arms' length. He took aim and high-kicked at the probing wrist. The needle sailed away into the room and pinged down behind him.

Bond came in closer. He examined the position. Yes, the woman was held firmly against the wall by the four legs of the chair. There was no way she could get out of the cage except by brute force. Her arms and legs and head were free, but the body was pinned to the wall.

The woman hissed something in Russian. She spat at him over the chair. Bond bent his head and wiped his face against his sleeve. He looked up and into the mottled face.

'That's all, Rosa,' he said. 'The Deuxième will be here in a minute. In an hour or so you'll be in London. You won't be seen leaving the hotel. You won't be seen going into England. In fact very few people will see you again. From now on you're just a number on a secret file. By the time we've finished with you you'll be ready for the lunatic asylum.'

The face, a few feet away, was changing. Now the blood had drained out of it, and it was yellow. But not, thought Bond, with fear. The pale eyes looked levelly into his. They were not defeated.

The wet, shapeless mouth lengthened in a grin.

'And where will you be when I am in the asylum, Mister Bond?'

'Oh, getting on with my life.'

'I think not, *Angliski spion*.'

Bond hardly noticed the words. He had heard the click of the door opening. A burst of laughter came from the room behind him.

'*Eh bien*.' It was the voice of delight that Bond remembered so well. 'The 70th position! Now, at last, I have seen everything. And invented by an Englishman! James, this really is an insult to my countrymen.'

'I don't recommend it,' said Bond over his shoulder. 'It's too strenuous. Anyway, you can take over now. I'll introduce you. Her name's Rosa. You'll like her. She's a big noise in SMERSH — she looks after the murdering, as a matter of fact.'

Mathis came up. There were two laundry-men with him. The three of them stood and looked respectfully into the dreadful face.

'Rosa,' said Mathis thoughtfully. 'But, this time, a Rosa Malheur. Well, well! But I am sure she is uncomfortable in that position. You two, bring along the *panier de fleurs* — she will be more comfortable lying down.'

The two men walked to the door. Bond heard the creak of the laundry basket.

The woman's eyes were still locked in Bond's. She moved a little, shifting her weight. Out of Bond's sight, and not noticed by Mathis, who was still examining her face, the toe of one shiny buttoned boot pressed under the instep of the other. From the point of its toe there slid forward half an inch of thin knife blade. Like the knitting needles, the steel had a dirty bluish tinge.

The two men came up and put the big square basket down beside Mathis.

'Take her,' said Mathis. He bowed slightly to the woman. 'It has been an honour.'

'*Au revoir*, Rosa,' said Bond.

The yellow eyes blazed briefly.

'Farewell, Mister Bond.'

The boot, with its tiny steel tongue, flashed out.

Bond felt a sharp pain in his right calf. It was only the sort of pain you would get from a kick. He flinched and stepped back. The two men seized Rosa Klebb by the arms.

Mathis laughed. 'My poor James,' he said. 'Count on SMERSH to have the last word.'

The tongue of dirty steel had withdrawn into the leather. Now it was only a harmless bundle of old woman that was being lifted into the basket.

Mathis watched the lid being secured. He turned to Bond. 'It is a good day's work you have done, my friend,' he said. 'But you look tired. Go back to the Embassy and have a rest because this evening we must have dinner together. The best dinner in Paris. And I will find the loveliest girl to go with it.'

Numbness was creeping up Bond's body. He felt very cold. He lifted his hand to brush back the comma of hair over his right eyebrow. There was no feeling in his fingers. They seemed as big as cucumbers. His hand fell heavily to his side.

Breathing became difficult. Bond sighed to the depth of his lungs. He clenched his jaws and half closed his eyes, as people do when they want to hide their drunkenness.

Through his eyelashes he watched the basket being carried to the door. He prised his eyes open. Desperately he focused on Mathis.

'I shan't need a girl, René,' he said thickly.

Now he had to gasp for breath. Again his hand moved up towards his cold face. He had an impression of Mathis starting towards him.

Bond felt his knees begin to buckle.

He said, or thought he said, 'I've already got the loveliest . . . '

Bond pivoted slowly on his heel and crashed headlong to the wine-red floor.